AGE OF GLASS

- RISE OF MANKIND 6 -

JEZ CAJIAO

CONTENTS

Thanks	5
Prologue	6
Chapter One	11
Chapter Two	25
Chapter Three	39
Chapter Four	51
Chapter Five	63
Chapter Six	71
Chapter Seven	81
Chapter Eight	89
Chapter Nine	98
Chapter Ten	108
Chapter Eleven	116
Chapter Twelve	124
Chapter Thirteen	133
Chapter Fourteen	143
Chapter Fifteen	154
Chapter Sixteen	163
Chapter Seventeen	170
Chapter Eighteen	178
Chapter Nineteen	194
Chapter Twenty	203
Chapter Twenty-One	210
Chapter Twenty-Two	218
Chapter Twenty-Three	227
Chapter Twenty-Four	237
Chapter Twenty-Five	248

Chapter Twenty-Six   256

Chapter Twenty-Seven   264

Chapter Twenty-Eight   272

Chapter Twenty-Nine   284

Chapter Thirty   295

Chapter Thirty-One   307

Chapter Thirty-Two   316

Chapter Thirty-Three   325

Chapter Thirty-Four   337

Chapter Thirty-Five   344

Chapter Thirty-Six   358

Chapter Thirty-Seven   370

Chapter Thirty-Eight   382

Chapter Thirty-Nine   390

Chapter Forty   401

Chapter Forty-One –   413

The Last Chapter   413

Epilogue   424

Thank you   429

Patreon   430

Rise of Mankind 7: Age of Expansion   431

Theft of Decks   432

Quest Academy   433

Wandering Warrior   434

Knights of Eternity   435

Scarlett Citadel   436

Facebook and Social Media   437

Battleforged: Conqueror   438

Legion 439

Recommendations 440

LITRPG! 441

Facebook 442

THANKS

Hi everyone! Well, that's it, The Age of Glass, another book finished, and the third of the year so far, which seems insane, considering for me it's the end of August, as I write this.

My thanks section is always a strange beast I know, mainly because I'm always at a loss as to what I could and should say.

There are so many people that I want to thank, that I want to reach out to and that I want to acknowledge that I can never do them all, and it just seems... well it seems like a wasted opportunity at times.

Regardless, I'm going to thank just one person this time around.

Chrissy; my wife.

Chrissy you make the sun shine, the flowers bloom and the fire burn, you are my life. You gave me two beautiful boys, a wonderful life, and today, the day after our wedding anniversary, despite all that we have going on, despite the hospital runs, the scares and more, you've still moved heaven and earth so that I can have the time to hit my deadline.

You are my sun, moon and stars, and I love you. Thank you, for I could never be all that I am, without you being all that you are.

I love you.

-Jez
29/08/2024

PROLOGUE

Robin gently drew her fingers down the small boy's face, closing his eyes a final time as she shook from the emotions raging inside her.

Twenty minutes ago, maybe less, she'd seen him going to the ration counter to beg for more food. She'd known what he was doing, and what he'd do when he was refused. They all had.

His little sister and his mother were sick; just one more of the unnamed infections, plagues, or maybe even venomous bites that came with this new world had gotten them both.

Now their only advocate was dead, and all for the cost of no doubt trying to steal some food for them. The worst thing was that their story, the mother and sister, was so common that it was barely even noticed.

That was why she'd seen him—Jonnie, she thought his name was—and she'd just shrugged it off.

She knew if they said no to him—which they always would—that he'd try to steal the food. She'd still ignored it—not her problem, too caught up in trying to survive the day herself—knowing that he'd not listen anyway.

Once, she'd not been like that. Only a few weeks ago, buoyed up by the new strength and power that came to her from leveling, she'd have stepped up. She'd have defended him.

Hell, she'd at least have tried to talk him out of it.

Now, instead, she slowly stood, looking down at the twisted body thrown out like garbage behind what had once been a supermarket. He wasn't the first, either. A few days ago, it'd been a kid called Mark. Before then an older woman…Dianne? And before then Peter, then… The tears blurred her vision as she stared down at the little face laid on the cold rock. Their bodies were found here as well…broken, discarded.

This was *wrong*.

It wasn't supposed to be like this!

Only a handful of months ago, she had a shitty job; she'd finally found real friends—online, but what did that matter; they still wanted to spend time with her—and she'd finally earned her own gaming rig.

Her life was getting straightened out. She was *fixing* it. She had her own apartment, she had some money, new books to escape into, a week off work on vacation and she'd been ready to spend all of it gaming.

She'd even been thinking of saving up for a flight, to go to one of those conventions in America. It was no longer a "one day maybe" but an actual plan! She'd been getting there; she'd been making it work.

That was all done now, though. Since the end of the world, there was nothing left, not of her old life and certainly not of her hopes and dreams. There were no more airplanes. There were no gaming rigs, no games, no…there was nothing. Not for her, again.

Where once she'd dreamt of being a Paladin or a spellsword, now she found that the world was giving her that chance, and she'd both hated and loved it.

The first part—*well*.

Her house had been one of the thousands that went up in flames in the Great Fire, as people were calling it now.

The entirety of Sunderland had gone up in smoke. The bucket brigades that people had been reduced to forming were no match for the creatures that leapt and danced in the flames.

Once the fire was too large, too out of control, she'd joined others in streaming from the remnants of the city, heading inland. There'd been no choice, after all: it was abandon everything and run, or stay and be burned to death.

On that journey, which felt so long ago, and yet only weeks or maybe months ago—it'd all become a blur—she'd been helping someone, a family, she dimly remembered, and some assholes had started a fight.

A thug had been robbing people, and she'd decided that she couldn't just let it go. She'd bought a telescopic baton online before the end, thinking a young woman living on her own needed some protection. That day, she'd finally found a use for it.

After that, it was a small step, a single guy who'd stepped up to help her with the next one; then a few others joined her. They encircled their small group, protecting a handful of families in the mass of slowly trudging people as they all streamed inland and to what they prayed was safety.

It wasn't to be.

By the time they'd covered the distant miles to Washington, they found the dozen or so small villages that formed the town, ringing it in some strange plan that the designers in the '80s had proclaimed the "wave of the future," had been turned into armed camps.

One or two would have probably been allowed in. It was only a few miles, after all; most of the refugees knew people who lived in the nearby town, or had family there.

There weren't a handful of them, though.

There were thousands, tens of thousands marching inward like locusts, starving, stripping the area as they desperately searched for food, for weapons, and for a new home.

The villages closed their doors to them all, and they formed their own groups, banding together to fight off the "invaders."

Suddenly, before Robin knew what was happening, she was responsible for a group, one that had hundreds of families in it. She'd gathered her little handful of fighters—if they could even be called that—and they'd made a decision.

They'd pick up the pace, move out and around the villages where everyone was fighting to find space.

Instead, they'd get up onto the main roads, the highways that ran through the center of the town and on toward Newcastle and Gateshead.

They'd head for the main shopping center nearby. It was huge, with hundreds of smaller shops and a dozen much, much larger ones, including a DIY center.

They'd hit it, loot what they needed to protect their people, and move on, heading farther inland. It was a terrible situation, but they'd already had proof that people weren't going to help them, so it was time to help themselves.

They'd tried that, only to find that they'd been beaten to it.

An hour's walking found them outside of the Galleries shopping center—what the Americans would have called a mall—and the force facing them was not only ready for them, they were armed.

It was made up of the local police force, some army, and the screws from the local prison. They'd offered them a place to stay, but under strict conditions: they handed in their weapons, they pooled their resources, and until the government came to help, the rule of law was that might made right. They did as they were told, or they were booted out. No warnings.

They'd not liked it, not at all, but considering the children were exhausted, the elderly were literally dying or being carried, and the healthy, supposedly working-age people were on their last legs as well?

They'd held a fast vote, and they'd decided to accept the terms in exchange for safety.

That'd been a *terrible* mistake.

It'd been less than an hour before they'd realized that the group in charge of their new home weren't the remnants of local and trained authority…

They were the escaped prisoners and gangs who had killed them.

By then it was too late, though, far too late. They were disarmed; the guards who supposedly were "watching over them" were just there to watch them.

The weeks passed in a blur, and unarmed, there was little the refugees could do. At first, there was talk of moving on. A family had gone to their appointed overseer and had asked to be given food to leave with—they were producing it and working for the group, after all; it'd seemed reasonable, and the ex-prisoners were making an effort to look like they were reformed.

The family vanished, and the next day, well, when the bodies were found, that was the end of that.

It was clear that they'd died hard, and although there was no proof—monsters was the story that was told—but everyone pretty much just got all quiet and accepting.

Robin and a small group had kept talking about moving on, about stealing away in the night perhaps…leaving without anything, sure, but getting away. There were only a few exits from the building that hadn't been sealed up, but there were ways out. They were locked in at night, but there had to be another way.

That'd come to an end when more refugees had arrived. Now it seemed like every day, more and more came. The tales of the collapse of civilization outside grew darker and darker by the day.

Roaming undead and mutations, terrible beasts, flying monsters…they were growing more and more common, and Robin and her people realized that if they were to run? It'd be out of the frying pan, and into the fire.

There was no hope outside. At least here, inside the walls, there was a chance.

Classes began to appear, people earning them through their efforts. And with the classes came new strength, new potential…but it was tightly controlled.

Their overseers apparently knew something, because it wasn't long before Robin and the others found out the downside to the class system they were given: you only got classes you'd *earned*.

There were no wizards, no warriors nor specialists offered to her and the other refugees. Instead, they were left to choose from classes like Drudge, or Serf.

Worse still were the prettiest among the group, those forced into the Whore or Slave pathways.

It wasn't all women, either. In fact, there were more men in that one than women. And there wasn't a day that some family wasn't left sobbing over the remains of a loved one who was "attacked by a beast."

That it was a human one, was never said aloud.

Now, though, Robin had reached the end of the road.

The body before her lay broken on the ground. The rain swirling a stream of bright-red blood into the nearby choked and overgrown drain was a line to her, and it was one that once she crossed, it led somewhere that you couldn't come back from.

"No more," she whispered, staring down, unable to look away as the steadily falling rain plastered his hair to cold flesh. "We can't let this go on."

"We've got no choice," said someone behind her.

She didn't know who. She didn't care, either.

"We've always got a choice," came another voice, and she turned, recognizing that one. "We can die on our feet, or we can die begging."

"Jakob." She greeted him, having not seen the man in weeks.

"Robin." He nodded once. "You going to do this?"

"I have to." She glanced at the one who'd said they didn't. "We've always got a choice..." she repeated. "And I'm making mine."

"We've got no weapons," another man said.

"They do." Robin shrugged, looking over at him. "All we've got to do is take them."

"We'll die." The first man shook his head, clearly afraid.

Robin looked at him—his filthy clothes, the worn-through sections on the knees and elbows, the streaks of mud that clung to his face and the lank hair.

She also saw what the man clearly didn't.

They were all being forced into hard labor: breaking buildings and roads down and piling the rubble; then one of the mages used a skill or a spell to smooth it into walls that slowly rose.

A fortress was growing here, and the ground they painstakingly uncovered was then being tilled and planted. The result was that the group that stood around currently were half starved by their captors, but also far stronger and fitter than they'd ever been in their lives.

Their overseers were running out of alcohol. They'd already eaten all the "luxury" foods, and although they were gaining classes that the rest weren't, they weren't all combat classes.

Robin turned slowly, looking at the small loading dock—the piled scrap, the wasted, twisted metal that had once been fencing—and her eyes gleamed.

"Everyone dies," she pointed out, striding over to the scrap heap and grabbing onto a pole. "Maybe it's time to stop being afraid."

She dragged the pole free. The metallic sound of steel on steel filled the air as she hefted the meter-long pole appraisingly.

The end of it was encrusted in a double fistful of concrete. Dirt still covered it from where it'd been ripped from the ground.

"I'm not... I won't..." One of the men backed away.

"I will," Jakob snarled, stepping up and grabbing another length of metal. "It might not be one of my girls laid there now, but it will be sooner or later!"

"Give me one," another voice ground out, shouldering the small handful of people aside. "What have we got left that they've not already taken from us?" She was petite, and had probably once been pretty.

Certainly prettier than Robin had ever been, she silently acknowledged to herself. But as the woman pushed her way forward, selecting a section of piping and lifting it with a grunt, they exchanged a nod.

Being pretty in this new world wasn't the boon it had been, once, and she was clearly doing her best to hide it now.

"Anyone else?" Robin raised her voice slightly. The eight people who had been nearby, who had drifted in by ones and twos while she checked the body, were evenly split now: four who would go, and four who were edging away.

It was now or never, she knew. If they waited, if they took the time to plan, some of these would sell what they knew in the hopes of better treatment.

No, it had to be now, and it had to be the four of them.

Nations had fallen from smaller beginnings.

CHAPTER ONE

The hand scanner that had released the lockouts for the dungeon had also released a faster exit from the "boss room," fortunately. In the seemingly solid wall behind the now-melted golden throne, a portal was slowly appearing.

The stones collapsed inward, like a sandcastle crumbling, and steps reformed, leading upward to the exit, even as Drak turned and ran in the opposite direction.

"Drak!" I shouted, glaring after him.

"The reliquaries!" he shouted back. "It's loot!"

"My people are dying!"

"Healing potions!" he replied, scrambling across the rocks and clamping a hand onto the nearest. "Weapons, blueprints—it could be anything!"

"Fuck's sake!" I snarled, hesitating for a second, then shaking my head and starting to run, heading for the stairs. "Grab me those goddamn daggers!" I shouted over my shoulder, even as I picked up the staff that the mage had been carrying. I examined it quickly, before dumping it as soon as I was at the top of the stairs and outside of the trial dungeon, and back into the main building.

It was metal coated and had a hell of a lot of random text, something about it being a ceremonial weapon, but bugger all of use beyond that, except perhaps as a way to tell the time. The deep "bong" as it bounced off the stone seemed to hang in the air longer than necessary.

It didn't matter, though, because I was already checking the details on the shotgun as I ran for the nearest stairwell, cursing the mess that the change had wrought on the ancient building.

The trial dungeon had been a variation on our usual training dungeon, which in turn had been inside the old building that had once housed the Empress bar, one of my old regular haunts in my earlier heavy drinking days.

It was built on a long slope down to a lower section of the city, on a steep hill, with a roughly triangular layout. Meaning that the building—it'd been office blocks, restaurants, and more, as well as a bar—varied massively in size and design from one end to the other.

At the western-most point, it was once five floors high, while at the eastern-most point, where the ground was the lowest, it was eight or nine floors high.

That might not sound like that big a difference, especially if it was my American cousins looking at it compared to the monstrous buildings they constructed over the pond. The difference was this building was nearly as old as their nation, and the ceilings were high, randomly maintained, and owned by hundreds of different people and businesses over the years.

That meant that when we'd torn out the insides and tried to make use of the building, we'd found floor levels that didn't match, rooms that were virtually rabbit warrens, and sections where the roof or floor—and in one case both—had been sagging close to collapse.

We'd massively rebuilt the entire place, not least because we turned the roof and the next floor down from the top into farms, and the weight was incredible.

I sprinted through the lower sections of the dungeon as fast as I could, racing up the stairs to the next floor, and then headed due north inside the building, already reaching out to what had been, until a few seconds ago, a solid wall.

Now it collapsed. A section two meters square vanished into a cloud of dissipating motes of light, as I ran at the gap and launched myself into the air.

My mana hadn't recovered yet. Neither had my health. And my armor? Hanging together by a thread in some places, covered in blood and battered to shit.

I'd not had a shower or a bath in days. I'd been covered in blood—usually my own—and sweat, bile, and worse. I was a mess, having literally just fought my way through the dungeon and into the open air, and now?

As soon as I reached the outside world, I was surrounded by screams, roars, and gunfire. This was *not* what I'd been expecting when I won the goddamn fight!

It was icy cold outside, and I blew out a plume of misted breath as I sensed Kelly nearby in the dungeon sense. I arched up and over the cathedral, staring as more of the devastation came into sight.

The dungeon was laid out in a bit of a mess, if I was honest with anyone about it. We'd claimed buildings as we could, and rebuilt as the need arose, which meant that coming out of the training dungeon, on the edge of Dean Street, we were close up against the outer west wall of the territory we claimed.

Directly north of the training dungeon, and literally a handful of meters from that wall, was the old cathedral, and on the other side of the road from that was the new housing block.

It was a literal ziggurat, heavily armored and luxurious inside, as well as having the space to house thousands. We were expanding it floor by floor. As each one came online, the need for additional space seemed only to grow.

Moving counterclockwise from there, there was the military building—again, one that was in progress, as we didn't have enough mana, *ever*, for all the things we needed.

For now, it was essentially a handful of offices and a public gym that the soldiers and trainees both loved and hated with a passion.

From there, moving farther to the northwest, a large warehouse type of building held the remains of the crashed ship that had brought the dungeon core itself, and then continuing around, the crafting area.

Next came the dungeon "proper," another of the multi-use old terraced buildings that had grown into one another over the years since it'd been built. I'd deployed the original dungeon core into it, and it'd grown from there.

Kelly and I—and most of the leadership cadre—had quarters in there, and there were also things like the canteen and some living areas, as well as my own smaller gym.

Next, continuing counterclockwise from there, came the mage's tower—or mancers, as some called themselves—and damn was that impressive. Five floors aboveground and four below, with the ground floor being a general one, and each of the other eight dedicated to a specific form of the eight elemental forms of mana.

It was huge, imposing, and hopefully to be our trump card when it came to the future wars we'd fight. For now, though, it was coated in a steady drizzle and almost lost in the fog that drifted from the pool.

The pool formed the heart of the dungeon territory here, a massive structure that'd been a quest reward. I had no clue what it was intended for originally, but as it was, with shallow zones, deeper ones and variable temperature sections, it'd become a giant open-air hot tub and swimming area that our people loved.

If the pool was in the dead center of the dungeon, and the mage's tower the bottom left—or seven o'clock, if imagining it from a clock perspective—then the six o'clock around to the three o'clock point held the last two main buildings. Closer to the center and directly between the entrance to the dungeon and the rest of our people was the castle.

The remains of Newcastle's literal castle had been repaired heavily, and a wall grown around the entire dungeon, with the only entrance from the outside right here.

Step through those massive gates, and you came to an internal courtyard, still surrounded by walls, giving us an area to greet people from the outside and deal with them, rather than just letting them in through the gates.

Finally, on its other side, in the space between the secure little greeting area and the edge of the cliff that dropped down to the river was the Parthenon.

It wasn't the real Parthenon, of course. The Greeks would be mighty pissed if I'd somehow stolen that, after all—and no clue how I'd get it here, nor what use it'd be in the current state.

Instead, it was an example of what we could do, as well as the heart of our little government. Where the great columns of stone in the real Parthenon were open to the world, between ours there stood clear sheets of thick anti-fogging glass in acknowledgment that it's Newcastle, not Athens, and it's cold as shit most of the year here.

The entire building was marble, but inside, the interior was beautiful, and half was dedicated to our people and their needs.

There were great rugs, tables, coffee stands and libraries, places where our children were taught and where they could cuddle up with a toy and nap.

Nurseries and lessons filled their days while their parents, be they biological or adoptive, worked to protect them and the dungeon. The rest of the building was given over to a medical facility, research sections, council chambers, war rooms, and more.

It was the shining example of what could be achieved here, and as I rocketed up out of the gap between the cathedral and the training dungeon, with that Parthenon on the training dungeon's far side, I snarled as the promise of what could be, met the reality of life in the apocalyptic war zone that was Earth.

The wall that protected the dungeon to the east, between the far end of the cathedral section and the southern-most section of the housing ziggurat, was down.

A huge section of the wall had fallen, with the nearby crossbow and siege weapon emplacements that had been built to defend the dungeon and crewed with corpse lords, already reduced to smoldering ruin.

Even as I slowed, hanging there and turning slowly, staring at the devastation, I saw additional rockets in flight, streaking past me to hammer into the remaining weapons emplacements.

A handful of our human and kobold allies raced across the farm atop the dungeon, taking up position and firing down into the figures that sprinted through rolling smoke toward the buildings, and...

I snarled.

They were using smoke bombs to cover them from my people, who were in turn coming under fire from snipers who were hidden farther out.

Glancing around, I realized there were even fewer of those people than there should have been. The walls were practically deserted apart from undead, and the kobolds that ran here and there were mainly dull-eyed and unaware.

Kelly was summoning more even now, but this was going to be a close one.

I slid sideways, moving to my left on instinct as soon as I spotted another fall to the incoming sniper fire. A half second later, a round passed right by where I'd been.

Twisting and diving downward, then rolling to the left, I dodged two more shots, presumably dropping too low for their line of sight by the petering off of fire.

That didn't stop shots from the incoming soldiers, though. I twisted again, this time firing off an Incinerate at a figure as they opened fire on me. Their scream barely registered.

There were at least a dozen here I could see, several busy in a pitched battle with the kobolds, who were firing back again and again, though mainly only using crossbows.

What the hell had happened? Where were the elites? The heavily armed squads? I knew we were low on ammunition, but still... Were they all at the park or with Mike? I twisted and fired, still trying to get my head around what was going on, as a handful of kobolds to one side, crouching along the edge of the roof and firing down, were taken out by a grenade. I cursed.

I could dimly make out other figures through the smoke on the other side of the cathedral. They were headed, as one, straight for the dungeon building.

My home, and the home of the core!

A notification flared. I almost dismissed it, then forced myself to open just that one, hoping against hope that it was what I thought it was going to be... Yes!

Quest!

Incursion (1)
***An unidentified enemy incursion has begun! Secure the borders of the
dungeon, and defend your territory to receive the following bonuses:***

- *+1 to top three Attributes*
- *2,000 XP*

Glancing around, I saw more kobolds and some undead streaming inward. I
twisted and raced for the dungeon, determined to make sure the enemy didn't
reach the core.

Ahead, I was already seeing the tell-tale blur of class skills from figures in the
distance who were leading the way. Well, the one thing I was sure of was that
considering the bodies that lay broken and bleeding here and there—both kobold
and dungeon resident human—was that anyone headed for the core couldn't be
allowed to reach it.

Knowing how powerful I'd been warned the shotgun was, I decided to make
the most of it. I headed for the ground, planning to shoot into the attackers from
behind and hopefully taking more of them out that way.

I flipped up the shotgun, the fléchettes already loaded. I dropped to the ground,
skidding and taking aim, before firing once; then, a slight shift of aim…then again,
and again, clearing the enemy out.

The shotgun had been designed by Aly. Although it was rough, and the
dungeon description of it had "complete, with issues" as the main descriptor, the
one thing it had going for it was sheer lethality.

It was a tri-barreled monstrosity of a rail gun that fired fléchettes, thirty or so
tiny darts that opened out as they flew and shredded anything fleshy they
encountered.

In this case, they took down a stealthed figure I'd seen hints of, and two more
I'd not, before sending horrifically dangerous shrapnel ricocheting off the walls
of the dungeon and in all directions.

Gunfire slammed into the wall next to me from behind. I cursed.

Spinning, I pumped the action and fired in the direction of the breeched wall.
Three blind shots burst in return, each vanishing into the smoke, before a swirl to
the right resolved into a figure in full British Army battle rattle.

He'd been hidden until the last second—some kind of ability, I guessed—and
he ran at me as I pumped the shotgun again. He fired a fast burst at close range,
and I snarled, twisting my shotgun up and between us, taking most of the incoming
fire on that.

The rest were mainly caught and deflected by my armor, even as damaged as
it was. But three got through. One pierced my lower right side, punching into the
gut above that hip and tearing out the far side. The other two were on my left side,
and a stinging line that tore itself across the inside of my left arm, between my
arm and chest.

I hissed in pain. The rail gun shotgun I was holding now emitted a sudden cloud of glowing steam, as one of the shots had apparently damaged something.

I lunged forward at the same time the soldier did. He was a big guy and clearly expected to bowl me over. That didn't work out the way he expected.

For a start, my left arm was injured, not out of the fight, and I was holding a damn big bit of metal between us.

I drove the shotgun into him, shoving with all my enhanced strength, and knocked him backward, tumbling to the ground. Then I flipped the shotgun, looking at the underside and seeing the clear blue glow, hearing the hissing, and feeling the heat that was growing from the damaged mana crystals it used for power.

Snarling, I twisted and threw it in the direction of the breeched wall, then kicked the rifle aside as the dickhead on the ground tried to bring it to bear on me.

Instead, as my gun vanished into the smoke, I dropped onto him, pinned his rifle down, and punched him as hard as I could through the narrow gap in his helmet.

He grunted, head banging—cushioned by the helmet—off the asphalt under him, even as he dragged a handgun free with his left hand.

He angled it upward, shouting. Blood ran down from his broken nose and covered his teeth, before he screamed as I activated my lightning shield. Shaking and hissing, he was essentially tasered by a stationary lightning bolt.

I ripped the handgun and assault rifle free, lifting the handgun on instinct as something resolved from the nearby smoke...only to cut the shield and jerk the gun aside as I spotted an advanced kobold bounding forward.

He kept coming, and I ducked as he leapt over me, hitting someone I'd not seen and taking them to the ground in a clatter of limbs, weapons, and screams.

Fighting in close quarters battle was second nature to British soldiers, I knew, but for an advanced kobold? They literally started out smarter, stronger, and better in almost every way than a baseline human.

Then add in the draconid legacy, along with the claws, fangs, and enhanced musculature? You needed to be damn lucky and highly skilled to fight one up close. And the screams that came from behind me made it clear whoever that'd been, they'd not been one of those things at least.

I quickly checked the unconscious figure below me, seeing I'd snapped a finger as I'd wrenched the handgun free. I shoved it, getting no response from him, before nodding as I clambered to my feet again. More kobolds were coming out of the gloom.

They were armed—most with spears and shields, some with swords. But the way they stooped low, keeping close to the ground and moving, I could see the animal or reptilian side of them a lot more here.

"Matt?" a familiar voice called, staggering out of the smoke farther down the street and waving a hand in the air. The mixture of steam and fog from the outdoor pool and the smoke grenades made it hard as hell for anyone to see anything.

"Here!" I shouted, before shaking my head and ordering one of the nearby kobolds to go for him.

I was seeing partly with my eyes, sure, but I was also sensing in the dungeon sense, allowing me to see a lot clearer in the smoke than Drak could.

"Here," I repeated, grabbing another of the advanced kobolds and pressing one of my bags into his clawed hands. "Take this to Kelly," I ordered, getting a nod before he bounded away.

It was a handful of the mana crystals I'd looted from the dungeon on my run. I knew that she'd be able to make better use of it than I could.

"What the hell kind of a place is this?!" Drak cursed as the other kobold led him up. The pair of us took shelter behind an outbuilding used to hold robes and so on, at the edge of the pool.

"What, you never saw a pool before?" I asked absently, reaching into the dungeon sense and searching, then sensing Kelly draw my attention to another trio who were in motion already. "Dammit!"

"What?" He twisted his head left and right, trying to see in the mess.

"Someone's given them a damn map or something," I snarled. "This way. Stay close!"

I set off running, trusting in the kobolds who were even now forming up as more shimmers of light in nearby windows spoke to Kelly summoning additional defenders.

I hissed and gritted my teeth. The gunshot wounds damn well hurt like hell as I ran across the old road, heading to the side entrance that ran between the main dungeon building and the crafting hall.

It was an old alleyway, one that ran east to west, and had once been used as both a place for people to relax on a night out, seats and heaters dotted around, and for those bars and offices that didn't use it, as a storage area for bins and more.

I'd long since cleared it of anything like that we could absorb, but it was still a long, narrow alley, and one that had direct access to the dungeon.

The doors were sealed and locked to anyone who didn't have permission to access these areas, but a shitload of explosives tended to make their own rules.

I reached the edge of the alley, turning to look inward just as the explosion went off. The narrow alley funneled the blast both upward and along, staggering me, before a barrage of gunfire drove me back into cover.

Snarling, I rolled back out into the alley as soon as the fire stopped, sighting down the stolen assault rifle and opening fire. A fast chatter of automatic fire filled the space and another figure fell, even as two more vanished into the building.

I started to stand, only to hit Drak, who'd tried to step over me, his own shotgun aimed into the alley. His shot went wide, flooding the narrow space with the flash of metal sparking off stone and cobbles. Flaming debris already gave the space a macabre air, and we both cursed.

A gun angled around the corner of the door and rang out again—this time a handgun, fortunately. Three bullets made it clear that although unaimed, they really didn't want us following.

We didn't take the hint. Untangling ourselves and exchanging a glare, we raced forward. His slightly stubbier legs and tail granted him a side-to-side run that slowed him as I pulled ahead. I threw myself down, skidding in a sliding tackle as I passed the smoking hole the fuckers had blown in my wall.

17

I leveled the assault rifle, aiming…and found nobody waiting. Then I scrabbled to my feet and headed into the hole, blinking as I figured out where I was.

Their intelligence wasn't perfect then, I realized, as they'd broken through the wall into the set of rooms two down from the area that would have led straight to the more secure zone, rather than farther along through the doors there.

Instead, they were into a set of rooms that held Life converters and a set of beds, basically a place for people to recover if they'd been overdoing it.

The Life converter made you feel a hell of a lot better when you were around them, increasing your healing. And the beds that had presumably been for comfort?

Crap, no.

I burst through the swinging door and into the corridor, hearing shouting, curses, and gunfire ahead. I took off, realizing that although yeah, this area had been used for that, the real and "official" use for it?

It was the triage area for the medical suite we'd had in this building.

My eyes darted all over, seeing traces of blood and random details, but fortunately no bodies. I dared to hope that, based on the medical suite being moved to the other building, nobody had been in this one at the time.

Instead, with Drak huffing and following me, the shotgun held awkwardly in his arms, I ran on.

The corridor wasn't long—ten meters, a turn to the left, then a second corridor, take a right—and I burst into the middle of a fight between a corpse lord and the two soldiers I'd seen heading inward.

One of them was already dead, the other emptying his magazine into the face of the boney monstrosity as it closed on him.

His mag ran dry. He dropped it out, slapping in a second and yanking the charging lever almost as fast as I could see it, and opened fire again.

The corpse lord held a hand up, trying to block the incoming fire, only to have the arm wither under the hail of gunfire. A second arm came up and was blown apart; then four shots slammed into the skull.

The corpse lords were huge creations, humanoid in design but around twice the size of a man, with three eyes, horns, a chest that was layered over and over with bones to form a rudimentary armor, and four arms that extended from dual shoulders. They could command the dead and spend their own health to raise additional minions from nearby bodies. And now, as the soldier before me triggered some kind of ability, spell, or skill, it used its final power.

The rifle suddenly glowed golden; the bullets that hurtled down range toward the corpse lord gleamed bright. Each hit detonated, sending the corpse lord careening backward…but as soon as they started, the golden glow was snuffed out.

"Wha…" The soldier gasped, clearly having been thinking it was his trump card.

But as the corpse lord fell, its suppression field collapsing as it died, I plowed into the fight.

I drove into him from behind, lifting him and ramming him into the wall, then twisting and running at an ornate banister that ended at the foot of the stairs.

It was oak, a meter high and carved in fancy fluting designs, as well as being at least two hundred years old. That was a shame, really, as the cracking sound of the oak breaking matched the sound of the soldier's legs breaking as I drove him into it.

He screamed, and with my left hand gripping the front of his battle rattle, I grabbed his chin with my right and yanked to the right as hard as I could. The air filled again, this time with the dry wood sound of bones snapping.

I dropped him, dead, to the ground and spun, panting as I checked the rest of the room. Drak skidded and bumped off the wall, before firing a blast into the body of the other soldier, where he lay on the ground, to make sure.

I reached out, hissing in pain, and checked the dungeon sense. The mana count bounced fast as it refilled. I summoned a healing potion. Then—after biting the cork, yanking it out, and spitting it onto the ground—I chugged it, not wanting to waste the high-end one.

I hissed again in that weird pain and pleasure mix as my body was flash healed. Bullets and random links of armor, cloth, dirt, and who knew what all were forced out as I straightened.

That I'd been able to summon the potion here meant that the nearby area was a "safe" zone. Essentially, there were no enemies in proximity nor close contact with it, and I let out a long breath, before turning to Drak.

"You okay?" I asked him.

"Not so's you'd notice, no." He snorted. "Considering the crap we just went through, I was expecting at least a bed and a drink before I had to fight again."

"Me too." I grunted. "Keep your eyes open, all right? This area should be safe. I'm going to seal it all up, but don't shoot at anyone who doesn't shoot at you."

"Wait!" he snapped.

"What?"

"Who the hell are we fighting?" He shook his head. "I thought you lot were in the dungeon. This a coup?"

"Humans," I spat. "The ones dressed like this…" I kicked the nearby body. "They're from another group, trying to take over."

"So, do I shoot them if they turn up?" he asked.

"Just…stay as hidden as you can. If anyone shoots at you or me, kill them. Otherwise, stay hidden. I'm going to get us some reinforcements."

"Joy," he muttered, moving around and searching, clearly looking for a corner to hide in.

I moved to the stairs, shoving the broken banister and railing aside, and sat down with a grunt. Leaning back against the wall and closing my eyes, I slid into the dungeon sense.

"What's happening?" I asked Kelly, finding her hovering over the middle of the dungeon, a hundred or so meters up.

"Matt, goddamn you scared me!" she snapped, before reaching out and taking my hand in hers, more or less.

The dungeon sense was weird. You could touch each other, a bit, but it was more a sharing of feelings, of senses. And here, floating above the dungeon as the smoke drifted away, I felt her fear, her anger and shock over what had happened.

19

The east wall of the dungeon was down, and oh boy was it down. A huge section was just in ruin, great stone blocks shattered and tumbled this way and that, with the rear of the cathedral and the nearby buildings—the training dungeon and the living quarters—damaged.

Beyond that, and leading up to the pool, were dozens of dead, mostly ours. They were advanced kobolds and humans.

The weapons emplacements that had been set up to protect the dungeon had been taken out in the first wave as well.

Even as we looked, a handful of soldiers took up positions, settling in and apparently getting ready to advance again as a second force moved in.

These were soldiers as well, and I could clearly see the snipers moving up on the buildings nearby. It took a few seconds for me to understand what the hell had happened, and when I finally got it, I let out a relieved breath.

"We're a wild card," Kelly said, realizing it at the same time, if not before I did. "They had no clue what we could do, after everything we've done. So while they needed to take the dungeon quickly, they couldn't risk throwing their entire force at us all at once."

"So they sent in a strike force to take a foothold, and here comes the real deal," I growled.

"They were probably worried we might kill them all with some magic, so they sent the strike force in. If they managed to do…whatever they were trying to do, then great. If not, and they died? It's bad, but not as bad as if the entire force dies. Lastly, if we'd hit them with a bomb or something, or magically killed them all inside the walls, the main force could retreat."

"So they sacrificed the advanced force for intel and to gain a foothold, not knowing just how close they came to taking the dungeon," I finished for her.

"Exactly, and now they're inside the walls." She shook her head. "They're too close for me to be able to summon right there, but they have to know this isn't going to work, right? I mean, we can summon more minions now…"

I checked the mana and nodded, also verifying the local situation. The team that was sent to Saltwell Park—apparently under Chris's leadership—was running back already. They were fifteen minutes or so away, but they were coming fast.

Jack was on his way as well. The damn automaton was always in the wrong place at the wrong time. He was a mile and a half to the north, but moving quickly. I winced at the reading I was getting from him.

37% operational. Combat capacity severely degraded.

There was more, though, as we had dozens of other dungeon creatures, advanced kobolds and not, ranging from Starr the shaman, who was even now creeping through the farm, casting a spell at the incoming human forces, to Beta, who was gathering her forces to slaughter them all.

Impai were flying inward, spawned in their dozens. Kelly had set a hundred of them to be summoned and sent in, knowing that although they were easily killed, each bullet one caught was a bullet that one of our people didn't have to worry about.

We had forty-seven thousand mana, and although that wasn't a huge amount, it was more than we needed for this fight, I knew.

I reached out, summoning ten lesser ghasts and sending them around the outside of the ziggurat, letting them stream down the side of the building that led between it and the destroyed outer wall, in stealth.

That was four thousand mana, that was all. Sure, they were the "lesser" variants, but they were also terrifying and had chameleon-like stealth abilities.

Kelly added in ten more advanced kobolds, at two and a half thousand each. That was another twenty-five thousand. But they were at least twice as strong as the average human, and both faster and more deadly. They sprinted out of sight of the incoming enemy, even as another series of small glittering collections of light appeared.

This was the goblins, five magelings and five smashers, with the magelings racing toward the enemy. Two triggered their signature spell Disgust, drawing all the fire that wasn't being directed at the impai. The other three hid in readiness to disrupt any advances attempted.

The goblins were so cheap it was barely worth noticing the cost. All told, it was less than a single advanced kobold. But the smashers weren't there to fight.

They lumbered forward, grabbing the dead soldiers and dragging them out of sight, dumping them where Beta and her kobolds could strip them, gathering the weapons and making sure they were ready.

Beta and the core of her small team had already trained with assault rifles. Although they were awkward for them—their claws barely fit in the firing guard—they could use them, and they were incredibly pissed off right now.

Then we summoned a brace of ten wraiths and sent them all winging their way toward the snipers.

Four hundred mana a pop, but that was still only four thousand points. The cost was negligible.

I could feel it as Barry appeared, joining us in the dungeon sense.

"What the hell happened?" He stared down, aghast at the damage.

"Looks like the army lads don't want to be friends," I spat.

"Fuck's sake." He shook his head. "This makes no sense! Why wait until now and then attack?"

"Because we were at our weakest," Kelly snapped. "Someone knew, and they told them!"

"What happened?" I asked again, having gotten only a very bare-bones account of the recent events as I left the trial dungeon.

"A marine made it to the walls yesterday, injured and broken, the only survivor of his platoon," Kelly summarized. "Mike and Griffiths believed the risk of trying to capture some of the enemy and see if they could save them was worth it. But just in case, considering it was another group of soldiers in full battle rattle who'd attacked them, we decided that if they were to go, they needed to take overwhelming force."

"Right?" I agreed.

"He said that they'd passed Otterburn garrison." Kelly went on. "We knew from Griffiths that something was going on there already, so knowing that they were ambushing incoming troops that passed there, we needed to know what was going on. Because the soldiers were grey skinned, with black eyes and seemingly

21

not thinking straight—not zombies, but close to it—we decided that the best thing to do was to try to capture some of them and see if we could learn more."

"Uh-huh," I agreed, watching as the impai were taken down in a hail of fire, and just as quickly replaced.

The wraiths were sliding around the outside, headed to the snipers' positions but taking a wide swing to try to get to them unseen.

"So we agreed to send them. We didn't know how long you'd be out of it in the dungeon. I mean, what the hell!" Kelly finished, gesturing at the training, and now trial dungeon in disgust. "It locked me out, locked all of us out, and you in! We can't use it anymore, not when we can't trust it, and then—"

"Kelly, it's okay!" I interrupted her, wanting to hold her, to make her see that it was all okay, when I knew that it really wasn't at all. "It's a trial section, just for the Dungeon Lord, as near as I can tell."

"Well, it's a stupid trial!" she snapped, gesturing out at the smoke and fire, the shouts and gunfire. "We could have lost everything while you were in there, and, and..."

"And it's my fault," Barry added.

"What?" I asked, confused.

"It's my fault," he repeated. "Chris and the others...I suggested coming here. I didn't think there was any risk to the dungeon. After all, there's fuck all left in the area that we knew about, certainly nothing that could make it in to attack before we could get there from here, anyway."

"So you suggested leaving the dungeon undefended?" I asked grimly.

"No!" he snapped. "Well, yes..."

"It wasn't his fault." Kelly sighed. "He asked me if I thought it was a good idea, and while yeah, sure, there were issues and concerns with the others being away, it just didn't seem like a big thing."

"It shouldn't have been," I agreed, frowning. "What happened to the roaming patrols? I mean, we'd just gotten them back up and going, hadn't we?"

"We did." Kelly nodded. "We had them going, more corpse lords on the walls, wraiths, the works, and then suddenly, literally over about a handful of minutes, they were all killed."

"A coordinated attack?" I asked.

"A very well coordinated one, one that kicked off right as we were at our very weakest. And at the same time, the communication boards in the park were sabotaged," Barry admitted. "We caught one of them, but there were at least three others involved, and someone here had to be in on it as well."

"Who?" I asked grimly.

"Do you really need to ask?" He shook his head. "Merriman, or at least his friends who stayed."

"You've got them still?" I asked. "Arrested, I mean?"

"One of them, and two others being watched." He waved a hand in the direction of the incoming forces. "It was one of them who suggested the event at the park, to show the people who stayed behind, who didn't volunteer, what they'd missed out on." He paused, sucking in a breath and going on. "Well, not one of them, anyway. It was a daughter, and she'd been saying it publicly, making it sound like she was trying to help recruit for us. It seemed...shit, it seemed like a good idea, all right?"

"It's my fault," Kelly said firmly. "I made the final decision."

"It is," I agreed, realizing that we were just wasting time, and got a look from them both. "Hey, I've done worse," I pointed out. "This is leadership. It's what it means to be in charge. It's shitty and people die, but the thing you both keep saying to me? It's about how many you save, not how many you lose."

"This was an assault. It was going to happen one way or another. As it is? At least we know about it, and they weren't expecting it to go the way it has. If we can take these fuckers down? We get a load of guns and we're a step closer to making the area safe, so fuck it. Let's deal with it and move on."

I hated saying it, but they'd said it to me, and it helped at the time.

When the shit hit the fan, if everyone said "there, there" and made out it wasn't your fault, you just blamed yourself more. You needed to be an adult and step up, accept the responsibility and move on, or else you learned nothing and you got stuck in a spiral of self-doubt.

I'd discovered that the hard way.

"So, now what?" Barry asked after a long minute of silence where we watched the forces moving in.

"I need to get out there…" I muttered.

"No, you don't," Kelly snapped. "You need to lead the dungeon, and they've got snipers. They used them all at once to take most of the defenders down—the corpse lords, then the wall. They planned this, and they're going to be waiting for you to show up. There's no way this ends well if a sniper takes you down with a headshot. This is a fight you win by staying in here."

I struggled with it, but ultimately, I agreed, as much as it made me feel like a coward.

The wraiths were being taken out now, as were the impai, and as quickly as they were, it was clear that the enemy didn't have unlimited ammunition. The delays between shots grew longer and longer.

As we watched, we marked up the sniper roosts, and ten more wraiths were created for each spot, then sent winging their way forward.

Kelly gave them specific orders: if the enemy surrendered, they were to take their weapons and wait, and one of us would take over; otherwise, it was kill time.

It wasn't long before the snipers pulled back. Flares were fired into the air and the advancing soldiers slowed, having just moved into the dungeon, leapfrogging from cover to cover.

That was when the ghasts arrived.

The team of ten hit from the side, shredding through the first few soldiers before being taken down by concentrated fire and a handful of grenades.

The element of surprise was gone, sure, but as we summoned more and more? It didn't matter.

Ghasts, skeletal archers, corpse lords, goblins, impai, and more—all were sent against them to drain their reserves and gain us the time we needed, as the people of the park absorbed more and more to power our summons.

Fifteen minutes after I'd burst from the dungeon and into the fight, the soldiers tried to retreat, cut down to half their size by their losses. That was when Beta and her kobolds marched out, stolen assault rifles cradled in their arms, with a clear desire to kill the interlopers.

A single wraith floated down from above toward them, holding a simple whiteboard in its hands, a message hastily scrawled on it.

Surrender, or die.

The whiteboard probably wouldn't have done it. Neither would merely being surrounded, with weapons running low on ammunition.

No, what did it was the sight of the humans who stood up on the rooftops on all sides, weapons raised, alongside their kobold counterparts, ready to open fire, showing that it wasn't in fact a dungeon full of monsters they were assaulting.

CHAPTER TWO

An hour after the attack had been stopped dead, I was at the table in the "real" council chambers, the one that we used rather than the public-facing one that Clarissa and her team had. John was on my right, Kelly on my left, Barry and Chris on either side of them, and a dozen more, including Clarissa, Ashley, Dante, and Markus. We faced the leader of the prisoners, who stared straight ahead, back ramrod straight, as he refused to tell us anything beyond his name and rank.

He was also clearly bothered by the fact that both Kilo and Beta sat at the table, and on entry had been noticeably trying to avoid looking at them at all.

"Well." I sighed after a few seconds. "This wasn't what I had in mind this morning when I got up."

"That's an understatement." Chris snorted. "I was on watch. You looked downright cheerful when you first woke up, and having seen you greet a day before, that was practically unique."

"Before we get diverted by the witty repartee…" John sighed. "I'm going to make a suggestion. The major here clearly feels he's been taken as a prisoner of war—"

"Which he fuckin' has," I interrupted.

"Which he has *not*," John corrected. "He attacked us without warning, any formal declaration of hostilities, or any legal basis. As such, before he and his entire team are executed for murder and attempted murder, he deserves the chance to speak up in his defense."

"Murder!" The major gasped. "We—" He slammed his mouth shut and glared at us, and this time it was Aly who spoke up.

"You attacked both the human and non-human residents of the dungeon, without reason, without warning, and without any explanation. *Murdering* them as they went about their lives. If Captain Griffiths, one of the members of this council and a soldier of the Coldstream Guard, was here, I've no doubt he'd be ashamed of you. God knows that as the wife of a special forces soldier, I'm disgusted that you were ever permitted to wear that uniform."

He stood there for a solid minute, jaw clenched and staring straight ahead, not responding, before I finally took over.

"Okay then, Major, let's see how much of this I can guess, shall we? We've already had a conversation with a few members of your little cabal, so how about this…you stop me when I get one wrong?" I suggested.

"You were approached by a group of those we banished from the dungeon, not sure when or how, but they made you aware that not only were we here, but

I've no doubt that we were doing something terrible. Considering they were banished from here when they tried to carry out a coup, and in the process injured a heavily pregnant woman, before refusing to serve in any way to make amends, I'd guess I was eating babies or some such?" I quirked an eyebrow at him in sardonic amusement, as I went on.

"At some point, they—or you—made the plan that you'd attack the dungeon, probably to try to take it over for yourselves, and that after that, you'd, well…" I shrugged. "Fuck knows what you'd do, really. The first thing you'd probably do is panic, considering that if I die, so does the dungeon."

That bit wasn't true, but it was a convenient lie to try to keep people from trying to take over.

"Then, once I was dead and the dungeon dies, you'd definitely panic, considering one of the primary jobs of the dungeon is to purify the mana in the area. What that means, if you're not up to speed on the new realities of life, is that all the creatures, the monsters and crap that are roaming and killing people in the area currently? They're at that level where they're suppressed and kept at a lower level by the dungeon.

"They'd jump in number and strength by a massive margin. Then, with no dungeon, the walls would start collapsing, the creatures all around going mad and rising up, and several *thousand* people who were being protected and fed by the dungeon no longer having that, I'm guessing you'd be trying to set yourself up as a warlord."

"I'm no warlord!" the major snapped, finally glaring at me. "I'm Major Albert Stevenson of the British Army, Fifth Fusiliers—"

"You're a fucking disgrace!" Barry snapped, slamming a palm down on the tabletop before him and sitting up, glaring at the officer. "*I* served. Hell, at least half of the dungeon has, or is related to someone who did! I'm in charge of Saltwell Park, thousands of people who, until this man…" He pointed at me.

"Until he led the way into the park. Back then, he didn't have a damn dungeon. And without weapons or anything else, we were all starving! He took out the gangs! He gave us a place to raise crops, created the beginning of a community and made us band together. Then you know what he did?"

"Do tell," the major sneered.

"HE FUCKED OFF!" Barry roared. "He fucked off and left us to make our own goddamn decisions, to survive or not by our own hand. *After* he'd given us the means to make sure we stood a chance! Not like you shitebags, hiding with your families all nice and safe in the barracks! You had the weapons, the gear— fuck's sake, you had the legal authority and the *responsibility* to help back then!"

"We have that authority still—" the major started, only to be cut off.

"No!" Barry shouted. "No, you fucking don't! Authority comes from us giving it to you, from the agreement that you'll do your part. Authority not exercised does not exist! We believed that you'd come and you'd help. You had *everything* we needed, and where the fuck were you? You were hiding! Looking after yourselves when all the world went to shit!"

"He left you—" the major started, gesturing to me.

"HE HAD NO RESPONSIBILITY!" the former marine thundered, slamming his hand down on the desk again and making drinks bounce all across it.

"Barry…" I said softly. "It's okay, mate."

"No!" he snapped. "No, it goddamn isn't. You left us, yeah, but you fought for us all first. You owed us nothing and you still left us weapons, and set us up to make a damn settlement. When I needed you, when we all needed you, you came back. You fed our people and you built all of this! You fought and bled for us all, and this streak o' yellow piss did nothing! He came out when he thought he could get something for himself and that's it!"

"WE came out to save YOU!" the major bellowed back eventually, turning and gesturing with his manacled hands. "We came to protect you, to save you, from HIM!"

I looked at the finger pointed at me, and I snorted.

"Tell me, anyone want me to step down? To try to hand the dungeon over? I'll fuck off right now…"

"Don't you dare." Clarissa was the first to respond. "I mean it, Matt. Don't you dare." She cleared her throat and looked from the major to me, and around the room before going on. "Right, I think we can all see what's going on here. So, let's lay it out from our side, and the major can explain himself and we can address what we learn. Or he chooses not to, in which case, he accepts that he will be treated as a murderer and a warlord, and whatever punishment the Dungeon Lord declares is just." She took a deep breath and went on.

"Matt and his friend Chris here rescued us, several hundred in number, from the Hillsong Church, several weeks ago. He recruited us to fill roles in the dungeon, and he provided food, lodging, and mainly he's provided safety. I say mainly because a significant number have died."

I winced at that, and she went on.

"He has, however, never asked us to take a risk he wouldn't. And had we not taken his offer of safety and protection, we'd *all* be dead. All of us, I have no doubt. So, is he a saint? No. Is he a warlord, carving out his own personal fiefdom? Yes, he probably is."

I sat up straighter, opening my mouth to object, and she waved me to silence.

"You don't hold democratic votes, Matt, therefore you're forcing your authority on the people. That's a reality of life. The difference is, however, you don't *need* to. To hold a vote, I mean. The old world, as much as I miss it, is gone. The place we live now is ruled by different beasts. So, tell me, if we turned up to your barracks, Major, and asked to be allowed to come inside, would you let us?"

"It would depend on what you could bring to the community," he hedged. "There are limited resources, after all."

"Exactly. And let's say, hypothetically, if you decided that several hundred of us, without anything to bring to the table besides hungry mouths, were to be allowed in, and we then insisted that you run an election to have the right to tell us what to do, inside your barracks and that we would not be contributing in any manner unless you agree to our demands, what would the response be?"

"We'd offer you the choice of leaving or rethinking your actions," he said firmly. "If you choose to live under our roof, you accept that you live by military rule, and—"

"And that's okay for you but not for us?" Barry growled. "We don't even enforce that level of discipline on people, and we take all that come to us, as long as they're willing to follow laws they can vote on, and are willing to contribute."

"We are soldiers of the British Army," the major snapped. "We have the legal authority to—"

"Well, that's a very good point, actually. You have the legal authority to detain, imprison, and punish members of the specific armed service that you belong to, and to enforce those rules upon civilians who trespass on your bases," John said formally, straightening up. "What you do *not* have is the authority to enforce military rules, doctrine, or martial law on the public."

That was a point, I realized, as I looked from John to the major. That fucker had literally no authority to do anything off the base or inside the country, did he? I'd never looked at it, but for example, the American army couldn't be deployed inside the continental US, as far as I knew. Sure, there'd be ways and means, and it wasn't like they'd be just sitting on their hands over there, illegal or not, but if this dickhead wanted to go down that route, he'd picked the wrong crowd for it.

"Whereas I, as a member of the police force for the public authority, have the right and responsibility to enforce any rules that are legally bearing on any and all individuals in areas that the public authority extends to." John went on, staring daggers at the major.

"That's a mouthful," I muttered, before grunting as Kelly elbowed me into silence.

"I was a legal advisor for the Gateshead court," Kelly said next. "Before all of this, before the literal end of the world, I advised the judges and magistrates of the local authority on the punishments that were available and appropriate. So, let's look at this from a legal point of view."

"Go on," the major said slowly.

"I don't need your permission," she snapped at him coldly. "First, I have a background in law, and the application of it, specifically in this geographical area. Second, we have a member of the local police force, who agrees the laws we have are just and correct, and applies them equally to all. This includes the Dungeon Lord, who—and I'll be clear—wanted to execute the same people I believe are advising you, and who set up this entire situation."

"Gerald and whatsherface?" I asked, looking at her and getting a nod.

"Sharon, yes," she agreed. "Those two and Merriman, according to the information we have." The mention of their names caused the major to narrow his eyes as she went on. "Regardless, the Dungeon Lord *wanted* to enforce his own brand of justice on them, and instead agreed to banishment when the legal points were raised."

Chris shook his head at that. "Shoulda fuckin' hung 'em," he muttered under his breath.

"So, legally, outside of your barracks, and without a formal declaration of martial law, you have no authority. Here we, legally, do. Be that under our own rights as citizens, or as members of the dungeon of Newcastle. That's the first point. Secondly, you attacked us. Without discussion, without any attempt to establish peaceful contact, you attacked—and killed—dozens of our people. There *will* be an accounting for that, Major, believe me." She paused to glare at him.

"Lastly, we won," she said. "Possession is nine-tenths of the law. And we're not stupid, Major. We could have killed you all three times over with ease. The reason we lost as many as we did was that we were trying to capture you, to find out what was happening. If the tables were turned, I have no doubt that we'd not be standing there, justifying our actions. At best, there'd be a show trial for some of us, but for those of us who can control the dungeon? We'd have been executed quickly and quietly."

"So what's your point?" the major said after several seconds. "I can see your position—it's ridiculous, but even with that legal framework to back it up, a court would laugh it out. In our case, we were attempting to rescue innocent women and children being prepared for sacrifice. The gang members and self-styled Dungeon Lord who have been raping and pillaging the area were to be captured if possible, and killed on the spot if not. Those were the orders I issued, and I stand by them."

"And that you hid and waited until your fellow soldiers left on a rescue mission? One that you could have damn well helped with?" Barry asked.

"Common sense," he said firmly. "We don't know if they're real soldiers or not. If they are, when they returned, and found us in place and our authority laid down, they would have had the choice to rejoin the fold, albeit under strict monitoring to ensure they had not committed any crimes.

"If they were found to be imposters, they'd be executed...again, should they have committed crimes. Otherwise, they'd be assessed on a case-by-case basis. Facing them while they were here? Even with our authority to act, there would have been losses on both sides. No reason to permit that," he finished, and I stared at him.

"Do you even understand what happened here?" I asked him, and he cocked an eyebrow at me, waiting for me to go on. "Those idiots tried to seize power from us, then came to you and lied. 'Innocent women and children,' that's what you said. There's plenty here, innocent men too, and they're living the best life they can under the circumstances, especially considering the war that's coming."

"They lied to you, or you're lying now to justify your actions. But, regardless, you attacked us, when we were at our weakest, and we still steamrollered you. Want to guess what's going to happen when we're at our strongest?"

"You'll attack us. Then, should you survive, you'll attempt to inflict your rule across the area," he said.

"'Inflict.'" I snorted. "Fuck's sake. All right, I don't know if you're intentionally wasting my time or just like going around in circles. Let's make it simple. You attacked and murdered my settlement and people. Regardless of your good intentions, if you thought you were rescuing people, all you had to do was send in one goddamn person to see what was actually happening. You didn't bother. You chose to attack us. Do you have anything to say in your defense?"

"Fuck you," he said, with a faint sneer. "I refuse to accept your authority. I am a member of the British Army and—"

"Fuck it." I grunted, focusing and summoning a corpse lord directly behind the major.

The reflected light and brightness appearing behind him shut him up as he spun around. His jaw dropped at the sight of the massive skeletal construction towering over him.

"Take him to the jail," I ordered it, getting a wince from John as the corpse lord reached out, and he quickly interjected more orders, primarily to do with where that jail was—I still hadn't bothered to find out what we'd been using for it—and the treatment of the prisoner now that the corpse lord had him.

The summoned minion looked to me, and I nodded, interjecting the need to follow John's added details, before grinning as it slammed one large hand down atop the major's head and dragged him, struggling, from the room by that handhold.

That hadn't been intentional, but I also didn't correct it, and neither did anyone else.

"Well, now what?" I asked into the sudden silence.

"Now you tell us what the hell happened, boy, and we make plans to deal with the soldiers on our doorstep, our new prisoners, and anything else that's come up since you left to run the dungeon," Clarissa suggested gruffly.

"Point." I sighed, shaking my head as I glanced after the major. "Right, this is going to take some explaining, but I'll go over the highlights real quick, as I don't think we've got long to sort this shit out." I took a deep breath, wondering where to begin.

"So, the trial dungeon, let's start there," I muttered. "Essentially, the Cinthians considered that the Dungeon Lords might not want to play once they gained their own dungeons, so as an added incentive, they added the trial dungeon."

"It's literally what it sounds like, a dungeon that's a fuckin' hell of a trial, but where in the normal dungeon you can leave at any time, in the trial dungeon you can't. First of all, on entry you get the option to run the dungeon on your own for a massively enhanced reward, or as a Dungeon Lord, I can summon a handful of minions using a limited pool of points."

"In my case, that was ten thousand, and I decided I'd try to do it alone. That clearly didn't work out, as any of you watching would have seen. Secondly, and the main reason that didn't work out, was that the beings summoned to fight in the trial dungeon aren't the usual minions. Drak, for example? The kobold I summoned and left the dungeon with me at the end of the run? He's a criminal. All the souls that are bound to the trial dungeon are."

"What?" John straightened up, looking just as concerned as the others suddenly did.

"It gets better," I assured them all. "So, first of all, criminals. They're offered a choice of death when their crime is bad enough, or the dungeon. Then, once in the dungeon, they get to die over and over until their crime has been atoned for. Sure, the first thought is that it's death regardless—what more have you got to lose if you just choose death? Well, it's simple. You serve for the requisite number of deaths, and then you're released. From what he said, I got the feeling that his 'real' original body is on his home world somewhere, and that he'll be released once he hits those deaths but that might be me missing something." I shook my head. "He wasn't exactly happy talking about all the details, and we didn't have a lot of free time in there."

"It looked like a bad one," Kelly acknowledged, reaching out under the table to take my hand in hers.

"It wasn't fun," I admitted. "So, all the minions are criminals, and all have souls. For each death, they lose one of the markers on their soul. If, say it's ten markers, they die ten times, or help a Dungeon Lord to the end of the dungeon twice, and they're set free. Alternatively, if they're a defender and they kill the Dungeon Lord, that's five deaths off their total as well."

"And how many does this Drak have outstanding, and do we know what his crime was?" John asked.

"He apparently fucked and got his imperial princess pregnant. The emperor took that badly, and when he couldn't have him executed in a painful way, changed the usual death count for him to a thousand."

"He has to die a thousand times for that?" Chris whistled, shaking his head. "I mean, I know sometimes you think it's worth a risk to get——" He broke off at the glare Clarissa was giving him, then winced as his girlfriend Becky apparently grabbed something under the table. "Okay! Okay!" He mimed zipping his mouth shut.

"Thanks." I smiled, leaving it to them to guess who I was thanking. "So, yeah, he basically fought alongside me, as did Ciara, the fairy I summoned, who——"

"She seemed to take issue with you summoning her?" Markus asked.

"Oh yeah." I nodded. "She was one of those I'd literally just killed. I'd stood on one of her friends, and she took that personally."

"I wonder why," Becky muttered.

"Well, I figured that, first, she was my damn enemy, and second, she was mortally wounded and I couldn't heal her, so it was better to put her out of her misery." I shrugged. "Apparently that didn't go down well."

There were a few winces around the table at that, and I went on.

"So anyway, we did the run, looted what we could, including this…" I lifted the bag of holding and shook it, grinning as Finn looked at it blankly, then gasped, his eyes going wide.

"You're shitting me!" He reached out, and I laughed, tossing it to him. "Holy crap, it's real!" he whispered, turning it this way and that and looking it over.

"For those who haven't figured it out, or don't have an identify skill or spell, that's a bag of holding," I explained. "Literally a magic bag that can hold hundreds of kilos of weight and an incredible amount of gear, all in a tiny package."

"Can we reproduce this?" Finn was asking, and I shrugged.

"I hope so, and I'll try, but after this." I reached out, and he reluctantly handed it back, only for Kelly to snag it and start looking it over before I could reattach it to my belt.

"So, as I was saying, there was a lot of fighting, and when we reached the end, this was one of the rewards, as was access to a new race for the dungeon—Dvorks, who are apparently the dungeon version of dwarves, incredible ship builders and engineers, but high-gravity beings. They've been driven to extinction by the Orcan. As such, they're basically a race of seriously depressed alcoholics. Incredible potential, but hard to keep off the drink long enough to get the job done."

31

"Two rewards, and those mana crystals?" Kelly nodded. "Not bad, but still, a hell of a risk."

"I also got a skill boost," I admitted. "Thirty levels into two skills of my choice, so I could add, say, twenty-nine into something like firearms and become a legend with them, and one into anything else, or whatever mix I want." I shrugged. "It'll be a useful bonus."

"Any skill?" Chris asked, before wincing as Becky moved to grab something again, I guessed. "Wait!" he implored, looking from her to Clarissa and back. "I'm not being an idiot—honest question!"

"Yeah, I think so?" I shrugged again. "Why?"

"Can it be any skill," he repeated, "or does it have to be a skill you already have?"

"I…I don't know." I frowned. "I'd not thought about it."

"So check it out," he suggested. "Try getting a point in a skill you don't have, like, I don't know, doing anime-style tattoos."

"And just like that, we're back to the stupid suggestions." I snorted. "Seriously, though, that's a good point." I nodded. "Thanks, dude."

"You were looking at Glassblowing," Aly suggested. "Could you take that for, say, ten points? That way you've not wasted the skill, and…wait, no!"

"No?"

"No, take it for one point," she suggested. "Take it for a single point. Then practice the skill naturally for a few days…get the first few levels, the ones that are the easiest to get that way, and then boost it using those points when you reach a plateau."

"Or, and I'm just putting this out there, could you give it to another?" Finn asked, looking hungrily at the ball that I'd pulled from the bag of holding. "I'm not saying me, don't worry, but could you give it to a crafter and boost them? I know you're not going to want to—you could gain a lot, after all—but do you have time to do glassblowing?"

"We need a glassblower," I said. "And I mean a dedicated one, not just someone who'll put up with doing a bit of it in order to get this." I pressed the button on the top of the ball. The sides folded down, sliding into the lower half, and revealed a monocle in the middle of the ball, ready to be used.

"Yeah, but what if you gave that to, say—" Finn started to ask.

"If I give it away, it'll be to someone who doesn't currently have an ability as a crafter," I clarified. "That way we're not losing a crafter in one of the other positions. Seriously, though, I don't know if I could give it away, and I'd be tempted to give it to a fighter if I could."

"A fighter! But—"

"But we could take a gifted sniper and make them into a god," I explained. "A really good sniper could make all the difference in this war—if we had a damn sniper rifle, anyway. You saw the damage they did to us."

"We've got a few," Aly admitted. "The wraiths managed to kill two snipers, and we already had a rifle in storage. We'd just ran out of ammunition for it."

"And the others?" I asked.

"Driven off. We think we captured or killed three-quarters of the assault force. But, looking at the potential numbers that a full barracks would have, and the things that Mike's said before about that base, there could be another hundred or more soldiers there, plus their families. It won't be easy to take it over." Aly sighed.

"What about a nuke?" I joked bitterly. "Fuck them, they started this—"

"And we're not finishing it like that," Kelly said firmly. "Come on, Matt, we know you. You'd not want that either."

"Maybe not, but they started this shit," I groused.

"Maybe they did. But if we'd gone to them before all of this, maybe it'd have never come to this," Kelly said.

I looked at her in shock, remembering that she'd argued against going to them before.

"Or maybe they'd have attacked us then." She went on. "Matt, we don't know what could have been. All we can do is deal with the things that are in front of us, and that includes that idiot of a major. So, is there anything else we need to know about the dungeon? Are you unable to use it, or it'll be a trial dungeon, or is that the case for everyone?"

"I don't know," I admitted. "When I entered it, I was given a choice to do the trial dungeon, and I had no clue what I was doing, so I said yes. Chances are, I can avoid it in the future, but the one thing that's definitely happening next time is if I do it again, I go in loaded for bear."

"Or don't go back in," Chris suggested. "Or take a team."

"If I go in on my own, I get better rewards," I replied. "And next time I do it, I do it with a lot better equipment. That's no slight against the armor you made me, Aly." I nodded to her. "It kept me alive, but next time I go in with a rail gun and a load of healing potions. If I could summon Ciara or her sisters? I would, though. She was helpful and while, yeah, she's a criminal, it seems like a lot of the galaxy that have access to the dungeon are using it to put people they don't like in there as well."

"Can we trust her?" Kelly asked. "Or any fairy?"

"Apparently, I'd need to give her the cybernetic implants to grant her access to the dungeon controls, and without those, I'd still need to intentionally put her over me in the control hierarchy. I'm not planning on doing either of those things, ever, so I guess we could look at summoning the fairies if we want," I admitted. "Moving on, though, the main advantages of the trial dungeon are that we can get things like this…"

I reached out and summoned one of the health potions I'd gotten in the dungeon.

It was a deeper red and gleamed more than the usual ones we'd managed to produce ourselves. But it was the description that really stood out.

Healing Potion	Potion
This is an average healing potion. It provides 2000 points of healing across 60 seconds and can be poured into a wound to directly concentrate the healing process and stop bleeding. Due to the strength of the potion, it will also have limited effect upon status modifiers, including but not limited to: poisoned, infected, gangrenous, and envenomed.	
Beware, stronger potions can be addictive…	
Durability 25/25	Potion Strength: Average

"Two *thousand* points of healing?" Ashley gasped, and I nodded, passing it to her.

"That's just one of the potions I got. The downside is that I was blocked from the dungeon sense while I was in there, until I got to a safe room. Once I was in there? I could make a copy into the dungeon, though they cost fifty goddamn thousand points of mana to create from just mana. I'd also gotten a pair of mana potions while I was in there, but I needed them or I'd not have gotten out alive, Sod's Law."

I reached into the bag when Kelly gave it back to me, and I pulled out the golden gem-encrusted necklace that I'd taken from one of the Daoine Sidhe. "I also got this, and a collection of weapons, including a set of daggers that steal mana." I laid the necklace on the table before us, then went on as I examined it.

"It's nothing special—the necklace, I mean—but it grants plus two to agility, which I guess is why they were wearing such gaudy shite."

I'd deliberately not lifted out the vampiric dagger, having already quietly taken care of that, reabsorbing it into the dungeon, then marking it as "restricted to Dungeon Lord only" and hiding it.

The few times I'd used it, I'd developed a need to use it again as quickly as possible. And even Drak, my damn ally, had looked like a viable target to me at that point.

I was making damn sure that fucker wasn't seen again.

"Anything else to add?" Aly asked, clearly making notes.

"Just that as much as it was a pain in the ass, and you can't leave straight away, if you reach a safe room, there's a lever you can pull. Once that's pulled, you can leave the dungeon with the loot you've gained. But if you make it to the end, you get a much better reward. There are also dungeon rewards, things that occasionally come attached to my quests.

"I had two of them for that run, and when I reached that end, that was when I got them. They were broken down into a set number of choices, and I picked from them, getting that monocle, the pattern for the Dvorks, and the bag of holding. Those things alone make it worth the run and the risk. But I'll need something that helps me deal with stealth fuckers before I'm willing to try it again.

"Oh!" I shook my head as a detail came back to me then. "There's also the option to 'chicken out' with the dungeon run. Basically give up everything you've got, including clothing and armor, etc., to the dungeon and it'll let you open the door. But anything that you sacrifice to the dungeon? It's wiped from the dungeon's memory and needs to be rediscovered. So armor and so on? All of that would be erased," I finished.

"Glad you didn't pick that," Aly muttered, then winced. "Sorry, Matt. If you'd had to, obviously…" She looked up at me, and I shook my head.

"If I'd had to, yeah, of course I would." I shrugged. "But I didn't. And considering the whole point of going in is to get experience and loot, sacrificing it is a bit of a crapshoot. Regardless, that's the trial dungeon. I don't *think* it'll be offered to others, but just in case, we make it clear that if it is, then they damn well say no."

"Would they get better rewards if they did it?" Chris asked. "I mean, if I took a team in, and…"

"You might." I nodded to him. "But considering the risks, I don't want to do it again. And if you do, then you're a fool, mate."

"Just being realistic." He sighed. "Anyway, glad you got out of there."

"Me too," I admitted. "Right, so that's the dungeon. I'm sure you'd have spoken up if there was any word from the team sent to the north, besides the goddamn firefight that could be distantly seen, so let's cover the park."

"Nothing to report." Barry shook his head. "I've got those who we think were involved in the destruction of the signs under watch or lock and key, and the rest of my people are either confused or seriously pissed off thanks to it. The parade— I don't know what else to call it—but the showing off of the trainees? That might have been done to try to cause issues, but it sure as shit failed at that."

"Really?" Clarissa asked.

"Oh yeah, people loved seeing the teams that only left them a week ago as they are now. Some can already do a little magic, but the difference in their lives is what got the majority excited. As soon as you're ready to take more, you'll have the volunteers. But regardless, we do need to talk about the improvements to the park sometime soon."

"Soon," I agreed with a sigh. "I'm sorry, Barry. I'm not pushing it down the road needlessly, but the—"

"The army, the damage to the dungeon, and the fucking way things are at the minute all mean we need to," he finished for me. "I know, Matt, and I understand. But if you don't want my park to become a penal colony, then you need to start sharing the wealth some more."

"We're looking at moving manufacturing or something similar," Finn admitted unhappily. "Something needs to be based in the park, and while I don't want to move, or travel back and forth if I don't have to…" He finished with a weak shrug that said all it needed to.

"We'll look at it," I promised. "Okay, with those sorted…Aly, Kelly, what's the situation with the dungeon?"

"Research is going as discussed. Upgrades to converters are being rolled out; conduits have been upgraded as well. It's taken us to almost two hundred and fifty thousand mana coming in a day now, not counting the absorbed mana from tearing the surrounding buildings apart, which is stable at around a hundred and fifty thousand a day."

"So four hundred thousand mana a day." I nodded. "That's impressive."

"It is," Aly agreed. "As discussed, though, to get the uncommon level of the crafting facilities researched and built, that's a hundred and fifty-five thousand in the cost of research, followed by another fifty thousand per setup. So that's two hundred and five thousand mana a day going to that project..." She paused, checking her notes as she went on.

"The blacksmith's is done, as is the glassblower, and the mechanist finished the day before yesterday. The armorer's was yesterday, and the tinker's should be done in an hour or two."

"It would have been," Kelly corrected. "While you were in the trial dungeon, it allowed research to continue, but it locked out the summoning of creatures, presumably to prevent us doing anything that might have helped you somehow. Instead, while food, general construction, and research went ahead, our forces stalemated. Now that the dungeon's unlocked again, we need to resummon our forces and repair the damage we've suffered."

"How are we with that?" I asked her.

"The wall is in progress," she admitted. "I started it literally as soon as I could. It should be done in roughly another fifteen minutes. As to the damage done to the buildings? That's something we'll address later. It was all minor, which is a testament to the buildings themselves."

"Oh?"

"The same weapons that were used to take down the outer wall were used on the buildings—thankfully not the cathedral, as that'd be a ruin if they had—but the housing and the edge of the training dungeon. The training dungeon repaired itself enough to make sure you weren't going to accidentally escape, then left the outside, which is fine, but the living quarters?" She gestured in the vague direction of the ziggurat.

"That place could hold off a nuke. The damage is basically scratches and soot marks more than anything." She shook her head. "We need to change all the walls to use that level of technology. Then, if the army tries again? It won't matter."

"My walls too," Barry added quickly.

"There's always fuckin' something," I muttered. "All right, we'll look at that. What about our forces?"

"That's the stumbling block," Kelly admitted. "We all spent a load of points in a rush to get the place defended again, but now what do we do? We've got hardly any forces again, quality ones I mean, and that means we can't just march on the army barracks now either. Unless you want to leave the dungeon undefended?"

"No," I said. "And the recruits..." I shook my head.

"They're not ready," Sarah said firmly. "You're not taking them into battle, not until they've had at least a month of training and they've run the training dungeon a time or two as a minimum."

"Exactly," I agreed, summoning another can of my energy drink and cracking it open as I thought. "We need to gather more forces, and fast, so it'll have to be the dungeon-born."

"And that's the issue," Kelly said. "We need to do that, but who do we summon, and how many?"

"Kobolds," Kilo suggested, holding a hand up uncertainly. "We help."

"You do, and I agree, Kilo." I nodded to him, noting the way that Beta still disliked talking when she could avoid it. "I'm thinking we summon two more teams of kobolds. We've got how many currently?"

"Twenty-three." Beta spoke up when I looked at her, and I waited.

Kilo spoke again. "We have Beta. Three magic…Starr, me, and Frost. Then nineteen kobold warriors."

I hesitated before asking the question. "The warriors…"

"All freshly birthed," Beta said with a growl. "All the experienced? Dead."

"Except for Psy," Kilo interjected and Aly nodded.

"Psy is the advanced kobold with the researcher perk. She's currently in the Parthenon."

"Fuck!" I banged my fists on the table; then, resting my elbows on it, I put my face in my hands and took a deep breath, mastering my instant response and need to fly to the goddamn barracks now and rip the fucking roof off.

They'd killed my experienced soldiers, depleted almost all the skilled teams I'd built and…

"Wait, what about the kobolds at the park?" I lifted my face from my hands, looking around. "Don't get me wrong, I'm glad Psy is okay, but the fighters?"

"They are common," Kilo said, and I glanced from him to Beta and back. "Unaware. All those who were aware, and alive? Dead."

"Fuck." I groaned. "Okay, so let's say two teams of advanced kobolds…"

"Three," Beta growled. "Asssssassssssins."

"Three teams," I agreed after a pause. "Five assassins, five mages, and another twenty advanced kobolds, with their gear…what's that costing?"

"Two and a half thousand for the standard kobolds, with another two hundred or so each for their gear. Assassins cost three thousand, and another five hundred for their gear. Mages…" Aly paused. "Are you wanting them to learn naturally or be boosted by the focal orbs?"

"Focal orbs," I said. "Don't get me wrong, I don't like that as a shortcut, I'd rather we learned the right way and didn't possibly stunt their growth an' shit, but as it is, we need them yesterday."

"Then we summon twenty-five fully aware advanced kobolds," Aly said. "Check the stats and affinities of the twenty-five and choose the most appropriate out of them for magic."

"Works for me." I nodded. "How much?"

"Twenty-five advanced kobolds comes in at sixty-two thousand five hundred mana, with five thousand more for gear. The kobold advanced warriors with their gear, which is a hell of a lot better, are five thousand each, though, so let's do them instead. Five assassins plus their gear at another…it's a hundred and forty-three thousand all told." She changed what she was saying as she leaped ahead in the working out.

"And we have that available now?" I asked, not bothering to look.

"We do."

"Do it then," I said, and Kelly nodded, settling back in her chair and reaching out to the dungeon. As the Mistress of Minions, this was more of her job now, I

37

guessed, anyway. "So, that's in progress, and so's the research, with the building under control. What's next?"

"Upgrades to the dungeon," Aly said, and I frowned.

"I thought we just covered that?"

"We covered the sensible stuff, repairing the walls and so on." She nodded.

"And?"

"Now we get to talk about the *fun* stuff." The smile that Aly gave me was anything but pleasant. "Next time some asshole comes looking for a fight? I want to be very sure they'll regret it."

CHAPTER THREE

"Go on." I settled back, watching her.

"We've been building and maintaining the dungeon with the plan that we're trying to look after everyone," Aly started with, and I nodded. "Well, I think that's where we've been going wrong."

"Oh God, Aly…" Kelly whispered, staring at her sister-in-law.

"No, Kell, they started this," Aly snapped. "They came to our home and they killed our people. We're going to be having more funerals, and all because some assholes can't get it in their heads that we're good people."

"Uh-huh?" I agreed. "So what's your solution?"

"We make it clear that they don't fuck with us under any circumstances in the future." Aly tapped one finger on the table. "Look, we can literally build anything we want here, right?"

"Yeah?"

"And people in the area think we're evil?"

"Apparently so." I nodded.

"So let's be evil." She shrugged. "They think we're evil? Fine! What's the one thing all evil overlords have?"

"Aly, this is madness, all right? We can't!" Kelly snapped. "Fuck's sake, give me a minute…" She waved at us as she clearly wasn't finished making the adjustments to summon the kobolds.

Beta stood, along with Kilo. "You ssssummon more?" She looked from Kelly to me.

"Yes." I nodded. "Kelly is summoning more kobolds."

"Where? We go."

I checked the dungeon systems and found that Kelly was summoning them in sets of five, along with their gear, directly outside, and I told the kobold. She nodded and left, with Kelly sighing and dismissing the interface a few seconds after the door had closed.

"Okay, that's most of the available mana gone, but it's done. Beta will have them in place and sorted in a few minutes, but the mages won't have a clue."

"Dante?" I looked across at him. "Can you go and see to that, please? You know where the focal orbs are, right?"

"I'll set the storeroom to allow you access," Aly offered. "It's downstairs here, third door on the left with the red banding. Go see what you need and find the orbs that'll suit best."

"I'll go." Dante nodded, clearly looking forward to playing with the orbs as much as anything else. "Ash?"

"Do you want me to go as well?" Ashley asked, looking from me to Kelly and Aly.

"No," I told her. "I'll have a job for you soon."

"Okay, I'll, uh, go sort the kobolds." Dante shrugged. "Should I teach a few of the humans as well? We've got some who're skilled in Fire, and it's not like I can't help them to learn with that path at least?"

"No more than five," I said. "Pick five out for a fast track and get them ready. Spend what you need to within reason and get ready for a fight as well, Dante."

"Got it." With that, he was off and out of the room.

I turned to the others, looking from Kelly to Aly. "Right, now what's this plan?"

"It's not a plan," Kelly said. "It's wish fulfillment and a dark joke more than anything!"

"It's not, and after this morning?" Aly replied hotly. "After this morning, anyone who's got a problem with it can go fuck themselves. Kell, Amy was out there this morning, walking around with Guido—*again*—when the shots started. She could have been killed, and that's the difference!"

"She's a child. She wouldn't have been a target—" Kelly tried to argue, and Aly cut her off.

"She could have been!" Aly shouted. "Fuck's sake, Kell, you're not a mother, not yet—you don't get it! She's my baby, and she was walking around the dungeon thinking she was safe, while she could have been shot! She was probably in the sights of at least one of those snipers this morning. She could be grabbed by some flying beast, or blown up by some asshole. She *could* have been a target or just collateral damage…I don't know. But what I *do* know? My plan means she couldn't be!"

"And it's not realistic!" Kelly snapped. "Aly, she's your daughter, and my niece! I love her and I'll damn well stab anyone who hurts her, right in the face, you know that! My point is the risk to everything we've made and the cost—we can't do it!"

"What's this?" I asked.

"Nothing!" Kelly said.

"A fortress!" Aly countered.

"It won't work!"

"It could!"

"We can't afford it!"

"We're getting closer by the day, and we do it in stages!"

"Fuck's sake, WHAT?!" I shouted, shocking them both out of their little private argument. "Shit, you both want to argue over this? Fine, you can go do it elsewhere, but tell us what it is first!"

"I…" Aly closed her eyes and took a deep breath, before going on. "I'm sorry, Matt. It's been a hard day, that's all."

"I'm sorry too," Kelly agreed. "Look, Matt, it's a solution. It's not one I like, and for good reasons, but listen to Aly. And when she's given you the brief version, I'll explain, all right?"

"Well, with that glowing recommendation…" Aly muttered, before holding a hand up and going on. "Okay, so look, my argument is twofold. First, we're getting shit on by people, such as the army dickheads, because they don't know us—they don't believe we're good. They decided that we have a dungeon, so we must be monsters. Sure, they were apparently egged on by your old neighbors and that councilor, but they jumped at the chance. They believed we were evil, or at least stupid and they could take what they wanted from us. That's the first point. They heard about us from others, and they made up their own mind, then attacked, okay?"

"Right," I agreed, not sure but curious where this was going. I shifted on the chair, wanting to just go get a goddamn shower.

"Well, they saw the high walls, and they climbed up in other buildings in the area and looked over. They used them as sniper nests and they attacked us, because they believed they had a chance and decided to take it."

"Uh-huh."

"So what I'm saying is that we need to make it clear that they damn well don't have a chance, okay?" Aly went on passionately. "I don't like this, Matt, to be clear. I thought we were doing the right thing before, but this? This just sent me right over the edge into 'mother bear mode.' Amy could have been killed, and it'd have been easy for that to happen. All she had to do was step out of the wrong door when they were attacking, and that's it, she's gone.

"They had assassins inside our walls, okay? They planted explosives on both sides of that wall. That means that stealthed goddamn assassins were inside our walls and we had no clue, Matt!" That last bit came out shrill, and by the look on her face as she composed herself, she knew it.

"All I'm saying—and I didn't like this, I still don't, but I think it's right—is that if they think we're evil, then we embrace that image."

"What?" I had not been expecting that at all.

"Like I said before…what does the evil overlord always have, Matt?" She went on quickly. "Not just the jackbooted thugs, I mean. They've always got the armies and the goddamn fortresses! All I'm saying is that we need to quit it with the half measures! If the walls were two hundred meters taller? With towers at each corner, armed guards, and something more like antiaircraft guns or rail guns, instead of the crossbows? The real bad guys wouldn't *dare* start shit with us, okay? You say you want to help people?" She stopped, shaking her head and dashing tears from her eyes.

I suddenly realized where all of this was coming from. She was terrified, and barely holding herself together.

"You want to help people?" she repeated. "Fine! We help them. We don't just do that here either—we do it at the park. We give it big walls as well, and we help *our* people first! We make them safe. We stop helping other people. We draw a goddamn line around the land we've got and we say 'this far and no more' and we damn well protect that! Fuck the rest of the world!

"They want to fight and be assholes? They want to be terrorists and rapists and murderers? That's their choice! It's not our place to goddamn save everyone, and I'm sick of it, Matt! I can't sleep, I can't eat… Mike might be dead. Right now he might be…" She broke off with a sob, and tears started to stream down her face.

Before I could react, Kelly was there, already taking her in her arms as Aly broke down.

41

Silence reigned as Kelly held Aly, whispering to her and stroking her hair while her sister-in-law literally fell apart, sobbing her heart out.

We all looked at one another, not sure where to be, if we should all get up and leave, or send her away, or wait for her to get over things on her own.

As usual, it was Clarissa who was the voice of reason in this. She stood, moving around the table and drawing Aly's chair back, helping the younger woman to her feet and taking her hand.

"Aly, you and I are going to go elsewhere, have some tea, and talk. Then, when you're ready, you can return. But for now, there's nowhere else you're needed. Come with me, please, dear."

Aly could barely speak for the tears, and with Kelly's help, the three of them left the room, the door clicking as it closed behind them.

"Don't you dare say a word," Becky whispered to Chris.

"Don't be ridiculous," Chris whispered back. "I play the clown, but I'm not a fucking idiot."

"We know." I said it for all of us. "There's times when you put your foot in your mouth, brother, but I know a lot of the time you do it deliberately, to defuse things."

"Don't tell anyone. It'll ruin my damn image." He grunted. "Damn, I knew she'd been pushing herself, but still…"

"It's the stress," Markus said. "Stress can be the straw that breaks the camel's back. A tiny thing, nothing in the great scheme of things, can be all that sends us into meltdown at times, and she has incredible stress right now."

"And having that attack this morning and her husband out there isn't a small thing," I finished for him. "All right, people, I don't think the whole 'let's be evil overlords' was a serious suggestion, but just in case, let's take a minute to think it over. Knowing Aly, she was saying it that way to make us consider it, and to show the mental images. A fortress? That's tempting," I admitted. "Especially with everything that's just happened. But in all honesty, there's two ways to make our walls the highest around."

"Oh?" Chris asked. Then he grinned as he got my meaning.

"Either we build higher than everyone else," I said for the others who didn't know me as well, "or we go out and knock every other fucker down."

"That's…not a very nice way to think," Ashley suggested, looking at me in disapproval.

"No," I agreed. "And normally I don't like that way of thinking. It generally signals a race to the bottom. But in this situation, if we plan to raise the walls and build a parapet all the way around, station undead on the walls every few meters with an order to press an alert button if they see anyone, it's not like they'll get bored, so they'll do it. Then we send out Clarissa's teams to expand into the bigger buildings on all sides. They'll be modern ones, so it's no loss when we then knock them down. We gain mana and a clear skyline. No more snipers looking in, at least."

"Okay, and then what?" Chris asked. "I mean, I get the whole 'no more sniper nests' plan, that works. And increase the height of the walls, put watchers on there all the way around? Works, I suppose. But I'd imagine there's a better solution than making the place look like a necromancer's spare parts bin. Either way, though, sure. That's *a* solution. What about the area?"

"Diplomacy." Markus spoke up, at almost the same time that Ashley raised one hand.

"I think that's my job," she offered. "Though I think this time I'll need to be more appropriately dressed, and maybe hide my tits."

"That's what I'm thinking." I winced. "Not about your tits. They're great but—" I shook my head and went on. "I'm going to rephrase that."

"I think that's wise." Becky snorted.

"Ashley, yes, I agree that you need to be making overtures to the local area. Please come up with a plan to do that. And yes, less distracting clothing would work better than the methods you used on the space station," I said carefully.

"Well done," she murmured, and I grinned at her, knowing that she'd not taken it the wrong way.

"I try," I admitted. "Okay, so if you're going to do that, you'll need an escort, and it'll need to be one who can take care of things if the shit hits the fan."

"Okay," she agreed. "What are you thinking?"

"I'm thinking it needs to be impressive and fucking terrifying," I said clearly. "So, with that in mind, I think it's time to go back to the creatures of the dungeon, and to start the next phase."

"Oh damn." Chris laughed. "Aly is gonna murder you if you change shit as soon as she's outta the room, you know that, right?"

I waved that aside, pulling up the menu and the various creature descriptions, as well as their costs, reading through. The others did the same; the screens appeared from the center of the table, projected into the air before each seat.

Alongside the screen, an image of each of the listed creatures slowly rotated, and damn.

They were impressive.

Monsters

Fey: The Fey, or Tuatha De Danann, are an unusual group, sub-divided into many species. The Fey as a group are often misunderstood. From the playful sprites to the solemn dryads, to the capricious Daoine Sidhe and the thousands of variations in between, the Fey are as likely to hinder as to help, usually anyway.

Beware, Dungeon Lord:

Although the Fey have donated their essences to be included in the core, they may yet take issue with your use of this...no two Fey regard their inclusion in the dungeon core program the same way. Some "wild" or "free" Fey may ignore your dungeon-born variants; others may include them joyfully...while some may declare war on you for your effrontery in summoning such as they.

You have been warned.

Fey: The most common of the Fey is the **Fairy**, and although the common variant is somewhat unreliable in many ways, they grow more advanced and powerful with each evolutionary level.

43

Cost: Fairy (Common): 100 Nature, 400 Pure Mana, 5 Control points. Maintenance is 5 mana point per day, per individual.
Current Level: Common.

Already existing research boost detected!

The Fey "Fairy" class has already been absorbed into the dungeon with integrated cybernetics and nanite upgrades. Although cybernetic and nanite upgrades still require numerous prior technologies to be researched to make them available for general production, the original variant is available now.

Dungeon Fairy: [Enhanced] This specifically augmented dungeon variant of the fey designated [fairy] can greatly improve on the dungeon's reliability, production, and expansion rates.

Cost: Dungeon Fairies spawn individually for 250,000 pure mana each. Maintenance is 500 mana points per day, per individual; control points are not required.
Current Level: Advanced.

Fey: Dryads are less common than the fairy folk, but are still plentiful in the universe. A literal Nature elemental, the dryad is uninterested in anything beyond land entrusted to its care, but it will defend said land with its life should any seek to despoil it.

Note: Be wary in harvesting land cared for by a Dryad.

Cost: Dryad (Common): 400 Nature, 1600 Pure Mana, 10 Control points. Maintenance is 15 mana points per day, per individual.
Current Level: Common.

Fey: The Daoine Sidhe, or "people of the mounds," as many refer to them due to their preference for underground halls and homes, are often also referred to as the "lords and ladies." A graceful and glamorous creature, the Daoine Sidhe live for their revels, their pranks and parties, but this is not to say that they are useless to a Dungeon. The Daoine Sidhe are rogues and infiltrators without compare. Their natural affinity with glamours and mind-altering magics have firmly established them as some of the most powerful—and hated—rogues in the cosmos.

Cost: Daoine Sidhe (Common): 300 Light, 1200 Pure Mana, 15 Control points. Maintenance is 40 mana points per day, per individual.
Current Level: Common.

Mammal: The Dvorks, Dvorkian, or People of the Deep, are the ancient enemies of the Orcan, a people who were recently disabused of their final world by the Orcan expansion.

The Dvork are shipbuilders and engineers beyond compare, but suffer from two significant situational modifiers.

1. The Dvorkian race is now formally acknowledged as extinct, and those summoned through the dungeon and given artificial life are unavoidably aware of this. As such, they suffer from significant emotional and physical issues, including uncontrolled aggression and a desire to render themselves insensate through external means. Commonly alcohol.

2. Dvorks as a race evolved on high-gravity, mineral- and ore-rich worlds, resulting in physical differences from most races. They are shorter of stature, broad and enormously strong. These are all minor issues compared to the fact that no Dvork can successfully mate outside of such a location. This results in an extremely high likelihood of Dvorkian breeding programs failing.

Cost: Dvork (Common): 500 Earth, 1500 Pure Mana, 20 Control points. Maintenance is 45 mana points per day, per individual.
Included Level: Common.

Mammal: Goblins as a species have multiple variations, ranging from the lowest caste, who are barely sentient, to the High Grenai, a race that suffers little interaction with "lesser" species, due to the enormous gulf of grace and beauty between those races and their own. The most basic can be spawned as Dungeon Monsters. Utilizing their species' polymorphic tendencies results in greater enhancements than are commonly available.

Cost: Goblins spawn individually for 5-30 mana each. Maintenance is 2-25 mana points per day, per individual.
Current Level: Common.

Mammal: Orcan, or as they are more commonly known, orcs, are a muscular, thick-skinned race. Similar to the goblinoid races in that they share a highly polymorphic tendency, resulting in as many versions of the Orcan as there are worlds, the gift of life to Orcans is a costly and highly risky decision that few Dungeons are willing to make lightly.

Note: The Orakai sub-species is blocked from reproduction by any and all Dungeons due to treaties and enforced by magical interference.

Cost: Orcan spawn individually for 25 mana each. Maintenance is 25 mana points per day, per individual.
Current Level: Common.

Mammal: Scepiniir are rarely seen, and are proud warriors. Only through a life debt were the Scepiniir convinced to permit their essence to be given to the dungeon core program. The conditions were made clear, and are passed onto you here as well:

- No Scepiniir may be forced into a bonded pairing against its will.
- No Scepiniir may be sacrificed to another species, nor consumed by any through any bond or partnership with the Dungeon.
- No Scepiniir can be forced into servitude, nor arenas for the purpose of entertainment.

Any breaking of the Three Edicts will constitute a declaration of war by the Scepiniir Empire.

Cost: Scepiniir (Common): 400 Nature, 1600 Pure Mana, 10 Control points. Maintenance is 15 mana points per day, per individual.
Max Number of Scepiniir you can summon: 4 per hut.
Current Level: Common.

Monster: The Lesser Ghast is a misnomer, considering the reality of the breed. Whereas most "monsters" are simply scared or confused members of races other than the one observing and identifying—example, goblins—certain species are quite rightly defined as monsters through their excessive bloodlust and violent natures.

Cost: Lesser Ghasts spawn individually for 100 Shadow mana, 400 Pure Mana each. Maintenance is 40 mana points per day, per individual, and requires 7 points of control.
Current Level: Uncommon.

Monster: Harpies are rarely used in dungeon settings, mainly due to their unpredictable and violent natures. Harpies will happily feast on their fellow dungeon-born unless forced to leave them be and are one of the most aggressive and antagonistic of the dungeon's innate catalog.

Cost: Harpies are 100 Storm Mana, or 400 Pure Mana each. Maintenance is 40 mana points per day, per individual, and requires 7 points of control.
Current Level: Common.

Reptilian: Kobolds are a common, highly structured, caste-driven species. Semi-sentient kobolds are a standard sight in Dungeons, due to their advanced trap-making skills and low cost.

Cost: Advanced Kobolds spawn individually for 2,500 mana each, 25 control points. Maintenance is 100 mana points per day, per individual.
Current Level: Advanced.

Dinosauria: The Triceratops Horridus is an ancient herbivore, specifically evolved to be as unpalatable and difficult to consume as possible. Where many herbivores are peaceful, and even cowardly creatures, the Triceratops evolved with a slightly different design. Be this through nature or nurture, the Triceratops, through its many variations, became a highly feared sight in the late Cretaceous era.

Cost: Triceratops spawn individually for 12,500 mana each, 50 control points. Maintenance is 150 mana points per day, per individual.
Current Level: Common.

Avian: Impai are simple creatures, easily distracted by their own hungers and difficult to control, but they excel in two areas: randomized destruction and threat detection. The Impai as a species are widely viewed as unreliable and unstable, resulting in repeated attempts to eradicate their species.

Despite this, they remain a popular choice for lower-level Dungeons and lower-scale conflicts.

Cost: Impai spawn in packs of three for 25 mana each. Maintenance is 10 mana points per day, per individual.
Current Level: Common.

Undead: The various forms of the undead are as numerous as grains of sand or stars in the sky; they are matched only by their antithesis, the forces of Life. Undead can be split into two basic categories, Sentient and Non-Sentient, with the simple Skeletons, Zombies, Ghouls, and so on beginning with non-sentient forms, while the average Wraith, Vampyr, or Banshee begins with a form of rudimentary Intelligence and awareness.

Cost: Variable.

Skeletons (Uncommon): 10 Unlife, 40 Pure Mana, 1 Control point.

Maintenance is 1 mana point per day, per individual.

Zombies (Basic): 20 Unlife, 70 Pure Mana, 1 Control point.

Maintenance is 2 mana points per day, per individual.

Wraiths (Basic): 100 Unlife, 400 Pure Mana, 5 Control points.

Maintenance is 5 mana points per day, per individual.

Corpse Lord (Uncommon): 500 Unlife, 2,000 Pure Mana, 10 Control points.

Maintenance is 250 mana points per day, per individual.

Special: Due to your Lightning affinity and the effect that your species change has on your Dungeon, you may summon a single Raiju at a time. Raiju are exceedingly rare beasts, and as such cannot be summoned in large numbers. Their playful nature means that many underestimate them, to their peril.

Cost: 150 mana per summon, 50 mana per day, 10 control points.
Current Level: N/A.

Vermin: Rats are a common pest that are ubiquitous across the universe. Vermin of this type vary in size and limb count, but often conform to similar local design.

Note: Flying variants have now been unlocked…cost remains identical.

Cost: Vermin spawn in packs of three for 5 mana each. Maintenance is 1 mana point per day, per individual.
Current Level: Common.

"So, what's the plan?" Chris asked me, after a few seconds, and I pulled up the creatures I had in mind.

The Scepiniir were essentially tiger-men, big fuckers, like the advanced kobolds, and they were lethal fighters, especially when they were roused and ready for it.

They were also arrogant, and assholes from what I'd seen, both in the dungeon system's description and in the actual trial dungeon when I fought them. My hope was that they could be reasoned with, or at least beaten into shape.

If they could, a scouting force that was made up of a pair of advanced kobold assassins, six to ten kobold warriors, a pair of Scepiniir, and four mages, preferably with a couple of human fighters as well?

I had the brothers Jimmy and Andre in mind for that role, but they were with Mike currently, meaning I needed an alternative. That force combined would be more than enough to take down any small threats that they might encounter, though.

Add in that they would act as Ashley's escort, and that could massively change the deal with the locals. If she turned up on the doorstep with that multi-species group of warriors who treated each other as equals and allies, armed to the teeth, and clearly carrying technologically advanced weaponry and equipment?

I had to think that attitudes would change, and not just because, yeah, she was incredibly attractive. If she, as a human, turned up, clean, well fed and well equipped, with a team of alien allies—not servants, not beasts that were under her control, but a clearly operating team, acting as the dungeon's representatives— that would change the game for most, I guessed.

That could start the whole "Is it these fuckers who brought about the end of the world" argument, I guessed as well, but that was something she would have to deal with.

The doctors and medical professionals camped out in the Queen Elizabeth hospital still? Their attitude would change, I'd imagine, and so would the gangs', if they came across a team that was strong enough to tear down a medium-sized settlement on their own.

Especially when Ashley made it clear that she was a representative of the dungeon, not that she was all we had.

Then we create two more teams like that, and send them out, with others we could trust, on a rotating patrol. They'd get experience; we'd get the area safer. And if they had a bag of holding for each member as well, they'd be able to bring back a fuckload of loot, not to mention extra creatures for the dungeon to absorb.

The only issue was the Scepiniir.

If they were arrogant fucksticks as common-level creatures, what would they be like as advanced?

That was a good argument to keep them as common, but…

Well, that was the point. Common kobolds were weak and barely useful as shock troops. The goblins? Annoying and disgusting little creatures.

The uncommon were a lot better. And the advanced? The advanced kobolds were a different species entirely, and they were born self-aware most of the time as well.

I checked through the lists. The uncommon kobold had cost ten thousand mana; the advanced? Two hundred and fifty thousand to research. The jump in cost for the Scepiniir was significant, but not crippling, I decided, even if I winced looking at it.

Fifty thousand to research from common to uncommon, and seven hundred and fifty thousand to advanced.

That was a mad amount of mana to me, literally three-quarters of a million points of mana, but…but it was less than two days' production of mana for the dungeon now.

Looking at it, and thinking about the cost and timescale, I took a deep breath and changed my focus. No choice really, I guessed, as I dove into the dungeon system again.

Our choices were clear, and none of them were easy, regardless of the end plan.

If we want to prioritize responding to the army base—which I couldn't see any options beyond dealing with that, and right now—then we needed mana. We needed mana to summon creatures from the dungeon to form our forces, and we needed to make sure that the other buildings in the area that overlooked us weren't a threat anymore.

"Okay, we need to sort out the army base," I said after a few seconds' thought. "Don't get me wrong, I know we need to do that, and right damn now, but to do it? We need forces to fucking back us up. If I go there now with a handful of us, they've already shown they're against us. They'll shoot first and ask questions never, so that's out."

"A surgical strike then?" Chris suggested. "A handful of us, maybe some of the trainee mages and the kobolds Kelly just made? We hit them hard and fast, take down their walls and try to dig them out before they're ready for us. Then we pull back, leave them with no defenses—they'll either have to spend the next few days digging themselves out of that shit, or move on. We don't need to kill them all, after all."

"No, it's too risky." I shook my head. "Don't get me wrong…we can't leave them alone to just plan another attack, but we haven't got the forces until Mike and the others come back. I don't like it, but we have to wait on them getting their arses home before we'd be able to launch a full-scale attack. If we went straight for them, even if we win, we'd be leaving the dungeon defenseless while we do it. We did that once already and got attacked as soon as we did it. We can't make the same mistake twice, not when there's no need."

"So what, we just let them grind out some more levels and get ready for us?" Chris asked, clearly disapproving.

"Fuck no." I snorted. "You think I don't have a plan? What we're going to do is…"

CHAPTER FOUR

"I hate you," Chris said to me a few hours later.

I snorted in dark amusement. He'd been saying the same thing for the last hour almost constantly.

"I know, mate. I hate you too."

"No, I mean it, man. If I'd known how boring this was, I'd have never agreed to help, not a chance, not even when—"

"Not even if I told you I'm thinking we need to work on the living quarters soon?" I interrupted him. "Maybe get better showers and so on?"

"Yeah…" He paused, clearly weighing his options before going on. "Even with better showers, we're only going from hatred to outright dislike here, dude. Seriously, this is fucking mind-numbing bullshit."

"Clarissa and her team have spent weeks doing it," I pointed out.

"And they don't have to fight on the front lines," he countered. "They don't need to get their enemies' blood and shit all over them as well. That's how they contribute, man. I work my ass off day in and out, and this is the thanks I get? I'm supposed to be your mate! There has to be some perks to putting up with your shit, right?"

"Kelly puts up with me." I lifted my right hand and smoothed it through the air, slowly and steadily, the move Zen-like and almost meditative.

"Yeah, and believe me, I feel sorry for her enough as it is. Not only does she put up with your shit jokes, but she had to make do with your tiny todger. I mean seriously, it's what, the size of a breath mint?"

"It's why your mother's breath was so fresh," I countered on autopilot.

"And there we go. Shit jokes." He nodded. "Look, mate, I'd *love* to help some more, you know I would, but the farms need me, all right? Magic skills are in demand. Too bad, so sad." He grinned at me and took a step back in the dungeon sense. "Toodles!"

And with that, he was gone, leaving me with only the peace of the work as I sighed and kept going.

He was right about one thing, I reflected, despite his shitty way of putting it. This was a boring-ass job.

I, and until very recently, Chris, had been working on expanding the dungeon's influence.

Basically, we were pushing out—incredibly slowly—the area that the dungeon could affect with its powers. In this case, anything that fell within the dungeon's territory was a space I could summon a creature, item, or structure into.

What I'd not thought about, until I had to, was that the dungeon had very set views when it came to the territory it held, and what that meant. Views that had been programmed into it by a fuckin' alien race.

So, first and foremost, was the knowledge that as aliens, they didn't know us very well. That meant that a lot of the dungeon's methods and rules had to be based on us, what it identified we thought and what we were doing.

That was why I was very carefully thinking only *nice* thoughts about our '*allies*' and their territory, the barracks and army base.

After all, Mike and Griffiths were members of that group, even if only loosely, and as such, their friends and any unknown family who happened to be inside the barracks couldn't possibly be our enemies, right?

No, It was all sorted out, and we were all *allies* now, with them accepting my authority as the Dungeon Lord.

That was what I was pushing at the dungeon all the time as I stepped slowly forward in the dungeon sense, carefully claiming inch by goddamn inch of territory, even as Clarissa and her people worked on claiming more and more all around me.

I was heading straight for the barracks, like a goddamn laser.

We'd already claimed a good portion of the distance between there and here, and it was only dumb luck that they'd not been picked up traveling through the sections we'd claimed before. That was for two reasons. First, we'd not had the time nor spare mana to build a mana collector, nor an alert tower there to watch over the area.

Had we done that, we might have noticed the troop movement, but mainly, as I'd already acknowledged, I'd gone in a straight line, claiming the territory.

Secondly, even if we had, they'd have marched up to the main roads and traveled at least part of the way on those roads, while my route went through houses and buildings.

Now, though, that was changing.

Two of Clarissa's people were moving northeast and southwest from the little parking lot we'd previously claimed near the fusiliers' base. They were going to claim a ring that led all the way around the dungeon at the one-mile marker. Dotted all along it would be alert towers, making goddamn sure we knew if anyone was coming in.

The rest of her team were currently working to expand a line out to the nearest tall buildings.

There weren't many, fortunately, but each and every one of them was being claimed or torn down.

The one that'd be left out there available? Cale Cross.

It was close enough to our walls that we should have thought about this before now and taken it down or claimed it, considering that it was less than a hundred meters from our nearest wall. It was also tall enough that it towered over said wall, but in light of the local geography, it'd not been an issue.

After all, there were relatively few guns in the area anyway, and what there were, were mainly in our hands, right? We had an army contingent, and most of our enemies were magical or undead in nature until now.

Well, Cale Cross was ours now, or would be soon. The dungeon's own automatic expansion had gotten us up to the edge of it, anyway. Once we'd taken all of it, we'd seal it up and put a team on the top floor, possibly even growing it a lot higher first to make damn sure that *nobody* was sneaking up on us again.

Regardless, though, the point I was working on, and that Chris had just so kindly abandoned me with, was the expansion to our *allies'* barracks.

And once we were there, if the dungeon accepted that I knew best and this was my territory?

Well, then I could adjust it, just like anywhere else in my fucking reach, couldn't I. Walls? They were coming *down.* Soldiers? Well, that's great! They're going to be just overjoyed when their *allies* the kobolds are summoned in places, ready to jump out and give them a lovely hug, weren't they?

This might not work; I knew that. The dungeon was in my mind, after all. It might understand what I was doing—or it might not. But even if it didn't let me, if it somehow assessed me and decided that no, we were enemies, that was fine as well.

I couldn't summon my creatures in a territory that was being contested. So, in a house, for example, if my enemies held each room, I couldn't repair the house, change the walls, and summon more creatures inside it, if they were too close to the enemy.

I could summon them in a different room, though, if they were far enough away from them.

In this situation, that wasn't an issue either. Sure, most of the rooms would have people in them, I imagined. The barracks was housing a lot of people, after all.

However, when creatures such as orcs kept appearing out of the blue and charging their walls, fighting their forces, and forcing them to expend all their ammo?

That was going to make it damn hard for the bastards to get the time to attack me ever again.

Then, when Mike and his people finally got their arses in gear and got back here, they could go make peaceful overtures to the base.

I say "peaceful" because one of the pieces I wanted in exchange for fuckin' peace was Gerald, Sharon, and Merriman's heads.

I'd even summon the silver platters, all nice and polished ready.

That thought was enough to keep me going as I kept working, smoothing the dungeon's expansion with both hands, like pushing out a soap bubble, gently but firmly: push, smooth, stretch, and step forward.

Rinse and goddamn repeat.

Aly was back in the dungeon now, along with Kelly. Neither of them were happy with my request, nor my plan for it, but they'd agreed with the need. And yeah, increasing the creatures we have access to was always part of the plan, after all.

So, for now, they were working on rebuilding our defenders and continuing the research—the crafting rooms had been put off for a few days, to many complaints from those who knew they'd been about to get the shiny new toys.

Instead, the common to uncommon upgrades were being carried out first, with regard to the creatures.

We'd taken it back to the basics, starting with the goblins. As much as I really hated the little bastards, that was probably the best idea, I'd agreed.

The goblins had been at common, so that was ten thousand in mana to go from common to uncommon, and another two hundred and fifty thousand mana to go from uncommon to advanced.

I didn't like them. Nothing that happened was going to make me like goblins, I'd decided. And considering the little sneaky one that I'd spawned into the civic center dungeon had been one of the casualties of the attack, I didn't have a single one that was self-aware, *again*.

They were short, smelled terrible, were vicious as sin and twice as ugly, and if you didn't keep a close eye on them, they were constantly fiddling with something. Rarely, it was something like an item they shouldn't be. Mainly, it was under their filthy loincloths, and I was damn glad they wore them, at least.

The common ones… I was going to summon them out of curiosity once they were unlocked, but I decided against it.

Instead, we agreed that the uncommon goblins would be researched, then the common and uncommon wraiths. That was another ten thousand mana. Once we'd done that, it was uncommon fairies—we weren't summoning a dungeon fairy, just a normal one, and I'd be damn ready to shoot it in the face as soon as it spawned, just in case.

Then it was the Scepiniir's turn.

I'd decided that we weren't going to go for the harpies, the trikes—triceratops—the impai nor the vermin. There was just no damn point.

I also looked at the Dvork, and saw that for them, it was the same as the Scepiniir—fifty thousand for the jump from common to uncommon—and decided that they were worth researching, but not summoning yet.

The others were to be summoned around the barracks for now, and literally as soon as we'd encircled and claimed anything and everything we could of the ene—*friendly*—base, we'd be back to the crafting.

As soon as the crafting was done, we'd be working on the upgrades to the mana collection systems, which was a half a million points, but that was life.

No matter what we did, there was always more that needed to be done.

Kelly wasn't happy about me "wasting" my time in expanding the dungeon's reach here, not when there was so much else to be done, and she'd literally barely seen me for days. But as I pointed out, if I could constantly make it clear to the dungeon that the soldiers were our *friends*, this stood a much better chance of working.

Plus, if I saw something, I was in the position to do something about it straightaway.

There was about a hundred meters left to go now. Yeah, that was, even with the upgrades that we'd managed, another day's worth of work yet to go. But it needed to be done, and so, I did it.

Clarissa slid across on occasion, or one of her people, checking on me, offering to take over. I politely rebuffed them, making it clear that they needed to focus on their jobs. Soon enough, Chris was back, standing at my shoulder silently, working his ass off as well.

I sensed the others coming and going, shifts changing, but in the end, my mind was worn to dullness by the time that Kelly finally dragged me from the dungeon. She forced me to accept that I needed rest, and that I couldn't do this on my own.

Then, being the woman she was, she showed me that she'd planned for this, as Finn and Patrick stepped up, taking my and Chris's places.

"There's only a dozen meters left," Finn pointed out. "If we need to, we can wake you, but as it is, we'll be pushing out and into the barracks by the time you return—that's eight hours, okay? If you take eight hours and get some real sleep, not just chasing her around, you'll be feeling a lot better for it."

I nodded, not intending to follow those directions at all, thinking I'd have four, maybe five hours at most. And then, when Kelly finally woke me after nine solid hours of sleep, I had to admit it'd been what I needed.

Drak had stuck around, it turned out, mainly eating and apparently chasing the female advanced kobolds. He'd tried suggesting a mutual scale cleaning to Beta with his cleaning tool, and was now sulking with a black eye and a half-eaten meal in front of him when I set my food down at the same table he occupied.

"So, you look like you had fun." I nodded to him, grabbing the ketchup and salt as I laid my breakfast out. I couldn't help but grin at the annoyed and embarrassed grunt I got in response.

Kelly had told me about it when she'd woken me, right after absorbing the original scale cleaner into the dungeon when Beta brought it to her.

The kobolds now had access to them whenever they wanted, and Drak had apparently not been able to tell the difference between his own one and the copy that Kilo had dumped on the table for him just before I'd arrived.

"I don't want to talk about it." He grunted, looking away.

"Fair enough." I shrugged, pulling a seat out and dropping into it, smiling unthinkingly at the metal creaking under me.

"You ready to make me an offer?" he asked suddenly, now staring at me.

"What do you want?" I picked up my cutlery and got started on the meal, even as I reached out, checking on the progress of the dungeon's expansion.

"Gold."

"How much?" I asked.

"How much are you paying them?" he countered, nodding to the group of kobolds running laps under Beta's eye we could see through the window.

"I have no idea," I answered. "We created an economy, and I know people are paid. There's a copper, silver, and gold coin base in use, but honestly, I'm not involved. Aly, my chief researcher, and Kelly, my partner and the Dungeon Mistress, deal with it."

"You just trust them to deal with it?"

I nodded.

"Fine, how much are your...what race are you again?"

"Humans." I shrugged. "Well, I was. Now I'm a Storm Titan, so yeah, slightly different when I get examined, I guess."

"Yeah, saw that." He nodded, rubbing at his bruised eye, then sat forward. "So how much are you paying your own kind?"

"I'm the only Storm Titan, as far as I know, and the kobolds and humans and everyone else are on the same wage. It goes up for the more skilled and dangerous jobs, but that's all I know. You want to bargain with those details, tell me what you're offering and I'll take you to Kelly or Aly. You can bargain with them."

"I want to sort this with you, not your people."

"And I want a goddamn week off to relax," I countered. "You want something I can give, ask. You want to bargain over something I'm not involved in, I'll take you to those who are. But I'm too busy for this shit, Drak."

"You want me to stay?"

I nodded. "Yeah, I do," I admitted. "Look, Drak, you helped me in there, and you didn't have to, but we both know that was a different situation. I set you free. Sure, you owe me for that, but you don't owe me your life and freedom. You want to stay? Fine, stay; we'll be thankful and we'll make sure you're well paid. You'll get somewhere that's yours to live, food, and a wage. You'll also be expected to work your damn ass off and to do dangerous shit on occasion that might get you killed. The other choice is you leave."

I gestured to the window with my fork, the sausage on the end of it dripping a little molten yellow yolk as I did it.

"Out there, you're free, mate. Go where you want, do what you want. But understand this: the world just ended. My people? Humans, I mean? They don't know what's going on. I'm one of a handful of Dungeon Lords on the planet. If you strike it lucky, maybe you'll meet another. Most likely, someone or something will kill you inside of a day."

"So you think I should stay here."

"Of course I do." I nodded. "Damn, I want you to stay. You've got skills, and I trust you, more or less. That's a decision you need to make, though, and you need to make it by the end of the day."

"Why so soon?" He straightened.

"No offense." I shrugged. "But I'm not damn well feeding and housing you for free if you're not one of us. You want to go to the park? It's a few miles that way…" I pointed. "It's part of the dungeon, but run by Barry. He's a good guy, and he could definitely do with the help as well. If you don't want to be there, though? Just keep going."

"I want a good wage if I'm going to stay," he muttered after a few minutes of silence, broken only by me eating.

"And that's fine." I nodded. "You're a skilled adventurer. You could be useful to the dungeon and me in a dozen ways. Hell, the least of them would be as a trainer, and it'd be one of the most important as well."

"It'd mean I don't have to go out there though, right?" He jerked a thumb in the direction of the wall outside. "Not that I'm scared, but if there's food and safety in here, I don't need to go fucking around out there."

"Tell you what," I offered, cracking a can open. "Either you can take a training role—for now—and yeah, mainly you'll be inside, but you'd need to help out, if we need you outside. Such as if we end up in a real fight, a big one, and your trainees are out there fighting, I'd expect you to help, okay? Or…"

"Or?"

"Or you prove yourself to me, and maybe you help with the more specialist training."

"I've not proved myself yet?" he asked sourly.

"You have, but there's always going to be different things we need. You want a nice, sweet job? I need specialists. You know a hell of a lot about the outside galaxy that we just don't. You want a nice safe job, one that pays well and keeps you more or less out of the shit out there?"

"Yeah, I do."

"Well, you've only got my word for what it's like out there, I know, and yeah, you were probably saving that comment for negotiation, so let's do a little deal now. My people are to the north. They were headed to this point…" I summoned a map and laid it on the table next to him, absorbing my half-eaten breakfast as I focused on what we needed instead of the meal.

I tapped the garrison at Otterburn on the map and traced the way down it to where we were now. "This is a map. It shows—"

"I know what a map is." He grunted, poring over the details.

"Well, I wanted to be sure," I replied philosophically. "So, a load of my people went here, and they're people I damn well trust to sort this shit out. If they've been captured, killed, or they just found a shitload of beers and strippers, I need to know. Chances are, they're totally fine, just dealing with whatever it is that's going on. But either way, we need them back, and fast. You take one of the other kobolds, one that they know, like Kilo, so that if you get there and they need proof, they know they can trust you, all right?"

"Then what?" he asked. "I go here for you, I find them and bring them back…then what?"

"Then you've proved yourself out there." I shrugged. "If you decide to move on? I'll give you a pack load of whatever supplies you want that I can make, and you go with my thanks. You want to stay? You've proved you're useful outside of the dungeon."

"So I get better pay and good quarters," he suggested.

"We'll negotiate." I nodded. "I don't know what you'll consider good and what you expect. Drak, you do this and I'll trust you with a training role, if that's what you want. We have people teaching different things. You're an adventurer, though; you can teach a shitload of skills. All low level, you said, sure, but everything from lock picking to spotting, I don't know, mimics? The survival shit that you had to learn, that could help my people, okay?"

"So that's it? I do this, you'll trust me and I'm a trainer?"

"For a trial." I nodded. "If you're a shit trainer, or don't teach people anything, don't turn up and put in any effort, we'll look at your future here, don't get me wrong. But you work hard? That's all I ask, man. We're all in the shit here, and the Orcan are coming. We need to be ready, or we all die. You get that, right?"

"I do." He grunted. "I'll do it, but then we negotiate."

"You find them and bring them back, and the woman you'll be dealing with will be either the wife or sister of one of those you bring back," I pointed out. "You get Mike singing your praises and bring him home? I bet Aly or Kelly will be happy to negotiate."

"Why not you?"

"Because I don't deal with the economy." I shrugged. "You want me to set you a wage? Fine. A gold coin a day."

"Why do I feel you didn't mean that?" he asked skeptically.

"Because for all I know that's an incredible wage, or a shit one. I don't know. I pay you too much and it destabilizes the economy; too little, you feel undervalued and you'll quit. So I stay out of that, all right? Food and lodging is taken care of if you're helping out, so just do as I ask please, mate—take Kilo and go find Mike and the team. Bring them home."

"How far is this?" he asked after a brief hesitation, staring at the map again.

"About forty miles, about twenty times the length we were worried the dungeon was when we were in it," I guessed, measuring it roughly. "They were going to try to capture some of the enemy and then come back, so they shouldn't have gone that far. But they might have decided to attack…I don't know. Chances are, you'll bump into them an hour after leaving and they'll laugh about me sending you. But if they don't? I need to know."

"Fine." He sighed, climbing to his feet. "I'll go."

"Thank you." I meant it. "You need anything?"

"Potions." He shifted from one foot to the other. "Health potions, and a lot of them."

"Anything else?" I asked. "Food? Supplies?"

"Just the potions." He then grinned. "I already stole the food, just in case."

"Ha!" I grinned back at him. "I should have known. All right, I'll give you one of the higher strength potions…"

"Ten."

"One," I said. "It takes the dungeon's entire mana production for something like four hours to make that, so you get one. I'll also give you ten lesser ones, weaker, but they should help deal with the addiction at least. Don't you fucking drink the high-strength one as soon as you leave, all right?"

"I'm an addict, not an idiot," he snapped. "I'll need the potions—one for me, the rest…well, just in case."

"As long as you're not drinking the good one," I repeated, checking the dungeon's mana, and wincing. "Gonna need to get some mana in first." I cursed.

"How long?"

"An hour, maybe," I admitted, thinking quickly. "So you get ready and go stand by the gate. I'll have Kilo join you with the potions as soon as we've got them ready."

"And it keeps them outta my claws." He snorted. "Give me the ten then."

"Five," I said. "That wasn't the plan, but I can summon five at the minute of the weaker ones. There's enough mana for that at least. Here."

I gestured to the table, focusing and summoning five potions and setting them there, sighing as he picked the first up, examined it, sniffed that it was trash tier, then downed it anyway.

He collected the rest, then moved out, and I stood slowly, letting him get ahead of me, before heading up to the roof. A little flight across the middle of the dungeon later, and I was alighting before Beta as she hissed orders at the newborn advanced kobold warriors that ran back and forth before her.

"Beta." I greeted her, smiling as she bobbed her head at me, clearly happy to see me. "Is Kilo around?"

"Training." She gestured to the mage's tower.

"I need to send him on a mission. I want someone I trust to go find the others. He'll also be watching over and evaluating Drak."

"Good." She grunted. "Judge him harshly."

"You don't like him?" I asked.

"Not trust. Dislike? Not sure," she said, with a little bob of the shoulders and tail, presumably her attempt at a shrug.

"Okay, you okay with me sending Kilo?"

"Send him." She nodded. "Trust Kilo."

"Me too." I nodded, then, smiling at her—although more at being able to do this at all—I leapt into the air, flitting across the dungeon to land near the entrance to the tower. I jogged a couple of steps and slowed, before bracing myself on the wall, and pressed a hand to the large door.

It was like a lot of the doors in the dungeon: set only to open if a member of the dungeon's population asked it to. I frowned, wondering whether we needed to increase that security now, considering that some assholes inside the dungeon had to have helped with the attack, I was sure.

There was just too much that'd not been addressed yet, and I didn't like it. I also didn't know enough to act yet, though. As much as I wanted to string the entire group up by the balls who had tried to set up that coup, I didn't know for sure they were all involved.

I walked inside, the cool air outside giving way to a pleasant warmth as I closed the door behind me again.

The mage's tower was one of my prouder moments, I had to admit to myself.

Sure, there were a lot of things that made me proud: events, achievements— hell, saving people meant a lot more to me. Honestly, it did. But the mage's tower?

That was just incredibly cool, and something that, if I'd not designed and created it? I'd still be in love with it.

The outside was marble, striated with dozens of colors and just insanely cool looking. Five floors were above the ground and four beneath, and each was created to be dedicated to a specific form of mana, like Fire, Water, or Life.

The only one that wasn't was the entrance level.

Each floor had dedicated mana converters on them, and each and every one changed their local area in little ways.

As a perfect example, the Fire floor was hot as hell, and yet for Dante? It was home. He loved it. Ashley, his partner, was apparently getting used to the heat, and increasing her Fire affinity by spending time there.

It probably also helped because the pair were very new to their relationship, and the heat meant that clothing was less of a necessity there, and more optional.

However, I'd instituted a rule that if they were taking clothes off, they had to lock the door. I wasn't stupid, and the last thing I needed was an irate parent complaining their curious eight-year-old had walked in on the pair making the beast with two backs.

The other floors were similar but very different.

The Death floor, for example, had an almost permanent resident in Catherine, a woman who had a natural affinity for Phantom mana that was at seventy-six.

She'd touched her mana core before we could even find her, though she had no clue what she was doing with it. The only instinctive skill she'd discovered so far was that she could sense the undead, and know which were naturally occurring and which were dungeon creatures.

That wasn't much of a skill so far, but it was a start, and it was promising.

It didn't take long to find Kilo. The rule that we'd put into place was that if the mages wanted to summon a mana converter for a specific floor for themselves to work with, they could. They had to personally earn the mana, though.

They could do that in the dungeon sense, literally absorbing enough bricks and so on, and that was it, but they had to earn it for the converter they wanted, *and* another.

That still wasn't exactly a hard job. I mean, they could do it in a few hours of hard work, no stress. Or, if they managed to find high-tech items like a server stack or whatever, which were worth more than bricks, it was sorted in minutes.

That wasn't the point, though.

They got what they wanted, they felt that they were earning it and were proud of that, and they added to the dungeon as well.

The individual mana converters took in the corrupted and "wild" mana of the area that we were dragging in, and they converted it to their own aspect.

That was then stored in the converter, Fire mana in the Fire converter for example. Once that was full, they then converted it into pure mana, and fed that into the dungeon.

That meant that every mana converter that say, Dante and Ashley made for their own studies, earned mana they could use, strengthening them, then earned the dungeon mana as well, which was awesome.

The exception to the dedicated floor rule was the entrance floor, which had a mixture of all mana converters. Light battled Dark, Fire against Water, Earth against Air, and Life against Death, making this one floor an absolute madhouse of swirling mana.

It was also fantastic for those who were learning, or those who just needed to rest and recover their mana. You wanted to train? This could be the place for you because as you focused on your core and growing, you'd find yourself naturally drawn to certain aspects.

From there, you'd be able to find others who were drawn to the same things and get lessons. This was where the next generation of mages was coming from, and I just loved it.

This floor was covered in rugs, chairs, and more. Great wing-backed ornate fucking things that people had looted clashed with tiny little Z-shaped office things that others preferred.

Great dark monstrosities of ash and oak, ancient heirlooms plundered from the castle nearby sat next to sheepskin rugs that others stretched out on, and in the middle was a raised stage.

From there, I—or Dante and the others—led the lessons, guiding people to find their core and do simple exercises, hopefully preparing them for when they hit level five and got their class choices.

Once they hit that, they'd be able to choose a class, preferably a magical one, and then they'd be able to grow, learning a handful of spells and gaining access to their abilities.

When they had a class, they'd earn quests that taught them to use their abilities and it was all full steam ahead.

Now, as I strode into the room, Kilo stood with one arm resting on a Water converter, talking to a mixed bunch of humans and kobolds, guiding them in a lesson. I paused for a few minutes, watching and listening.

He sensed me, unfortunately, and drew the lesson to a close early, coming across to see what I wanted. As soon as I told him, he nodded, understanding the reasoning and the need.

"I'll find them," he assured me, taking the potions as I summoned them and handed them over, making it clear that the last one, the most powerful, was only for emergencies, and Kilo was to carry it. "And I'll watch *him* as well." The way he said it made it clear that although Beta was unsure about how she felt about Drak, Kilo wasn't happy with him.

"Thank you," I told him. Then I apologized to the rest of his impromptu class for stealing their teacher, and directed them to go find Dante and tell him I said they could ask him questions.

It was both reasonable for me to do that as the Dungeon Lord, and funny for me, because I could be a bastard at times, and I had no doubt that he'd be trying to have fun with Ashley one way or another.

By the time I dropped into the seat next to Kelly and Aly in the Parthenon, I felt like I'd been all over the place, and that I'd accomplished precisely fuck all as well.

Bringing the girls up to date on my actions, I got a pat on the head for the thoughtfulness of sending Drak and Kilo to check on the others, and a telling off for spending so much of the mana on a potion—it was fifty thousand, after all— without warning them.

The current plan was confirmed, and I got a glare from them, affirming that if I tried to change the research plan again, I'd probably get stabbed. And finally, *finally* I shifted around, then settled back in the chair and reached out to the dungeon properly.

Kelly had made it clear when she woke me—without any fun on offer—that the local army base that the assault had come from was under watch, partly absorbed into the dungeon sense, and they were apparently currently doing their best to stay small and quiet.

That had been a relief and the only reason that I'd managed to do as much as I had without diving straight back in. But now that I was free to do it, the first place I went was to the base.

Hovering over it in the dungeon sense as an incorporeal spirit, I found it'd not changed much from the images we'd had before.

It was on the river, a single large building that ran perhaps a hundred meters by twenty or so, and it had an extensive fence around the exterior.

The parking lot inside the fence had been painstakingly dug up. Literally, all the cars—and a few military vehicles—had been pushed out, and the entire space had been returned as far as possible to arable land.

They'd then planted it heavily, and clearly with the help of someone who knew what they were doing. There were several "waste recycling facilities" nearby according to the map, and they'd been hit by teams, I had to guess, judging from the depth of the compost and the sheer number of random planters and so on.

The fence had been, or was in the process of being, replaced by a makeshift wall. Here and there, actual concrete had been poured, forming a much more impressive barrier.

All in all, it showed a determination that, if it was anyone but the British Army, I'd have been overjoyed to see. Knowing soldiers, and the way that they could put literally anything and everything aside to accomplish a goal, though, and that it was the end of the world? I found it a strangely lackluster and half-arsed attempt.

I pondered that for a few minutes, wondering why I expected so much better from them. Then I snorted. I was comparing them to me. That was it.

I'd built a full-on community, and I was just, well, *me*. I'd gotten the dungeon, and that'd helped incredibly, sure, but that was something I'd made the most of, and as it was "just me," I had expected the professionals to have done *much*, much better.

They'd not, though. They'd basically turtled up and waited for orders, and damn that pissed me off.

I stomped that down, forcing myself to think of the lovely surprise that my *allies* in the base here were going to get. Then I reached out and summoned a small bar of chocolate, letting it fall to the ground near a slowly patrolling soldier.

He'd been walking the perimeter. At first, he missed it, sweeping his gaze back and forth, before finally spotting it when he reached a literal arm's length from it.

Sure, if I gave him the benefit of the doubt, I'd probably have to admit to him guessing it to be rubbish. There was plenty of it stuck to the chain link fence, after all, and more blowing aimlessly down the streets nearby. But the way he leapt on the chocolate bar?

Oh, that was a treat all right.

He spun in place, his prize clutched tight in one hand as he looked around, trying to see who could have dropped it. Then, after making sure he was alone, and apparently unobserved, he tore the top of the wrapper off and practically inhaled it.

I nodded happily to myself, before summoning—a little farther along, and again, waiting until he was looking in the other direction—a single goblin wretch.

It was time to make these fuckers regret their shit.

CHAPTER FIVE

"What are you doing?" Kelly asked me suspiciously when I got her attention and dragged her over to the relevant area, pointing out the hiding goblin wretch and the oblivious soldier who was even now searching the area, sure, but it was for more chocolate.

"Oh, nothing…" I smiled at her. "I just thought they'd find this little joke really funny."

"What 'joke' is it?" she asked after a few seconds. A new hardness came into her voice as she figured out exactly where and what I was doing.

"Well, considering you're the Mistress of Minions, and you get bonuses for dealing with them, much like I do to running the dungeon, I thought you might like to send this little guy around the base, and see what he can learn."

"Okay…" she agreed slowly. "Any rules?"

"He can't hurt a child or obvious civilian," I said, and she snorted.

"You should know me better than thinking you needed to say that."

"I do, but you asked for rules, so here you go. No violence if at all possible as well. Sure, if you see Gerald and the others, all bets are off, but that's a short-term gain. I want a lasting impression, and for that, you use him to scout the base."

"Then what?" She was already checking the area.

"While you're doing that, I'm going to get a small team of dedicated assassins ready." My smile widened. "We're going to use this situation as a leveling opportunity. They're going to be given missions, and you're going to practice guiding them. Both you and they'll gain some levels, and we get the entire base, or as much of it as possible mapped out."

"We can do that in the dungeon sense," she pointed out.

"We can, but we won't always be able to do that, so let's practice while we get things ready. Scout the place, then get your people into all the areas we need— the armory, the commander's office. Fuck, I don't even know what rank they might be, but we've got a major here, so there has to be someone higher in there."

"You want them all in place and ready?"

I nodded. "I was thinking that we needed to wait for the others to get back here first, but when I sent Drak out, I realized that it's forty miles to the Otterburn base. If they've gone all that way, it could be a day or two before they get back, or longer. I don't know. But what I do know?"

"Yeah?"

"The mana density," I said. "When I was looking at the best place to put the dungeon, I realized that where I put it was the best site in the local area, right?

Well, there were places with a lot more mana available as well, and one of them was up there, near Otterburn."

"I remember," she said after a few seconds. "You think that's why the others haven't come back yet? That they ran into something they couldn't handle?"

"I don't know," I admitted. "I might be totally wrong. Hell, I sent Drak hoping that he'd get to the end of the street and find them all coming back and he'd lord it over me that he did what he was asked and now we owe him. I'm really hoping that's the case. But if it's not? We need to be ready to move."

"And we can't be ready to move in that direction unless we're ready to move with this one," she finished for me, nodding. "Okay, I get that. So, you want me to get some experience with this goblin sneaking around, right?"

"Yeah. Then you'll be able to better guide the more advanced ones when they're ready."

"And if they tighten security because I screw up?" she asked. "If they see him three seconds in and the dungeon decides this wasn't a funny prank after all?"

"Then we do it the hard way," I growled. "Fuck's sake, Kelly, I know—"

"No, Matt," she snapped back. "I know what you're thinking and why, and I agree, all right?" She glared at me, and I forced myself to not say anything, waiting for her to finish. "I understand, Matt," she repeated, her voice softer. "But we can't waste the element of surprise here. We need to train and to get an idea of the base, you're right about that. All the reasoning behind what we need to do? You're totally right, and I'm a hundred percent behind you."

"Right?"

"It's the last hurdle I disagree on. We can't risk our one chance with this as a training op. We need to plan better, and yes, definitely use this opportunity to 'prank' our 'friends.'"

"So how do we train them?" I asked her, and she smiled.

"I do a dungeon run." She shrugged.

"Oh, hell no—" I started, shaking my head.

"A dungeon run, as a Mistress of Minions." She clarified, "Not a trial dungeon run, not the shit you just went through. Instead, I do a normal, if high-level dungeon run, and I guide the same team that we're looking at using for the mission."

"And how do we keep the base under control until we've got what we need?" I asked her.

She smiled at me, and it was oh, *such* an evil expression.

"Well, that's easy," she offered flippantly. "We just seal them in."

I stared at her, my mind whirling. Then I couldn't help but nod. "Yeah, yeah...that'll work," I agreed.

The next hour passed quickly as I worked with Finn and Patrick, as well as two of the expansion team who worked under Clarissa, making damn sure we had a ring of influence around the army base. We expanded it a little way both up and down, testing the ground to make damn sure that it was solid and there weren't any tunnels or anything in place.

This was the regimental headquarters for the area, and after a little searching nearby, we found that a bunch of the close-in houses had all been taken over, and more soldiers apparently lived there with their families.

I had no clue what had happened to the original inhabitants, nor whether they'd always been military. But if I had to guess, I'd say the reason we'd found the other nearby bases empty was because everyone had come here at the very start.

Now we proceeded to expand the dungeon's control, working in relays to make sure all the occupied housing was inside the new boundaries.

While I worked on that, Kelly was out talking to Barry, setting things up and calling for volunteers.

By the time she came to get me, I was more than ready to stop the expansion, sick of the slow, constant strain.

A handful of minutes later, I stood—in the dungeon sense—in the middle of the park, looking out over around five hundred people, people who were supposed to be on their rest period, sleeping, eating, and spending time with their loved ones.

They'd all come when we asked, and I couldn't help but feel honored by their dedication.

"Thank you all," I started with, nodding and forcing a smile. "I know this is your downtime, so I'll be brief, but thank you for making the effort and coming. So, first of all, a lot of you will be wondering why I ended up trapped in the dungeon a few days back—if you heard about it, at least. I'll explain quickly, as otherwise that'll be hanging over the conversation. Basically, that was a trial, something that the creators of the dungeon system instilled in it, to force me as the Dungeon Lord to still work to grow.

"I'm guessing that they didn't expect me to be doing as much as I already was, or they'd not have tried that shit. But, essentially, it gave us an opportunity to learn and to improve, as well as a chance to gain some new bonuses for the dungeon. I'll be speaking about the bonuses and the new opportunities soon.

"The issue, however, is that as I finished the trial dungeon and came to escape, and I don't mind admitting, expecting a little goddamn celebration as I emerged...we were under attack."

I paused at that, holding off as the muttering and rumbles started, before raising a hand and waiting for silence from the incorporeal mass before me.

"Now, that attack was, as near as we can tell, orchestrated by several assholes hiding in our community."

That set off the mutterings and worse mounting, and I waited until they'd really started to build—while being very careful not to look in certain directions— before I waved at them to calm down.

"It's okay. We caught them all. There's no more traitors in our midst, but you might remember their faces if I showed them to you. You remember the 'vote' to elect a new council that was carried out? One that only included a small group, and that if you voted for any of them, they tried to swing it as a vote for their group to form the council?

"Well, that wasn't a real vote. I know I've said it before, but I'll say it again. I had no knowledge of it until it was done, and didn't endorse or agree to any of them being members of *my* council at all. They essentially decided that they had the right to carry out a vote, and expected that we'd all just let them take over.

Clearly, considering half of them were banished and the rest are helping our armed forces, that didn't work out too well for them."

I let the chuckles and nods die out before I went on.

"The thing is, that little cabal—and understand this, they *were* a cabal—they weren't trying to carry out a fair election. There was nobody but their own people on that list, and not one of them were working in any of the ways you do every day. That little cabal went to the nearby army headquarters. Now, you know a lot of our army is made up of ex-armed forces personnel, from the marines to the army, the navy and hell, even the RAF.

"The thing is, our serving army personnel recommended we wait before contacting them directly. This was because they were close enough that they had to know we existed, and yet *they still didn't come to help.*"

That drew some angry muttering and glares.

"We don't know why," I clarified, lifting my hands into the air and making a calming gesture. "We don't know why they didn't help, but we were advised to wait until we had the forces strong enough to make it clear we weren't a ragtag bunch reaching out, but a solid community.

"That's what we were doing. And that little cabal I mentioned? When they were given the option of help us, work hard, and pay off the damage they'd done in trampling and nearly killing a heavily pregnant woman and her babies, its leaders instead chose exile. No great loss to us, I'm sure you'll all agree."

I looked around, seeing nods and hearing the rising anger of the group.

"Well, that's where they tried to fuck us again. Instead of leaving, taking the supplies we gave them and moving on, they ran straight to that army base. And according to the survivors of the army assault on our base, they told them a pack of lies. Sacrifices." I said it loudly.

"They told them that the dungeon runs on the sacrifices of innocents. That we were killing people to gain personal power. They waited until not only were most of our forces out on a goddamn rescue mission, but until others were visiting the park to show you how far they'd come in their short weeks of training. What should have been a joyous celebration ended with those same people running like hell to come and help defend the dungeon, as our own defenders—human, kobold, goblin, and undead—were murdered in cold blood by snipers."

Silence fell.

"They blew up the wall of the dungeon and sent assassins in. They murdered our people and tried to blow up the dungeon core with a shitload of heavy explosives!" I roared.

"They attacked us. They risked us losing everything, and they did it without warning. No discussion, no fact-finding, no attempts at communication or negotiation. No, they believed what they were told by those we'd banished, and they tried to take us all out. Everything that we have—the walls, the floors, and the goddamn lights, the food and the dungeon creatures that help defend us?

"All of those would be gone as if they'd never existed, and all because a small group couldn't accept that they weren't in charge. We captured some of the group, which is why we know as much as we do. But at the end of the day, we're left with two choices. Either we ignore the army base and let them attack again, with impunity, or we do something about it."

I turned slowly, looking at them all as I took a deep breath, and let the tension build.

"I'm not asking you to fight," I said clearly. "I could, especially considering those bastards murdered so many of us. But no. I'm asking you to do as you have been. I'm asking you to help us to gather and process as much as possible to ensure that we have enough mana to rebuild and to deal with the base *for now*.

"As much as I want to go storming in there—literally—and kill them all, I know, and you know, that most of those involved won't have been even aware of the real plan, nor the consequences. Sure, the leadership will have known that there was more to the story, and most likely that the sacrifices they heard about were bullshit, but the story that they passed onto the soldiers who did the actual deed? That was that we were evil and they were going to save people.

"I could go storming in," I repeated. "But if I do that? A lot of innocent people will die. They have families, and I don't doubt they have damn honorable men and women in there. It's the leadership and the banished who are responsible. So what we need to do is deal with them in a way that gives us the best chance for survivors, and as little collateral damage as possible.

"We have a plan." I said that part loudly, seeing the relief on a lot of faces. "We have a plan, and my advisors agree it should work to contain them until the time comes to cut the head off the snake. We have limited time, though. They could launch another attack at any moment, and that one could be with all their forces. We don't know what's coming, so by necessity the plan is simple.

"We need to finish repairing our defenses, and summon more dungeon creatures to defend us. That's in progress already, but because they did so much damage and they killed so many, we have nothing to spare to deal with them.

"That's where you all come in," I said. "I know you've just finished a shift...I know I've asked for your help before, with the tower and other projects, but hell, I'm here asking again, for a few hours of your time.

"Help me to build a new wall, one that rings their base. One that's higher and stronger than they can deal with, and help me do it now. We ring their base in a high, solid wall, and we make it so that they can't climb it. We make it so that the only way they can get over it is with a hell of a lot of difficulty and effort, and we gain the time we need. They'll be able to prepare for the next stage—of course they will—but they'll be contained, and we won't have to kill them. Then, when our own forces return, we can sort this out.

"This is the only way that we can see this working without bloodshed. But again, the mana that's coming into the dungeon now is desperately needed. That's why I need your help. They used tall buildings around the dungeon as sniper nests, to rain down fire on our people, and that can never happen again.

"We've pushed out our influence to them all, almost, and although the one closest to the dungeon will stay, so that we can build on it and use it, the others have to be torn down. We need to claim them, tear those bricks and beams apart, and feed them into the dungeon to help us all. So the question is, will you help me?" I paused, then went on. "Will you help defend us all? I know I'm asking a lot, but there's simply nobody else I can ask. Will you all help?" I finished it honestly, the speech—as always—turning my back into a river of nervous sweat. And yet, as soon as I finished?

The first cheers and shouts started.

It swelled quickly, hundreds agreeing, and I treated myself to a long breath as I relaxed slightly. That was the first stage done; now we just had to watch for...

I turned, looking for them. A few of the watchers I'd put in place were still there, but three were gone, and I grinned darkly. The rats had taken the bait.

I left then; Kelly had already gone as well. And while I was making the point of being seen, and to be both helping out and clearly too busy to be watching over people, she and the others were drifting through the dungeon sense already. We had advanced kobold assassins in place, and second by second, we'd gain more mana, ready to summon more.

It was time to hit back.

I took a hundred people with me, moving northeast of the dungeon, and taking the commercial building that had sprung up in the last days before the fall, right next to the 55 Degrees North apartment block that Kelly's ex had lived in.

Others were working on that building, but the one I had before me? That was seeing the sun on its last day.

The group that drifted in behind me were a mix of experienced and new, many of them having only worked on already torn-down buildings before now, and the sheer scale of this one had to be daunting for them.

"Remember!" I called. "We're in this for the mana, not just to remove the threat from the snipers. So we start at the top, literally—go brick by brick, and block by block: absorb, break down, and then down to the next. If we start at the bottom, the building comes down fast, sure, but it'll block the sightlines from the walls, and it'll take forever to clean up. Slow and methodical, and we'll get a lot more done today, rather than rushing and making a mess, okay?"

With that in mind, I led them all to the roof, drifting through the concrete, cabling, and more, floating upward and alighting on the roof, before grinning to myself at the sight of the pigeons that wandered here and there.

Little bastards were in for a surprise.

I reached out, laying a hand on the gleaming metal of an air conditioning unit. The slowly spinning metal, driven by a gentle breeze, barely registered as my hand brushed against it.

Permeate?

Yes/No

I didn't need to think about it; the prompt barely flickered into view before it was gone, and I flicked away the next one as well.

Repair/Absorb

Absorb was obviously what I wanted. It took a handful of seconds to shift. The molecular structure of the metal broke down, transforming to motes of light, cascading away as they were drawn into the dungeon.

Not bad, I reflected. Ten points of mana for that, though the raised plinth underneath it was only worth three. It was all a start.

Fifteen minutes later, I sensed a presence by my side. I glanced over from the elevator I was working on absorbing, nodding at John as he reached out, laying his hand on a control panel and getting to work, even as he spoke.

"We got them," he said. "Three more made a break for it, and each of them were known to each other."

"What happened?"

"They tried to sneak away." He snorted. "Literally, as soon as you were done, they left the dungeon sense, fleeing to their buddies, and met up. There was one more, one who was working on another shift, but thankfully they left him a helpful note, in 'the usual place,' and it detailed exactly what they were doing before they left."

"Idiots," I muttered.

"Oh, well and truly." He grunted a laugh. "Seriously, they'd stop every few minutes and check the dungeon sense to see if they were being followed, but they'd argue over who should do it first, so we had plenty of notice and time to hide and to make sure Jack did as well. Thanks for letting us use him for this as backup too."

"Fuck's sake they're that incompetent? And yeah, no worries, then what did they do?"

"They ran straight toward the army base." He shrugged. "Well, I say 'ran'—they're complaining and whining all the way currently. Obviously I couldn't follow them all the way in the dungeon sense, so instead I dispatched the Sharons and a very annoyed pair of fighter trainees who have a lot of stealth skills, with Jack as backup as if they catch sight of him, they're used to seeing him roaming the area anyway. With the fighter trainees and the Sharons, considering their friends died in the attack, you better believe they're incentivized to catch anyone else involved."

"They know not to get seen, right?" Then I shook my head. "Sorry, that was a fucking stupid question. Of course they do. What's the next step?"

"I'll drop in on them when they approach the line we expanded along toward the hospital. It's not up to there yet, I know, but it's in progress. And unless they get lost, they should cross it in about an hour."

"And there's no way they can warn them, right?" I asked. "The barracks, I mean?"

"Not that I can see. Might be that there's an outpost hidden nearby and they're watching the park. I mean, I'd do that, so it seems common sense. If there is, then the kobolds will find them. And let's face it—while there's magic means that might work, I don't see it. I think any scouts will still have to run back to the base to warn them. We'll soon know, though, if anything changes. We've got people watching the base."

"Fair enough. Anything else to report?" I got a shake of the head but he stayed, absorbing and working for a few more minutes.

"John, I know you're busy as fuck," I pointed out. "So if you're here now, there's a reason. You aren't needed to absorb shit as much as you're needed on other jobs, so what gives?"

"I want to know what you're planning for the base and the banished when we take it," he said after a few seconds.

"A show trial and an execution for the banished and any leadership who were in on it," I said. "Then hopefully break the base up and absorb anyone into our ranks who's worth the effort."

"And you're really going to execute their leaders?" he asked me. "That doesn't bother you?"

"What?"

"Killing them in cold blood," he clarified. "Gerald, Sharon, and Merriman…whoever is in charge of the army base. You're happy to order them executed?"

"John." I turned to look at him, waiting until he faced me. "I don't like it, don't get me wrong, but there have to be consequences. They killed our people. They knew what would happen, and they did it anyway. I won't order them executed." I paused, making sure he was paying attention. "I'll do it myself."

"That's cold."

I snorted. "They attacked us. As far as I'm concerned, they deserve it, and more. You say 'cold blood'—that's just ridiculous. If I have to do everything in cold blood and without emotion? I'll never get anything done because there's shit hitting the fan every goddamn day.

"They started this, and later tonight we're having a goddamn funeral for all our people. They chose this, and they're not the ones who'll have to stand there tonight and talk about the people we lost to grieving fucking families. Believe me, it's taking all I have right now, not flying to the base myself and making this very, very personal. So yeah. My blood will be as cold as I can make it, but that won't be saying much."

"You need to be careful, Matt," John replied. "All this anger and rage? I get it. I feel the same way at times, but I've seen what it does to people, and how easy it is to go from defending your rights and other people to punishing those who cross you, because you know they're about to break the law. From there? It's a short step to tyranny."

"I'll remember that," I told him, and promptly dismissed it as soon as he'd gone.

They came to my home and they tried to kill those I love. Fuck them, fuck their rights, and fuck the horse they rode in on.

If I didn't need the extra soldiers and equipment, I'd have given the women and children the chance to leave; then I'd have turned the place into hell.

CHAPTER SIX

By the time Kelly came to me, reaching out a hand and disturbing my mindless work, between the hundred plus of us, we'd reduced the building by half. When we took into account the work that the others had managed as well, we'd earned enough with the dungeon's mana intake to build a simple wall that would ring the entire base, even if it'd not be as tall as I wanted it.

Five meters, that was all—barely bigger than three men standing atop each other's shoulders—and yet it was enough for now. Each day the wall would rise, until they realized that they had two choices: they could stay inside, or they could try to escape. And considering how high and strong that wall was going to be? Good fuckin' luck with that.

No, they were in for a surprise, and I deliberately waited until the three assholes had reached their rendezvous point with the army, two hundred meters down the road from the base, before I made it clear that we knew about them.

Kelly had the assassins capture both soldiers who had been waiting for them and the three traitors in seconds. Then they trussed them up like turkeys, and Kelly summoned a pair of skeletal laborers, having the mindless monstrosities pick up the terrified bundles and carry them down the road to the base.

The guards went ballistic as soon as they saw them. Thirty seconds later, the laborers were being ordered to halt, to surrender and more.

I ignored that, making them march closer, the struggling forms in their arms clear to see, before dumping them to the ground, from several meters up.

Then they about-faced and walked off, while we watched in the dungeon sense.

The soldiers on gate duty called for others. Several more struggled out into the dreary dying light of early evening. Winter made itself known in the plumes of breath they released as they ran across the frost-covered ground.

They grabbed the bodies and dragged them back inside, before an officer ordered the laborers be fired upon, and I growled at the senseless waste.

They were walking away, their backs shown to the enemy and still, fuckin' *still*, they had to do it. Well, that was why I'd not used the kobolds for this.

They were alive and aware; the laborers weren't.

They fell, collapsing under the onslaught, and I snorted at the thought of how much ammo had just been wasted, before the guards finally got the five back inside the rough walls.

Then, when I was damn sure that they were all inside, and any forces that were left outside were well enough hidden that I wasn't going to be finding them, I gave Kelly the nod.

She wanted to do it, and I didn't blame her, considering the work she'd put in to design and fix the wall. So when it began, I made sure that I was in the dungeon sense and inside the walls, watching the base commander's face as his little fiefdom was suddenly ringed in bright, drifting motes of light.

There was panic at first: shouting, orders being passed back and forth that included things like using grenades on the light to "kill it." Grenades were dutifully pulled, activated, and thrown. The walls solidified and bounced them right back into the base, sending their murderous gifts flying back at them.

The light gradually died away, printing as always from the ground up until the very top was finished. A wall was revealed, five meters high and one deep, made of solid granite. Then it was sheathed in a single piece of steel that ran the entire length of their territory.

There was more panic as they realized the reality of that, which slowly broke down into nervous laughter as someone pointed out that a ladder and a bit of effort was all that was needed to get over the wall.

That was when Kelly made phase two clear to them.

The section directly before the gate on the road—the gate was still there, as was their wall; it was just two meters further in than our wall, meaning they had to climb up and over, then down.

That section, though, began to glow, and slowly, oh so slowly, a platform started to grow.

Twenty meters high, it gradually extended, until it stopped. A single corpse lord appeared atop it, glaring down at them, holding a simple whiteboard in its hands, with a handwritten message on it.

We're watching you.

As threats went, it was a bit of a shitty one, I knew, but it wasn't meant as a real "I'm gonna get you" threat. It was a tiny little marker to make things clear. And the appearance of the fresh walls when they'd lost most of their attacking force only a few days ago?

We were making it clear that the power differential was bigger than they thought.

Drifting through the dungeon sense into the base and following along, I got to watch as the base commander—who was wrapped up against the cold, with ruddy cheeks and a nose that looked to be constantly running—gave a speech about "driving the evil from our lands" and "rescuing our people" and more.

Then I got to see the bluster fall away as soon as he was inside his own quarters, collapsing into a chair and dropping his head into his hands.

Two others came in, both sergeants, and he spoke to them for a few minutes, cursing "that damn fool" before agreeing that they needed to keep up their people's spirits.

I waited, giving him a minute after they left to get his head back under control. That was when I summoned a dagger. It was printed in midair; the light alerted him to finally look up, before he screamed in shock. It fell as soon as it was completed, point first, slamming into the table and sticking there, quivering, while he ran for it, bellowing for his guards to "bring me those idiots."

It was enough for me. I wasn't going to waste any more time on them. Instead, I handed it over to a pair of volunteers Clarissa had drummed up.

One was to follow the commander all day, making notes and passing the word along if he started doing anything. The other was to follow the sergeants, since in case the army started mobilizing, it'd be them who ended up doing it.

That handled, I was free to get back to actual important work.

Leaving the dungeon sense, I found Kelly standing nearby, looking away and stretching. I paused for a short while, admiring the view.

"Behave yourself, Matt." She sighed, before snorting and looking over one shoulder. "I could *hear* you perving on me."

"Hey, I just finished a job, opening my eyes, and you're bending over right in front of me...what am I supposed to do?" I asked. "Not look?"

"Yes, actually." She sighed, straightening up.

"Nope, never gonna happen." I laughed. "If I ever don't want to look, or if you ever ask me if I want to join you in the shower or whatever, and I say no? I want you to just shoot me in the head. Clearly I've given up on life and I want it all to be over."

"Don't tempt me." She shook her head. "That'll make me the Dungeon Lady, right?"

"You already are."

"I'm the Mistress of Minions, not the formal Dungeon Lady yet." She said, using her seductive voice, "So all I have to do is kill you, right?" She leaned in and kissed me.

"In bed," I clarified quickly. "Through strenuous sex and my heart has to give out."

"So, promising you sex while you're on a running machine and just upping the level won't work?" she joked.

"Fuck cardio," I replied with a look of horror. "You're my only cardio!"

"I don't know, you've been working on that rowing machine a lot..."

She broke off into a laugh as I grabbed her and dragged her into my arms, kissing her soundly and making it clear that yes, I was far more interested in cardio with her, and no, I wasn't too tired.

That, of course, was when Aly cleared her throat and gestured to the door.

"Seriously, you two, if you can't keep your hands off each other, you can go to your room!" she called.

"Sounds good to me," I replied, winking at Kelly, who laughed again as I nuzzled in and kissed her neck, before she pushed my face away and stood.

"As much as yeah, I'd love that..." she told me, "we have responsibilities. I have more work to do with the freshly summoned kobolds, setting their routines, and you have classes to teach."

"What?" I groaned. "Ah fuck, Kilo."

"Yeah, you sent him out, and with him, Ramnik, and almost all the actually half-experienced mages gone, we're down to you and the trainees. Either that's no classes until the others come back, or it's you as the teacher with Dante and Ashley helping."

"They're actually doing well," I pointed out. "Or they were."

"They really are." She nodded. "But they're still learning, and they don't have a real plan for the lessons yet. You were teaching them, and then they were teaching the others."

"I'm still learning," I admitted. "You've got a point, though. I think it's time to start the mana manipulation lessons properly."

"Sounds like a plan." Kelly leaned in for one more kiss. "I'll sort the kobolds, and get to work on the research for more of them, and…"

"And?" I saw the way she and Aly shared a look. "What's this?"

"We've got a theory," Aly said slowly, reluctantly.

"Go on," I encouraged, settling back in the chair, before smiling and mouthing "thanks" at Kelly as she slid back into her chair, summoning me a can, and herself an espresso.

"Well, what do we need from the people who are absorbing the bricks and so on?" Aly asked me, and I shrugged.

"Their time, really. A solid effort, but not much more."

"So, more of a slogging mentality than a thinking one?" she prompted.

"Yeah, but I don't want to start using people on it as punishment duty or whatever," I said. "If we do that, then it's a slippery slope, and…"

"Not what we were thinking," Kelly assured me. "So what you're saying is that we need a low level of intelligence and basically a mindless obedience?"

"And there we go." Aly smiled at me, clearly seeing the lightbulb moment.

"You think we can use minions?" I asked.

"We can." She nodded. "The kobolds can be let into it, and we already know they can summon things, like the cat calendars and food and so on. We'd just not considered the undead."

"I'm not sure how I feel about the undead being able to control the dungeon," I admitted uncomfortably.

"That's the point," Kelly said quickly. "We felt that way as well, but to absorb? Treat them as simple AI, or computers. They can only do what they're told, so we set them very specific commands, and we set a human to watch them. Plus we use specific undead—no wraiths, for example. We make some very simple undead, like the uncommon skeletons. We already did the research, but we never really thought about giving them orders beyond the mindless ones."

"Right?"

"We want your permission to try," Aly said. "Start with a single undead, literally just set them to work in a building and absorbing something, a wall or a table or whatever, then we'll experiment with the commands."

"You don't need my permission for this," I pointed out. "You've got the authority already."

"Yeah, we have the authority, but this is a seismic change. If this works, it could be incredible," Aly pointed out.

"And if it goes tits up, it'll be terrible," Kelly added quickly. "They'd have access to break things down, so if they decided to take the outer wall down, or the Parthenon, they could."

"I don't like it," I said slowly, imagining all the hard work that they could undo and biting my lip as I weighed it up. "But…they could make a hell of a difference to the mana we're taking in." I sighed. "Thinking about that side, they could be a boon."

"An incredible one," Aly agreed. "Look, Matt, we've got kobolds in the dungeon doing research. We had goblins and more. We know that there's ways that the dungeon creatures…actually, better to call them dungeon citizens, really…there's ways that they can be put to work, to be integrated that are just miles ahead of where we are."

"I know," I growled. "I just don't like it much."

"Any change is a risk," Kelly agreed, before taking a deep breath and going on. "But…I think it's worth it. Don't get me wrong, I don't like it at all, not even a little, but the potential? As long as the undead are monitored and are kept in certain areas, and for specific uses, then I think it'd be a good idea. For example, we make a hundred that are going to just dissolve buildings, or push the boundary of the dungeon."

"That's a thought," I admitted, imagining a hundred undead standing in a line at the edge of the territory in the dungeon sense, pushing outward and expanding our reach inch by inch. "Damn, that'd be useful, but that's Clarissa's job at the minute and—" I nodded.

"Clarissa and her people would be perfect to watch over the undead. Give each of them, say, twenty to lead, and have them work together. They could watch over the undead and be ready to cut them out if they do anything they don't like, but it'd mean that the teams could massively expand our reach." I nodded as I worked through it in my head.

"It'd also mean that as they work in shifts, three eight-hour ones around the clock, they could monitor them constantly. We could use this as a tester. Imagine if we moved from the people we've got working to individually absorb the bricks and so on themselves, and if each of them was say, monitoring twenty or fifty undead doing that job?" Aly suggested excitedly.

"It'd mean that we would be able to free people from the drudge work and massively increase our production," I agreed, warming to the idea.

"And it'd mean that those who want to craft, can. Think about it…if we went to each of the thousands of people we've got in the park leading fifty skeletons each, there'd be hundreds of thousands of undead. For numbers like that, we'd have the city of Newcastle stripped down to bedrock in what, a week? Two at most? Then we crash and burn because unless we've been building more methods of mana production, we'd be screwed.

"Instead, what we do is take, say, half of that…maybe less. We start with Clarissa and her people. They can guide and control the undead, and we trust them to watch over and report in. Then we scale it up to maybe three shifts of five hundred people who'll lead the skeletons—give them a title and a dedicated role. We make it something that's respected, because the job is going to be a hard one. Each individual is going to have to watch over twenty skeletons, making sure they actually work and don't fuck anything up…"

"And it doesn't have to stop there." Kelly gasped. "Oh my God, how the hell did I not see this before now?"

"What?" I asked.

"Armies," she said. "We need to raise armies to deal with our enemies, right?"

"Yeah?"

"Well, what if the skeletal builders are only the start?" She sat forward, excited. "Imagine that we have two paths for controllers, one that focuses on leading the skeletal forces to break down unused buildings and expand the dungeon out."

"Okay…" I nodded, wondering where this was going.

"What if that was just the beginning? What if the second path is that we take all the wargamers, the people who loved playing with those miniatures and studying wars and so on, and we train them?"

"I don't get it," I admitted.

"You know, the miniatures? The ones that you paint and have entire armies and stuff?" she asked excitedly.

"Yeah?" I'd had friends who loved it, but when I'd been interested, I'd not had the money to consider it, so I'd just sort of moved on.

"Well, there's two shops that sell them here in the city. I know because an ex tried to get me into it."

"You didn't like it?" I guessed.

"No, I *loved* it. But I kept whining when he tried to teach me to play, and all I got when I went to the war games on my own was looked down on for being pretty, or perved over, and not in a good way. I never went back. That's not the point, though. What if what we do is go hit those shops? Clean them out?"

"Right?" I agreed, not really seeing how her plastic crack addiction—I'd heard it referred to as that—was going to help us.

"Then we have someone like Griffiths lead the battles," she said. "We get volunteers. They get a box of like twenty or whatever, and they can paint them and relax doing it—don't look at me like that, it's fun," she said sharply, noticing the smile.

"Sorry," I said quickly, banishing it. "I was just enjoying seeing you so interested in something so geeky."

"Uh-huh. Well, they get a set of their own, and we come up with set rules, but we base them on real life, okay? Then Griffiths oversees and teaches them, and we have mock battles. Battles where they have to do things like survive ambushes, big team battles, wars and more."

"I don't get it," I confessed. "Is this just for them to relax or…?"

"They do it as training," Aly answered, smiling at Kelly. "I see what you're getting at, I think."

"It could work!" Kelly agreed. "Look, Matt, the one thing we can't replace is our people, okay? Anything else? A little time and effort, and we've got it back. Our people are our real treasure here. So what if we take them from the drudge work of breaking down the buildings, and instead we train them to fight battles, but using undead troops?"

I paused, thinking it through as she went on.

"I don't mean that they fight on the front lines, and I certainly don't mean we stop our warrior training program—we'll always need *real* frontline soldiers. But what if we make an easily replaceable segment of the army? Like the way the US was starting to use drones for everything and looking at bringing in those robot soldiers and stuff that made us all talk about Skynet. What we do is train people to be controllers. I'll guide them in basic exercises to help them to control the dungeon undead more effectively, and they'll be there, guiding them back and forth on the battlefield!"

She had a point—hell, a brilliant one, I had to admit. Having real people who could guide the undead to fight, making the most of their replaceability without the drawbacks of their innate stupidity? Hell yes, that was a wonderful thing. The only problem, as I saw it, was that for those people to be able to see the battle and help, through the dungeon sense, we needed the battle to take place in the dungeon's claimed territory.

That was a problem, and one I pointed out, making their faces fall as they realized the single flaw in the whole plan, until I started to smile evilly.

"You've got a solution," Aly accused me.

"I do," I agreed, then waggled a hand in the air from side to side. "Well, I sort of do. It's a solution that might work, but it'd need a lot of damn work."

"Is it worth the effort?" Kelly folded her arms, settling back in her chair. "I mean, if it's a lot of work?"

"It could be." I shrugged. "Depends on what you're thinking. But if we use the solution, we'd have to make serious investments to keep it being usable. The upside? We'd be able to create reinforcements."

"The dungeon seed." Aly suddenly snapped her fingers, sitting forward. "You're talking about the dungeon seed!"

"Yup." I grinned. "If we use the dungeon seed, then any area we claim is now part of the dungeon. We just have to make sure we can pick the battlefield, and we choose a high mana density area. Then we have our controllers push out their skeletons to expand the control area of the dungeon, and make sure we fight inside it. That way, we can also absorb the dead. Our enemies become resources for us to pay for reinforcements."

"We could build fortifications in minutes," Aly breathed. "Control the battlefield in ways that no army ever has."

"Exactly." I nodded. "Create pit traps that we can activate when we want…let them march half their army over them, then they give way. Slaughter their forces."

"That only works if we're facing large forces, though," Kelly pointed out after a minute of thought. "What if they break into smaller groups?"

"Then we look for another solution," I said. "We work to push out our control as far as possible, and we secure the area. It might be that none of this works, that what sounds good in theory is impossible in practice. But if we can make it work, it could be incredible."

"It'd also mean that the people who want to assist but just aren't capable of fighting as soldiers on the front line, or as mages, could still help," Kelly added. "We need something for people to do once they stop working on absorbing the buildings. Don't get me wrong—I'm not saying that we take them off that…put a small team in to monitor the undead as they work and then the others all just sit and drink beer all day.

"We free them up from the crap jobs, so that they can improve themselves and help the dungeon as well as live better lives. They and we always knew this stage was a short-term one. People won't work seven days a week, around the clock, and put in their top effort forever.

"It's human nature that they'll want to improve themselves. Some will want to do dungeon runs. Others—" She grinned. "They could do *dungeon runs*."

"Yeah?" Aly agreed, nodding; then she covered her eyes and shook her head. "Matt, you need to watch yourself. I always knew Kell was quick, but that's just sneaky!"

"What am I missing?" I asked, confused.

"If we can get a large enough area claimed and put aside, and enough mana coming in, then we could hold weekly war games. Make it a replacement for TV, or football. We set aside a large space, like a valley, and the teams that win in the daily war games get to put together a team that can run the dungeon and fight while everyone watches. We just make it an outdoor dungeon, one that everyone can see, and the controllers get to learn 'on the job.' That way, they get bonuses as well, like the winning side gets, say, half the coin split between them from the reliquaries. The rest goes into the economy. And any magical loot? Just like the dungeon runs are now—we get to make copies. That way, you'll end up with people who are really good, who win regularly, creating elite teams and kitting them out with all magical gear, and it costs us nothing."

"Beyond the dungeon setup and the summoning of the creatures," I pointed out.

"That's a training expense," Aly explained. "We do it for, say, a small valley, and the cost of the first setup, expansion across it, and the breaking down of everything will more than cover the costs. Then we use the rest to build the converters, have them put the mana they generate into a special pot or collection point. You can use it the rest of the week, but on the weekend?"

"It pays for the dungeon setup." I nodded. "It'll train our people, give them better morale from the entertainment, and gives people something to look forward to."

"It's a win-win." Kelly grinned. "So, that's the plan: essentially, we train people to watch over the skeletons in the dungeon sense; that gives us a massive burst in productivity, and we trial it with a small team first. Then, once the concept is proven, we reduce the teams that have to absorb the bricks and crap out of that side, and have some of them start studying war games, those who want to.

"The others can watch over and guide the skeletons in their day-to-day work, and they keep the dungeon growing, as well as massively speed it up. We start making dungeon seeds just in case...are they expensive?"

"A million mana each." I nodded.

"*Very* expensive, but okay, they'd be linked to here still. We can make dungeons at each location as we grow, anyway—pick the really high mana areas, and it'll both cut out the growth of monsters in those areas and give us footholds. Then we can take in more and more people, increase the dungeons, and it becomes an exponential growth surge."

"In the beginning, we keep people to certain jobs," I said slowly, thinking about it. "Make it clear that when people are accepted into the dungeon, they work physically, say, sorting the things we recover or whatever. Then, as they earn more trust, they get low-level access to help guide the undead. Make it a tier system so they have to earn our trust before they get real access. That way, if there are any more like those three shitbags, they can't do real damage."

"That works," Kelly agreed. "So, can we do it?"

"Do it." I nodded. "But include Clarissa in it. As I said, I want her watching over it, and use her people to guide the undead at first."

"As much as it's not polite to say it, the elderly citizens have pretty much taken to working under her exclusively, and they're split at the minute. Those who want to work absorbing things and expanding have formed one side, and the other watching over the kids we have. This will give them a third choice," Aly said softly.

"Thing is, with access to the Life converters, a lot of the older people are recovering memories and more that were thought lost for good. Most mental conditions have either been cured or are in the process of it. It means that we've got a handful of centenarians who fought in the Second World War, and who now have access to their memories again. They could be invaluable in this."

"*War never changes,*" I quoted. "Okay, yeah, go for it. Okay, do you need me for anything else?"

"Nope, go play." Kelly grinned at me, reaching over and patting me on the head. "Go on, run along."

"I'll leave you to play with your new toys then!" I nodded and climbed to my feet, before leaning in and exchanging a kiss with Kelly. Then I put my lips to her ear and whispered that we could play with some other toys later.

That earned me a look I recognized. Grinning, I headed for the door, before pausing as Aly called out a reminder that the funeral was tonight for those we'd lost in the attack. I nodded, then left, jogging along the corridor and down the stairs, hearing the rising noise of the children below.

As I came out into the main plaza of the Parthenon, I slowed, glancing around.

This was something that had come about almost accidentally, considering we'd created the Parthenon as a governmental building and to sort of show off more than anything, adding in things like places for people to gather as an afterthought.

Now, as I looked around, seeing a smiling octogenarian sitting with a dozen small children and singing the alphabet, I couldn't help but think that this was the greatest accomplishment we'd managed as a group.

Magic and everything was incredible, but at the end of days, when the dead walked the earth and literal monsters roamed, slaughtering the innocent and guilty alike, having a place like this?

Somewhere that parents were bringing their children and leaving them to learn and play, knowing they'd be safe—it was incredible.

I sped up as one of the groups spotted me and started talking. Before they could say anything, I hurried across the floor, giving them an awkward wave and leaving.

I'd been caught out by that once already, a woman having her little class all stand up and chorus "thank you, Dungeon Lord." It had been both a heartwarming and incredibly awkward feeling, and I'd resolved to never let anyone catch me like that again.

Now, as I pushed open the door, I winced, stepping out into traditional Newcastle winter weather, which was to say, it was pissing down.

Literally, the rain was washing across the dungeon in great sheets, not helped, even I had to admit, by the sheer number of Air, Water, Lightning, and Storm converters up on the buildings around me.

They affected the local environment, and as I walked across the wet roads, the steam and fog of the heated pool only increasing the gloom, I thought seriously about adding in some Fire converters as well.

They didn't make a huge difference, but if I was to add one every ten meters or so around the perimeter, it'd raise the overall temperature inside slightly. That, in turn, would cut down on the fog as the air and water wouldn't be at such a massive difference and…

And I resolved to ask Aly and hand it off to her after a little more thought. Fucking with the weather was probably a massive mistake, more than I already had anyway. And at least if she did it, it'd be with reasoned-out consideration and solid plans.

I was just going to chuck a few things out until something changed, after all, and that was definitely not the way to deal with this.

Jogging around the pool and heading to the tower, I had to admit it'd be nice to be able to see clearly, though, as the mist, steam, or fog—whatever it was classed as—was getting annoying.

Approaching the tower, I slowed, cursing myself for not even thinking about the lessons before now, and frantically racking my brain on what I could do, while simultaneously thinking that there was almost certainly going to be nobody about anyway, so it'd be an easy one.

Oh gods, was I wrong.

CHAPTER SEVEN

As I opened the door and slid in—gripping the edge as a sudden errant gust of wind tried to rip it free—I was hit by a wall of noise, and I winced instinctively.

It was manic. When I'd been here earlier I'd found a comfortable hum filling the room, now it was bedlam, with people talking over one another and practically shouting to be heard.

There had to be at least five hundred people here. Glancing at the raised stage, I saw Dante, Ashley, and a handful of others standing there talking or moving through the crowds. The handful of kobolds, that had presumably been given focal orbs, stood in a tight group, staring around and trying to come to terms with things.

I pushed through the crowds to the center and jumped up onto the stage, finally getting the attention of the small group who hurriedly shut up, turning to face me.

As they did that, and more and more people saw that I was on the stage now, the silence spread.

"What the hell's going on here?" I asked the small group, noting the way that Ashley's friends Emma and Jenn, the wives of the two massive new recruits Jimmy and Andre who were with the advance team, were backing away quickly.

I let them go, glancing from Ashley to Dante and back again, pointedly not commenting on the focal orbs that I'd noticed were being clutched in both of the girls' hands.

"You asked me to give out the focal orbs..." Dante started.

I nodded, glancing around the room, and back at him pointedly. "Yeah, I did, and I can totally understand the kobolds and five very carefully chosen people being given orbs. But this isn't five people."

"Ummm, word got out?" Dante tried, his cheeks crimson with embarrassment.

"This is my fault," Ashley said, drawing my eye. "I asked Dante if we could check Jenn and Emma, see if they had a high enough affinity to make it worth training them with the focal orbs, and he agreed. I told them what we were doing, and they had some friends with them, and..."

"And there were a lot of people here already," Dante finished for her. "The classes are usually on now, after all, so there were people here who were trying to study others who were here because they didn't know where else to be..."

"It wasn't that long ago I was here," I pointed out. "Kilo and a small group were here, but not that many others..."

"They were spread across the floors," Ashley explained. "Now that there's more converters, people are going to their floors, and they like being there even when there's nothing else going on."

"You just naturally feel drawn to the converters that suit you." I sighed. "I get it. And they all left there and came here because word spread you were giving out focal orbs?"

"Basically, yeah," Dante whispered, looking mortified.

"Great." I cursed. "Okay, how many have you given out and who to?"

"I gave two to the kobolds," he said quickly. "It's Inferno, and the kobolds are really good with Fire magic. I think it's something to do with their draconic lineage and—"

"And Kilo is a cryomancer," I said. "It's more that we were lucky, I bet, but go on."

"Right, crap." He closed his eyes, thinking about it, and went on. "The other is Tar, the Earth-based spell. I was thinking that both crowd control and working with that and Fire would work well, as well as a single healing spell."

"And that's the kobolds?" I asked, getting a nod. "Great. How many to the humans? And I really hope that those two didn't just get them because they're your friends, Ashley." I clearly nodded in the direction of the pair who looked to be trying to hide in the crowd.

"They did and they didn't," she conceded. "Jenn got a healing spell as well. Her Life magic is at sixty-eight, which we've given that spell out on a focal orb before for less."

"Uh-huh," I agreed. "And Emma?"

"Thunderbolt," Ashley admitted.

"That's a hell of a spell," I pointed out slowly. "A powerful one that hurts if her affinity isn't high enough. What is it?"

"Sixty-three."

"That's high, but not high enough," I said. "Kelly was hurt when she used Inferno at that level. Yeah, it was only minor burns, but she was sixty-eight. For Emma to have Lightning high enough to even think of using the Thunderbolt spell is great. She'll probably be offered a class that will boost it and then she can—"

"Matt, trust me," Ashley said quietly. "Emma wanted that orb. And if I need to find anyone hard and focused enough that they'll still do what's needed, it's her."

"It'll hurt her," I pointed out forcefully, still seriously considering taking it from her and to hell with the hurt feelings.

"It will. And her first words, when I told her that, was that it was fine. It'd give Jenn a chance to heal her and improve her skills. Trust me on this, Matt. Jenn has an absolute heart of gold, and she'll do anything to help anyone. But Emma? She'll crawl over broken glass to protect those she loves. She'd watch the world burn if she had to. She's hard—I know that's not a good thing, but that's because she's been hurt, and hurt a lot. I remember when Ramnik and the others wouldn't touch that orb, out of the fear of what it might do to them. I told her that, and she took it anyway."

"That might be because—"

"Because she wants to jump the line and just take advantage of the situation," Ashley finished for me. "Matt, you asked me to help, and to guide you when I know something. You promised to listen. Well, now's that chance. I know Emma was rude to you when you first met her, and she's…well, she can be a bitch."

Ashley took a deep breath, reaching up and tugging an errant hair free of the corner of her mouth as she spoke.

"Trust me, though. She'll earn this spell ten times over. And if there's anyone you can trust at your back, to protect the dungeon because her family is going to be living in it, it's her. Please."

I hesitated, still not sold on the whole concept, especially considering how many others were here waiting in hopeful silence. But she was right.

There had to be a level of trust here, and I trusted Ashley. If she was saying that Emma and Jenn were worth this little bit of extra trust? Well, I already let them in. Ashley and Dante did a shitload without ever complaining. I had a sudden mental image of the way that she'd changed to show herself off before the nexus meeting, acting like a dumb bimbo to distract, divide, and conquer, knowing exactly what she was letting herself in for, and how the other Dungeon Lords and Ladies would see her.

She'd done that without pause, because it gave me an advantage.

Well, now she was asking for my trust.

"Fine." I nodded. "You've earned that."

"Thank you." She let out a long breath, smiling shakily.

"No, Ashley, you earned it," I repeated. "Frankly, I trust you, both of you. But now we've got three more orbs to give out—"

"No, we don't." Dante spoke up suddenly.

"What?"

"We've...we've only got four," he explained.

I closed my eyes, taking a deep breath. "I thought we had more?" I racked my brain for why I'd thought that.

"I know, I thought that as well." Ashley bit her lip. "The kobolds...they've got two, Tar and Inferno, and Jenn and Emma have Healing and Thunderbolt. You said you were going to train them all with the orbs, so I guessed..."

"Wait, I thought we'd emptied the damn orbs anyway?" I frowned. "Weren't they reset to Healing because we needed Healing ones so much?"

"The Inferno was; I just put it back in that one," Dante admitted. "The others were kept. We were going to wipe them, but even Jo agreed that it was better to have the other two spells ready if we needed them."

"Right." I sighed. "Okay, give me a goddamn minute," I grumbled, before settling into a chair and closing my eyes, reaching out to Aly and Kelly, who were fortunately working together still.

"What's the problem?" Aly asked abruptly when I appeared before them in the dungeon sense. "What did you break?"

"Nothing!" I protested.

"What did you lose?" Kelly asked, and I glared at her.

"Considering I've seen you searching our rooms for your clothes, it's not me who's always losing shit," I growled. "But..."

"Told you." Kelly snorted, looking at her sister-in-law.

"Dammit."

"What's this?" I looked from one to the other.

"We bet that if you came running, it'd be for a reason, and we each picked three questions." Kelly grinned. "So, what did you lose?"

"I didn't lose anything," I grumbled. "I thought we had more focal orbs though, and we've only got four."

"Six," Aly corrected.

"Four according to Dante," I countered. "That's all he could find, anyway."

"There were six," Aly replied slowly, looking worried.

"Jo took one," Kelly pointed out.

"Okay, that's fine. And the missing last one then?" I looked from one to the other.

"I...don't know," Aly admitted. "Which spells do they have?"

"Thunderbolt, Tar, Healing, and Inferno, but the Inferno had to be put back in by Dante," I reeled off.

"Then we're missing another Healing," Aly replied as Kelly suddenly vanished. "It was Nature's Glory that was put in the other one, and Chris was using it to boost the growing speed of the farms."

"That heals as well, yeah?" I asked, wondering whether we'd used it already.

"It does...makes an entire season's worth of healing and regrowth happen in a short timescale." Aly looked distracted as she struggled to remember. "If I'm right, it doesn't heal so much as speed up time. So if you'd lost a finger, it'd not regrow it; it'd just heal over the stump maybe? I don't really remember."

"Either way, we're down one." I sighed.

"No, we're not." Kelly reappeared. "Chris has it at the farm."

"Why the hell..." I started, then shook my head. "You know what, I don't need to know."

"He's got Starr with him, and the kobold is using it. I think they're trying to boost the growth of alchemical ingredients."

"Damn," I muttered. "Another perfectly good reason to shout at Chris for being an idiot, lost."

"He'll give you another reason soon." Kelly smiled. "Okay, so was that it?"

"No," I said sadly, shaking my head. "I need another kobold."

"For?" Aly asked, all business.

"To work in the glassblowing room." I resigned myself to it. "As much as I want to use it, we need someone who can work in there, and I just don't have the damn time. We got someone who's a natural with Sand mana, right? She had over a hundred affinity, uh..."

"Alison," Aly supplied. "She's started your magic lessons, and she's at a hundred and four."

"Okay, well, she's going to be learning to work in the glassblowing area as well," I said. "She had no clue if she could help or not, but with an affinity that high? She needs to spend all her time working with sand in one way or another. If we give my monocle that had the thirty levels of skills to the kobold we summon and have him take twenty in Glassblowing and ten in Magical Artificing, or whatever it's called, then she can work with him. They should be able to figure out a focal orb in pretty short order with one to examine. Or, failing that, they should at least be cheaper to produce through the dungeon."

"Why not give Alison the monocle?" Kelly asked.

"Because if she's at a hundred and four affinity, we need her to evolve naturally," I said. "Whatever skill she's going to develop is going to be insane, and if it's even just building fucking amazing sandcastles, I want to see what it is without us guiding her off course."

"Okay, are you sure about giving the monocle away?" Kelly asked after a few seconds. "That's a hell of a boost you're giving up. And not only did you literally fight and bleed for it, but it could boost anything. I agree we need magical artifacts and having things like potion tubes that concentrate and purify the potion instead of breaking as soon as you look at them would be amazing, but…"

"But we could have a sniper, or a magical researcher who's incredible," I agreed. "I could leapfrog my mana manipulation skill through the roof, or my teaching skill. Anything, really, could be fantastic for us as a community." I took a deep breath, then went on. "But a perfect plan a week from now is useless; a plan now gains us something. We'd gain a lot more by holding off until we have the perfect situation, but fuck it. We can't afford to wait."

"If we could get the focal orbs, we could produce mages by the hundreds. And even if that stunts their growth one day, it might be the difference between them being around to complain about it at some point and not," Aly added, clearly not happy, but seeing the sense. "Okay, I'll summon one. Where should I do it?"

"Next to me in the tower." I sighed. "Might as well get it done as soon as possible."

She nodded, and I felt a ghost of a kiss on my cheek from Kelly, before I was blinking my eyes open, looking around as people gasped, nudging and pointing at the stage.

The kobold that started to appear from the motes of light was almost generic-looking by now. Each advanced kobold was slightly different; they weren't like the other creatures that were summoned from uncommon down. Instead, at advanced, you got a mixture of traits and affinities, and remembering that, as the kobold started to appear, I cursed inwardly, steadying myself and sliding into the dungeon sense again, then flitting across to the girls.

"How do we know if he's going to have an affinity for crafting?" I asked them both, getting dismayed swearing as my only answer. "Great," I grumbled, then left again, blinking as the line of light rose higher and higher.

The crafted kobold was stock-still, lifeless until the last motes slid into place, dimming and leaving a slightly mottled pattern across their scales.

"Can you hear me?" I asked the kobold, and he blinked, seeming confused, before slowly nodding. "You understand me?" I tried again, and he nodded, again. "Good! Welcome to life and the fight. What's your highest affinity?"

Dante had to step in and explain how to find the affinity menu, but when he did, the answer, although I'd been expecting it, wasn't what I'd hoped.

"Gardening."

Not that I'd expected gardening, of course; it was just that I'd expected anything bar fuckin' crafting.

"What's your Glassblowing affinity?"

"None."

"That makes sense," Dante said softly, clearly hesitant to interrupt, but knowing something.

"Why?"

"If he's never tried it out, he might not have anything to compare it to. The system seems to give people one skill, and then anything else you learn on your own."

"All my high affinities and skills are things I work at," Ashley admitted next. "I've got random affinities, but they're all linked to things I've done, even if I don't agree with the title."

"Korean cooking," I remembered with a grunt. "Kelly has a high affinity for it," I explained when I got confused looks from some of those nearby. "She's never done it, but she cooked enough that was similar that the system assigned her that as an affinity. Okay, crap."

I scratched my chin, then nodded. "What's your highest crafting affinity?" I asked the kobold, and snorted in grim amusement at the answer.

"Woodwork, seven percent."

"And just like that, we found a soldier." I sighed. "Sorry, mate, that came out wrong." I examined him, double-checking, then nodded. He had no particular perks, wasn't good enough at any skill or affinity that he stood out, and was basically average in every area.

"Okay, Dante?" I turned and glanced at him, getting a nod as he straightened. "I want you to take our friend here, go check the affinities with the other group of kobolds, then head out and find Beta and her trainees. I want the very highest-leveled crafter you can find. And if they have Glassblowing or Magical Artifice or whatever as well, that'd be a bonus."

"On it." He nodded, drawing the confused kobold aside and leading him down the steps from the raised stage.

"Now what?" Ashley asked, looking around at the still watching crowd.

"Now we try to teach a goddamn class, and explain to people that they don't all get to jump ahead." I sighed. "Damn, I wish you'd been more subtle about that."

"I'm sorry," she whispered, forcing a smile and looking confident for the people watching. "I'll do...I don't know, but I'll make it right."

"You're fine." I smiled, joining her in pretending everything was under control. "It was an innocent thing, and it wasn't you who spread the word. Next time, we just need to be a little more careful, that's all."

And with that, I turned and clapped, addressing the crowd. "Okay, people, time to talk about magic..." I started, taking a deep breath and going straight for it.

"So, first point, and I'll get this out of the way fast. No. I'm not skipping the plan I already discussed with you all, and I'm not forcing a focal orb on you to boost your chances of getting a magic class."

There was a wave of groans and complaints that rose at that, and I held both hands up placatingly.

"There's a reason!" I called out firmly. "If we do that, you'll be offered a class that's appropriate to the experience you've got. In this case, that means that one of you who may have received a class that would have guided you in making magical artifacts could end up as a warmancer.

"Alternatively, one of you who wants to fight, to be there marching out to battle with us and defending their friends and family, not to mention the much more rapid growth in power that comes with it, might end up casting spells to help the plants grow instead."

I finished looking around as the complaints dropped off sharply.

"Now, yes, there are a small number of those here who will be provided with focal orbs to cast spells through, and the reason for that is that we lost so many recently! We're asking these people to make sacrifices, to give up the possible unique classes that could have propelled them to incredible power.

"They might still end up with gifts to rival the gods, but it's much more likely that they'll end up stunted in their growth…" I paused, noting the sudden worried look on Emma and Jenn's faces. "Just like me," I finished, seeing the now popping eyes at that.

"Yes," I clarified. "I used artifacts to force my path…in this case, the dungeon core. My gifts are in Lightning, in the Storm, and I'm a Storm Titan in ascension now. Without the time lost to the dungeon, and the changes wrought in me there? I might be very different—far more powerful, for a start. That's what the paths that lie before you can guide you to.

"Lastly, to be very clear, those who wish to sacrifice and are brave enough to ask to use the focal orbs, there are two things you must understand. One is that you *must* have a high affinity for the spells being offered. That means if, for example, you have a low affinity for Fire, and you used the Inferno orb, you'd be horrifically burned by the backlash. That's a very, very well-known consequence. It's why certain people are being given that chance, because their natural affinities are appropriate."

That closed down a lot of the last grumbles, and more people slowly drifted back, giving us all some more room.

"The final point is that in accepting this, in accepting the orb and saying you'll use it? You're giving up your right to back out. If you have a Water affinity and Growth, perhaps, as I've said, your future lies in spells of rain that boost the growth of food production.

"If, however, you take Thunderbolt, you accept that you will become a living weapon, and you'll come to the fight when I call." I made the point of looking directly at Emma as I said that. "If you do this…" I said it to her more than any other now, "then if I order you to the wall, to stand in the path of incoming fire to defend the dungeon and those we love, you damn well do it. Or, by my word, I'll make damn sure the ability to cast any kind of magic is burned out of you. If I can't trust you, I'll not be leaving you at my back with magic."

"I'll fight," she replied, her voice clear in the silence that fell. "I accepted that risk, and I still do. My husband is out there fighting for us all right now…I'll not do any less."

"Then I'll take you," I agreed. "And thank you for your trust and bravery." I turned around the rest of the room, looking and waiting, letting the silence grow longer and longer before I spoke again. "We have a very limited number of focal orbs, and frankly, there's no point in even looking at it, unless you're willing to risk the possible consequences. Those, in turn, are pointless if you've got less than a sixty-five percent affinity in Earth, Fire, Lightning, or Healing."

Silence fell like lead as people checked their affinities.

"If you have sixty-five, that is the MINIMUM I will accept. And be warned—that level will leave you injured. For Fire? That's likely to take the case of third- or even fourth-degree burns. For Ramnik, when we experimented and she tried it, she got fifth. For those who don't know what fifth-degree burns are, it's essentially when the skin is gone, not burned—it's been rendered to charcoal, and the muscles are in the third- and fourth-degree burns stage.

"That's the level of burns that cannot be recovered from, without magic. Understand this—magic is fuckin' dangerous!" I called out. "If you fuck about, you will find out. Not *might*…WILL."

I looked around slowly before going on.

"Now, if you have an affinity above that point, and are willing to make this choice, come and see me at the end of the lesson. Ideally, it'll be in the seventy-five to eighty range, as we believe that will mark you safe. For your information, if you hit a hundred, anything over that is how much you will be *healed* by that element. In my case, using lightning against me literally heals me, so yeah, that's been a nasty shock for a few of my enemies. In each case, it was the last surprise they ever received."

A little nervous laughter greeted that as I grinned around.

"So, with that in mind, and now that I'm betting you're looking at me a little less like a side of meat, as the one who has control over the orbs, it's time to begin the lesson! First of all, mana manipulation! So, as you should have all learned to sense your mana core by now, we're going to teach you about circulating your mana. Either way, though, partly because we have new members…" the kobolds straightened at that, "and because we will no doubt have people who would forget they have a head if it wasn't attached, we're going to go over the basics first…"

CHAPTER EIGHT

It took two hours, and by the time I'd finished, we gained eight new kobold warriors as well. I shook my head in disbelief that it'd taken nine attempts to summon one that was worth using up the damn monocle on.

That wasn't fair, I forced myself to accept. They were all compatible; it was just that until the ninth, not a single goddamn one had a crafting ability higher than ankle high on a damn toddler.

When the ninth appeared and was examined, Dante, punched the air and shouted out, totally disrupting the goddamn lesson I was leading, before apologizing to everyone and bringing her over to me.

"Crafting is fifty-nine!" he hissed at me in a stage whisper that carried halfway across the room. "Jeweler is sixty-four!" He went on, as both I and the freshly spawned kobold stared at him, waiting for him to elaborate. "It means that she's naturally adept at working with heat, fine details, and careful, valuable work. She's as perfect as we could get without finding an actual glassblower!"

"Okay, thank you, mate." I nodded to him, then smiled a greeting at the new kobold. "Dante, can you take over the lesson now?" I asked him, getting a shrug and a nod, before I led the kobold away, noting the looks the other kobolds were giving her.

I looked at her and couldn't figure out what they were looking at, and dismissed it, guessing that the details of kobold sexuality could stay damn well opaque as far as I was concerned.

"Okay, first of all, I'm Matt, the Dungeon—" I started to explain to her when we were off to one side, and she cut me off.

"Dungeon Lord." She nodded. "How do I serve?" she asked abruptly.

"I desperately need a glassblower," I replied honestly. "But you have to be interested in the skill, and want to do it. You'll be learning a lot, and you'll have to teach yourself most of it, experimenting and figuring things out as you go. I have a monocle that should bestow thirty points of skill on you, split across two skills. That's the good news. It'll give you a boost to start off with, and make things a little easier on you, but..."

I paused, looking at her carefully, as she cocked her head to one side, birdlike.

"But I don't know for sure this will work on you," I went on quickly. "I want it to, I *need* it to, but it was a quest reward, and honestly, this could help us out massively in a thousand different areas. If you're not willing to dedicate yourself to learning about and growing as a glassblower, then I'd rather know now. It won't be held against you. And if you don't want to be a crafter, I guess you can work as a fighter or..."

"I want to craft," she said softly, then louder. "Crafter. It...it calls to me, though I don't know why."

"Well, that's a good start." I sighed. "Okay, glassblowing, that's where I summoned you to work, but I need you to understand that it's likely to be boring and repetitive, at first at least. And I'd really recommend you use the monocle sparingly."

"I can do it," she said slowly. "If this is my calling, I can grow to embrace it."

"It's why I summoned you," I admitted again. "Okay, look. First, I think you should use the monocle to get a single level in the skill, Glassblowing, I mean, then..."

"Then save the other points until I hit a threshold," she whispered, obviously seeing it as clearly as I did. "Learn, then use the skill."

"Exactly." I sighed. "Okay, once I give you this, I think you can use it as much as you want. I won't be able to guide you, so I guess, just don't waste it, all right? I had to fight and bleed a lot to get it."

"I will earn your trust," she said. "What is my name?"

"Uh..." I thought for a second, then blurted the first thing that wasn't specific to crafting, as that was all that I could think of at first, and that seemed a bit shitty to do to her now that she was conscious. "Sierra."

She nodded, reaching out and taking the monocle from my outstretched hand and examining it, before looking around in curiosity. "And I am to craft here?"

"Shit, no. This way." I shook my head, waving to Dante to finish the lesson.

He nodded, giving me a wave of acknowledgment and going on, as he spoke about the joy of finding your mana and your first spells.

I stepped up to the edge of the platform and dropped off, barely noticing the six-foot drop as I did it, bending the knees and straightening, before nodding to myself as the advanced kobold that I now knew as Sierra landed next to me.

She, like all advanced kobolds, was impressive as all hell, looking more like a humanoid dragon than a lizard or beast.

The original kobolds were unthinking creatures of the dungeon, literally upright lizards that could carry out the most basic of tasks, and little more. They were gifted the basic knowledge they needed from the dungeon—much as Sierra had been, I guessed, with her crafting affinity—and yet, they'd been mobs, without a doubt.

They were created as cheap—compared to the new costs, anyway—mobs to fill the dungeon. They could live and die without making any real effects on the world around them, deeply replaceable and unidentifiable.

The "advanced" creatures, and even the uncommon ones, were a hell of a different level.

The dungeon-summoned creatures ranged from "basic" or "pathetic" to common, uncommon, advanced and then higher, though advanced was the highest I'd reached so far.

The creatures that were summoned at basic and common were clones, male and female, but beyond that they were identical. At uncommon and scaling up from there, they started to have differences, though, especially in the affinities and awareness levels.

It'd taken a while for Beta to grow fully aware, developing from a bland cookie-cutter mindlessness to a fully formed sapient, self-aware, and now one of my most trusted companions.

Sierra, like all advanced kobolds as far as I knew, had awoken on summoning, self-aware and both stronger and smarter than the average human.

Where our stats started at around five to ten, at most, the advanced kobolds had twelve as the average stat, and climbed from there.

Ten to twelve as a difference might not sound much, but when you considered that an Olympic bodybuilder who spent their entire life working to get to that level—or an athlete of any kind, really—might be very lucky to hit twelve at all, and this was the average for them? As a starter?

It meant that the average advanced kobold could match or even outrun the fastest human alive if they were both level zero. That the same kobold could then go on to compete in every single goddamn other Olympic category was incredible.

Sure, there was a big difference between capability and skill, and the mind and mental drive was always a massive part of it, meaning that if they were both, again to use the running analogy, twelves in say, agility, but the human had years of practice as a sprinter, they'd beat an unskilled kobold.

The issue there was that the kobold would have strength, endurance, and more all at twelve as well.

The reason all these things went through my mind then was because it'd taken me multiple levels to be able to ignore dropping six damn feet without even noticing, and she just did it easily, her wings flaring and tail bouncing as she did.

As we started to walk toward the exit, I waved to Alison, the Sand mage, and gestured for her to join us, getting a confused nod as she clambered to her feet from sitting, listening to Dante as she had been.

I also couldn't help but see the way the handful of kobold mage trainees were still staring after Sierra and winced, hoping that wasn't how I looked to them when I was watching Kelly.

Passing out into the street and into what was now a heavy damn rainstorm, I cursed and ran, keeping our speed down so that Alison could keep up easily enough.

The distance was short, thankfully, but as we rounded the dungeon building and headed into the crafting one, I heard more raised voices as soon as we stepped inside. This time it wasn't from happy people engaged in general conversation either, much to my annoyance.

The crafters under Finn were arguing, as Finn tried to calm them all.

"Seriously, what the hell?" One of the figures, a man I didn't know, was complaining. "One minute, it's that we're getting a crafting station, then we're not; then we all get better ones, then we're not till next week, or next month. Does he have a plan or is he making this shit up as he goes?"

"I do have a plan, yes, thanks for asking," I said loudly, hiding that childish surge of satisfaction as the random complainer turned around, then went white as a sheet.

"Matt!" Finn grinned at me. "Great timing there, buddy. Want to take the floor and explain a few things to our people?"

"Not particularly." I forced a smile as I strode forward, nodding to the people I knew, and noting the way the complainer was moving to hide in the middle of the crowd now. That was when I noticed that what had to be the glassblowing setup, an entire section on the far side of the people who were standing around complaining, had been stripped.

Seeing that, I took a deep breath, trying to maintain my calm as I looked it over. What Aly and Kelly had shown me as the overall design was now nothing like what Sierra was going to be working in.

The room was large—hell, the crafting area was now in the building that had once held the local newspaper printing press, one that had produced tens of thousands of papers a day.

Once we'd taken it over, the dilapidated and scrap-filled building had been cleared out, and it'd become a dual-use facility. The walls had been reinforced, as had the roof, and much to my constant chagrin, I'd once again forgotten that the damn harvesting facility was up there as well.

It was in the smaller northwest portion, on the second floor of the building that we still had the basic gathering facility, though that had long since outlived its use even there.

The ground floor was a rough triangle and massive, which was fortunate, as the design that Aly and Kelly had gone with for the crafting area was essentially grouping each craft into its own area with complementary units nearby.

That meant that so far, with the machinist, armory, blacksmiths and glassblowers all complete, that took up about a quarter of the available space.

That was great and all...plenty of space to expand. But what I'd not considered? The people who didn't have anywhere built yet had been making use of the "unused" facilities.

So far, that was the machinist and glassblowing setups, with the equipment that was built and seriously important for those jobs being moved the hell out of the way. In the case of the really sensitive and fragile stuff that both areas needed, they were now piled up in a mass, and looked to have been looted.

There were two makeshift stations set up inside the damn glassblowing section that I could see from here!

"Okay, people, I didn't catch much of that, but I did hear that there were complaints about the building schedule and concerns that I keep changing it." I paused, looking at the figure who was apparently now really interested in his shoes, and reminded myself that they were trying to help, and not to scream "Who the fuck did this shit" at them.

"There's a very simple reason for that. I know you don't like the changes, but believe me, neither do I," I said, after a deep and calming breath. "So, after the recent attack, once again, we've lost a significant number of our defenders, both human and dungeon-born, and the priority is always to make sure that we're safe here. We need to summon more defenders, arm them and make damn sure we're all safe before we spend mana on infrastructure. With that in mind, I made the decision to change from making common or even basic crafting facilities, to making you all uncommon-grade ones.

"That's not cheap...it's around the entire production of the dungeon in mana, for a full day, to do that—and that's for each individual station. So, let's look at it. Considering the dungeon also needs mana for food, light, and to use the doors, not to mention keeping our summoned allies alive, we had two easy choices to make.

"First, we could make you a basic station, like this…" I gestured to the crafting station Finn had been working in: a table and a simple area to house it and little else in a self-contained unit. "And then later on, we could upgrade to a slightly better one, and then again, months down the line we could repeat that process."

I paused, looking around, and smiled at the genuine nods as a few people remembered that there were authentic needs that had to come first.

"Or, I could do what I'm doing now and get you the very best we can afford, as quickly as I can." I tucked my thumbs behind my belt as I spoke, forcing myself to relax and not glare at the complainer. "I know you need the facilities, because frankly we need the things you'll be able to make if you have access to them. That brings me to why I'm here now. I'd like to introduce Sierra." I gestured to the kobold, who stared at them all impassively.

"Sierra is our first kobold crafter, and she's agreed to study glassblowing." I looked over at Alison and gestured at her as she smiled hesitantly, understanding her place here. "And this is Alison, who will be learning magic, as a highly gifted natural mage, with experience with Sand. The reason she and Sierra are here should be clear. And yes, I know you want different crafting stations each. I'm focusing on the glassblowing one as part of strengthening the dungeon, as focal orbs and potion containers are literally going to keep people alive when the shit hits the fan. As such, they need to be able to work here."

That the space they'd apparently recently torn up and taken to squatting in was clearly intended for someone, and something that was desperately needed, made a few people nearby wince as I went on, and Finn made the point of speaking up then.

"Then they're very welcome to join our little family! Sierra, do you have experience with glassblowing already?" he asked, clearly thinking to ingratiate her with the crowd.

"No," she replied shortly.

"Ah…" He bit his lip. "Well…"

"She's getting a station and doesn't know what she's doing?" came the question from someone, and I didn't bother to look to see who'd said it.

"Yes," I said unequivocally. "Again, for two reasons. First of all, as soon as she can, she's going to be learning to make magical artifacts, and we desperately need them. Secondly, and I don't like making this point, but apparently it has to be made now and then, she gets it because I *say* she gets it. Am I clear?"

There was a rumble of assent; a few people looked pissed that I was throwing my weight around like that, while others nodded that it was common sense.

"Seriously, people, you don't get to know all the details of the things that are going on each day, because you don't *need* to hear it, that's all. We know there are other bands of people in the area, ones who have attacked us already without cause. There could be dozens or hundreds more out there, and we know there's already groups that are clearly hostile to us, including the goddamn undead army that's headed this way. I have to juggle the day-to-day costs that we can afford with the long-term options to make sure as many of us can grow as strong as possible.

"The blacksmith's is done, as is the glassblower; the mechanist and the armorer's was yesterday. The tinker's will be done soon—" I broke off as Finn let loose a whoop and high-fived a friend nearby.

"Yeah, yeah." I waved at him, unable to help a smile at that. "I know that suits you, mate, but the main thing here, people, is that we're moving in the right direction, okay? That's five different crafting stations there, all done to an uncommon level. That means that they'll not be getting upgraded again for a long time. What you get is what you get, so make it work.

"That being said, though, there's nothing to stop you from improving your stations, okay? You want a better bit of kit? You make it, trade another of your fellows for it, for their help in making it, or you come to Finn and talk to him about it. If it's minor and we can see a point to it, no stress.

"When it'll improve production or learning for the entire group? Sure. If it's just useful to you and it's a cosmetic thing? It's not gonna fly. You've got access to real magic now, and the capacity to reproduce things ten thousand times over with ease. The crafting station is here to help you, to help keep us all alive. Everything that's made in here is important, and I know that. Please don't think that I'm just changing the plan for shits and giggles, alright?"

I got more nods and apparent good feelings at that, letting them know there was a plan, before I moved right on.

"So, with that in mind, and that Sierra's station here is vitally important to the short-term survivability of the dungeon as a whole..." I paused, glancing around from one to another. "We need to rebuild her damn station! Any equipment that's been 'borrowed' from the glassblowing area? I need it back, *all* of it, and right now please."

"Shit." Finn groaned, stepping forward and moving in closer to me as others beat a hasty retreat. "I'm sorry, Matt. I told people that it was okay to borrow things and use the space. We're so used to making do with anything, and not having anyone in there... I'm sorry, Sierra. That's my fault."

I opened my mouth to assure him it was fine and to make sure it was all put back, when Sierra spoke up instead.

"Mine," she said firmly.

"Excuse me?" he asked.

"That place, and all that is in it, it is mine, yes?" She paused, looking to me for confirmation and getting a nod. "Then I need all out of it. No more must be stolen."

"Stolen...?" Finn asked, then shook his head. "No, Sierra, you don't understand. It's just that—"

"They are in my place, using my tools, yes? They have not asked the Dungeon Lord's approval? Then they are thieves."

"Crap," I muttered. "Okay, Sierra, Finn here is, uh...he's in charge of the crafters, all the crafters. Do you understand?"

"He is my master?"

"No," Finn said. "I'm just, well, I'm the, uh..."

"The master of the crafts." I winced as I tried to make an official title that wouldn't sound damn stupid.

Congratulations!

You have filled the role of Craftsmaster in your Dungeon.

Any Crafters or Dungeon Creatures under his command will now use his Control Points rather than your own, where possible.

Remember to increase the Craftsmaster's team whenever possible!

The notification was a fast pulse that washed out across all those nearby. I guessed that the dungeon chose to share the details slightly differently for everyone, but clearly the others were reading it, as Finn straightened up and grinned to himself.

"Craftsmaster, eh?" He nodded. "I can work with that."

"Yeah, well, you needed a title and rank." I grunted. "I need to make the point and do that a little more around here."

"Yeah, well, maybe give me a week or so, all right?" he joked. "Let me enjoy it a bit before you name another like that."

"A day," I countered. "Then I'm naming Chris 'Village Idiot.'"

"I can accept that." He nodded, the smile tugging at the corners of his lips. "So, ah, Sierra, with the crafting area…"

"I'll leave you to it," I said to Sierra, making the point by looking to the monocle in her hands and nodding. "Make use of the advantages you have but remember that Finn here is Craftsmaster. If you need anything, he's most likely the best to talk to."

"I shall claim my territory, then begin experimentation." She nodded. "What is my focus?"

"Ah, crap," I whispered, reaching up and rubbing at the bridge of my nose. "You need a damn focal orb to reproduce, don't you?"

"Uh, just to be clear, why can't you just copy them in the dungeon as is again?" Finn held a hand up as if he were asking a question at school.

"We could." I sighed. "And it might come to that. But they're horrifically expensive, and they'll only ever produce the most basic version of the orbs. They'll never get stronger, or improve. Now, with Sierra here working on them, the cost…" I checked in the system and nodded to myself. "They're expensive still, fifty thousand a pop, but they're a fraction of what they were."

"Damn, how much were they?"

"You *really* don't want to know." I snorted.

"Okay, well, maybe starting off smaller would be better?" Finn suggested. "We've got a few jobs that could benefit from some glasswork. And either way, the first stage would be simply learning the very basics…how to create glass, for example? Then we can go to the more complex things, as I don't know if you know, but failures? They teach a little bit, sure, and they get you a small amount of XP, but learning something earns a lot more. If you want her to get good, fast, she needs to go level by level. Learn things properly."

95

"That works." I sighed. "Finn, you're in charge." I stepped back, gesturing to Alison to walk with me.

"Dungeon Lord," she greeted me, falling in alongside as I started to walk around the crafters, heading for the old stairs that ran up one side of the building toward the second floor. "I, I don't know what you want from me?"

I sighed, not really knowing her and wondering what rumors she'd heard about me, considering she was young and female and I already knew there were some tales about me and harems going around.

"Sand." I looked at her. "Look, it's Alison, right?"

"Yes, Lord." She nodded earnestly, her short-cropped light-brown pixie-cut bobbing and the row of freckles across her nose giving her an elfin appearance.

"Just…ah, whatever." I sighed, shaking off the need to tell her to call me Matt. "Okay, so what we're doing now is heading to the gathering room."

"Okay?"

"It's a basic facility for the dungeon. Do you know how the dungeon works?" I asked, and she shook her head. "Okay, no stress. It's fairly simple. Basically, the dungeon can make anything. It was built by the same assholes who ended our world, in the hope that humans could learn to use them and get strong enough to fight and defend the galaxy against the incoming Orcan."

I glanced back and took in the bewildered and terrified look on her face, and changed what I was going to say.

"All you need to know is that the dungeon can pull in the corrupt mana that makes the monsters in the area, and it can produce pure mana that we can use to make things—items, buildings, food, and the summoned creatures, okay?"

"Okay," she agreed nervously.

"Well, as part of that, if we want something, we can make it from the mana, such as the focal orbs, the things we desperately need from the glassblowing."

"Right."

"We can, though it's damn expensive, make those items without building everything first. I could have had the dungeon make a focal orb before I assigned Sierra or even before I built the glassblowing section." I led the way up the stairs, speaking over my shoulder as we went. "The issue is that the creators of the dungeon wanted things done a certain way. If I try to just make the focal orb without a glassblower and a facility to make them, it's anywhere from three to a hundred times the cost.

"If I make the facilities and then just ignore them, I can produce what I want much, much cheaper, but…" I held up a hand to forestall her question. "If I do that, and just cheat the system essentially, we get the most basic and shitty quality version of it. If we think of a pane of glass, we can—or we could, before the fall—make glass that could deflect high-powered rifle shots. That's still fucking glass, and it can deflect that." I snorted at the madness of that.

"The building over there?" I gestured vaguely toward the ziggurat. "That's got glass that can take small rocket fire directly to it and still hold together. Don't get me wrong—they won't do it for long, but they can do it. The reason they can is that they're perfect, or as much as can be. No impurities and ten inches thick."

"Lord, I don't get it?" she said quietly. "I want to help, but I don't understand."

"It's okay, just listen," I assured her. "So, the glass is that strong, because it's thick, okay? But the thing is, it's not strong because it's well-made, or that it's made by skilled crafters. It can be made as thick as we want—I could make a wall of it—but it's pointless. And once it shatters, it's fucked. A skilled crafter, though, can make better and better versions of things. I'm hoping that Sierra will be able to make things like potion vials that concentrate the effects of the potions that are stored in them. Windows that regulate temperature, that protect and more.

"Most of all, at this point we need focal orbs, but they have massive side effects, especially if you have low affinities. My plan is to have her make these things, and learn. She'll level up, and we'll make copies in the dungeon. The glass we used to produce in the Middle Ages was warped as fuck and you could barely see through it unless there was a high-level crafter involved. That's where we are right now."

"Okay."

"Do you have a question?" I asked, as we reached the second level. The rickety metal stairs shook as we climbed them, the paint flaking off the handrails.

"I don't know what you want me to do," she admitted.

"Your gift is Sand, right?"

"It's my affinity," she agreed. "It's, well, it's what I like?" She winced. "That makes me sound so dumb. I just really always felt happiest at the beach, no matter the weather."

"And I bet when you go on vacation, you always pick somewhere you can lie on the sand?"

"I tried to," she admitted. "Tenerife was my last holiday last year—no sand at all, just rock and I felt sick the entire time."

"Hah, Sod's Law." I grinned at her. "Well, the point I'm trying to get to is this: you like the beach because it's sand, it fills some need in you, and we desperately need the glassblowing to work out. What I'm hoping is to help you to unlock your abilities, and to do that, you're going to be spending a lot of time in here."

The door before us opened into an absolute mess of a room, one that still stank of goddamn chicken shit, and was just pandemonium.

"Oh gods…" she whispered, covering her nose and mouth. "Why does it smell so bad?"

CHAPTER NINE

"That's...well." I sighed. "That's my fault, and it's something I need you to bear in mind as you do your job."

The room before us was roughly square, with four large box-like structures against the east wall, to our left as we entered the room.

Each of the boxes had a large conveyor belt that led from it past a dozen small bins, presumably that had been intended for sorting and collecting the various goods the harvesters found.

Unfortunately, it'd been a long time since anyone was in here, and not only were the bins full, but the conveyor belt ended in a massive pile of random collected items, which had spilled to the sides, filled the belt, and was slowly choking off the outlet from the drone boxes as well.

Walkways between the belts, and that led to much larger and clearly marked storage bins that circled the room, were generally only identifiable by the slightly lower mounds of crap that filled them. Everywhere I looked, it was chaotic and generally a goddamn mess.

"Watch where you step," I said over my shoulder as I led her deeper into the room, cursing as I heard a distant "cheep" followed by a terrified squawk, and then silence.

"If that's you, Thor, I hate you!" I called into the sudden silence, before sighing and moving deeper. I dismissed it as just one more fucked-up thing in here as I went on.

"I decided, when I first set this room up, that we needed, amongst other things, food samples, so that they could be fed into the dungeon and we'd have them for when we needed them."

"Okay."

"Well, what I did, was order the gatherers..." I gestured to the boxes, and on cue, one started to rattle. "That's one taking off, I think. The boxes hold gatherers, essentially giant drones, like the ones that the various delivery companies were experimenting with. They go out and collect whatever we tell them to, searching the area for things; then they bring them back here and drop them off, before going back out."

We both looked around, seeing the massive piles of general rubbish at the ends of the conveyor belts.

"What happened here was that I asked them to gather up seeds and chickens, thinking they'd both be useful, and then we came under attack and I forgot all about this for a week or two. The entire place was overrun by chickens.

"They ate the seeds and crapped everywhere—that's where the smell came from—and they started breeding. One of the side effects of the end of the world was apparently a faster breeding cycle for creatures like that, as when we checked it, we suddenly had hundreds of chicks and chickens running amok."

"That's actually kinda funny," she admitted, when I paused and looked at her, and I grinned at the nervous smile she gave me.

"Yeah, well, I wanted you to understand how easily a little mistake gets out of control, but also how easy it can be to fix it." I moved to lean against a table nearby.

"I need this place sorted out, Alison, but I also need you to learn to harness your ability, so we're here for you to do something for me." I paused at the half-terrified look she gave me, and I quickly went on. "The gatherers, okay? They can roam a few miles, maybe farther in any direction you want. A little focus and you can guide them individually. What I want you to do, and I'll arrange a few helpers in here for you, is to guide a gatherer to collect sand samples. Lots of them."

"Ah!" She got it at last. "And you want me to get the sand?"

"I want you to *find* it," I clarified. "I'm betting with your affinity so high, with a bit of focus you'll be able to sense details that the rest of us will totally miss. Also, you'll know where the cleanest sand is—the purest, I should say. Wherever you always felt most comfortable in the area? That's where I need you to send the gatherer. It can go and collect samples, and you examine them, see what you think and feel, and make notes on them."

"Notes on them," she repeated, nodding seriously. "I can do that."

"The plan is that you find us places that have good sand. Essentially, we're prepping for when Sierra is ready to start production. Once you find good sand, we absorb it into the dungeon and reproduce it for her. That solves the production issue in the short term, but I'm betting that there's going to be 'good' sand and better versions…like the way that there are variations of quality, we'll find better and worse samples of sand. You find them, make notes, and gather up what we need."

"I can do that." She nodded, seeming happy to have a job.

"Thank you. Also, as well as that, you'll be meditating and attending magic lessons. So don't get me wrong, I don't want you to spend your time just playing in the sand here."

"Oh no, unless the drones are really fast, I'll need something else to do!" She nodded.

"Glad we agree, because all of this?" I gestured to the room and grinned evilly. "This is now your problem to sort."

"Oh…" She winced, looking at the mess.

"It's not that bad," I reassured her. "I'll summon a few of the dungeon's workers for you, and you get to just guide them as well, but I want you to sort the room out. There's a lot of gold amongst the crap here. Not real gold," I amended hastily. "I mean things like ammunition."

Reaching down to a pile on the floor, I plucked a rifle round out of it and held it up. "We desperately need ammunition, and it was one of the things the gatherers were sent to get. Aly and Kelly changed the orders so that they'd get the essentials that we all need, but we've been so busy that we've not had the chance to sort through them yet. The gatherers are great, but pretty basic—I'll upgrade them as soon as we can. But for now, you need to sort the ammunition, the plants, the…"

We both spotted the bottle in the middle of the pile between us, at the packet of little blue pills marked "mydicksafloppin" and the cherry-flavored lube next to it.

"Essentials." She nodded.

"Yeah," I agreed, closing my eyes and reflecting that there was no way that I could address that without it going wrong. "I don't need that" for the medication would just sound like a denial; joking about it made it clear I knew what it was and would just help the rumors spread.

Offering to prove that I didn't need it wasn't going to end well, and telling her to ask Kelly wouldn't work out well either.

So I did the manliest thing I could.

I took the bull by the horns, took a deep breath, and totally ignored it, moving on.

"You've already got basic access to the dungeon for now, though we can look at higher authority if it's needed, and these will obey you." I summoned a pair of skeletons, leaving off armor and weapons, and held a hand up as she gasped and started to back away. "It's all right!" I assured her, before grabbing the nearest thing…and tossing the lube aside, gritting my teeth as I snatched up a lipstick instead.

"Watch!" I said quickly, drawing a dick on the polished skull.

"Why…why would you do that?" she asked me, appalled, and I winced.

"I just wanted you to see that it wasn't scary." I apologized to her, considering the bright-red lipstick dick in the middle of the skeleton's skull before closing my eyes and wishing I'd invested a bit more in intelligence.

"I mean, do you know how *expensive* that is?" she asked, horrified.

"What?" I asked squinting at her.

"The lipstick!" She jabbed a finger at it. "I could *never* afford that brand, and you just wasted it."

"The lipstick?"

"Really, *really* expensive lipstick!" she corrected.

I snorted before starting to laugh.

Somehow, that really made my life these days clear. I wasn't getting told I was ridiculous because I'd drawn a cock on the skull of a magically animated skeleton; it was because I'd used some lipstick brand I couldn't even pronounce and that looked like it was cheap as all hell.

Fuck it. I shrugged, then tossed it underarm to her.

"Well, make good use of it," I suggested. "Either way, though, there's a control terminal there…" I pointed to a table almost buried nearby that held a dimly lit map of the area. "If you use that and select the gatherers, you should have no issues. For now, I need you to sort through all of this crap. But remember, most of the things on that collection list were needed. Alchemical ingredients, for example…Ashley and Starr need them, so if you find any, send them over to them."

"And other things?" she asked, so obviously and carefully not looking at the lube and soft-cock remedies that she might as well have jumped up and down, pointing.

"Sort a box for them and put them all in," I said. "You've already got basic absorption and creation authority as well, so make sure you permeate everything first. That way, the dungeon can make a copy, then store it."

I slid into the dungeon sense, checking and confirming the lowest level of authority, before blinking back into the room and nodding.

"Do you need anything else?" I asked, before grinning and pointing at the skeletons. "Just literally order them," I promised her. "They'll listen and obey."

"Okay, ummm, do you really think I can help?" She smiled nervously. "It feels good to be busy and useful, you know? My affinity always makes me feel a bit stupid. Like, if it was that high for Fire, Dante told me I'd be a real powerhouse and an asset to the dungeon. Having Sand instead just made me feel a bit of a joke."

"Truthfully, I'm betting you'll be able to do things that could make all the difference," I assured her. "Sand is going to have grades, purities or whatever. The purer the first stage, the more likely the glassblowers will be able to make things that make a difference. You'll be able to adjust things for them, fix them, and I've no doubt, create wonders. Just trust your instincts, go to the classes, and make damn meticulous notes, all right?"

She nodded seriously and I left her to it, deliberately not pointing out the reason we needed the notes was just in case she was killed in the weeks ahead.

It was a shitty way to have to think, but that was life in the fucking apocalypse.

I beat a hasty retreat, leaving the poor woman standing in the middle of the room, staring uncomfortably at the two skeletons. Was it right that I passed the job off on her like that? Probably not, no; I had to admit that. But was it something I had time to do?

Fuck no. She got a lot out of this, including magic school basically, so yeah, a little extra job like sorting that place out was only fair. Or so I told myself. And who knows. Maybe she'd be good at that kinda thing as well. Organization and so on.

I hurried down the stairs, waving to Finn as he stood with Sierra on the far side of the room, working on rebuilding the glassblowing equipment.

That was going to be painful to figure out, I just knew…but again, not my problem. The buggers who had disassembled it all could figure it out.

A few minutes later, I stepped into my little gym, closing the damn door and looking around at the mess.

Clearly someone had kept using it while I was in the dungeon, and just as clearly, they'd not been introduced to the brothers ugly, that were Jimmy and Andre.

They were men-mountains and they'd not been shy about teaching me proper gym etiquette when they thought I was doing things wrong. Now, looking around the room and seeing the sweat stains on the limited machinery, the empty cans, and rubbish in the corner, as well as—goddammit—the full ashtray, I couldn't help but curse.

The room reeked of cigarette smoke, and that just made me snarl in fury. There wasn't much I hated in life besides people who were intolerant of other people's cultures and the French, but smoking?

101

I hated it with a passion, and now everything in my meditation and exercise room reeked of it. Dragging the rowing machine into the middle of the room, I summoned some workout gear and got changed quickly, before getting onto the seat and strapping myself in.

It was time to start making the most out of the place, I reflected, and to do that, I might as well start by splitting my attention.

I'd proved I could access the dungeon sense while standing or sitting, after all, and I didn't fall over or collapse generally, so simple movements should be possible as well. Or so I hoped.

I started off small, going slowly and gently, no great exertion but enough that I could feel it, while looking through my mind and into the dungeon sense, moving around the room and tagging and absorbing everything as I went.

All the rubbish, the ashtray, the piles of cigarette ash, and yeah, the goddamn sweat-stained cloths and more—all were absorbed and used to feed the dungeon.

After the first pass, I picked up speed slightly, feeling a little strain in both my mind from twisting my attention in this way, and from my body as I built up to a comfortable rhythm.

Ten minutes or so passed as I searched the room from top to bottom, trying to find whatever was still holding the stench of ash, before starting against one wall, and working my way across the room instead.

Everything was tagged in the dungeon sense and repaired.

It cost me six *thousand* mana by the time I'd reached the far side of the room. I knew it was a bit of a waste, genuinely I did, but the room had reeked, and now, finally, when I finished, I had a room I could work in again.

Also, nice bonus, all the general wear and tear that had marred the room was gone—from the scuffed paint on the walls to the scratches and wear on the machines, the cracks in the skirting boards, the window that wouldn't open…everything. It was all restored to pristine condition.

As I drew in a deep breath, I let it out with a sigh. Damn, that felt better.

One last job to do, then I could move on, I reminded myself: notifications.

I'd been avoiding them for a while, not needing the shit. But now, I was damn well ready for it, that was for sure.

Congratulations!

You have killed the following:
- **1x Scepiniir Dungeon Boss [Advanced], Level 25, 5,500 XP**
- **4x Daoine Sidhe [Uncommon], Levels 19-21, 1,300 XP**
- **1x Scepiniir [Uncommon], Level 19, 310 XP**
- **6x Lesser Ghast [Common], Levels 21-24, 1,145 XP**
- **7x Local Military [Common], Levels 4-11, 605 XP**

Total XP earned: 8,860 XP

Total XP awarded: 8,860 XP

Current XP to next level stands at 35,413/50,000

I couldn't help but stare at that. I'd gotten the credit for killing the dungeon boss, which was great, sure, considering I'd forced the crazy Daoine Sidhe's spell around to point at him. I'd have understood if I hadn't gotten that as I didn't cast the spell, just twisted it, so that was nice.

What wasn't nice, though? I'd not gotten a single point from the dungeon defenders fighting off the assault, just my personal kills. I'd forgotten about that minor detail, and it annoyed me. Then, the knowledge that I was pissed because I'd not gained from the deaths of those soldiers...it made me want to vomit.

The changes in the world since the fall were weird. One minute, I was totally fine with the killing, viewing it as they came after me and my people after all, and then the next... I shook myself free of that thought, and fought on, picking up speed as I continued to exercise, pulling up the next prompt to distract myself. There was a quest notification, followed by another two, part one, repeating the class quest notification I'd already earned, and then offering me the next step.

You have completed a Quest!

Quest!

Incursion! (1)

You have defended the dungeon; then, upon questioning the attackers, found a short-term solution to the problem.

You receive the following bonuses:

- **+1 to top three Attributes**
- **2,000 XP**

Quest!

Incursion (2)

The source of the incursion has been identified, and a short-term solution found. However, a permanent solution must be enacted. Deal with the enemy base however you see fit...
Deal with the enemy base to receive the following bonuses:

- **+1 to top three Attributes**
- **+1 Class Skill Point**
- **5,000 XP**

Congratulations!

You have successfully crafted your first signature spells. These spells are unique to you, and although others may display highly similar versions, they are different. Each personal spell you create is an amalgamation of your knowledge, your abilities, and your affinities. They will evolve as you

do: the stronger you grow in the relevant affinities that make up these spells, the stronger your spell will, in turn, grow.

Know this: each unique spell you create will gain you a five percent [5%] increase in their relative affinity up to one hundred percent [100%]

Your Spells have gained you a fifteen percent [15%] increase in your Lightning affinity, but as this affinity is already at or surpassing the maximum affinity level, the bonus has been assigned to the lowest of the component mana forms.

In this case, your [AIR] mana was the lowest affinity of the contributory mana forms, and has been selected for advancement.

[AIR] mana has been increased from [72%] to [87%].

That was the same as last time, and checking over the affinity notifications proved that it'd not changed. But the next prompt was a bit more positive at least, as was the one after.

Congratulations!

You have gained an additional Stat Point in the following area through constant effort.
- **+1 Dexterity**

Continue to work hard to increase this or other stats…

Congratulations!

As an Arcanist, you have gained access to the secrets of creation itself, or at least the ones not very well hidden. Magic, mana, and mysteries fill your mind, and you are finally ready to move on and prove yourself.

You have completed the Foundational Tier of your [Arcanist] Class Quest! You have now gained access to the Apprentice Tier, and the chance to walk a path less trodden. Beware [Arcanist], with great power comes great danger, as the higher you ascend, more powerful opponents will seek to remove the competition. There can be only one Deity of the Elements.

I had no clue what the hell the Deity of the Elements was, and frankly, I didn't give two shits. I had enough on my plate without aiming for that as well, but it made something clear. As I reached the higher ranks, people would apparently come gunning for me.

I blinked, the sweat starting to run down my face as I pushed harder, baring my teeth. I decided that if they came looking for a glass cannon, they'd be in for a goddamn surprise.

Moving on, I read the next section carefully.

Crafting the signature spells of the Apprentice [Arcanist] is a hurdle that many sapiens fail to clear, as each spell completed not only limits the paths available to the mage for their future growth, but is also correspondingly more difficult.

Choose to create three separate spells of any two of the following categories to reach Apprentice Rank as an [Arcanist]. Alternatively, create a single spell in each category to receive an increased boost to your selected affinities and a bonus magical item:

- **Animation: 0/1**
- **Blood: 0/1**
- **Divination: 0/1**
- **Elemental: 0/1**
- **Enchantment: 0/1**
- **Mental: 0/1**
- **Rune: 0/1**
- **Temporal: 0/1**
- **Spatial: 0/1**
- **Summoning: 0/1**

Looking over the options, I winced. Any and all of these could be awesome, or could be nigh-on impossible to complete. First of all, Animation—I guessed that it wasn't creating manga, but instead dealt with creating and guiding golems or other creatures.

A burst of knowledge from the dungeon side of things had made it clear as soon as I laid my eyes on it, that the dungeon's way of summoning and the way that the spell needed to be created from scratch were very different.

That was out, as far as I was concerned.

Seeing that "minor" detail made a few other things click for me as well as I stared at the list. This was why fewer mages—or mancers, dammit—reached apprentice. If you needed to learn six elemental spells...well, that was probably easy enough for someone like Dante.

He was fire obsessed and would want to create all the spells he could in the elemental category. But if he had to create, just as a guess, an animation magic as well, he was gonna have to damn well learn and study rather than going all-in on instinct.

It'd also give you a solid foundation if you didn't know what kind of mage you wanted to be. If you went for the bonus to your affinities, which I already knew I was going to have to go for, then you'd have to learn one of each spell.

I bit down on a grumble as I noted that my already created spells in lightning—which *had* to qualify as elemental spells, for shit's sake—weren't counted. So it was only new spells that were included and the counter was reset at each level.

That was okay, though. I only needed to teach myself...ten spells. *Fuck.*

Thinking about it, though, I could differentiate from the different forms of mana. Although I wasn't good with a lot of them, I could use the bonuses to the affinities that I got from creating specific spells to increase those as well.

The sweat was rolling down my body now, and I kept going, looking over the spells and making a few more mental notes.

So animation was essentially bringing inanimate objects to life, and I already knew that blood could be using our blood or that of others to cast spells, or to empower them.

That was a bit funky, and not in a good way.

Fortunately, more or less, I'd already managed a little blood magic. Unfortunately, it was dangerously addictive when you were up shit creek to use it, and I'd already sort of sworn off it, more or less.

Divination? Telling the goddamn future was something I'd always believed was impossible, something that was maintained and sold to gullible fools by sneaky con men.

Thinking about it, though, divination was literally getting information from something through magical means, right? That meant that maybe I could, I don't know, create a spell that'd let me eavesdrop on some fucker in the enemy camp and that'd qualify?

Elemental was simple, and I bet that was the school that most people chose. It certainly seemed obvious enough.

Enchanting was fairly cool, and I'd already done a variation of it in the dungeon in imbuing things with my mana, then letting them take their own steps to create specific weapons, like the void blade.

I didn't get any kind of "hell no" mental message from the dungeon when I thought on that for a second, and I grinned that maybe I'd found a sneaky way to figure out the right path for that spell at least.

Mental was an interesting one, and as soon as I thought about that, I knew what I could do with it. A shield, one that would block off my mind from others, because I'd already had experience of mind magic, in that crazy vampyr bitch who hit me with whatever lust magic she'd had.

That'd been a weird experience, that was for sure.

A shield that protected me from that kind of thing would be incredible, so I resolved to make that a priority, though I'd probably need to have someone with that flavor—school?—of magic try to use it on me to test it.

Ashley did something like that, didn't she? I paused, thinking about that and winced. Yeah, that was definitely *not* a good idea.

Next was runes, magic writing of some sort that I guessed was similar to enchanting…magical coding of some kind? Again, no "hell no" sense, so I mentally marked that one up.

Temporal was— I broke off, suddenly coughing and hacking. My eyes fluttered open as my rhythm was totally thrown off. I twisted halfway through an extension, my lungs suddenly full of secondhand smoke.

The twist was at exactly the wrong time, and the effort I put in, in my shock and confusion, was at exactly the right—or wrong—angle, as the pedal I'd been bracing against snapped *again*. My left leg shot forward, the exposed metal digging into my inner ankle and tearing the skin and muscle, spraying blood as I carved a lovely long flap of skin free.

Just to add to the fun, as my other foot was still trapped in the strapping of the footrest on that side, I couldn't even catch myself. I fell to the floor, one leg up and over the machine, one on the floor pouring with blood—and the first thought that went through my head was that I was going to fucking kill someone.

This was the second time that this had happened, and although I'd not snapped the footrest entirely off last time, I must have put some pretty insane force at exactly the wrong angle to snap the damn thing, considering I'd literally just repaired it.

I twisted as another wave of cigarette smoke washed over me. I braced myself on the floor, glaring up and over the rowing machine, to see a short man who was almost all hair, staring wide-eyed at me from the far side of the room, as another ran for it.

I missed him, catching a glimpse of only the back of their highly polished head as they ran. But the hairball? He was backing away slowly, eyes wide, as he apparently tried to decide whether running was still an option.

"You," I growled.

He ran for it.

CHAPTER TEN

"A smoking ban, Matt, really?" Aly asked me half an hour later, as I explained my plan, glaring as Kelly covered her face with her hands and peeked out. She was clearly trying to decide whether she should laugh or commiserate with me.

"Any public area," I said firmly. "In their rooms? Fine, people want to smoke, that's their business, but in the fucking *gym*?!"

"It's a bit strange," Aly agreed. "Most people who are there to work out aren't the kind who smoke. And if they are, they at least have the common courtesy to know that not everyone there is going to want to breathe their smoke."

"I had to repair the entire fucking room earlier. They'd used it to smoke what had to have been half a dozen entire goddamn packs worth, and then they'd left them!" I went on, furious. "I repaired the entire room to get rid of the smell, and then they saw me working out, and still fucking lit up!"

"What do you want me to do?" Kelly reached out and checked my leg, nodding as she saw the damage was still there, blood running down my leg. "Matt, are you going to heal this?"

"No," I grumbled. "I figured it'd be good for Jenn to use the focal orb to heal me."

"Good plan. Have you asked her to come here, or are you just leaving blood trails all over the dungeon?"

"Blood trails," I grumbled again, fighting the urge to rant and rave about the smokers.

"Okay, I'll summon her." Kelly sighed, and I nodded, doing my best not to sulk as she slipped into the dungeon sense and communicated with the nearest kobold to Jenn, asking her to come to the room we were in and having Ashley, who was with her, bring her across.

"I really don't think you should be the one to speak to them about the smoking," Aly said. "But I think someone needs to, both to point out that rudeness, and to make sure it doesn't happen again. This does bring up an important detail, though, and it's one that Barry has been battling of late as well."

"What's that?"

"Intoxicants and…fuck it, can't think of the official word. Booze and drugs." Aly sighed, shifting and getting more comfortable as Kelly blinked aware, catching the end of the conversation. "Kell, you want to handle this?"

"Can do." She sighed. "Okay, so before the end, the north of England had a pretty bad alcoholism and drug problem…you knew that, right?" She quirked an eyebrow at me, as she tucked her legs under herself in the chair.

"Oh yeah." I snorted. "It's pretty common and obvious, and it's not like I didn't partake."

"Yeah, but as long as it was under control, well, it's your business and nobody else's. Well, in my last role for the courts, it meant I saw a lot of it. People tended to commit crimes around drugs and alcohol a lot, either because they were intoxicated or impaired, or they were in need, and committed crimes to fund the habit," she explained.

"When the end came, at least forty percent of the dungeon's population, those originally in Saltwell Park—and are almost all still there, I'll admit—had breakdowns of one kind or another. Of those, at least ten percent are still pretty much incapable. The return of some normality was massively helpful for many of them, but for those with specific issues, that's created entire new levels of problems."

"What?" I asked, and she fixed me with a look.

"The alcoholics, smokers, and drug abusers now have access to far more than they ever did before, and it's all free," she clarified. "Or most of it is, anyway. For most people, the way the world is now means that they've kicked old habits. They know that they need to focus, and work, and they're happy to do that. Many of those with long-term habits were dealing with horrific depression, for example, and being needed, respected, and useful in many cases has helped them to get clean. Others have found that in the apocalypse, the willpower to get clean is actually far easier to find than the bravery to go out and face creatures, for example.

"There's also the uncomfortable but clear correlation that those who abuse drink or drugs are impaired, and they miss situational clues. They die quickly, and while it's a horrible solution, it's a permanent one. All it takes is for that to happen to one of your drinking buddies and suddenly the group really wants to stay sober."

"Okay, that makes sense," I agreed.

"Well, the issue comes that now that there's a degree of normalcy and safety, those who haven't successfully dealt with their demons are rapidly losing to them. Smokers, for example, can summon a packet of cigarettes that would cost them the same as an hour's work earned them, for a single point of mana. They go into the dungeon, help out by absorbing things to offset the little luxuries, and then they summon the cigarettes, often by the carton, not pack."

"That's like ten packs, right?" I guessed.

"Yeah, but that's not the point. The issue is that they're doing nothing wrong, but they're also killing themselves and they're getting a bit out of control. It's nothing particularly bad. A few others have had things like your experience with the gym—people who are just acting a bit weird, but it's evidence of a larger problem, and it's one we have to deal with."

"I don't think we do," I said after a few seconds' thought, sighing and sitting up straighter. "Look, the hard drugs we banned, right? Weed is fine, as long as it's in moderation. The others, cocaine and so on, the harder drugs are just outright banned, yeah? John was dealing with that and you cut off the 'sugar substitute' method of creating it."

"I did, and he did, but there's still a lot of drugs in the park and to a lesser extent here," she admitted. "I don't know if it's down to stuff that was produced before we caught on, or if someone found a stash or…"

"A stash…" I muttered, a hint of something occurring to me, before I groaned. "Shit, did anyone think to check the police storage areas? They're not far away— the station isn't, anyway—and when we were there, we were only concerned with the weapons. If someone went there and thought to search for things like that…"

"That might be where our drugs problem is coming from," Kelly agreed. "That or the Gateshead police stations. There's one not far from the path to the park, literally across the road from the civic center, and that would be easily reachable. Barry searched it for weapons, but again, we didn't think to look for drugs."

"So we make it clear that anyone who's caught peddling hard drugs is put out," I said. "We can't force people to stop drinking excessively or smoking, as much as I'd like to because I damn well hate smoking. But we can at least stop the drugs and make it clear that the smoking is done in private areas or specific spots outside only. Set up some smokers' shelters like they used to around offices."

"A lot of people won't use them," Aly pointed out. "They'll just lean against the No Smoking sign and point out that it's the end of the world and to grow up, we've got bigger problems."

"Well, we create them and give them somewhere to go." I sighed. "As long as we deal with the common-sense issues, we can leave it."

"I don't like it," Kelly admitted.

"Neither do I." I shrugged. "But that's not the point. We can't make everyone act the way we want, so either we deal with that and move on, or we become dictators."

"Okay, well…" Aly winced. "About the plan that we turn the dungeon into a fortress…"

"You were stressed, and you didn't know what else to do," I said. "You were just panicking and didn't—"

"I meant it." She cut me off.

"I…oh. Right."

"I think we need to look at a fortress option," she clarified. "Not necessarily so much 'we're clearly evil and we need glowing red runes on the gates and massive black walls and crashing lightning' levels, but I still think a fortress is the way to go."

"Go on." I settled back into the chair, watching the look she gave Kelly and waiting, wondering whether they'd had the same plan I had.

"When you're healed," Kelly said as a knock sounded out. She called to whoever it was to enter and smiled as Ashley walked in, leading Jenn.

"Hi, everyone, I think you're expecting Jenn?" Ashley asked, leading the young woman in, and to nobody's surprise, her more abrasive sister Emma followed along as well.

"Yes, thank you, Ashley." Kelly nodded, sitting up straighter and unfolding her legs, smiling at the new arrivals. "Jenn, you've got the healing focal orb, is that right?"

"Yeah," she replied, smiling back and lifting it, the light catching it as she waved it vaguely.

"That's great. Have you used it yet?"

"Once, on the kobolds." She nodded. "One was injured in training and…ouch!" She broke off, seeing my leg and the trail of blood, before stepping forward. "Is this why you asked me to come?" She was already kneeling and looking at the wound.

"Yes, please." I peered down at her as she examined it.

"What happened?"

"The gym." I grunted as she reached out and gently pressed the sides of the wound, examining it.

"If this is what you get from the gym, then you're doing it wrong," she pointed out, moving on and checking that there was nothing in the wound that might cause issues later, before focusing and struggling.

It took several attempts, mainly filled with Emma and Ashley asking me questions until I explained the whole sorry affair, but eventually the wound was closed and Kelly was summoning a cloth and water for Jenn to clean her hands, while I swept the room clear of the rest of the blood using the dungeon sense.

"It sounds like Monty," Emma said suddenly, glancing at her sister.

"Who?" I replied absently, focusing on the last drops of blood.

"Monty Hall. Little guy. Looks like someone put a monkey in a suit. Hairiest man you've ever seen?" she clarified. "Mid-forties and smokes like a chimney. He's always with that other guy he plays darts with, uh…"

"Marko," Jenn supplied. "He's like the opposite of Monty—clean-shaven, well groomed, *always* shaves his head."

"I didn't see the second beyond the gleam off his head as he ran for it," I admitted. "The other one was a hairy little bastard, though. Why?"

"They're both married to women who are in the magic school with us," Emma admitted. "The pair just sit around all day and smoke or drink."

"The husbands do, she means," Ashley clarified. "I remember seeing them before this all happened. They were always in our local bar—it's why we know them."

"And they're just sitting around drinking all day still?" I frowned.

"I heard Sasha—that's Monty's wife—berating him that he was getting fat and out of shape, so he was going to join the gym, but beyond that I don't know," Emma offered.

"That's part of the point I was getting to." Kelly nodded to my leg. "Are you done there, Jen?"

"Yeah, all done." She smiled at me, wiping down my leg with a cloth that she summoned, then shook her head as she reabsorbed the cloth into the dungeon. "I swear, I'm never going to get used to that." She stood, stretching and cracking her back, before heading for the door as Emma led the way.

"Thank you," I called after her, before catching Ashley's eye and gesturing to her to stay.

She nodded and bade the girls goodbye, promising to catch up with them later, before slipping into a chair and looking around. "What's up?"

"Those two, Monty and uh…"

"Marko," she supplied.

"Yeah," I said. "Are they really just sitting around and smoking or drinking all day?"

"Ummm, honestly, I'd not be surprised at all. They've not worked as long as I've known them. Their wives do, but they don't."

"But they're contributing to the dungeon, right?" I asked, getting annoyed. "I mean, it's the end of the goddamn world, right? There's no room for people who won't help themselves."

"That's what I was getting at," Kelly said. "There's a small but persistent group who are either unwilling or unable to help the dungeon and the rest of us. And although we'd made inroads into rehabilitating them, the surge in alcohol, cigarettes, and drugs has reversed it.

"In the case of these two, we agreed that the people from the park who came and joined the magic school could bring their families. We didn't set restrictions on those people being contributing members of society."

"So what do we do?" I asked after a few seconds' thought. "I don't want to basically kick people out of the dungeon if they can't help for a genuine reason—that'd be shitty; we should help people wherever possible—but I'm also not happy about freeloaders."

"Are they freeloaders?" Aly asked suddenly. "I mean, is it just a case of we don't know what they're doing? It's not like we're monitoring everyone, after all."

"That's another good point." I sighed. "I think we're getting to the point where we need to enforce societal rules again. At first, it was only us, so we all worked to help each other. Then, as we brought more and more people in, everyone helped out. People just picked up the slack and worked to get the jobs done. It wasn't until Gerald and whatsherface refused to help that we realized that people who could help, weren't."

"Sharon." Aly smiled.

"So what do we do?" Kelly asked. "I mean, we're insanely stretched already. Sure, you have some time you could spend assigning jobs, Matt, but the reason you handed over as much of the day-to-day running of the dungeon to us as you did was so that you could study. That's the path to power for you and for the dungeon. We can't afford to take you away from that."

"No, we can't," I agreed, before chuckling evilly. "But you remember that woman, the one who took the idiots to task when we had the all-hands meeting, and who dragged them out? Dammit, I can't remember her name…"

"Pat," Aly, who had a better memory than me, offered. "Patricia. She's on one of the gathering teams."

"Fantastic. From what I've seen, she basically works her arse off and causes no issues, as well as helps people. Anyone heard anything that's not complimentary about her?"

"No."

"Nope."

"She's really good," Ashley added in. "She helps Clarissa a lot as well, and well, she's been really friendly with me. A lot aren't."

"Does she have any kind of official role yet?" I asked. "And what do you mean, a lot aren't friendly with you? I thought it'd be the opposite." I said that, thinking of the way that pretty girls were usually welcomed into any group from a male perspective.

"You'd be surprised," she said wryly. "As I'm sort of included in your inner circle, I'm excluded from a lot of groups, probably because they're not sure if I'm reporting on them."

"Who the hell has time for that crap still?" I groaned. "It's the goddamn end of days, we're fighting monsters, and that kind of 'mean girls' shit is still going on?"

"It's human nature." She smiled. "Seriously, though, as far as I know, Pat just likes to be busy and believes everyone should help out if they're able."

"She could be a lot more use to us making sure people are working rather than being part of the gathering team then," Kelly suggested.

"That's exactly what I was thinking," I agreed. "I know she was trying to meditate when I first met her. Do we know—"

"She's stopped that." Ashley shook her head. "Once she found her affinities, she gave up on meditating with people, though I know she really wanted to learn magic."

"Any idea why?" I asked.

"They were low," she said. "Pat wouldn't say more, but when I spoke to her, talking about something totally separate at the time, I asked her what she thought of the lessons—Dante and I are a bit self-conscious, after all—and she admitted she'd not been to any more lessons since she found out that her affinities were so low. She didn't want to waste everyone else's time around the converters."

"That needs addressing then," I said. "She's working her ass off and doesn't want to be a burden on us? Hell no. How about this? If she's willing to take over helping to organize everyone, making sure the various work-avoiders are kicked into shape, she can pick a converter and we'll put it in her office?"

"Office?" Kelly asked.

"Yeah, I think if she's organizing people to work, she's going to be in the dungeon sense most of the time, and there's spare offices in here, right? Give her one and set up a converter in there, much like the way we set up the Life converters around Clarissa and her people when they work to expand the dungeon's influence."

Aly nodded. "That makes sense, and it's something we've done before. Plus, to be fair, having someone everyone can come to, and a dedicated work assignment means that people will know what they're doing, and those who have been slipping through the cracks won't be able to anymore.

"I feel a bit shitty that we're doing this, forcing people to work, I mean. It's a bit despotic and all, but it needs to be done. It's really not fair when some people are fighting to defend us, or working their ass off around the clock, for others to be sitting around and smoking or drinking all day and not contributing. If it's alright with you, though, I think that we need a formal restructuring of the dungeon's ranks anyway."

"Uh, okay?" I agreed. "In what way?"

"Well, you're the Dungeon Lord, that's really clear to most people, and it gives them a figurehead to look up to. But you put Kelly and me in charge of most of the day-to-day arranging of things, right?"

"Yeah."

"Well, as we grow, I think we need to make it a bit clearer to people where we all stand in the food chain. And it'll make it a bit easier as we're getting interrupted by people who don't know who else to turn to."

"Finn's gotten the Craftsmaster title now as well, if that helps?" I offered. "It should mean that at least those with an interest in that area head to him, rather than you?"

"We can hope. That's really becoming a pain." Kelly sighed. "I'm trying to do a job and being interrupted a lot. It's not malicious—they're genuine questions—but most people don't know who to ask, so they tend to come to one of us."

"Me too." Ashley shifted around in her chair, summoning a hot chocolate from the dungeon and settling back. "God, it's gotten a lot colder outside as well, you know? So, people tend to save up their questions, and when you're trying to eat your dinner, there's like a dozen questions every day about why and what."

"That's what I'm finding too," Aly agreed. "And I'm getting more and more people coming to me telling me that they'd told such and such this, is that all right?"

"Yeah, dammit, I never considered we'd need a bloody organization chart," I muttered.

"Well, we're growing to the point that we do." Aly summoned her own hot chocolate and shifted, getting comfy. "It's simple enough, though, if we work off the standard model."

"Go on," I invited.

"Okay, so at the top of the food chain we've got you, as Dungeon Lord, right?" She went on before I could say anything. "Then, and I think we need to be clear on this, we've got Kelly, as the Dungeon Mistress, with the rest of us underneath her."

"No comments from you." Kelly leveled a finger at my nose, and I grinned.

"So, we need to split things into three distinct paths or sections from there." Aly went on, giving me a look that said any stupid comments would not be appreciated.

"So, under Kelly comes your council. She basically leads the council when you're not there already, and when you are, she has a standard vote on things, like the rest of us do.

"On the council, when it comes to important things we've got the military, which is Mike and Griffiths; diplomacy, which is our Ashley here; people, which is Clarissa; and crafting, which is Finn.

"Then we have religion, which I don't think we really need on the council…"

"Definitely not," I said firmly.

"Glad about that one," Kelly muttered.

"Less chance of Matt upsetting people." Aly grinned. "Training is covered by several people at the minute, but honestly, I'd say we have Markus and maybe Rhodes. She's fantastic at training."

"Dante as well maybe?" Ashley suggested, before wincing. "That's not me saying he's my boyfriend so he should be on there, but if we're going to help with the magic side…"

"It makes sense," I agreed. "It'll also be a case of a lot of us wear multiple hats—you're covering diplomacy and magic, he's doing magic, and I'm doing, well, everything."

"And Ramnik when she gets back," Aly added. "Okay, maybe this isn't the way we should be doing this. I'm sorry, I'm not exactly used to org charts either. Let's keep the council as it is, minus the religious lot."

"That works," Kelly agreed.

"We do have a need to have a group for people, though…think HR in a standard organization. I think it should be under Clarissa."

"I'm fine with that." I nodded. "I mean, she basically was the person we gave the jobs to originally when we were all too busy to do them. Just handed stuff over and told her to organize things."

"Me too," Kelly agreed.

"Good, so I think that Clarissa and Pat would make a great sort of HR team for us, maybe have Barry included in that or…"

The meeting was going nowhere fast, and my first reaction, when someone started banging a fist on the door and shouting, was a mixture of relief and irritation.

Relief because goddamn was this meeting boring, even if everyone bar me who was in it was pretty, but the irritation? We needed to sort this shit out, and if we were being interrupted for no reason…

The door popped open, letting in a worried Emma and Jenn, who helped an exhausted, clearly stressed and blood-streaked Drak in, notably without Kilo.

"Help," he gasped, looking directly at me. "They got ambushed, and so did we. Kilo needs your help."

CHAPTER ELEVEN

"We don't have a choice," I said over my shoulder as I grabbed more ammunition and I slotted the magazines into my bag of holding.

A handful of weak healing potions joined them, and I focused on a magazine, wanting it, and felt it slide into my hand as soon as I reached into the bag.

Nice that it worked the way that the games always said, that.

I kept grabbing things I figured I might need as Kelly tried to dissuade me for the fourth or fifth time from leaving. "It's not like we can leave them there to cause more goddamn problems!" I snapped back at her.

"Matt, it's the British Army!" she hissed. "You can't just march in and tear them a new arsehole!"

"Watch me!" I glared back. "Fuck's sake, Kelly, you heard him—Drak is exhausted. He had to have a dozen of those little bastard coronaughts cut out of him before we found that healing spells kill them!"

"Yes!" she agreed quickly. "And going after Mike? Taking a team to rescue him, knowing that the kobolds are resistant to them is sensible. We need it and they need us. But taking care of the army problem first is just stupid! It's a risk we don't need to take!"

"We left them intact before and they waited until you were defenseless before goddamn attacking us!" I roared. "I'm not leaving them in there to do it again, not unless we make it a real goddamn cage!"

That had been the other option, the one that Kelly and Aly had shot down in short order already.

I'd suggested that we grow a stone mesh up from the walls and across the space over the army base, literally enclosing them in a stone prison that they'd only be able to escape by blowing up.

My point that, if they did that, it'd all fall inward and solve our problem for us wasn't taken well.

They'd said that not only did we not have the mana we needed to enclose over a square mile of territory to create a massive stone cage, but the knock-on effect would be worse: making it clear they were our prisoners would practically guarantee we couldn't negotiate with them later.

I'd taken that on board, and decided that in that case, I'd deal with this shit personally.

"Twenty-four hours," I said grimly to Kelly. "You've got that long to get me an army to rescue the others. Now, anything you spend on containing the goddamn enemy base? That's coming off the amount you can spend on backup for me to rescue your brother, so you decide how you're going to spend it. But I'm telling you now, I'm doing this."

That's what power came down to in the end, as the Dungeon Lord, regardless whether she liked it, or my plan, or not. I was damn well going to do what I decided was for the best for my people.

"Fine!" she snapped. "You're doing this? You do it. But you'll take the forces I have ready for you, and we're canceling the funeral! I don't have the time to do that, so we have to focus on the living."

"To rescue Mike and the others?" I agreed. "Damn right I will. For now, though, all I'm taking is Chris, Ashley, and Dante…oh, and the assassins."

"No you're…the assassins?" She broke off. "The trainees?"

"The fastest way for them to level is to get experience." I nodded. "And despite everything, I'm not a fucking idiot. I'll take those three with me, and four assassins as well. If the shit hits the fan, they can be a distraction and help cut our way free. But either way, all we need is that room ready."

"I'll start summoning them into it now." She threw herself down on the bed, clearly feeling a lot better about the whole plan as I slid weapons and equipment into place.

"Is Aly—" I started to ask.

"Already working!" Kelly called, clearly working in the dungeon sense by the distracted look on her face.

"Well, that's a good thing I guess," I muttered to myself. "Is it…?"

"It's working!" she said, annoyed. "Now stop goddamn interrupting me!"

"Yes, boss." I smiled.

We were in our bedroom, underneath the dungeon's original building, and I finished checking my gear.

Fortunately, my armor had been repaired—again—and although it'd not been heavily upgraded, the addition of the armorer's workbench had apparently allowed Finn and Aly to make a few minor upgrades, which included a layer of anti-ballistic fabric under the main steel plating.

Originally, it'd been bronze instead, then high-grade iron. Now, with having access to any material in the Steel tier of the dungeon, Finn had plans for a full-on titanium set, with aramid underlayers and more—possibly being powered later on as well, but that was months away, at least, if not years.

For now, the upgrades we'd made had gone from bronze to iron and steel, and now to nickel-steel alloy, over a layer of leather, which in turn had silk as a base layer.

It was both stronger and lighter than the last set made, but as it was as simple as replacing components in the dungeon's memory for the creation, it'd been a relatively easy upgrade.

The dragon scale was still the overall look, with heavier body armor for the chest, thighs, shoulders, and shins, and bracers that concealed a blade on either arm.

There was a dagger in my right boot as well, and just in case, a pair of handcuff keys in the belt of my pants.

You never knew, after all, and they unlocked real police-issue handcuffs. I literally remembered they were attached to the headboard and grabbed them as I passed it.

117

Then I added my void blade over my right shoulder, and the handgun on my hip, making sure it was full, even if it was just a goddamn standard-issue handgun rather than my 1911.

I'd looked at that, sitting there in my personal storage area, and damn well decided that one of the first things we'd do when we got the ammunition side up and running was make some 10mm rounds for that.

Regardless, thanks to the efforts of Alison in sorting the ammunition out, and the looted ammo we recovered from the dead and captured soldiers, we had enough that I could carry three magazines for the assault rifle, and Chris should be getting the same, along with a fuckload of spare rifles.

Lastly, and because I just didn't feel right without one these days, I'd summoned a hammer, and hung it on my hip.

As soon as I had five goddamn minutes, I'd be imbuing that damn thing and seeing what I could manage with it as well, I decided.

The final weapon I had access to was a last resort only, and that was the shotgun. It'd been a great weapon in the fight to defend the dungeon, mainly because it was a case of "point and destroy the entire area." But precision wasn't its strong suit, and I really didn't want civilian casualties if I could avoid it.

Instead, the kobolds were armed with captured assault rifles, and with the prototype shotguns in a sheath on their back, just in case. That was expensive as hell, and adding on their armor, shields, and a dagger, not to mention spare ammo, they were costing me a fortune to equip. But on the upside, if the shit hit the fan? They'd be able to clear the board, all right.

Finally, I was as ready as I was going to be. I looked down at Kelly laid there on our bed, eyes closed as she manipulated the dungeon, and because I was a bastard, I took two extra seconds to try to stack three playing cards on her forehead.

Then I snorted as she twitched and they collapsed, kissed her and headed for the door.

"I felt that!" she called after me, and I grinned, leaving the room.

"I should fucking hope she did," Chris shot at me, as I exited into the small private sitting area we had, finding him straightening his boots. "Damn, man, I know you're quick, but still…"

"Sod off." I sighed, walking over to him. "You ready for this?"

"Are we ever?" he countered. "What's the plan?"

"Diplomacy."

"Ah." He nodded sagely. "So we're fighting them all then."

"No, we're going to try diplomacy," I repeated.

"No offense, mate, but you're a bit shit at it," he pointed out.

"That's why it'll be Ashley doing that side of it," I growled.

"Well, she's better, I'll agree, and a lot nicer than you to look at, but what's the plan there then? We just being bodyguards or what?"

"We're going to try to sort this shit out diplomatically," I ground out.

"Them attacking and killing our people?" he asked me carefully. "How's that going to work?"

"I'm hoping it's a fucking misunderstanding," I said. "But considering that Major Dickhead we have in the brig, I'm not hopeful."

"Yeah, I wouldn't be either." He grunted. "So what's the backup plan for when it all goes tits up?"

"Assassins," I admitted. "I've managed to cobble together a shield spell, so if we need it, I'll activate that and hold on as long as I can. Kelly's already found a room in the middle of their base that's not in use. We've absorbed and permeated our way into control of it, and she's locked the door."

"So's that a place for us to hold up, or…?"

"She's summoning assassins into it." I shook my head. "If the shit hits the fan, we back up, use the shield, and we close off the exit we'll make in the wall. Then the assassins go to work."

"Kill everyone?" he asked grimly.

"No. There's a load of families in there. Hell, there's a shitload of innocent soldiers we damn well need, not to mention the gear. I think we can all guess where the trouble with them started, with that fuckin' shower of shite Gerald and his lot. I'm hoping that we can cut that cancer out and at least get a non-aggression pact going. Failing that, we eliminate their leadership and try to integrate them."

"How the hell do we do that?" he asked curiously as we started up the steps from the dungeon, heading out into the back alley.

"For now?" I shrugged. "If we have to eliminate, then we'll also lock away their access to their armory and more. Basically, we'll strip them of weapons and gear, then leave them locked inside, make it clear this is a short-term solution. Then we give them some luxuries…you know, real food and so on. Heat. The little things."

"Shit, I'd not thought about that." He grunted. "The barracks is going to be colder than a witch's tit, right?"

"Probably. They've built a chimney and they've already got extraction from their kitchens, but they're not geared up as accommodation. Hell, this is a reserve battalion headquarters, not a full-on one. The fusiliers' main headquarters is at Catterick."

"So there's an armory and a training area, as well as a couple of offices and that's basically it, considering the garages that hold things like the heavy transports and artillery." He sighed. "Damn, thinkin' of wee kiddies having to sleep on the floor in a big garage just ain't right."

"It's not," I agreed. "And considering they'll not have much to burn or anywhere to burn it, they've all got to be used to the cold by now. Sure, it's not snowed yet, but it could at any time."

"So they're low on food, no heat, and considering the way things have been off and on here, I'm betting they've got a few malcontents." He nodded. "Then add in Gerald and the other two, probably mouthing off about how we've all got all the food we want and more, then a little push that we're all spanking each other in a big gang bang every night and Bob's yer uncle, Fanny's yer aunt. They attack."

"Is there a name for what's wrong with you?" I glanced back over my shoulder at him, then snorted as I saw the grin.

"Oh yeah, sorry, you're right, it's the army we're off to see, not the navy. I was thinking if the navy lot were involved, they'd be wanting to join in the spanking more than the heat and food," he tossed off casually, as the pair of us walked out into the alley, before I cursed.

"Goddammit, I had to open my mouth, didn't I?" I reached out and batted aside a melting snowflake as it drifted past.

"It's not that bad." Chris shrugged. "Barely sleet."

"In here it is," I agreed. As we started along the road, the kobold crew that Kelly had summoned jogged over to join us, along with Ashley and Dante. "The temperature in here is higher than out there, remember?" I gestured to the pool. "If that's made it to the ground in here, out there is gonna be a mess."

"That's not that big of a problem, though, right?" Dante pointed out, attempting to cheer me up. "Sure, it'll not be fun for us jogging in it, but once we explain that we can provide heat, light, and food, that's going to encourage the other side to join us, isn't it?"

"Possibly," I agreed. "But I'm more concerned about the effect on people in the area who haven't joined us yet. The holdouts, and the people who just don't know we exist. They survived the last few weeks of the autumn all right, but there's not been the time to have much of a crop yet, and the snow coming this early?"

"It's going to be a hard winter," Ashley agreed. "It'll kill a lot of people."

"Not if we can help it," Chris said. "Look, Matt, all joking aside, she's got a point about the cold, and so does he."

"I know," I said, about to go on when he cut me off.

"No, you don't." He shook his head. "You're thinking from a commander's point of view, thinking of weakening the enemy, right? And the cost of the heat for us, slowing down expansion and so on?"

"Yeah?"

"Well, think of it as an *opportunity* instead." He gestured upward as we picked up speed. The kobolds, led by Beta, fell in behind me in a double line, ten on either side, with what looked to be ten more assassin-class kobolds ranging out to all sides. "There's a handful of people like the doctors in the old QE hospital who didn't trust us, right? They don't want to join us, but they sure as shit tried to get Griffiths to jump ship and join them."

"Yeah."

"Well, give it a day, let it get fuckin' cold. Then send Ashley up there, have her create a space that's warm and safe for them, food and more, then leave again. No questions about paying us for it. Show we're not all dicks the way they're worried we are."

I kept looking ahead, thinking about it as the gates opened. We picked up the pace again, starting to run, despite the thin covering of slush that was rapidly turning to snow ahead. We'd not be able to keep this speed up for long, but we also had sod all time left to spend fucking around with this shit.

Twenty-four hours, that was all we had before I needed to leave. I'd only agreed to wait that long because, knowing what we had to face, we needed resources that couldn't be produced any faster, even with the undead being guided in the dungeon sense to tear down buildings at speed.

Jack would take a further nineteen hours to complete his rebuild, and it'd been horrifically expensive, but we just didn't have an option.

I knew we'd need him for the trip to Otterburn if nothing else and with the damage that had started to mount up.. I'd had to pull him in set to work.

I thought on the changes I'd selected as we continued. The drop-off of the cliff to the east of the wall meant we actually had to use the old stairs to head due south first of all, jogging down to the river, before taking a left and heading east along the quayside.

Jack was a hell of a weapon, and a damn useful platform, considering he wasn't actually sapient, not really. There was a clearly upgrading core to him, one that I was quite sure would come with a fully aware level of personality sooner or later. But considering the last upgrade I'd given him was to Panthera, and had been at the Iron core level, there was definite room for improvement.

I'd not really done much with him, not lately, and the reason for that had been simple. First and foremost, I was trying to protect my people, our home, and our future.

Having a giant robotic panther crossed with a damn saber-tooth tiger that could patrol the area almost constantly, eliminating the various creatures that sprang up on a regular basis was too valuable to take away.

That was true, right up until it wasn't.

I'd not upgraded him partly because it wasn't worth the cost—at Glass he got access to the greater species designation list, while for now he was limited to "local species only"—and partly because for now, he'd been fine as he was.

He was getting more and more battered, sure, but he was also a goddamn robot tiger. Almost anything he went up against was in for an incredibly bad day, and that included asuras.

No, it'd been worth keeping him as he was, especially when I was also trying not to put more pressure on the core, but…I needed to be fast and deadly, and I needed my people to be the same.

I could burn mana and fly, basically leaving the others behind as I flew straight after Mike and the others. But then, whatever had happened—and we knew the coronaughts were at least involved again—I'd have to fight on my own.

Anything that could take all our people down, and that quickly, as well as a full army base, wasn't going to be an easy fight, not even slightly, and I had to be realistic. Chances were, it was well beyond me—without a force that could back me up, at the very least—which was why we were so desperately pushing people now to strip the area.

We needed an absolute buttload of equipment and more fighters, as quickly as possible. To get that, we needed mana, and we needed a trump card, something to keep us in the fight when everything else seemed hopeless.

That was Jack.

The upgrade tree for him wasn't a complicated one, thankfully.

Dungeon Lord Automata detected:

Automata designated as "Jack" is eligible for form upgrade. Do you wish to upgrade this Automata?

Yes/No

121

I'd selected Yes again, obviously, and was greeted with a second screen.

Please choose Automata physical form from the following:

- Avian
- Canis
- Insectoid
- Reptilian
- Equus
- Ursus
- Panthera
- Homo
- Elephas
- Pongo

Please note, these are restricted to the local species variant examples until this Dungeon Core has reached Glass.

Even knowing this was a short-term upgrade, and that as soon as we reached Glass, we'd be upgrading him again, I'd still refused the insectoid and reptilian options out of hand.

Sure, dinosaurs were reptiles, more or less—or birds, apparently, which was still weird for me—but they just freaked me out.

Homo was a no. I was tempted by a humanoid Jack, mainly to be able to march him into places I didn't want to go and see whether he got shot, etc., but that was still too close to the asuras. And if they got the chance to take him, it'd just cause all sorts of problems.

Not to mention, if people saw me with a robotic follower, there'd be someone who'd immediately decide it proved I was working with the aliens or something, and I just didn't need that.

Avian was a possibility, if it could be made big enough to carry cargo, and still be able to fight. There were also always those goddamn flying shitbags as well, and I had no clue what they were up to, so that might be useful.

Equus was basically a horse. I'd never been interested in one before, but if there was a warhorse option, like those big bastard shire horses, that could have been a good one. Unfortunately, the options were mainly stubby little buggers, and frankly, the loss of the combat potential to have a transport just wasn't worth it.

Elephas was pretty awesome, considering the current situation, and even more so as it was a genus of elephant that was closer to mammoth than anything else.

That had me seriously tempted. Like, insanely so. It was large enough to transport things, and the tusks and general weight and power in the frame meant that Jack would still be a lethal fighter.

The issue there was speed, as it came with a warning of "reduced mobility in this design."

Pongo was monkeys, various versions, but mainly orangutans and similar. Again, tempting for the power, less so for the mobility side of things.

Canis was a dog, which we'd tried and had been great, but not that effective long-term in this situation.

The option I'd gone for in the end—and that was taking a whopping two hundred thousand mana to complete out of the dungeon—was Ursus.

The bear was a hell of a template when I looked at it. Although it wasn't great for mobility traditionally, that was down to the natural bear's design for short but fast bursts of speed to catch prey.

In the natural world, bears were designed to fight and be more plodding than endurance creatures like horses and humans.

The thing was, though, this wasn't the natural world, and the power core that made up Jack's heart was designed to run on the ambient mana around us. The more mana, the more power he had, and thanks to the storage facilities I'd found in the plans, even when there was no mana in the area, he could do some serious damage for a short period.

The decider for the Ursus design, though, was that not only was it powerful and lethal, but that I wasn't limited to current bears.

The giant short-faced bear, Arctodus simus, had apparently gone extinct relatively recently in geological terms, a mere ten thousand or so years, but not only was it bigger than a polar bear, it was also capable of running at more than thirty miles an hour.

It weighed almost a ton in the wild, and the robotic version was even cooler, coming in at damn near three times that, with storage options included.

They were limited, admittedly, but it wasn't like he needed space to process his dinner or fat reserves.

Nineteen hours it'd take to complete him, and while that was being done, we weren't wasting any time.

Aly had already started the process of absorbing the missiles that the army had in their base, sitting atop huge launchers that were hidden and immobile in the middle of the giant garage.

Without power, they were literally impossible to move. But what the soldiers didn't know was that they were also mere shells of their old selves—literally in this case, as the high-tech and explosive components that had made them up were currently vanishing into the dungeon.

Now, as I led the way, blinking as a random snowflake landed in my eye—right in the goddamn eye, for fuck's sake—I glared at the drifting snow ahead.

It was time to deal with Gerald and his friends, once and for all.

CHAPTER TWELVE

By the time the wall we'd built around the army base came into sight, I was already snarling in absolute bloody fury, though I was doing my best not to show it.

The one thing I'd never considered—not in all of this fight to come, nor in the plans I'd made to take the fight to the enemy to our north at Otterburn—was that as the snow got heavier, the kobolds would have serious problems.

They were goddamn cold-blooded. That was probably why Drak had been so fucked up when he'd gotten back with the news. Well, that and blood loss, admittedly.

I'd not even considered it, putting it down in part due to stress, and partly down to the injuries, but damn, cold-blooded was a kick in the teeth.

Back at the base, we'd had the undead on the walls on permanent patrol, so the kobolds hadn't been stuck up there, and this was the first real cold snap of the year, meaning although we'd seen them in "cool" temperatures, they'd also been wrapped up and fully dressed, as well as around the dungeon and the pool area with its slightly raised temperature.

Beyond that, we'd not had them anywhere that it was cold at all.

I'd always known, though I'd not been paying a great deal of attention to it, that the kobolds were identified as reptiles in the system, not mammals. It was there in black and white, after all. But seriously? We were going to have to massively invest in the other species now, and as a priority, or some kind of high-tech suit heater option.

It'd be great come the summer, or whatever passed for summer in this country. After all, we basically had warm rain or cold rain as our main seasons in England. But for the winter? We had issues.

"I've got the Scepiniir up to uncommon," Aly assured me. *"We're going to get the first of them ready by midday tomorrow, but the restrictions on them mean that we won't have many. And I doubt that their fur offers the same level of protection that the kobolds' scales do from the coronaught infections.*

"Do we have enough mana to get us up to advanced?" I asked, already knowing the answer.

"We do, but not and produce anywhere near the numbers we'd been hoping for. The cost of reaching advanced and then the huts they need means that we're going to be really down to small numbers.

"Plus…" She audibly took a deep breath. *"If we spend everything we've got on setting you up with an army, there's going to be nothing left for your surprise."*

I heard the concern in her mental sending, and I nodded to myself. We'd make it work; we had to, after all.

"Phase two will still work out fine," I assured her, feeling the silent presence of Kelly as well as I closed on the distant wall. *"So focus on that for now. I'll take a small team and we'll get as far north as we can. Then I'll set up as close to their base as we can get, and we can work on things from there."*

"Thank you."

I knew it wasn't so much for the things I'd said, as it was for making it clear that I wasn't backing down or putting it off. It just meant that this was going to be an elites-only mission now.

I left unsaid that if need be, I might have to launch myself ahead and damn well abandon everyone else, leaving them to catch up when they could.

"Be careful, be respectful, but firm," Kelly said suddenly, speaking up. *"Remember that they're the military. As far as they're concerned, they're here to protect people, and they're used to being spoken to as either too stupid to understand simple things, or looked down upon. Don't do either of those things, for God's sake, but also don't forget that they started this. You're the Dungeon Lord of Newcastle, and you damn well deserve respect for that."*

"I'll play nice," I promised.

"Liar," she replied, and I could feel the ghost of a smile. *"But whatever you have to do, do it and come home to me, okay?"*

"I will," I assured her, jogging down the long bank that led to the base. *"What's that?"* I asked, as a sudden burst of lights sprang up, swirling in that distinctive dungeon way that told me something was being created just ahead.

"A rest area for the kobolds," Aly explained. *"The colder it gets, the less useful they'll be out there. So even though you've probably kept them warmish by running all the way, go in there and rest for ten minutes. Let them recover, then go and make your play. Also...good luck."*

"Thank you," I sent her, and directed a burst of love at Kelly. They both faded back from my immediate consciousness, as I guided us toward the low building ahead.

It wasn't anything special, oblong and a single story, about three meters by six, with a door in the middle of the narrow end closest to us. It had a gently sloping roof, and no windows, but the closer I got the more I was impressed with that thought.

"That building?" I called over my shoulder as we closed on it. "It's a warm place for you to catch your breath." That was all I said.

Not one of the kobolds were ever likely to admit to it, but they damn well hurried to get in the door, that was for sure.

Dante led the way, the Fire mage having even less liking for winter than the kobolds. As soon as the door was open, he ran to the far end of the room, hands already conjuring twin firebolts. The crackling heat that washed off them was almost pushed away by the panting a little half an hour run in the snow had brought about.

Ashley and the others joined him at speed, with even the assassin kobolds happy to get out of the cold wind and drifting snow.

Chris shook his head in amusement at the others, insisting on holding the door and making me get inside before he would. Once we were all in, the temperature jumped noticeably.

Bulging up from the ground, and running down the middle of the room, with simple benches growing out from the walls on either side, was a long fire pit.

The middle was filled with glowing coals, sitting in a metal trough that was then ringed with a stone area, presumably to make it safe to lean against or whatever.

I moved in close to the trough. The kobolds were spreading out along its length, standing shoulder to shoulder and reaching hands out over the rising warmth.

Crouching, I squinted along underneath it. A single plinth rose from the ground, then a metal trough that radiated the heat, and a protective mesh extended outward from it that looked to be stone.

Coming back to my feet, I couldn't help but be impressed. The building was simple, but the combination of the mesh underneath and the metal sections meant that heat would radiate outward from underneath as well, and yet there wasn't the risk of people shifting and accidentally burning themselves if they huddled too close.

It also wasn't a complicated design, and the extended stonework around the trough meant that people could lean on it, eat food, and essentially those who had access to it would be comfortable.

It'd have made me a fortune if I'd introduced it as a product for cold temperature places back before the end of the world, and probably even more if I'd hired a celebrity chef to cook along the line.

In the long term, it wasn't that efficient. Once the coals cooled down, they'd need to be replaced, and a simple heating system that ran on ambient mana would be a lot better. But the argument whether this place was worth that long-term investment wasn't one that was worth having today.

For now, though, it was clearly helping the kobolds, who were letting out groans and gasps, huddling in closer than was probably advisable to the heat.

"How the hell did we miss this?" I wondered to the other two. *"I mean, they're desperate."*

"We've been functioning in the late summer and autumn," Kelly replied. *"It's been getting colder, but the snap overnight was a lot colder than we'd been expecting. It's the first snow of the year, combined with the majority of the kobolds having been stationed inside the dungeon's perimeter. Then those who have been out were mainly either with us but higher levels, like Beta and Kilo, or they were on patrol on their own."*

"So the higher levels can deal with the difference better." I nodded to myself as I eyed Beta, seeing the way she glared at the others for their weakness. *"Probably endurance playing a part in it."*

"Probably, but even higher-level kobolds will be susceptible to the weather changes. How's Drak holding up?" Aly asked.

"No clue. I couldn't find him after he made his entrance. Just got healed up and fucked off to hide, I think." I looked over the kobolds before me, then compared them to Dante and Ashley.

"I'll find him," Kelly said.

Ashley wasn't really having any noticeable issue with the cold, not really; neither was Chris. But Dante was still holding his firebolts and bringing them close enough to himself, he was probably in danger of toasting his robes at this point.

"Thanks," I sent absently. *"Okay, looking at this, and I can't believe I'm seriously considering it, but what do we think of upgrading the goblins in place of the Scepiniir?"*

"Honestly, I don't think it's a good idea." Aly came back after a few seconds' silence. *"As much as I want you to have the best backup possible to go and rescue our people, the goblins are just too weak in comparison. The kobolds were always a clear better option than the goblins, even at the lower levels. And while there's an argument for the difference in uncommon and advanced creatures, I think a warrior race might be a lot more help."*

"The orcs are a warrior race," I pointed out, and I felt the wince.

"They are, and this might be a mistake in summoning the Scepiniir as well, considering the way the orcs look at everyone, even you. Do you want to look at the goblins instead?"

"Not really," I admitted with a heavy sigh. *"I just damn well wish there was a better option than this shit."*

"You and me both," Aly said.

While I waited, I pulled up the quest notification I'd gotten on Drak's return and read it over again. I cursed the damn situation that left me where I was, not to mention the shitty stupidity of Gerald and all his kind.

Evolving Quest Discovered!

Part 1: Investigate Otterburn Camp:
Tragedy has struck! Many of the dungeon's inhabitants have vanished, and reports suggest they have been captured by the insidious Coronaught Queen.

The Otterburn military camp has fallen under the control of this vile creature and her minions. Your first task is to locate the camp and gather intelligence on the fate of your missing comrades.

Complete this part of the quest to receive the following bonuses:
- **+2 to Perception**
- **10,000 XP**

"Five minutes, people," I called out. The kobolds straightened and tried to look as if they didn't care and were fine with that. I snorted a laugh at the look of horror that Dante gave me, even as Ashley put a hand on his shoulder and kissed his cheek lightly, before moving around the kobolds and heading down the line to stand with Chris and me.

"Do we need to give them a little more time?" she asked, pointedly making it about the kobolds, and not her boyfriend.

"No." I shook my head, even as I checked my gear, making sure I was as ready as I could be. "We've got people who are in the shit already. Their reaction to the cold is a pain in the ass, and not one I'd considered, but it is what it is. We need to deal with it and move on."

"Okay, what's—" she started, only to be cut off as I raised a hand to stop her.

"Found him," Kelly said to Aly and me. *"He's in the pool. I missed him the first time around as he's only got the tip of his nose above the water. I've sent for him, and we'll find out how they deal with colder climates."*

"Thank you," I said. "Sorry, go on." I nodded to Ashley.

"It's okay," she assured me. "So what's the plan?"

"We go in and try to sort this shit out." I grunted. "First of all, we know they're on the bare bones of their arse. We've been busily permeating the base, accepting it all into the dungeon, which either believes we're friends and it's allowing us access for that reason, or it's accepted that we're not currently at actual war, which is the same thing as far as it's concerned.

"It means that we can both create inside their walls, and absorb, so we've been busily checking the place out in the dungeon sense. They're down to about two weeks' worth of food, and that's on short rations. They've got almost no heat as they're rationing the wood, and they lost their assault force, or most of it at least. Then we surrounded them with a big fuck off wall, and made it clear they're on our shit list.

"I'd imagine that the lower ranks are desperately willing to negotiate right now, but it's the higher ranks that are going to be a problem, and…" I paused.

"Did we ever confirm if they're here?" I asked Kelly and Aly in the dungeon sense.

"They are," Aly replied. *"The three of them are here, though Gerald is the only one who's not in the base stockade at the minute."*

"Merriman and Sharon in a small, enclosed space?" I winced at that thought. *"Thanks."*

"Aly just confirmed," I said aloud. "The three we kicked out are here. Not sure about any of the others, but Merriman and Sharon are in the base prison, and Gerald is skulking around somewhere as well. With that in mind, that they're here I mean, we can guess we were told the truth about how things started out. Best-case scenario, we march up to the gate and they apologize, we sort this out and all go on our merry way."

"After they attacked us?" Chris asked skeptically.

"I don't think it's likely," I admitted. "But that's the best case. Worst case, they tell us to go fuck ourselves and start by trying to shoot us in the face. Then we kill the nearest threats, and we capture those we can, forming something between a penal colony and an outpost here, until Mike and Griffiths get back, and they can sort these shit-heels out."

I shrugged. "Honestly, the reality is probably somewhere between the two. But regardless, what we need to do is step up and start it. It's only from there that we can find out the next step."

I glanced at Beta, who stood nearby listening, and I raised my voice so that the others, including Dante at the far end, could hear.

"Listen up, people!" I called. "The plan here is simple. We march up to the front gate, and Aly will open a small section of the wall for us. We hold there, shields at the ready, and we demand the base commander comes out to explain himself."

I glanced from one to another, noting how much more expressive the advanced kobolds were compared to their simpler brethren. Their tails and wings gave as much away as their faces did, twitching and lashing from side to side as they tightened grips on their new rifles, making me wish we'd had time for more training with them than we had.

"You've got new weapons," I called down the line. "Use the assault rifles, first and foremost. I know, with your claws, they can be awkward, but use them over the shotguns where you can. The shotguns are prototypes. Some will break. Some, though I don't like it, will probably jam and even fail entirely. I don't want you to use them unless you have to, all right? There's no middle ground. You've had very little time to practice with these weapons, and there's no way to use them on a target that isn't going to be lethal to them and those around them, so don't fire unless you have to.

"That being said, if you need to? Do it. You're our people—they're not. If one side has to die to end this, I intend that it's them." I glanced at the assassins, who watched me silently, waiting. "Assassins, while I and the rest are marching up to the front door, I want you climbing up on the walls. The Mistress of Minions is watching. If she judges you can make it over the wall and to a place you can be better help, unseen, she'll direct you. Otherwise, stay hidden and be ready.

"We—and that's everyone who's not an assassin—will be taking the front door. You're to be a show of strength from the dungeon, a reason for them to take us seriously and explain shit. Failing that, you're there because we'll be killing or capturing them, and I can't kill them all myself. It wouldn't be fair."

I paused. A notification popped up before me, and I took a deep breath. My eyes drifted over the damn thing, and I prayed it wasn't once again using my goddamn XP to power it.

Quest!

Incursion (2)
The source of the incursion has been identified, and a short-term solution found. However, a permanent solution must be enacted. Deal with the enemy base however you see fit...
Deal with the enemy base to receive the following bonuses:

- **+1 to top three Attributes**
- **+1 Class Skill Point**
- **5,000 XP**

It wasn't exactly earth-shatteringly worth it—the quest, I mean—but it was something that I had to do anyway. Seeing the others were clearly reading something, I took a chance and spoke quietly to Ashley and Chris.

"What rewards is the quest offering you?" I asked.

129

"Five hundred XP, plus one point to invest in any attribute and a class skill point to spend," Ashley said promptly, and I winced.

I had thirty-odd thousand XP currently, and I was damn well hoping that the quest didn't take that from me to "pay" everyone else, as there were ten assassins and twenty kobolds, plus Chris, Dante, and Ashley, which came to sixteen thousand five hundred points.

If it was a choice between them getting that reward and the quest or not getting anything, I'd definitely rather give that XP up. It was a hell of a bonus, after all, and for the freshly "born" dungeon creatures, five hundred XP was a good three levels, and that was before they included any kills they got. But still…

That was *my* goddamn XP!

I was still getting five thousand as a reward when they were getting five hundred, and that was a hell of a difference. Plus, that class skill point was far more valuable anyway. I took a long breath.

"Be ready with the shields, and remember, the shotguns are area of effect weapons: you use them, you've got a good chance to kill your friends, or me, if we're in that direction. Only use them if you damn well have to!" I looked them over, making sure they understood I wasn't fucking around with this, then nodded. "Okay, people, let's go get this done."

It didn't take long to leave the longhouse, though the kobolds and Dante were clearly unhappy to be leaving the warm and pleasant building, to walk out into the driving snow.

The wind had picked up and it'd gone from drifting snow, the world around us silenced by its constant fall, into a heavy and steadily building blizzard.

"Is this normal?" Ashley shouted to me as we started to walk. "The weather, I mean?"

"How long have you lived here?" I called back, as we slogged down the narrow street that was left between our wall being grown, and the original other buildings in the area.

"Most of my life?" she replied, looking confused. "Well, a year in Dubai as well as some time in London, but that's it—"

"Why the hell are you asking me if this is normal then?" I shot back, cutting her off. "It's fuckin' Newcastle—it should be raining!"

"I mean, is it magical?" she said, exasperated.

"How the hell would I know?" I lifted my face to the low and heavy clouds above. The whiteness made the world seem smaller as it fell.

"It's a storm, right?" She went on. "Can't you do anything with it?"

"I… Fuck." She had a goddamn point. I was a Storm Titan, and this, as much as I really liked lightning, this was a storm.

I took a deep breath, reaching out and extending my senses, feeling the pressure that came from the heavy snowfall, as well as the rising water content, always my least favorite element.

Air was there, obviously, and the wind was making its presence known. But the water had made ice crystals, which had grown as more and more fractal patterns were formed, developing into snow.

They were increasing second by second, and I drew in deep breaths, searching for anything, and finding…only wild mana.

"It's natural," I guessed after a few seconds as the kobolds bunched up around my small group; Dante looked miserable, already shivering. "I don't sense anything controlling or guiding it, do you?"

"All I know is that if I don't get back inside soon, I'll die of cold!" he called over the swirling snow. "Can I summon my firebolts?"

"Yeah, fuck it. Release them when we get in position, though. Then you can resummon them when I say." I nodded, and he was already casting before I'd finished speaking, both hands bursting with flames as he dual cast.

"This is going to have to be a quick one…" I muttered to myself, noting that the kobolds were already looking lethargic.

Less than a minute later, the wall before us shifted, burrowing inward, forming a passage through, while a second section, directly above the growing hole, appeared as well.

I grunted, then grinned, amused by the inventiveness of the ladies' design. The section above the entrance was almost exactly matching the second one below that was vanishing, creating a plug that hung suspended over the entrance, resting on a pair of wooden braces.

All that had to be done was smash the bracer out of the way and the plug would drop, sealing the wall again.

A nice touch that, just in case the enemy were in contact with the wall and the dungeon wouldn't let us reseal it.

Through the gap into the base, I could see a wide-eyed soldier staring at me as I moved up to the edge of the ten-foot square hole in the wall, stopping there and waiting.

He started to blow long blasts on a whistle that hung from his neck. As the shrill notes carried even with the snowy air, I had to admit it wasn't a bad way to make the base aware that the shit had hit the fan.

"Identify yourself!" a corporal—I guessed—barked at me, even as the other soldier—probably a private—started to move sideways, staying low and switching his rifle from one of us to the next.

"I'm Matt, Dungeon Lord of Newcastle, here to see your base commander," I called back.

"Lower your weapons!" his companion shouted suddenly. "All of you! Drop them!"

"No," I called back. "And if you open fire, I'll erase your soul."

"I…what?" he asked, a squeak making its way into his voice at the end.

"The base commander, get him, NOW." I folded my arms in a fair imitation of someone who had no issues standing here all day, despite the shitty weather and my kobolds getting closer and closer to naptime by the second.

"Do it!" the one on guard who had demanded identification snapped at his companion. "Go get the colonel!"

"Drop your weapons!" the second guard bit out again, and I looked at him…and really looked for the first time.

The pair of them stood beside a makeshift building on the right and a small wall on the left, obviously designed to both keep the soldiers safe from an attack and out of the weather. But it was also presumably made by people who had very limited access to skills.

It was basically a small self-contained, square building that stood to the right of the gate. That gate had been chained shut with some heavy-duty chains and a padlock, while the fence that ringed the base was topped with razor wire.

That was fine, except that the gate was twisted. Clearly someone had hit it with something hard at some point, and it didn't lock any more, hence the chains. There was a small, poured concrete wall at hip height to the left and the building...

I glanced from the pair of them to the building and then back. It'd been constructed, from the looks of it, from paving slabs that had been concreted into place, and then a tarp pulled over it to protect it further from the elements.

Concrete doesn't usually need that much protection from the elements, until it starts to break down. At that point, it generally dissolves and the makeshift building there was just a mess of cracks.

The tarp itself had a hole cut through for a gleaming metal chimney that stood from the top. I noted the snow that was piled atop its cap.

It wasn't being used, that was obvious. And if two people were sitting in a cracked building in the middle of a snowstorm, without using a heater of any kind, then there were definite issues.

The pair were in cold weather gear, admittedly, but it was worn and damaged-looking, and for one of them, clearly several sizes too big as well.

The private looked worse than the corporal, with his lips tinged blue and purple and bloodshot eyes. His rifle shook, making me wonder if he pulled the trigger whether any of the rounds would head where he intended.

The ground behind them, and what had once been a parking lot for the barracks, had been torn up at some point and they'd attempted to grow food.

Whatever plants they'd been trying to grow didn't look very big, and the snow that covered them just made it even less likely that there would be viable food for the winter. Between that and the drawn look on his face, I was sure that they were on short rations as well.

Lastly, I saw that the corporal looked nervous, but clear-eyed and focused, while the private really didn't.

"DROP IT!" he screamed at me.

I reflexively triggered my shield into being. Unfortunately, the Lightning mana I'd used instinctively flared into visibility as the snowflakes touched it.

I should have used Air mana exclusively—I *knew* it. I damn well mentally cursed myself as the shield formed; I'd done it with bloody fire before, and it wasn't that complicated to change the primary mana used.

But I'd not done it; I'd created it with Lightning because that was what I was used to using the most, and it was my instinctive go-to form.

That meant that the shield burst into being with a crackle of blue-white light, and a half second later, the other side opened fire.

CHAPTER THIRTEEN

"CEASE FIRE!" the more reasonable of the two guards screamed at his companion, as the three-round burst hit my shield, making it flare even brighter.

"STOP!" I barked, feeling Kelly pushing out the same command to the others as I was shouting, even as the kobolds lunged forward, shields up and assault rifles leveled.

It was too late, as they'd already opened fire. Bullets shredded into the private; the corporal dove to the ground, shouting for backup.

"FUCK'S SAKE!" I roared. "CEASE FIRE!"

The kobolds had stopped firing as soon as the order was given, and it was only thanks to the effect of the cold weather on them that the corporal was alive and unhurt still.

The delay between them lifting, firing, and switching targets was only a few seconds, but damn was it enough for the experienced soldier to get out of the line of fire.

He hit the ground, rolled behind the short wall, and screamed at his companion. "Jeet!" he bellowed. "Fuck's sake, Private, you dead?"

"Arghhhh!" the private screamed, writhing on the now blood-spotted snow, pressing one hand to his abdomen. "Fuck!" he howled, before twisting around and reaching for his gun. It lay on the ground just out of reach, and as blood sprayed from his wounds, he frantically tried to grab it. The scream tamped down to a hiss of breath as he caught the strap, and he dragged the assault rifle closer.

"Hold your fire!" I shouted again, as Chris, who stood on my right glanced at me, his own large metal shield up and held at the ready, repeated the order.

The kobolds were hunched behind their shields, holding them up and in place. But considering the narrowness of the pass through the wall, my own magical shield had stopped the fired bullets getting anywhere near any of our side.

"Mother… fuck…" the private—Jeet, apparently—hissed out, forcing himself back upright, his rifle held in a shaking hand as he tried to line it up on us.

"Private!" the corporal screamed at him. "Cease fire!"

"Mother…" he hissed again, pointing it vaguely in my direction and managing a single shot that spanged off the shield and vanished into the blizzard.

Shouts came from the barracks behind them, and steam rose from the blood lost already as the private tried to get his gun back on target. The recoil and his palm being covered in blood gave him some issues.

"Stop him," I called to the corporal. "Or I will."

"Fuck's sake!" he snarled. "Hold your fire!" he bellowed, leaving it uncertain whether he meant us, his own guy, or the running soldiers banging the distant base door almost off its hinges in their hurry to get outside.

"We are," I assured him.

He peered around the edge of the small barrier, then back to his companion, and at us again, seeing that we'd not moved.

"Lower your weapons, everyone," I called, with Chris again echoing me. I noted, but said nothing about, the blurs of the two assassins who moved closer to the two soldiers.

He cursed, then rose quickly, rifle in hand and pointed at us, moving slowly to the side and back. The barrel was fixed on us unwaveringly as he moved back, glancing down; then he released his weapon to hang from the retaining strap as he grabbed the private's weapon again.

A third burst ripped into the air, vanishing again, as the corporal dragged him from sight.

"Stay where you are!" he shouted.

It took long heartbeats as the new soldiers made it from the building on the other side of the makeshift field. The first of them skidded to a halt nearby in standard-issue Kevlar and battle rattle, rather than cold weather gear, with rifles leveled, as the corporal started shouting orders and for a medic.

"Identify yourself!" a sergeant, this time, barked at me, and I snorted.

"I'm Matt, the Dungeon Lord of Newcastle, here to try to sort this shit out. If one more of your people fires on me? So help me God, I'll tear your walls down around your ears."

It probably had more of an effect because I called it in a calm voice, rather than being angry.

The NCO glanced from me to the blood trail, then to where the corporal was crouched out of sight from my position, trying to stanch the bleeding.

"I can save him," I called clearly, my mind whirling. "Probably, anyway."

"What?" the sarge snapped.

"Your man, the one who fired on me when I asked to speak to your base commander." I held my rifle across my chest, ready, but trying not to be threatening with it, and I reached down to the bag of holding on my hip.

A weak healing potion came to hand as soon as I slipped it into the bag, the much more expensive one not being brought out and wasted in this situation.

I drew it out, hearing a little grunt of surprise as the red potion seemed to shimmer in the light. "Give him this." I tossed it over the fence to the sarge, who caught it left-handed, his rifle staying fixed on me like it was on rails. "Pour a little into the wounds and have him drink the rest, then do your usual triage. It'll help."

"What is it?" he called back suspiciously.

"Shit, man, you've not seen a healing potion before? You've got some levels, right? I mean, you didn't send everyone with a single goddamn skill out after us already?"

"We have levels," he replied shortly. "Fire on my people again, and I'll make sure you find that out the hard way."

"There's two snipers sneaking out onto the roof of the barracks, far right side," Kelly whispered into my ear through the dungeon sense. *"We already*

summoned three more assassins, and they're on the roof with them. When the first shots were fired, we were locked out of summoning inside the walls, though."

"Did you get many in place?" I asked her.

"The storeroom we were looking at is full. Two assassins, four warriors, all armed, and a corpse lord that's having to fold itself up to fit."

"That's going to be a nasty surprise for whoever goes to replace the printer cartridges then," I sent to her, the room we'd found having been full of stacks of untouched papers and print supplies.

"How do we know if this is safe to use?" The sarge passed the bottle back to a nearby soldier and told him—quietly—to take it to Jeet and make use of it.

"Because I could have killed them both, or all of you easily enough. I don't need to poison you."

"Keep telling yourself that." He grunted. "We're the British Army, my son. Plenty have picked fights with us—not many are still around to tell the tale."

"How many of those could summon creatures from myth and legend, and own a dungeon?" I countered. "Listen, pal, you already told your guy to make use of the potion, so either you know what it is and you're playing for time, or you're really that far up shit creek that you can't afford to ignore a chance. Either way, how about we sort this out?"

"Go on," he replied briskly.

"You sent a team and attacked me and mine," I ground out in just as friendly a tone as he'd made to me. "Assassins, murderers, and snipers—you assaulted my goddamn home when I was busy, and took the lives of my citizens. I want to know why!"

"You're a threat to the civilians of the United Kingdom, and our oath of service required it!" a new voice called.

I glanced across at the figure slogging his way through the snow in a full set of snow gear.

"Who the hell are you?" I snapped back at him.

"Colonel Ptolemy, commander of the Fifth Fusiliers, most decidedly not at your service!" he shot back at me. "You're the Dungeon Lord?" He looked unimpressed.

"I am." I nodded. "You're the base commander then?"

"I am!"

"So it was you who decided to attack and murder my people?" I asked again, wanting to be sure before I gave the order.

"Matt, don't," Kelly whispered in my ear. *"If you have the assassins kill him now, it'll kick off a bloodbath."*

"He started this," I sent to her, forcing myself not to snap.

"He did. And if we need to kill him, fine, but for now, he's just an idiot. Remember who's really behind all of this."

"Gerald, Sharon, and Merriman." I said it aloud, before snorting. "And look, there's the walking shit stain right now." I lifted a hand and extended one middle finger in the direction of the wide-eyed Gerald, who stared out of an upper floor's window.

"You admit to knowing them then?" The colonel followed the direction of my gesture. "You sent them to us?"

"I kicked the greedy troublemakers out of the dungeon," I clarified. "That they came to you? Well, it's not what I wanted but that's my goddamn life these days, isn't it."

"They brought us evidence of your actions, your degradation."

"Really?" I countered, looking him up and down. "What the hell did they bring you that convinced you that launching an unprovoked assault was a good idea?"

"We're responsible for the safety of—"

"Oh, give it a fucking rest!" I snarled at him. "You're really going to try to claim that you were forced into it because you were trying to protect people?"

"We were forced into action—" he ground out, sounding like he was struggling with it before I cut him off.

"You were hiding in your fucking beds, wanking over the lingerie catalog, you mean!" I snapped back at him. "Even if I was attacking and subjugating the local populace—which I fucking wasn't, by the way—you'd still have fuck all right to intervene! You *hid* here!" I roared that last bit at him.

"We were battling monsters, murderers, goddamn vampires and undead by the literal thousands, and the only group in the area with the skills, training, and equipment we needed? You were trying your hand at fucking gardening!" I leveled a finger at them. "WHERE WERE YOU?!"

"We were constrained by our oath of service to secure the local area and—"

"Bullshit!" I roared again. "There's fuck all in the oath you took to say you get to hide and leave the civilians to it. If anything, you broke your oaths. And while you were doing it, I was building a safe haven for people. I got stabbed, shot, and damn well blown up. I've been responsible for these people, feeding them, keeping them safe and making the decisions that kept them alive, or condemned some to death!

"Where the hell were you! I could have handed this all over to you and left. I could have been free, or at least just responsible for me. I could have had *help!*"

That last bit came out almost strangled, and I snapped my mouth shut on it, as more words tried to escape.

I'd not realized, not until right now, how furious I was with them, and it wasn't just because of the assault on our base. I'd been raised by Mama Aurelia and by my own, now long-dead parents to respect the forces, to respect the police, and to know that if you needed help, they'd always come.

I'd been told, though I'd had a harder time going along with it, that even the local politicians were actually good people, and that if push came to shove, they'd be there with the rest of us. That the reason they'd gone into politics wasn't to fuck over everyone else, as all the damn evidence suggested.

It was because they were good people trying to make a difference, and that was what we all were.

Mama Aurelia never had a bad word to say about anyone, and since I'd lost her, and then the end of the goddamn world, I'd just realized that what I was really looking for was someone who could help me.

Someone in a position who I could turn to and ask for advice, for help and to hand everything over to if need be.

Now, as I fought the words that desperately tried to escape, I came to the realization that I'd been battling with all this time. There wasn't anyone out there I could turn to. The army wasn't coming to save us, the politicians would turn it all into a shit-show if they came out of the woodwork, and the police had no more of a clue than I did.

If I was going to save myself, and get to a point where I could hand everything over to an outsider to take it on and just live again? I'd have to damn well fix it myself first.

Never rely on anyone else; they just fuck you over.

As all of that went through my mind, the colonel was watching me, and he seemed to come to a decision.

"We need to talk," he said. "You and I."

"What?" I asked, distracted and trying to reboot my mind.

"A talk." He grunted. "That's what you came here for, isn't it?"

"Yeah."

"Then we need to talk, privately." He nodded. "Inside my barracks," he suggested. "Just you, and oh, one of your people. The rest stay outside."

"Tell him no," Kelly whispered into my ear. *"The undead are tearing buildings apart with abandon so we've got the mana to spend. I'll make a room next to the wall. Oh, and I'll sort the kobolds as well."* She added that as almost an afterthought, and I nodded.

"I agree," I called to him. "But not to your base…there instead." I gestured, having seen the first of the swirling lights starting to appear.

"What the hell are you doing?" He snapped, "Stop it."

"It's a warm and private room," I assured him. "And I'm not so stupid that I'll just walk into your base alone and unarmed."

"I said you could bring one other," he offered, sounding caught between angry and tired. "I, on the other hand, will be alone, as a gesture of good faith."

"Sir!" one of the soldiers snapped. "I don't think that's wise."

"It's my decision to make, Captain," the colonel said. "Stand down."

"And I say no to others as well," I agreed. "I could bring my diplomat, or one of our mages, but I think this is a conversation better had between us."

"Very well." He accepted after a few seconds and nodded. "You'll need to remove your monsters. While we talk."

"My what?" I asked flatly.

"The only thing we'll be discussing is the removal of your forces and monsters from the city," he declared, raising his voice.

I glared at him, seeing the look in his eyes that didn't quite match the words.

"Matt…go along with it." Aly spoke this time. *"There's something going on here, and you're right to go and speak privately. Just…don't cause any more issues in public with him, okay? Give him a chance."*

"Why?" I shot back.

"I think he's terrified," she said. *"I think he desperately wants something. I saw his face when you said about searching for help. It wasn't clear and he covered it quickly, but I think there's more going on here."*

The building was climbing: a single story, square building with a sloped roof and a simple door, matching the simplistic design that I could sense blooming out from the wall as well on the outside of the perimeter.

Instead of the kobolds and the others being forced to stand in the cold—which, if they had to do it much longer, would probably result in unconscious kobolds, if not dead—Kelly was building a second longhouse. One that ran along the wall on the outside, with a similar heating system as the first.

"What do you want me to do?" Chris asked me in a low voice. "You sure you don't want me to come in there and watch your back?"

"Thanks, man, but no," I said quietly. "Take the kobolds and the others. Kelly and Aly are watching over us in the dungeon sense; you take everyone else and get them back in the warmth."

"I can stand a bit of cold," he muttered, still not taking his eyes off the soldiers, who were darting glances between us and the rapidly growing building.

"I know you can," I agreed. "But the damn kobolds can't." I shot that to him in an even lower voice, covering my mouth with my left hand just in case the other side had any lip readers. "Get them inside and be ready if I need you."

"I don't like it," he admitted.

"Neither do I, but if the shit hits the fan, I can kill him. It'd take high explosives to get in at me if we don't want to open the door. I'll just create a tunnel and fuck off. The risk is to you all if you're out here."

"Got it." He grunted. "Never realized how shit-scary fighting us must be for other people, especially in our territory."

"Oh yeah," I agreed, before grinning. "But I'm going to have the snipers taken off the roof before I have the assassins get out of the cold, though."

"Good plan."

"Already on it," Kelly assured me. *"I'll have them take the snipers inside the building and hide them."*

"Thank you," I sent to her, before stepping forward, and making the entire group of soldiers snap their weapons up again. "So, you want to have this chat or not?" I looked at the colonel.

"Of course. This way, please." He gestured to the small building, even as the sarge snapped out orders to stand down and to keep their eyes open.

"Sure, as soon as your damn snipers stand down," I agreed, staring into his eyes.

He hesitated, then nodded. "Of course." He whispered something to the nearby captain.

"He told him to get the snipers down, but to have them ready by the windows. If need be, they can open them and fire, as we already know they're there," Kelly whispered into my mind, and I nodded.

I stepped through the wall, carefully shrinking my shield and tightening it around me as I wove between the soldiers, trying to make sure I didn't touch them with it.

Snow occasionally hit it as I moved, so it wasn't like it was hidden. The flare of light that came each time made it clear I was surrounded by a bubble of light, but still. I guessed that brushing the other side with the equivalent of a walking taser wasn't going to win me any friends.

The private who'd been shot was laid on his back still. Blood covered the ground under and around him, and I slowed, staring at him.

"Keep moving, killer!" one of the men standing over him snarled at me.

For an instant, I contemplated pulling out the much stronger healing potion I had in my bag. That'd save him, I was fairly sure, even if the weak one I'd already handed over wouldn't.

"Is he—" I started.

"None of your concern," the same one who had called me killer snapped.

I glared at him, noting the way that some nodded and stood with him, while the others...

"We're in the middle of a faction war," I sent to Kelly and Aly, slipping slightly on the snow as my lack of attention betrayed me.

"Oh fuck." Aly groaned. *"I knew there was something wrong with this!"*

"I don't see it," Kelly admitted, sounding confused as I strode into the small building, the colonel following me.

"Just listen," Aly told her.

I tuned them out. A pair of seats were set on either side of a small table, one that had the same coal-filled center and mesh design underneath as the longhouses had.

There was also a plate of biscuits, which made me smile. I made the point of drawing the massive sword from over my shoulder, the shotgun and the hammer, then setting them down against the wall, which slid out small prongs to hold each item in place.

"Thanks," I whispered, knowing it was one of the girls watching over me.

"What was that?" the colonel asked.

I snorted and shook my head, settling into a seat and gesturing to the plate of biscuits. "Not important," I said to him honestly. "Want a drink?"

"No." He made sure the door was shut, but could be opened, then shut it again. "Do I need to suspect these?" he asked me grimly, gesturing at the biscuits. He took off his helmet, revealing a short but well-maintained head of salt-and-pepper hair and small glasses.

He looked more like a professional accountant than a soldier, but that look he gave me... I got the feeling I'd just been weighed and measured.

"Again, no." I stared at him. "If I wanted you all dead, that'd be a hell of a lot easier to accomplish than being here, so believe me, there's nothing sneaky going on."

As I said it, mentally added "inside this room," considering that his snipers were being stalked by my assassins, and the soldiers outside the room were surrounded by the buggers as well.

Oh, and there was a room in the middle of his barracks that was currently jam-packed full of my people waiting for a go signal as well.

"I see," he said noncommittally before seating himself across from me. "What, no tea?" he asked in a poor joke, gesturing toward the biscuit plate.

"I was waiting to see what you'd prefer," I replied, showing a lot more teeth than a smile needed, and doing my best to play nice.

"Oh, let's see, an espresso, followed by a black coffee, Italian blend." He forced a smile onto his face, leaning forward and starting to speak before cursing and jerking back.

The lights that spiraled into being on his side of the table, printing a small cup full of high-strength espresso, as well as what was—from the look on his face as he sniffed it—a damn good coffee, made my mood lighten slightly.

Slightly.

"Anything else?" I asked.

"Is there a limit to this?" he asked instead, sipping at his coffee and closing his eyes. "Gods, I missed that," he whispered, apparently unconsciously.

"Energy," I admitted, still not sure where this was going. "What looks like magic is basically energy—different flavors of it, for want of a better term. Mana is just a form of energy, I guess. In this case, the mana is absorbed by the dungeon and we can create what we want, inside of its territory."

"And you view this as inside your territory?" He stared at me over the lip of the second cup.

"I do." I nodded. "Until you attacked us, I was extending our reach out to here in an effort to try to work with you. That's why."

"In what capacity?" he asked.

"What?"

"Working together, in what capacity?" he asked again.

"I'd wanted your goddamn help," I said. "There's a hell of a lot of people who need defending and more threats out there than you can shake a stick at. We need to band together."

"And you still think that?"

"Personally? No," I admitted. "I want to nail you to the goddamn wall by your balls for attacking me and killing my people."

"And professionally?" he asked, without missing a beat.

"What?"

"You said 'personally,'" he pointed out. "That implies there's more than one position...for example, professionally."

"And what makes you think I want a professional relationship with someone I can't trust?" I asked bitterly.

"Realism." He settled back, staring at me as he spoke. "I spent more than half my life on deployments and training exercises with the army. I lost track of how many warlords and arseholes I had to play nice with in the sandbox. So, I ask again, what about professionally?"

"What the hell happened here?" I asked him after gaping at him for a few seconds. "Out there you're all hard ass, in here you want to work with us?"

"I wasn't in full control when the attack was made," he admitted. "Since the fall, there've been some...issues with discipline and leadership that have been difficult to stamp out."

"Like what?"

"Like your friends coming to us, and a major who disagreed with my orders, leading half my damn soldiers out on a fool's errand," he snapped, before taking a deep breath and going on. "Look, it's Matt, right?"

"Yeah."

"Okay, Matt, well, I'm Colonel Adrian Ptolemy, commander of this base, though barely in name only these days with many of them." He kept going, watching my eyes as he explained his position.

"I formally relinquished command over this garrison, and the barracks, on a Friday at 1700 hours. Or, I was supposed to—that was what my orders said—and I was leaving the army. My final day, as it were, I was supposed to wake up a damn civilian on Monday, having spent the weekend helping the new commander—Colonel Stevenson—get acquainted with his command."

"Colonel? I met a major…" I started to explain, and he snorted.

"Is he still alive?" he asked, and I nodded. "Pity, that would have solved a lot of problems." He sighed.

"Anyway, I was to hand over command to him, but he was late. Supposed to arrive on Friday, and instead—through some snafu, that, if you're familiar with the army at all, was almost laughable—resulted in him not only being unable to receive his promotion, but being stuck in Leeds."

"It took him three days to make it to us, using a combination of pedal and foot power. But once he arrived, he immediately tried to assume command."

"And you didn't want to let him, I'm guessing?" I summoned a cold soft drink and cracked it open, guessing that a beer wouldn't go down well.

"He's a political appointee, with the bare minimum time served in each slot before he's promoted. He has no understanding of the debts we owe to the lower ranks, nor that we extend to the higher. As such, when he turned up without his promotion paperwork, and with the situation as it was…well. I used my prerogative to refuse handing over command, and enforcing his old rank.

"I remained in command of the base, but he's spent the time since he arrived steadily eroding my position, along with a few malcontents. Your friends—"

"Don't call them that," I spat. "Gerald, Sharon, and Merriman? They're assholes of the highest order."

"I agree." He nodded. "They arrived and spun some fantastical tales of both your dungeon's power and your sinister deeds."

"Let me guess, am I roasting babies on a spit yet?" I asked him darkly. "Consorting with otherworldly beasts? Summoning succubus?"

"I haven't heard those tales yet, but I have no doubt they're simply awaiting the right time to share them." He nodded. "Major Stevenson was determined to lead an expedition to contact you, and to take you under our control. I tried to stop him, but frankly, in the end, the only way to stop him and his people would have split the base down the middle. More than it already is."

"'Contact.'" I snorted. "They attacked without warning, snipers picking off my people as they went about their business."

"So I heard when the survivors returned," he admitted.

"Well?"

"Well what?"

"Not even a fucking apology then?" I snapped, glaring at him.

"Would it do any good?" he asked me. "Matt, they're my people. I'm responsible for them, regardless of that waste of a rank Stevenson. I can apologize, if that'll make any difference, but we both know you came here for blood. There's a price here, but there's also something you're after. Otherwise, as you say, you'd have attacked. I'm here to negotiate."

"What?"

"Negotiate," he repeated. A sad smile lifted the corners of his mouth. "From what your fr—sorry, from what your acquaintances say, it's a long word and you're unlikely to be able to understand it."

"Are you actually trying to piss me off?" My fist closed on the can I'd been drinking from, making me curse as I crushed it. "Fuck's sake!" I wiped at the table, then took a deep breath and gestured instead, reabsorbing the crushed drink can and the spilled soft drink, replacing it with a can of my usual brand of energy drink.

"No, I was trying to interject a little humor," the colonel replied tiredly. "Look, Matt, as I said, you came here for blood, and I understand it. I'd probably be looking for the same in your position. Hell, you killed a hell of a lot of good soldiers of mine, friends I've been through literal hell with. The difference is, I have to rise above it."

"And I don't?" The constant switching of the conversation left me off-balance.

"You do." He nodded. "You need to decide what you want out of this, while I've got a hell of a lot of civilians I'm responsible for. Let me ask you a question."

"Go."

"If something happens to you, what happens to the dungeon?"

"It dies." I lied instinctively, then I paused, guessing he might be able to tell that I was lying, and deciding to play it safer. "We think, anyway. Certainly we'd lose control of it, though."

That was true enough, as "we" in this situation was me, and I'd be losing control, because I'd be dead.

"And what happens if a dungeon doesn't have someone in control of it?" he asked. "Is that what happened in Gateshead?"

"You heard about that?" I asked, then nodded. "The dungeons were set up here by an alien race, the Cinthians, and they're here to sort of clean up the mana so it doesn't go out of control and just keep mutating things into monsters, and also as centers to help us get stronger for the incoming invasion. The Gateshead dungeon decided that the best way to achieve that was to kill everything nearby to get as much power as possible as quickly as possible, then use that power to protect and guide people. Kill us all but for a good cause, I guess."

"Invasion?" The colonel had sat up straighter, if that was possible, at that point.

"Hah...yeah, lot's going on in the wider galaxy, apparently." I nodded. "That's not important right now, though. What is, is what we do from here."

CHAPTER FOURTEEN

"That's what I'm leading toward." The colonel eyed me warily from where he sat across the small table. The heat made it warm enough in the small building that he had to be sweating under all that cold weather gear by now. "So, just to be clear, if I was to kill you, we'd have lost control of the one thing we were desperately trying to gain control of?"

"Oh, right." I nodded. "Yeah, killing me wouldn't get you control of anything. Also, depending on how the dungeon dealt with it, the various creatures and so on that we have would have either died instantly or gone mad and rampaged. So yeah, not a happy time for you, that's for sure."

"That matches the details that Merriman gave me, though I had to push for that." He took his glasses off, then rubbed at the bridge of his nose, sounding exhausted. "Look, I'll lay it on the table and then we can talk about where we go from there, all right?"

"Why?" I asked him again. "You say the soldiers aren't under your control. But you're the colonel, and if the major was the issue, well, he's out of the picture for now, right? How've you not regained command?"

"I have, partly, but that's a long story, and one that I'll cover after this, but it's heavily dependent on your decisions here, Matt, so please, listen while I explain things, all right?"

"Okay." I grunted. "Go for it."

"We have three hundred and forty-three people on base." He gestured to the building hidden on the other side of the wall. "In a space that's meant to be a local headquarters only, no accommodation beyond a small kitchen area and training facilities."

"Uh-huh."

"My soldiers who were based close by brought their families. Others based at the various sites around Newcastle brought their families into their sites as well, then secured their weapons and brought them here as a central rally point. We took control over the local area, and stockpiled food and equipment, awaiting orders."

"While everyone else died," I interjected.

"Do you want to listen or complain?" he snapped.

"I don't want to do either. I'd rather be helping my goddamn people who are under attack right now, fighting for their lives, but instead I'm here," I snapped back. "I'm having to sit here and talk this shit out with someone who attacked my home and murdered good people, while my friends fight for their lives, so yeah, by all means, take your goddamn time."

143

There was a long silence after that.

He nodded and went on. "That's fair," he said softly. "Okay, cards on the table, I have near three hundred and fifty people living in a space that's impractical for them, and we're starving. We're on short rations as it is, and if this is the new normal..." He gestured vaguely at the wall and ceiling.

"If the winter is starting like this and to continue on, not just a very strange cold snap, then we're fucked. I'm here to ask you to take my people in."

"That...that's not what I was expecting," I admitted. "Not even close."

"And that's one of the secrets of negotiating." He smiled sardonically. "Never give your opponent what they're expecting."

"Yeah, well, you get a point for that," I muttered. "You acted all Billy Big Balls out there...what gives?"

"If I asked for this out there, half of them would refuse to follow my orders," he said. "As I said, I've got a hold on the base, but it's a weak one thanks to that fool of a major. I lost more of my support in sending good people, men and women I trusted, to make sure that if he took the dungeon, he'd not be surrounded by his own. Instead, as many of his fled, I'm left with a weakened support base here.

"We're starving. We've got people desperately in need of medical and emotional support. And while we're having to limit the amount of resources we burn to stave off the cold, you can create these things with a wave of your hand." He nodded to the table, the heated coals and the drinks. "You can do that with food and drinks for more than just us?"

I nodded. "We can recreate anything we need," I said slowly, reaching out a hand and focusing. The weak healing potion that appeared on my palm glimmered softly in the gentle illumination, and I set it down on the table before him. "That's a healing potion, weak grade. It's barely above a stiff drink and being told to pull your finger out, but I don't trust you enough to give you anything else."

"This is the same as the one you gave my people before?" He picked it up, swirling the liquid as he glanced from it to me. "Why does it glow?"

"It's a healing potion." I shrugged. "It's magic. I mean, why does any of this shit work? Some is technology, like the dungeon, just so advanced its indis—"

"Indistinguishable from magic." He finished the quote. "Arthur C. Clarke."

"Exactly. A cocktail shouldn't heal you, not really, so there's some form of magic involved, but alchemy is real now. You follow the painstaking steps, and you can make a healing potion. The stronger grades are much more effective. This one? Like I say, it'll heal a bit."

"But my soldier out there, Private Jeet, you have something that could have healed him?"

"I do," I admitted. "And it costs. That's not me being a dick—that's the grim reality of the situation. He fired on me, and he got shot for it. If we heal him and use a much more powerful potion, that costs us a hell of a lot more to heal him, and we're out a valuable resource when he just attacks us again."

"So what was the point of giving him the potion you did?"

"That's a lot slower acting but it's still powerful." I shrugged. "I've had to survive a hell of a lot worse than he's dealing with right now, without the potion.

"If your people follow their usual steps in triage and work to heal him, surgery, blood transfusions, careful infection control, *and* they do as I told them, pouring some of the potion into his wounds and having him drink the rest? He'll pull through. But it'll take time, that's all."

"Impressive," he said softly. "So, back to it. I have nearly three hundred and fifty souls, and they need a home. They need safety, food and supplies. What will it cost me?"

"What the hell do you think you have that I want?" I asked honestly. "I mean…"

"Only my life."

"What?"

"My life," he repeated. "I'll not fight you in any way. You erect a gibbet and I'll step up and put the noose around my neck myself. Bullets are expensive and a limited resource…or perhaps they're not for you." He sighed and went on. "Matt, I understand the need to be seen to enforce discipline; it's a large part of the structure of the armed forces. There must be consequences for actions, and they must be seen to be paid.

"Knowing that the rules have been broken and the perpetrator is dealt with is important in any situation. If you choose another way to punish me, then that's fine. I'll face any death you choose, but I ask that you limit it to me. My officers and my soldiers are, for the most part, good men and women.

"They'd be an asset to you, and the members of the forces you already have working and living under your control may be able to vouch for them. But even if they can't, they'll be able to confirm the value of bringing them under your command."

"Just like that?"

"No," he admitted. "There's a little more to it actually, including that I'll require an oath from you." That was when he did smile, even if only slightly. "I'll warn you now as well, it'll not be an oath you can break without consequences."

"Explain that."

"We're not unaware of the new realities, Matt," he said. "You might think we've not been busy here, sitting around and hiding in the base, but in reality, what we've been doing is clearing out the monsters of the area, and sending expeditions out.

"While you secured the center of Newcastle with your dungeon, we were reaching out to local leadership—most of whom, regrettably, were either already missing, or made…poor life decisions." He looked at me significantly at that comment.

"Several of the local leadership accepted our invitations to move into the nearest houses, while others joined the expeditions. Unfortunately, those haven't reported back, but due to the distances to be traveled, that's understandable."

"What expeditions?" I asked. "Hell, what oaths?"

"We've been gaining classes and leveling up, too, Matt," he said. "I've dispatched two long-range expeditions, each of two sections, led by a lieutenant, to make contact with both the Otterburn garrison and our main infantry hub in the north, Catterick Garrison.

"The Otterburn section is overdue, but not by enough that it's a concern. The Catterick garrison, on the other hand, aren't expected to return for several days,"

145

he explained. "As part of my class, Protector, I have the ability to make, take and enforce oaths. Breaking an oath sworn to me is, at the very least, unpleasant."

"Unpleasant?" I asked. "Wow, oh no…"

"You know two individuals who swore to be completely honest with me." He allowed himself a little smile, as I replaced his coffee and he took a biscuit this time. "The three you sent to us were unpleasant individuals, and although they'd convinced the major of their story, I was less sanguine about it. Using my oaths, as it was, allowed me to tell that they were hiding things, but not that they were making deliberate attempts to lead us astray…more that the details were incorrect.

"That's normal. If you're not aware, the oath enforces itself, so if you believe a lie to be the truth, you can tell it, unfortunately. That means that instead of black and white, I'm learning to deal in shades of grey, as intent is highly important.

"As a perfect example, Sharon told us quite truthfully that you were a vile and evil man, and that you made completely unreasonable demands of your people, as well as insinuating that you were…making demands of the ladies of your group."

"That fucking…" I hissed, my blood boiling. "I would never!"

"That was what she believed!" he said placatingly, holding one hand up as I visibly seethed. "I'm telling you this for a reason, and I'm trying to cram a lot in here as I'm aware you've got limited time. So, listen to what I'm saying, Matt."

"Go on." I sighed, rubbing at my temples. "Gods, I'm gonna kill her…"

"She believes that, and as such, could say it without triggering my abilities. Once the attack failed, and many of the particulars she and the other two had told us proved to be, at the very least, incorrect given the new information we had, I managed to piece together the important details about shades of grey in perception. Asking much more detailed questions resulted in the growth of my skill, until I made them swear a new oath, one that required them to be completely honest with me, on pain of being ejected from the base."

"And?"

"And her attempt to break that oath is why we know it's such an unpleasant process. The only reason that Gerald isn't locked away as well is that he saw the result from the other two's actions, and decided to be completely honest.

"They've started to recover now, but it's taken several days, and they've needed to be hosed down regularly. Have you ever had food poisoning? Or a real bout of norovirus?"

"Both." I winced.

"Well, consider that this will not only make those incidences appear as a fond memory in comparison, but that it will be accompanied by a full body rash that combines the worst traits of severe sunburn with chicken pox."

He smiled wryly. "Believe me, it's the most effective method of ensuring honesty I've ever seen. It costs a lot of my mana—yes, we know what that is as well—and stamina to take an oath, so it's not something I can just do whenever, but it's well worth it."

"So you learned the truth from them," I guessed.

"We got a version of it," he countered. "Even with the higher-leveled version I gained recently, they must know and understand it's incorrect for the oath to take hold. That is a mid-range effect of breaking the oath as well, with much more severe consequences dependent on the situation."

"So my people dying wasn't enough to trigger 'severe' ones?" I glared.

"It would have been," he agreed. "Except that the oath was bound simply to her being honest about questions asked after that point. Had she knowingly lied beforehand and that had led us to the unfortunate deaths…" He saw my face and changed what he was going to say.

"Matt, there's a lot gone wrong here on both sides. Had you come to us, we could have addressed our concerns before, and had we come to you… Regardless, that's water under the bridge now, and both sides are going to have issues trusting the other. We need to learn to, though."

"And now you want to join us?" I asked flatly.

"I want you to take my people in as full citizens," he said. "They'll work just like any other, and they'll be granted the opportunity to grow and develop. You're in a unique position, Matt."

He looked at me, making sure I was listening as he went on.

"Without my ability, I wouldn't countenance this. And even if I decided I wanted it, I probably couldn't bring myself as an officer of the Queen, to hand over my forces to another. The reason I can is the oath I'd have you swear."

"And what would that be?"

"The oath I swore when I became an officer was to the Queen, she however, was struggling with her health even before the end, as such a decision was made in the barracks more recently. In an attempt to bind the group together more, we repeated our oaths, and included a secondary oath that upon her death, a replacement oath of allegiance would be included to His Majesty the King. I will be faithful and bear true allegiance to His Majesty King Charles the Third, His Heirs and Successors, and that I will, as duty bound, honestly and faithfully defend His Majesty, His Heirs and Successors, in person, crown, and dignity against all enemies. I also swore to accept the orders of those placed above me—which has occasionally been an issue, I'll admit, but that's a separate matter.

"On activating my Protector class, and the Oath ability specifically, I was made aware that should I break that oath—and yes, it's holding me to oaths I swore in my life previously—then I'll die. Highly painfully."

"Right." I nodded. "Go on."

"So, if you swear to take in my people, and swear to uphold the same oath to the Queen, followed by the King, and—"

"No." I cut him off.

"Then I can transfer them into your care and…what?"

"I'm not swearing to follow the Royal Family!" I said firmly.

"Matt…"

"I know what you're going to say," I growled. "That you want me to swear to follow them, but that as I'm up here and the world's gone to shit, I'm not likely to ever have to have anything to do with any of them, right?"

"That had crossed my mind," he admitted.

"Well, I already agreed to lead or at least enable an expedition by members of the Coldstream Guard to reach London and look for the royal family."

"You did?" He looked so relieved I almost punched him in the face on general principles.

"Yeah, I did, and I'll damn well do it, but I'll tell you now I'll not be swearing to goddamn follow them if I find them! Your oath, that one you want me to swear, is to obey the Queen, the King, their heirs and any successors. That means if they name some shower of shite politician or other criminal to take over for them, then I'll be magically forced to obey them as well. Fuck no."

"Matt, if you do this..."

"No."

"Think of the advantages!" he tried instead. "The royal family would never enforce an oath of—"

"Still fuck no," I snapped. "Look, I like the royal family, I really do. Would I want to live in a glass bowl the way they did before all of this? Fuck no. I think the next generation are good people. They're genuinely trying to do right, and old Charlie-boy wasn't that bad, despite the whole situation with his wives. At least he didn't try for eight in the end."

The colonel tried to interject, and I spoke over him as I went on.

"And old gingernuts who fucked off to the States? Fair play. You want out? Go for it. I get it totally. I wouldn't want to live in a fuckin' fishbowl either. Don't like the way he fucked his family over to make a buck, but that's the way it went. Every time they needed some cash, a new story was out and bang, a great big wheelbarrow of cash arrives for them. I get family fallouts, and I get looking out for number one, okay? The Queen? She's a fuckin' institution. She's why they called it 'The Firm,' because she's hard as nails and a good one, but she takes no shit, I bet. Her, I could work with. Her, I get, but we've no way of knowing if she's still around. For all we know we've got one of those thirty-first cousin's twelve times removed that's just all over-bite and no chin!

"The issue with following anyone, though, is that if I'm magically constrained to do it, I'd *have* to do it. If once they got a taste for power—real power, I mean, instead of being a figurehead—and decided that they needed a new wife a week and to chop the old one's head off? I'd have to do it.

"I'm not swearing an oath to obey anyone." I fixed him with a glare. "Because the Orcan are coming, and when they find Earth—which, by the way is supposedly directly in their path of invasion across the galaxy—they'll fucking slaughter us all. I need to continue to grow the dungeon, to unlock more and more advanced tech, to be able to face them.

"That's why we are where we are." I jabbed a finger into the hard surface of the table before me—avoiding the coals—as I went on. "The Cinthians tried to make peaceful contact, apparently, and it went badly. If that's true or not, I don't know. But I'm telling you what I do know is that the orcs I've had access to are absolute dicks, and that's when they're magically forced to put up with me and mine. When they're not, and they're more advanced than us? It's not going to end well, I can promise you.

"They're coming, they're bringing armies, and they've already eliminated entire civilizations. The only chance we've got, and this is what the Cinthians are relying on, is if we can bootstrap ourselves into space, and fucking fight them. Personally, I'm not into space shit—I don't doubt that if I've got to fight them in space, we're going to need admirals to do it, because I don't see how I can help there, but what I can do?

"I can fight them on the planet, and I can rip their goddamn heads off. That's why I need to be in control. Not because I want to be, but because I can sense the dungeon. I can unlock greater technologies through it, I can create armies and weapons, and I can use them to defend us, *especially if people would stop fucking me over for five goddamn minutes!*" That last came out in a furious hiss, and to his credit, the colonel winced.

I sat back, glaring at him, and we had a few seconds of silence.

"Let's say I believed you..." he replied after a few more seconds of contemplation. "Perhaps a slightly different oath would enable us to work together, and with some trust after all."

"Go on," I offered, not intending to swear anything of the sort.

"If instead you were to swear to protect the direct royal line, the heirs and successors..."

"And if they're dicks, it won't work," I snapped back. "Also, define protect. I mean, if one of them gets a boo-boo and I don't kiss it better, I've failed then."

"You agree to try to protect the current Queen or King and their direct heirs for one generation," he suggested after a few seconds. "The family who you can reasonably reach and protect, you agree to try to save if you can, providing them with a place of security. That's what you've already said you'll do," he reminded me. "If the Coldstream find the Queen and her family, you'd need to protect them or you lose the army. If they're enforcing that you help them to reach their families and the Queen as a condition of them joining you, if you find them, then refuse to help them, or whatever members of the family survive, then they'll leave you...you have to know this."

"I already agreed that I'd offer help," I admitted. "I'll *offer* help to the royal family, just like I would any survivors who aren't assholes."

"So now it comes down to the details." He nodded. "What will securing that, in the form of an oath, cost me?"

"Why the hell would I give you an oath?" I snapped. "I still don't see why I'd do that."

"Because if you give me an oath, I'll give you one." He smiled.

"Nice offer but you're not my type," I quipped unthinkingly, before covering my eyes and taking a deep breath as he burst out laughing. "Shit, that came out wrong."

"I certainly hope it did!" He chortled. "That wasn't the intended offer. My wife would have killed me."

"My girlfriend wouldn't be happy either." I rubbed at my face, then sat back. "All right, seriously, why do I want an oath from you?"

"Because it binds my people to obey," he said. "It'd have to be simple. I could either bind a small number with larger oaths, or a great many with smaller, but it's all in the wording and the consequences. I could bind them to tell you first if they decide to betray you. To enforce an oath that would prevent them betraying you would have to take into account all possible betrayals, and it'd cost all the mana I have to bind one person. Two would kill me. I'll do it, though, if that's what it takes. And if the other two agree, or, if you can provide me with the mana, I'll do as many as I can. Literally, I'll burn myself out to tie them to you."

149

"In exchange for an oath from me that I'd try to look after the royal family."

"And my people here," he clarified. "My wife and children…" He took a deep breath and struggled to keep tears from coming as he went on. "They are…gone, so that's not an issue, but my soldiers and the civilians we accepted into the barracks are my children now, one way or another, and I need to know they'll be safe."

"What about the dickheads?" I asked. "The soldiers who have been undermining you all this time and the major?"

"That's for you to decide. But in all honesty, one option I would put forward is that you give them what they want."

"Which is?"

"In the case of the major, to return south. Once he realized that I wasn't handing command over to him, he wanted to return to the south and his family. That, I can respect and understand. But he wanted an escort, and not to reach the barracks at either Catterick or Leeds, but to march all the way to Buckinghamshire, where he's from.

"I couldn't expect, in good conscience, a section—and certainly not four as he was asking—to go with him on what would be essentially months of travel by foot. Especially not when they're needed here."

"So he started causing trouble," I guessed.

"He did, though not all is down to him. There are always those who are glad for a change in leadership for other reasons. When it didn't come about, nor did the retiring of other soldiers I convinced to stay…well, that went down poorly."

"Plus short rations and short fuel." I grunted. "The politicians you found added to it?"

"In part. None were as inflammatory as Merriman, admittedly, but most were firm in their belief that we needed to contact the local bases, gain heavy support, and then secure the area. We were aware of you and the nigh-on miraculous feats you seemed to be creating, but it seems that the creation of the monsters and your dungeon were linked in most of our minds. That was then exploited by the three you banished, and was taken up as a solution. 'Kill the Dungeon Lord, remove the monsters, and take control of the dungeon' was their plan. Although I opposed the attack without more observation, I did believe the monsters were coming, in part, from you."

"What changed that?" I asked.

"We saw your people battling them, as well as received reports that you were working to protect Saltwell Park." He set his empty coffee cup down again, looking at me. "Look, Matt, we can go around in circles all day, but the truth of the matter is that we need you, and you need us. Accept my people into the dungeon, give them the chance to earn a place, and promise to try to save the Queen and her family if you can. I'll have those soldiers I trust swear to follow you, and to warn you if they're going to betray you. That's the best I can do.

"Then you send Major Stevenson and the other troublemakers off to London. Give them a similar backpack of supplies that you gave Merriman, and they'll take it. You get to be free of the troublemakers, additional soldiers you know you can trust, and an influx of willing workers. These people are desperate, and they know, as do we both, that without help, they'll be lucky to see spring.

"You need a public punishment for the attack on you. We both know that's the case, so I'll offer my life. Kill me however you want, make an example if you need to, but protect my people," he finished, staring at me.

I stared back, mind racing.

"What do you think?" I asked Kelly and Aly, knowing damn well they were there listening still through the dungeon sense.

"Can we afford to say no?" Aly asked.

"We've only got his word that he can oath-bind them," Kelly pointed out. *"And for all we know, this is a trap."*

"It's not," Aly said softly. *"Look at him, Kell. He's broken. He's barely better off than Griffiths and the others were. Think about how much help they've been. And he's got a point that he's only asking you to swear to do what you already promised, Matt. This could really help us."*

"Or it could be a trick," I agreed with Kelly. *"I've got no idea how, but it could. Half the soldiers out there hate me—there's no way I want them inside the walls—and they fucking attacked us!"*

"And he's offering to pay whatever price we decide to make up for that," Aly said quickly. *"Matt, can we really say no? And that's without considering that we'd be leaving these people to starve. You might as well kill them yourself. The food they've got won't last much longer, and with the snow as it is? If it gets much colder this winter, they'll simply freeze to death. The trees around here are already cut down and used, and the nearest buildings all have anything that'll burn stripped out."*

"So it comes down to we're damned if we do and we're damned if we don't," I sent to them. *"If we let them in, we've got people we don't trust inside the dungeon. If we allow them access to the systems, they can fuck us over. If we don't and we keep them locked up but feed them, not only is that a cost to us for no gain, but we ensure they'll attack us later."*

"Or we refuse them and we'd be responsible for starving children," Aly said.

"You're right," Kelly said after a brief pause. *"As much as I hate this, we all know we can't turn the kids away. And if we accept the kids but refuse the parents, what kind of people are we? Who'd look after them? Then, once the parents are in, and their brothers, sisters and family? We take them all…we can't not."*

I listened to both sides, while watching the colonel, aware that although the ladies were giving me their advice, and Kelly was saying we were going to do it, it always came down to me agreeing.

There was more to add, though, before a decision was made, and in this case, it might offer a solution as well, of sorts.

"There's something you need to know," I said aloud, watching the colonel's face. "The squads…you called them sections?" I queried.

"The British Army uses sections traditionally, though more modern soldiers prefer squads," he said and shook his head. "Showing my damn age."

"Well, the groups you sent off to Otterburn aren't coming back," I told him. "Or at least if they do, you don't want them back."

"What?"

"You ever fight a coronaught?" I asked.

151

"No?"

"They're a hive mind, spread by little worms, a bit like a mix between a leech and an eel. They numb the skin, so you don't know you've picked up a passenger; then they burrow under it, and go for the head. Once there, they hijack the body as near as we can tell, keeping you alive, but a puppet of the queen. We had a group come through there to join us, the Coldstream Guard that I told you about.

"They reported that there was something weird going on, and they kept going, intending to continue on for London. By the time they'd reached us, they knew that, without help, they weren't going anywhere, so they agreed to help us.

"Then another soldier made it to us through Otterburn, and warned us that the shit was hitting the fan. Most of my forces went to try to sort it out, believing that we had enough trainees and creatures that the base would be secure, and that it was better to go in strength and make sure they got out of there intact.

"Instead, when we lost contact with them, and we'd just been *attacked…*" I glared at him, "then we sent a smaller and much sneakier team after them. One made it back to us, and he told us what we're facing—a coronaught swarm."

"And your people are all dead?" he asked. "Mine too?"

"No," I replied flatly. "Or, at least, we don't think so. The kobolds have scales, they're highly resistant to the worms, and our healing magic enables us to literally burn out the coronaught worm infection. Long-term, 'I don't know' is the more honest answer. The worms apparently take up space in the brain. I can't think that the survivors aren't going to be missing something when something that was living in their brain is removed—there's limited goddamn space, after all—but I've got hope."

"And Catterick?" he asked after a few seconds' worried thought.

"No clue," I replied honestly. "If we're lucky, they've weathered the storm better than us. There's heavy agricultural land nearby, so in theory, there should be a fuckload of food available. And it's a main barracks and training center for the infantry, so they should have both the capacity and the ability to survive. It's just time and whatever unknown shit they might be facing that's there."

"Then we do what we can and we address the problems before us," the colonel said decisively. "First, will you accept my people?"

"Will they accept you handing them over and swearing allegiance to me?" I countered. "Let's face it—at least half of them clearly fucking hate me."

"Those are the most vociferous of the troublemakers, and they'd be the ones I'd recommend we dispatch to the south at the earliest opportunity," he countered. "Plus, they lost friends to your people hardly five minutes ago"

"So did I," I growled. "And believe me, my people aren't going to be exactly happy either. And we still need to sort out those three shit birds."

"I think both sides will have to learn to adjust and accept, though mixed missions will help with that, I suspect. And as to Merriman and his ilk, what do you intend?"

"Hanging," I said grimly. "They tried to raise a coup in my own dungeon against me, and I gave them a chance. Then they took that grace I gave them and came to you, knowing what the outcome would be. Personally, if we weren't so busy with everything, I'd spend the next month researching and building a giant catapult, then I'd fire them into the fucking sun, but that's just ridiculous."

"It is, somewhat…"

"Because knowing them, they'd find some way to put the sun out or something, so yeah. Hanging. Old-fashioned and quick. It's that or I put a round in their head."

"I cannot approve of that," the colonel gruffly replied after a few seconds of silence. "But due to the situation—and their actions—I also have no better suggestion."

"Yes," I said after a few seconds' thought. "I'll accept the civilians, and the soldiers…we'll see."

"Will you accept those I'll vouch for?"

I snorted. "I don't trust you yet, so no," I said honestly. "But now that you know if you try to kill me, you'll be killing the golden goose, as it were, maybe there's an opportunity to earn a little trust."

"Oh?"

"What we're going to do is…"

CHAPTER FIFTEEN

The last day had been a hard one, and I still wasn't sure what I was doing was the right thing. I slogged over the hill, the snow underfoot making the footing treacherous as we climbed higher and higher.

"Goddamn, this blows." Chris huffed next to me, shaking his head. "Next time, we need snowshoes, all right?"

"Who the hell would have thought we'd need them in England?" I asked him, getting a snort of amusement back.

"Fair point. Usually, it's a goddamn snorkel and goggles." Chris groaned. "Remind me again why we weren't on vacation when all this shit happened? I mean, we could have been in the Greek islands, right? I could have dealt with all this shit with much better grace, if we had the sun and sea as well…"

"It's colder there, too…beginning of winter, remember?" I told him absently, as we crested the top of the hill, looking out over the heavily snow-covered valley ahead.

We'd set off some six hours ago, alternating between walking and running, a "dogtrot" as I'd been told it was called, to try to cover as much ground as possible.

The secret was apparently to just not stop, running until you were almost out of breath, then slowing to a fast march, then running again. Ten minutes of each or thereabouts, and I'd been assured we could cover as much in a day as a man on a good horse could.

I was calling bollocks on that. I'd much rather be damn well flying rather than walking—or better yet, not out in the damn snow at all.

It'd stopped snowing about half an hour ago, but it was deep enough here—especially farther inland and higher up as we were—that the snow had been heavier than in Newcastle itself.

We'd made our way through what were rapidly becoming blizzard conditions, and it was only down to the magic of professional cold weather gear that we were still going.

I'd not considered snowshoes, though; we'd just copied the gear the soldiers had.

Now, standing at the crest of the hill, staring down into the picturesque village that lay at the bottom, I couldn't help but curse as damn well.

There were no signs of life; not a single chimney sent smoke into the air, and considering the nearby woods, that wasn't because they had nothing to burn.

Underneath the snow, admittedly, there were great fields as well, many that I knew had fall vegetables in them because I'd visited a restaurant near here that rotated the menus regularly, only using stock grown in the attached farms.

The entire area should be self-sufficient, in terms of heat and food, so seeing the houses that lay silent a mile and a half or so away meant that something else had cleaned the area out.

Still, it gave us a chance to get inside, and perform the checks we were due.

"Tell me we're not getting naked again." Chris huffed, bent over and leaning on his knees as he recovered from the climb.

"You know you love it, really," I assured him.

"I've had enough people staring at me tackle to last me a lifetime." He snorted. "Look, man, I know I should have taken that opportunity to make my career in adult entertainment, but I still don't like gettin' naked around other blokes, all right?"

"The only way you'd have had a career there is as comic relief, or to make others feel better about themselves," I replied halfheartedly, before shaking the concerns for the silent village out of my head. "Seriously, you know why we need to do it as much as I do."

"Goddamn worms." He grunted, straightening up. "All right then, Sparkles. Let's go check it out."

"I hate you," I told him conversationally, as we set off following the giant tracks that Jack had left in the snow for us.

He was ranging ahead again. The new Ursus class design was a hell of an upgrade. Not only was he fast and insanely strong, but his AI had been upgraded as well.

He wasn't quite aware, not as much as a real person, but between my link to him and the upgrades he'd received, I was confident that he wouldn't be misunderstanding anything he was asked to do.

In the blizzards, for example, he'd been invaluable. A simple rope was attached to him, and he led the way, able to sense and follow the road even when all we saw was whiteout.

We then used the rope for guidance, and if I was honest, to help us run and walk as well. The bugger was massive, after all, and had the strength and endurance to match.

There'd been talk of us stopping until the storm cleared, though nobody had taken it seriously. Both me and my small team, and the soldiers who had accompanied us from the base, had people we cared about up here somewhere.

Neither side wanted to leave their friends in the shit for a second longer than necessary, though the eight Scepiniir that accompanied us apparently felt rather different.

They wore modified cold weather gear, and apparently most of their versions came from a hot climate, naturally.

They sure as shit hated the cold, though one of their breeds—variants, sub-races? Fuck, I didn't know what to call it—but one of them had snowy fur and seemed quite content with the weather.

They were currently spread out around Chris and me, watching the surrounding area and the soldiers with equal distrust. Their leader, or at least the more vocal one that the others hadn't stabbed in the face yet, was called Cryseth.

He stayed closer to me as the others roamed; they were rarely out of sight, and yet weirdly, rarely in sight as well. Basically, they were like all goddamn cats in that they liked to stay close enough to annoy me, and yet far away to be as little use to me as possible.

Just when I thought they'd buggered off out of sight, I'd spot one, and realize that they were all *right there*. They just blended in so well that they were a bugger to keep sight of.

Cryseth, on the other hand, stayed close, watching over the other soldiers. I got the feeling that the conversations that Kelly had with him before we set off had been about slightly more than "This is your job; go help out."

I had the nasty suspicion I'd just acquired a bodyguard.

He was about six foot, fairly broad across the shoulders, but lithe as well, fast on his feet. And I just knew he and the others would be unholy terrors if anyone taught them Brazilian jiu jitsu. They had that smoothness to their movements that was so graceful it was almost unnatural.

I'd made the mistake of using my Dungeon Lord access privileges to check their starter stats precisely once.

I was so unnerved that this was their level-zero version that I just didn't want to look any more.

Name: Cryseth				
Species: Scepiniir		Bonus: Advanced Variant		
Spells: None		Class: None		
Level: 0		Progress to next level 0/10		
Available points: 0		Perk: None		
Stat	Current points	Description	Effect	Progress to next level
Agility	16	Governs dodge and movement		0/100
Charisma	12	Governs likely success to charm, seduce, or threaten		0/100
Constitution	16	Governs Health and Health Regeneration	HP: 16x10 = 160	0/100
Dexterity	16	Governs ability with weapons and crafting		0/100
Endurance	12	Governs Stamina and Stamina Regeneration	Stamina: 12x10= 120	0/100
Intelligence	10	Governs base manapool and	Mana: 10x10= 100	0/100

		standard intellectual capacity		
Luck	10	Governs overall chance of bonuses and critical hits		0/100
Perception	16	Governs ranged damage and chance to spot hidden items/traps	+16 damage to Ranged attacks	0/100
Strength	10	Governs damage with melee weapons and carrying capacity		0/100
Wisdom	10	Governs mana regeneration and memory	100 mana regenerated per hour	0/100

Not only did the fucker get five points per level to invest, not only was he naturally at around double the stats of an average human, but they were just...they were goddamn cats!

That was it!

I instinctively wanted to boot them up the arse as soon as look at them, the way he was all cool and relaxed about everything, the way that you gave an order and they looked at you like they were doing you a favor by allowing you near them...

They were like the dickhead jocks and pretty girls in all those damn movies I'd seen, the ones where the reasonable people were just picked on constantly. The ones where the smart as shit people who were going to end up changing the damn world were given wedgies and picked on all day long, while those bastards just floated through life and never had to work!

Every instinct in me said that I couldn't trust them, that I couldn't rely on them or let them behind my back. That the very least they'd be doing is taking the piss out of me because I was poor and...

I stopped, choking off that line of thought, and forced myself to look at it, to really look at it, and then at them.

This was fuck all to do with them, really. This was me being on edge and stressed, then projecting all my insecurities and low-grade paranoia onto them, and I needed to damn well deal with that.

"We have found tracks," Cryseth suddenly said.

I jerked as I realized the fucker was right by my shoulder. "Goddammit!" I cursed. "What?"

"Tracks, Lord." He smiled. "You instructed us to search for them, yes? We have found some."

"Where?" I glanced around, seeing nothing.

"Y'meren," Cryseth said in explanation, gesturing down the valley to the left, and I followed his gaze.

The Scepiniir that he was gesturing toward, Y'meren apparently, stood near a hedge, or what I guessed was a hedge. It was a large mound of snow from this angle, one of dozens that crisscrossed the snow-covered fields. Here and there, roads were visible in the distance; the centuries-old trees that lined them stood in silent watch.

Nothing moved, nothing stirred, and nowhere that I looked was there so much as a sign of life. The only movement now that the snow had stopped was the occasional "thump" as snow fell from an overburdened branch or bush.

The Scepiniir was crouched in the lee of one such hedge. But as I watched, he stood and gestured to the distant farmhouses, presumably meaning "they went that way" as opposed to "look, a house we can all see."

Goddamn cats.

I throttled that thought again and asked the most obviously stupid question in the history of questions.

"What did they find out?"

"There's tracks," Cryseth replied slowly, as if talking to an idiot. "They go that way. Anything else, I'd need to shout and make the prey aware of us, or go to them and examine the tracks myself."

"Uh, yeah, fair point," I agreed, berating myself internally as Major Dickhead staggered up the hill to join us.

That was the second part of all this, and the reason I was really feeling all out of sorts, I knew.

When we'd sorted the details out—and there'd been some fun ones to sort, that was for sure—the major had flat out refused to head south until "his men" were safe.

Normally that would have been a point in his favor in my book. Clearly, he cared about his people, or at the least felt a sense of duty and honor.

Well, that was what I thought for about half a second, until I realized that there was no goddamn chance I could leave him behind me in our territory and free, to just sit around and plot.

It was either we kept him in the stockade—or jail or whatever John was calling it this week—or I shot him in the face. The only other choice was that I took him with me. And every mile we covered, I regretted not making shooting him in the face my decision.

Colonel Ptolemy had turned out to be something of an asset. His people who weren't the troublemakers in the barracks actually seemed to respect him, and the civilians loved him. He was a sort of father figure to many of them—stern, and a bit of a stickler for the rules, admittedly—but still they respected that.

Although I wasn't happy about things with the soldiers, I'd had to be realistic. And besides, the ones I really had on my shitlist—Gerald, Sharon, and Merriman, as well as their various assistants and spies—were all locked up now, on a strict diet of, well, a diet.

They got unlimited eggs and beans, though, mainly because I was petty and the thought of them in a small space constantly arguing over who had farted really amused me.

I was still bound and determined that I'd be stringing those three up, but I was also enough of a realist to accept that doing it on the first day when everyone was still unsure about who I was, wasn't the best idea.

Instead it was to be a treat to myself. As soon as I'd gotten things all sorted out, got the dungeon straightened up and things in order. I would probably give them a chance to redeem themselves.

The orcs couldn't be the only training dummies that people got to fight in the dungeon, right?

The base had been folded into our control, and the look on Ptolemy's face when I'd revealed the assassins outside, and then the team inside his own base, had been priceless.

The people there were a bit afraid of me and mine, given that they'd heard all kinds of tales—mainly from Gerald, who'd still been free at that point.

As soon as I reintroduced them to the wonders of magic heating, unlimited hot food and cold drinks—not to mention the magic of hot showers—I was basically Father Christmas and Keanu Reeves rolled into one, in the way they thought of me.

I'd taken the six troublemakers Ptolemy was most concerned about, and I'd taken fifteen others he said were actually trustworthy as well to even things out.

The two groups of soldiers—they were distinctly groups and blatantly distrusted one another—were careful to maintain their position in line, and yet stay clear of one another wherever possible.

"What...did that...creature...say?" Major Stevenson asked, huffing as he tried to breathe.

I snorted, looking at Chris and Cryseth. "Tracks," I told him flatly. "We're following them."

"And...if they're...a...trap?" he asked, unable to speak, we'd been pushing that hard.

"Damn, man, you need to invest in stamina." Chris chortled. "You look like shit."

He got a glare from Stevenson, before the other man eventually responded when it was clear we were both waiting on one.

"I...did," he growled, forcing himself straighter, while barely being able to stand. Clearly it was pride or nothing for this one.

"You already did?" Chris cocked his head as he looked the older man over. "Damn, how low was your stamina when you started?"

"It's not important." I cut them off before they could really get started arguing. "And if it's a trap, then we'll kill things." I shrugged. "Okay, Cryseth, let's move out. Straight to the village, please. Let's follow those tracks."

He nodded, making a series of hand gestures that must have made sense to the Scepiniir scouts, as they continued on their way.

"This way, people," I ordered the soldiers, hiding my amusement at the glare that Stevenson was giving me.

159

Apparently, most of his team weren't much better off than him, but he was notably the weakest. By the time he'd staggered up, both Chris and I, neither of whom had focused on stamina, had returned to full and were feeling good.

The road that led down the hill—we were sticking to the roads as a matter of general principle—was a winding route into the village below. The closer we got, the more we could pick out little details like the battered state of the houses, the overgrown sheds, and more that seemed to be being strangled by plant growth.

The river as well, when we got close enough to make it out, was almost buried underneath a layer of brown vegetation—vegetation that was in turn mainly buried under snow, making it hard to identify at a distance.

It was only the slow breeze that had started to pick up again that was even uncovering that.

"I don't like this," Chris muttered to me, drawing closer as we jogged together. He kept his voice low enough that although Cryseth could clearly hear us, Major Dickhead, who'd already fallen behind, couldn't.

"That asshole?" I asked him, about to apologize to Cryseth about not collaring the fucker for the "that creature" jibe.

Kelly and Aly had recommended that I didn't pick a fight with him and just put up with things, Ptolemy had stressed that I needed to take the Major with me on this, and while I didn't like releasing him from the little jail, I wasn't left with much of a choice.

The deaths of our people and the assault on the dungeon had been pinned quite firmly on Sharon, Gerald and Merriman and their cronies. That meant that when things were all settled, I was going to publicly hang those fuckers, but when it came to Stevenson, being an unlikable dick wasn't enough to justify adding him to the mix.

Under orders and Oath from Colonel Ptolemy he'd made it very clear that while he didn't ask enough questions or do any kind of research, the assault came about through their actions.

That'd meant as much as I wanted to stab him in the face, in the interests of absorbing the base and its personnel in with our own, I had to set him free.

We'd all discussed the deal with the Scepiniir as well, making them understand—I think—that I was honor-bound to accept the fool into my party for a short period of time, and that I couldn't, and neither could they, kill him.

Not unless he started it.

Kelly had also stressed that the idiot would try to provoke us—all of us, no doubt—and again that it was an honor situation, and we just had to put up with it.

Then Chris went on, and all thoughts of apologies faded.

"No," he said firmly. "These plants…they're wrong."

I glanced at the plants on either side of the road, buried under the snow, and squinted, wondering what he meant.

Now that we were farther down the valley and the wind had begun to pick up again into what one of the soldiers had assured us was the next half of the storm, the hedges were starting to lose their deep covering of snow.

The first hint there was something wrong for me wasn't the brown and fading green foliage that poked through here and there. No, it was the *roots*.

The roots of the hedges, when I looked down and where I could see them infrequently, were the way I assumed hedges would be. Not too thick, not too thin, just a fuckload of small to medium branches essentially that wound up through the soil until they were high enough to instead be covered in leaves and so on.

That was a plant for me. I couldn't tell one from another, nor tell what was a weed or a flower or whatever, beyond that some of it was in the ground, some of it wasn't, and some bits had bright colors attached.

Oh, and some bits were edible. That was an important detail as well.

That meant that it'd taken me a bit longer to notice than it took our resident druid. But when I did see it, I slowed. "What the hell is that?" I stared wide-eyed at the thick root.

Where I could see the base of the hedges, they were obvious. As we approached a massive old oak tree, one that had been caught with half its leaves still, now bound in a snowy prison, the roots were even more clearly wrong.

They rose from the ground, having slid along it, not burrowing beneath the earth, and where the roots I'd expect for a hedge varied from as thick as my little finger to perhaps twice the width of my thumb, these were, at the smallest, wrist thick.

The thickest were larger around than my thighs, and they were wrapped around the tree and rising into its branches as densely as they roamed through the hedges.

Here and there, they twitched, as evidenced by the sudden cascades of snow on a branch or bush until at last Cryseth grabbed us both by the shoulders, slowing us as he peered ahead intently.

"What's up?" I asked him, and he shook his head that he wasn't sure, as Chris spoke.

"You sense it too?"

"Yes," he said.

"What?" I asked. "The roots?"

"The death," Cryseth corrected.

Chris and I stared forward. Chris held one arm up in the simple "rally on me" gesture, one of several that we'd learned recently with the help of Reedy—or, as he was officially known, Sergeant Steve Reed.

Reedy was the one the colonel had chosen to make sure we got through this without a bullet to the back of the head. Most of his trip so far had primarily consisted of teaching us idiots the basics and watching his erstwhile colleagues, to be sure that they knew they were being watched and not to try to start shit.

The rally one was a simple one: left hand clenched into a fist held up and circle in a short gesture.

It worked, though, as the others fell in around us. Even Major Stevenson, dick though he might be, said nothing as he stood, watching with a keen eye.

"There," Chris said suddenly. His eyes glowed with a golden light as he apparently triggered some druidic ability, and he gestured forward at one of the trees, then another, then the hedges. "Holy shit, they're all around us…"

He whispered it, and I stared, my gun at the ready, rifle stock braced, even as my left hand was held clear, ready to grab onto the rifle if I decided to shoot, or to cast a spell if that was what was needed.

Instead, it took a few seconds to make out what he'd seen. And when I did, it was clearly after the Scepiniir did. They were all on alert, prowling as I stared wordlessly at the skull of a small child.

It'd finally resolved itself into what it was, and now as I glanced at the bumps and ridges that lay all around us, blanketed by the snow, I couldn't help but swallow hard at the realization.

"They're all around us." That was what Chris had said, and as I spotted a few, I saw more and more.

A femur here, an ulna there, skulls that had roots woven through them, in one eye and out the other, tearing jawbones free, showing how they'd choked their victims to death.

The plants were all around us…and so were the dead.

CHAPTER SIXTEEN

The moment of realization was a harsh one: we'd wandered into the middle of the plants like lambs to the slaughter.

Weapons were raised, spells readied, and in the case of a few soldiers, grenades were held in hand, ready, watching the surrounds, until, after a long minute, Chris finally spoke again.

"I think...it's asleep?"

"What?" I asked.

"Make sense, man," Dickhead snapped. "It's a plant, yes?"

"Yeah, it's a plant," he snapped back.

"Then how does a plant sleep!" The major shook his head. "Stand down, everyone. It seems the children were playing." That last was added in a withering tone, and my fists itched.

"Just shut it and listen, you idiot," Chris said scornfully. "I'm a goddamn druid, all right?"

"A druid?" He scoffed. "Of all the choices out there, you chose to be a druid. That explains a lot."

"Yeah, I did," Chris growled. "It means I'm in step with the natural world. And who was it who spotted the plants in the first place, or that we're surrounded by dead and goddamn hidden bodies? Oh yeah, that'd be me, so shut it!"

"Chris," I said warningly. "Fancy telling us what's wrong now, and arguing later?"

"Yeah, sorry, *Dungeon Lord.*"

The way he said it let me know he wasn't taking the piss out of me, but was instead making the point to Stevenson that I had a real-world rank, one that he didn't.

"It feels like it's asleep, or—crap, no, wrong word—it's in hibernation. That's it, I think."

"What?"

"It's a plant," he explained quickly. "Some kind of an ambush predator. It eats meat...no, it's the compost!" He clicked his fingers as he went on excitedly. "It's a damn plant, all right. It's gone into hibernation because the temperatures dropped so far. However it hunts, it draws people close to its roots. Where they fall, that's by a root, every time. Then they decompose and boom. Plant food."

"A plant killed this village?" Reedy asked, and Chris nodded to him.

"Probably a lot more, actually," he mused. "There's a lot of bodies here...probably killed anyone coming past. Sorry if I sound a little vague. It's not a direct data download, you know? It's hints, feelings, and scents as much as anything else I get, but this is definitely a predator."

"How?" I asked.

"No clue, man. Something in the air...poison berries, apples? I can't get all of it, but I can see the plant; I can sense the life that flows through it."

"How dangerous is it?" I asked.

"Right now?" He shrugged. "Not very, I guess. In the summer? Probably lethal. There's got to be a hundred people just here, all dead. The only good point is that it's here, up in the hills of Northumberland, well away from the city. If it gets the chance to grow all the way there, though, or some decent summer weather to spread? It could be serious."

Then, being Chris, he went entirely in the other direction. "Or you know, could be shite. I mean, it's not like there's a lot of visitors this way, anyway. Might be that it never kills again as no fucker bothers coming this way beyond the animals and some monsters."

"So it could be deadly, or no threat at all. Well, thank you for that electrifying insight." Stevenson rolled his eyes. "With your *kind permission* then, oh great and powerful *Dungeon Lord*," he gestured to the path that led through the village, "shall we pass through? We've got people to rescue, after all, even if you're more interested in the flora."

"You need to shut your cock-holster," Chris said to him with a wide, friendly smile. "Or I swear, I'll shut it for you."

"Leave it, both of you!" I snapped, before it could get any further out of hand. I knew Chris was one heartbeat from punching the soldier, and I didn't doubt that would start a fight, as well as quite possibly a firefight. "We're going to explore the village before we move on."

"I refuse," Stevenson snapped. "We have soldiers missing. I refuse to waste more time while you search for bugbears or imaginary monsters in the village. Light is fading."

"Well, you do you, pal, and fuck right off." The words were out of my lips before I knew it, and I saw the gleam of triumph in his eyes. Before I could think to say anything else, to change what I'd said or to make it clear that I knew he'd set me up, he was calling for "his" soldiers to follow him.

Sergeant Reedy looked to me for confirmation, and I spoke up loud enough to be heard, while glaring at the major.

"Looks like we've come to the parting of the ways sooner than I expected," I said. "It's up to you. Those who believe in me *or* accept that the colonel had a reason to order you with me, stick with us. Those who don't, feel free to go with Major Dickhead."

That brought a few open smiles. Although about half the soldiers I'd expected to stay with me out of the fifteen did, the other half were clearly torn between following one of their own or a stranger.

"I mean it," I said clearly. "If you want to leave, I'd rather you went. This plant creature is a menace, and if it's in hibernation now thanks to the harsh start to winter, we're not passing on the chance to kill it off before it spreads."

"And there you have it." Major Dickhead snorted. "He's going to spend time here killing off a plant, while the rest of us go and rescue our fellow soldiers. With me, people! That's an order!" he barked, starting forward while glaring at me, clearly waiting for me to do something.

Instead, I smiled and waved him on.

"You sure about this, *sir*?" the sarge asked me quietly. "He's got a point, you know. The plant will be here on the way back with our people as well, and the losses while we hunt and dig out a plant..."

"You're thinking old school," I said in a low voice. "Trust me on this, Sarge. If they want to leave, better to let them. That's part of the reason you're here. And we don't need to share the XP with people we can't trust."

When Chris had been talking about the threat, I'd seen the flash of a new notification come up; I'd deliberately kept silent, letting Major Dickhead and his people leave. I couldn't wait to see the sneers turn to chagrin when they realized there was a quest they'd just missed out on. And if it looked like it'd take more time than I was willing to spend, which was literally a few minutes at most, then the plan was, indeed, to leave it for later.

"There's also the issue that if we leave it, and the weather breaks, and then we have to come through this way with wounded? It's going to be a nightmare," I pointed out, watching as more and more of the section gathered their gear and left.

"Finger," the sarge snapped instead of replying to me, as one of the lance corporals made to stand up. "Don't be a fool."

"I'm not, Sarge," he replied, looking clearly conflicted. "But our people are out there. Maybe they're dead, but if there's a chance they're not? We've lost so much time already..."

"Do you trust me?" the sarge asked.

"Finger," as I'd heard a few call him—or Efinger as his uniform declared him to be—paused, then nodded.

"Well, I trust him, and neither of us trust that streak of piss." He gestured with his chin in the direction of the major, making a few others who were standing suddenly nod and settle back into place.

In the end, we were left with eleven soldiers. The other side had nine leave, along with the major leading them. As soon as we were sure they were out of earshot, I turned to the section.

"Thank you for trusting me, or the sarge," I said. "Don't worry, we're not going to be staying long, and remember that while the major is leading the way, as soon as that storm hits..." I pointed in the direction of the almost blue and grey incoming clouds that covered the horizon to the north. "They're going to have to either turn around, or march on in a blizzard."

"They'll keep going, sir," one of the privates said flatly. "You're planning for us to stay here until the storm blows over?"

"No," I assured him. "I'd like to, don't get me wrong, but my friends are somewhere ahead, and I want to save them as much as I want to help yours. No, my point is that we had to follow my automata Jack to be able to even find the road in the last bout of snow. They won't be able to do that."

"You'll refuse to help them?" another asked.

I shook my head. "No, but I'm not going to go out of my way either. They were happy to leave us, and that has consequences. They'll have to wait for us to catch up to them, or, when they end up staggering around in the blizzard, unable to find their way, they can try to find our footprints and follow them."

"We've got a compass, sir," another pointed out.

"And you tried using it recently, Reeves?" the sarge asked bluntly. "In those storms, it spins like your mother on a pole, so shut it."

"Aye, Sarge." Reeves winced and nodded. "Sorry."

"It's fine." I smiled. "Second point, and this is a biggie—has anyone opened their notifications recently?" I pulled my own up and started to read.

> *You have generated a Quest!*
> *Quest!*
> *Recover the Village.*
> *You have discovered a small, lost village, and upon closer inspection, you've discovered it is not only an abandoned village but also an active monster nest.*
> *Leaving the dead unburied is a crime in many cultures, and due to the rampant mana of the area, it's only a matter of time before the undead rise.*
> *But of more importance is the source of the spreading infection.*
> *The Anadromus plant is both rare and dangerous, renowned for its life-enhancing properties when prepared correctly. If, however, it is left to run rampant, the Anadromus will spread unchecked, drawing in any and all life-forms in the area to fuel its expansion.*
> *Beware the potent kiss of the seeds of the Anadromus plant, also known as the "Breath of Sleeping Death."*
> *Eliminate or gain control of the Anadromus to receive the following bonuses:*
> - *+1 to top three Attributes*
> - *+1 Class Perk*
> - *500 XP*
>
> *Note: Rewards have been decreased on this quest due to level of difficulty.*

Most of them hadn't seen anything and had nothing showing in their notifications tab, while Chris and I, and the few who were clearly remaining, all had the quest.

"I think…" I started, then I shook my head. "Fuck, this sounds ridiculous. Okay—Finger, right?" I looked at the lance corporal.

"Yessir."

"Are you staying with us?" I asked him. "Do you choose to trust me and follow my orders?"

He hesitated, glancing at the sarge, then nodded slowly. "Yessir," he agreed, before blinking. "Hey, uh, I see it now?" he admitted.

"That's it." I sighed. "Look, people, for better or worse, I'm sort of the only authority figure in the area that the system seems to be recognizing it for this kind of 'protect the area' quest. Or, at least, if it is recognizing others, I don't know about it. If you're loyal to me, you get extras. That's the top and bottom of it. So make a decision. If you want to stay here and trust in me, then say it, a public declaration. Believe me, I know how stupid that sounds. If not? Jog on after Major Dickhead."

The naming of the major like that aloud again to the rest of the group drew some laughs. While I stood there, feeling ridiculously self-conscious, they all muttered or said the words—or, in the case of Finger—who I realized was the squad joker—declared his undying love.

Sergeant Reed glared at the corporal, clearly promising he'd pay for that later, while the ice was well and truly broken between that and Chris joining in with even worse shit.

We gave it thirty seconds more while everyone read the quests and accepted it, before I spoke again.

"Thank you all for that…even you, Finger—though I'm now going to ask you to stay the hell on the far side of the section from me when I'm sleeping. Right, Chris, where's the heart of this thing?"

I turned to my friend, and he nodded, starting to lead us deeper into the hamlet. The Scepiniir had watched over the little event with some confusion, but now, as we started to move again, Cryseth stepped up.

I eyed the large humanoid tiger, seeing the way that he moved, the easy grace and confidence, and I briefly thought about how terrifying facing an army of his kind would be.

"Y'meren is nearby," he said. "Tracks lead to a building ahead, on a low rise overlooking the village."

He drew the word *village* out, clearly not one he was used to, and Chris repeated it for him, helping him to get it right, as the group set off, deeper into the houses.

Chris led the way, though Cryseth agreed to point out if we started heading away from the house we needed to investigate.

For now, we were headed in the same direction, and I looked at the houses and main street.

The village was an old one, and small—perhaps a dozen houses, that was all—with a postal box recessed into a stone wall, and a shop that was clearly long closed even before the end of the world.

The main road led through the bottom of the village, and onward, up the hill on the far side, with houses on either side of the road, and a single tributary road that led off on the left, curving around out of sight.

The houses, like the walls that hemmed the road in, were old, made of stacked fractured stone; then, in more modern times, they'd had little refinements like additional reinforcing and damp-proofing, as well as more cement and so on added.

From the outside, as we passed, they looked solid enough to resist a nuclear strike, though, the craftsmen who had built them having passed the tricks of the trade from father to son for centuries. The roofs were of slate, angled more sharply than in the city and surrounding areas, as with the higher elevation came harder snowfalls. As we wound our way through the village, taking the left and heading deeper into the houses, we could hear the nearby river growing closer.

At the end of the road, with smaller houses on either side, was a large house. It was clearly a converted commercial building. The old waterwheel that had once upon a time driven some machinery—way back, centuries ago—had been locked in place now for presumably longer than it'd ever worked.

Regardless, as we approached the end of the street, Cryseth spoke up.

"There." He pointed at a house over the river and perhaps twenty meters farther on. The rise of the land meant that on that side, the house loomed over the river with a garden that looked to be so sheer that cutting the grass would require a mountaineering setup.

At the side of the house, I could make out Y'meren crouched and watching us, with a second of the Scepiniir behind them, watching the other way.

"That is where the tracks lead," Cryseth said, and I nodded, peering up.

The way the street wound back and forth to get to this point, and the way that the houses were built with walls literally against the edge of the road on this side, meant that there was nowhere to hide, if we wanted to move on.

I nodded, looking to him. "Have they entered the building?"

"No." He shook his head. "They wait for permission to hunt."

"Tell them to check it out, but carefully. Remember, we're missing people, and it could be an enemy who's hiding in there as easily as a friend. They won't know your people, though…" I hesitated, then cursed.

"We can't have you lead the way." I decided after a brief time to think. "Sarge?"

"Aye, sir?" He stepped closer.

"Take a team and check that building out, while we search this one."

"Sir." He agreed with a nod. "Finger, you're in charge. Keep the Dungeon Lord alive."

"Yessir," the corporal agreed, stepping up closer and gesturing to his team, who stayed close, while the sarge led a second team of five with himself back to the main road, to loop around to the house.

As I was issuing orders, Cryseth was doing the same apparently, all through hand gestures. By the time I turned to Chris, the Scepiniir were already on the move, heading down the almost vertical garden, and toward the building before us.

"What are they doing?" I asked Cryseth.

"Moving to encircle," he said softly, his eyes never leaving the building ahead. "Something is there. It watches us."

"Where?" I squinted.

"Inside."

"Chris?" I asked, knowing he was seeing more than I was by the golden sheen to his eyes.

"That's the heart of it." He nodded. "All the roots lead to here."

The issue, for me at least, and presumably for the others, was that in the more recent past, when the building had been converted into an admittedly beautiful house, someone had applied some mirror-like film to the windows.

From the other side, whoever or whatever was inside—presumably the anadromus planty-thing—would be able to see us quite clearly.

"You're sure we're being watched?" I asked in a low voice.

"The plant…" Chris whispered. "Get ready…"

I cursed, speaking quickly to the soldiers who weren't used to fighting with us. "Give us plenty of room and only use ammo if you have to. It's going to be fuck all real use against roots."

As I said it, a faint creak came from nearby, and I glanced to the sides, judging the distances from the roots.

"Looks like I'm bait," I muttered, stepping forward slowly.

My rifle was connected on a sling to my armor, so that—as I did now—I could simply release it and the retractable sling dragged it in close, keeping it there.

I drew my longsword, cursing to myself when, thanks to the resize, the last few inches once again caught and I had to shift my grip to draw it free.

I heard a low comment from one of the riflemen to another and chose to ignore it as I gripped the sword and swung it slowly, loosening up in preparation.

The houses on all sides were covered in the roots. The way they clambered up and over, winding in through broken windows and displaced doors spoke of either fast and heavily powered movement, or slow and steady advancement.

I didn't know which it was, but if they'd needed to smash through doors and windows, I was guessing it meant that they were flexible.

Snow covered everything, piled in drifts here and there; my breath fogged the air as I moved closer and closer, the house right before me.

"Which way?" I asked Chris, who was a few meters to my left.

"In," he said firmly. "The roots are coming out from under the house and around from behind."

"In it is then," I whispered, stepping slowly forward.

The front of the house was clearly either the heart of the infection or close to it. The road ended in a small turning area for cars. Each house had space for a small garage down the side of the building and a narrow garden at the front, and they all looked inward into the cul-de-sac.

The building before us, though, had a larger garden, with two steps that led through a wider gap in the garden wall, and a path that led across the garden and up to the front door.

The path was bordered by what had once been a meticulously trimmed pair of hedges, the remains of some fanciful animal shapes almost lost to the growth and snow, mirror images on either side. The front door stood ajar, with roots as thick as my torso laid one atop the other and filling the entrance.

As soon as my foot touched the first step, leading up to the front garden of the house, though, all hell broke loose.

CHAPTER SEVENTEEN

Cracks and the retort of smashing stone on all sides rang out. Roots buried in snow tried to move and found that winter's harsh grip wasn't willing to let go.

As many roots shattered as managed to move; splinters filled the air as they tried to respond, only to find that winter had cold-welded them in place.

Still, on all sides, the roots tore free, and I lunged forward.

"Focus on the big ones!" I barked out the order as the smaller, and apparently less fixed ones, rose on all sides, lancing inward to remove me.

The soldiers behind me opened fire. Short, sharp bursts tore into the biggest roots as they tried to pull free of the houses. Bullets ripped holes through the biggest roots, severing them before they could tear free, and where the roots managed to rear up, shots rang out, cutting them down as soon as they did.

That was a hell of a nice surprise for me, as I'd half expected the rifles to be fuck all use against them.

I moved forward, with Chris behind me grunting out something I couldn't catch. Strange sounds filled the air, almost musical, as fully half of the roots around us slowed, as if they were trying to burrow through stone.

"Can't hold them for long…" The big man grunted, and through it all I danced.

The changes to my agility from when I'd first been taught the sword by Markus meant that to an outside observer, it was graceful and smooth. But to me, knowing how far I'd come, and knowing in truth that I was still a bare novice with the longsword, I gritted my teeth and kept going.

Chris stayed back, the instinctive response from so many hours of training and fighting side by side, as he knew to leave me room for my sword.

Wielding a longsword was more about balance and footwork than Hollywood would have people believe, namely that it was just swinging a sharpened piece of metal and shouting catchy things.

I took two quick steps forward, bracing my left foot, my right back behind me and facing out at a forty-five-degree angle, both knees bent slightly as I blew out a breath, focusing.

Roots flashed in from all sides and I spun, with Markus's comments in training on circular footwork constantly running through my mind.

The sword slid through the air. My mana and health powered it as the void blade cut effortlessly through even the thickest of the branches, sending them tumbling free without so much as a tug on the blade.

It dipped, rose, and slid through the air. The zornhau diagonal, downward-leading cut severed more limbs before me, and I twisted. The regular standing bushes on either side of the path through the garden crashed to the ground as I spun, sweeping the blade around at ankle height in a clearing cut. Then the blade rose as I faced back the way I'd come. The first strike had been made from the right shoulder diagonally down to left, then the sweeping circle, followed by the blade returning up to the left shoulder. Now I switched my stance, leading with the right foot and left braced behind me.

Chris stepped slowly as sweat ran down his face, the effort of holding so many of the striking limbs back.

I felt the strain now as well. The cost of powering the void blade was high, the equivalent of taking multiple tiny wounds constantly, even when cutting what was essentially a mobile damn tree.

Lifting my blade and inverting it, I swung in a circle. I swept my right foot out, pirouetting as I cut downward. The magic of the blade enabled me to slice through the limbs as they attempted to strike.

I stomped down, bringing an end to the spin and straightening as severed limbs all around me tumbled free.

More creaking and cracking sounded on all sides as the limbs tried to move forward. Burst of fire from the soldiers cut the thickest from the air, as Chris worked to slow them and I cut and sliced.

Houses nearby exploded as windows were smashed through. Thick roots and vines lashed out, driving at the tiny food that dared to trespass in their territory, and the fire from the soldiers ramped up.

Reaching the front door, I switched to a motion Markus had laughingly called "beating the grass" followed by the "eggbeater," a fast up-down cut that then had me twisting the hilt to make the tip spin in a circle, the leading edge slicing more and more from the air as I led the way.

"Entering!" Chris called from behind me, and I shouted back to let him know I'd heard.

"Check the rooms!" I called, and heard him passing it on, even as I advanced through the house.

The effect of cutting through the roots and vines outside in the garden had been stark. Most of the growth led from here, meaning that everything I severed, once cut free, simply collapsed and lay still.

I had no clue whether they could regrow, but I needed to make my way down to the basement, I could see, and the damn carnivorous plant was trying to get to me instead.

As I approached the stairs ahead, the roots lifting and rearing back, ready to strike, I lunged and stabbed out, then twisted to the side as the woody mass collapsed.

Whatever else it was, the damn anadromus plant was a shitty fighter. I guessed that most of its attack was from that sleeping death thingy that the prompt had warned against. Fortunately for me, it was winter, and if this was a real plant, even a magical one, it'd have cannibalized its seeding process, to give it the strength to last to spring.

A few more cuts, and the stairway that led downward was revealed, though admittedly, the damn thing was so full of roots that it was going to be hard to get down there.

"Incoming friendly!" came a voice from behind us, quickly followed by, "I think..."

I didn't have time to look. The roots surged forward and the sound of cracking rang out from below as I stabbed and cut, until I heard Chris's voice.

"Kilo, my dude!"

That got my attention, and I turned.

The kobold hurried up to Chris, grinning widely. His blue-tinged scales looked battered, but he was positively glowing with health.

"Chris." He nodded, before sliding past the big man and punching out with his left fist, followed by his right.

A blue blur flashed past me, impacting the roots as I spun back, momentarily cursing myself for the distraction, before grinning evilly.

"Kilo, you got much mana?" I asked him.

"I was saving it." He grinned back. "Glad to have friends to kill this with, and share the XP."

"Oh yeah." I nodded to the gaps that were rapidly being filled by the panicked surging of the plant. "Can you slow that down?"

"Easily." The limbs that he'd hit with the spell already were blackening and curling in on themselves. He stepped up and shifted his spell, locking his wrists together and projecting a blast of icy air that, even free of the cone of devastation as I was, I could feel was harsh.

Judging from the effect on the plant, as it immediately slowed, the sound of creaking and cracking, followed by splits that radiated down the limbs, it was a hell of a counter to the fucker.

"Chris!" I called over my shoulder, seeing he had one hand extended and was still battling to keep the plant slowed, and I shook my head. "Sorry, man, I'll do it." I stepped back and passed him with a clap on the shoulder.

The drinks cabinet was clear in the room on the right, just a few meters back before the stairwell. I strode to it, grabbing bottles as I called to the soldiers.

"Pass the word—we're about to kill this fuck. Do as much damage as you can so that you get the XP."

There was a pause as the soldiers apparently passed the word, before the sound of gunfire ramped up.

I saw the Scepiniir moving in as well, their guns—they'd accepted the rifles from the base, but really didn't like them—slung in favor of short blades that gleamed and stabbed.

Beyond them, I could see the snow had already started to come down again, slowly falling as I looked through the door and out nearby windows. I nodded to myself, lugging the bottles closer to the stairs.

"What's the plan?" Chris forced out, frowning as he kept his abilities extended, even as around us more creaks rang out and the building shook slightly.

Clearly the roots were looking for another way up to us.

"Simple." I twisted the top off the bottle of whisky I'd found, then spit it on the ground, as I began to pour. "We flood the basement with this shit, and we light it. Between the heat and how cold the stone is, the whole thing is gonna shatter—all the stonework will—then it collapses. Once it's down, we can cut the plant out easier and Kilo can freeze it to death."

"You got a lighter?" he asked me, before cursing and snagging a bottle from my hand. "Not that, man…that's good shit."

"Fuck the lighter, I've got a lightning bolt," I pointed out, before moving back to the cabinet and grabbing a few more bottles.

There were dozens, and I deliberately didn't take them all, noting the cases of cheaper but still good booze stacked nearby. Clearly someone had been prepared, or had raided somewhere recently.

I dragged a case from there and set it in each room, making sure they were spread out, but taking the tops off the bottles as I went.

Two minutes later, just as Chris sagged and let out a groan, I was ready.

"Can't hold this any longer, man…" Chris called to me.

"Fuck it, run!" I replied, stepping up and pouring two more bottles into the stairwell, this time cheap-ass vodka. I shook my head; Kilo was looking the worse for wear as well.

"Go on." I grabbed his shoulder and pushed him toward the door. I picked up the last bottle, intending to lead a trail to the doorway with it, until Sergeant Reed stepped in.

"Can I interest you in a thermite grenade, sir?" He held it like he was offering me an expensive bottle of wine in a restaurant. The narrow cylinder was clearly old and looted from some forgotten military dump of the past. It was bright red and marked all the way around with warning symbols. "I particularly recommend the L84A2, sir. It's a *classic*."

The evil grin on his face made me grin in return.

"Why don't you do the honors, Sarge?" I suggested, tossing the bottle back toward the piled and frost-withered, blackened roots.

"Why, thank you, sir." He pulled the pin and shouted: "Stand clear, fire in the hole!"

Then we ran like buggery out the damn door and into the street.

It was almost instantaneous that as the grenade flared and sparked to life, the thickly poured liquid and drifting alcoholic fumes caught. The resulting *wumph*, I felt in my chest as I was picked up and thrown along with the others across the street, hitting the snow and rolling, before twisting and looking back at the house.

My notifications were flaring already. I couldn't help but grin, after glancing to the sides and making sure that everyone was okay, as not only the flames rose high, but the crackle and pop, followed by streaks, lit the snowy air.

The previous inhabitants of the house apparently, at some point, had not only a fuckload of fireworks stashed, but also from the fierceness of the blaze, clearly had loads more booze hidden downstairs as well.

The screech and whirr of Catherine wheels, the fizzing, the crack and pop of dozens of different creations, not to mention the sudden booms as high-power rockets exploded in the bowels of the building, all combined to make it almost festive, despite the situation.

"Fuck me, we'd be in deep shit if this was any other situation," the sarge said to himself, before offering me a hand. "On your feet, sir. I think we just butt-fucked the element of surprise."

"What elephant?" Chris pressed a hand to one ear and wiggled it. "Fuck me sideways, that was a bit…excessive."

"Did we get it?" I accepted the hand and climbed to my feet, even as I checked the notifications.

The first one was minor: I gained a single point of luck. And although I liked that, the real bonus was the next one.

You have completed a Quest!
Quest!
Recover the Village.
You have discovered a small, lost village, and upon closer inspection, you've discovered it is not only a village but also an active monster nest.
Leaving the dead unburied is a crime in many cultures, and due to the rampant mana of the area, it's only a matter of time before the undead rise.
But of more importance is the source of the spreading infection.
This source has now been eliminated, and the bones of the former inhabitants and the victims of the anadromus plant are being rendered to bone dust.
You receive the following bonuses:

- *+1 to top three Attributes*
- *+1 Class Perk*
- *500 XP*

Note: Rewards were decreased on this quest due to level of difficulty.

"Fuck me, I know it wasn't exactly a ten-hour battle, but that could have ended badly," Chris said aloud. "And bone dust?"

"There." Finger gestured to a skeleton that had been exposed in the fight. Most of the vines and roots were woven through the dead, meaning that as they curled up in death, they were shattering the bodies as well.

It also meant that everyone got the same prompt this time around, more or less, which was interesting.

"I got two levels…" someone nearby called.

"Three!" Another laughed. "Fuck me, the guys are going to be pissed when they realize they missed out on this!"

I glanced at Cryseth, who stood nearby, his gaze distant as he clearly assigned points, and I nodded, before turning back to Kilo.

He was doing the same, I guessed; certainly he was looking at the system prompts, as he had "that" thousand-yard stare. Either way, though, I was damn glad to see him, and I looked him over quickly.

His armor and gear were tattered, a lot of small tears, and here and there were wounds that were still healing—both scales that were broken and cut through, and what looked to be a few bullet wounds.

These were rimmed with frost, and that made me look a little closer, seeing the glimmer of what I guessed was an active spell.

His pouches were gone, as were most of his weapons, beyond an empty handgun, the slide jammed back, in its holster on his hip.

His knife and spears were missing, his rifle was gone, and the strap to secure it was dangling, broken. His backpack, with what I guessed was all his food as well as any camping gear, was gone too. And yet, he looked...healthy.

As if he'd grown in stature as well as power. It suited him.

I pulled up my own screens, reviewing my stats page, nodding to myself as I saw the improvements.

Quickly working things out, and checking over the details I could see, I found that I'd gained two points in dexterity, three in endurance, and a whopping four points in luck, which I wasn't sure how I felt about.

If I'd gotten any points in the other areas, I always felt like I could see a difference. Endurance was my stamina; the longer and harder I could, uh, *run*, with stamina upgrades, for example, was noticeable.

Luck? It was always a guessing game. Was it really helping or would I have done that anyway?

Fuck it. Didn't matter either way, really, because the damn system had allocated the points for me. Three times I'd gotten a plus one to my top three attributes of late, and clearly I'd been coasting on luck as the system saw it.

Fortunately, now that my mana regeneration was back, I wasn't suffering the way I had been. And even better, now that I could draw from the four primary elements of mana, and I had those goddamn gates rebuilt and filtering, it meant that they canceled out the issues I was having.

Admittedly, I still wasn't getting more than ten times the damn stat number, so in this case I was getting ten times forty-seven, so four hundred and seventy points an hour.

That was nowhere near the amount I really needed, considering I was at over four thousand mana, but I was confident that I'd be able to advance that with improvements to the gates and meditation. At least now it was less than eleven hours to fully restore my mana...which was several lifetimes in a firefight, as I already knew.

Name: Matt, First Lord of the Storm				
Host Powers: 1 (Enhanced Regeneration)				
Species: Thunderstorm			**Bonus**: None	
Level: 26			**Progress to next level**: 40,913/50,000	
Stat	**Current Points**	**Description**	**Effect**	**Progress to Next Level**
Agility	42	Governs dodge and movement	Heightened chance to dodge attacks 84%+20%= 104%	81/100
Charisma	32	Governs likely success to charm, seduce, or threaten	48% more likely to succeed in events that	83/100

			require seduction, persuasion, or threats ((22x2) +10%= 48)	
Constitution	52	Governs Health and Health Regeneration	HP: 52x60 = 3,120	97/100
Dexterity	45	Governs ability with weapons and crafting	+45% Increased chance of improved result +17 to melee damage	22/100
Endurance	46	Governs Stamina and Stamina Regeneration	Stamina: 46x50 = 2,300	85/100
Intelligence	61	Governs base manapool, standard intellectual capacity	Mana: 61x70=4,270	98/100
Luck	45	Governs overall chance of bonuses and critical hits	+70% increased chance of positive outcome	17/100
Perception	43	Governs ranged damage and chance to spot hidden items/traps	+33 to all ranged attacks	94/100
Strength	40	Governs damage with melee weapons and carrying capacity	+60 to all damage with Melee weapons	98/100
Wisdom	47	Governs mana regeneration	470 mana regenerated per hour	90/100

"What happened to you then?" I asked Kilo, after banishing my stat screen, deciding to assign the class skills later. I damn well knew I'd need them when phase two went active.

Even the thought of that had me double-checking the pouch that held the seed, before glancing back at Kilo.

"Much fighting, more running, and until this glorious weather, I was using my mana more than air." He smiled. The draconic muzzle made him look far more disturbing when he smiled than normal, given the teeth.

"You're okay with the weather?" I asked, before shaking my head. "I mean, yeah, of course you clearly are, but…"

"But my kind are not usually so sanguine about the cold." He nodded. "I learn as I go, but some knowledge, it comes to me through the great system. My magic grants me more. Though my blood is colder than yours, the gift of magic sustains me, and lifts me when I flag."

That was it apparently, all the explanation I was getting as to why a cold-blooded creature was totally fine in the snow where others were literally on their knees, barely conscious.

But hey, that's life in an alien apocalypse with magic, I guess.

"What changed with the weather?" I asked him, wondering whether it was just that it was easier to hide, or…

"The weather? The gift of the cold has changed everything." Kilo smiled. "Had the cold not come to us, then you would have been suffering slavery by now."

"Slavery?" My balls tightened in unease.

"The coronaught … You have seen them?"

"No…" I admitted.

"You should have. And had the cold not sealed them away, you would," he said seriously.

It took a second for me to work my brain around that. Then I turned slowly, staring out across the ground, ground that was being uncovered by the flames that rapidly melted the snow and ice.

"RUN!" I roared. "Back away from the house!"

CHAPTER EIGHTEEN

I'd been a little paranoid, it turned out, when it came to the coronaughts and the weather. The cold didn't send them into hibernation, as it so easily could have. Instead, it killed them, and fuck me sideways with a traffic cone was I glad about that.

I was also glad about not being fucked by a traffic cone, if it came to it…but that wasn't the point.

Jack finally arrived back over the top of the valley—which was already growing hard to make out—and just behind him were more of the soldiers who had gone with Major Butthurt.

They were willing to leave us to explore while they soldiered on to try to rescue their friends, but as soon as they'd heard the gunfire behind them, and that it was ramping up, not cutting off, they'd been unwilling to leave us behind.

The result was that we now had all the soldiers the colonel had said were trustworthy, and none of the ones he wanted rid of, which massively cheered us all up, in the short term at least.

It was almost tempting to leave the idiots to get caught, now that we knew that the coronaught worms had made it this far south. But as much as I was an asshole, I didn't want them dead.

Also, as Chris pointed out while I was considering it, there was always the risk of the fuckers giving intelligence away once the worms had them. We really didn't know enough about the coronaughts' capabilities.

We gathered up all we could, as well as several frozen and small buds of the anadromus plant—I put them in the bag of holding, just in case—then we set off, heading uphill.

I'd deliberately not put the seed in the bag, because that was far too valuable to risk. But the plants? Well, I wasn't sure about those fuckers as it was. If they died, that was a risk I was willing to take.

It took about ten minutes to make it to the top of the valley, and from that point, with the snow starting to fall heavier, we could only just make out the village below us.

That I could still do it, though, and that I could clearly pick out the still burning remains of the house, which had now spread to the other houses nearby, was all that I needed to see.

The major had clearly been able to see from here that we were in a firefight, and then had to have seen the explosion, then the spreading flames. The fucker had decided to continue on, regardless.

I took a final look down at the flames slowly reaching out to engulf the village, before turning my back on it.

The houses were mostly stone and shingle; the storm and deep snow should have stopped or at least seriously hindered the spreading fire. Instead, the flames greedily licked their way along the dead roots that ran literally everywhere, and the entire village was a lost cause.

The only redeeming feature, as I turned my back on the conflagration, was that at least I could be damn sure that nothing of the plant beyond the small sections I'd saved in my bag of holding would survive.

Heading onward into the storm, we quickly tied a rope around Jack, to act as a guide, and connected a carabiner on our armor to the rope, keeping us all together as we set off.

The only excitement of the next hour was that after twenty minutes, having found the tracks of the others almost buried in the snow, we paused to debate leaving them to get lost.

In the end, Chris was outvoted in our little management meeting that consisted of him and me, Sergeant Reedy, Kilo, Cryseth, and Finger.

It was a damn close thing, though, and had Kilo not just blatantly voted as I did—bless him for that loyalty—it would have been more than a little awkward. Chris and Cryseth accepted it with good grace, but had it come down to three against three, that would have been awkward.

As it was, we followed the tracks and found them after another few minutes. The idiots had decided, as they couldn't see, they'd hunker down and ride out the storm behind a wall.

They were halfway through setting up their tents when we arrived and booted them back out to play.

We now had some very surly and untrustworthy people in the group again, but we'd found Kilo. That alone had made everything a little better than it had been this morning...plus, I made them share out their ammo so that everyone had the same again.

That was a win for our side right there, as were the looks on their faces when some of the soldiers started to talk about their levels gained.

The next hour, and the hour after, was boring as all hell though. Literally, it was the group trudging forward, the snow surrounding us and whipping in random directions as the wind picked up. The most we could see in any direction was a matter of meters. As the minutes stretched into hours, we grew more and more brain-dead to the world around us.

The Scepiniir were clearly suffering, most of them anyway, but they were also—as the description of their race had made plain—a damn proud people.

As long as the "real" humans and kobold weren't complaining, neither were they.

Though it probably helped that Chris had explained the major and his people to Cryseth as a sub-race, one that was slightly stupider and weaker than the rest of us, but that we were required by the bounds of honor to be sort of nice to "our poor dumb cousins."

That meant I had somewhat of an excuse for not realizing, until it was almost upon us, what the sensation that finally woke my tired mind was.

Mana.

I could sense it in the air, and as soon as I recognized what it was, I ordered a halt, moving into the lee of Jack—even on all fours, he was two meters tall now—to crouch down.

"What's up?" Chris had to practically shout it into my ear.

"Mana!" I shouted back, pushing my hood out of the way, then holding it to block some of the wind. "I need a minute!"

"Got it!" Chris nodded to me, straightening up and turning to the others. "Kilo, you good for mana?" he asked, and the kobold nodded. "Can you make a wall?" he asked then, gesturing with his hands as he explained what he wanted.

The kobold nodded again, then set to work. Chris helped him and the others fell in as they saw what he wanted.

While they created a small shelter, I reached into myself, and into a section of the dungeon sense I'd rarely touched since I'd first set the original core up.

The ambient mana levels for the area weren't something I'd looked at much, mainly because I'd set the dungeon up in the highest mana concentration I could reach in a reasonable time, an area that was mid-blue in color, while most of the area around me at the time had ranged from green all the way to red.

The center of Newcastle, where I'd decided to set up, had been spotty with various colors and depths, but it'd been the best choice by far.

I'd looked at the map later on again, and when we'd extended it as far as we could, we'd seen that the mana density at the very edge of the map, about halfway to the barracks, had been deep, deep blue.

That'd been "as the crow flies" though.

We'd been using the roads, so now, searching over the map, and finding that—while I was outside of the dungeon itself, I had a fraction of the range it'd gifted me—I could still see a hell of a lot more detail.

The area I was in now was, as I'd guessed it would be, dark blue. That was why it'd caught my attention. As I checked, I couldn't help but grin. My own mana regeneration had taken a leap as well, to nearly four times what it had been an hour ago.

I had a mental range of about three miles now. The map I was used to accessing in the dungeon since interfacing with the dungeon core gave me a rough topographical layout of the area in my mind. I zoomed all the way out, looking down, then spinning it slightly and snorting at how bloody stupid I was.

The map wasn't "real time," unfortunately—not in the sense of being able to zoom in and see myself—but it was accurate. I could zoom in and see that we were almost slap-bang in the middle of the road, marked with a pulsing dot.

What that meant, as I zoomed out, was that the surrounding area was shown as well, and it was shown as it presumably had been recently. I could make out the fields and rivers, nearby buildings and more.

There was a blurred filter on the ground, which I guessed was to indicate the snow, but I could dismiss it easily, and see the area as it was a few days to a week ago, when I supposed that the dungeon had last updated it.

Drawing back, I could see a nearby farm and collection of outbuildings which was hidden from me by the swirling snow, as well as the village of Otterburn, maybe a mile and a half from here.

Passing along the village, at the far end from where I huddled now, I found a wider track that led north-by-northeast, around half a mile to the edge of the barracks.

That meant that we were close enough, and almost as close as I'd wanted to get, before beginning the next stage.

I needed to be close—close enough that we could expand to it; close enough that we were in this area of high mana density, which I had to guess was what had led to the coronaught outbreak—and yet far enough back that we had the time to set up.

I wanted materials to salvage, but also to be hidden...

Scanning the area, I went back and forth three times. The worry about what had happened to Mike and the others constantly drew my attention as I looked at the map. Finally, I decided to take advantage of the storm and the weather to get closer than I probably should.

"Okay, people, so... What the...?" I blinked as I opened my eyes again. Not only was I now a lot warmer than I had been, but I was out of the wind and snow. For a second, I panicked, looking around to make sure the storm hadn't blown itself out.

Nope, thank fuck. Instead, while I'd been focused, and presumably that'd taken longer than I thought, Chris and the others had made an igloo.

More or less.

On three sides, we now had walls of packed snow, snow that Kilo was busily turning into thick ice, while several soldiers were following along behind him and packing snow hard against that.

The result was a steadily increasing internal temperature, and as someone had thought to string a tarp from the top of Jack's back—he was the fourth wall still—and all the way to the ground, we even had a sort of roof in place.

That was great and all, but as others started to break out all the things we needed to camp, I spoke up.

"Hold up, people. We're not stopping here," I said quickly. "This was a break to check the local area, not a camp."

"*Sir.*" Major Annoyance's tone made it clear *sir* was being used instead of *Listen, you fucking idiot.* "Clearly you have limited experience leading people. In conditions such as these, a soldier requires regular rest and recovery stops, not to mention food and shelter. If we push on, the men will be in no shape to fight, and there's no way to know how far we need to cover yet. As such, I've made the call to camp here. Now if you and your creatures wish to keep going, feel free, but we'll be staying here."

The way he said it made it obvious he knew I'd have to back down and shut up. After all, it was that or march into the snow without the soldiers who were all looking at me with varying degrees of hope and derision.

"Not going to happen." I smiled. "Pack your shit up, people. We're moving on."

"I think not," the major replied. "As an outsider, not an officer of the British Army, you have no rank here beyond that which we grant you. Our respect for the colonel aside, I will not endanger my men one step further. Sit down, shut up, and learn, or leave."

"I'll leave," I said. "Thanks for your time, dickhead." I stood, with Chris, Kilo, and the Scepiniir standing as well, along with Finger and Reedy, who both moved in close, trying to speak privately, despite the cramped conditions we were in.

"Sir, I know the colonel gave you command, but I really think—" Sergeant Reed started, only for me to cut him off.

"Sarge, *trust me.*" I winked when the major couldn't see it. "I have access to more details about the area than you know, and this is not the place to camp. We can set up in an hour, two at the most, and we'll be a lot better off."

"Sir…" This time it was Finger. "We understand the drive to move forward, to try to rescue our people, but the major has a point. We're *done.*"

"I agree," Reedy said firmly. "Sir, if you insist on this, we will follow you, but please understand, I have a responsibility to my men. I won't allow you to put them in more danger through a misunderstanding of your—and our—limits."

"Sarge, Finger." I lowered my voice. "Trust me on this. I know more than I'm willing to share here, and while I'm not leaving anyone here in more danger than you know, the potential for the next stop is much higher. You don't want to be here. I'm asking you to trust me on this, but if you choose to stay, that's your choice. We're going."

Sarge looked at me for a long minute, then nodded. "As you say, sir."

"Fuck's sake!" one of the soldiers snapped, and I deliberately didn't look around to see who.

"As I told you all!" The major sneered. "No command experience, no understanding, and happy to leave you behind. I don't even need to order you to stay, though I'll do it, to make our positions clear when we return. I hereby relieve the colonel's choice of commander of his authority for gross negligence and dereliction of his duty to his soldiers. With that done, I order you all to settle down. We need to eat and rest, before we mount the rescue of our comrades…if there's even a risk to them."

"Then I'm happy to say my responsibility to you is done." I smiled at the major. "Anyone who chooses to stay with you as well, remember that you made the decision here."

"Sir… I really think…" Finger tried to interject to me quietly, and I held a hand up to stop him.

As I did that, Jack moved, rising to his feet and breaking himself free of the ice, to shouts and curses.

Apparently that if I left, so would Jack hadn't crossed most of the soldiers' minds. But looking at the hate-filled and triumphant look in the major's eyes, he'd seen it coming.

"You see it out there?" he shouted above the sudden howl of the wind. "You want to be in here, following orders, or disobeying a direct order and following a fool? Anyone who leaves is turning their back on the army as well as their families!"

That made a few hesitate, as we started moving, until the sergeant spoke up.

"You know the difference between us and you, sir?" he called loudly.

"That I'm a soldier and you're getting a dishonorable discharge, Sergeant?" He sneered.

"Nossir," the career NCO replied with a grin. "I'm following the colonel's orders, not just looking out for myself. And I remember that it's down to following those orders and *him*..." he jerked a thumb in my direction, "that my wife and kids are warm and dry now, with all the food they can eat. Me being stuck in the snow up here, so my bairn has a full belly and is safe in a warm bed is a trade I'll make any day."

"That's it! Dereliction of duty! You're no soldier in my army!" the major screeched. "You're done! Dishonorable discharge!"

"Then, as you're no longer in my chain of command, let me tell you, from the entire company: you're a useless streak of piss and when you were born, they should have thrown you away and kept the afterbirth!"

"Yeah, see you, dickhead!" Finger called, grabbing his ruck and weapons, standing and fastening the clips and latches. "Come on, lads. Better out there than stuck with this wanker in charge."

"Go on!" the major roared as we started off. "Discharged!"

I shook my head, catching Chris's eye, and connected myself to the rope that was still attached to Jack. I started off again, the majority of the soldiers fortunately following along.

I gave it five minutes, judging that was long enough both to get some distance from those who stayed behind, and for anyone to have made a decision, before turning and gesturing to Chris and Reedy.

"Sir?" the soldier called. The wind battered his hood back and forth as he stared at me through his goggles, the snow already building on his uniform.

"Phase two?" Chris asked, and I nodded, getting a grin from him as he took the lead, while I explained the situation to Reedy.

"Sarge, I needed to know where you stood, as well as the soldiers who came with us. I'm sorry, but there?" I gestured back behind us. "It's too open for what we need. As soon as the weather breaks, we'd be shit out of luck if we set up there."

"For the night, it'd have done well, though, sir, and no offense, I can see you and your people are fine, but we're a lot lower leveled than you, and this storm..."

"The storm doesn't matter, Sarge. If anything, it's given us a hell of an opportunity to get even closer than I dared hope! We've got a seed with us, all right? A seed for the dungeon!"

I saw the confused look in his eyes, and I went on.

"We can create a secondary offshoot of the dungeon, all the way up here, somewhere safe, where we can not only start building defenses and check the area out, as well as summoning reinforcements, but everything that I could summon back home, I can do there!"

"You mean...?" He started, eyes widening.

"Food, drinks, heat, and shelter—all the comforts of home. And with the weather killing the coronaughts off, we can do it right under their noses," I agreed.

"Holy shit..." He shook his head. "And the major?"

"I didn't trust him to not shoot me in the back of the head as soon as it's set up and try to take over," I admitted. "I'd have let him in, but I'd have kept him under guard the entire time. As it is, he made his decision, and I don't feel bad about it in the slightest."

"A few damn good soldiers stayed back there with him." Reedy shook his head. "If I'd known..."

"If you'd told them, they'd have all come, and if they choose to stay with him, then that's their decision, Sarge," I said. "We're never going to get a better chance to get in close to the base than this, and we have to take it."

"How far is it?"

"A mile to a mile and a half along this road to the town, then a right and half a mile up the road to the base." I grinned. "There's what looks to be a small collection of houses halfway up that road. That's where I'm thinking to set up."

"The luxury lodge?"

"The what?"

"In the woods, on, uh...the left side of the road?"

"Yeah, that's what I found," I agreed. "I saw that it was a collection of buildings. Didn't have time to go looking around much more than that."

"It's a luxury lodge...bunch of wood cabins and a wedding venue." He grinned. "Believe me, when they have a wedding and the soldiers just happen to be walking past..."

"Bridesmaids?" I asked, with an answering grin as we stomped along in the snow. "Let me guess, they march back and forth, all dressed up and hoping that drunken bridesmaids come out at the right time?"

"Oh yeah." He nodded. "Damn nice place, that."

"Well, that's the target. It's probably too close to the base, but that's the deepest and heaviest concentration of mana in the area, and we need it."

"You're gonna need to explain that to me sometime."

"Probably not." I smiled to take the sting out of the refusal. "No offense, Sarge, but to do that, I'd need to talk you through a lot of the internal details of the dungeon, more than I'm comfortable with right now and a lot more than any save my closest team know."

"Of course, sir. I didn't mean to pry," he lied.

"It's fine. You're curious, totally understandable, so I'll say this: the mana in the area matters, all right? Here it's a hell of a lot higher density than Newcastle. There's less we can absorb from the surrounding area as well, but that's life."

"Okay..." He nodded. "Maybe we can talk about it another time."

I shrugged, stomping on and reminding myself that there was a reason the colonel had sent this sergeant with me instead of any other. He was a nice guy, sure, but he was also here to get info as much as to earn their place with me and watch my back.

I had to remember that.

I wanted us to run, or to jog at least, but the sarge had a point in that the soldiers were dog-tired now after such heavy going through the snow. Plus, with their rucksacks, a full loadout, weapons, and the weight of the winter gear, along with the snow...

It took us an hour to cover the last section, with the blizzard fading as we drew nearer and nearer, of course.

It got to the point, as we crested the last hill, that the snow had almost stopped, and that was when the sarge, with his better knowledge and experience, took over.

"I take it you have access to a map, sir?" he asked, having flagged us all into the safety of the lee of the trees to rest. "By my estimate, we should be in the village by now."

"It's just over the next hill, maybe two hundred meters to the edge," I told him, focusing on the dungeon sense and checking the area on all sides. "Yeah, literally, we reach the top of the next rise on the road, and then it's a dip down to the edge of the village."

"Then from here on in, I'm going to insist my people lead, sir," the sergeant said. "In this situation, you're an officer. You might not know what that means, and please don't be offended, but we train for this a lot. Please, give me the orders, and trust me that we can carry them out. You leave the details to us."

"I...shit, you're right." I nodded. "I can't share the map with you, Sarge—not because I'm being a dick. It's a personal ability, that's all."

"Okay, then, sir, is it real time?" he asked. "What I mean is—"

"No." I cut him off. "It's a general map. I can zoom in and out and I can track our location relative to the map, but I can't see us on it, or anyone else."

"Damn." He struggled to be heard above the wind and snow. "Okay, then, sir, from my recollection and the map here..." He pulled his own out and showed me the folded paper. "We have a field here, then a small wooded area. I suggest we head north right there, leave the road and follow the line of the trees for as much cover as we can get. Between that and the remaining snow, we should be able to make it to this point."

The map showed a line that ran due north of the road just ahead, a forty-five-degree angle leading from the walls that bordered the road. I nodded, watching as he traced along that wall, to a joining one a hundred or so meters along, that ran northeast.

"We follow this one, heading away from the target, but it keeps us in cover from the village still, then we follow this point."

The next field was roughly oval in shape, before heading on an almost direct line straight for the wooded area we wanted.

"It gives us an extra half a mile to cross, and for about seventy meters we're in the open. That's a shitty way to move here, but it's the best choice we've got. The base is set up to remove any cover the closer you get to it, so we have to hope the bastards aren't maintaining a full watch. If they are, we're fucked."

He shook his head. "This is the worst part of the plan, sir, but you said they're essentially zombie worms that are controlling them. We need some luck."

"We need a lot of luck," I muttered. "But yeah, that looks good."

"Then here we go. From here on in, no unnecessary talking please, and when we tell you to run, you run." He looked from me to Chris, then Kilo and the Scepiniir.

"We understand, Sarge," I said for everyone, before squinting at Jack's armored bulk. "Though Jack might have an issue being stealthy."

"How much can it understand, sir?" he asked.

"Probably more than you expect," I said honestly. "I can communicate with him remotely, and give him any orders we need to. That's why as soon as we didn't need to be tied to him, I had him off scouting. I think he can probably pass for a bear…"

We all looked at the massive form, and there was a long silence.

"No, sir, not to anyone that's seen a bear before," he replied.

I had to admit he was right.

Jack *looked* a bit like a bear, especially now, with the snow and all, but if you actually paid attention, he was obviously not.

His eyes glowed with an eerie blue, and occasionally, as he moved, a soft blue light could be seen glimmering out from deeper inside him. He was two meters tall when on all fours, and perhaps four and a half meters if he stood on his back legs.

He was shaped generally like a bear, the same rough build as a bear that I'd seen in the zoo and in other places, but the key difference—beyond that he was literally made of high-carbon steel, bronze, copper, and a dozen other metals, woods, and materials—was that he was based on the extinct short-faced bear.

His legs were longer, his build more upright, and his face was shorter—the muzzle, anyway. It was *wider* too, with bigger teeth that were in nature designed to make a carnivore's life easier, but was now a horrifically upgraded slaughter machine version over what the extinct version had been.

Then, yeah, okay, you had the whole steampunk and cyberpunk aesthetic he had going on.

From a distance, when snowing? Sure, he could pass for a bear. Or, considering the way the world was these days, as just something fuckin' weird out there.

Now it was stopping, and for anything that actually looked—which sure, worm-infested brains in soldiers may or may not qualify as that—but if they were looking? Nope.

"So what's the plan for him?" I asked. "I don't really want to leave him here."

"As powerful as he looks to be, and considering he's immune to the worms, no sir, neither do we. But if there are unfriendly eyes out there, better they watch him and then see him leaving, rather than following us."

"Leaving?" I asked.

"Yes, sir." The sarge nodded. "He's a damn big target, and better anything here watches him and not us. If you can have him follow the road, and then head wide of it, looping out around the village and heading west, before looping around to join us once we're in the target area, that's the best bet. If he's attacked, you said you can repair him even if killed?"

"Well yeah, but it's fuckin' expensive," I commented.

"More or less expensive than my men, *sir*?" he asked pointedly, and I winced.

"Yeah, all right, I'll give you that one," I agreed with a sigh. "Jack, you heard him."

That was all it took. Truth be told, I could have just mentally prodded him, but it felt more natural to at least send him off to his possible death with a word, rather than sending him without. "Good luck, mate."

That was that then, I guessed, as Finger got the soldiers moving, and the sarge chivvied us along as well.

The side of the road was like all roads in this part of rural England, in that it was originally a very, very old road, so what was under it was generally more road.

As soon as you moved off it, there was a minimum of two meters of grass—now that we were outside of the village limits and back to the higher speed limits—and then a dip. It was basically a ditch that ran on either side of the road right before the farmers' walls.

Some said that it was to catch run-off rainwater from the road; others said it was to stop shitty drivers from punching into the old stone walls the farmers then had to repair.

The thing I knew, and by God knew from experience, was that they were an absolute pain in the arse when you were drunk and staggered in the wrong direction, because you then fell into a filthy, watery ditch that was full of whatever had been washed off the road.

That meant that as the soldiers clambered down and tried to make it across the half a meter or so of ice without breaking it and punching into the freezing water, I was oh so goddamn happy to just jump and provide a little boost from my mana, allowing me to fly—while staying low, of course—over the ditch, grab the wall, and vault over, landing smoothly on the far side.

I had to stifle a grin, just knowing I looked awesome and impressive. And that, of course, was when Chris threw a snowball at me.

"Show-off," he said in a whisper that carried.

"God dammit, Chris!" I snapped, knowing my image was ruined.

He just let out a low laugh, before quickly shutting up at the glare the sarge gave him.

We set off quickly, hurrying along in single file to the edge of the trees that ran along the next wall, running due north. We then followed the next wall, looping out to the northeast, until it slowly arced around again to point due west.

The snow hadn't been disturbed until we started crunching our way through it, and the first two sections of wall were easy to navigate, even if the snow was deep.

The unseasonal snowfall, never mind the damn blizzards, had deposited drifts that ran along the sides of the walls, with the trees still wearing autumn's colors providing a little break as they towered over the old stone walls.

That meant that the drifts were sloped and ran halfway to the peak of the wall, and our little group was leaving a trail a blind man could follow in the pristine blanket as we went.

The wind and snow were dropping by the second, in that weird way the snow did sometimes. As more and more distance became clear, the stress levels of the group rose.

Still, thanks to the wall, and the trees, we were still reasonably well hidden from the worms, as we had to hope that the frozen little fuckers were all the early warning the hive had thought it'd need.

The next section of the wall, though, where it went from north-by-northeast to north-by-northwest, was far less covered.

187

The fields here that extended to our right—to the east and away from both our target and the enemy base—were silent. Not so much as a sheep in sight and covered in snow. But they were also five hundred meters on a side, and exposed as all hell.

Where we crouched and ran along the wall, all it'd take was a single eye pointed in our direction, and we'd be fucked.

That only got worse as we ran along the next section of wall, as the trees that had bordered one side of the field had been long ago cut down.

Instead, there were long fields that were normally filled with grass and horses. A sign half-hidden by the snow proclaimed a stud farm somewhere close by. A glance over the wall when we paused to reorganize—one I was glared at and told off for—let me see half-buried show jumps and training areas covered in snow on the far side as well.

The path along the wall changed here. The snow drifts got smaller and smaller as we went, until eventually it was down to bare inches deep, and beneath that, a hard-packed dirt road as the wall curved and we came out of the protected leeward side.

We hurried on for a few minutes. A feeling of eyes on me made me paranoid as all hell until I finally managed to convince myself that it was all in my imagination.

No, there was a logical argument for the worms to have been the only watch set up out here. If they were genuinely as thickly spread as they seemed to have been, then why the hell would you have anything else out here?

That made me feel better for almost a full minute, before the nearest soldier tackled me and shoved me down into the snow, hissing at me to be quiet.

I kept the automatic urge to shove him back down. Then, when I realized what had happened and that my own distraction had made me miss an order from the lead, I stifled more curses as the sarge crawled past, heading to the front of the line.

I almost crawled up to follow him, then thought better of it, staying down and waiting, until a nearby black spot caught my eye.

It was on a plant. A vine, more accurately.

The thorns of the vines were draped across a sign proclaiming the road to be private property and threatening something that couldn't be seen thanks to the snow, to anyone who also couldn't be seen by the snow.

That wasn't the point, though. The thick covering of thorny bushes and vines were normal for the area; they grew rampant across the summer and died away in the winter, before being cut back heavily in the spring. And in this case, they'd managed to colonize halfway up the simple post and the sign that hung from it.

No, nothing about that was unusual…until you looked at the icicles that hung from the plant, and in particular one that shivered ever so slightly in the breeze.

It was black, about six inches long, and the frost that covered it, that glittered and had caught my eye, covered a coronaught worm.

I stared, transfixed, before slowly pushing a handful of the snow that lay inches from my face away from the path under me. Dirt, I was relieved to see, dirt and…

Dirt and frozen mud in a depression that had probably been caused by tractor tires bouncing along the road, and right in the middle of the frozen ridges was another worm. It, too, was dead, curled up and frozen. The skin had split in places and fluids had presumably expanded as they froze, breaking the body more so, but damn.

If they were this closely laid…this many? I swallowed hard, hoping that the slightly raised temperatures that lay underneath the snow all around us hadn't left any survivors, and more so that the warmth of my own body wasn't…

"Hssst!" came the sound, and I glanced over, seeing the next soldier along gesturing to get my attention. "Move up!" he snapped in a low voice.

I winced, having gotten distracted again.

I crawled up past the next few soldiers in line, before eventually reaching Finger and the sarge, who were carrying out a very low argument.

"What's up?" I asked, stopping nearby.

"Firstly, *sir*, you need to pay attention," I was told in no uncertain terms by the sarge. "If you're going to woolgather instead, then you need to stay here, or move on, on your own. I'm not willing to lose my people because you think you know best and don't have to listen. Is that clear?"

It wasn't a question, not at all, but I nodded I understood and he took a deep breath before going on.

"Secondly, at the edge of the path here, the wall continues on. There's a sentry braced against the wall, and I need to know more about these worms."

"What about them?" I asked, shitting myself that there was a sentry already. "They're a hive mind, so what one sees, they all see."

"How resistant to the cold are they?" he asked instead, and I hesitated before answering.

"I don't know," I answered honestly. "Considering there's so many frozen in place around us, and they died in the first real snowfall, not very, I think?"

"Is that a guess or do you know?" he asked me.

"A guess," I admitted. "Why?"

"The sentry," Finger replied, nodding in the direction of the edge of the wall.

I raised my head and peered ahead, but couldn't see anything.

The road we'd been following was barely a dirt track, just hard-packed earth that ran alongside the stone wall of the field, and that ended close by with a large gate in the wall.

The road looped around here. Presumably it'd been made to let the tractors and horse carriers get up here, collect or deposit and turn around, as from this point we were down to snowdrifts again, as the walls shifted back around and the field was less exposed to the wind.

Creeping forward at the sarge's gesture, I stopped by the lead soldier, who was watching something through the drooping and frost-browned bushes that ended the road.

I edged up to the bush, making a hole in the snow as he had, and stared through. I saw nothing at first, just the bushes poking out of the snow drifts, the walls, the lichen that covered the stones that had been scoured free, and…

And the sentry that sat slumped against the far wall where another wall joined the one we were following.

He was hard to make out, thanks to the mixture of camouflage gear and the snow that covered him, but it was clear he'd not moved in days, and presumably never would again.

"What's up?" I whispered to the sarge as he crept up to join me. "He's dead, right? He's got to be?" I pointed out.

"Yeah." He nodded. "He's dead, but is the worm?"

"How the hell would I know?" I asked. "I mean, if the soldier is dead, it'd have to be, right?"

"The internal temperature of that body is going to be higher than the surrounding area, inside his uniform, under the snow..." He shook his head. "Is it *definitely* dead?"

"Two minutes." I squinted through the trees and triggered my Examine spell, reading quickly.

Corpse	Human corpse
This human has died. The life force that animated it in life has left the body, and due to the lack of any mana to interact with, you cannot glean additional details.	
HP 0/????	Special Abilities: ??/??

"Well, he's dead," I said after a few seconds, then shook my head as I looked at the sarge. "Sorry, I'm not being disrespectful, but I've got a spell that lets me see additional details on things. Literally, I've gotten names and family details from people I've examined before. Trying it with him, all I'm getting is 'dead human.'"

"Well, at least we're getting that." He grunted. "Would you be able to tell if he was about to get up? If he was undead, I mean?"

"You've seen them?"

"A few," he admitted. "Could you, though?"

"Yeah, they'd show as undead." I nodded.

"Then I guess we're down to blind luck and hope then," he whispered after a few seconds. "Toby?"

"Sarge?" the soldier, Toby apparently, responded.

"Get your arse up there. Check the body and turn him over, face down."

"Arse up, aye, Sarge." He grunted, then checked on all sides, before rising to a half crouch and hurrying ahead.

"Face down?" I asked the sarge, who nodded.

"If the worm can see out, it'll only see him and he'll turn it away. If it's dead and couldn't see anything? No loss for the effort."

"He's checking the body," I said after a few seconds, seeing the way the Scepiniir were talking in a series of hand gestures again, as Kilo practically buried himself in the snow, looking quite comfortable.

"Recovering tags and ammo," Sarge said with a nod. "At least we'll know who he was."

I stifled the urge to apologize again; I'd never even considered that the soldier was unknown. For me, he was hopefully not a threat and beyond that, well, I'd seen a lot of bodies by now. I might have thought to take the ammo, but not the tags, not right now.

Less than a minute later, I was on my feet again with the others, hurrying forward to pass the now hidden body and vaulting the far wall where it joined this one.

This was the riskiest part, I knew, as I landed and started to run, racing to catch up to the others.

The large field we were in now was open to the elements and slightly higher than the last one, meaning we were even more exposed than before. But worst of all? The land rose into a small hill to the north now, a small wood to the northeast, and a straight run of maybe four hundred meters to the west before there was any cover.

That meant that anyone on that hill, or in those trees, would see us easily. I gritted my teeth as I kept slogging forward, trying to run through knee- to thigh-deep snow.

It was a nightmare, one in which the lead soldier kept falling back and letting the next in line trudge past. The effort of trying to run in such terrain wore on everyone. And the entire time we were doing it, we were exposed.

The Scepiniir had to be ordered to let the next one take their place, the stupid proud bastards forging ahead with a "I can do anything better than you" attitude that resulted in them being ordered into the rear guard quickly.

Every instinct in me cried out against running like this in the open, and also against the goddamn trail we were leaving behind us, but, at the end of the day, I knew there was no choice.

We were in cold weather gear. We could have laid down and crept along in normal circumstances. Hell, as deep as the snow was, we'd be able to keep out of everyone's view and we'd leave less of a trail than we were now.

The issue was time.

If we crawled this section, with powdery snow, this goddamn deep, I'd been told in no uncertain terms that the best time we could realistically expect the group to make was an hour to an hour and a half.

It was that the snow was so powdery, so freshly fallen, and as deep as it was that made this such a nightmare. If it was still snowing? This wouldn't be nearly the issue, as we could afford to take the time and we'd be more hidden, but that was life, wasn't it.

We were stuck with a limited window of opportunity as we literally raced against the coronaughts being sent back out, and we had to take the chance we had.

Running on, we staggered, slipped, fell, and clambered to our feet again. Each and every single one of us tripped over hidden roots, got caught in half-frozen, buried bramble bushes, and lost skin, blood, and had our clothing shredded as we went. But eventually, after passing two more frozen bodies of soldiers slumped in death—the sarge and Finger grabbed their tags—we finally made it to the far side, and I cursed the sick, suffering-loving bastard that was the sarge.

He didn't ask us to do anything he wouldn't, but the sight of him sliding down the slope to the almost frozen river, then splashing into it up to his knees made my balls shrivel in terror.

The Otterburn Camp was named for the Otterburn River that lay nearby, before it joined a larger river on the far side of the village. It wound its way through the land, having cut its way down at least five meters into the soft loam and moors of the area.

As much as I hated the crazy bastard for making us do this, I understood it as well.

The river was in a narrow gully, one that ran between the fields and ranged from five to ten meters farther down out of sight, not even considering the depth of the water itself.

That meant, as he shoved his way past a few low branches and hurried upriver, he and the rest of us were now well out of sight of all but the most insane of possible watchers.

We didn't have long, though. The army-issue gear was good—waterproof to a degree and certainly warmer than normal clothing was—but the water here where we followed him, even at the edge of the stream, ranged from up to our thighs to past our shins.

There was no way that we could stay in water like this for long. It was half frozen already, and it was only the speed of the water as it raced past that kept it unfrozen.

If we tried? Hell, my legs were *already* going numb. A few more minutes and we'd be in serious frostbite territory. And that wasn't even considering that if we were caught down here by the enemy, at the bottom of a gully, we were fucked.

It sucked ass even more, in my opinion, because I could fly.

I could have lifted above the water and flew along it; I didn't have to get in the water. I could have just flashed along and left the others behind.

I kept telling myself I *should* do that, I really should!

It was wrong, though. First, I couldn't abandon them like that. And second, I was already an unsure factor to the soldiers, one that at least some of them didn't like and a lot more didn't trust at all. Me flying along and not suffering with them? That was just going to make that disconnect even worse.

So, I gritted my teeth and I splashed onward.

It ran north for about fifty meters, then wove left and right for another fifty to a hundred, before finally, after nearly twenty minutes of hard damn work, we emerged from the snow-racked gully and saw the trees ahead of us.

The forest that surrounded our target was deliberately tended so that it looked wild and natural. The river we followed led down from that forest, and under a small bridge; the road across the river took us to the—thankfully—out of sight camp.

We splashed onward, all of us shaking. The cold had worked its way deep into our bones, and at least half of the party could barely stand. We moved under the bridge, checking for anyone who might be watching, and headed into the cover of the trees.

As soon as we found ourselves in the wood, and hopefully far less exposed to view, I felt the relief pouring off us all. The last fifty meters to the first of the cabins, and beyond it to the bar and restaurant that lay behind it, were covered at a staggering run.

The Scepiniir had gone from trying to lead the way to lurching and limping, their fur sodden. They were clearly suffering.

The buildings were…well, they weren't anything special, not in the way that some in the area were, great old manor houses and country estates of the rich and shameless.

Instead, they were a collection of luxury log cabins, grouped around and laid out carefully within reach of the central buildings.

There was a pub and restaurant, along with a small shop, that squatted inside a collection of Victorian buildings.

The red bricks and ornate gables were now half buried in snow, and a large tree that had clearly fallen recently in one storm or another crushed a wall inward.

When it'd been open, and well maintained, it was probably impressive, luxury even. But as it was now—dark and silent, laid under a blanket of snow and utterly dead in the middle of a forest—it just made my hackles rise in instinctual fear.

"There!" I heard one of the soldiers snap. "Contact!"

"Fire!" the sarge ordered grimly.

A series of loud gunshots rang out, as the first body stumbled into sight, making my stomach clench in fear.

CHAPTER NINETEEN

The dead soldier, because that was what she had been, and certainly what she was now, collapsed without a sound. Their body hit the snow and thrashed, as the sarge turned to me.

"If they're a hive mind, then they know we're here now. Do we stay or run?" he demanded.

"We stay." I pointed to the nearest large building. "That one! Get us inside!"

"Stay close," he ordered Chris and me, before barking orders.

As soon as he gestured, I started to run, my dungeon-born up and leading the way.

The soldiers ran on either side of us, rifles up and ready, in a half crouching movement that suggested an ability to dive at any second. But it was the sudden movement on all sides that really got my attention.

Whatever the coronaught queen might be, it'd clearly recognized that its drones were dying from the cold and exposure, and it'd apparently had the same plan that we had: to hide in the buildings.

The first few had been slow to emerge—the one that we'd killed first had been a scout, I guessed. But movement from inside all the buildings made it clear that they were goddamn occupied already.

"You sure about this?" Sergeant Reed yelled as he fired on another form that shuffled forward out of the trees.

I nodded, my own rifle pointed down as the soldiers on either side and ahead of me opened fire. "Yes!" I replied. "Get me inside and some room to work!"

"How long do you need?" Finger asked, and I snorted, glancing at him.

"As long as you can give me."

"Seconds it is then!" he replied with a manic level of cheerfulness, before opening fire at a sudden movement nearby. "They're on all sides, Sarge!"

"Closing in!" another agreed from my right, as more bursts of rifle fire rang out.

"Fucking better make this worth it!" one of the soldiers snapped. "These are our own people, Sarge!"

"Light them up!" he shouted. "All right, everyone, we clear that building!" He gestured to the old Victorian one ahead.

It wasn't the one I'd have chosen if we'd had more time, not looking as run-down as it did. I could distantly see a much more imposing manor house through the trees on the far side. But its one advantage was that it had four relatively intact walls and a roof. It also had a broken table out the front and Private signs on the walls, making me guess it was part of the hotel's administration.

The first soldier in the door opened fire before his rucksack was out of sight. The flare of light and the vicious bark of the rifle echoed as we followed him in. I couldn't help but curse as it rang out again and again. My Scepiniir shoved inside right behind him; me next, and Kilo right behind me.

We were quickly into the building, and as soon as we made it through the doors, I kept up a low level of swearing. The full corridor that was headed our way made it clear this had been a shitty goddamn choice on my part.

Cryseth had been right in front of me, and he was out of the fight already, another soldier having shoulder-charged him from his feet from a side door. I tracked, firing three times as his opponent carried him into the room on the opposite side of the corridor, where he screamed and fought.

Before I could follow, another of the Scepiniir had, bounding into the room and firing the shotgun. The boom and crash filled the air as screams rose on all sides.

Kilo cast spell after spell, slowing the enemy as best he could, while the soldiers ahead of me fought to clear a space. Another of them went down, pinned as a coronaught soldier buried his teeth in the screaming man's neck while ignoring the rifle fire being pumped into his stomach.

I shoved out my left hand and shouted as loud as I could. "Down!" I roared.

One of the remaining soldiers listened and reacted. The other two totally fucking ignored me, making me snarl and lift myself into the air using my mana instead.

The building was a big one. No clue what it was originally used for, but it had high ceilings and a corridor that ran at least ten meters back from the entrance, before reaching a large stairwell that rose upward and down.

Once I was in the air, I threw the bolt of lightning I'd summoned into the middle of the figures that were reaching for us, sending it hurtling over the heads of the terrified soldiers.

It punched its way through the first, and picked up the second, slamming them backward. I pointed my rifle into the room that Cryseth had been carried into. He was gone, so I opened fire to my right, spraying the feeding figures that filled the narrow room.

As I did that, the guy who had dropped to the floor ahead of me continued to fire. The standing pair of troopers opened fire as well, staggering and cutting down the onrushing figures from ahead.

Kilo sent great winds of freezing air at the figures that tried to reach us on the left, from another room, but I knew instinctively he couldn't keep it up for long.

"My turn!" Chris shouted, barging past me and running forward. The soldiers cut off fire as he raced through like a raging bull. His shield held high, he slammed it into the oncoming figures that were already reeling.

They fell like bowling pins, the bodies of the soldiers emaciated and weakened by what had to have been months of ill treatment and poor management, and he ran on and on, battering them from their feet.

I landed behind him, my rifle released to drop to the sling. I yanked my hammer out, using that to smash back anything that came too close.

"Fuck!" I heard Finger yell. "Get back behind the line!"

"Fuck no, follow us!" Chris yelled back, still driving his shield into people, before he screamed and started thrashing. "Shit, shit, get them off me!"

I lunged forward. One of the figures he'd hit had been different from the rest: where most were skinny and looked to be on the verge of death, this one had been bloated.

As it'd fallen—I couldn't tell from the purple and black bruising that covered their face whether they were even male or female—they'd apparently been swollen, ready to burst.

Now, along rips in their flesh, dozens, possibly hundreds of coronaught worms started to roll free, as Chris tried to frantically leap free and stamp those that were already on him into the ground.

I gasped, horrified. More and more dropped from the ceiling overhead as well, landing on his armor, as he twisted this way and that.

"This way!" I roared, heading for the stairwell that led down to the left. Racing for it, I grabbed the harness on the back of his ruck and yanked it hard, pulling him off-balance as he panicked.

He was screaming in horror, and the soldiers were doing the same. I dragged him off his feet and the pair of us tumbled down the steps, banging into one wall, then off the other, rolling arse over tit as we went.

After hitting the bottom of the stairs and crashing into a closed door, one that was clearly made of metal, I shoved myself to my feet and snatched free a worm crawling across the side of Chris's head. It had clearly been aiming for his ear. I crushed it, then threw the body to the ground, before stomping on another one. There were dozens on him, and the shouts that came from the others…

I batted at my right leg, seeing the little wriggling black thing at the last second, just as it started to drag itself through a gap in my armor, then screamed in joint fear and horror as it vanished.

It was *inside* the armor, under it, between it and my skin. I slapped hard at my leg again and again, frantically trying to crush it, before screaming in mingled pain, horror, and rage. I twisted around and swung my hammer, smashing it into the door where the large lock stood proud.

I did it again and again, shouting to the others to run, to come to me if they wanted to live, until the fucker gave way, banging open to reveal a frightened face that gestured to me to run, to move.

"Leave him!" the man before me shouted. "He's infected!"

"No!" I roared, grabbing onto his armor and dragging Chris through the door, as the sarge, Finger, and three others ran down as well. "Close it and burn it!" I shouted to the sarge, who was already slapping at a bulge under the skin on his left cheek, scrabbling fingers that were encased in gloves failing to dig in enough to stop the worm.

"BURN IT ALL!" I roared in his face, and he screamed even as he apparently agreed.

He spat, wild-eyed, biting and slapping at the side of his own face with one hand, trying to force the worm into his mouth to kill it…as with his other, he dragged another incendiary grenade free.

I ripped it from his hands and pulled the pin, tossing it literally just outside of the door into the small area at the bottom of the stairs as the worms continued to pour down.

Then I dragged the door closed. The flickering light of a candle on one wall was all that gave us any light to see by. The older man desperately backed away, as Chris started to convulse on the floor. The others ripped at clothes and tried to reach the worms that were already burrowing deep into flesh.

I dumped my rucksack onto the floor, along with the hammer and anything else. I dragged the focal orb from my bag of holding, frantically shoving mana into it, and shuddering as I felt the stored spell activating.

It washed through me. The healing spell literally burned out anything that the magic viewed as an "infection" and healed the damage left behind.

The one in my leg, I felt, and I was incredibly glad to feel vanish. But the one on the side of my neck? The one that had been eating its way through me from a joint on my armor at my waist?

Those were even more horrible because I'd had no clue they were even there until the healing magic made it clear.

Two hundred mana it cost me, and it was worth every goddamn point. Fortunately, I'd not been badly injured beyond that. I spun, dropping to Chris and pressing the orb to his forehead as he thrashed wildly, a blackness rolling behind his right eye.

The orb flared again. The mana cost this time was higher, as no less than eleven worms were torn apart and their entry and passage wounds healed.

He stiffened, gasping as the magic scoured him from tip to toes, before collapsing. Then I cursed, stomping down hard on another worm I'd just spotted, then lunged to grab the sarge.

He fought me without meaning to, not understanding. But Finger was there a second later, grabbing his friend and pinning him in place, staring at me with mixed panic and hope as I burned the infection out of them quickly, one after the other.

With them and Chris clear, the others didn't take long to be pinned and healed as well. After that, it was literally the work of a minute to make goddamn sure the room had no more unwelcome visitors, helped in large part by Kilo blanketing the walls, floor, and door in a layer of glittering frost to make goddamn sure of it.

Then we were backing away, hurrying to the other end of the room, and finding a second door that was already being barricaded against us.

"What the hell?" I called. "What are you doing?"

"Surviving!" came the cry. "I... I'm sorry, but you're infected. You're turning, even if you don't know it!"

"Fuck's sake!" I snarled, leaning back and kicking the door down the middle, hard.

In the end, it took four kicks to break it, and when I did, the first thing I saw was the older man stabbing at me with a kitchen knife.

"Drop it," the sarge ordered, his rifle leveled at the diminutive figure on the far side, before coughing. "Shit, smoke!" he got out before he coughed again.

"We're all going to die because of you!" the older man howled, before Finger grabbed the back of his wrist and half dragged him through the shattered door, twisting it expertly to make him release the knife.

"Tell me you can fix this," the sarge shot at me.

197

I took in the tableau, everything from the half-destroyed interior of the building, to the fact that the grenade had already set fire to the building overhead and heat was radiating in, along with smoke, around the edges of the door.

"Gonna do my best," I agreed. "I need as much room from that as possible, though, and the seed needs to be in a safe spot."

"Where?" he asked.

Chris grabbed a section of the door and yanked, snapping it free before tossing it behind him to widen the opening down the middle. "In there."

I nodded.

Finger shoved the man he'd been holding in place backward, then clambered through the gap after him. Two of the soldiers followed in short order, and we cleared the door while they checked the other side and made space.

"It's clear!" one of them called quickly. "Not much space, though…"

It was a storage area and the old building's heating boilers, I guessed. Then, seeing the piping and the layout, I corrected that. The building might look older and worn down, but the sheer mass of piping here made it clear that this was the center of the water supply for the entire site.

That meant we had a fuckload of water here, even if it was in pipes, and thanks to some twists and turns that hadn't been clear at first, a few more rooms with large, solid-looking doors.

That was going to give us…oh, at least a few minutes before we choked to death from the smoke that was already drifting in.

I pushed through, heading as deep in as I could, covering my mouth and nose as I passed the room that was clearly the old survivor's toilet. Cursing, I realized that was the best room to be doing this in.

It was literally a square room that had been used as the toilet. A drain in the corner had backed up and overflowed, and a bin that had once held his other leavings in ziplocked bags…now overflowed with what had to be months' worth of shit.

It utterly reeked, and I coughed as much from the thick smell of piss and shit as I did from the drifting smoke. Mold climbed the walls; clearly, a single spark in here would level the room.

The seed needed the best location, though, and this one…it'd be cleanable once things were up and running.

I dragged the seed free of the pouch on my waist and held it before me, focusing on it. Text flowed across my vision.

Do you wish to activate this Dungeon Seed at this location?

You will have 36 seconds to place the Seed and activate it before it becomes unstable and detonates.

Dungeon Lord detected. You have a sufficiently high enough level of Control to be able to assume full command privileges over this Dungeon Seed. Do you wish to assume control?

Yes/No

Estimated area consumed by Dungeon Seed detonation: 0.473sq miles.

Unsurprisingly, I hit the Yes with a mental flick of my will, and whimpered at the screen that came up next.

Current Level of Seed Activation: 0%

Dungeon Core Seed has been placed and is absorbing mana. Full control privileges will be released at 100% charge. It is recommended the Core is not disturbed until primary activation has occurred at 10%.

Current Charge: 1%

Estimated time to full charge: *calculating...* **147 minutes**

Basic functions will be made available to the Dungeon Lord in 7 minutes.

"Seven minutes!" I called to the others, many of whom were fucking coughing and had watering eyes, and not just from the smell in here. "We've got to survive for seven minutes!"

"We won't last two!" one of the soldiers cried. "Fuck's sake, Sarge—look at the smoke!"

"Cloth!" the sarge snapped, looking around. "Get all the cloth you can and wet it—pack it around the edges of the doors!"

That set the soldiers off running. And as they did, I got out of the room as well. The stench was horrific. It wasn't just that it was smelly; it was actively noxious. Standing in the middle of it, trying to ignore the literal piss and shit on all sides of me, I'd seen my health ticking down by one point after another the longer I was in there.

It didn't take long, literally two minutes, and by then we were all gathering on the far side of the room farthest from the doors that led out. The old man had moved right to the farthest end of the small underground complex from us, to sit next to a grate by the wall.

"Holy crap..." Chris whispered, shaking his head as he jerked his head back in the direction of the door to the toilet. "Seriously, dude, that's a nasty place to set up anything, and you're dumping our fucking future success in that?"

"Gotta be done." I grunted. "Solid walls, and it's the farthest point from any threat that I can see. There's a drain in and out, but I'll block that up once things are more sorted."

"Who...who are you people?" The older man whimpered. "What are you doing here?"

"Sorry, sir." The sarge explained he was a soldier and had a mission to check out the garrison.

"They're dead," he replied when the sarge was done. "The whole garrison, the locals, even my cat! They're all dead..." He seemed to deflate, before shaking his head and settling back, staring around hopelessly. "It's okay, you know. It will be, it will..." he whispered, as if trying to convince himself.

"Dead?" I looked at him: the bloated belly, the general pallor to the skin, but the awareness in the eyes that was massively lacking in the faces of the infected.

199

"Walking around, but they're dead… The worms got them. I… I ran. I shouldn't have. I should have let them take me, but I was so scared!"

"But they didn't get you?" I asked.

"They don't like me," he muttered. "Not the way I taste. But they'll let me join them soon, they say."

"They don't…*like*…you?" Chris cocked his head to one side.

"They die," he admitted. "Sometimes they come in, and they bite me, but all I get are the dreams…"

"What dreams?" I shook my head, getting up to move over closer. I grabbed his arm, pressing the orb to his chest and focusing.

"Just the dreams of her. She speaks to me, sometimes." His voice drifted off.

I stared at him in horror, seeing that he wasn't at all as I'd assumed—clear of the damn worms because he'd stayed far enough back. I triggered a reflexive pulse of mana through the orb, slamming it into him and making him scream as he collapsed, even as I was shouting to the others.

"Keep back from him!"

"What?" the sarge asked, only to have Chris moving in fast to stand next to me, ripping his hammer from his belt and holding it ready.

"Stay clear," he ordered the others. "Infected?" he asked me.

I nodded, gritting my teeth as my mana was torn out. The world around me started to spin as I realized my mistake, right before I collapsed to the floor, shaking, as more and more mana was ripped from me.

"Shit!" I heard shouted from somewhere, followed by pain…then a gunshot that echoed in the small room.

The orb was kicked from my grasp. It clattered across the floor, the sound of glass bouncing and rolling nearby reverberating.

The world was spinning for me: up was down and down was sideways at the sudden use of my entire damn mana pool in a matter of seconds.

"Wha…" I groaned, before coughing and sagging onto my back, staring up, my head ringing as Chris leaned in.

"It's all right. I'm here, dude," he said. "Relax, I've got this."

"O…kay?" I groaned, having been utterly unprepared for it, and closed my eyes. I decided it was better to trust him, and try to hold onto the last meal I'd eaten, rather than make an impression of a fountain and vomit it up into the air.

I could distantly hear Chris explaining, and instead of joining in, I focused on my breathing, then started to meditate, pulling in the mana that flooded the basement.

"Infected," Chris was saying. "Matt tried to heal him, and the mana was too much, I'm guessing."

"What happened to him?" someone asked.

"Matt?" Chris snapped. "It's mana fatigue. He's bottomed himself out, literally drained himself dry to try to save that guy. And he'd have kept going if I'd not done what I did."

"Shooting him in the head," a flat voice called. "Yeah, real fucking nice guy, aren't you."

"Fuck you!" Chris said vehemently. "You don't know what it's been like, hiding in your fucking base while we fought to survive. That man's my brother. But more than that, he's the only goddamn hope we've got. If he dies? We're all screwed. And what was he doing that nearly killed him? He was trying to save that old fart!"

"That's enough, everyone!" the sarge snapped. "Until this dungeon is up and running, we need to stop. Stop fighting, stop moving, just stay still and rest. The less energy we use, the better until we've got a plan. You...Kilo, is it?"

The kobold stared at him for a second before nodding.

"I need you to make sure any air vent, any dark corner, any way at all that the fucking worms or the smoke can get in here is sealed off. Do it now."

The kobold looked at me, and I nodded, then winced as the motion made it feel like my head was going to explode.

"Finger, go check the doors. Everyone else, lie down, breathe slowly, and hope to fuck that the Dungeon Lord pulls some magic out of his arse," the sarge finished.

I almost forced myself back upright at that comment. Instead, I blew out a long breath, and forced myself to relax and meditate.

Chris crouched down next to me; I felt his hand on my chest a second before the pulse of healing energy washed through me.

"Just hold on, dude...few more minutes and we're up and back in business," he assured me.

I agreed. But given that there was nothing I could do to force the dungeon core seed to activate any faster, I instead sank deeper into my mana channels, searching for the star that formed my core, feeling its dim and guttering pulse growing slowly, oh so slowly stronger.

I needed my mana, either to give to the dungeon, to use to heal us, or just to stop the pounding headache that threatened to split my skull, so meditation it was.

The flow of mana around my body was a river normally. But now, drained as I was, it felt wrong, weak and empty, like I was falling through a misty jet of air, rather than swimming through a fast river and over rapids.

The gates, mana gates I'd painstakingly reconstructed, flashed past, one after another, until eventually, I burst free, floating into the darkness of the void.

Here, both inside my stomach, and somehow a billion light-years away at the same time, I found the core.

As always, the core seemed to be a silvery star from a distance, flaming with light, but the closer I came, the more the heart of the core resolved into a collection of pillars, incomprehensibly vast and moving with ponderous inevitability.

They rotated around the central pillar. One end of each pillar dipped into a stream of mana that flowed around the outer area, drawing more and more mana up and into the core.

I watched for long seconds, just breathing as my mind gradually recovered. The shock and pain that I'd fight through if I had to, and I had on other occasions, just gradually faded this time. Instead of fighting it off, I just took the sarge's advice and rested.

Kilo came back; he was out of mana. Although he'd tried to close off the spaces around the door, I'd half hammered it from its hinges before the old guy had given in and had unlocked it. It wasn't going to stand for long, and as soon as the ice formed over the gaps, the insanely hot flames melted it.

Minutes passed in incredible slowness as we all started to find it more difficult to breathe. Coughing got more and more frequent as someone—the sarge, I was betting—spoke again, his voice distant.

"Here, it's soaked in water. Breathe through it."

A cloth was pressed to my mouth, and I reached up, taking it and continuing to meditate. The mana flowed faster and easier, even as the air grew fouler and my headache returned with a vengeance.

I slid into the dungeon sense, watching the counter as it dropped oh so slowly.

One minute.

Fifty seconds.

Thirty…

It was getting harder and harder to breathe now, and my head was pounding, even as it grew fuzzier.

Twenty seconds.

I was deliberately not moving now, focusing on slow, even breaths through the cloth, even as I started to notice an increase in the heat.

Ten seconds.

Someone nearby coughed long and hard. Then, unable to stop, they retched, then vomited. The splattering sound of an almost empty stomach redecorating the room was suddenly clear, even above the coughing of the others.

Five seconds.

Four…three…

I focused, knowing that I needed to move incredibly fast with this, if I was to save everyone.

Two.

One.

Zero.

CHAPTER TWENTY

As before, when I'd first activated the original dungeon core in Newcastle, hidden in the basement of my old favorite bar, the world around me flared to life, and yet froze.

I found myself in a clearly defined "out of body" experience, inside the dungeon sense, as all sides the building expanded away from me.

The walls were wireframe drawings. Everything from the pipes to the piles of stinking excrement were picked out in glowing lines, and yet the detail that should have made that disgusting also robbed it of the personal aspect.

As I'd once told Kelly, long before we'd "bumped uglies," yes, in the dungeon core at its original level, it would have been possible for me to pass through walls and accidentally catch a peek at her when she was changing.

The difference between seeing her naked in reality, though, and seeing the wireframe outline of a rough humanoid form, was a massive one.

There was absolutely nothing sexy about it, that was for sure.

As time had gone on and the core was upgraded, things had changed significantly, and yeah, all right, now I could have caught her and been a Peeping Tom and have seen things very differently.

The difference was that I'd never have done that to her. Sure, I had a split second of *what if* like everyone does, but it'd have been wrong on every level.

The reason all this flared into my mind, though, in that split second of broken time, was because as I stared now, everything was reduced to the very base level of detail, again.

The dungeon flickered, and I moved in a panic, as I saw one of the group, a soldier whose name I didn't remember, started to vomit again, in slow motion.

That was it…time to work.

The dungeon seed was hovering in what could only be called the poop room. A thin spike of glowing metal extended from the ground and lifted toward the fist-sized core as more and more aspects activated. On the ground all around it were fragments of the housing; as I reached out, a pulse washed over me, heading in the opposite direction from the core.

It was the first of many, and they came faster and faster as the spike of metal stabilized and thickened. Its base grew to a star shape that narrowed all the way to a sharp point.

That point ended several inches from the core, which had started to spin, slow at first but moving with increasing speed.

Dungeon Seed Activated – Permeate area? – Yes/No

I stared, pushing a query at it, and frantically choosing No when I got the answer back. Essentially, when it permeated an area, it shoved its essence out and infiltrated everything and everyone around it.

That was fine, but the permeate option had a secondary setting, and one that I really, really wasn't looking to activate here.

This one was a sort of fast-track approach to building the dungeon. I damn well knew I'd found why the Gateshead dungeon had done so well, so quickly.

As part of the area permeation option, it'd rip the mana from the entire area and feed it into the core, jump-starting its growth and expansion—not to mention that it'd be able to physically absorb the nearby materials as well to increase its power.

It sounded good, and would have been, if I'd thrown the dungeon seed into the distance and ran in the opposite direction like fuck at the time.

As it was? It'd kill us all, or the others at least. A small certainty pulsed that I'd have been kept safe from that, so there was a thought for the future maybe.

For now, though, as soon as I told it no, the next option flashed up.

Confirm: Manual Permeation and expansion selection.

"Fuck yes," I whispered, triggering that. Another pulse of energy sparked out from the core, as the systems began to unlock further.

The first thing I had to do as the various options opened up to me was get the air sorted. That, of course, required me to have enough reach to damn well do something.

Fortunately, I had a plan for that.

The manual expansion option came with some issues. First of all, it was slow as hell, and secondly, yeah, it was entirely manual. But the biggest advantage?

I already knew how to use it.

The bubble that the core had already deployed was slightly larger than the room I'd put it in, which had been three meters wide by five deep.

The bubble was just under five, which covered half of the corridor, and I nodded to myself as I reached out with fingers made of soul-stuff.

The bubble that surrounded the core always felt like it was about to pop—a stretchy film of silicone, or perhaps spandex. It also made me think of a soap bubble. But no matter how hard I pushed, it'd never yet popped.

Now, as I shoved frantically and twisted, smoothing it across the remaining half meter of the corridor with my left hand, I "pulled" with my right, drawing up a fresh wall of stone to fill the passage from wall to wall, cutting it off.

It wasn't as fast as I wanted, nowhere near. As much as I desperately wanted to do a million things all at once, such as purify the air, I couldn't, not in the time I had, so the first step was to stop more smoke getting in.

As soon as I had a solid covering of stone across the passage, though, I was off, blurring across the space and back into the poop room.

That, unfortunately, was the only room I'd found so far that had a drainage system, and we needed the fresh air coming in. I selected all of it—the shit that covered the floor and the bin, stacked high, and the pools of stagnant piss, the darkness and the reek of ammonia that told of dehydration—and I absorbed it in a great wash of light.

It collapsed into motes. The motes were sucked into the core, strengthening it, providing a tiny burst in mana to use to expand further. More and more of the core began to unlock.

Seed Core Stabilized. Please select from the following options:

1. **Form symbiotic link with parent dungeon.**

2. **Form secondary associated/unassociated dungeon.**

3. **Specialize dungeon core for subsidiary action.**

I barely read them, moving as quickly as I was to clear the drainage passage, pushing into it and absorbing the crusty goddamn shit that filled it, having to select inch after inch of the disgusting mess to ensure I didn't accidentally take the pipes or more with it as I broke it down.

I selected the first option after only a heartbeat's hesitation.

It was good to know that we could create a totally new, and free dungeon using this if I wanted to. But it was also goddamn terrifying. If I'd lost this damn seed? Anyone could have used it! Worse yet, if people figured this out somehow?

They could literally kill me and take the dungeon seed to start a new one up if they wanted to.

Fuck, that made the seeds even more dangerous and terrifying than they had been originally!

The secondary unassociated dungeon was interesting, mainly because, from what I could tell, it might be linked to the main dungeon, but it'd be sort of like a city-state. I'd have limited access to it, and a degree of overall control as it was me setting it up, but not total.

It might be an option later on to use that, to provide people with their own little fiefdoms.

The subsidiary action, though? That was even more interesting.

It was more or less a brainless dungeon that it was offering up, instead of forming a "real" dungeon. I guessed that it would make something like the mana purification systems that the main dungeon had, but that would be it.

Basically, it was for the times when we decided "This area is a shithole of epic standards; we don't want to be here, but we need to make sure nobody starts spawning monsters." Plunk one of these down there and fuckoffski; it'd work on cleansing the area of corruption, and pushing out pure and clean mana, stabilizing it.

It was tempting in some ways, as that would massively cut down on monster threats. But the thought of wasting a million mana in growing a seed, then just selecting that and wandering off on my merry way?

Madness.

No, the symbiotic link with the parent dungeon meant that I could reach it, and it could reach back to our home. As soon as it was up and running, Kelly and the others would be able to reach through and help. And, more to the point, the mana that it generated would be available to spend here.

Symbiotic link selected: Estimated time to full activation: 37 days, 16 hours, 47 minutes, 12 seconds.

I glared at that, then forced the irritation away. It had a tiny space that it could draw mana from currently, and anything it did was based off that, so the estimate was just that, an estimate based on incorrect data, as the next pop-up made clear.

Activated and fully charged Dungeon Seed housing detected. Please select from the following options:

1. **Break down and absorb Dungeon Seed housing, providing an immediate mana boost to the new core – Time limited**

2. **Store Dungeon Seed housing and begin growth of secondary Seed.**

3. **Consume Dungeon Seed housing for a one-time boost to this dungeon.**

I read the options, actually glad of the distraction from the knowledge I was practically bobbing for apples in another man's toilet bowl, and considered them.

The first one was what I'd expected to be doing. Basically, it meant that instead of me starting a brand-new dungeon from scratch and having to go through all the tedious crap that I knew was coming, I could cheat and jump ahead.

It was a supercharge for the dungeon—a few hundred thousand points of mana to get things like the link with the main dungeon underway, and possibly more, like securing the immediate area.

It was certainly the one that I needed the most, considering the air around us was still contaminated.

The second option was a much nicer long-term plan, though, if we weren't so utterly up the creek without a paddle as we were right now.

I had to guess that the replacement core in the seed would be a much cheaper option than a full regrowth from scratch, and that was tempting.

The third option? That was more like the one I'd gotten when I captured and fragmented the Gateshead dungeon core, though.

I'd basically get a one-time boost that I could choose. The last time I'd done that, I'd goddamn supercharged the mana collection conduits and made the dungeon far, far more efficient.

That was tempting, and for a long, few heartbeats I frustratedly debated it…until a wracking cough tore through me, and I forced myself to choose the option that I knew I had to take.

The seed housing was broken down and absorbed into the fledgling dungeon core. The cracked-apart fragments flickered and then collapsed into light that streamed upward.

The core shuddered, the spin interrupted. Rather than speeding up as it had been, it slowed. What had been a gleaming ball the size of my fist and spinning so fast that it appeared smooth and uniform from the outside, slowed until the clear patterning I remembered from my own core started to appear.

Again and again, it shuddered, seeming almost to wobble off its axis as the mana and light streamed into it, imprinting on the surface.

As the last fragments vanished into the core, a final pulse pushed out, shoving my incorporeal form backward by a few meters. I realized that the influx had increased the claimed area of the dungeon by a good ten meters in all directions.

"Thank fuck," I muttered, selecting the remainder of the drainage pipe and absorbing the last of the "blockage."

That done, it was the work of only another handful of seconds to clear the remaining blockages, allowing air to flow more freely.

I left the dungeon sense then, racked with another bout of coughing, and forced myself to stir, reaching out and shaking the others, most of whom looked at me blearily, as I gestured to the former toilet.

"In there," I gasped. "Get in there."

Then I was back in the dungeon sense. My body sagged and panted roughly, the breaths interspersed with coughs that now tasted of smoke and blood, as I started to try to purify the air.

It wasn't as easy as it could be, that was for sure.

There was no option to simply highlight the smoke and whoosh, rip it all from existence. Instead, it was more like painting with an eraser.

I dragged my focus through the thick clouds and selected everything I could, absorbed it, then started again. Only the flaring of the motes let me know that I was achieving anything at all at first.

I felt my body being pulled and with a twist of focus, I saw Chris, always Chris, had hold of me by my armor and was dragging me.

Focusing on him, I selected, absorbed, and attacked, clearing the air around him as fast as I could.

Long seconds passed as he healed himself and me, then set off moving again. I cursed myself, wondering whether I was just naturally stupid that I'd not considered using the healing spell in the focal orb to clear our lungs...

Then I checked my mana and let loose a mental chuckle.

Unless there was a mouse that really needed that help from me, it wasn't happening.

Mana always refilled from absolute empty far slower than it did regularly. And even with meditation and the increased mana density in the area, I could see this was going to take a while.

That was fine, though. I might not have much mana for me, but I damn well did for the dungeon.

The core had stopped spinning, I saw, as Chris staggered back out of the door, before appearing again, helping Finger to pull the sarge in. Then the pair headed back out again, as he lay there, unconscious.

The last influx had apparently been enough to activate the mana conduits. They began to snake free, three to a quadrant, the top and bottom of the core split into four each.

That gave me twenty-four conduits, and as I focused, they extended into the air and sucked down the smoke, breaking it into individual motes of energy that again, pushed the influx of mana to the core higher.

That was a relief, and I quickly selected the conduits one by one, imparting a target to each, then grinning as the core started to push.

Why the hell hadn't it goddamn occurred to me before this to do that? I'd dragged the conduits out manually each time before, burrowing through the stone to feed them into the areas where people were, so that they could absorb additional mana from them.

Now, as I mentally wanted to slap myself, I simply designated a target, and a route, and they got to it.

Fuck's sake, no wonder I'd broken the first ones I'd tried this shit with!

I shook my head and went on.

Now that the twenty-four conduits were twisting free and the room was quickly being stripped of smoke, I focused on the far wall, wondering whether this was genius, or utter stupidity.

Airflow required a through-draft, I knew. What I had in here was air, but it'd be a pain in the arse to keep it going unless I had that.

In the old dungeon, I had extraction built into the ceiling. It'd been an underground nightclub, after all; it was built with the expectation of hundreds in a small space.

This was an engineering space in the pipe room and boiler of a small private complex, so where they could save some money, they had.

That meant now that the corridor was sealed up, I had the airflow from the drain in the core room, and the vent at the far end of the rooms we had access to.

That was great, and should give us some movement in the air, but that was all. It *should* but I couldn't reach that vent yet. For all I knew, it was connected to the goddamn queen's bedroom and a billion worms were feeding through it right now.

That meant I needed a third option. What was really important about airflow was that one end needed to be pulling, essentially, to make the air…well, flow.

There was a great big fire in the corridor farther down right now, and directly overhead I suspected, so all I needed to do was create a little hole and make sure that neither the flames nor the smoke could get in, and the air would be sucked through to feed the fire.

That'd get the breeze moving, all right, and my sneaky and yet oh so simple plan was either inspired, or madness.

I couldn't decide which.

The first stage was finding the fire, and that didn't take long. A quick check of the area showed me the others were all inside the room, apart from the old guy who was obviously dead. A further search around made it clear now that I'd burned up all the worms, there were none about to burst free of his corpse, either.

The others nearby were being healed by Chris. Although he was getting tired, it was also in terms of the magic that was needed to achieve it…not that big a deal, as the damage was actually minor.

That meant that I left them talking as I slid through the wall and out into the smoke-filled corridor beyond my firebreak.

Thirty seconds later, I was at my limit, unable to go any farther without pushing out the dungeon's influence. But I'd found the fire.

Oh my fuck, had I found the fire.

Whatever else this building might have been, it'd been a storehouse of some rather nasty chemicals, probably intended to paint, preserve, or otherwise improve the area. But the one thing they all had in common?

They were *flammable*.

The incendiary grenade had been a panicked action on my side, setting fire to basically everything in an effort to get rid of the worms.

That fire had gone on, though, hot enough to set fire to the paper coating and plaster that covered the internal walls, to eat through the skirting boards, the wooden floorboards and more. The building above was very much ablaze now, and nothing short of a full-on thunderstorm downpour would slow it down.

That was fine. A three-inch pipe extended out and up into the flames, then looped over and pressed almost flush against the floor, literally in a U-bend with a half inch of space between the flat ground. The pipe started to pull the air through from this end as soon as I opened it.

The smoke that had half filled the room even after my cleaning attempts was sucked out in a fast burst, as the fire at the far end greedily devoured the available air. I grinned to myself, before creating a razor wire mesh over the far end, just in case anyone tried to feed a worm into it.

That done—with the entrance and exit secured, the airflow set up, and the core establishing—I finally opened my eyes and looked around, expecting to see a little relief and possibly even some good cheer.

Instead, I saw Chris get punched in the face by one of the soldiers.

Chapter Twenty-One

"**M**otherfucker!" Chris bellowed, lunging for the smaller soldier. The sarge leapt to separate them; the other soldiers piled in as well while Finger jumped on his companion, pinning him to the wall.

"Stop!" Sergeant Reed bellowed. "Fucking idiots, stop, dammit!"

"He's killed us all!" the soldier shouted. "You fucking idiot!"

"I've killed us?" Chris shouted. "Fuck you, you little bastard! I saved you!"

"You're a lapdog for that bastard!" the soldier shouted back. The pair of them were restrained now by their companions, both sides being pinned by multiple people. Chris was still wading forward, his massively enhanced strength making it clear that even if they all piled on him now, they might not be enough.

"Get off me!" Chris shouted. "Back off, or I'll do you next!"

"He killed him and almost killed us all!" the soldier repeated, lunging at the massive druid, who was getting closer and closer by the second.

"Stop…" I croaked, before clearing my throat and trying again. "Stop!" I called. "Fuck's sake, Chris, it'd be like fighting a toddler. He's not worth it."

"Who are you calling—" the soldier started, before Finger balled his fist up and punched him solidly in the face.

The shock of his own corporal punching him, especially without a warning and through the front of his helmet so perfectly aimed, flattened the formerly struggling soldier. Before he could recover, Finger had twisted him around, dropping onto him and pinning his arm behind his back, whispering in his comrade's ear.

I missed what was said in the noise as the sarge calmed the others, and Chris broke free, glaring around before moving back to squat next to me.

It took a minute or so for the group to settle again, but the fight had made one thing very clear, as I sat there watching them.

The former group was now splitting, with Chris and me on one side, and everyone else on the other.

"I think we deserve an explanation," the sarge said a little while later, once everyone had calmed down and the food we'd carried with us had been broken out.

"You promised us a hot shower and food as well. Was that a lie too?" A soldier next to Finger spoke up grimly.

The corporal glared at him, but didn't stop him.

"No," I said. "None of it was a lie, but what do you want explained?"

"The old man," the sarge said flatly. "Sure, he was a bit of a pain, but you killed him—no warning, no explanation. Why?"

"Shit." I grunted, not having had time to deal with it before and not really considering how it must have looked. "All right, you saw me try to heal him, right?"

"I saw you press some glass to him," one of the soldiers muttered. "Maybe you healed him, maybe you ate his soul."

"It's a focal orb," I said acidly. "If you'd been out helping instead of hiding behind your walls, maybe you'd know that. The spell in it is designed to heal *any* injury, but it needs power…mana, in this case." I went on, looking around at them all. "As Chris told you, I gave too much in trying to heal him, and that's why he died and I nearly did as well."

"He looked fine until you grabbed him," another soldier mumbled.

"Aye," I agreed. "He did. But when he said that the worms didn't like him, but the queen talked to him, I wondered what the fuck was going on. I scanned him. I used the orb to find any issues with him, anything that was hurting him, and you know what I found?"

"Clearly not," another muttered.

"He was immune," I said angrily. "Immune to the coronaughts."

"So you killed him?" Finger cocked his head to one side. "No offense, *sir*, but that sounds like a useful gift to have."

"And it would have been," I agreed. "If he hadn't been infected by the coronaughts and turned into a fucking walking worm factory!"

"You said…"

"He was immune, somehow, *to their mind control shit.* Yeah, that would have been great to have if we could figure it out. But when I scanned him? He had hundreds of the worms *inside* him. Literally goddamn hundreds, and they were moving. They were awake, alive and eating him from the inside out. When I tried to heal him? As they were burned out of him, they bit and tore at his insides. He was literally a bag of blood at the end. And in trying to heal him, because the spell in the orb doesn't have goddamn limiters on it, I drained all my mana and started using my life force to power it instead.

"I was trying to rebuild an entire fucking human from scratch, do you understand that? The mana needed to create something from nothing is an order of magnitude higher than to say, heal a fucking broken bone. I tried to save him, and it almost killed me. So yeah, you want an explanation? That's fine. Now you know."

Silence fell as the soldiers looked at one another and from me to Chris and back again.

"What about the showers?" one of the soldiers asked suddenly. "I don't know about you fuckers, but a steak dinner and a fucking shower would make me like you a lot more…" He tried to summon a smile, but it faltered.

I snorted, unable to help myself. "Yeah, that we can do," I agreed. "The food, anyway. The showers might take an hour or two longer."

"Seriously?" The same soldier stared at me in shock. "I was…sir, I was joking. We're underground in a fucking burning building."

"No," I corrected, smiling a bit evilly. "From the outside, it *looks* like a burning building. For us? It's a newborn dungeon. Chris, you mind sorting that food?"

"On it." The big man reached out his right hand, rolled his wrist theatrically, and summoned a cold beer that dropped into his hand. "Ah, civilization at last," he murmured, lifting the bottle to his lips and taking a swig, before winking at the sarge. "What's your poison then, Sarge?"

"That." He nodded fervently. "A goddamn cold one, and then that steak Davison suggested. I need both."

"Coming right up," the druid assured him, rubbing his hands together as the others started to ask for specifics. "Whoa, guys, just give me a minute." He grinned and got to work.

As he did that, though, I was back in the dungeon sense, looking around.

Two hundred and seventy-eight thousand mana. That was what we had. And the portal back to the dungeon that I wanted to set up? Well, that was showing as a cool million mana in cost all on its own.

We had a portal at that end already, a nexus gate or whatever the fucker was called, back at the main dungeon. We could create a second for "free," it'd said. I guessed that the free part was the cost of the tech, not the cost of construction, but that was fine. After that, I needed to unlock more through my class upgrades.

I could set one of those up, and that'd sort the minor issues out for us straightaway when it came to reinforcements, as we'd be able to march them straight through.

The symbiotic link had updated, and I was tempted to push it along.

Symbiotic link selected: Use available mana?

Yes/No

That wasn't to use all the mana, I sensed; it'd use half of the mana we had left, roughly. And as soon as it was up and running, I'd have access to the main dungeon's mana, which was what we needed.

I selected Yes. A hundred and twenty-four thousand and twelve points of mana was suddenly all we had left, and I winced, as the next screen popped up.

Symbiotic link boosted: Estimated time to full activation: 1 day, 27 minutes, 13 seconds.

That was a kick in the tits that it wasn't instant, but it was what it was. And that also gave us time to get started with work. I just needed a plan.

I lifted upward through the dungeon, hovering overhead as the flames spread outward. I stared at the rough outlines of the buildings, the collapsing trees, the damaged stone, and more.

The location was actually perfect for us, I decided suddenly. We'd been seen, we'd been found, and then, as far as the coronaught queen knew, we were dead.

If they captured Happy Harry and his team of misfits, they'd have learned about us anyway, and then the thing would have gone nuts trying to find us, considering it was clearly at least sentient, if not sapient.

Now, if it found them, it'd decide we were dead, hopefully, and that would be it.

That gave us time, probably. Although that took a weight off in that way, it didn't help at all with the real reason we were there.

We needed to find the others and rescue them.

To do that, we first needed to be sure that they were indeed being held by the coronaught queen, and whether they were dead or alive. Once we had intelligence, then we could move on with making a plan. But until then?

We were stuck in the most boring of all dungeon activities.

Expansion.

The building we were in the basement of was still blazing\merrily, but the steady expansion outward from the core gave me access to more and more of the surrounding area, an inch at a time.

"I'll let them eat," I decided, talking to myself in the dungeon sense. "Let them rest as I get the first stage online, and then they can work for their breakfast."

The rooms on the other side of the wall ran primarily to the left; the pipework and boilers sat there in the darkness. I reached out into the thick packed earth and concrete that lay on the far side of the walls, finding little life, but plenty of room to grow.

It was time to get to it.

The first step was mana. We needed all the mana we could get, and a little effort was all it took to seal off the pipes where they arrived into the building, before absorbing the rest where they ran here and there in the room.

Half an hour later, the boilers, control facilities, water purification, and more were all gone, absorbed into the dungeon and powering the first new rooms to appear.

The very first was a barracks, more or less, because there was no fucking way I was leaving the soldiers in here when I finally went to sleep. So I expanded out into the earth and formed the walls and floors, the ceiling and finally, five bunk beds, each two high and wide as a normal double bed.

The width, I just knew, would have some people asking questions, but fuck it. There was no way Chris or I were going to fit on a regular single bed these days, and we needed sleep as well.

I then created a second room, exactly the same, just in case people wanted to spread out, as we were going to be in here for a good few days at least.

Though I'd probably sleep in here, I had to admit, even if only to myself.

Once that was done, I reached the next section, expanding a small part of the room beyond and making it wide enough to fit two of the shower cubicles from the living quarters we'd unlocked in the main dungeon.

Fortunately, I had access to all the same tech I had there, so that made things a lot easier.

Five minutes after that, I was blinking and sitting upright, before theatrically summoning a mirror and examining my face from all angles.

"You're still the prettiest princess in all the land," Chris assured me, and I snorted.

"I was just making sure you didn't draw a dick on my face when I was working," I explained, still checking.

"One time!" He clutched at his chest. "I did it one time and you still don't trust me?" He pretended to be hurt.

"Never again," I assured him, before dismissing the mirror and turning to the others. "Okay, people, the barracks is finished next door...first two doors on the left as you go out. The shower cubicles are beyond them, next two doors along. So unless you want to cuddle in there, I suggest you take turns."

"Showers?" One of the now sprawled soldiers perked up. "Real showers?"

"Yup." I nodded. "Shower gel, towels, and shampoo as well. Let me know if you need more. And if you hang your clothing in the first section, then close the door, I'll give you a minute to get out of sight before I work on them."

"What?" One of the female soldiers frowned.

"Look, I'll say it because you'll realize it sooner or later, but I can move through the dungeon in a sort of incorporeal sense, all right? It's like being a ghost, but everything is all wire drawings, no detail."

"It's like everything is a rough drawing by an artist." Chris grunted. "No detail in anything but you can make things out like that's a person, that's a wall, that's a gun."

"Yeah, well, once you're no longer attached to your clothing, it becomes a separate item. I can then fix it—think laundry service and repair all rolled into one."

"So we leave our clothes in the changing room, then we go into the shower, and you promise not to peek, while fixing our clothes?" Finger cocked one eyebrow.

"Basically, yeah." I nodded. "Believe me, nothing in there is sexy. There's no detail, and I was doing this for all my group until I managed to unlock their access. You can't get that yet"—*little white lie there*—"so either I can do this for you and you can trust I'm not peeking, or not, and you put back on dirty and wet clothes. That's your choice."

"I've lived around these perverts for years." The female soldier snorted. "There's not much they've not seen. And for a chance at clean clothing and a goddamn hot shower, peek all you like."

"Thanks for the trust, but I won't, don't worry. My girlfriend would kill me, though, and as I say, it's about as sexy as an architectural blueprint."

"I don't give two shits," one of the soldiers declared. "First!"

With that, they were all allocating turns, with the first of them moving to the showers, while the others generally started looking at the barracks rooms.

The only three left in the room after a few seconds were the sarge, Kilo, and Chris. And the way that Finger closed the door after showing one of the others out made it clear this had become a private meeting.

"So now what?" The sarge sat forward as Chris absorbed all the empty crockery and leftovers.

I summoned a fajita and bit down, chewing as I thought about the next stage, before swallowing and speaking.

"We expand," I said. "This is the pain in the arse stage. I'd hoped that we could avoid it, but apparently not. Basically, we gain control over the area by pushing the area of influence out. It's annoying, but it takes more time than anything else."

"We can help," he offered, and I grinned.

"Until a week ago, I'd have been over the moon to hear that," I assured him. "Fortunately, though, one of the team realized that not only do we have the perfect dungeon creatures for such a mindless task, but they're actually good at it as well."

With that, I focused and summoned a skeleton. The uncommon level was my first choice, but after a few seconds, as the swirl of motes began to print the creature from the ground up, I pulled up the options and looked at their system details again.

Uncommon was the highest I'd managed to unlock so far in the skeletons' chain. I quickly considered whether it would be worth upgrading them to the advanced level—we were working through upgrading the various creatures already, after all. The wraiths were the ones that Aly had intended to continue working on out of the undead, mainly because they were powerful mages. But they were also a bit lower in level, so they needed to be taken step by step.

The skeletons' standard version, as in the basic "I'm a fucking skeleton not a wraith or corpse lord," etc., was at uncommon currently. And damn if I didn't want to summon something that had a bit of a brain, but the cost was just too high.

Two hundred and fifty thousand mana to reach advanced, the same as it was for the goblins, the kobolds and more. Could we afford it? Sure, we could add it to the list. But for the mindless tasks, for the ongoing plodding "just get it done" side of things, I had to accept that these were better suited at this level.

Fuck it.

I checked the goblins; a notification waited for me there and I guessed it was the goblins having hit advanced—which was great—but I forced myself to ignore it and deal with the situation before me.

The skeleton stood there now—hell, standing over me, in fact—as I looked up at it. It slowly turned, examining the room, before returning to staring ahead, blankly. The sarge stood, handgun at the ready as I watched him.

I'd been thinking that I might be able to create a skeleton mage, which was why I'd looked at the level the design was at. But to get a mage that was repeatable, we needed to either permeate and destroy a living one, or experiment. If I was going to experiment, I'd much rather have created a Scepiniir mage.

Then again, considering how painfully they tended to die when I did this experimentation, and that they were self-aware now…maybe not.

"You've got control of it?" he asked me in a terse voice as he stared into its eye sockets at the little flare of magic that glittered back at him.

"It's a dungeon creature," I explained, putting my fajita down and reaching out to undo my boots, pulling them off and setting them aside, wincing as the now-tepid water that had gotten in there earlier now flowed out. "Damn, that's better." I groaned, wiggling my toes after pulling my socks off.

"And what does that mean?" the sarge asked sharply. "I'm not one of your people, remember?"

"A dungeon creature? They're literally created to serve me. The dumber ones can't imagine working against me. The brighter ones know they only live as long as I do, so yeah, they're under my control." I felt a little shitty saying it like that in front of Kilo, but it was the truth.

"And you summoned this because?" He went back to staring at it.

"Because the ladies managed to figure a way to make them able to push out the influence of the dungeon for us," I said. "They can absorb matter around us into the dungeon and feed the core as well. And they don't get bored, or forget things, and they don't need breaks."

"Perfect workers." Chris grunted. "Believe me, Sarge, the manual labor side of the dungeon is all mental—beyond the fighting, I mean. It's all done in the spirit side, but it's just as boring and exhausting as the normal one."

"And so you're going to teach this creature to do it for us?" the sarge asked me, getting a nod.

"I'm going to try," I said. "Add to that, if we need a sentry, we've got more of these we can summon."

"I'll set my own watch," he said firmly. "Use your things if you want, but we'll be setting a human on watch."

"Your choice," I agreed. "One last thing, Sarge. The core is lethal to you if you touch it. Think of it as the main relay at a power station—touch it and you're dead. So this room will be locked when I'm not in it, and only Chris and I will be entering in the future. No offense, but the last thing I need is one of your people touching it and blowing themselves up."

"And I'm banned as well?"

"You can't touch it, or interact with it in any way," I clarified. "So why allow the risk when a slip could kill you? I'll sleep in here, as I'll be working on the dungeon around the clock."

"And you?" he asked Chris, glancing over at the big man as he summoned a little party hat and put it on the skeleton.

"I'll be in the barracks." He smiled. "Unless there's a reason not to, anyway."

"It's not that I'm being a dick, Sarge. There's no reason to allow access, that's all. I'm starting to trust you, and you're starting to trust me, but let's face it—a worm gets in one of us somehow, and all a soldier needs to do is roll a grenade in here and boom, the mission is over."

"So for now, we all just try to get along, while you do what?"

"I'll extend the dungeon's area of control, and link up with our people at home. Once that's done, we should be able to find a way to upgrade it and then add you in, and you'll be able to meet the colonel again if you want to.

"While you do that, we'll be extending our influence to the camp and the queen. We'll go room by room, searching it out and making goddamn sure that when we can see things properly, we can get a good idea of the infection and what happened to our people."

"I don't like it," he admitted after a few seconds of thought. "Not this thing, not the sitting around while our people are out there, and certainly not that all I've got to do is rely on you. No offense, *sir*, but as you say, we're still learning to trust each other. I don't know you well, and you don't know us. For all we know, you're lying about everything and working a totally different angle. How would we know?"

"That's a fair point." It was Chris who said it, and I looked at him in question. "The access, the situation, all of it—he's got a point. There's a lot going on trust here," he offered.

"There is," I agreed. "I'll do my best to get access to the system for you tomorrow, all right, Sarge? There's basically a day from now until the link is stable and we can reach out—there's a burning building above us.

"There's no choice in what we do, not really, so just take the time, relax with Chris in the barracks, eat hot food and drink a beer or two if you want. Have a shower and recover—you earned it, and I need the time to work. You could have shot us both in the head as soon as we were out of sight of home," I pointed out to him. "We took you on trust. Now maybe try to get to know Kilo, see us for who we are and give me a little trust in return. I'll make sure you don't regret it."

"Thank you, sir," he said after a few seconds, before nodding to Chris and Kilo, then heading out of the room.

"Well, that was fun." Chris snorted. "Now what?"

"Now you go do 'hearts and minds' while I work." I grinned at him. "Come on, how many times did we want to have drinking beer and eating good food as a job?"

"It's less fun than it used to be." He shook his head. "Somehow I thought I'd be interviewing strippers or something, schmoozing them, instead of heavily armed soldiers. How weird that I never considered that was my future, eh?"

"Yeah, weird that." I snorted. "Chris?"

"Yeah, man?"

"Thanks, mate. You knew what I needed straightaway there."

"Friends for a long time, that's all." He shrugged. "Also, you're not that bright, so it wasn't hard." With a last wink, he stood and nodded to Kilo. "You coming?"

"Yes." The kobold nodded, flowing to his feet in a fluid gesture. "Safe sleep and a cleaning would be good."

"Enjoy." I waved to them as I settled back to lean against the wall, looking around, before finally realizing what I'd missed earlier.

"Now where the fuck am I going to fit a bed?" I asked myself, staring at the three-by-five-meter room, and the still growing dungeon core in the middle of it.

CHAPTER TWENTY-TWO

In the end, I'd gone for a hammock, suspended from two hooks I extended from the walls, then clambered into, promptly falling out the far side.

On the third attempt, though, I'd managed to get in and stay in, and that was where I was now, half asleep. My body certainly was anyway, while my mind was deep in the dungeon. The skeleton next to me had been joined by three others, and all four were now working in the dungeon sense, expanding its influence.

It hadn't been complicated in the end to "bring them in"; it just wasn't something that I probably would have ever considered if Aly and Kelly hadn't suggested it. All I had to do was be in the dungeon sense and reach out to them. It was a variation on the way I gave sapiens access to the dungeon, just sort of select them and say "Bob gets this" to the right part of the dungeon.

In this case, I selected the undead foursome, then gave them basic access, and simply ordered them to do it.

They were either born with the knowledge inbuilt, or gifted it as part of the order, and boom. Ten seconds later, the four of them were standing—for values of standing—in the dungeon sense, pushing the bubble of influence out through the walls and up toward ground level.

I'd split them into two teams.

The first pair were headed north-by-northeast toward the nearest point of the camp. I'd outlined a rough path around the camp that I wanted them to take, bringing more and more under our control by the minute.

The other two were working to permeate and include the entire area around us, starting here and heading down at the lowest point to three levels below. They were working inch by inch, meter by meter, until the building and everything around it was entirely inside the dungeon.

Hour after hour passed as I worked around the rooms we had control over, reinforcing them, sealing them from all sides, then expanding as soon as I knew they were safe, making sure the worms couldn't crawl along the drain or anywhere else.

A room was created below the one I was in, and inside it, five Dark mana converters were set out at a cost of twenty thousand mana each.

That sounded horrific, and bloody expensive to do, considering how little we had. But the converters here were producing three times as much as they had back in Newcastle, and where the lower-grade converters had earned us ten mana per hour, each, per day originally, these could earn a hell of a lot more.

If ten was the base, then, with them being built in appropriate areas, they'd earn more. In this case, the ten points had worked out closer to fourteen to sixteen an hour. That was great.

That was the original "basic" level of converter, though.

The next level of converter, "common," had earned twenty officially, and because they were in the perfect position for them, they earned just over half again the standard.

That worked out at thirty-three points an hour, per converter, and that was when the converters were upgraded—which they were still in the process of doing in Newcastle, but I'd not had the chance to double-check things, beyond vaguely seeing that the mana had jumped at the time, and things were "probably" all okay.

We'd then upgraded the design again, going all the way to uncommon, which should be pulling in thirty points as a base, and around forty-five points for the top end.

Obviously, I was creating the new ones here, so those five units should have given me five thousand, four hundred mana a day coming in between them all.

Again, that really wasn't much in the grand scheme of things, but it didn't need to be. That was the mana that was being generated on a *normal* basis.

Normal being the condition that we were used to back in Newcastle—and this wasn't that area. The mana density here was over triple the density that it was there, and that meant we were earning around sixteen thousand a day.

From there, we would be paying off the cost of each new generator in practically no time. But again, that wasn't the point.

I'd done all five generators as an *experiment*.

Could I have done it with one? Sure, but that one might have needed a second to verify the results—could two be the same; sure—but considering they'd be paying off the cost in short order and we didn't have the space to summon reinforcements yet, it seemed the more reasonable expenditure of the mana we had.

The mana system was a complicated one, and one of the main reasons that dungeon fairies were created to manage it, and not goddamn humans and other species with manuals.

Well, that and the instinctive human urge to open the window and throw any manual out of it when you started a job.

We were now earning nearly seven hundred mana an hour from those converters. As we gained more and more space down here, I was viewing that as the spend we had to play with.

But before I could do that, I needed to double-check one little detail, and this was why I needed the five converters.

Reaching out, I mentally selected one of the conduits, and then the nearest converter, and pushed "tab A" into "slot B."

It took less than a minute, but when it connected, I was torn between swearing, shouting and screaming, and celebrating.

I'd been right. We'd been missing half the damn system. I connected up the others quickly, testing each time, and saw that it worked. Clearly, this was the way it was damn well meant to be set up.

Adding the conduits to the converters made it clear that all this time we'd been wasting an incredible amount of mana. Mana that was increasing exponentially now that we had the systems fully connected.

I was furious and relieved in equal measure. But fuck it, time to move on, and I'd explain this little detail to Aly and Kelly when I got the chance. I only had twenty-four conduits available here currently, so I'd be a bit more limited until I could get more working.

Back to the situation at hand, I decided.

Inside, I was chafing at the bit, desperate to get out there and search for our friends, ready to bum-rush the base and fight. But I had to be smarter about this.

We had no information, none at all, and the only thing that would be guaranteed if I ran at the base and threw myself into the fight was that it'd end badly.

The others had most likely been captured. There was no sign of them out there on the road on the way here, none at all. Even Kilo had found little before the snows had come, facing other creatures and finding traces of fights and tracks while running and fighting.

What we knew was that they met with the soldiers from here, and that they went back with them.

Most likely that meant that they were converted into the coronaught's prisoners and slaves. Although that sucked ass, we knew we could *probably* capture them and heal them. The issue was going to be that once we started, the queen would *have* to see what we were doing, and then all hell was going to break loose as she tried to make sure we couldn't.

That gave us two options.

One was to grab anyone we could, heal them and basically accept that once we got to the point of diminishing returns and the coronaught queen caught on, we'd probably gotten as far as we could, and to return with those we could save. Just writing off the others.

If we could somehow find our friends, that would be great, but in doing that, we'd end up with an enemy up here that now knew we existed, that knew we had a method to kill them, and one day it'd come to a fight, no matter what happened.

We'd also be leaving a fuckload of good soldiers up here, and all the ammunition and equipment as well. Lastly, the chances of us just rocking up there and magically finding everyone was basically zero…so, that left us with option two.

We build the secondary dungeon under their noses, we expand and push through their base, we find the others, but in the meantime, we accept that the enemy has them, and that we might lose them all because we wait and study, work and expand.

That sucked, but it meant that there was a better chance in the end to free them, to free them *all*, and all it'd cost was time.

Time and the possible lives of those we loved.

I hated every goddamn second of it, but that was life. In this situation, I wasn't Matt, the ex-IT dude who had a great girlfriend, whose brother and my friend, along with a load of our other people, were stuck up here, captured and possibly dying.

Instead, I was the Dungeon Lord of Newcastle, and I had to take the long view, see the bigger picture and be realistic.

I hated it all, and I was damn well doing it. We needed to get this place sorted out, and we were doing it right.

That was why the mana converters had been the best use of the mana I had. It was expensive, and it'd not pay off for days. A hundred thousand mana spent, at a recovery point of sixteen thousand a day gave me six days...well, six and a bit.

In normal terms, that'd be stupid.

In this, though, when I was making sure of a damn theory before I moved ahead and invested much more heavily in it, I'd needed to be sure.

Now, as the hours slid past like they were being carried by asthmatic ants with heavy shopping, I worked doggedly to capture and make use of more and more space.

The rooms beyond were enfolded into the dungeon, and inch by inch they were scoured of the original equipment. The walls were sealed as each room came under our control. Although we absorbed the levels above, on the surface and all around into the dungeon, so that we had access and visibility, it was downward that we built, staying hidden.

Another room was eaten out of the earth, and then sealed up. The walls, floor, and ceiling were created, before another ten skeletons were summoned into it. They stood motionless in the utter darkness, unaware and uncaring of their future, as they were permitted into the dungeon and set to expanding its borders.

Hour after hour slid by, until finally, after what seemed like a month or more after I'd set the damn thing away, the last seconds ticked over, and finally, the system linked to the dungeon.

Symbiotic link countdown to completion: 2 seconds... 1 second... complete.

It was like being plugged into a lightning bolt. The entire system around me suddenly went haywire. Counters for mana, construction countdowns, research progress meters all appeared, flipped, and vanished.

I saw markers that showed the maximum control capacity of the dungeon. I saw the current capacity in use. Images of kobolds, goblins, skeletons, and more popped up and twisted with their details alongside.

I saw power ratings, estimates; I saw ranges and input designations. Data appeared faster than I could focus on it. Some of it showed a thousand tiny sections of metadata while others...

Blinking at a sudden graph section—that, like most of this, I'd never seen, as it went from stable, to fading into black and white, then flaring so far into other colors that I thought I might be on a bad acid flashback—I almost pulled out. Then, with a snap of resizing images, the dungeon was back, intact, like the entire system hadn't just acted like its dick had been stuck in the power socket.

"Matt?"

It was Kelly, and I let loose a sigh, twisting myself around in the dungeon sense and focusing on traveling to her.

She stood before me suddenly, in the council room of the Newcastle dungeon.

She flew into my arms, our incorporeal selves seeming to fuzz and join for a brief second, before we settled, holding each other.

"Are you okay?" she asked me quietly.

I nodded, still holding her to me, amazed that even the touch of this wonderful woman's out-of-body avatar made my heart leap, then settle, like it'd been put back in the place it was always designed to be.

"I am now," I admitted, squeezing her tight.

"What happened?" She pushed back after a brief embrace and stared up at me. "Was that the dungeons linking?"

"I think so. Must have been, I guess. What happened for you?" I asked.

Before she could answer, Aly was there, and a half second later, the others were popping up on all sides.

"Did you find him?" asked Aly, her voice hungry and desperate for news of her husband, Mike.

"No." I shook my head. "I'm sorry, Aly. There's no sign of any of them, beyond that they were probably taken to the camp."

"Alive?" she asked, clearly unable to stop herself from asking, yet terrified of the answer.

"I don't know," I clarified. "Literally, I've seen no evidence he was ever here. Kilo said they were headed in this direction, but the snow…did you get the snow?"

"We got a heavy snowfall," Kelly admitted.

I suddenly realized that the first thing she'd asked about was whether I was okay, even though her brother was up here and missing. Looking at her, I recognized it wasn't just that I was incredible and the center of all reality; she'd been petrified that I was going to tell her he was dead.

"Was it bad for you?"

"Blizzards." I nodded. "Worse than the ones in Newcastle when I was at the base there. Worse than I've ever seen."

"And my people?"

I heard the voice and looked over, nodding to the colonel as he appeared with several of the council around him, notably Clarissa and Markus, apparently teaching and stabilizing him.

"I've got some of the group that came with me," I said.

"Some?" he snapped. The look on his face was clearly a mix of horror and fear that he'd failed them in trusting me.

"Some wouldn't follow me and stayed on the road outside the camp, setting up their tents and planning on riding out the storm. I don't know what happened to them, but we lost two soldiers in the fight here…"

I focused, dragging them all with me until we hovered in the air over the still smoldering remains of the luxury campsite, the nearby log cabins reduced to flinders, and the trees still burning.

"This is the dungeon, as it is currently, and yeah, we had a hell of a fight to get in."

"What the…" He looked around, frowning and clearly trying to get his bearings.

I lifted them all up as high as I could, giving the group a view of the surrounding area from about twenty meters up in the air.

Next to us all, a skeleton slowly toiled, forcing the bubble of influence still higher, and Aly stared at it, then nodded.

"Figured out my trick, eh?" was all she said, but I could see the way she barely took it in, instead searching in all directions.

"The camp is that way." I pointed to another forest some six hundred meters to the north. "I think, and listen when I say this, I *think* the others are there."

"Why?" Aly asked quickly. "What makes you think they're there?"

"The coronaught queen pulled everybody she had into buildings. There's nothing else in the area beyond the houses to the south, and I think she'd want to see freshly captured people, but beyond that I don't know," I said. "There's fuck all cover in the area beyond those houses and the occasional farmhouse. All her worms that were outside in the cold have died, so I'm betting she'd be pulling everyone back to her, but…"

"But?" She latched onto it, glaring at me as if daring me to give her bad news.

"But…there's a change from the coronaughts we saw," I admitted. "We came across humans who were turned into worm factories, their internal organs consumed as the host broke down. I tried to heal one of them, but I didn't have enough mana."

"How much mana did you have?" Dante asked.

I quirked a smile that he'd want to know such an esoteric bit of data. "Four thousand and change."

"Whoa, now *that's* a mana pool." He whistled.

"It wasn't enough." I shook my head. "Not nearly enough."

"Then we level it up," Aly said harshly. "Did the healing work? And…where's the dungeon?"

"Okay, let's sort this out." I took a deep breath. "So, first of all, yes, the healing worked. When we were infected and did it, it burned them out of us all. Next, the dungeon is under all of *that*." I gestured at the smoldering ruin, and people dutifully looked down.

"Now that's smart," Dante said with a sudden smile. "Setting fire to it to hide the evidence that you were ever there? Wow."

"Yes…" I said after a pregnant pause. "I totally did that. Intentionally."

"Oh God," Kelly whispered, covering her face. "What did you do?"

"I set off an incendiary grenade." I shrugged like it was nothing.

"They're insane!" Dante gushed. "Like six thousand degrees plus. They'll burn *anything*!"

"Yeah, nearly died of smoke inhalation." I grunted, before closing my eyes and cursing my loose lips. When I opened them again, it was to find Kelly hovering right in front of me.

Waiting.

"What. Happened?" she said slowly and clearly.

"You know who would really help us here?" I said suddenly, getting a burst of inspiration. "Chris! And Reedy! I'll be right back…"

I backed out of the dungeon sense so fast that my head was still spinning. I tried to sit up, reaching out to haul myself to my feet and head to the door…

Only to remember that I'd been in a fucking hammock, as I fell out of the goddamn thing and smashed my face into the floor.

"I know you're there," I mumbled, lifting one hand skyward in a "wait one" gesture, my face still smushed into the concrete that until recently had been a worm-infested old man's toilet.

"Then get back in here and explain what happened."

I sensed as much as heard Kelly through the dungeon sense as I forced myself to my feet, blinking and scrubbing at my face, before straightening my nose and wincing as it popped.

Leaving the room, I found Chris in pretty much the usual state for him when I needed him—which was to say he was sprawled across one of the barracks beds, snoring loudly, and dead to the world, while most of the soldiers and Kilo were crammed into the second barracks room, trying to sleep through the god-awful noise.

"Chris," I called, kicking the bottom of one of his feet where it hung off the bed, then stepping back.

He opened one eye and extended a finger in my direction. "Pull my finger."

"Hell no." I snorted. "I'm not falling for that. And we're connected again. The others are waiting in the dungeon sense, so wake up and get in there, or at least drag that blanket over your tiny shame."

With that, I turned to the sarge, who was eyeing me from his own bed, and we exchanged a long look. "You want in?" I asked eventually.

"Yes, sir," he replied slowly, sitting up and blinking, as if unsure what I was offering.

"Okay then, what you need to do is this…"

A few minutes later, we all stood in the council chambers back in Newcastle, more or less, in the dungeon sense, as we discussed the events that had led up to the dungeon seed being placed, and the plan moving forward.

"It wasn't your fault," the colonel was telling the sarge, and I agreed, right up until the pair glanced over at me and shut up.

At that point, I realized who they were blaming for their losses and I sent a mental "fuck you" in their direction, before turning back to Aly.

"Go over that again for me," I said.

"As near as we can tell, the storms are rolling in, one after another." She gestured vaguely upward. "I went as high as I could, and all I can see on all sides are storm clouds, so either it's a massive, once in a century natural event, or it's something to do with the mana or… Look, I don't know, okay? The only thing I do know is it looks like this is just a break in the storm, not the end of it."

"They're natural as near as I can tell, but yeah. So we've got a chance to hunker down and make some progress while the coronaughts are stuck inside." I nodded. "That I got. I mean about the research system."

"Oh, sorry, I thought that was obvious." She blinked. "So, the research system is limited by the mana put in, more than the time. If we put in a billion points of mana in one go, we could unlock everything in less time than it took to click the options."

"Uh-huh."

"So, I'm saying what we do is set up a secondary research spot there with you; then you can focus on separate research from me here, and we can literally research at twice the speed." She said it like it was obvious, and I shook my head.

"That's the issue," I pointed out. "Why set up a new slot, when the mana is all that matters? If a hundred thousand points of mana could unlock two techs in a half second, from there without setting up a new site, why bother?"

"It could," she agreed. "But remember that the research can only be boosted by researchers."

"Uh-huh?" I tried again, not sounding any smarter the second time around.

"So, if you have your team working on a higher-level tech, or guns, or sharp pointy sticks, that's fine," she said as if explaining it to a particularly dense child. "If you have the researchers working on it, and they get a breakthrough, you can produce something wonderful. While they're doing that, though, we can still be feeding in the automated stuff!"

"Like…we could have the next level of mana converters being auto researched, and armor designs being worked on by living researchers?" I tried.

"Exactly!"

"Why aren't you doing that?" I asked, confused.

"I am!" she shouted. "I am," she repeated, more quietly. "Matt, that's where the designs for the shotgun and more come from…your armor, that kind of thing. While I'm working on those things, the mana for say, the advanced Scepiniir, is being absorbed and it's unlocking *them*. We use the automated system for the things we can't unlock, because I can't design a better damn space-cat, Matt. I *can* make a better spear, or a gun, or a football or whatever, but I can't alter the genetic code of a species I'd never heard of a week ago!"

"Okay." I nodded, gesturing to her to calm down, and wondering why the look I was getting was like I'd just tried to baptize a cat.

"*Okay!?*" she asked in a brittle voice.

"Why don't we take a break from this, and move onto the plan?" Kelly suggested brightly.

"Right." I nodded, relieved I seemed to have dodged a bullet there. "So, the plan…"

"We need to make a better one anyway," Aly snapped. "We can't just leave them in there for the next few days and hope they're okay."

"Of course we can't," Kelly agreed.

"That's not what Matt was considering, was it?" Clarissa directed that last bit at me, as she looked from Aly to me, then to the table that took up the middle of the room.

"Actually, that's exactly what I'm planning on doing, and maybe for a few more days beyond that as well, once the storms clear," I admitted.

"What?" Aly growled.

"I don't like it either, but watch this and listen." I brought up the overhead plot on the map.

The first thing that I showed was the dungeon buried in the burnt-out forest. The lines of ghostly buildings underground shimmered into existence in response to my will.

It started with the central core room; then it built outward, the rooms on either side and more below appearing as the seconds passed.

"So what we do is this." I nodded to the map. "We treat this as our second base, and as a farming outpost…"

"Farming?!" Aly practically yowled, only to go quiet when Clarissa shifted to appear next to her, resting a hand on the younger woman's shoulder in silent support.

"Farming," I repeated, fixing Aly with a stare. "What we do is set up as many of the mana converters that we can create underground, and we expand. This area is incredibly saturated in mana, and for some reason, it's drawing more and more in. We set it up to take advantage of that, and build as much as we can."

Aly opened her mouth, and I held a ghostly hand up before she could speak. "Trust me, Aly, I don't like leaving them in there any more than you do, but listen to the plan first, please, all right? If you disagree, you can try to explain why and how we can improve on the plan then."

I waited as she struggled with it, before nodding and folding her arms as she glared at the table instead of me.

"We're not going to get two chances to do this, so we either view this as a full-on cleansing, where we take out the queen and secure the base, in which case we need to seriously get ready for a fight, one where not a single worm can be allowed to escape, or…"

I looked around and waited, making sure everyone was listening and understood the stakes.

"Or we do a raid, one that will alert the queen to the potential threat that we are, and we try to grab our people and run. But it's a literal crapshoot, because we won't have any way of capturing them all to heal them. It'll be a 'run in and trust to blind luck' affair. One where we try to heal them, and just hope they can run away with us afterward."

I let that hang there for a minute, before going on.

"This would also mean that we're grabbing a few of our people and accepting that most of them will be left behind. No way to know who. And as they'll be under enemy control, we might have to kill the people we want to save, to try to escape."

"So it's impossible," someone said, and I didn't even dignify that with a look.

"No, actually, it's not, because…get ready, people… I have a plan."

"Oh fuck," Chris muttered, reaching up and covering his eyes. "Well, there goes the neighborhood."

CHAPTER TWENTY-THREE

They'd agreed in the end, as I'd thought and hoped they would. Nobody was happy about the wait, but for the best chance of success, it was all we could do.

The plan hinged on three main points. First, surprise. As far as the queen knew, we were dead. The last thing that the infected old man had seen—and we had no way to know whether she'd seen through his eyes or whether the last thing she'd seen of us was the flames from outside—was us all choking in an underground room.

That meant that, hopefully, she thought we were dead and no threat to her.

The second point was that we could literally burrow through the world to her, and we'd be in the dungeon sense all the time, not in reality. Unless she had some sort of magical spirit senses, I was confident that just as it'd worked against the soldiers at the barracks in Newcastle, she'd have no clue we were coming, nor that we were observing her and getting ready.

The last point was that because we were in the darkest and deepest concentration of natural mana I'd ever seen, we had mana to burn, more or less, provided we invested in it right at the beginning.

The dungeon was now earning almost a million mana a day. That was thanks to the upgrades being rolled out to the mana converters at home, and the upgrades that were going to be sorted in the next day or so.

Though to reach that, I'll admit, we needed to add the ongoing and indefatigable march of the skeleton resource armies.

As always, that million was split between the production side—which paid for the buildings, the infrastructure and summoning more creatures, food, light, heat, and basically everything else—and the research side.

The research, now that it'd reached a solid half a million points a day available, had started to roll on at a ridiculous speed.

It wouldn't do it for long, I knew, because the costs for the next level, when we hit Glass, were going to be insane. The jump in mana research costs was getting crazy already, and that wasn't even reaching that kind of level. We were going to make the most of it while we could, by researching in a totally unexpected direction.

First, because I had a plan, I focused on the wraiths.

They were assholes, generally…not in the same way that the orcs were—just in the whole "the only reason they're here, instead of moving on after death, is because they're such dicks they could never rest in peace."

The first time I'd encountered them, the information I'd gotten from examining them had been…memorable.

Wraith	Undead Creature
Wraiths are the magically active spirits of the unquiet dead, those who refused to accept their eternal rest. When given the power to rise again, rather than the prior possessing soul refusing and moving on, leaving an empty vessel to rise, the Wraith has seized the power and embraced it.	
Wraiths are generally the souls of those who know the great beyond would judge them harshly: murderers, rapists, and worse. Each Wraith is unique, yet their power comes from another, forcing them into subservience that they hate almost as much as they hate the living.	
Ability:	
Plague! **Wraiths, like all undead, are composed of the decaying forms of the once living. Once per day, at a cost of 90% of the Wraith's life force, they may create a plague that will infect the living and the dead alike, draining the living of life, forcing them all to rise and serve the Wraith; area affected and effective time is determined by the health invested.**	
Ability:	
Shield! **Wraiths are more magically active than most and have the ability to form that magic into a simple shield.**	
Ability:	
Command! **Wraiths retain much of the cunning they had in life, allowing them to act as leaders of their lesser brethren.**	
Ability:	
Deathbolt! **The Wraith fires a bolt of necrotic energy across the battlefield, dealing 5-50 damage depending on the target.**	
Weaknesses: Fire, Light, and Life Magics	
HP 500/500	**Special Abilities: 4/4**

That was a hell of a résumé, after all, basically saying that they were such dicks in life, such scumbags that had no redeeming features, that they knew they would be cursed even in the next life, if one existed.

The ones we summoned weren't entirely like that. They were dungeon-born, and had no evil spirit asshole pasts. But still, something about them always set my damn teeth on edge.

It wasn't just that they stared at everyone like they were from a certain island that billionaires liked to play on and we were innocents, either.

I'd not wanted to upgrade the wraiths to this level because they were just like that slightly weird guy at work who always stared at everyone and made them generally uncomfortable.

The reason I'd changed my mind, though, was threefold: They were powerful magic users, which gave a lot of strength and depth to our forces. They could fly. And their third ability was that they could command their lesser brethren.

Basically, a wraith could act as a company commander or a section leader, and we were going to need that ability. In the future, I wanted real people leading these sections, the teams that we'd already discussed building. But for now, we'd be splitting up the command of the wraiths and their attached forces between a small group of older dungeon citizens, led by Markus.

The wraiths weren't cheap. The upgrade cost was coming in at yeah, you guessed it, two hundred and fifty-thousand mana, but using them would drop the cost overall. The best chance we had of taking our people back was to use creatures that the worms—if they were rereleased back into the wild—couldn't affect.

Also, the undead didn't matter in the same way that the living did, or at least not to me.

The math was fairly simple. If we set out say, twenty companies of undead soldiers, with each commanded by a single wraith, that meant that we could field massively different numbers of undead in each company for the same cost.

An undead army...well, it wasn't happy making, I'll admit. But half a million mana for a day that could, if we needed it, be channeled into summoning standard undead meant that we could have twelve thousand five hundred normal undead. Or, if we upgraded them from uncommon to advanced, five hundred advanced undead, as they jumped in cost to a thousand each from four hundred.

The wraiths were a lot more expensive than the standard undead, admittedly—ten times, in fact—with the basic wraith coming in at four hundred; the common had leaped to a thousand, the uncommon to two and a half, and yeah, the advanced at ten thousand.

Twenty of them came in at a whopping two hundred thousand, which reduced the available to spend on the undead "line soldiers" to three hundred thousand.

But that total divided by the summoning cost gave us a total of seven and a half thousand undead to spread out, or three hundred and seventy-five soldiers each to twenty companies.

Although we'd come up with that plan for wargamers to help guide the companies, there'd not been time to implement it, so that was why we needed the wraiths.

The wraiths at advanced were going to be a hell of a lot different as well, hopefully an order of magnitude stronger and more powerful. But that was going to be balanced with the need to watch the fuckers like a seminary alongside a daycare all the goddamn time.

That, in turn, was going to be offset by the class skill points I was going to be spending though...or so I hoped. But more about that in a minute.

The main reason for the undead army was twofold. First, the worms could infect anything living, but I didn't see what they could do against the undead apart from smash them up. They certainly couldn't take them over, so that was one bonus. The next? Well, that was easy.

I frankly didn't care about their losses, as long as they got the job done. I could send waves of undead in from all sides, burrow along under the base and come up in places they didn't expect with forces that could be summoned and left standing in the dark, waiting patiently for the order to attack. There were no concerns like air or whether they'd be ready when they were needed.

They could run straight into withering fire, and unlike when the idiots who attacked the dungeon with the undead last time had come, I had a second phase to the attack, not just "overwhelm them with dross."

The undead would have one simple—ish—order, and that was to *capture* the enemy. That was it: grab them, pin them, remove weapons and bring them to set places, where they could be healed and stripped of the infection.

If we lost a hundred undead to capture a single human? That was still a win as far as I was concerned. Not only could we increase the size of our side with those humans we liberated, more importantly, we were making this many undead in a fucking *day*.

That meant that if the fight raged on more than a day? We could replenish our forces—no muss, no fuss. The soldiers would, worst-case scenario, run out of ammo before we ran out of bodies.

Sure, I wanted that damn ammo, I really did, but the people were more important.

The third option, and one that I was discounting heavily, was that the coronaughts would do suicide attacks to try to counter us attacking. Basically holding the humans they already had captured as hostages, and threaten to kill them if we didn't stop.

That was a possibility, one that Aly had raised, but I didn't think it was likely. And, if they did that, they were weakening their side. Plus, the whole, "I need to kill myself to win," wasn't really a viable strategy as far as I was concerned.

If they went down that route, then we were going to have to zerg them anyway.

That was the main plan, nice and simple: burrow deep beneath, set up additional spaces that were ready for us to expand into, and launch attacks on all sides and from within when we were ready.

It sounded a lot simpler than it was going to be, though. Because even with more and more undead expansion teams planned to come online and our people now able to help them, there was a fuckload of "fiddly bits" that needed to be addressed.

First and foremost, there was the time it was going to take to reach the base and map it all out, not to mention the hollowing out of the areas for staging, and the building of the needed infrastructure for mana generation and control facilities. A load of little issues needed to be worked out—not least was that the queen had apparently sent her drones or whatever into the buildings nearby to rest and hide from the weather, which was understandable.

Great even, because we wanted to get our people back alive after all, but the "minor" issue there was that, for the time being, they were inside and out of sight, so we had to check each and every goddamn building.

They might have all been recalled to the camp, and that was what we were hoping, but chances were they were just ordered to the nearest building and told to huddle up.

If that was the case, there might be pockets of additional coronaught infections springing up as soon as the storms blew themselves out.

That meant we needed to extend additional scouting runs to the nearby buildings as well. And for that, to do it in any kind of speed, considering the dozens of miles in all directions we'd need to check, we needed more fliers to reach and search the farthest points.

They'd need to be upgraded, and that cost mana, control points, storage and…the list went on and on.

All the millions of small jobs that needed to be done, basically, were going to take, we estimated, a minimum of three days.

The storms, we were guessing, would give us at least another day, possibly two while they raged. But after that, it was going to be touch and go. The longest we could agree to give our people in enemy hands was three days.

Longer could give us time to gather larger forces, and make sure we won with less losses—or breakage—of the targets, but they might all be used as breeders by then and/or be dead as well.

No, this was it. Three days to D-Day was the agreed plan.

The first stage, now that we knew the mana generation was literally three times the average, was to start to accumulate.

Looking over the mana that we had available from both dungeons, we had just under a million points per day coming in. If we cut the summoning of new creatures and all the research entirely out for now, the ongoing daily maintenance cost was around a hundred thousand.

That gave us nine hundred thousand mana for three days, or two point seven million, at the current generation rate.

We had just under nine hundred "in the tank" and available, so the first steps were the research area here at the new dungeon, which we decided to call the north dungeon for ease.

It was long and large, and that wasn't a euphemism: ten meters across by twenty long, with five sections laid out, each three meters wide for the first four, and the last a much bigger one designed for multiple people to work in.

The first four each had a single reclining chair, similar to the original dungeon research post that we'd created. But the new, upgraded post also had room for two more in the large bay and plenty of space to work.

The risk here was that we needed to either summon kobolds or whatever race, then dismiss and resummon until they were all filled with those that had the research perk, or, as was much more realistic, the soldiers all got to wear new hats.

That was the approach we'd decided on in the end, despite the sarge's concerns that some of the section shouldn't be allowed to walk and breathe at the same time, never mind do research.

I didn't point out that in some ways they were filling seats as much as working, but I had hope for them.

Aly gave them orders and explanations, and hovered over them in the dungeon sense as soon as they were integrated, both to make sure they didn't do anything dodgy, and to help them acclimatize.

That cost us a hundred thousand, which dropped us to eight, but it meant that we could run more projects. That was going to help overall, as each project that was being worked on could then be brute-forced by pouring additional mana in.

While the brute-force option worked, the others were helping along the road to techs we needed as well.

We started with the basics.

Mana conversion was being researched currently for the five hundred thousand level, and that was just on the Bronze tier still. We'd agreed that we were going to get that done, then check the next level that was available.

I had a nasty suspicion that the next level of it was just going to be insane. It was already half a million, and if it "only" doubled to a million, it was going to be out of our reach in the short term.

As it was, though, as soon as it was done, we were going to start on the next stage straightaway, and build more mana converters.

If they followed the path that we'd figured out, then the new ones would cost around fifty thousand mana each. It was an incredible sum, but they should bring in around forty-five to fifty mana each—even back at Newcastle—per hour, and the upgrade process wasn't as expensive as just building new ones.

Better yet, here in such a rich mana area, they'd be pulling in between a hundred and thirty and a hundred and fifty mana an hour.

That was astounding, and yet it wasn't even half the story.

The mana converters were converting the mana of the area around them into a specialized form, so a Fire converter created Fire mana, and stored it. That was great…but they also created pure mana once the internal reserves for storage were filled.

We'd been trying to figure this out before, and we'd found half the story was true. Basically, we'd made a massive mistake in thinking that certain tech was closed in and when you left that tier, such as Bronze, you lost access to it.

What we'd been doing until recently was researching *Bronze Age* levels of tech in this area. The converters went from basic, to common, uncommon, advanced, rare, legendary, and artifact.

Then we'd realized that if we went further back in the tech tree, we had an option to leave the Bronze Age path, and start on the next available one to us. As Iron was now locked—we'd not tried to research it at the time and had missed our chance—we had to move to Steel instead.

Aly and Kelly had spotted this literally about a week ago, and we'd started factoring that into our plans. But at some point, when I was trapped in the trial dungeon, I'd come to a realization that maybe the conduits had more to do than just wave around in the damn air to suck mana in.

Making and proving that connection—I'd not had the time to try it before I got this new offshoot up and running—had made me curse, and celebrate.

Basically, the mana converters produced differing levels of mana depending on how they were set up, and the models that had been researched and unlocked. And I now had proved we'd missed half the damn system.

"WHAT?!" Aly had half screamed at me, and I'd nodded, knowing exactly how she felt.

"Look at it from here," I said, when it was just the three of us a little later. "The mana system jumps in tens, right? So one converter that's drawing in the mana provides ten points per hour, that's at the basic level. Jump to common, it should be twenty. We know that damn system bumps up at ten points per unit, per hour of research done."

"But we get around fourteen to fifteen," Kelly pointed out.

"We do," I agreed. "But that's the goddamn problem."

"What?"

"We started upgrading the mana converters. They should have started at ten, then gone to twenty, then thirty, right? I mean, we got all the way to uncommon, and we're doing advanced now. But the mana we've been getting? It doubled, not fucking tripled."

"Uh…"

"We've been looking at it and seeing 'oh we should have ten, then twenty, then thirty' and we've seen that we're getting roughly that, so we didn't ask any questions.

"The mana we're getting, though, as the converters are optimized for their locations, is forty-five points from each on average. And once the new level is done, that's going to go to forty as a baseline, and sixty for the optimized. That's great. But why do we have research available in unlocking mana converters, mana conduits and generators? Why not just one general 'mana upgrade' or something?"

"Gods, I just know I need a drink for this," Aly whispered, covering her eyes with her hands.

"Yeah, well." I shrugged. "This is where it gets fun. Each of these systems are part of the whole; each bit is upgradable, and when you do all of it? It makes a hell of a difference."

"Go on," she whispered.

"Hey, you spotted this the last time…I just found the next step." I grinned at her. "The conduits are just to feed the core, right? They pull in mana from everything around, and they feed it in."

"Yeah."

"No," I corrected. "What's a conduit actually for?" I asked them both, looking from Aly to Kelly, and seeing that Kelly had already made the connection, while Aly was staring at me, wide-eyed.

"It's to connect things, to draw something from one end, to the other," Kelly whispered.

"Exactly." I nodded. "I connected up the five Dark mana generators in the area below me, to the conduits, and now they're drawing in double."

"DOUBLE?"

"Double," I said. "What was happening before, I think, is that we were drawing in the same but losing it by the time it was somehow transported to the core to be used. There was no physical link, after all. Think of a super conductor and a semi—there's a world of difference in the power that gets from one end to the other, and that's why the systems are broken up."

"But that's stupid!" Kelly said. "Why assume we'll know that? Why not just put it all together?"

"No clue," I admitted. "Cost in parts, I guess, probably because doing each level as we have will bring in more and more mana and be cheaper to upgrade individually. Means we can do it sooner. Honestly, I don't know. Might be that being assholes is a sacred alien responsibility. But what I *do* know is that this is going to double our mana input."

"We need it," Aly chimed in after a few seconds' thought.

"Yeah, I know." I nodded.

"No, you don't." She shook her head, gesturing as a new screen popped up. "Let's take this further, now that we understand a bit more."

The screen was blank, then populated with a stylized core on the left and the converter on the right, with a conduit attached to them.

The core had "Bronze" written above it and the converter had "Advanced" above it, with the equation below reading: 60 X 24 = 1440.

"Okay, that's pretty obvious. Sixty points per converter, per hour works out to fourteen hundred and forty per day."

"Exactly," she agreed. "Now, we think that the next level is going to be at least a million points, right?"

"Yeah, so we probably need to work out if it's worth it, then either do it or jump to the next tier instead."

"Exactly, a million mana. Yeah, it *will* be worth it, mainly because the next tier—we missed the chance with Iron so it's Steel, remember—will double the previous level. So, if say, we're getting an average of sixty, and we get the million points level of 'rare' researched, we go to fifty, which is going to hit seventy-five as optimized.

"Then, when we start the next tier of research, we close the Bronze one off, and instead we start that tier at seventy-five points, doubled." The image changed to one that showed "Steel" above the core, and "Basic" above the converter, with a hundred and fifty written below it.

"That means that if we're damn lucky, the jump from basic to common is going to cost us anywhere from a million to five million, and that'll only gain us a ten-point increase."

"Damn," I whispered. "It's almost tempting to skip the rest and go all the way straight to Glass after getting the basic level in Steel, doubling it again."

"It is, for the short-term boost. But long-term, that would fuck us all," she said. "Remember, this is worked out on the old data we had. So if we change this by adding in the upgraded converters…"

The space below the converters gained an "x2" additional marker, and the overall math changed to three hundred, then a new equation replaced the old.

300 X 24 = 7200

"Damn." I whistled. "That's a hell of a change."

"It gets even better when you add in this last detail," Aly whispered. She added in the overall number of converters we had currently, clearly considering my new ones and some more that had been added while I was out of the loop.

300 X 24 X 204 = 1,468,800

"Fuck me." I grinned.

"I'll leave that to Kell," Aly distractedly tried to joke, before clearly giving up and just moving on. "So, it means that we can stay in the game, rather than essentially cutting ourselves out of the running. If we skip this and just went straight after the jumps in core level? We'd get access to great tech and quickly, but we'd be unable to do anything more.

"The core costs to upgrade are massively more expensive each time. And lines of research like this? Unless we really invest, and invest now, we're going to be fucked farther down the line, compared to where we could be."

"And the other dungeons—" I broke off, realizing the massive advantage they had over us.

"They'll have known this, with them having the fairies to guide them. They might have still leapt ahead, but they'll have plans to deal with it all."

"We're stuck at Steel for a while then," I said slowly, thinking about it.

"No," Kelly countered. "We need to reach Glass as soon as possible."

"Kell…" Aly looked at her sister-in-law. "You know why we can't."

"No, I know the arguments why we *shouldn't*," she replied. "We shouldn't because we'll miss out on potential benefit. We shouldn't because we'll miss out on this or that. But if we take too long, we all *die*. So I think we need to balance it out.

"Matt, the next few days? Yes, of course everything is on hold to save our people. But then we need to massively invest in the mana generation side…like, exclusively," she said grimly.

"We can't allow anything else to be a priority, not for at least another week. We research the mana we can get access to, then we build the infrastructure to access it. We do that for a week, solid, and we get everything we can. We focus on the lines of technology that we know are limited to a core level, then we draw a line under it and move on."

"Why?" I stared at her. "What changed?"

"Your focus did," she said softly, before gesturing around. "Look at all of this. Matt, I love you, and I desperately want my brother and our friends back, but you're fighting fires, not aiming for the end goal, which you were before we all came along."

"The Oracan," I said.

"Exactly," she agreed. "If they show up next week, can we survive?"

"No."

"Next month?"

"No," I admitted again.

"Can we beat them with a Steel core?"

"You know we can't."

"Glass?"

"No."

"So it has to be the top one?"

"Neutronium." I sighed. "Yeah, and even with that, it's not a guarantee. The Cinthians have them already and they're getting their asses kicked, I think, reading between the lines with the details we get about the universe."

"So as much as I want to take our time and plan this all out, we have to balance it." Kelly looked from me to Aly and back again. "A week, then we need to close the doors and focus inward, starting to move to Glass."

"Or we go all out on expansion," Aly suggested.

"I guess I need to get to work then, and we'll figure the next step out once we've won," was all I could say.

CHAPTER TWENTY-FOUR

The next three days passed in a blur. As we'd agreed, we worked first to unlock the advanced level of converters, before moving onto the wild card, then finally upgrading the wraiths.

The wild card was a plan that we came up with as a real Hail Mary pass. Although it paid off, more or less, it didn't work entirely as I'd hoped.

The focal orbs were incredible technology—or magic, depending on your point of view—and now that we finally had a glassmaker and the systems set up, the replication of the basic focal orbs was possible in the dungeon through normal dungeon means.

Chris and I had brought five of the orbs between us, each freshly summoned and each loaded with a healing spell. But the real trick came when I'd been eating with the soldiers at one point, and trying to explain to them how the orbs worked, planning that we'd have to have people ready at set areas for the undead to bring their captives, for us to heal.

Finger had hefted it in one hand, tossing it up and catching it, before staring in its depths, curiously. "Could you not make a big one?" he'd asked, and I shrugged.

"Possibly, but it'd be a ballache to carry. Why?" I'd replied.

"Just thought it'd be cool if you could set one up in a hospital, and connect it to the mana generator thingies, that's all. Then you just walk people past it."

"If it was connected up, would it work?" the sarge had asked. "*Could* people just walk up and touch it and be healed?"

"It would, I think," I'd said, staring at Chris as he stared back at me.

"Or..." he'd said slowly, "we could look at powering my mending spell."

"This was based off that, right?" I asked.

He nodded, then shook his head. "No, wait, the *original* one was—then Jo put a proper healing spell in. Mine doesn't regrow shit; it just speeds up the body's natural healing cycle."

"But could you do AOE with that?" I'd asked him, and the pair of us had turned to stare at the orb in stunned hope.

After explaining the thought to Aly and Kelly, we'd all dove into the system, searching through the options, desperately, until we finally found something that could work, but not where I'd expected to find it.

The dungeon had a dedicated spell list, ones that could be cast by the dungeon so long as the mana needed was provided, and the first spell available had been Fear.

Dungeon Spells

Fear:

Fear is a standard general-purpose spell, used primarily to drive away low-level adventurers or monsters while the Dungeon is being remodeled.

Cost: 100 mana to cast, with a further 10 mana per minute active.

AOE: 5 meters, but can be increased for a further 10 mana per meter, per minute active.

That spell had been the first I'd unlocked, relatively recently, and it'd been followed by Burning Hands, a spell that sounded way more awesome than it really was.

It basically taught the spell to all dungeon creatures, and somehow provided them the ability to cast the spell—if they had the mana—while inside the limits of the dungeon.

One step beyond it, and they couldn't cast it anymore, and it used a lot of mana for some reason.

The Fear spell, on the other hand, was designed to be emitted from dedicated "Fear Generators" that would subtly guide anyone we didn't want near the dungeon, away from it.

It was expensive to keep up all the time, and a bit indiscriminate, so we'd not really bothered before. But the one thing I did like about it?

It was basically a spell generator that covered a set AOE.

Area of effect spells could affect a literal area, constantly, as long as the mana needed was provided, and that was the secret…that was exactly what we'd been looking for.

Not on the medical side, though Jo was going to be pleased when she found out about the upgraded medical suite we'd unlocked at first, looking for a way to do this.

No, it was a little twist on a cheap system that simply needed the runes for the Fear casting spell removed, and instead a focal orb loaded with a healing spell attached in their place.

A little trial and error, and some reverse engineering of the Life mana converter, and boom! We had a simple creation that would radiate a healing aura in all directions, indiscriminately healing those around it, *and removing any infections.*

It also helped that midway through the second day, chance offered us an opportunity to test things out, as several of the infected were roaming around aboveground still, on a roving patrol. One of those nearby had recently fallen through a damaged section into an underground room that was already under our control.

They'd tried to escape, dragging themselves back up and out of the rubble and debris, but the ground had collapsed beneath them. They had both a compound fracture in the leg and were apparently dying of exposure.

After a few minutes of trying to escape, the others aboveground, that had been looking in, apparently decided that they were too busy for this shit, and all at once, turned around and wandered off, resuming their patrol.

The trapped one had continued to try to escape, but with absolutely no success. It had, though, provided us with a great opportunity.

Growing the orb on a plinth, attached to the dungeon and feeding it mana all the time, it quickly rose up behind the dying drone, the wash of light barely noticeable due to the collapsed rubble.

Then, it started to radiate the healing spell.

The effect was slow to take hold. We'd deliberately limited the mana being fed to the pedestal so that it didn't just send out a great big flash of power and alert the queen that something was weird.

Instead, it slowly healed the nearby figure, keeping them from dying from the compound fracture at first, and then, as that priority was taken care of, breaking down all other infections in the body.

The hope was that the gradual destruction of the worm in the infected drone's body would just look like they'd succumbed to their injuries, and boom. That was it.

What happened was that they slowed, more and more, no longer trying to climb out as much, and then keeled over and sagged to the ground, unconscious.

We quickly opened a passage into the room, grabbed them and dragged them through, before sealing it all back up.

They were put in an empty room—no light, no contact—and we had an undead watching them, with the order to tell me as soon as they stirred.

It took a while, but when they finally did? They were awake, and *aware*!

That was a bit shitty, admittedly, as we literally couldn't risk telling them anything—just in case—and summoned some food and drink, a candle and matches, and a bed, then had to leave them to it, in a small room with no visible way in or out and an Air converter to keep the air breathable.

The skeleton was in the dungeon sense—not there physically, but still. We couldn't risk the person in there seeing us, just in case, but leaving them in a black room with no food, water or light was pretty nasty, so we compromised, and left them with that at least.

Then, I forced myself to move on, and focused on unlocking the wraiths, moving all the way to advanced.

They were terrifying creatures now, I had to admit. The originals had looked like humans that had been amputated at the waist, still wrapped in the rotting remains of funeral clothing, and flying as they cast spells and tore at their enemies.

They were nasty fucks, and yet, the new version made them look positively cheery.

These latest versions were more intact—humanoid still, in that they had a head, arms, torso and now legs—but they were closer to Nazgûl than dead human.

They could fly or walk with equal ease, gravity seeming to have no claim on them, and they stood at an impressive seven foot in height. They were thin, their flesh a mixture of greys and black, seeming withered, as if they'd been left for years in a cave or something, and yet their muscles were powerful.

They had three eyes now; each gleamed with a bright-blue flame. Their mouths were filled with needle-sharp teeth, when they chose to open them.

When closed, their mouth vanished, leaving a seemingly unbroken line of dead flesh. And when they chose to open them again? It looked like they tore the flesh apart each time.

They wore long robes, the fabric seemingly made out of night, and their fingers were long and skeletal, tipped with bone claws at the end that they clacked together regularly, apparently pleased with the sound.

And the effect on those around them?

Nobody liked being around them, literally nobody, and that included me. There was something fucking uncomfortable in the way that they stared at you, as if they were considering ripping your soul free and eating it.

The damn things gave me the willies, honestly.

I'd summoned the first of them, and based off the look the fucker had given me, I'd immediately pulled up my class skills, and started hunting for the best way to spend those two points I'd gained.

Class Skills:

Class selection: Arcane Dungeon Lord

Imbue: You may choose to give freely of your own mana pool to imbue an item or creature of the Dungeon with magic. This ability can fail, and spectacularly so; however, creations of wondrous might can also be brought into being. Be wary. (Selected)

Evolution: Foresight: No longer are your creations the chance things they were...now see the true potential of a creature! (Selected)

Monster Master: No longer do the creatures of the Dungeon view you with apathy or irritation when you pass by. Now they are devoted to you! This skill ranks in levels from 0 (Interested) to 5 (Worshipful). (Current level: 0, Interested)

Evolution: Lord of All! The creatures of your Dungeon know their true master, and those who follow willingly can now receive arcane gifts that match their level of devotion! (Selected)

Arcane Breeder: Some Dungeon Lords wish for only the purest strains to survive, while others enjoy the randomness of evolution...select the genes you wish to see and promote them!

Artificer: You may gift magical artifacts to your creations, and when combined with Foresight, these creatures will gain significant bonuses to magical item creation and replication. This skill ranks in levels from 0 (Curiosity) to 5 (Legendary). (Current level: 0, Curiosity)

Arcane Pets: Your sentient Dungeon inhabitants can gather and breed pets, but where before there was an element of random chance, now you may lure those you wish into the range of your tamers. This skill ranks in levels from 0 (Magical) to 5 (Legendary Creatures) (Current level: 0, Magical).

Insatiable Curiosity: **Random Sentient Dungeon Creatures will now have the chance to be spawned with an Insatiable Curiosity. These creatures can be put to work in your Research Nodes to increase Research by a staggering degree. This skill ranks in levels from 0 (Incompetent) to 5 (Genius). (Current level: 4, Gifted)**

Evolution: Magical Researcher! **Before, your researchers were generalists, plodding along at their task, be that a better toilet seat or a converter; now they stand a chance at developing true magical gifts, and at learning the secrets of creation! This skill ranks in levels from 0 (Novice) to 5 (Master). (Current level: 1, Apprentice)**

Manafield: **Your Dungeon's Manafield will now passively expand at 10% more than the previous rate, enabling greater growth in a shorter period of time. This skill ranks in levels from 0 (Restricted) to 5 (Expansive). (Current Level: 1, Limited)**

Evolution: Tides of Mana! **All life creates mana, as do elemental interactions. Now through the wonders of gravitational magic, you can start to draw more mana into the area of your Dungeon. This skill ranks in levels from 0 (Gentle) to 5 (Vortex). (Current Level: 1, Steady)**

Reach Out and Touch Me: **Your Dungeon is no longer only controllable when you are within its own environs. Now you can interact with it at increasing distances. This skill ranks in levels from 0 (Local) to 5 (Interstellar). (Current level: 0, Local)**

Evolution: Gates! **No longer is the Dungeon a distant creation. This skill unlocks the creation of the Gates, transportals that can be built inside the Dungeon and activated at a remote location to provide a stable link between the two points.**
**This skill ranks in levels from 0 (Single Gate) to 5 (Unlimited)** **(Current level: 0, Single).**

Looking it over, there were a few things I _wanted_. Mana fields, for example, I _really_ wanted, as that'd help with everything. A second gate unlocked beyond the one I was going to make here? Yup, that'd be cool too.

Magical researchers? Upgrading that from the low level it was at would really help with a lot of things, or adding in the artificer higher levels would massively help with magical artifact creation.

Any of those I wanted. Any and all.

What I took, though, was two levels of Monster Master, and that jumped me from Interested, first to Befriended—which was a shitty name, to be honest—and then to Revered.

I was guessing this was the starter level for all creatures, though, and I damn well hoped it stuck for the orcs as well, because the difference from the wraith's original attitude to the new one was marked.

It'd been staring at me like it wanted to eat my soul, but couldn't be bothered before. Now, though? As soon as the skill was upgraded and activated, the wraith dropped to one knee, its arms clasped together across its chest, hands placed on opposite shoulders as if a vampire in a coffin.

I stared, then gestured for it to stand, which it did quickly.

It didn't speak, though I suspected it could now. Instead, it simply stared, waiting to hear its orders.

"Wait here," I said after a few seconds. "You're to command a company of undead foot soldiers, and your aim is to lead them to capture the enemy, not kill."

It nodded, almost bowing, as I pushed a load more information at it, making the reasoning clear, and the need to capture and contain the enemy, not rip their heads off.

That done, I couldn't help but pull up the new data on the wraith.

Wraith Lord	Undead Creature

Wraith Lords are leaders of the undead, minor lordlings that, although not granted true power, are still fearsome enemies. They know that most of their kind understand only pain, fear, and lust, and they regard them with a hatred that is barely held in check by their own avarice.

As a Dungeon-Born Wraith Lord, there is no past to drive its baser urges, but make no mistake, this creature is still filled with them. Leave it to its own devices at your peril.

Wraiths are generally the souls of those who know that the great beyond would judge them harshly: murderers, rapists, and worse. Each Wraith is unique, yet their power must come from another, forcing them into subservience that they hate almost as much as they hate the living.

Ability:

***Plague!* Wraith Lords, like all undead, are comprised of the decaying forms of the once living. Once per day, at a cost of 90% of the Wraith's life force, they may create a plague that will infect the living and the dead alike, draining the living of life, forcing them all to rise and serve the Wraith; area affected and effective time is determined by the health invested.**

Ability:

***Shield!* Wraith Lords are more magically active than most and have the ability to form that magic into a simple shield.**

Ability:

***Command!* Wraith Lords retain much of the cunning they had in life, allowing them to act as leaders of their lesser brethren.**

Ability:

Deathbolt! **The Wraith Lord fires a bolt of necrotic energy across the battlefield, dealing 5-50 damage depending on the target.**

Ability:

Wither! **The Wraith Lord expels a harsh breath, drenching the area around it in the cold of the grave, before ripping this breath back into itself and tearing the life force from those caught in the area of attack spell. This life force can be used to either heal itself or raise additional minions from the bodies of the recently deceased.**

Ability:

Grasp of the Grave! **The Wraith Lord designates an area to hold, reaching through the veil that separates life and death, and forcing other undead to join it, reaching their limbs through to try to capture the living, dragging them through to feed upon.**

Weaknesses: Fire, Light, and Life Magics

HP: 2000/2000

Stamina: 0/0

Mana: 2000/2000

Speed 7/10

Level: 0

HP: 2000/2000	Special Abilities: 6/6

I read it all, and vowed that once they were no longer useful, they'd be killed. They couldn't be left to level, to grow beyond my control. I just knew I'd come back to find they'd set up a church and started recruiting altar boys.

The wraith looked to the side as the first of its minions began to appear. Its claws clacked hungrily as skeleton after skeleton resolved from the bright glow of the dungeon's motes.

"These are for you to lead, to capture the enemy," I said, and it nodded hungrily. "Your goal, and the one thing you have to do beyond anything else, is to protect the dungeon," I said slowly and clearly. "I'm the Dungeon Lord, and I work to protect my dungeon and my people. You exist to serve me and to protect them. Do you understand?"

It nodded again, and I swore under my breath, then turned around, walking away from it.

I'd created this as one of the closest caches of undead to our base, mainly because I wanted to see one of them before I released them to cause havoc, and damn.

I made the point of sealing up the chamber as soon as I was on the other side, then hurried along back to the others, climbing two sets of stairs up from the lower level I'd been on, before entering the core room again and settling down to work in the dungeon sense properly.

We'd spent most of the time focusing on the research side of things as well as pushing out the dungeon's area of influence.

One of the things we'd done, as we went, was create pockets in the ground, growing an influence generator inside them, and then moving on, leaving them to gradually permeate the area around them. They weren't that expensive, after all—two thousand a pop for the directional one—and although they didn't do their best work underground, they still worked steadily.

Setting them down here and there, underground with a single direction activated to expand in, they labored slowly, claiming the area around them.

It had taken the first day to get a path all the way from where we were, to the tip of the camp's southern boundary, then the second day to get all the way to its northernmost edge. As the undead worked in relays, Clarissa and her team monitored and guided them, as more and more were summoned.

By the end of the second day, with a thousand undead now summoned and being guided, we were claiming hundreds of meters an hour. By the start of the third day, we finally began to feel that we had a real chance, when, of course, the storm front started to clear properly—meaning it was almost certainly today we had to attack, or not at all.

The base was separated into three sections. To the northwest and separated from the majority of the "working" side of the base was the accommodation section: nearly thirty large buildings, each a modern barracks, split into rooms for sections of ten soldiers.

Each section had a communal bathroom, bunks, and a small space for the individual soldier to store their personal effects and gear, but very little in the way of luxuries, which was pretty much expected.

There was also a small on-base store, a larger storage area, and both a canteen and three bars: one for the rank and file, one for the NCOs, and one for the officers.

The same river we'd slogged through, half freezing and that would have probably left us all with nasty frostbite if we didn't have healing magic, ran between that section and the "working" area of the base.

That was from the northeast, running to the south, and included the rest of the main base, the armory, vehicle bays, radar, and exercise areas...the lot. This wasn't a dedicated training base, not like Catterick garrison to the south; this was a working military base, with the weapons and systems that would be expected.

At the very south of the base, and leading toward the Otterburn village, were the administration blocks and facilities, and medical.

We'd gone up the middle, claiming everything we could, then split left and right, seizing every damn inch as we went. We were determined to make sure we missed nothing, and yet still, despite all of that, we'd nearly missed the damn queen. That was because the sneaky bastards who built the camp had a hell of a lot more in the base than could be seen from above.

The middle of the base, where the east and west sections were separated from each other, had the river running through it, a forest, and some small hills—hills that were used daily in more normal days for the soldiers who had annoyed someone to be ordered to run up and down.

All very traditional.

What wasn't traditional, and we only found when one of our people stumbled onto a passage that was sinking downward, was the more secretive areas of the base.

An entire sub-ground complex that we later found out was accessible only from certain highly controlled areas.

There was a second armory, one that had a smaller number of weapons stored, but they were apparently there to serve the defenders of this more exclusive area.

Searching it, following corridor after corridor of the maze-like layout, we finally found something. I just damn well knew it was both the thing we were looking for, and the very last thing we wanted to find.

The corridor had ended abruptly, behind a large, unmanned guard station, with a pair of solid steel doors that looked designed to hold off Godzilla.

They were cracked open, but try though we might, there was just no way to move ahead.

A line of distortion, something similar to a heat haze, grew stronger the closer I got to the doors. As soon as I stopped trying to push ahead, I felt myself sliding backward.

It extended all around whatever was generating it, in a rough circle, and no matter how hard I tried, I couldn't get any closer.

It was Kelly, though, who spotted the symbols, and that changed everything. As soon as she'd seen them, she sent the team who had discovered this on to work in a different area before she'd explained what she'd found.

Signs were hard to read in the dungeon sense, even now that we'd integrated the north dungeon with the main one, upgrading its sensing abilities automatically.

Still, they were resolved as a sort of block; symbols and text weren't clear, and I'd just grown used to ignoring them, considering they were written without a Dungeon Lord or an alien invasion in mind, after all.

What Kelly had found, in addition to the signs that promised consequences if you were there, not just if you went farther—promises of death and life imprisonment—were two signs I never expected to find here.

One warned of the dangers of trespassing around nuclear weapons. And the other? Biohazards.

What kind of biohazards were going to be stored with nuclear weapons, you might ask. Because I know I did.

And Kelly's response was a disgusted one. "The weaponized kind."

With the line of distortion forcing us to keep our distance, I'd gone looking for the colonel, with Aly and Kelly waiting for me to bring him back.

Something about the place prevented us getting any closer than fifty meters or so. But even from here, we could see creatures in the distance that were insanely different from the humans patrolling above.

If our people above were the drones, these were the soldiers, the warriors, and finally, some kind of guardians.

That was all that we could tell from a distance, one that gave us little more than rough outlines, but it was enough.

"It's the queen, it has to be," Aly had announced on seeing the other creatures that surrounded the nest, before rounding on the colonel as well. "Why the hell didn't you tell us there were nukes here!" she snapped, as soon as I'd dragged him in.

"I wasn't sure the queen would have found this place," he admitted after a few seconds of staring. "I wasn't sure and my oath is binding still. You have neither the need to know, nor the clearance to discuss the nation's nuclear arsenal with and—"

"Fuck the nation," I growled. "It's gone, dead, kaput!"

"You don't know that," the old soldier had shot back. "As long as a single member of—"

"I know that *we're* the only authority here," I rumbled. "And in there, there's a fucking worm queen that's got access to the nukes and *goddamn bioweapons* that we as a country definitely don't have!"

"I can't discuss them with you," he said almost woodenly, before shaking his head and fixing me with a glare. "Not, 'I don't want to.' I *can't*, Matt...do you understand? My oath forbids it."

"Fuck your oath," Kelly snapped at him. "Those signs—we can make them out from here, and so can you!"

"I can't discuss them," he repeated.

"Bioweapons," she said flatly. "They're illegal and everyone knows it. Fuck's sake, they're illegal for a reason! If they got out..."

"They will have," Aly said slowly, staring at the darkness ahead. "If there's anything in there, the queen has to have found them, right? It's not like she'll have read the signs and backed away."

"Fuck knows," I ground out. "We can't get any closer." I reached out to show the colonel.

He stared at the way my hand—seemingly solid, more or less, if ghostly—started to fuzz and break down as I reached further toward the heart of the distortion.

"You see that?" I asked him. "I *need* to know, Colonel...I need to know what's in there, how many, and why."

"I can't discuss it with you," he said again woodenly, before leaving the dungeon sense.

"Motherfucker!" I whispered, staring in disbelief at the space he'd occupied. "That's it, I'm gonna hang him."

"You can't and you know it," Kelly snapped. "Matt, this is serious."

"You think I'm not?" I muttered, before turning back to stare into the darkness ahead with the other two. "What do we do?" I asked at almost the same time the other two asked me the same question.

"We leave the colonel," Kelly said suddenly. "If it's an oath and one that's magically enforced, like John's are, then if he tries to break it, it'll kill him before he can. He was right to leave. And we can already see everything that we need to. There's shit in there we don't like, but more importantly, we need to deal with it."

"We keep this quiet," Aly said after a few seconds where we all looked at one another in dismay. "We've got healing magic, all right, so we don't need to worry about the bioweapons. We just need to kill the queen and get back out."

"And the nukes?" I asked disbelievingly. "That's what this has to be, you realize that, yeah?"

"What?" Kelly shook herself free of whatever dark thoughts she'd been wrapped up in.

"The distortion." I waved a hand at it. "It has to be the nukes, something that's fighting against the dungeon's influence. I mean, it can't be a bioweapon that's doing this, right?"

"It could be an ability," Aly suggested. "I mean, it could, couldn't it? The queen could have some ability that stops us observing her?"

"Probably," I admitted after a few seconds. "No clue what, though. And if she's aware enough to be choosing passive abilities like that, then we're in for a world of hurt."

"So what's changed?" Kelly asked.

"Uh…" I gestured in the direction of all that shit, and she shook her head, ponytail bouncing.

"As far as we're concerned, *nothing* has changed," she repeated. "We can't get any closer than this? Fine. We still need to find and save Mike and our people. We can't see what's going on in there, not from here, so the best thing we can do is deal with what we do know about, and make a plan to deal with this."

"Fire," Aly suggested. "We might not be able to get any closer in reality, but there's a slope here."

She indicated the way that the corridor was still canted slightly downward. "How about we get a load of barrels of flammable fuel, some of the incendiary grenades you liked, Matt, and we throw them in?"

"We don't know who might be down there," I pointed out.

"If the nuclear matter is pure enough that it's affecting us in the dungeon sense from here, and there's bioweapons in there, I think it doesn't matter," she said.

"No human could survive it, not for long, and even if they did, they'd be dying slowly. We can't risk anything escaping, so how about this? We roll the fuel down and set it off. If the distortion field stops, and we burn them all? Great. We can go in, in the dungeon sense, and check it out.

"If it doesn't work, though, we build a barrier, ten meters thick and with a shitload of lead in it. Then we encircle this whole area, and you can put Fire converters in and make lava or something. Let it all burn."

"Magma," I replied absently, thinking it through.

"What?" Aly asked.

"Magma… it's magma underground, lava above." I shrugged at the look Kelly was giving me. "What, I'm a massive nerd. You knew this."

"You really are. Can we do that?" she asked me after a long look, and I nodded.

"Yeah, actually, it's probably the best method to deal with it all," I admitted.

"Okay, well, with the—" That was as far as she got, before Clarissa popped in, startling us all.

"We've found them."

CHAPTER TWENTY-FIVE

It was heartbreaking to see.

Mike, Jo, Griffiths—hell, dozens of our friends could be seen easily from here, all standing, swaying slowly as if pushed past utter exhaustion. They gathered together, along with over a thousand other living creatures, and each and every one of them were infected.

As soon as we saw them, Aly let out a scream, rushing forward, reaching out to Mike, and Kelly collapsed to her knees. Her hands covered her mouth in horror, tears already starting from red-rimmed eyes.

Mike stood like a zombie in one of those old movies, staring straight ahead, unseeing in the darkness of a huge warehouse.

He was dressed in his full gear; though his backpack was gone, he still had his rifle. Dried blood covered one side of his face, leading in a crusted mess from his right ear.

He had no helmet, and it was clear from the state of his armor and clothes that the worms had no clue about bodily eliminations or cleaning.

Standing with him on all sides were hundreds of others. Many were human, but just as many clearly weren't. And some were badly mutated.

The humans, it seemed, were some kind of favored class, as the vast majority were left as human as possible.

Others, though—the cows especially—were only identifiable by the tattered skins that had once covered their bones.

Now great tentacles and chitin-tipped claws erupted here and there. Some rested on a single massive foot that had grown from the stomach, something like a slug's, while others stood atop a dozen smaller spider-like limbs.

Again and again, I saw what looked to have been settled upon as a preferred design. Their bodies were covered in pulsating, fleshy tentacles that sagged now, but looked to be able to whip and thrash with incredible speed and strength.

The cows' eyes had been replaced by clusters of smaller, insect-like ones grouped together seemingly without rhyme or reason, but granting them 360-degree vision. Their mouths were mutated into gaping maws filled with rows of jagged teeth, perfect for tearing flesh from bone, and great tendrils of saliva had drooped and pooled from them.

Looking around, I saw maws that slowly dripped out blood and mucus; pus and saliva were common. Worst of all were what had once been pets.

I saw a small dog, something that had to have been a much-loved member of the family, gasping. Its eyes bulged from their sockets, the neck grown impossibly thick, and a stylized choke-chain driven deep into the meat of it.

It was embossed with fake jewels, and proudly proclaimed Muffy to be the "best dog in the world," even as it choked him—or her—to death.

More and more, I saw that "man's best friend" had become a nightmarish predator. Dozens of different breeds, most probably freed from kennels right here in the base, had been warped into quadrupedal horrors, their bodies elongated and their limbs bent at unnatural angles. They glowed in the darkness, their fur replaced with a thick, leathery hide that pulsed with bioluminescent patterns, while others lay on the floor, dead or dying.

I moved through the mass of bodies, finding one woman who had apparently walked in on a badly broken leg, before collapsing and slipping free of the nightmare. Her compound fracture had been worn to a nub, and a trail of blood she'd left behind showed that the queen couldn't care less about the individuals who made up her army.

Horses, once symbols of grace and beauty, were now perverted into towering, centaur-like beings. Their upper bodies were vaguely humanoid, with long, sinewy arms that ended in scythe-like claws, while smaller arms that jutted from the stomach were covered in something that looked like thin tentacles.

The remains of clothing on some of the bodies told the tale that they'd possibly started out as two separate creatures and had been melded together, somehow.

The horses' heads were replaced with bulging, chitin-like craniums, complete with compound eyes and twitching antennae. And their legs? They looked almost comical, the muscle that had once been slim and graceful now bulging and mismatched.

Hundreds of the bodies, perhaps thousands, bore the twin markings of frostbite and mold. Fungus that had apparently been in the process of colonizing those all around us was only stopped in the process of inflicting death by the cold instead.

Necrosis was everywhere, and the more I looked, the more alarmed I became by it all.

I turned slowly, details blurring as I saw the true horror of the coronaughts. For long seconds, I couldn't decide whether this was something we could actually fight.

Something that had such a level of control over the creatures around it, such a spreading horror and adaptability… We'd faced this before in the coronaughts in the center of Newcastle: the old Idols bar had been burned to the ground to make sure we got the fucker and rooted out the infection. But what I was seeing here was that it had been a tiny, tiny fraction of the true evil.

I had to hope, desperately pray, that the ones I fought before, as strong and potentially deadly as they had been, were actually an offshoot of this same hive.

If not? If there were separate infections springing up everywhere, I genuinely didn't know what we could do.

They might not be spreading as quickly, if they'd found places with less mana or a smaller breeding pool and more threats. But the possibility that I'd faced two unconnected hives so close together?

Statistically, that meant that there could already be a population in the country alone that was in the millions.

Billions worldwide.

The only thing that might have given us a goddamn chance was the onset of this unseasonably early and harsh winter.

I stared for long seconds, until I felt a hand on my physical shoulder, a hand that shook me and drew me out of the dungeon.

I blinked, looking up at Chris, who stood over me.

"What's up?" I croaked, before swallowing hard, then straightening as I saw his face.

"You need to take charge," he said.

"What?"

"People are scared, mate."

"Fucking hell, of course they are," I agreed. "I'm one of them!"

"You can't be," he said quickly, shaking his head. "Matt, we're fucked if this goes on. If this spreads, if we lose heart, we're fucked—not just as a group, but as a species. You can't let that happen."

"Jesus Chris—" I started.

"Close—I've got a beard, yeah, but I'm sexier," he replied without breaking eye contact. "That's not the point, though. If we can't win this fight now, then we need to run, and I don't mean to fucking Newcastle and hole up. I mean pick the dungeon up and run, or start doing a full new underground society and hiding away forever."

"We can win," I said slowly. "What's got you so spooked?"

"You know as well as I do." He snorted. "If the winter hadn't killed a shitload of the worms off, we'd have had no chance getting this close. And by this time next year? Fuck no…Britain will be an island of the dead."

"I know, but—"

"No." He stared down at me, as I still lay in my hammock. "My point is that I can think that, and I can see the threat, but you can't."

"I can see it, believe me."

"No, man. You, Matt? You can see it, sure, but the fucking Dungeon Lord of Newcastle can't!" he snapped. "That's the point. Dammit, I should have explained it better, but everyone's panicking, all right? We're all seeing that, and it's like, all right, we can do this… But when you start thinking of the possibilities, of the possible other areas this shit could be going on?

"People are freaking out, and if you don't nip it in its arse right now, they're gonna start running. Aly's screaming and having a breakdown. Kelly can't speak for tears. Half our people are in there…our friends from the dungeon are right there. People are looking at them and for the first time they're seeing we could lose, so get your fucking arse in there again and make it work!"

I stared at him for a brief second, then cursed and laid back. My mind raced, realizing that we'd be losing support by the second as people considered how to get out of here.

"Back me up," was all I said to him. But I saw the answering nod as he dropped down onto the floor, shoving the door closed and stretching out in here instead, his words the last thing I heard as I closed my eyes.

"Always, brother."

I dove back into the dungeon sense, rocketing across to the warehouse. More and more of our citizens who had access were there, hundreds of them, staring in horror, as wails and panicked shouting filled the ether.

Someone had spread the word, and every second, people popped in from the dungeon or from Saltwell Park, searching for their friends, their family.

I saw what he was saying now. He'd been trying to make me see, to shake me out of the head fuck I'd been in, and it was almost too late already. I could practically feel my support base eroding away as people saw their loved ones standing in there, being consumed and puppeted by the coronaught.

"That's it, everyone!" I barked. My authority as the Dungeon Lord dragged everyone inside the dungeon sense to me. I yanked them all back, forming them into a wailing, confused mass that congregated outside the dungeon as it was, currently in Newcastle, to the east, where twice now the walls had been shattered and cast down.

"SILENCE!" I roared. The shouts, the demands, and the cries died away to a low buzz. That was the best I could hope for, I sensed, and I forged on, before I could lose the momentary respite.

"We're launching the attack in thirty minutes!" I shouted. "Access to the northern dungeon area is locked down. None of you, save the leadership team or those who are already organized with a specific role to play can access it..."

That started a rising roar of panic as people feared losing access to find or see their loved ones.

"SHUT IT!" That was Chris, bellowing out across the mass. "HE'S TRYING TO EXPLAIN, SO SHUT THE FUCK UP!"

"Distractions by anyone who's not there for a strategic reason might be why people die," I said flatly. "When the fighting starts, I'll set a section away that you can watch it from, but you'll be above and apart from the fight. If you try to interact, if you try to interrupt or get involved, if you fucking distract us, when we're fighting and trying to save lives, I will ban EVERYONE. So, if you're a fighter, if you're involved in this, then gather with me in the council chamber. If you're not and you want to help, even a little? Get out there and tear the scrap piles apart. Every single point of mana you can get us is going to matter in this fight!"

With that, and before they could do anything, I gestured out around us. "Remember this!" I bellowed. "Remember the times these walls fell, the people who died here, fighting to protect us all, and remember that we're still here! We're here because we don't panic, because we fight and we win. So take a long look around and pull your fucking finger out of your asses. We've got a fight to win, and friends to save."

With that, I flexed a mental muscle and the dungeon around me blurred. A half second later, I stood by the table in the council chamber, staring down at it as people arrived, taking up spaces around me and the table.

I hesitated, then glanced over at Chris.

He caught my look, frowned, then winked, gesturing in a circle with one finger extended. "You want me to watch over the meeting?"

"Kick any lookie-loos out," I agreed. "Any you see, cut off their access entirely for now. We can deal with shit later."

"On it." That was all he said, then he vanished.

251

As he did, I crossed one more issue off my mental list, knowing he was off checking the nearby rooms, making sure nobody was trying to get in.

To my right were Kelly and Aly. Both looking tear-streaked, horrified, and resolute, even if they were clearly barely upright.

To my left were Clarissa, Markus, and Barry. Beyond them on both sides were Finn, Tulio, and a handful of the team from the older meetings, as well as Ashley and Dante. Across from me, on the far side of the table, spread out and seemingly ill at ease, were the colonel, the sarge, Reed, and Finger, waiting for orders.

"All clear," Chris said after a second, before fixing Ashley with an annoyed look. "Your friends Jenn and Emma are gonna be pissed. I had to boot them out."

"Fucking idiots." She cursed, looking mortified as she turned to me. "I'm so sorry. I'll deal with them."

"Do that," I said grimly, tamping down the surge of anger, even as I understood it. Their husbands—the man mountains that were Andre and Jimmy—hadn't been found yet, so I couldn't blame them for searching and wanting to hear it from us first.

"First step," I said loudly, looking around. "We've got no time, and with everyone panicking, we can't hold this off longer without things coming apart here as well. So the assault is starting early. Half an hour—that's all the time I think we can safely take before anyone can do anything to fuck it up. I'm only holding off that long because we need to summon more undead, and we desperately need the time to cheat."

"Cheat how?" Aly wiped her face.

"By being the sneakiest fuckers in the game," I said with an evil grin. "Colonel, as we discussed, you're to watch, and point out issues you see. Don't fucking interrupt unless you seriously need to. But this is a watch and learn situation. If you see an improvement you can make, speak up by all means. But if you interrupt to fuck with my people, you'll be evicted, understood? I don't have time to deal with anyone playing games or trying to undercut me."

"As you say, Dungeon Lord," he replied formally—which could be agreement, or a shitty way of saying "what*ever*" like a '90s girl movie, I guessed.

"Markus, you have the northwest, so get it moving. I need you to clear it out and capture anything and anyone you can. When it comes to the monsters? Kill them. Don't try to capture and take them to be healed—it's a waste of mana. Humans only, and any of our kobolds, etc., obviously."

I'd not seen any, but I had to hope they were still there.

"Barry, you've got the northeast, twelve around to five o'clock. Leave the admin buildings and shit until we can get to them. I don't see them being as full as the rest, but I could be totally wrong. I'll raise two healing towers in the agreed locations."

We'd already mapped out locations as part of the plan. As soon as things started to kick off, the healing towers would rise there, ready to act as fallback positions for the living, and for the undead to bring their captives to and have them hopefully cleansed of the infection.

"On that note, Matt." Clarissa spoke up, and I glared at her for interrupting, before smoothing my face and nodding. "Just a thought, but you said that likely most of the healed people will be exhausted and unconscious afterward?"

"Yeah?"

"Perhaps a building where the undead could lay them out to recover? One with solid walls and a light inside, as well as a sign or something that they're safe? Just in case they wake?"

"The building, yes," I agreed, wishing I'd thought of it. "The rest, as and when we can afford it, all right? And it needs to be made strong enough to hold the worms off if they try to retake them, or to kill them."

"Won't the towers…?" She started, before nodding as she realized the truth. "The towers won't see them as an issue; it's when they start damaging the humans that they'll be seen as an infection to be cured again. Thank you," she murmured.

"Right, moving on. I'll lead the team that'll take on the warehouse." I noted the way that everyone stiffened. "I'll not be there in the flesh," I said quickly, seeing the headshakes that were already starting, and smiled grimly.

"I know you were all thinking I'd just run in and start hitting shit. Well, that's fine when there's something to be gained by that happening. And yeah, when the fight with the queen comes, I'll probably need to do that. For now, though, it's a remote fight. We guide; we watch and lead. We let the undead take the injuries, and we've got a better chance of winning this.

"Clarissa, Finn, Tulio?" I glanced at them, making sure they were ready. "I need you working with your people. Clarissa, you're support for Markus—Tulio, for Barry."

"And me?" Finn asked, looking uncertain.

I forced myself to nod again. "You're with me. But Finn?"

"Yeah?"

"Patrick is going to be okay, or he's not. You stay with me and you do what I can't, all right? The best way you can help him is to use your skills to build what I need, and to help me capture and secure the spaces around us."

"And us?" Kelly asked me, clearly meaning her and Aly.

"Aly is going to manage the mana flow and make damn sure that we can build the healing towers when we need them. God, that name is so stupid…" I muttered.

"We've not got enough mana," Aly replied suddenly, her eyes wide. "We were still at the spending to expand our influence stage, the research has barely been completed, and—"

"How much do we have?" I asked.

"Five hundred and fourteen thousand points."

"That's plenty, isn't it?" Markus frowned. "We were only going to be spending five hundred, right?"

"No, no, not at all!" Aly groaned. "The healing towers cost fifty thousand each, and that's to *build*, not to run. When they start running, they're going to take up all the mana we can generate and more."

"And that's why we cut the forces we're taking in," I said. "Kelly, you're the Mistress of Minions. The majority of our people, and we think the colonel's people as well, are in that warehouse. You'll be helping us all to guide the undead. I know we'd expected to have more forces and multiple teams. Instead, I think we're each going to be guiding a specific set. These four"—a set of four of the locations we'd picked out as the summoning points for the undead pulsed, closest to the warehouse—"will be under my direct control."

I gestured to the table. It changed to show one of the locations: a long, narrow room, four meters wide, three high, and twenty long. In it, there were already sixty skeletons in the room, along with a single wraith lord that stood ready to lead them. But as I gestured to it, that began to change.

"We've barely had time to summon half the forces we wanted," I explained, "and we've not got them located where we wanted either, but shit happens, so here's the new plan.

"I'm going to run these four, and I'm going to summon more undead into these rooms as soon as the first ones leave. Before, I'd been intending on each of us commanding multiple columns or so, each of which could be commanded by a wraith lord, and with nearly four hundred in a section. Now, we're going with the 'summon as you go' method…at least, until the dungeon stops us.

"In a space this large, as it's underground and away from any direct contact with the enemy, I should be able to fit in nearly two hundred undead, along with a single wraith." As I spoke, they'd already started to appear.

I looked around and went on. "We didn't have the time or the opportunity to get everything done that we wanted to, so the new complement, for me at least— you all do you—is going to be two hundred standard skeletons, led by a wraith lord, with ten regular wraiths under it to provide firepower and mobility. Then, because we're going to need to be both hard-hitting and fast, I think ten corpse lords."

"What's the difference in cost for that?" Aly asked for the others, as she was clearly already doing the math by the look on her face.

"The original cost, for each of us to have six or so wraith lords, was sixty thousand for them. Then we were each getting two and a half thousand soldiers— that came to another hundred thousand. Instead, because we've not got the time to set up the extra spaces to summon underground, and we'd need to waste a fuckload of time to go farther out…"

"Can't you just summon more in the same spaces when they move?" the colonel asked gruffly.

"No. We can't rely on that now," I replied. "Once we're in a fight, the dungeon area becomes contested. Anything that's too close to the fighting is locked out, so, we're looking at securing the area first. The original cost was about a hundred and sixty thousand mana each for the three teams.

"Now, with four sets of two hundred skeletons coming in at thirty-two thousand, the wraith lord at ten thousand, and the ten lower-level wraiths, say uncommon at a thousand each, that's another ten. Then ten corpse lords at twenty thousand more in total, we've got…"

"Seventy-two thousand," Kelly said, as she was apparently faster at math than me.

"Less than half the cost, but can you do it with that?" the colonel asked.

"That gives us two hundred and sixteen thousand, and with the mana that's coming in, it gives us enough for four healing towers," Aly pointed out.

"I'd rather summon that for each contingent, as we'd planned, and have the two hundred undead in each bunker of four, with them, then the wraiths, the ten corpse lords and the single advanced wraith lord, but that's not going to happen," I said grimly. "That'd cost a lot more—"

"A hundred and ninety-two mana," Kelly interjected, having clearly worked the figures out just in case.

"Yeah." I shrugged. "But, we can do it with this, *if we cheat*," I repeated. "This is the plan…"

CHAPTER TWENTY-SIX

We'd had to allow a dozen more of our people to flit about the area. Explaining their roles to them had taken some time, but by the time we reached the kickoff for the fight—forty-seven minutes later, but it wasn't like the enemy was timing us—they struck, all at once.

Across the base, the sappers—as we were calling them—all leapt into action. I got a mental peck on my cheek, and then I left Aly and Kelly to watch over the overall battle, while I took direct control over my smaller teams.

My four "storage areas"—each of which held two hundred undead soldiers, along with the rest of the forces spread out among them—had been created as literal boxes. They were similar in shape to a shipping container—if larger—and between them and the ground level was a ramp, ready to drop for them to charge up and out.

At "go-time," one end of the ramp dropped, leading from the ground above down to the entrance of the container, and the undead started to stream toward the fight.

As soon as they moved out, making room, fresh motes began to congregate behind them, printing more and more dungeon creatures. The first of the ten uncommon wraiths were already racing forward at the heels of the departing skeletons, even as the first corpse lord began to appear.

The advanced wraith led the way out into what was currently gently drifting snow. That snow that was up to knee-high almost everywhere you looked, but where they appeared was at the south end of a huge parking lot.

The warehouse lay at the north end, a recently—in terms of army buildings—completed and cavernous structure that held most of our people. I was determined to get as close to it as possible before starting the construction of the healing tower.

The infected—as we were increasingly coming to call the humans under the queen coronaught's control—were armed still, and they apparently could use those weapons, suggesting at least some muscle memory, if nothing else.

That meant that if they saw the healing tower rising, and thought about it in time, they might blow the fucker up—which meant it needed to be built back outside of their sight and reach.

It couldn't be too far, though, so we'd come up with an easy solution.

The walls of the warehouse were sheet metal, but we'd guessed at them not being that thick or strong, so the four sappers on my team were split into two groups.

One would be reinforcing the walls of the warehouse, to prevent breakout anywhere we couldn't handle, while the other would be sealing up every way in and out of it, except for the south doors.

That southern exit, they'd rip open, pulling the whole thing down, and the healing tower would be built as close to the western wall of the warehouse as possible, but on the *outside*, and out of sight.

I had a theory, one that I was increasingly sure would be proved right, that the limit for my building anything that the dungeon viewed as "mine" was going to be up to a section that was in contact with the warehouse as that was clearly an enemy structure.

So if the healing tower had a radius of say, ten meters for the AoE, then the closest the tower could be built to the warehouse was ten and a bit meters, so that the edges didn't touch.

I'd considered that until the first punch or whatever was thrown, the dungeon wasn't locking us out, so in theory I could probably summon a healing tower in the middle of the warehouse and just not power it yet...

Then I'd considered what the rest of the infected and all the monsters would likely do to the healing humans we were there to capture and save.

No, the best option was for the skeletons to capture and drag clear our people, and as soon as we could, we'd be building additional towers.

The plan, therefore, was for the enemy to be "managed" as best as possible.

The rest of the sappers, and mine, as soon as they were done with their job, were going to be working to seal entrances and exits from other enemy locations, hopefully slowing their advance and managing the paths they'd take.

They'd close off specific buildings, and force the enemy to attack us in waves, keeping us from being overrun, as we essentially worked to capture, subdue, and cart off the humans.

Each who could be carried to the healing towers would be. Then, once they were cured of the infection, they'd be moved into a storage area as we continued.

The plan was both elegant and simple, as the undead could be summoned as long as we had both the space and mana to do it. And if it cost us ten or a hundred undead per human to rescue them, it was worth it.

The enemy would grow weaker by the minute, and we'd be able to claim and secure territory, making it easier to summon more undead as we went.

Lastly, any dead or destroyed undead could be dragged back into our territory and absorbed to power the next wave.

It was a plan that had little that should go wrong, once we were in place, but we desperately needed to secure space to work. And that, of course, was where it all went Pete Tong.

As soon as the first wraith lord reached the outside and hovered there, the drifting snow clean and white against the ground, pristine and unsullied, it fucked the element of surprise right in the butthole. It paused, then screamed a challenge to the universe in general.

I froze as the entire camp turned from open and available for me to work in, to fucking locked down and bright goddamn red.

"ARE YOU FUCKING KIDDING ME!" I screamed in the dungeon sense at the dumbass bastard, who spun and cocked its head, apparently utterly unable to understand why I was annoyed.

257

"We're locked out!" Kelly called. "That stupid... Shit! Matt, we've got movement!"

The warehouse before us and presumably the other areas around the camp had started to buzz like a kicked anthill. I cursed as I realized that try as we might, the area that we could build was now reduced into a space no more than a meter from one of our undead. A distance that would only reduce as soon as the enemy was up close.

The people hovering above, watching, had already been forced back, as something in the dungeon's system now identified the enemy camp as a single location. One that we were not permitted into.

It was only goddamn luck that we were allowed close enough to command our minions.

"Fuck!" I grabbed my hair and pulled hard, before releasing it and taking a deep breath. My mind raced as I tried to figure it all out. "Fine. All forces, fall back on me. We're backing up and establishing a safe location. Sappers!" I felt them streaking toward me as I scanned the map. "Thirty meters back and ten to the east, I want a star fortification built there and—"

"Diamonds." The colonel was there by my side. "Sir, allow me to help. You need *diamonds*. They're cheaper and faster to build..."

"Do it!" I snapped after a brief hesitation. "Do it and don't forget the healing towers!"

"On it," he agreed.

I glanced ahead, already seeing the greater monsters bounding out of the warehouse.

The queen clearly guessed we were a threat, judging by the way everything was coming for us.

I barked out orders. "Wraiths! Fall back. Get your forces moving..."

"We need weapons." Kelly was there, and I nodded grimly.

"Yeah, spears and shields. We need to kill the monsters first."

That was a problem now, considering that the wraiths had magic, and the corpse lords were armed with hammers and shields, but the normal skeletons were unarmed. My plan had been that the skeletons were to basically mob the infected, grab them and run; the wraiths and corpse lords would use their magic and weapons to take down the monsters, and we'd summon more of what we needed on the fly.

The skeletons were to carry the infected to the healing towers, then pin them until the worms were burned out; then they'd run back and grab another.

It sounded stupid, basic as all hell, but if we'd been able to limit the numbers coming at us, that was all we needed.

I'd intended that we'd race as close as we could and form up. We'd start the building right next to the warehouses because that'd count as us claiming that space; then we'd be able to start building more from there.

Sure, there was the risk that waiting until the last second wouldn't work out, but as soon as we started building it, shit was going to kick off.

We'd needed to wait until our forces were moving, just in case this had happened and we'd been locked in, instead of locked out, but this was still an incredibly bad start to the fight.

"Don't you do it," Kelly whispered in my ear.

I sent her a mental peck on the cheek, not saying anything. She knew me too well. If the shit hit the fan? Yeah, I'd be going in.

For now, though, it was leadership time.

The corpse lords had already begun to be summoned so it allowed them to be completed, but I couldn't summon any more, not until I was on "safe" ground again. I snarled as I directed the wraiths to lead their forces back into the new defensive fortifications.

More and more of the enemy raced outward, and because I'd planned on the skeletons being used primarily to grab and run with the people they fought...they were unarmed and therefore pretty much useless in a fight against most of the monsters.

They were also a significant portion of the cost we'd just had to pay to kick the fight off, so we couldn't afford to lose them...

"Fuck!" I screamed, before taking a deep breath and looking at things as calmly as possible.

"Markus, Barry! Take your teams and loop around. Fall back on me. We already know that most of the people we need to save are here, so fuck it. Staying as we are would have worked if we could bottle them up. As it is, we're going to be defeated in detail."

"Got it. Pulling back." Barry grunted.

"Already engaged," Markus responded. "I can't pull loose—I don't think, anyway. Going to try to take the first target. Then, if the dungeon lets me, reinforce it, set up a tower, and start summoning reinforcements."

"Good plan," I agreed. "Good luck, Markus. I'll send Jack to you...use him to help break the line. Barry, can you make it to me?" I asked, changing the direction I had Jack heading. The massive automata had been planned to arrive once we were decisively engaged. I'd decided he would pound in from the side and take out anything we needed dead—they were flesh, after all, and he wasn't—but now he'd be more useful helping to hold what we had.

"Yeah, limited resistance here. We'd managed to close a few of the exits before the plan all went to shit, so we're moving now. What's the new plan? And is there any point or should we just accept it's 'make shit up as we go along'?"

"No plan survives contact with the enemy," the colonel muttered, and I nodded grimly.

"Okay, new plan is..." I checked, seeing the layout that the colonel was creating, and I nodded my approval. "Right. The colonel is creating diamonds."

There were five diamonds in the layout he'd suggested, and I frowned, looking them over, as a second alternative occurred to me.

They were laid out like on the playing card design, two-one-two, with each diamond being constructed with simple stone walls that rose to shoulder height.

That was it.

"Uh, not to tell you how to do your job, but a star..." I started, trying to figure out the reason for it, when he explained quickly.

"A star fort would be much better if we had ranged weapons, as it would be a larger wall. As it is, the walls will slow attackers, but those that can jump over will be able to.

"The diamond shape funnels the enemy into specific routes, and as soon as we have the mana, we can summon a healing tower in each diamond, giving us an overlapping field. The outside walls will be raised higher as soon as we have the mana as well, then angled outward to prevent anything climbing or jumping them.

"The inner paths that lead between the diamonds then slow the attackers. We can grab those we want and drag them over to hold. Those we want dead will be stabbed by spears that come out of the gaps here and here…"

I saw narrow slits carved in the walls that I'd not noticed before, and he went on.

"We can then leave the spears in them, forcing them to gut themselves to get away, or they're trapped in place." He gestured upward. "While that's hopefully slowing the big guys, these wraith things…you said they've got magic?"

"Necrotic bolt." I nodded. "They basically rot an enemy apart. Good call, but the enemy have assault rifles as well."

"We can duck," he replied simply. "If they use grenades, well, that's going to be an issue. But there's only so much I can fix on the fly."

"Fair point, and well done. If they do use grenades, dedicate one person to dealing with them. Grow a steel dome over them…fuck it. Okay, people, here's the new plan. Form up on me. We hold the diamonds, use them to bleed the monsters, and hopefully to waste the ammo that the soldiers have in the short term.

"As the diamonds are going to count as our territory, we should be able to summon inside them, so hold the outer wall, absorb anything we can, and start summoning inside. Then we build the healing towers and use them to take down the humans.

"Once they start to fall, we advance into the enemy and claim as much territory and rescue anyone we can. This fight just changed from a sprint to a marathon, but that's fine. We can do this," I finished.

"What do we do about the queen?" Kelly asked, appearing again at my shoulder.

"It was always going to come down to a fight with her. If we're lucky, we can find out what the hell is in there with her. If it's nothing we care about, we seal her up, apart from a small hole, and we pour napalm in."

"Cookout." Chris grunted. "That'll teach the bitch."

"Damn right." I nodded.

"Mind you, knowing the weird stuff you Americans eat, you'll try and eat it no doubt. What's it called? Gumbo?" He grinned at me, and I stared back.

"Showers," I said. "I foresee showers breaking in your future."

"Evil bastard."

"Love you too." I turned back to the streaming figures below me.

My forces were split in two now. The advanced wraith was leading the eight hundred skeletons in the direction of the diamonds, while the ten uncommon wraiths and the ten corpse lords stood beneath me, as the mass racing from the warehouse started to resolve into clear figures.

As they exited the building—some smashing their way out of goddamn windows and from other exits we'd not managed to seal yet—to loop around, they broke up into set ranks.

"That's not good." I grunted. "They're forming ranks and charging!"

The centaurs were in the lead, drawing ahead naturally due to their different speeds, but the monstrous cows were forming up between the humans and the rest.

Clearly, not only were they virtual biological battle tanks, they were to be bullet magnets as well.

Joke's on them, I thought. *We've not got the fucking bullets to waste.*

Between the centaurs and the cows came the dogs, running and staggering in untidy lines. Their massive jaws and tentacles dragged them off-balance with every step. One fell, rolled, and came to its feet again every few seconds, so frequently it seemed almost a design feature, rather than a flaw.

Then, behind the humans, streaming up from holes that had appeared and presumably led underground came the itopedes, making me curse all over again.

They were much slower than the others, but the humans were slowing for them, stepping aside to allow them through. I'd faced them before, back when I first met the Newcastle infestation of these fuckers, and I'd hoped they weren't here as well.

They had an ability called Mesmerize, I remembered, something that basically hypnotized people, letting them get close enough to capture their prey and…and I suddenly felt so much better as I saw the new way the lines were folding out.

The centaurs raced into the lead, then the dogs, then the cows, then the itopedes and then, and only then, the humans.

That meant the queen didn't understand what the undead were, nor what our plan was.

If she had, she'd have had the humans hammer us with bullets, then send in the rest to mop up. Instead, she was trying to run us down.

The centaurs could grab targets, but most likely they were to break our lines and do damage; then the dogs could do the same. Once they're down and our forces are battered, the bovine tanks soak up any damage we can deal out, and the itopedes mesmerize us, letting the humans come in and capture the survivors.

It'd work on humans well, I reflected. The undead? Not so much.

"Chris, I need you to watch over them. Back out as far as you can from the fight and watch things from above. Make sure they're not flanking us with a second force, or that there's nothing else incoming."

"On it." He flitted away.

"Okay, here we go," I whispered, spreading them out—the wraiths in the air, and the corpse lords standing a few meters apart—getting ready.

The centaur-looking motherfuckers were in the lead, outdistancing the others, and I squinted, examining them.

Centaur Coronaught	Mutated Creature
Coronaughts are unusual and frequently deadly predators that are often underestimated. The true coronaught is a parasitic vurm less than three inches long; however, they are naturally transgenic and as they grow, they collect mass as well as genetic templates.	
The centaur variant appears to have originated from equine lines, and has been forcibly evolved for running down prey for the hive.	

Coronaughts are often underestimated because in their most basic state they are simple creatures to defeat, needing only a high-enough-pitched sound to render them immobile.

Beware: To combat this weakness, as the coronaught evolves, many discard any and all auditory functions.

Shock:

The centaur variant has developed the ability to unload high-voltage shocks to their victims, through the lower "false hands" and their attached cilia.

Burst: For brief periods, the centaur can focus additional energy into its limbs, highly increasing its maximum speed, at the cost of long-term survivability. Note: This ability will render the centaur sluggish upon expiry, and greatly reduces its reaction speed.

Weaknesses: Fire, Death, and Metal Magics

HP: 700/700

Stamina: 1500/1500

Mana: 0/0

Speed 9/10

Level: 7

HP: 700/700	Special Abilities: 6/6

"Okay, people, heads up," I said quickly. "The centaurs have a shock ability. Basically, they grab you and unleash a fuckload of it to stun their prey. They can supercharge their sprints, but it tires them out fast and makes them sluggish after."

As I said it, I started to work on a counter, grinning evilly as I did. I barely had the time to do it, and I really didn't have the mana to waste, but fuck it, I couldn't resist.

I created a dip in the ground, six inches deep and the same wide, then ran it in front of my forces, running left to right, half again as long as the force I was holding here.

Then I repeated it six inches farther out, and another six inches after that.

The end result was something like a cattle grid, but large enough that anyone wearing shoes would have a reasonable chance to step over it. Anything with hooves, though, was going to have issues.

I ordered the corpse lords to hold until the centaurs got closer. Then they were to step back as if retreating, leaving a handful of meters between the centaurs and the corpse grid, as I now decided it was called.

"Those bugs…" I called out, watching the incoming army. "They can mesmerize you, or hypnotize or whatever. If they start dancing, don't look, but the undead should be fine."

I pulled the itopedes' data up as well, then cycled through the others. There was nothing out of the ordinary for any of them; each save the humans had a shock ability. I bet the humans would have had, if they weren't armed to the fucking teeth instead.

Still, the queen had a lot to learn, I guessed, as the corpse lords started to move, and the wraiths each summoned a Deathbolt, ready to throw.

"Hold…" I whispered. "Wait for it…"

I glanced inward, searching out my link to Jack. He was already accepting orders from Markus, cutting through several of his own monstrous foes.

"Wait…" I muttered, switching back.

The centaurs suddenly blurred, clearly activating their ability. The nearly thirty, in a mixture of sizes and shapes, started screaming forward. Their hooves sent sparks flying and the clatter across the parking lot grew louder by the second.

"Wait for it…" I whispered, not considering that the undead weren't nervous, but I sure as shit was. I added a single order to the wraith lord to add its grasp of the Grave spell to the trap.

The last few long-abandoned cars, parked between them and my forces, were passed by. I glanced back. The running undead behind me were two-thirds of the way to the diamonds by now; I turned back and blew out a long breath.

"Now!" I shouted, and the first cast spells howled their passage to the enemy.

CHAPTER TWENTY-SEVEN

The Deathbolts tore through the air, aimed at the leading legs of the centaurs. The corpse lords backed up quickly—their long legs covered the meters easily—before they crouched. A series of small spikes jutted from the ground a meter ahead of them, and right between the corpse grid and them.

"Just a little help…" Finn muttered, and I grinned, as the centaurs encountered my little surprise.

The best bit about the corpse grid? It was buried in the snow.

That meant that the centaurs had no warning, no chance nor reason to avoid it. The first hooves slammed into the gaps, plunged down and caught. A quarter-second later, the popping sound of legs breaking in their dozens filled the air, even as ghostly hands lashed up and latched onto them.

Most lost their grip almost instantly, the speed being too much, but it was enough. Their phantom forms burst and dissipated into corpse-lights.

The centaurs' speeding bodies transformed into hundreds of kilos of hurtling mutated meat. Others flipped end over end, bouncing, crashing and rolling.

"Well done!" I called to Finn. The incoming tidal wave of meat then hit the spiked wall and slammed to a halt, and damn was I glad he'd had the foresight to think about that.

Then I was issuing more orders. The corpse lords stepped back up to the line, driving fists and claws down, tearing their enemies apart.

Not all the centaurs were caught. A small handful had made it through the gauntlet, or the angle they'd been coming in at was oblique enough that they managed to clear or leap the now exposed trap.

They rammed into the corpse lords, each vaulting at them and sending several of their opponents crashing to the ground, bones splintering.

Others leapt straight into massive boney fists coming the other way; their bodies ripped apart in hellish meetings of muscle and mass.

The corpse lords fought and bit, and the centaurs responded in kind, before unleashing their shock attack. Where a living creature might have been paralyzed, though, the undead merely hissed in fury and pummeled them harder.

While that was going on, the wraiths were casting. Deathbolts screamed through the air again, this time into the oncoming mutated canines.

The dogs began weaving back and forth, but fully a third of the wave were hit. Seven of them were struck full-on by the wraiths' necrotic energy.

They faltered, their flesh already sloughing free, rotting as muscles broke, eyes rotted, and tendons snapped. The other fifteen kept coming, winding through the second wave of flung spells, then bounding through the corpse grid.

Where the centaurs had hit it full speed, the dogs clearly took its positioning into account and adjusted, jumping over it.

Most made it, though two didn't. One leapt too early and landed inside the farthest edge, front legs snapping instantly. And the other skidded on some ice and slid straight into it.

That left thirteen to leap at ten corpse lords, seven of which were still standing, while three battled on the ground.

Fists flew, smashing the dogs from the air, but each impact, although killing the dog, staggered the corpse lord. Two more fell, crashing to the ground with limbs broken free. Those that stayed on their feet were damaged, most losing a limb or covered in radiating fractures.

The wraiths cast again, this time ignoring the dogs, as the corpse lords worked to finish them off. Instead, they fired one after the other of their Deathbolts into the oncoming next wave: cows.

Again they struck with visible effects: the frost-bitten flesh that covered these living tanks was blue with cold, bruised and torn, but where the necrotic energy hit, it blackened instantly.

The flesh failed, pocking inward and running; pus streamed free. Legs collapsed under the running monstrosities. Heads rotted away, eyes withering. And one after another, the mountains of flesh fell, to lie still.

That was the end of the free XP though, as the racing itopedes came into view.

They raced forward, giant centipedes that ranged from a meter to almost two long. Side to side, they came in lines, their heads barely lifted from the snow. Thousands of chitinous legs clacked down as they approached, maws like a sinkhole given teeth and a terrible hunger…but over their heads, as the wraiths prepared to cast again, came the gunfire.

Bullets ripped through the wraiths, dozens hitting each, even as hundreds missed—and that was just the first volley. Thousands more came after, as the humans marching in a mass fired again and again.

Their front line was thirty or more strong. As they ran out of ammunition, they simply stepped to the right; the lines opened, and the next row pushed forward, firing in their place.

As the rifles ran dry, another took their place, then another. The "empties" didn't reload; instead, they simply moved to the rear of the pack and continued marching.

That was a small relief, that they didn't appear interested—or able—to reload, but all the wraiths were torn from the sky, and most of the corpse lords fell as well.

Of the ten that had started the fight, two were still alive —or functional, anyway. I grinned evilly as I ordered them to activate an ability I'd not had them use in a while.

Raise! _The Corpse Lord can sacrifice its own health to raise the dead around it, replenishing its master's forces when needed._

The mass of dead flesh on all sides suddenly quivered. A sickly green wash of energy rolled out from both creations. Then they fell still, as I sent them very clear orders, before flitting back from them, headed to the diamonds.

It took two full minutes for the humans and itopedes to reach the line. And as soon as they did, the enemy started to rise again—though, this time, they turned on their former allies.

The itopedes were the closest. The remains of dogs leapt up, biting down hard; their mangled, overgrown teeth crunched through carapace.

The centaurs rolled over, bones jutting from shattered legs, but their bladed arms flashed out, rising and falling as they carved into their victims.

A single cow twisted and rolled on the outer edge of the corpse lord's field of effect. Claws that should have been on nothing living on land lunged free, latching onto the nearest bug, snipping it in half—before, in turn, the undead were overrun.

More bullets crashed into their resurrecting ranks, shattering bones and robbing them of their second, or possibly third, lives.

"That was…effective." The colonel shook his head next to me. "With twenty undead, you managed to remove what, a hundred?"

"With the element of surprise, sure." I grunted, as I hovered with him, in the dungeon sense, over the central diamond. "We spent it, though, and now the real fight begins."

"Well, that's life as a soldier." He gestured to the walls that were rising still. "You took down their cavalry. Now it's slogging through to take the majority of their forces."

"True, but don't forget the advantages we have."

"I count three," he said after a brief hesitation. "Defensive fortifications, reinforcements, and the healing towers. Normally I'd include morale, but that's not a factor for either side. And their weaponry is a significant force multiplier, one that's not going to be entirely offset by the fortifications."

"I was thinking of terrain." I smiled.

"We're on flat ground, but… I suppose, in theory, we could lift the fortification?" He rubbed at his chin. "I don't see the advantage. We could have increased the size of the walls at any time. I thought we were keeping them low for the opportunity to slow the enemy, so that the undead could grapple and capture them?"

"We are," I agreed. "But we can build, or more to the point, *burrow*, up to ten feet from any of our forces, provided what we're touching isn't in contact with the enemy."

"Go on," he said slowly, adjusting the walls and raising the section he'd left lowered to allow the undead to enter.

"We burrow under them, then hollow out a space, and fill it with more undead. Then we give them a ramp up and out and have them attack from the rear," I suggested.

"They'll be cut down as soon as they appear, and it'll allow them entry to the diamonds," he countered. "Without defenses, their fire will tear through the ranks, unless they can be brought up right at the rear. And even then, most likely their companions will fire on them and kill their captured brothers."

"You're still thinking of both sides as people," I said. "Ours can all be lost—to the last one, if need be. All it costs us is time. But theirs?"

"I know what you're saying, but if they get into the diamonds, we can't summon more undead. We lose that facility, we lose the fight. Sure, we can come back again later, but any humans we've managed to save will be either recaptured or killed. We can't take the risk."

"The rear soldiers are unarmed," I said quickly. "I know what you're thinking—that if they're captured, they're still lost, but the wraiths come with another useful spell. *Shield.*"

As I spoke, I checked the mana available to the dungeon, and cursed.

"Or they would, if we could afford to summon any," I corrected.

"What were you thinking?"

"Simple. We send the undead through tunnels behind them, have them pop up and grab people, and then have the wraiths form shields around their target. That protects them as they're carried into the tunnels, and wastes the enemy's ammo advantage as well."

"Not a bad plan." After a few seconds, he said, "But perhaps needlessly expensive."

"Go on..."

The humans and the remaining surviving itopedes hit the first diamond as we talked, and it felt damn surreal watching them. I couldn't help but look for the people I knew, seeing, then being forced to look away from Mike as he strode forward, his rifle raised.

He fired over and over. The bullets, like those of the infected marching by his side, slammed into the walls and undead repeatedly.

"Damn," I muttered, seeing how quickly the stone walls were being worn away. "That's...not good."

"Definitely not," the colonel agreed, glaring at the incoming soldiers and civilians as if they personally offended him. "At this rate...the walls are likely to fail before the remaining healing towers come online."

The first, in the central and largest of the diamonds, was already standing tall, but the AoE was...well, it was crap, frankly.

The spell tower was fixed and it was doing well. The idea was solid and the potential was massive, but it was a botched-together system and the enemy would not be inside its AoE until they practically cleared the damn wall.

The others were slightly smaller and they'd have the AoE projecting out a little over the edges of their walls, meaning that they should mesh together between the diamonds and have a solid effect on the incoming enemy.

That was the theory, and it should work well, or so I hoped—right up until a new enemy joined the fray.

They came from the middle of the base. Barry's forces fell to it, as his force of mainly standard skeletons was taken from behind and above as they exited the trees. They had been streaming toward the diamonds from the east, as the infected bunched up around them from the north.

Instead of wandering obligingly into the middle of the diamonds, the infected stood well back and pounded them with concentrated fire.

That shouldn't have been an issue, considering they didn't seem to have figured out how to reload—until you realized that there were over a thousand of them.

That many rifles all blasting away were tearing the walls down. And because the bullets hitting them counted as them being in contact with the enemy, we couldn't repair them.

Barry's forces raced to flank the infected, and I'd started to think that might work out nicely, right up until Chris shouted a warning.

"Incoming!" he bellowed, flitting back to me. "They just burst out of the forest. They must have been hiding and…"

That was as far as he got before I saw what he was talking about.

The new force was a nightmare given form and flesh. They boiled out of the trees where they'd been hidden, launching into the sky in their hundreds, before diving to slam into the running undead. They shattered bone and ripped free skulls and limbs.

Searching them, using my spell, I swore.

Spawnskull Coronaught	Mutated Creature

Coronaughts are unusual and frequently deadly predators that are often underestimated. The true coronaught is a parasitic vurm less than three inches long; however, they are naturally transgenic and as they grow, they collect mass as well as genetic templates.

The spawnskull variant appears to have originated from avian, and specifically the Laridae genus. They have been forcibly evolved to provide huge quantities of biomass for the hive, as well as to provide perimeter security.

The spawnskull has a unique attack: they will frequently swoop in, using its razor-sharp beak and talons to rend and tear at its victim, allowing the parasitic worms within to burrow into wounds of the unfortunate prey.

Coronaughts are often underestimated because they are simple creatures to defeat, needing only a high-enough-pitched sound to render them immobile.

Beware: To combat this weakness, as the coronaught evolves, many discard any and all auditory functions.

Infliction:

The spawnskull gestates vurm in specialist pouches dedicated to the ability, and depending on the needs of the hive, will turn on one another, tearing their brethren limb from limb and scattering the vurms held within across a large area.

Weaknesses: Fire, Death, Ice, and Metal Magics

HP: 50/50

Stamina: 50/50

Mana: 0/0

Speed 8/10

Level: 1	
HP: 50/50	Special Abilities: 1/1

"Spawnskulls," I read aloud. "They're fucking aerial hunters for the goddamn hive!"

"What do they…oh my God, *seagulls*?" Finn asked, before shaking his head. "Fuck no. If they'll even recruit the beach bastards, then that's just wrong."

"Well, call them what you will," the colonel said grimly. "They're making short work of the contingent coming in, and they'll be here next."

"Shitfuck," I growled. "Okay, options, people!"

"Our own avian forces?" Kelly suggested, until she saw the way they were dive-bombing the skeletons. The majority of the spawnskulls weren't trying to fight; they were literally killing themselves to take out the undead. Hurtling from the sky into our forces when needed.

"She's realized we're a threat," the colonel said. "That's why she's keeping her infected out of range, why the birds are dive-bombing. The counters you used against the monsters were successful, but probably too successful, as it made her take us seriously."

"Well, dammit," I whispered. "Okay, plan B."

"I thought we'd be on F by now." Finn appeared next to us. "What's the plan?"

"You know the healing towers?" I asked.

"Yeah?"

"Stop building them."

"Uh, okay?" he agreed, as I smiled coldly. "What've you got in that evil mind of yours, boss?"

"Terrain," I said. "Just fucking terrain. Chris? Get back up there and keep watch for her next surprise, please."

It wasn't elegant, or inspired, and there was the threat of doing more damage to our people in there, no matter what we did. But the only way I could see to do this without backing off and coming back another day, without the element of surprise, was a very simple adjustment to the battlefield.

All our available sappers were rerouted, as the damn spawnskulls started to dive-bomb us. While they began to cut out our skeletons inside the diamonds, the sappers began work underground.

The colonel and the rest of us worked as well; the skeletons found shields and spears appearing by their feet, and swept them up, bracing.

The wraith lord manipulated them, dragging them in to protect it over anything else. But that was fine; they were a lot more expensive to summon as well, and I wanted my money's worth out of the fucker.

They managed to kill more than they lost. The last few diving spawnskulls fell only a few minutes later, but as one remained on overwatch, the infected resumed fire, even if it was now sporadic.

The solution, as I'd explained to our people, was to form a room, directly below the infected, and then to work from that point outward.

The restrictions on us building anything that was in contact with the enemy was negated in the ground, beyond a meter, so the first stage was to dig a fresh tunnel outward to where we needed, with a skeleton trooping forward along it.

Then we started to lay out the room, one that was five meters across, three meters tall, and that ran around and underneath the massed troops. Where they were carefully staying out beyond the diamonds.

It had stone for the walls; the floor was soft earth, and the roof, as we hollowed out our way upward, was thin earth as well.

As we got closer and closer to the touching point, we lost the ability to absorb the earth, but that was fine. As we absorbed it in great swathes, we gained a tiny amount of mana—not enough to actually cover the costs, but our people were working hard.

That meant that as the earth vanished beneath their feet, the suddenly weakened and hollowed-out structure was no longer able to hold the massed weight of the enemy overhead, and they fell.

Crashing to the bottom of what was essentially an empty moat, the infected fell atop one another—hard enough to trap them, but not hard enough, nor far enough, to do real damage.

Sure, some were hurt—there was no way around that; we had to be realistic—but the sides were coated in stone.

They could neither dig their way out, nor could they reach us, and that trapped them, out of any angle they could attack from.

Sure, it wasn't a permanent solution. But that was fine as well, because it gained me enough time that we could start building again.

Some of our people were already hard at work absorbing the dead, and the mana that was coming in was bouncing like a hooker's ass.

As soon as it went up, it was smacked down, and damn was I planning on using it and abusing it.

The first thing to do was get rid of the overwatch. The wraith lord we'd had staying under cover was dispatched to do just that. The fucker seemed to take an inordinate level of pleasure in killing the damn seagull, or spawnskull.

Mind you, I hated the bastards as well.

The healing towers couldn't be created in an overlapping field, not to cover the enemy, which I'd thought was likely the way it was going to be before. But that was okay, because there was an interesting, and minor thing I'd not noticed until Finn asked.

It turned out that the issue was, as we'd hoped, *active* effects.

Turn the healing tower off—it was a simple enough thing to do—and suddenly it could be built pretty much anywhere I needed, as it was no longer rolling over the enemy.

I laid three out, one on the left, then three meters on, one on the right, then three meters beyond that, one on the left.

Then I created a second moat that meandered between them, narrow and twisting, making sure it was only wide enough for two abreast. The wall that connected to the enemy's section of the moat was a problem, but only right up until I spawned a corpse lord with a sledgehammer.

Then I created a second corpse lord with a new section of stone, this time in a runner groove, ready to slide along to close off the entry when I decided enough had made it into the trap.

The last job was simply to create two more ditches, much like the first, but this time on either side of the ten-meter section I wanted to feed into my new moat.

I left a slope that led up on one side, carefully pointed away, so that the infected could run or walk or whatever in that direction, but only a limited amount of them could walk down into my new moat.

Then I smashed the wall free, and let them in.

They streamed in, and in seconds, gunfire rang out. The corpse lord fell to the ground, dead, as they hammered his skull with concentrated fire, which he didn't bother to try to hide from.

The others watched as the new group rampaged forward into my little trap, finding to their clear confusion that the new moat just wove in and out, around the healing towers, while not exposing them to fire at all.

The field that was projected through the walls was weaker than aboveground and partly blocked, but the overlapping effect made it more than strong enough when combined with the zigzag pattern.

The queen couldn't see what was going on in any way that I could be sure of, and when the first of the infected humans suddenly staggered, falling to their knees, hands coming up to grasp their heads, a cheer rang out across the dungeon.

It didn't take long for the second, then the third to fall. By the time the last in line fell, I could feel the stress pouring from me.

It'd goddamn *worked*!

All but one of the figures was unconscious, as the "gate" was slammed into place, cutting off the intake. But the one that wasn't, predictably, was Mike.

He pushed himself half upright as a skeleton materialized next to him. The bright light of the motes washing over him, and he grinned.

"About…time you…fuckers…showed up…" he whispered, before collapsing face-first into the dirt.

"That's it, people!" I shouted. More skeletons appeared next to each of the bodies, turning them over, checking them and lifting them. A ramp at the far end opened up, leading downward to a room that was even now being created.

"Time to get to work!"

CHAPTER TWENTY-EIGHT

It took two hours for the queen to figure out what was going on, or at least to lose her temper to the point that she threw caution to the winds.

Markus and his team had been able to close off the section of the building they were in, although it'd been touch and go for a while. They'd managed to hold off the incoming monsters and infected, long enough to get the healing towers up and running. Then, after a little judicious retreating, sealing off, and advancing through new sections they'd turned the lower floors into, they'd managed to rescue almost a hundred humans.

He'd have managed to rescue a lot more, had the queen not apparently realized what was going on and pulled her forces back.

Silence had reigned for a while, as we continued to open sections up. As soon as the infected stopped playing ball and roaming around, we simply created more turned-off towers on either side of the moat and closed sections off, leaving them trapped inside.

Then we turned them on and started clearing the space.

Two whole hours it worked for. And had we had the mana, we probably could have saved them all. But it wasn't meant to be.

Even with us absorbing the "old" healing towers as soon as their position was no longer viable, even with the people helping to absorb more and more as they—and the undead—worked like, well, the undead.

Still, we'd barely managed to save half, when the tide turned.

More spawnskulls had appeared, presumably flying in from further afield. This time they'd stayed high, well out of reach of the wraith.

For a little while, I considered summoning other creatures—the impai, for example—but it just wasn't worth it.

By the time we'd spotted the fuckers, as high up as they were in the cloudy sky, they'd already seen exactly what we were doing, even if they didn't understand the details of how it worked.

When we tried to close off the next section, those nearest to it suddenly started screaming, then collapsing to their knees as they shook. They clutched at themselves, writhing; blood sprayed free as flesh ripped and tore, then extended. Others nearby pressed themselves to the screamers, their skin melding like hot wax to seal up.

They grew, while all around them, the rest stared on impassively.

I tried to get the towers up and running in time, but as soon as the first of the new creatures was complete, it attacked.

It stood nearly three meters tall, warped and twisted with a great chitinous claw on the left arm and tentacles on the right. Twitching mandibles clacked from the face, and the woman next to it didn't have a chance.

It spun, raising the club-like claw overhead, as the other woman moved in place, providing her head like a sacrificial virgin; then the creature struck, again.

The force must have been like being hit by a wrecking ball, as she practically melted under the impact. Then it did it again with the next in line…then again, each time with a fresh victim.

I was panicking, until it turned to the fourth and paused. The others in that section of the moat had calmly lined up and were moving into position one at a time to be killed. It stopped, the claw raised, ready, and it pointed in the direction of the healing tower.

The message was unmistakable.

Keep doing that shit, and you won't be able to save them.

I hesitated. Then, despite the risk that I'd misunderstood, or that it was bluffing, I broke down the tower, needing to know whether I'd misinterpreted. Instantly, the creature responded as well, lowering its arm and stepping back, as it gestured to the wall.

The hint was clear.

Let me out.

Again, I hesitated, but this time only for a second, before breaking the earth on the far side of the wall down and installing a ramp that led upward.

Then a corpse lord was summoned on the far side with a hammer, and it smashed its way through.

This time, as the hole was opened up, the infected didn't attack. Instead, they marched through as the corpse lord stood aside, moving up the ramp and out into the dimming light.

They gathered together, then started to head back to the base. Markus quickly reported the ones around him had done the same, pulling back.

An amalgamation paused, at the back of the group, and gestured to the wraith lord as it floated there, watching it. It drew a claw along the ground, making a line and pointed at the wraith, then the line, before walking away.

The meaning was unsubtle: *This is mine—that's yours. Fuck off.*

"Now what?" the colonel asked, and I snorted, glancing at him.

"Now we count the win, and come up with a new plan," I said. "The easy shit is over, and we're gonna have to fight for the next round."

"Daylight's wasting. What's the plan?" Barry asked.

I turned to him. "Get ready to summon a quick response force. You're going to keep an eye on things for a bit while I get to work," I said after a little thought. "I need to check on the others, make sure they're healing up and that they're clean. If they are, we're moving to the next phase: recover anyone we can and start expanding into the camp. Capture, contain, and kill what we have to."

"How many in my force?" he asked.

I rubbed my chin as I thought. "Ring the camp. Make sure they're not trying to sneak out, and have volunteers watch over them in the dungeon sense. As soon as we've got the mana, we summon undead to surround it, and they can watch while we prepare. This was only the first round."

"On it. Hey, Sarge, you got some of your people we can use?" he asked, and the sarge, after glancing at the colonel for approval, agreed. "Great, let's get together and…" They drifted aside.

Instead of walking or flying all the way there, I paused long enough to read the prompts I'd gotten and check the XP.

You have completed a Quest!

Otterburn Camp (1):
You have found the camp and learned the location of some of your missing inhabitants. Although you succeeded in rescuing some, you are far from saving them all.

For completing this part of the quest, you receive the following bonuses:
- +2 to Perception
- 1 Skill Point
- 10,000 XP

Quest!

Otterburn Camp (2):
Your investigation has confirmed the worst: your missing inhabitants have been taken captive and are being controlled by the coronaught queen's parasitic powers.
The very warriors you have trained to defend you are being corrupted against you, and are now forced to do her bidding. Your mission is to infiltrate the camp, locate your enslaved people, and free them from the Queen's clutches.

- Inhabitants rescued: 757/1843

Complete this part of the quest to receive the following bonuses:
- Additional Forces/Inhabitants
- 2 Skill Points
- 50,000 XP

Optional Additional Quest:

Quest!

Otterburn Camp (3):
Locate the queen and the heart of her hive, then decide: will you conscript her to add her forces and their capabilities to your own, or will you eradicate her, removing this valuable piece from the board?

- Eliminate/recruit Coronaught Queen

Complete this part of the quest to receive the following bonuses:
- +1 Class Skill Point
- +1 Tech Upgrade (Random)
- 25,000 XP

That had been a surprise, that the damn system was viewing the entire population of the base as possible members of the dungeon, and also so many had been rescued and still so many left to free.

Congratulations!

You have led your forces to eliminate the following:
- 247x Coronaught Spawnskulls, Levels 1-7, 2,470 XP
- 27x Coronaught Centaurs, Levels 2-5, 1,080 XP
- 19x Coronaught Bovine Monstrosities, Level 1, 4,050 XP
- 21x Coronaught Canine Aberrations, Levels 3-9, 1,050 XP
- 11x Coronaught Itopedes, Levels 1-11 820 XP

Total XP earned: 9,470 XP
Total XP awarded: 9,470 XP

—Due to the nature of this quest and the threat to your dungeon, you as Dungeon Lord receive full XP from all enemies killed—

Current XP to next level stands at 60,383/50,000.

***

Congratulations!

You have gained two additional Stat Points in the following areas through constant effort.
- **+1 Intelligence**
- **+1 Perception**

Continue to work hard to increase these or other stats…

***

Congratulations!

You have reached Level 27.

Current XP to next level stands at 10,383/55,000.

You have 9 unspent Stat Points and 12 unspent Skill Points.

That was damn nice to see—another goddamn level at last. It'd been, oh, a week since the last? Considering how damn hard I'd fought in the dungeon, if nothing else, I felt I deserved that.

I eyed the points, then put it aside, resolving to deal with it as soon as this was sorted.

I shifted, focusing and blurring through the darkening world.

I'd not realized it until the other day when I'd needed Kelly and with a thought, I'd been able to vanish and pop up there next to her, but on reflection, it made sense. After all, in the larger dungeons, to do anything, it'd take forever if you couldn't "fast travel" like that.

Now I stopped inside the still expanding, buried bunker. Rows of people were still being arranged in their dozens and their hundreds—filthy, battered, and hopefully, now free.

Aly and Kelly were there together, with Finn and others, working to improve the space available, while unsubtly searching for those they recognized, as I drifted closer.

Mike was laid on a cot-type bed, his eyes closed, his clothing filthy, his beard and hair matted with blood and dirt.

As I came to a stop near Kelly and Aly, others nearby were being rearranged. Some were being carried aside, and others moved around to free up space, with new ones being set up in their place, including the guy we'd left in the dark hole when we'd rescued him as a test.

Admittedly he was currently catatonic, and totally unresponsive, but, well, he was alive and that was an improvement on where he would have been if we'd not intervened.

"What's this?" I asked Kelly quietly.

"Our people," Finn said softly. "We're moving our people in close, so that we can get them on their feet as soon as possible. Then we need to get them ready for transport."

"Transport?" I asked, startled.

"Well, yeah?" he replied, frowning. "I thought you said you wanted to build a nexus gate? So we could transport our people through it?"

"No," I said, then winced, hearing how it came out and the way people around me flinched. "Shit, let me try that again: 'not yet.'"

"Why?" Finn asked, even as Aly nodded nearby. "Our people need to see them, Matt. Aly, you want him home, right?"

"Yeah, and we need to be damn sure he's healed," I said. "Jo is one of the unconscious, and when she comes around, we're going to have to come up with a way to make sure she's clean. Then she can gather a cadre of doctors and test everyone else.

"Until we know that they're all clean, and I mean fucking *know*, then we're not letting them move from here to the dungeon." I shook my head. "Aly, I know you're not gonna be happy with that but—"

"You're right." She cut me off.

"We need to be sure he's…what?" I broke off.

"You're right. I need to know he's safe before I can have him near Amy." She sounded stricken, but her eyes never left him as she went on. "But the only way that we'll know is if we examine him, and we won't be able to do that from here. The healing might have just made sure the worm's effects are healed—we don't know if it's been removed. What if as soon as he's removed from the area of effect, it can start the infection again?"

"Then…I don't know," I admitted. "Then we look at surgery."

"Who do you know that can do brain surgery?" she asked me with a brittle little laugh, and I winced.

"Well, no one, but…" I admitted. "But there has to be a way, right?"

"There is," she agreed, glancing back at me then reaching out and gripping my arm, holding it tight as she went on; the feeling of ghostly fingers gave me goosebumps. "But you're not going to like it."

"Oh?"

"We upgrade the core."

"Aly, we've been through this," I responded, staring at her. "You know why we can't. Hell, you were just telling Kelly that!"

"I know why we *have* to now," she countered, glaring at me. "If we reach Glass, we should have access to all human tech, right?"

"Pretty much," I admitted as she released me. I held my hand out with the palm flat, facing down, then tilted it to the left and right, wobbling it. "It's not an exact thing, but we should have. There's a lot of additional tech we've got to reach in the general tree before we'd be able to work on anything like high-tech shit."

"Well, what do we need for an MRI?" she asked me flatly. "Because that's what we need. We need to know for sure that these people are okay. And Matt?"

"Yeah?"

"We need that before you can return to the dungeon as well."

"Me? I've not been infected…" My mind whirled through the possibilities, before grunting as I realized that, if I had been? That was exactly what I would say. "Well, fuck."

"Yeah." She nodded. "And before you say it, yes, a heartbeat ago I wanted the portal open. I know I'm not being goddamn consistent, okay? My husband was missing, maybe dead, and now here he is, right there, lying unconscious. He *should* be fine. With the healing spell and everything like that? He *should* be *fine*!"

"Okay…" I agreed carefully, pulling up the details for the coronaught queen again and reading it over.

"But we don't know that for sure. We don't know if the healing spell just heals the injury, or if it kills the worm, or…"

"Vurm."

"Even if it…what?"

"Sorry." I cursed my mouth. "The system calls them vurms, not worms. I was just looking at the system notification recently and saw it. Sorry."

"I don't…" She stopped and took a deep breath before going on. "Matt, I don't care if the system calls them fucking orgasms, cheese sandwiches, or a fucking vurm. With everything that's going on right now, that's the least of my goddamn concerns, all right!"

277

"Yeah, like I said, sorry," I offered.

"Well, because I know how your mind works, Matt, I'm just going to say this, okay?" Kelly said suddenly.

"What?"

"Until we know for sure that you and the others from there aren't infected somehow, no sex—even if you decide you're going to ignore us and come back."

"WHOA!" I made a T sign with my hands. "Time out. Fuckin' time out here. I wasn't even saying anything about sex…"

"I know you weren't," Kelly agreed, forcing a smile. "But you need to understand that as much as I love you, and I know there's no way we can stop you from coming back to your dungeon if you decide to, if you do come? You won't cum, at least not with me."

I stared at her in shock, as she turned and stepped in close, taking both my hands in hers and looking into my eyes.

"Matt, honey, you know I love you, and us being apart is going to hurt me as much as it is you. But you can't tell all of these people that they can't come home, only for you to then come home regardless. I'm betting there's been a lot of times that you've been alone and could have picked up an infection when you were asleep or whatever? One that you'd not even know about?"

I thought back to when Chris, the soldiers, and I had broken into this section of the base, claiming it as part of the dungeon and that I'd healed myself. Remembering the multiple worm…*vurms* that I'd had burrowing into me, and I'd not even known they were there.

"Fuck," I whispered again. The rising urge to smash something made my fists itch.

It wasn't the threat of no sex, as much as we both knew she'd used that to soften the blow. I wasn't a damn child, not even close; she'd used that as almost a joke to force me to think about it. No, it was that she was right, and that she was being totally reasonable and responsible.

It was that I'd not even considered how that would look for the others, for those like Emma and Jenn, whose husbands were up here somewhere, and… "Wait." I frowned as that thought caught up to me. "Emma and Jenn…did we find their husbands?"

"I say no to sex, and that's where your mind goes?" Kelly asked me, her eyebrows rising in surprise.

"Oh for…no! I was thinking of the others, and how shitty this would be on them, and then I thought of the people there I knew were married!"

"And those of us not married as well, I hope," Finn said softly from nearby. "Just because we're not married doesn't mean I don't love Patrick."

"Finn…" I took a deep breath. "The married bit wasn't a dig at you, okay? I'm sorry—it was just the way it came out. Did you find him?"

"No." He shook his head sadly. "And some of the volunteers already absorbed and broke down the bodies of some of the dead, so…" He took a deep breath, his voice breaking as he went on, sobs building as he tried to hold it together. "If he died…out there, now…I might never know for sure."

"Finn, I'm so sorry." Kelly hesitated as she looked from me to him before blinking out of the dungeon sense, and a second later, so did he.

I guessed that she'd gone to see him physically, supporting him as best she could, and I turned back to Aly, who was staring at Mike.

"We need to figure this out." That was all I could say to her.

"Which bit?" she asked distractedly.

"The bit that gets you and him back together and makes damn sure that we're all safe as we do it," I assured her. "Where do we start?"

"Medical suites," she said after a few seconds. "That'd be the logical section to have access to things that we need. We've not looked, but I'm betting that the higher-leveled cores have better versions of the medical suites. It's not showing anything currently, but that's probably because it's a general level of tech, not a core-specific one.

"There's no way a civilization that can travel across the stars doesn't have a way to examine you internally though, so I'm hoping that the Glass core will either have what we need, or a way to power the tech that we can recover from the hospital," she guessed.

"Okay, but we need to get as much of the core-specific tech researched as we can," I countered. "There's no point in sorting all this out to get us all back together, only to have us max out at a lower level and die because of that."

"God, I wish we could ask the damn fairy!" Aly groaned. "That stupid fairy… If it'd just—" She shook her head. "I know it wasn't her fault. She'd have wanted to live, and she gave up her soul to save the dungeon, but…argh!" She grabbed at her hair and pulled, clearly trying to calm down and failing, as I had a "lightbulb" moment.

"We can't ask *our* fairy…" I said slowly. "But what about another?"

"Another what?" She froze, her hands letting go and dropping. She stepped back, her eyes shifting as she worked through details until she pointed an index finger at me. "You clever, clever bastard!"

With that, she vanished, leaving me staring at the space she'd been in. I waved generally and called out. "So, what now?" I tried. "Hello? Fuck's sake, are you dealing with this, or am I?"

Silence.

Utter goddamn silence.

"Great." I sighed, rubbing the bridge of my nose with one phantasmal hand, before gesturing vaguely. "Well, I guess I'll just go get all of this sorted then."

There wasn't much else I could do, as the tokens the fairies from the nexus platform had given me were all back at the dungeon, and I was here. Mind you, so was the access point for the nexus gate, but fuck it, it still felt like I should be the one doing it all.

I turned back to Mike, looking down at him, and the people nearby, then sighed, shaking my head. The best thing I could do for them, I was betting, was to win this fight. But in the meantime, the next best thing I could do was get them clean.

"Colonel…" I looked for him, then cursed and focused. I was about to blur to him, then I grinned. I was the Dungeon Lord, after all; surely there had to be a way to make the most of that?

A little focus, a bit of concentration, and a simple *"come"* thought as an order instead of a request, and the colonel stood by my side.

He ran on a few steps, passing through a gurney, and jerked back, then spun, his eyes wide. "What the..." Then he saw me and did a quick double take. "More magic, eh?" He took a deep breath, before nodding and going on. "I shouldn't be surprised, I guess. What's happening?"

"We have a problem."

"What's new or unusual about that?" he asked, and I grunted my agreement.

"Do you have any medical teams?" I asked.

He hesitated before answering. "Not entirely. We had a medical assistant, Jason Fieldworthy, a cadet who was showing promise, until Captain Roberts was killed. The captain was our base doctor, and his mentor. Since then, apart from the basic field medicine and training all soldiers receive, all we've had is Cadet Jason's assistance. Why?"

"Well, I was really hoping you were going to tell me you had a neurosurgeon hiding somewhere, but—" I broke off, then grinned. "But we have the nurses and doctors at the hospital. Oh, thank the gods. Right, what we need here is some army organization, please, Colonel," I said instead.

"Go on."

"The army isn't just about fighting," I said. "I've seen all those disaster programs, where the first people on site are the army and then ten minutes later it's all regimented lines, disaster relief and well planned out. Can you do that here?"

"Take over the management of the injured and maintain the perimeter?" he asked, and I nodded. "Son, I've been doing this for fifteen years, and I'd be damn pleased to do it here for our own."

"Okay, you've got this then." I gestured to the still expanding area. I turned, squinting at the walls, and nodded, checking the mana levels. "Looks like we're reaching the maximum size we can afford to run for now. But if you need more space, let me know."

The underground bunker was squared off, roughly a hundred meters on a side, and had rows upon rows of cot-like beds being summoned into place. Clearly the sappers were working well because...

I smiled, despite everything. The sappers in here were primarily those with military experience, and they were working with that same precision that characterized military life. Set lanes were appearing, clear spaces that people could move through, even as others directed the undead skeletons in collecting the unconscious and injured, carrying them inside and laying them on the beds.

They were being carried in, in shifts. Clarissa and her people guided the skeletons, I saw, and the military laid them out in patterns that they understood.

"Showers and clean clothing are the first stage," the colonel said. "It's not safe for so many people to be left in such a state, and the damage that level of...*filth* will be doing to them is incredible. There will be morale issues as well, of course, but primarily these people need to be stripped, washed, and put into clean clothing, then IV drips to feed them attached."

"Can your trainee do the IVs?" I asked.

"Remotely?" He shook his head. "In real life, any soldier could do it—we have significant personal emergency field medicine training. But to attempt to guide an undead creation to do such a thing? I genuinely don't see how it could be possible."

"Yeah," I admitted. "That's what I thought."

"So what do we do?" he asked.

"I'll set up showers, and you need to detail a few people to guide the undead to run people through them, strip them, clean them down and redress. I'll sort the authority to order the undead in here and to repair and clean the clothing."

He nodded, and I moved into the system controls, assigning that to the colonel and his people, before adding a small caveat that any orders given to kill or otherwise harm our people would trigger the undead to stop instead of carrying it out.

It took a little monkeying with the authority system, but I wasn't there for trusting the new people, not yet.

That done, and with the colonel giving orders, I expanded a new section out into the side, producing two additional rooms as the mana slowly increased.

This was the easy bit. The creation of the rooms wasn't cheap, but all it was, essentially, was creating blocks of flooring that ran out to a size I was happy with, then walls up and around, a ceiling, and then absorbing all the earth inside the new room.

Once that was done, some manastone lights were added. Finally, all the sections—from the flooring to the walls and ceiling—were sealed together and linked up, then smoothed out to ensure that nothing was going to be sneaking in.

Once that was done, benches were added with attached shower heads, and a drain that led to a space under the floor. I added in a detail to the colonel to make someone keep it from getting blocked up, as the dirt and other waste was washed away.

The clothes, when they were removed, could be hung on a simple hanger, and the difference between the clean and dirty ones would be obvious.

Lastly, I added a set of heating and some air recycling, and that was it. All the details crap was done, though I noted some of Clarissa's people working to fix my hasty creation.

That done, I was out, floating up into the air overhead, looking down at the base.

It was split now, with the dungeon recognizing that we were at war with the local queen. The territory was split into green and red sections, with green as ours and red as theirs.

The parking lot was split roughly into a third ours, and the rest theirs. The warehouse was clearly theirs, and a path that led through to the main base was mainly theirs as well.

The top left side had two buildings that were ours, held by Markus. But beyond that, the majority of the base was clearly in enemy hands.

That left us with a decision to make.

Chris appeared not far from me, drifting over, and I turned to look at him.

"How's it going, Superman?" I asked him, noting the way he floated in the air over the camp.

"All good in the hood." He nodded, then paused, thinking. "You know, I'd have made a better Superman than any they've filmed yet."

"A more confident one?" I suggested.

"Definitely."

"More handsome?"

"Oh, for sure."

"Smarter?"

"Yup."

"Well, at least I know you're still you after that fight...fuckin' delusional as always," I finished.

"Love you too, brother." He grinned. "So, what's the next stage?"

"I don't know," I admitted quietly, glancing around to make sure we weren't being observed.

"You want to talk it out?" he offered.

"I'd rather you just told me the answer." I grunted, then sighed. "If we start healing her drones to rescue the people, she's made it clear she'll kill them."

"Go on."

"So we can't do that."

"Wrong, but keep going."

"We can't," I said. "There's no point in healing people if she's just going to kill them."

"Snipers," he said instead, grinning. "If she's going to try to kill them, she's got to do something, right? She needs to create the monsters or whatever?"

"Well, no, not really," I admitted. "They've got guns..."

"Which are almost all out of ammo," he pointed out. "She didn't need to make that monster. She could have just made them all open fire on each other. Instead, she did that."

"Why?" I asked. My mind ran through the possibilities.

"Honestly, I think she doesn't know why the guns stopped working. Think about it logically: she's a creature, not a human. She's learning and learning fast, but her mind works differently. I'm betting that, for now, reloading isn't something she's seen much of. So instead, she's probably distrusting the weapons now. After all, some work, then stop at random. If she needs them to work, and they don't, she's going to panic. Can't figure out why they stopped working, so she does what she understands, and creates a monster."

"Then uses the monster to threaten us all," I agreed. "You're thinking we accept the, what's it called, the 'breakage'?" I asked.

"The ones who are turned into monsters are dead," he said grimly. "The healing spells—mine, at least—aren't going to be capable of fixing that, and I don't think any others will either. If I was being changed, I think I'd beg you to shoot me."

"So you think we build the healing towers as close as we can and we go for it, kill any we have to and accept the losses?" I said, working my way through it.

"Basically." He sighed. "Don't get me wrong, man. We've recovered about half of our people so far. The others? We know that some are in the other contingents around the base. Some, we've no doubt, just missed in the mass, but a lot are just gone. We can't fix that, as much as I wish we could. Now we're at the stage of do we accept it and honor their sacrifice to save those we can, or do we lose more people to save a few and blame it on conscience."

"We're damned if we do and damned if we don't," I translated, staring out over the base, before scratching at the back of my neck as I thought.

"Or, and just listen, *or...*" I said slowly. "We do what they're not expecting."

"How bad is this going to be?"

I grinned. "Bad," I admitted. "And the girls are probably going to kill us for it."

"That good?"

"You want kids?" I asked.

"No?"

"Well, if you go with me on this one, I can practically guarantee you won't have any," I offered.

"There's an upside." He nodded.

"Or if you do, they'll probably be ginger."

"Oh hell no, man. Why'd you say that?" He glared at me.

"Just warning you now, so you can't turn around later and complain."

"Besides, you know as well as I do, if either of us are having gingers, it's you, right?" he replied, suddenly grinning. "Dark hair on you, Kelly's got blonde hair—combined, that's a ginger!"

"Ah fuck..." I muttered, playing along and pretending that was it, he'd won.

"Yup, that's it!" he crowed. "You're screwed!"

"Ah well, I suppose that's a risk I'll run...unless my balls are irradiated, anyway, which was the direction all this conversation was going in."

"I...what?"

"Yeah, but look on the bright side—chances are, after the dose we're going to get, no kids at all."

"Uh..."

"And at least you're winning there, what with Becky's condition and all. At least you'll have one, even if this does go wrong," I continued on cheerfully. "Right, give me a few minutes, mate. I need to check something. Keep an eye on the enemy and don't leave your post, whatever happens!"

With that, I blurred and shifted, vanishing from next to him, only to appear under the trees and out of sight nearby. I peered up and watched him as he hesitated, then grinned evilly as I saw him panicking and trying to decide whether I was joking about Becky and her "condition" or not.

"Simple pleasures," I muttered, before shifting again, this time popping back into reality as close as I could get to the queen's chambers.

I was in Markus's building. The damn system had blocked us out of anywhere we didn't already hold, but from here, I could see the buildings we needed to capture to advance on her. And that was the only option left, I decided.

Straight into the lion's den.

CHAPTER TWENTY-NINE

"I don't like this," Chris muttered to me as we trooped along the well-worn and graveled path across the camp.

"Nobody likes this," I said in a low voice. "Put your big girl pants on and deal with it."

"I hate you."

"I get that a lot," I replied.

The pair of us lapsed into silence again.

I could feel Kelly by my side, hovering over me protectively as my little band headed deeper into the enemy camp. My little party stomped along in order.

"Is it working?" I whispered.

"What?" Chris asked.

"Not you." I shook my head, focusing, and tried again.

"Is it working?"

"Yes, but only a meter around you," Kelly replied.

I let out a breath and kept going.

That was going to make it close, especially as that meant we couldn't guarantee room to do anything. In theory, it would work. Aly and Kelly had finally agreed on that late last night, when I'd come to them with my half-baked plan and they'd worked to rationalize and improve upon it.

The dungeon's influence was determined by three things. First, claimed territory; that was obvious. If we'd absorbed it into the dungeon, and there was no enemy in that space currently, and it was linked to another section we owned, then we could build there.

Secondly, the level of contestation, which was an awkward way of saying that if there were more of us than them, or vice versa, then it changed what we could do.

Lastly, the level of influence in an area.

The closer we got to the queen, the more her influence worked to suppress my own. But in the areas we'd already taken, we had a prior claim.

Add in that I had a small but powerful force, and that I was the friggin' Dungeon Lord, and this was the result. We could move around inside the camp, and our influence was expanding.

A meter out from me wasn't much, and if that was all it was, when the time came to put the second stage into play, this was going to get messy. But honestly, try as I might, I couldn't come up with a better option.

I'd even swallowed my pride: I'd gone to the colonel with the options, explained the half-baked solution I had, and then I'd waited for him to shoot it down.

He'd not. Instead, he'd offered to come with me, claiming that if the system accepted my authority as a Dungeon Lord, then perhaps it'd accept his authority as a colonel in the British Army, as this was an army base.

I'd assured him that it was a kind offer, and that if he'd been closer—you know, rather than back in the fucking city—I'd have considered it.

It made it clear how little he understood about the real world, though.

With no better options, I'd gathered up those I needed and I'd just gone for it.

As soon as we'd left "our" section—marching up out of a tunnel we'd dug out—the nearby infected had come boiling out of the warehouse ahead, gathering up, ready to attack. At first, I'd fully thought that was going to be it, that we'd guessed wrong and she'd not be interested. But as we set off marching, and the ten of us were all that came out, they stopped.

The numbers, we now saw, showed the fucker had started heavily converting the living into those monsters as well. The sight of dozens more of them now than there had been yesterday made me grit my teeth and move on.

The path we were following led from the snow-covered parking lot into the trees. Then, after twenty or so meters, we were out, into what presumably had once been a manicured section of the camp.

The trees ringed a section that was filled with dead grass poking through the snow. The paths led north from here, before turning and heading into the camp proper.

The team with me were, pound for pound, the heaviest hitters we had nearby. Chris and I were in our full armor, rifles at the ready and additional magazines ready. Our secondary loadout—thanks to the soldiers who had been rescued—was the heaviest we'd yet carried.

In addition to the extra magazines, there were dozens of grenades, incendiaries, our upgraded homemade rail gun-shotguns, and of course, our personal weapons.

My 1911 magnum, hammer, and sword were matched by Chris's two toys, which were, respectively, a hammer, and the L111A1 heavy machine gun.

We'd found it along with a bunch of other damaged weapons in a transport that had crashed nearby. I'd been convinced it was trash, but he'd spent the time with the sarge to repair and rebuild two of them.

He carried one now, strapped to his back, and damn, the thing was insane.

It was built to be attached to the side of a ship, or onto a tripod and used at a squad level. Thanks to his size, Chris planned to use it with both hands, so he had literally hacked off and then smoothed the end of the barrel down to a third of the size.

The sarge had nearly gone apoplectic with rage, until Chris explained that this wasn't going to be a long-range fight, and he might need to be able to use it in the corridors.

Along with the pair of us was Kilo. There was no way he was going to leave us to fuck this up on our own, after all. And beside him was Finger.

The colonel had been determined that at least one of the army had to be with us, and Finger was both junior enough he was actually useful—without the mandatory lobotomy that most officers had on enlisting—and a damn good shot.

He was also the first to volunteer, and if we had to take one of them with us to probably die, best it was a volunteer.

Behind him came two corpse lords, then two advanced wraiths, two skeletons, and finally, Jack. The automata was almost as tall as the corpse lords, and wider. That meant that there was a bloody good chance we'd not be able to get him inside with us, considering the size of the doors, but I wanted him with us if we could.

The reason for this was basically for the look of it. I'd have rather taken an army in, but the only way we'd get anywhere was if we weren't obviously attacking.

We needed to be made up of a clearly different group than the attacking force. I was hoping that two of each of them, then the three humans and a kobold might look ceremonial or something. Jack? Fuck it, he was today's security blanket in giant form.

I didn't know whether that would help us or not, but we marched two abreast and moved steadily deeper, keeping their attention while behind us, the others worked.

By the time we'd come to an agreement for this fight, we'd managed to squirrel away just over a million points of mana, and we'd been spending that fucker like it was going out of fashion in the last few hours.

First was the "eyes in the sky." We needed them gone, but the beach bastards, as Finn had called the mutated seagulls, were fast.

They were significantly bigger than a normal bird, some a meter to two meters in size, massive wingspans, and had both long claws and acidic spit. Add in the jaws that could kill a lion, and the belly full of worm…*vurms*…and you had a serious threat to anything that lived.

The weather had broken again, starting to warm briefly. The snow turned to slush all over, and a warmer front moved in, bringing driving rain.

The first pass of that had broken a lot of the snow down, and that meant our time was up. No doubt, as soon as the queen could, she'd be pouring out vurms like water to try to recover her lost drones.

That meant we needed a solution to take down the flying bastards, and it needed to be fast.

A quick search through the dungeon catalog had netted us two species that were likely to be able to manage it. Although we had one already, I decided that the expense of the second was worth it.

Going from common to uncommon for the harpies was fifty thousand mana, but the visual of the creature that was offered up in the dungeon made it clear this was a short-term solution.

The harpy was female, that was abundantly clear—no male had a chest like that—but why that had been decided to be an evolutionary trait? Well, I had no fucking clue.

Reading over the details, I grunted, guessing that maybe the tits had come from the idea of seducing other creatures, but I really didn't get it.

Harpy	Avian Predator

The Harpy is a large, swift and deadly avian predator known for its vibrant plumage and razor-sharp talons. These creatures are predominantly female, with striking humanoid features that can captivate their prey. Harpies are closely tied to the elemental forces of air and storms, wielding powerful magic to control the winds and weather.

Abilities:

Gale Force! **Harpies can summon powerful gusts of wind to knock back enemies or propel themselves through the air at incredible speeds.**

Thunder Clap! **By infusing their wings with storm mana, then clapping them together, Harpies can create a deafening thunderclap that stuns and disorients their prey, though this results in damage to their wings.**

Storm Shroud! **Harpies can conjure a swirling vortex of storm clouds around themselves, obscuring their movements and protecting them from ranged attacks.**

Weaknesses: Earth, Fire, and Metal Magics

HP: 120/120

Stamina: 80/80

Mana: 400/400

Speed: 9/10

Level: 6

HP 120/120	Special Abilities: 3/3

I mean, I'm a breast man, and the sight of those things…sure, impressive, but what the hell? Considering the rest? There's no way I was going to ignore the whole "wings, pointy teeth and maw, and massive talons" just to ogle them.

The uncommon harpy stood nearly five foot tall, with wings that were covered in colorful plumage. Her head was the same, all shorter and longer feathers rather than hair, but a maw that was more vicious and predator than beak.

She had dozens of short, sharp teeth that were hooked inward, making it clear that she was evolved for biting and tearing, more than chewing.

Her eyes were bright and golden, larger than a human's and faced forward, with the chest…well, it was more like nature had decided that "bull's-eye" was the term to best describe them.

Each nipple was simply a collection of different colored feathers, signaling they were definitely for attention only. The legs were backward facing, the knees hinged away—they were probably designed to launch themselves and land fast, rather than run. And the feet?

They were more like an eagle's, huge and taloned.

She had arms that were spindly, ending again in claws. The wings came from behind her shoulders and started in the center of her back. But, all in all, the example the dungeon showed me made one thing clear.

If I wanted something that could hunt and kill a mutant bastard seagull, this was it.

The second option—because the smaller fliers were just not going to cut it—was another advanced wraith, though they were a lot slower. I decided to play it safe, and as the ten uncommon harpies were plenty fast, I only summoned one of them.

They were currently underground, waiting out of sight and ready to go, as were our other reinforcements.

Due to the situation, there was no way I could risk any of the squishier races in fighting with the infected. But, fortunately, the advanced kobolds were a hell of a lot hardier than most, thanks to their scales.

I'd summoned ten of them and outfitted them in basic armor and equipment, then gave them some of the captured assault rifles as well.

That came to a grand total—including the fifty thousand research fee—ninety-eight thousand, four hundred and seventy mana.

That left us with almost nine hundred thousand earned for the last twenty-four hours. To make sure we got as many people out and healed as we could, the next five hundred thousand points were exclusively split into summoning corpse lords and advanced wraiths.

That gave us essentially a seriously heavy-duty team that could plow in, take names and basically kick the shit out of anything.

The last thing I'd done before setting off with my tiny little "bait" team was line all the wraiths up and make my position fucking clear to them. I'd summoned them on a ration of four corpse lords to every wraith; that gave me twenty-two of the eerie monstrosities and eighty-eight of the corpse lords.

We'd had to summon the corpse lords in one of the spaces we'd set aside for the botched last invasion, but that was fine. Although they might not be fast, they sure were powerful.

"Listen up!" I'd said to the wraiths. "Your mission, your *only* mission is to help us to rescue as many of the humans as possible. They've been infected with a parasite that is controlling them and that can transform them into monstrous creatures. You will be watched over by one of our people at all times, and they will guide you. If you want to live through this, and earn the right to grow, to become more than you are now? You'll damn well work as hard as you can to save these people. If you can get them to a healing tower and hold them there, then the magic we have should—and I say this carefully, so pay attention—it *should* save them.

"We don't know for sure, though, so if you can knock them out? If you can pin them and drag them free, do it. Be inventive. Use your shields as a battering ram. Lead the corpse lords to work together more effectively, but do not, for fuck's sake, use the necrotic death bolts on anyone you expect to be able to save! You'll be given high priority targets—save these people above all others.

"This is your chance to prove that you should be given more, so earn it!" I'd finished on that. The wraiths watched me silently, and I'd turned away and moved on. What they thought I was offering to let them earn I didn't know, but there had to be something these undead fuckers wanted, and frankly, I didn't care what it was. They weren't priests, so there was a chance it wouldn't be twisted at least.

I'd also spent less than thirty seconds allocating my available points before I set off, simply because I was going to damn well need them to pull any of this off.

As much as I'd hated every goddamn second of doing it, instead of putting all nine of my available stat points into something that I felt would make a real difference outside of this situation, or somewhere I'd know that there was an effect...

I was down to only two choices.

Jump my luck by a solid fifth, or do the same in charisma.

I hated the luck stat—genuinely, I did. You never knew whether it was doing anything at all, and I could never work out how the hell it could actually make a real-world effect. But it was that, or charisma.

Charisma won out in the end. Not because I felt the need to be one of those pretty boys who spent all their time trimming their beard one hair at a time, but because of the other side of it.

Speeches were something I had to give more often than I'd ever like to look at. And when it came to the flip side of speeches that was intimidation?

Yeah. I needed to be better at that as well, as much as I didn't like it. Because if I could get the queen to listen to me, then maybe, just maybe I could get our people free.

Confirming the nine points in charisma made my skin itch a little for a few seconds, but beyond that? No real effect I could see.

I'd done it, accepted that it was done, and just hoped it helped somehow, though I had no clue how the hell it was going to.

Name: Matt, First Lord of the Storm				
Host Powers: 1 (Enhanced Regeneration)				
Species: Thunderstorm			Bonus: None	
Level: 27			Progress to next level: 10,383/55,000	
Stat	Current Points	Description	Effect	Progress to Next Level
Agility	42	Governs dodge and movement	Heightened chance to dodge attacks 84%+20%= 104%	85/100
Charisma	41	Governs likely success to charm, seduce, or threaten	68% more likely to succeed in events that require seduction, persuasion, or threats (10%+ (31x2) = 68)	88/100

289

Constitution	52	Governs Health and Health Regeneration	HP: 52x60 = 3,120	99/100
Dexterity	45	Governs ability with weapons and crafting	+45% Increased chance of improved result +17 to melee damage	23/100
Endurance	46	Governs Stamina and Stamina Regeneration	Stamina: 46x50 = 2,300	89/100
Intelligence	62	Governs base manapool, standard intellectual capacity	Mana: 62x70=4,340	17/100
Luck	45	Governs overall chance of bonuses and critical hits	+70% increased chance of positive outcome	54/100
Perception	44	Governs ranged damage and chance to spot hidden items/traps	+34 to all ranged attacks	4/100
Strength	40	Governs damage with melee weapons and carrying capacity	+60 to all damage with Melee weapons	98/100
Wisdom	47	Governs mana regeneration	470 mana regenerated per hour	97/100

I'd also rolled the dice; as much as I was tempted to, I decided against saving the skill points I had any longer. I'd wanted to save them for crafting, honestly believing that at some damn point I'd be able to make the most of them. But realistically, that was never going to happen.

Fortunately, it seemed that setting up my second dungeon had opened a new line of investment for me, as well as a new skill set when I opened the long neglected and ignored skills list.

First came the inevitable onslaught of notifications I'd been suppressing. Dozens, quite literally, of skill rises had been hidden away by my determination not to be overwhelmed with such things needlessly.

After a few seconds, I had them pared down to the important ones, though, and damn did they bring a bonus I needed.

Congratulations!
You have unlocked the Structural Design skill!
For joining the rarefied heights of dungeon society, as one of the top 2% in your system to gain full control over your second dungeon, you gain a basic understanding of dungeon architecture and construction. This skill grants you a 1% bonus per level to the durability of all structures you create within your dungeon. You can now design and build improved defensive features, such as reinforced walls and target traps. As you progress in this skill, you will learn to further optimize your dungeon's layout and maximize the effectiveness of your constructions.

Congratulations!
You have unlocked the Advanced Dungeon Management skill!
With the creation of your second dungeon, you have begun to grasp the fundamentals of advanced dungeon management. This skill allows you to more effectively, yet still remotely, oversee and control basic aspects of your dungeon from a central location. Your minions' efficiency in performing tasks and maintaining the dungeon increases by 5% per level gained. You can now designate specific areas within your dungeon for additional resource storage and distribution, streamlining your dungeon's operations.

Congratulations!
You have unlocked the Dungeon Warfare skill!
As you prepare to expand your second dungeon, you have gained a greater understanding of dungeon combat tactics. Your minions now receive a 2% bonus to their combat effectiveness when fighting within one mile of the dungeon's influence. You can more easily issue simple battle commands and formations to your forces, or choose to delegate this skill using the Battle Management tab, allowing for more coordinated attacks and defences. With further progress in this skill, you will learn to create and deploy more specialized minions with unique abilities to bolster your dungeon's military might.

There were more skills than this, mostly a point here or a point there, but reading this over, I didn't even hesitate a second.

For so long, the skill points I had access to were pushed aside, unimportant simply because I could still increase their level by practice as much as anything else. No more.

As much as I knew I should be saving the points for later, and earn the lower levels right now by doing the job, there was no way I was going to pass this opportunity up.

I had twelve points available, and I sank the first nine into the Dungeon Warfare skill, jumping it straight from level one to ten. And as I'd hoped, on hitting ten, I got a bonus.

Congratulations!

You have reached level 10 in the Dungeon Warfare skill! As you prepare to expand your second dungeon, you have gained a greater understanding of dungeon combat tactics. Your minions now receive a 20% bonus to their combat effectiveness when fighting within one mile of the dungeon's influence. You can more easily issue simple battle commands and assign simplistic formations to your forces, or choose to delegate this skill using the Battle Management tab, allowing for more coordinated attacks and defences. With further progress in this skill, you will learn to create and deploy more specialized minions with unique abilities to bolster your dungeon's military might.

Additional Bonus!

Due to leading more than ten thousand dungeon-born creations in battle since unlocking your first dungeon, you have gained the ability to nominate and create NCO classes.

Note: You gain the ability to raise and control 1 NCO class dungeon individual per level in this skill, along with one officer class unlocking for each twenty levels gained.

The remaining three points, I invested in the Advanced Dungeon Management skill, taking that from level one to four. It didn't make a huge difference at first, but it wasn't long until Aly was reaching out.

"*Maaaatt.*"

The long drawing out of my name let me know that I was in trouble already.

"Yeah?" I'd asked her, focusing more on assigning the first NCOs in the dungeon, and wondering what the difference in them being assigned in this way, rather than me simply naming them before, like I had with Beta, were.

Kilo was the obvious choice, after all, and I made him a sergeant, with Beta given a sergeant major role, despite her not being here currently. We had every other surviving advanced wraith as a lance corporal. That gave me seven positions filled, and I named another of the wraiths, the one that had been with me since the start of the disastrous attack on the camp.

When I'd checked, it was now level three, having killed a few of the enemy, and the uncommon wraiths were seemingly happily following its orders already.

We'd lost a few of them to the damn spawnskulls, but the others were ready and waiting as well.

"What the hell did you do this time!" Aly had snapped. "Seriously, Matt, I know this was you!"

"Uh…"

"Did you think we'd not notice, was that it?" she asked. "You thought, 'Oh Aly and Kelly, they're just women; they'll never be able to count' or something—was that it?"

"What?" I asked, totally fucking bewildered…until she couldn't do it anymore.

"Matt, I'm sorry." She broke off the clear attempt at joking, and instead forced a smile and shook her head. "I couldn't help it. How did you do it?"

"What?" I tried again, as Kelly appeared as well.

"It wasn't you?" Kelly looked concerned. "The increase was so sudden and unexpected, I thought there was no way that it could be…"

"Increase?" I'd asked, then smacked my forehead as I finally understood. "Ah, crap, that?"

"What did you do?" Aly asked again. "How did you break the system this time?"

"Is it, um…about a twenty percent increase?" I tried, relief rising as she nodded.

"The increase in mana from the skeleton teams is, yeah, twenty percent right on the nose. Though I can't tell why. Nothing else has changed."

"A skill." I nodded, then cursed. "Dammit, I should have put all the levels in that!"

"Slow down, Matt, and explain it." She moved closer. "What did you do?"

"I've been holding onto my skill points," I explained. "Not because I didn't want to use them, but I was going to use them to artificially boost my ability in crafting, doing glassblowing or something…once I'd learned the first few levels naturally."

"Why?" Aly frowned.

"Because I knew we needed more crafters to make things. We talked about this, right?" I pointed out.

"Sure, but then…ah." Kelly nodded. "I get it. You'd been saving the points and once we got Sierra to be able to do glassblowing, you realized you didn't need to save the points?"

"Pretty much, yeah," I agreed.

"Because you've got so much time to play at crafting," she agreed absently. "So, what was it? The skill, I mean?"

That had started the whole conversation off about the skills, and that had taken even more time.

The long story short was that the mana that any minions were bringing in, or any resource or task they were carrying out, just got a permanent boost of twenty percent—and that was massive.

Looking at the Dungeon Warfare skill, I still thought—after a little consideration—that I'd made the right choice, but damn. Knowing that I could have boosted the dungeon's income by such a massive margin made it a clear contender for every single point I could spare in the future.

I checked and sure enough, the two points that were there to be gained as a reward for killing or recruiting the queen were standard skill points, not class ones. And as such, I could spend them on this if I wanted.

I'd actually dismissed them as unimportant when I'd looked at it earlier, and now I was damn pleased. They'd just gone from a minor thing into a major boost for the dungeon any day of the week.

All of this had filled the last day, making a massive difference to the way the fight was building up. But now, as I marched across the melting slush, with the cold wind tugging at my beard and hair, I couldn't help but pray on the inside.

This was going to be a bastard of a fight, I just knew it, and the butcher's bill was going to be horrific.

CHAPTER THIRTY

The slap of wings nearby made their arrival clear, but damn, I couldn't help but stare at the sight of the things. As the first spawnskull arrived, dropping down from flying on overwatch up high, to literally hovering, watching over us, I slowed and stared up.

The creature was one of the most horrific mutations I'd yet seen, and that was including the eidolon and all the mad shit I'd fought since.

The spawnskulls slowly moved in closer—four in total, with two of them dropping in to examine us. The other two stayed up high, which I didn't like. But they didn't attack straightaway, giving me the chance to really see them for myself, in the flesh.

The two that came in for a closer look were clearly different in design, though both had the same rotten and diseased appearance. With the frost-bitten black and grey patches of skin, the missing feathers and bare flesh, they'd clearly long since left the realm of normal natural evolution behind.

Where most birds—all, in fact, as far as I knew—had feathers, these had a mixture of feathers and flesh. Although occasional patches of feathers hung on, they were clearly falling out. Their wings were more like those of bats or flying dinosaurs instead. The skin that showed through underneath was dying. The cold was clearly doing massive damage. And then adding on the bruising, the rotting mass, and finally the vurms?

Nope.

Even if the queen wanted to keep these alive for a bit longer, I didn't see it happening.

They had malformed beaks, a mixture of crocodile and seagull, all twisted, with teeth that jutted free in weird directions. Under its beak, a seething pouch of twisting, writhing vurms moved ceaselessly.

They eyed us as they flew in close circles, alternating hovering and beating those great wings, more than two meters across. They stared down at us through milky white eyes, and I shivered.

Of all creatures, of everything that the damn queen could have decided to use, why the hell would they base anything off the beach bastards?

They were the most psychotic and evil of all birds already, and that was before you considered the fact that even the more common and "normal" birds in the area—the goddamn pigeons—were basically rats with wings.

These were closer in temperament to trash pandas, or honey badgers with wings, and humanity was only still around because that state of affairs had never come about before.

Suddenly, one of them twisted, swooping in close and landing on the muddy, slushy grass with a ferocious flapping. A back leg snapped as it landed too hard, but the creature barely noticed, lurching to the right as the other leg compensated. It lunged forward, tilting its head side to side, studying us.

From this close, it was yet more obvious that even without the earlier fighting, these abominations were nearing their end. The spawnskull looked terrible. Its toast-rack chest rose and fell, tongue protruding from the side of its malformed beak. It seemed to be waiting for us to make the first move.

The queen's actions—if she could "think" at all—made me suppose she was confused at our behavior, which was exactly what we intended. More or less.

As we continued to march onward toward the local armory, the path arced to the right, flanked by towering trees that ringed the base. The lowest end of the hill rose to our left, narrowing the path.

From what we could see, the queen was oblivious to the difference between the guns her infected had and the point of the armory itself, considering the stacks of ammo left in boxes and the weapons that were left in place.

The power failure had apparently disabled the magnetic locks throughout the camp. Although secure areas had physical locks as a contingency, some "normal" areas like accommodations looked to have been in the process of upgrading. Keycard entry locks had popped open upon losing power, while older, physical key locks remained closed.

The armory had both keycard and physical locks, making sure it stayed sealed when the power failed. We'd talked about it and believed one armory had been open when the coronaught queen took over, so her drones found some areas accessible and others locked. Whatever passed for thinking for her apparently didn't include considering the significance of the locked areas, leaving the second armory untouched.

During our search, we'd discovered the base had two main armories in close proximity, apparently for entirely sensible reasons beyond my non-military understanding. It was obvious that they aimed to restrict access to a select few for this second one, though.

This armory seemed to be the specialist one, while the first contained the SA80 rifle family, basic handguns, and usual loadouts, which were probably more useful to us traditionally.

It had been frustrating to find that had been looted, when we saw it in the dungeon sense before the assault began, as a significant amount of the pre-loaded ammunition had already been used previously. But the secondary one was still intact.

Although the colonel and others had been seriously pissed to discover they'd apparently been storing loaded weapons, they eventually conceded that in the end times, scrapping the rules on not doing that kinda made sense.

However, the *real* treasure lay in the ASM units stored in the second armory. Despite warnings about their potentially compromised condition, we hoped that at least some of them would still function, and whoa boy, were we going to find out, as those were what the local garrison had used against our corpse lords and weapons emplacements when they'd attacked us.

I'd wrongly assumed they were all good for nothing for us. Now, the comments from conversations with Griffiths and others made me think that the shoulder-mounted systems were too high-tech, while things like the old school ones that you saw in the '80s movies would have probably still been fine.

That was…well, it wasn't wrong, but there were ways around it apparently.

The two units that Griffiths had when he was traveling down from the top of Scotland had been too high-tech; they'd been utterly useless. The aiming mechanism needed a distance to be traveled and input to the small warhead before priming, and they wouldn't track, activate, or detonate without it.

The one they'd managed to fire had hit their target and bounced off, useless.

The colonel had pointed out that this wasn't the case for all these units, though.

He'd not had any at his base, but the camp had specialist weapons. The L2A1 ASM was a rocket launcher that was basically a fiberglass tube, with a chemical propellant and a mechanical fuse—though, admittedly, they still needed arming.

The issue here was going to be deterioration. The armory was secure, but the systems that were designed to keep the temperatures constant were long dead.

I'd never even considered that a fucking bomb could go off, like an old cheese, but apparently that was normal.

If these missiles and shit that the government spent literally billions on a year weren't kept in just the right way, they went off and were slightly less dangerous than a wet fart. Or, apparently, they could go the other way entirely.

The sarge and Finger had told me about their experience in the sandbox, watching as the army's ammo techs set up a controlled detonation of over two billion quid's worth of ammunition and explosives, all because some idiot government official had decided it wasn't a good idea to "waste the taxpayers' money" on a specialist cooled and controlled ammunition storage area when the units were only going to be in the area for a few months.

The cost was apparently just over a million to build the needed storage area. That was an obscene amount of money to spend, knowing that as soon as they moved out of the area it'd be abandoned.

I'd nodded along with it as Finger told me, then winced as the sarge then explained that as all the weapons had to be assumed to have deteriorated, they'd not been possible to transport back at the end of the deployment, so they'd had to be destroyed on site.

Two *billion* quid's worth of gear lost, and that needed to be spent on replacements for the saving of one million that could have been spent. The army had tried to explain it, but all the government guy could see was the headlines of him approving the overspend on the original bases.

That second restocking fee hadn't been on him, and wouldn't tie back to him most likely, so he wrote it off, and even got a promotion to the cabinet over the next few years.

The sarge and Finger had watched as the ammo techs set the entire dump up, rigged it, then detonated it, and they'd said the destruction was terrifying.

Although it was also cool as hell, they admitted.

That was the thing here: the storage area was designed to keep these things in top condition, but they were also meant to be stored in carefully controlled temperatures.

That meant that the rockets might work, or they might not. We were gonna find out if the shit hit the fan, because at least the ones in the base in Newcastle had been maintained. These hadn't, making them far more dangerous.

The building that we approached on our left was the sealed armory, with its twin beyond it, separated by a few dozen meters.

The front of the buildings was like any military building in the world: solidly constructed, if dull, with a multitude of cameras and heavy doors.

As we approached it, more of the infected appeared, stepping out and blocking off the armory they had access to, apparently thinking that they'd let us go as far as the queen was willing to.

Some were monstrous, a handful of the figures misshapen with claws, tentacles, and jaws that drooled and clacked. But most were human still, or looked it, with only a handful of those that exited looking like they were too far gone to save.

We kept going, looking the party over; more were coming. A handful turned into dozens as more of them exited the buildings. I cursed under my breath as the first of a second group stepped out of the building we wanted as well.

Most of these were human still, but one that stood on the right-hand side was paler than the rest, with a protruding stomach that the body armor struggled to contain, and clear signs of vurms roaming under the skin.

"That one." I slid into the dungeon sense and focused, barely able to maintain everything as I sent it to Kelly. *"For Kilo…"*

"Got it," she agreed.

I banished the sense, hoping that I'd been clear enough.

I'd also been hoping that the front door into this building would be locked, and that we could break the lock in the dungeon sense, then just turn and burn, run inside—or better yet, walk calmly.

If the queen didn't know what we were doing, then she might wait until we got literally into the middle of the nest before stopping us from getting any farther. But as they all lifted their rifles as one, it was clear this was as far as we were going.

"Get ready." I lifted my left hand high. "We come in peace. Take me to your leader," I tried.

"Fuck's sake," Chris muttered behind me. "That's the best you've got?"

"Shut it."

For a long minute, we just stared at each other in silence, as sweat rolled down my back and tickled my ass crack. This wasn't going well, and I really hoped my shield was going to help when the bullets started flying.

It was an air one, something I'd practiced for a few hours, over and over before we set off, fine-tuning the spell for a minute, then meditating, then trying again.

The result was a shield I could make literally invisible. But as the first splatters of rain started to fall, the real issue became clear.

It was invisible, but any impact cost me mana, as did holding it at all.

In this case, I was down to half the mana I'd had on setting off, just over a thousand mana now. And not only were the few drops that had already hit my shield still hanging there, suspended atop it, but they were draining my mana more by the second.

"We…come…in…peace…" The figures all around us suddenly chorused as one. "Take…us…to…"

"I am the leader," I called out. "Who speaks for you?"

"I…am…the…leader…" they started.

I cut them off again. "Do you understand me, or are you just repeating my words?" I asked, before cursing as they repeated that entirely. "Okay, let's try this…"

I lowered my hand and waited, then raised it, holding it.

There was a long pause; then, as one, the humans with the rifles lifted their left hands free, holding them up.

I grinned, then nodded and lowered that hand. Then raised it, then lowered it. The copies on all sides did the same.

"Get ready," I said aloud, figuring it was getting closer and closer to kickoff. This time I let go of the rifle, letting it clatter against my chest on the restraining strap, and lifted both hands this time.

There was a pause, then the stupid fuckers did the same, and I grinned evilly.

"Okay, now this…" I tried, bending my elbows and putting my hands flat on my head. They did the same. I lifted them back off, extended them before me and interlaced the fingers.

The creature apparently had a lot of difficulty with managing that level of dexterity, before on the third repetition it managed it.

It was like leading a dance or an exercise session, but as I reached up and pressed my interlaced fingers to my head, I smiled, and spoke aloud as the infected all around me did the same.

"Okay, so is there anyone there?" I tried again.

Again the repeat and no sign of any understanding, which left me with three options. I noted the way that vurms under the infected carrier's skin started to move with more and more speed, clearly getting ready.

I could keep trying to communicate and ignore the obvious hints they were getting ready to try to take us. I could roll the dice and let the vurms take me—not a good idea, but if I could keep my mind free, more or less, I might be able to form a link with the queen and talk, somehow.

The hint about recruiting her made it clear there was a way after all, or…or I could accept that this fucking creature was a perfect example of everything wrong in the world these days, and that I needed to eliminate her entirely.

"Plan C, people. Battering rams and bracing on three," I said, bloody glad that the queen was this stupid, even if I knew that it was going to be damn costly in mana.

"Two…" I said clearly, carefully taking one large step forward, then another. "One…"

They all did the same, and the group behind me spread out. Kilo and Chris took station on either side of me, slightly behind, with Finger behind them.

The wraiths flowed back and the corpse lords stepped up, getting ready.

"Zero. Fuck them up." Then I started to run.

The corpse lords moved first. A mixture of my orders and my intent made its way into their minds to make it very clear what I needed.

They burst into motion. The two of them lumbered into the lead, as the wraiths screamed and cast their shields to both sides and above.

As soon as we moved, the infected tried to respond. Their fingers interlaced on their heads slowed them an extra heartbeat, as did freeing their rifles and getting them into position.

We covered the first few meters at a sprint. The left-most corpse lord hit the four figures that had exited the door to the target building, sweeping them from their feet.

The next two that were inside the door were left clear, but the path to the door was clean now.

They stepped forward, both of them firing—of course they would have the fucking ammo—and my shield held, though the mana was dropping incredibly fast.

The other fire that came in was sporadic and uncoordinated; most of it hit the corpse lords who raced ahead of us. They plowed into the middle of the mass, lashing out with fists and feet and slamming infected from their feet as I led the way instead, straight for the door.

The fire that did get through made it clear that the only reason we were still alive was blind luck. I smashed the rifle barrel aside and then ran into the figure in the door, shrinking and angling my rapidly diminishing shield to let me through, as the first bullets drew blood.

My shield popped and failed. The mana backlash made me snarl as I drove the infected from his feet and went down atop him, wrestling for the rifle.

Behind me, I sensed as much as heard Chris leaping into the fray. His hammer and physical shield combo let him run straight into the second figure, though the third was going to be an issue.

I'd not seen the other four inside the room, and as much as I'd have rather taken these fuckers alive…

Kilo was there then. Twin blasts of ice erupted upward from the ground, forming arcing shields that cracked and resealed as the gunfire from the other four poured in.

Then he was hit, falling sideways. The first advanced wraith leapt over him, landing between the twin shields. The two of us, on one side of the room, fought with the figures on the ground, and the four that stood waiting.

Bullets shifted from the shields and the downed kobold, and instead hurtled at the wraith. But they were stopped a half second later by its own shield.

It held long enough for the monstrous creature to lash out, talons rending as it beheaded first one, then a second of the infected. Then its shield went as well. Before the wraith could kill another, it was screeching in pain and anger.

I rolled to the side, shoving the barrel down and then wrenched it sideways, rotating it in wide arc that ended with a snap of bone as I yanked it back and around.

The infected soldier under me made no sound of pain, and instead shifted to bite at me, continuing to try to get the weapon into position.

I was dimly aware of the fight going on around me.

Outside, the two corpse lords were going down. The concentrated fire, even if more than half of the weapons no longer worked, was enough to take them out.

The two skeletons that had been at the back? Dead. They'd barely made it a handful of steps before they were down. One of the spawnskulls dropping like a rock had made sure of that.

It'd crashed into them both, half bouncing from the edge of the wraith's shield and sliding, then vomiting up an arcing spray of vurms as its arms slashed and tore at the skeletons.

The vurms had hit the wraiths' shields and slid free to coat the ground. But some of them had apparently hit the windows as well, and they'd done that at the same time that deflected bullets had hit them from the inside.

Outside, I could hear the madness that was Jack giving his all as well, racing back and forth, ignoring the counterattacks of the mere fleshy creatures that were trying to stop him, as mechanized destruction was unleashed.

Glass was shattering, infected were battling, and Chris and I were frantically trying to get a grip. Kilo twisted, hissing with a hand pressed over his right thigh to stanch the bleeding, and gestured to the windows, forming ice across the shattered sections and sealing them back up.

Finger was disarming another soldier. He'd shot one in the head—a single shot—then tackled another to the ground in a smooth roll that had taken the unsteady infected down with him, before breaking both its arms and ripping its weapons free.

Then he was cursing, rolling free and coming to his feet, handgun in a two-handed grip. He fired a single shot into the struggling figure's head.

"Vurm's trying to get loose!" he shouted.

The carrier—the vurm breeder or whatever it was—had somehow gotten around the corpse lords. As I finally wrenched the gun free fully, I saw that fucker grabbing the doorframe and struggling up the three steps to enter, with more behind him.

I reacted on instinct, pulling the trigger into the face of the infected soldier under me—the gun promptly jammed and did fuck all—at the same time that I lashed out with my left hand and slammed an Incinerate into the head of the carrier.

I promptly hissed. The world around me went white with overload and pain as the spell drew on my life force instead. The mana that I'd replenished since my shield failed and bottomed me out only was a few points—and that was when the soldier under me struck, smashing me in the face with his rifle butt.

The helmet I'd been wearing had barely fit; mine had gone missing and I'd just grabbed one of the soldiers' when I needed it before leaving. It tore loose now, the strap giving way.

I fell sideways; both hands came up to clutch at my head, and the rifle held in my right released. Tumbling sideways, I missed the infected that had been under me twisting around the gun and turning it on me, pulling the trigger again and again, clearly not understanding that it was jammed.

That was when Chris plowed into him from the side, lifting him and slamming him into the other wall; he bounced off, and then Chris hurled him to the ground.

301

He hit hard, losing his grip on the gun and totally ignoring the handgun on his hip. His head came up as he hissed…then snapped back in a spray of blood as Chris hit him with the head of his hammer, shattering the skull and killing him.

The big druid was moving again already. He bounded across the ground, shoving his left hand out and casting a spell outside, as the second wraith in the room finished the remaining infected off.

Finger ran to Kilo, dropping down and starting first aid then—no hesitation in dealing with a wounded comrade, even if the big kobold wasn't human.

Then it was Chris's turn to come under fire. His big steel shield rung over and over as he tried to hold off the incoming bullets from outside…while light sparked and spun from the ground before him.

Motes danced, climbing higher and higher as the others went to work. The room had been claimed the day before already, and the influence we pushed out now that we were inside was enough to claim it as dungeon territory again.

As such, either Kelly or Aly was hard at work summoning our reinforcements and securing our beachhead. The others, the majority of the expendable forces, streamed free of their hidey-holes and raced inward.

I forced myself to all fours, then to my feet, reaching up and dragging blood free from where it ran from my nose, then snorted and spat more onto the ground, glancing around.

The windows were shimmering, clearly being replaced with thicker glass where we could, and covered in either ice or stone as someone summoned it in place. But as the enemy were even now rushing the building, we couldn't make more changes for long.

The infected in the room were dead, and most of us were injured. In my case, it was minor; my health was already tracking upward again. For Chris, it was barely a scratch across his face and a few rows in his armor that were clearly the result of bullets landing. But for Kilo, it was worse.

He'd sealed the wound with ice, which even for a cryomancer had to be fucking uncomfortable, though a bulging light that filled the room, rising from the ground, made it clear that a healing tower was on the way.

One of the wraiths was down, a bullet-riddled mess, but the second one was still going. Or, more to the point, it was tearing bloody chunks free of the nearest dead, feeding them—still dripping—into its maw with every sign of enjoyment.

I nodded to Chris as he looked over at me, and he stepped back. The replacement "door" solidified before anything could get close enough to stop it.

It wouldn't hold long. It was literally a slab of stone, sealed on the ground and slightly shorter than the roof, which was Sod's Law. But as long as it lasted a hot minute, that was all we needed.

The room was wide, with a corridor leading off the left and right, and directly opposite, a second door…one that was much larger and with warning signs about who could enter, and why, as well as the consequences for those who tried and weren't permitted entry.

Reaching down, I checked Kilo, regretting that I was out of mana, as I couldn't use the focal orb and heal the poor fucker, but that was life. "You okay?" I asked him, waving Chris in.

"Yes," he lied, teeth gritted.

"Bullshit." I smiled. "Thanks for the save."

"Anytime," he responded, as Chris moved over, crouching next to us.

"I'll get it," he assured me.

I nodded, passing him the orb, and stood, moving around the wraith that was still eating, and headed toward the door. I stopped, then turned to it and pointed to the dead soldiers.

"Either eat their heads entirely, or leave them alone," I ordered it. "The vurms are in there somewhere, so either you eat them completely or we try to bury them later. No pulling them apart."

It stared at me, clearly not liking the orders, as I'd noted the way it was rooting around in its current victim's chest, the heart lifting free in one clawed hand. Then it bowed its head in assent.

I moved on without another word, approaching the door and hearing the click as someone—Aly, I was betting—intervened and sorted the lock.

Pushing it open, I found myself in a man trap, a small room that had a set of chairs against the wall I'd entered by, but beyond that and the multiple cameras in the room, there was nothing but the gate.

The gate—as the sarge had called it—was a narrow spot with steel bars on both sides, leaving a gap that was far too small for anyone to get through, but enough space to pass most weapons through.

As I approached it, the bars shimmered, then melted into motes of light. I continued on, stepping inside, before coming to a stop as I stared at the neatly organized weapons that could have once taken out entire battlefields.

This was the heavy weaponry playground. Racks of incredibly expensive shoulder-mounted rocket launchers were followed by carefully protected ammunition, though only a hundred or so were in here for these.

There were more on the base, I'd been assured, but they were in a second underground storage, one that was deliberately offset so that if something happened to this, that would survive.

I didn't know whether it was any more intact than this one, but I damn well hoped so.

One of these fuckers could have taken the necromancer Dickless's dragon form out with a single hit, and I was well aware that there were more threats out there that we needed heavy weapons for.

There were sections dedicated to the massive tripod-mounted, crew-served heavy machine guns, more that stored specialist rifles, and grenade launchers, as well as mortars and three tables that were covered in disassembled weapons.

There were things in there I had no clue what you could do with, things that looked to be part of tank-mounted weapons systems and handguns that were weird looking—apparently someone's fun and probably highly unofficial project.

Sights, specialist magazines, and more…each had their own places. As Finger stepped in behind me, he looked like a kid at Christmas.

"Man, I always wanted a go at one of these…" he said softly, reaching out and picking up the ASM rocket launcher. "You know these things can take out a tank? They cost nearly fifty grand a piece, so you don't get to practice with them. But damn, I always wanted to shoot one."

"Well, when we know they're safe." I shrugged. "As long as we've got some for the fight and some for the dungeon, I don't care if you steal one for shits and giggles."

"Seriously?" he asked incredulously.

"Yeah, but you make sure an armorer passes it for use first," I said firmly. "And even then, you fire it well away from anyone in case it explodes."

"Worth the risk." He chuckled, then stepped back, shaking his head. A dozen fresh lights all started to spark upward, as new dungeon creatures were being born before his eyes. "Man, I'm never going to get used to that," he admitted.

"You will," I assured him. "Well, you will if you live long enough."

"Yeah, on that comforting note, mind if I find myself a new toy?" He gestured in the direction of the weapons to one side.

"Feel free." I waved him off, moving to the nearest table and sitting down, sliding into the dungeon sense. *"Where are we with the plan?"* I asked Aly, who was waiting for me.

"Moving ahead," she assured me. *"The queen doesn't seem to have realized that we have anything in here. She's focused on pouring more vurms in, and seems to think that we're trapped, so she can turn her attention to the incoming forces."*

"And the fliers?"

"The harpies are vicious fuckers," she said. *"And they really don't like being told what to do. Kelly hates them already, but she admits they're great for clearing the skies."*

"She's guiding the minions?"

"She is." Aly nodded. *"The others are pushing to expand our zone of control, but we need to move quickly before we lose the opportunity."*

"Sounds good. You sealing this off?" I asked.

"Yeah, already done." She nodded. *"And I've got a pair of corpse lords ready to go as soon as the coast is clear. I'll give them a couple of deep containers on wheels, carts basically, and we'll load them up with a few of everything. They can run back and forth with everything we can loot."*

"Just in case my plan fails and we all die?" I asked. *"I mean, considering the armory is at the end of the corridor that I'll be in, when I set this shit off."*

"Well, I already got my husband out." She shrugged, playing like it meant nothing to her. *"If we lose you now, no great hardship."*

"Yeah, yeah." I snorted. *"Fuck you very much."*

"Seriously, though, Kelly will be tied up watching over the incoming forces, so I'll be here with you. No last-minute changes?"

"No, we need to close it down and fast. There was no response when I tried to talk to the queen through her drones. We make one more attempt, then we tear the camp down around her ears. If we're lucky, we gain control of it without too much damage and once she's dead, we can absorb everything in there. If not, we seal the fucker up in lead and move on with our lives."

"Good luck then and... Wait a minute." She vanished, and I snorted.

"Oh yeah, no stress, I'll just sit around with my thumb up my arse as we lose the element of surprise!" I called, before sighing and looking around, knowing she'd not be wasting time if there was a choice.

While she was gone, I started with the next phase, trying to keep busy, as I damn well knew how little time we had…but she was back before I'd summoned more than a handful of wraiths.

"We found them!" she told me excitedly. *"Rhodes, Andre, and Jimmy, as well as a handful of others. There's a group of them incoming from the north. They've been hiding out there, apparently!"*

"You're sure they're not infected?" I asked.

"If they are, we've got problems," she countered. *"They can access the dungeon, so I really hope not."*

"How the hell did they survive?"

"Salt!" She shook her head, mystified. *"There's a couple of small-scale salt deposits in the area, and there's something about the mineral makeup that the vurms don't like. They try to cross it, and they die."*

"Damn, that's lucky." I grunted. *"So they've been hiding out in a room filled with salt?"*

"In a cave, apparently. It's something the locals found a year or so ago, and they've been working to get it up to commercial production. There was a long section that they'd carved out, and as soon as the vurms get in there, they go nuts. The trio were drawing in small teams of the infected and trapping them, letting them out as soon as the vurms die."

"So we've got a way to get rid of them?" I asked excitedly.

"Yes and no." She shook her head. *"We can't be sure, so it's not a viable solution. We still need to be able to look inside. But it means we can take people there if we need to. There's nearly thirty of them. They saw the signs of the fight and decided to come looking. Rhodes and the twins saw the signs of the dungeon."*

"The summoning stands out." I nodded. *"Okay, you ready for the next phase?"*

"Give me two minutes," she said, starting back and looking around, clearly working through things, and I nodded.

"Okay, open the door as soon as you're ready."

With that, I left the dungeon sense and spoke up quickly. Kilo was walking again, and Chris was putting his armor back on, having presumably repaired the damage.

"Get ready, everyone. Next stage in less than a minute."

I was careful not to say what it was just in case, though they all knew.

At the back of the armory, in a section that was once again accessed by a keycard and physical key, was a large metal door, that in turn led into a corridor that was sloped downward. From there, it joined up with a second corridor that ran into the hidden underground base.

There'd been a few sections we'd still not explored but the majority we'd already been able to reach through expanding the dungeon's influence.

At the lowest level in the hidden base, there were the bioweapons and nuke sections, and that, we were sure, was where the queen was.

It was a long run from where we were, at the farthest possible point from there, but the most secure and closest entry point.

305

That meant that as soon as we could, we were going to set off running—sprinting, really—along the buried corridors, heading straight for the queen.

The plan was to try one more attempt at negotiation, but if not, then no stress. I was seriously hoping that our distraction of running and gunning down here would draw the queen's attention. That way, she might miss the rest of the plan.

There was a good chance the death of the queen would have an effect on the infected, but we had no way to know what that would be. They might all drop dead immediately; they might be freed and cured—or anything in between. So we needed to keep her attention fixed on us, and move it.

Also, if we were exposed as being the leaders that I hoped it would see us as, then there was no reason to try to do the whole thing with mutating and threatening to kill its minions if we didn't cooperate.

If the shit hit the fan, though, there were two options left. I fully intended to use them if need be: napalm and heavy weapons.

CHAPTER THIRTY-ONE

"Go, go, go!" I roared as the door ahead of us finally opened. Three lights had appeared one after the other on the right-hand side, each with a colored glass covering that made me smile, as I guessed at Aly's intervention there.

We'd gotten the message on the first red light, and as it hit yellow, everyone had tensed.

On green, we were moving.

The door collapsed into the corridor beyond. The first corpse lord was moving already; three more behind it ran in formation. One was an ammo carrier, but the other three were there to make sure that if anything fucked with us, there wouldn't be enough left to bury afterward.

They each carried the vehicle-mounted version of the heavy machine gun that Chris was lugging around. Although they had to stoop in the corridor, there was no way that anything that picked a fight with them was walking away afterward.

Behind them were ten wraiths, then my small team, and ten more uncommon skeletons. They, in turn, were each armed with the ASM launchers, or carrying ammunition, as they alternated between shooter and loader.

Lastly, two more corpse lords and two more wraiths. The corpse lords had grenade launchers and a fuckload of ammo, and the wraiths were ready to cast shielding spells.

This was a fight we weren't going to lose, nor let be put off to another day.

The sound as we all ran in the descending corridor was incredible, and that was down to just the clatter of bone, feet, and boots. I'd started to wonder whether I'd even know if the fight was joined, when I found out definitively that yes, I would.

The lead corpse lord saw movement in the distance—something that was neither one of the dungeon-born, nor an ally—and it opened fire without hesitation.

The chattering boom of the heavy machine gun echoed around crazily, filling the corridor and making me wince, but we kept running.

The fire cut off after a second, and almost no time at all later, I was slowing as I ran past a body in the corridor. It'd been a quadruped of some kind, but what it'd specifically started out as…I couldn't tell. The combination of mutation and heavy fire had made sure that the only description that was beyond doubt now was "that fucker be dead."

We passed a joining corridor and kept going, not slowing at all, knowing that it led up to the other armory building.

One of the wraiths broke off, taking up station. Its field of influence was just enough to hold the position for the shimmering motes to appear.

They burst from the floor, spiraling upward as the great invisible 3D printer of the dungeon began work. Then, in less than a minute, it'd been walled off.

A second burst of fire ahead, followed by another, more sustained one made me grit my teeth as we kept running.

We were one level down, that was all, and the area we needed to reach was on the fourth.

Each level that we passed had multiple offices, work and research stations, and even a significant guard post at the top and bottom levels with a small barracks area in the middle.

As we hit the first set of offices, dog-like creatures burst free of the concealing darkness and raced at us, only for most of them to be cut down by the lead corpse lord.

Four made it past his withering fire, as the HMG suddenly clattered to a stop and jammed. But Barry was guiding the boney bastards, and the massive creation simply stepped aside, pressing itself to the wall, and let the next in line take over, opening fire instead.

The creatures were small, barely a meter high for the very tallest, and although hairless, they didn't have the same frost-bitten and mold-covered look that their friends aboveground had.

Instead, they had strange heads that were all massive eyes. They ran with their stomachs distended, swinging from side to side with every step they took.

"Carriers!" I spat. "Kilo, you're up!"

The second corpse lord stopped firing as the last fell, torn in half lengthways by the bullets. But even as it slid to a halt across the ground, blood fountaining and body bouncing, the worms were breaking free.

They writhed and danced, and as we'd not stopped running, we were getting seriously close to them, by the time Kilo pushed past me and started to cast.

It was one of what was becoming his go-to spells, as the blue-white blast of ice and wind howled from his hands, hands that were pointed down at a forty-five-degree angle, as he tried to avoid freezing the wraith before him.

I heard the hisses of displeasure that came from the creature. I was forced to split my attention equally between watching to see whether it was going to turn on the advanced kobold, and making sure I was jumping over the damn vurms.

They were dying, and dying fast, as Kilo washed the ground back and forth with both hands, coating them in a deep layer of ice.

Soon enough, we were past the first set of rooms; a single wraith had peeled off to double-check the rooms behind us. By the time I glanced back, I saw it pausing by the nearest door and waiting as a second wall started to grow across the entrance to that floor, sealing it away too.

The floor canted downward again. I followed our team; Chris, Finger, and Kilo stayed close as we jogged in the middle of the mass of unliving matter. The passages switched back and forth, the ground angled in a way that suggested it was intended that carts or whatever could be used to transport things in here.

The next floor was silent. Nothing lay hiding there, and I dared have hope, before we took the next looping switchback and emerged right into the concentrated fire of something I'd never seen before.

They were multiple-legged monstrosities, fused remnants of several humans and at least one local animal. Though what it'd been was hard to tell, considering the darkness of the passage, the distance, and the fire from both sides that blazed away frantically.

The passage angled down at a gentle run, then flattened out, the passage vanishing out of sight. Two sets of assault rifles clutched in two sets of human-looking arms blazed away at our lead corpse lord, staggering it and blasting chips and fragments of bone free.

It returned fire. A chattering cacophony filled the air. The echoing reverberation made me wince, as it fired on and on in the enclosed area.

I only caught glimpses as the corpse lords before me and between the fight swayed and bounced in their run—a hint of chitin in the distance here, a flash of putrescent flesh there, with blood and bone exploding out and painting the walls as we pushed on.

Reaching out, I confirmed Jack was still active, crushing his way through the enemy. I'd ordered him to take out anything that wasn't human—so any monster he found—then to head for the armory entrance.

Then we'd found that the door was too small for him. He'd been about to hit it at speed, and Aly was going to change it so that the structure would fold under the impact. Then he was to hold it, as she rebuilt it with him on the other side.

If he managed that, and she was able to seal it again, then he would head down to join us. If not? He'd stay up there and make sure our escape was open and available later.

I triggered Examine, squinting and cursing as the latest monstrosity of the coronaught infection was made clear.

Drone Warrior Coronaught	Mutated Creature

Warrior Drones are the twisted remnants of human soldiers forcibly fused with local fauna by the insidious coronaught vurms. These parasitic creatures, each less than three inches long, gather mass and genetic templates as they grow, reshaping their hosts into nightmarish forms.

In the case of the Warrior Drone, the coronaught vurms appear to have combined human DNA with that of local animals, creating a grotesque hybrid that stands upright on four legs, with a body that is a patchwork of human and animal parts. The drone's central torso still resembles a human, and its arms bear weapons proven in battle.

The head is a twisted fusion of human and beast, with glowing, inhuman eyes and a simple hole where once the mouth lay.

Warrior Drones are not sophisticated creatures, driven only by the coronaught vurms' instinctive desire to defend the hive and destroy any threats. They attack in swarms, using their enhanced strength and speed to overwhelm their targets.

Beware: Soldier Drones have been observed to lack any visible auditory organs, suggesting that the coronaught vurms have evolved to discard this potential weakness.

Abilities:

Frenzy: When in proximity to a threat, Soldier Drones can enter a frenzied state, lashing out with increased ferocity and speed. However, this state is short-lived and leaves the drone temporarily vulnerable afterward.

Hivemind: Soldier Drones are linked to the coronaught hive through a rudimentary telepathic bond, allowing them to coordinate their attacks and share sensory information.

Explosive colonization: Upon taking excessive damage, the drone may detonate, choosing to spread its genetics as far as possible. Beware, as any flesh spread from this action may contain a vurm.

Weaknesses: Fire, Ice, and Lightning Magics
HP: 250/250
Stamina: 500/500
Mana: 0/0
Speed: 6/10
Level: 3
Special Abilities: 3/3

HP: 250/250	Special Abilities: 3/3

This was a new class of coronaught, something that I'd never even considered. Though, as soon as I realized it, I also knew that I damn well should have.

After all, if the queen could make the soldiers under her command use the weapons they had, even if she couldn't yet understand the need for reloading, and she could create melded forms...why not combine the two?

The one that I saw, for all of a third of a second, or so it seemed, was four legged, two humans joined together front to back, and staggering, their heads melded into one that was just nasty.

The flesh had run, waxlike, to seal the two bodies together with something that I couldn't identify, but it had three human legs, one that looked like a horse or a cow's, and two sets of arms that angled out wide. The heads of two humans were fused together, side by side, creating a beast with four eyes, two ears, and one mouth.

The shoulders of the upper body held the main arms, with the second torso seemingly pressed into the first from behind. This one's shoulders exited around nipple height, making the first arms stick out wildly and reducing their mobility.

That the creature had to hold the gun in two right arms and two left, at such angles, meant that it was slow to aim. Certainly it was slower to aim than the corpse lord in the lead, who rattled off another burst of .50 caliber ammo.

The bullets slammed into, then punched straight through the creature; it flew from its feet. The short hail of bullets slammed into the walls and floor of the passage before ricocheting onward.

We kept running; we'd slowed, but never stopped, and the bodies crunched underfoot as we raced over their remains.

Ahead of us were a handful more of the drone warriors. Each time they appeared, they were punched from their feet with ease, staggering sideways and crashing to the floor.

It was almost too easy, until one of the wraiths turned to me, and hissed a word.

"Listen!"

I blinked, then cursed, focusing and reaching into the dungeon sense, feeling it as Chris, the legend that he was, took my arm unasked, keeping me going as I slid into that second reality.

It was Barry, and he was clearly focusing more on the corpse lords than on me. But as soon as he was sure I was paying attention, he spoke up.

"I need to pull the other two corpse lords back," he said tensely.

"Why?"

"It's too easy." He shook his head. "Either the queen has no clue about tactics, or she's just that dumb."

"Right?"

"Or it's a trap," he finished. "They show up spaced out just enough that they've drained the lead two of all ammo now. If they keep doing this, we'll hit the main level with only a handful of ammo."

"Fire less," I suggested. "I mean, a single bullet does the damage, right?"

"It does, and I would," he agreed, "if they weren't shite shots. And they're running. You know how hard it is to stop them firing off the full belt? It's only because we're firing enough lead down there that I could walk on it that we're hitting anything!"

"Okay, so what's the plan? And make it quick. I'm trying not to get run over by wraiths here," I said.

"We kick the wraiths into the lead. Use one with a shield up to catch anything incoming; the second in line casts a Deathbolt. They can pass through the shields, right?"

"They can when they cast it," I hedged. "Not sure if they can if it's their mate that does it."

"Fuck it, they can take turns then." He grunted. "Seriously, you don't want them running out of ammo before we get there."

"No, do it." Then, just before I could leave the sense, I thought about it, and spoke up again. "Summon another back at the armory and have them grab more ammo, bring it with them."

"Already done." He grunted, then shifted forward to control the corpse lords more.

I blinked myself free and promptly staggered, my foot coming down on an outstretched dead hand.

I bounced off the wall. Only Chris's grip under my arm kept me upright, and I snarled as I straightened, gritting my teeth as my right ankle flared in pain.

"You okay?"

"Yeah..." I gasped, then cursed, nodding and clapping him on the shoulder as I tried to pick up the speed...only to stagger and curse again.

"Twisted ankle?"

I nodded, gritting my teeth again. "Just what I needed."

"Here." He hit me with a shot from the focal orb, and I used a little magic to lighten myself as well, holding on for a handful of seconds, half flying and half jumping, letting only my left foot touch down. "Dude, we've got no time for hopping along." He grinned, and I glared at him, before testing the ankle again.

It was sore still, the healing taking a bit more than a few seconds, but it held. A few steps later, I let out a relieved breath and took my own weight again.

"Damn, I love magic."

"Yeah, man, me too." Chris nodded. "What's happening?"

I looked where he pointed. The wraiths and corpse lords shifted their running order, and I explained quickly, raising my voice for the other two to hear as well.

The passage ran past three doors, two close together and apparently leading to offices, while the third, hanging open, led to a barracks. Several torn scraps of clothing and dried blood coating the walls made it clear that not everyone in here had given up the fight easily.

As I passed the barracks, I saw more shimmering. The passage around us was lit by a barrage of light, as once again, it was sealed away.

The wraiths ahead of us were firing bolts almost constantly now, their shields being drained second by second as incoming fire hurtled into them.

"Summoning more wraiths." I heard distantly, now that I was listening for it.

I nodded, as we approached the last corner, turning back on ourselves one final time as the passage again led downward.

This time, as soon as the lead wraith took the corner, it screeched in outrage, slashing with its claws.

I only saw the result—the angle I was at too extreme—but the wraith was grabbed by a huge beak and ripped from sight, its right arm already falling, as heavy fire tore into the one next to it.

As the wraith fell, the one behind it started to cast, only to be met with more concentrated fire. It jerked sideways; bullets ripped through its thin chest and tore out of the far side, hitting the wall and ricocheting toward us.

As it went down, the corpse lord next in line stepped up. Not hesitating in the slightest, it opened fire, walking the stream of .50 caliber bullets through its wounded comrade and into the first of the drone warriors that marched around the corner.

The gunfire was horrific, hammering into the enemy and back over and over. I threw up a shield on instinct, then almost cut it, thinking it was a waste of a spell, until the first round hit it.

The wraiths and corpse lords were suddenly in a point-blank fight, as both sides tried to take the corner. The larger heavy machine guns were too unwieldy; the drone warriors were taken down, one after another.

Whatever the thing was that had grabbed the first wraith, it'd dragged its victim from sight and then had vanished. Now, the incoming waves of drone warriors seemed endless.

Kilo stepped up, trying to cast an ice-based spell, only to have another wraith step up into the way and be hit from behind, this time spinning in place and raising a hand that glowed with a Deathbolt forming.

"STOP!" I barked, stepping in front of Kilo and grabbing his arm, which had already started lowering. I pointed my rifle at the wraith, glaring at it, until it hissed in fury and spun about.

I had a sudden sureness that had I not raised my control levels over the dungeon-born with those class skills, I'd have been up shit creek right about now.

The first of the corpse lords had been put out of action by the jamming of his heavy machine gun. The second had almost run out of ammo. Barry had ordered the third to hold back. And the fourth in line was basically a glorified porter, carrying a fuckload of ammo for the other three. But as the second corpse lord took a lucky round to the head, shattering its skull and sending it collapsing to the floor in an avalanche of bone, I started really swearing.

"Back it up!" Chris barked suddenly, and I nodded, seeing the sense. Barry was already shifting their order as well; the last two corpse lords stayed well back, considering the issues we'd have if they started firing high-speed grenades in here.

The third corpse lord fired steadily as it backed up, until the belt ran dry. Before he could be guided into the reload, a hammering hail of fire took him down.

The rest of the party were far enough back now that we were out of direct sight. But it also meant that we couldn't see them, as the corner angled back on itself and proceeded down at an angle.

Two of the wraiths were dead, two more were barely holding their shields, and one had been dragged around the corner and presumably killed as well.

Others were streaming forward now as we moved back; the passage was wide enough for two side by side to cover it with overlapping shields. Behind them, four wraiths were filling their hands with Deathbolts, getting ready.

"Give me that!" Chris snapped at the corpse lord with the jammed gun, only to have Finger shove him out of the way and start stripping it with impressive speed.

"Stay back," I ordered Chris tensely, knowing that he'd be straight up to the front if I didn't, and determined that the undead could take the brunt of this.

The first drone warrior to take the corner practically disintegrated under the hail of necrotic energy, followed by a second wave. Its flesh sloughed from horrifically twisted bones, eyes running like curdled milk.

As it fell, the second and third took the corner. That the last wave of spells had been wasted on overkill was suddenly fucking clear as they galloped forward, their rifles bouncing and roaring as they unloaded their magazines into the shields.

Four assault rifles, all firing over and over—three apparently full and one with only a few shots in it—hammered into the shields, all focused on the one on the left, as a second wave of necrotic magic was summoned.

I cursed as my mana started to bottom out again, and I cut the shield just in time.

The left-most wraith screamed in furious despair as its own shield popped. Then, demonstrating their wonderful nature, it grabbed one of those next to it and yanked that one in the way of the incoming fire.

Its sacrificial victim, one with almost full mana, howled and died. Bullets riddled it, before passing through into the wraith behind as well.

They both fell to the floor, as the next wave of spells poured over their targets, taking them down, gurgling and drowning in their own blood and fluids.

The fight was hard. More and more warrior drones raced forward; wraiths before me stepped up and held the line with their shields.

More were summoned, sliding around us, hands rising. The air shimmered as they took over from the last to fall. Those at the front held the shields as those behind let loose with spell after spell, until finally, seemingly ages after he'd taken it, Finger rammed the HMG back into the corpse lord's waiting grasp, a fresh and full belt attached.

It didn't hesitate, spinning to the front line and wading forward, its boney fingers tight on the triggers as a veritable hail shredded the incoming drones.

They'd pushed forward, and had been pushing us back from the corner. Their seemingly endless wave had been too fast and coordinated for us to stop easily, but now, we tore them down again.

Marching forward, with the wraiths peeling to the sides, the corpse lord cleaned the passage with massive bullets, and we followed.

It turned to the left as soon as it reached the switchback, gun held ready. Its lower hands were on the triggers; the upper supported the weapon. At the first hint of movement, it opened fire again. We stayed back for a few seconds, before Barry ordered the wraiths up in support; then we followed.

The ammo carrier corpse lord was down to a third of its original loadout. Chris grabbed the box, grinning at me as I realized he'd just snagged all the remaining ammo we had, for the gun he still had on his back.

The corpse lord, though, wrested the other gun from the inanimate remains of its brother, then stepped up to help clear the way. The wraiths slid aside again to permit its passage.

"Now what?" I asked aloud, as I sensed Barry close by.

"We advance," he said. *"The wraith that was grabbed? It's gone. I can't sense it anymore. They're falling back, though."*

"It's dead, isn't it?" I asked.

"No corpse," was all he said, but I cursed.

I knew the undead couldn't be converted with the vurms—they couldn't, right? I mean, the skeletons and the corpse lords were literally polished friggin' bone, nothing for the little bastards to bite into. But the wraiths?

I paused, glancing down at the nearest dead one, and saw something grey leaking from the skull. I cursed again.

"Any of you that are captured by the enemy are to kill yourselves immediately," I ordered the wraiths, unwilling to take the risk and hating how much of an asshole I was sure it'd make me sound to them and anyone listening.

Then I followed on, and we continued deeper into the hive.

The corner was almost impassable as we took it, the bodies were mounded that high. As we struggled through, one suddenly lunged forward, biting down on a wraith, trying to drag it down.

The wraith screeched its fury and ripped the offending head from its shoulders, but it made the point. Before I could order it, though, the bodies started to collapse into light. Our influence was enough that we could take the dungeon's range with us as we advanced, absorbing the dead.

The corpse lord in the lead exchanged sporadic fire with the retreating forces. Now and then, another would gallop into sight, pointing its guns up the incline, and detonate under the hail of HMG fire.

They kept doing it until the corpse lord ran out of ammunition again, and the wraiths took over. This time, as it let its companion take over its spot, the new belts that were added were the last we had.

"Save them," I ordered Barry. "If at all possible, we need to save this shit."

"I'm keeping mine," Chris added, making it clear he was both saving his ammo for later, and that he wasn't intending to goddamn share.

I nodded as the wraiths flitted forward again, hitting the bottom of the ramp, and holding their shields up ready...only to freeze in place.

We hurried after, finding the new passage led in a straight line, and not a single enemy was in sight.

The bodies were all vanishing, and ahead, at the end of the passage, was a downward angled one.

This passage—this was the one that led to the point of no return, to the ring of exclusion that the dungeon had enforced for what we guessed had once been a nuclear and biological weapons research facility, one hidden under an unassuming base.

All we knew was that we'd been able to see hints of something a fuckload bigger in the distance when we'd stood and peered down. Now, as we approached it again, the hairs on the back of my neck tried to stand up.

"What is it?" Chris rolled his shoulders.

"What?" I asked him back.

"That feeling, man...what is it?" He shot me a look, and I nodded that I understood.

"No fuckin' clue, mate," I admitted. "Could be radiation. Might be a bioweapon that's escaped. Might be that we know it's all down there and it's all in our heads."

"And it might be the queen," he finished, glancing at me. "You think?"

"I try not to," I replied unthinkingly, before shaking my head. "Time to go play." I waved the wraiths forward.

CHAPTER THIRTY-TWO

W here the passage tilted downward, it looked almost normal—apart from the bloody splatters and scuffed broken sections, anyway.

As the lead elements descended, we kept running. The party was now made up of four wraiths, followed by two more corpse lords with the HMGs, then four more wraiths. After them came me and Chris, Kilo and Finger.

Then came two more wraiths, and then ten skeletons, split into five armed with the ASM launchers and five carrying additional ammo. Then there were four more corpse lords. Two carried grenade launchers; two carried ammo belts for them.

Lastly, there were four more wraiths. These ones were kept back just in case, along with the extras that ran ahead of them, ready to step in when they were needed.

At first, we just ran, not sure why the others had fallen back. For a handful of seconds, I dared to hope that it meant the queen had run out of minions…right up until I remembered that I'd not yet seen the wraith they took, nor whatever had grabbed it.

Then I started to sweat.

"Approaching the cutoff…" I sensed as much as heard Aly and Barry, before suddenly they were gone. As each of the undead crossed the invisible line that marked the farthest we'd been able to reach before…they staggered, and then slowed.

It was only for a few seconds, but as I crossed it, and then Chris and the others, I felt the difference: I couldn't sense the dungeon anymore. I gritted my teeth.

We'd been afraid of this, and we'd planned for it, just in case.

Behind me, lights flared as the dungeon took control of the area as best it could. A single wraith was left behind to ensure that our influence was steady, as the rest of us raced ahead.

The passage ended at a large set of doors, the kind of incredible, insane-sized doors that you saw on entry to the American underground military and last-resort bunkers.

To me, here, they made no sense, until I reached level ground, and swore. A second passage led off at a gentler angle downward. It was large enough for vehicles, and we'd had no clue the fucker was here, concealed by the angle as it was.

Fortunately, I couldn't see anything down that way, but through the wide-open doors ahead, I could.

The darkness beyond was almost physical in its totality. Even with my magic, I could barely see a handful of meters into the gloom—a gloom that *moved*.

I slowed, then spoke aloud, when the undead didn't respond to my unspoken orders. The fourteen wraiths took up station before me and to either side, forming a semicircle as the two corpse lords ahead of me spread out to the left and right.

"What the hell is that..." Chris whispered, and I had to admit, I had no fucking clue.

The room was large, and obviously so. The doors alone were a good fifteen meters across. And, cracked open as they were, they made it clear that something had been occurring as the power went down.

Inside, three large vehicles—two were clearly military vehicles—were parked off to the side, where they'd presumably been somehow pushed. The pair were some variant of armored APC, and I heard the name whispered in shock from behind me as Finger saw them.

"Boxers!" he murmured, and I snorted.

"They named them after underwear? Where's the G-string?" Chris muttered, squinting into the darkness.

Finger hissed back, "Don't be stupid. The new line, they're all named after dogs for some reason. And I bet that one there? That'll be a mastiff." He nodded toward a barely hinted at outline farther in.

"Quiet!" I snapped at them all, and heard Chris shutting his mouth with an audible *clop*.

It was nerves, I knew it was, and it was whispered. Plus, it wasn't as if the queen wouldn't know we were coming. But still.

I glanced over at the third vehicle. Although the other two looked to be fresh out of a war zone—even if they were all clean, more or less—the mastiff was a very different beast, even barely visible in the gloom.

The boxers were eight-wheeled all-terrain monsters, and between their turret-mounted cannons and the armor, I damn well wished they were still able to be used.

Beyond them was the mastiff. Where they were clearly military machines, built to take incoming cannon fire and drive over trenches or whatever mad shit they had to put up with, this was a transport—a high-value transport. And judging from the six wheels, it was able to go anywhere as well. The V-shaped hull was presumably intended to take a blast, and had a gun turret and multiple weapons systems.

The weirdest part of the system had to be the grating. I didn't know what else to call it, but it was like someone had surrounded it, all the way around, in oblong metal boxes missing lids and bottoms. Then they'd been turned on their side and welded together.

Clearly nobody would be able to jump onto it and live, if it was in motion, and anything it hit would have a damn bad day as well. The only downside? Well, it was a high-tech bit of kit, and we had fuck all tech that worked.

Joy.

I opened my mouth to ask something, peering into the darkness and wondering what the hell could cause this, when the first voice rang out.

"YoU cOMe HoMe."

317

I flinched. The weirdness of the voice, the whole thing...the sonics, the timbre, the way that it echoed and reverberated...it rippled up and down my spine. I shook my head violently, looking around, trying to make out something, anything in the gloom.

"YoU fEaR... yOu Do NoT uNdErStAnD."

Chris spun around, staring off to the left behind us, spellbound, while Finger stared straight up, his mouth dropping open in awe. For me, the sound seemed to roll around me, to be ahead for a second; then it moved, like someone was walking around me, whispering, barely loud enough to hear.

"ReSt... Be SaFe... SlEeP..."

I turned my head, trying to follow it, then froze.

Kilo stared ahead, over my shoulder and deeper into the room. Beyond him? The corpse lords weren't interested, not even slightly, standing as still as statues and awaiting their next command. But the wraiths?

They were all listening, and I swallowed hard as I saw that.

"Baaad." That was Kilo, slipping back into a simpler way of speaking as he shook his head from side to side, as if trying to get a smell out of his nose. "All baaad."

"Dude, this is...you're hearing this shit, right?" Chris asked me, and I shrugged.

"Yeah, thinks we're home, right?" I muttered, distractedly, as I stared into the darkness, trying to spot whatever was speaking.

"YoU cAn Be. YoU cAn Be FrEe..."

"Home? What? No, man, it's offering...well, it's not a home."

"It's saying we can be free?" I suggested.

"No, no, not that at all." He shook his head, then grunted in pain as Kilo grabbed both him and me by the hands. His claws dug painfully into the gloves we wore, and I glared at him.

When I did, though, I saw the look on his face, and for the first time, heard the voices.

There was more than one, and as soon as he saw that I was realizing that and was apparently aware again, he spun, gripping Chris harder, squeezing then slapping him across the face hard enough to leave three narrow lines of blood bubbling to the surface faintly.

"You motherfucker!" Chris staggered back. "What the hell, Kilo!"

"You listen!" he snarled. "Both you listen!"

"Yeah?" Chris asked, and I nodded, only to have Kilo slap his hands together hard. The clap echoed in the darkness.

"Noise!" he shouted. "No listen!"

"Wha..." I started, only to twist as a new light illuminated the underground bunker, and it wasn't a good one.

Where the electro-chemical phosphoresce of sodium lights would have been a huge relief, these lights brought only fear. Twenty-eight sickly yellow-green glows shimmered into existence as the wraiths on all sides of us began summoning their necrotic bolts in both hands.

"What are you... Stop!" I barked the order.

The nearest wraith to me faltered, twisting to lock eyes with me, then hissed as if in anger and began to summon it again.

"Matt..." Chris whispered, eyes wide.

The wraiths slowly shifted, lifting into the air and drifting around. The semicircle of their threat no longer faced out. Instead, it faced inward.

"I order you!" I shouted. "I am the Dungeon Lord! STOP!"

It rippled through them. The command warred with something, but although they clearly recognized it, it wasn't enough to stop them, only delay.

"Matt, what do we do?" Chris called, staring as more and more of the wraiths apparently decided that the only threat here...was *us*.

"*Fuck!* Kill them!" I snapped my rifle up and locked the sights onto the wraith before me, right between its eyes, then fired.

A three-round burst tore into it. With both hands filled with necrotic energy, it apparently couldn't cast a shield at the same time, and its head came apart under the fire: the first impact in the top right of the left eye, the second the bridge of the nose, and the third the right cheek.

As it was flung backward, hands lifting and burning yellow-green fire bursting into dissipating clouds, I switched my aim, tracking to the right and lining up on the second, just as it threw its first spell.

I jinked to the left and it screamed past me. The feeling of that much necrotic energy so close made bile rise in my mouth. It hit Kilo in the back, right between his wings, washing over him. He screamed and staggered, before a second bolt slammed into him and sent him to the ground even faster.

He screeched, writhing as his armor started to bubble and fail, falling apart, and the wraiths started to hurl their spells as one.

"KILO!" I shouted, cursing that I'd ran out of goddamn mana and now couldn't heal him.

I dove to the right, landing and rolling as a pair of additional spells hit the ground where I'd just been. The floor started to bubble as I came to my feet again, cursing my stupidity for using my magic already.

I had practically nothing left. And that meant I had one goddamn option, though I knew just how stupid it was.

Blood magic.

I rolled to the right again, then locked eyes onto the next wraith in line, and screamed "Incinerate!" as our gazes locked, all the while bringing my rifle around to line up on the next in line.

I opened fire and coughed wetly. My life force was ripped from me to power a spell that I couldn't afford, and that sent me from jumping back to my feet...to falling to all fours.

The bullets ripped out, completely missing their target. But the other wraith burst into flames; its hands came up to grab at its head, as that charred to charcoal in a split second.

The burning wraith fell from the sky, and I looked up at the other one, the one I'd tried to shoot and had totally missed. Its mouth split open, the flesh tearing free to show pointed and sharp teeth, as it hissed in pleasure.

I heard the rest of the fight going on—the shouts, the screams from Kilo, the grunts, the zip and hiss of necrotic Deathbolts—but we stared at each other, its hands full of summoned magic.

I knew as soon as I spoke, as soon as it sensed the slightest threat from me, the tiniest start of a spell, it'd throw them.

It was toying with me; it was enjoying this, and I knew it.

"Fuck...you..." I ground out. The words made it smile, even as I knew the first syllable had nearly resulted in my death.

It knew, though—it had known—I wasn't casting.

It...*knew*?

My mind raced.

How the fuck had it known, and how did I know what it knew?

I reached out, feeling the oppressive darkness around us, the pressure, the sickness that filled me like an ocean of vomit, a feeling that rose as I did this. A need to empty my stomach rose as I reached, and strained, feeling...a very faint and distant something.

The corpse lords continued to stand as still as statues; the wraiths had moved in. I felt and sensed it as Chris was disarmed. The claws of the wraith before him rested against his jugular, as he stared at it in fury.

I felt it and I *saw* it, despite facing away.

Kilo writhed on the floor, panting as the two necrotic bolts that had hit him slowly burned their way through his armor and into his flesh. I felt the buckling and crumbling of his scales, the way that his wings twisted, the bones snapping as they turned in ways they were never meant to and drew screams from him.

Muscles cramped and squeezed. The wraith that hovered over him was enjoying looking down at his suffering, as he tried to reach out a hand, clearly about to cast, only to have it hit by a necrotic bolt and begin to crumble.

Finger?

He was already gone. His head and upper chest had taken multiple hits, despite her orders. He was almost a pool of gore now, bubbling as the organs of his chest cavity shivered and blackened.

I saw it all as we stared at each other, and I understood, at some level.

I knew what they were seeing because *we were still connected.* They understood me for the same reason, and I knew that *she* had ordered the wraiths to capture us, because...

I rolled sideways, then hurled my life force into my manipulation of the world around me.

Where I could fly normally due to the storm, the lifting of gentle and powerful winds alike, now blood magic powered my flight.

It was a blur; the more powerful, much more addictive magic roared and sung through my veins. Unused to it, I crashed into the side of a nearby parked motorbike, tipping it over and flipping myself. I hit the floor, skidded, rolled, and came to a stunned halt. Before I could get back up, a new hand crashed down on me from above, driving me into the concrete. It knocked the wind out of me and bounced my head off the floor.

The next thing I knew, as I woozily watched the trail of claret that ran from my nose drip out and splatter to the floor below, was that I was being lifted higher, high into the air, by a massive, malformed hand.

I blinked. Voices warbled on all sides, filling the air and making my head hurt even more as I flexed and shifted, heaving and trying to break free, to no avail.

"StOp... YoU sErVe Me!"

The words rattled around in my mind, echoing, reinforcing one another. They got louder every time they were repeated, until it was like the clap of tomb doors.

It was all I could hear, but as they got louder and louder, seeming to shake my very brain from the cadence, I was turned to face the one that held me.

It was a wraith, or it once had been, I saw. The darkness seemed to melt back and forth, growing darker and deeper, before lightening as the sound in my head approached the limits. Blood ran freely from my ears to join that of my broken beak.

Its skull was misshapen, melded into another, much larger creature that was, in turn, constructed of a dozen or more forms all pressed and joined together.

My eyes grew wide as I saw the madness, the hatred, and the desperation of the wraith. It was half subsumed into the flesh of the monstrous entity around it; vurms crawled under its skin as its mouth stretched in soundless screams. Inches away from it was the smoothness of tightly stretched skin over bulging bone. And below that, down to my right, bulged what looked to be a boil, if a boil had ever grown to over a foot in diameter and been filled with wriggling black vurms.

I stared. Not only was this amalgamation huge, looming at least eight or ten meters tall, but it wasn't alone.

Two others stomped forward. The world seemed to shake with each crashing footfall, and from their wide-open maws came the cacophony of voices. They echoed and rang, they whispered and screamed, and above all, they spoke madness.

I turned back, staring into the stark eyes of the wraith, seeing it buried between the plates of growing chitin, the hair and leather, the feathers... The queen must have melded together whatever she had to form this, and her control? It was almost all being expended on guiding them.

I saw it, I understood it; then, all in a wash of insight that just as I had sensed something before—as I'd sensed and yet not, the wraiths—so too was I still joined to this one.

I felt the difficulty in controlling something so large, something that was held together by bile and duct tape, hatred and fear, and I realized that they were *newborn*.

The queen's control was growing by the second. She was figuring it all out, as other new forms clambered up and down the walls on all sides.

I was running out of time. And from the sound of the hissing and pain, so was Kilo.

I had a single chance. It wasn't my magic, nor my muscles; it wasn't in action or in speed. *It was my link to the dungeon.*

I could still feel *something* from the wraiths, from them all, on all sides, and that meant that I'd not been severed from it entirely. I wasn't blocked from the source of my power. If anything, I was starting to feel it more, and...

My left eardrum burst, the sensation like a pressure building and popping, like a flight that had dropped or climbed too far, too fast. It popped and crackled, blood bursting free. The feeling of filling pressure and a receding tide, and at the same time, a wave of familiarity surged in me as the dungeon seemed to almost reach out to me, before vanishing.

It was gone as my right ear popped; the pressure equalized and the pain dipped. I shook my head, blood flying free; the sensation of up and down spun as my middle ear rolled.

The wraith before me screeched, and I heard it, then silence. Then it was back, and knowing nothing else, I twisted my head to where the hilt of my sword rose over my right shoulder, held tight in place by the monstrous grip.

The huge creature turned slowly, lumbering around as it began to carry me deeper into the queen's lair. As it did, I pulled my head to the left, then slammed my ear back to the right, full force—or with as much force as I could muster—into the pommel of the sword.

The pain that rang free stunned me for a second, long enough that I saw stars, wincing and biting my cheek, before it all rushed back.

As my mind cleared, I sensed it all. Though I didn't know how or why, I did damn well understand that what I'd been feeling all along was some kind of defensive siren-song of the queen.

That was what was keeping us out; that was what had been keeping the wraiths disconnected and letting them take their natural instinct to fucking murder and be basically shitehawks to heart.

They'd believed they'd lost their connection to me, to the dungeon, and all they'd known was that they didn't have to listen anymore.

That was enough—coupled with the confusion of losing their link to the dungeon at large, and the danger that we posed, as well as the danger that the queen in turn posed them—to convince them to swap sides.

That, and the queen, through her link, to this wraith had been able to reach others.

Now, though, as deaf as a post as I was, I could feel the dungeon again, although it was farther out from me than I wanted.

I couldn't summon anything, not in here. This space I was in wasn't linked to the rest of the dungeon, nor to a seed. I couldn't cast a dungeon spell, nor raise a wall, but the one thing I could do?

I could feel my minions.

The wraiths weren't cut off from the dungeon, not entirely. Instead, they were insulated from it. Something about the sonic weakness the coronaughts have—I'd read in other popups they discarded their ears to escape—had been turned into a weapon instead.

They filled the air with it, the frequency either so high or so low that we couldn't hear it, though the strange feeling suddenly made sense.

That meant that the wraiths were still connected to me, even if they thought they weren't.

I reached out, forcing the connection, digging deep into myself and searching, desperate for the bond I'd felt to the fairy and the dungeon before.

I twisted and tried to break free, flexing muscles, even as my mind dove deeper inside, searching for the place that I felt that ephemeral connection.

It was nothing new; it'd been with me since the dungeon first activated, after all. I'd used it day in and day out for what seemed like forever, and yet...when I was away from the dungeon, I'd lost access to it.

Or had I?

Reach Out and Touch Me was a skill I'd taken forever ago. It'd allowed me to interact with the dungeon when I was outside of it; even if I couldn't summon things, I could still feel them. I could reach back to the dungeon from outside and order changes or reach the others inside it.

I'd lost that ability when I'd moved far enough from the main dungeon, and as soon as I'd planted the seed, that'd started back.

I'd still been able to feel the dungeon creatures around me, and searching, I found it.

It was that skill—that low-level class skill, one that I'd taken for granted forever—that I found the link through, diving into it and connecting back to the dungeon, despite the suppression field the queen generated.

Feeling it, feeling the way that the dungeon around me existed still, yet seemed incredibly weak and distant, I realized what it was and why.

Whatever was causing this—and I was betting it was an ability of the queen, as opposed to anything that was coming from the nukes or more, as we'd first worried—it was pushing out hard enough that it made it difficult to feel the dungeon at all.

It was still there, just remote.

Now, reaching out to the wraith before me, subsumed into the wall of flesh and madness, I could distantly feel it, though it was damn hard.

That meant, though, that I could summon my trump card, more or less. And the combination of my stress and the call I put through made sure that when Jack arrived, he was going to do it at speed.

That also meant that the others were still there as well. As close to the dungeon as I was, I might even be able to push out a field of influence still, one that could link up to the dungeon a few dozen meters away.

I reached out, ignoring the feeling that told me the dungeon was gone, that I was alone and that I couldn't sense it, nor it me. Instead, I grabbed that link, that simple link that ran to the dungeon, and I filled my mind with it, focusing on it with all I had, before hammering my orders into those around me.

The monstrosity holding me lurched as one of its legs twisted in the wrong way, as all the undead around me tried to respond at once.

I didn't *ask* for their compliance—I *DEMANDED* it.

The wraiths had thought they were free. In their confusion, they'd reverted to their instincts and the terrible whispers of the queen and her minions had convinced them to change sides. But now?

They spun as one, hands rising. Spells that were inching closer to my friends were hurled into the nearest targets instead.

The wraith that had been subsumed into the massive titan screeched as it tried to obey the vurms that filled it, but had no choice in disobeying me.

It tore, muscles working against each other; bones broke, and its spells activated. The rubbery outer hide of the titan did nothing to protect it when the wraith summoned Deathbolts to hands buried under and within the flesh of its new form.

The titan screeched, already staggering and spiraling, trying to catch its balance as one leg unexpectedly twisted in the wraith's control. The new attack made it roll and squirm, trying to grab at the burning pain in its chest.

As it did that, it released me, and I fell.

CHAPTER THIRTY-THREE

Hitting the ground hard, my mind was still foggy as I tried to focus on controlling the others. I'd barely bounced, before a kick from a windmilling leg sent me flying into the side of the nearest boxer. I crashed back to the ground, stunned and winded.

I gasped, trying to get my diaphragm to release, to suck down a breath of air, but as I did it, I rolled.

Grabbing the edge of one enormous wheel, I dragged myself under the vehicle and out of sight, gasping and smacking at my own chest, trying to get my damn lungs to work. All the while, as I did it, I sent out diamond-hard orders to the undead.

The skeletons and corpse lords, on receiving no orders and being totally undead, instead of the kind of weird unlife thingy that the advanced wraiths were, had simply locked up, standing still, waiting for the Dungeon Lord to order them.

With them losing—or seeming to lose—the connection to the dungeon, they'd not been responding when I'd shouted their orders.

Now, though, as I sent the demand through the link, they sprang into motion.

The two with HMGs opened fire almost at the same time, the grenadiers ready but waiting. The wraiths moved as well, their pleasure at capturing and killing us forgotten. They spun—the one holding Chris dropped him—and they all leapt into the darkness, spells starting.

As they leapt, two of the titans lurched at them; claws and club-like limbs rose, swinging with ponderous and yet unstoppable inevitability.

The one that had captured me, and that the queen had been holding onto, writhed and thrashed now. It might not feel pain in the same way as a living sentient creature, but the wraith that was a part of it was summoning necrotic energy into its insides.

Muscles snapped…bones blackened, twisted… It shuddered and came apart.

But the titans weren't all the queen had left to guard her.

A dozen of the warrior drones sprinted out of the darkness, racing forward, some with guns blazing. Others, already spent on ammo, pulled the triggers anyway.

From the heights of the hidden ceiling and from the walls came a dozen creatures I hated to recognize, even with triggering my Examine spell. I ordered the wraiths to engage them, paying the price in life force.

Spawnskull Sentinel Coronaught	Mutated Creature

Spawnskull Sentinels are the result of the queen fusing multiple human soldiers into a single, already existing and incredibly insane monstrous form. These abominations combine human cunning with bestial ferocity, creating a terrifyingly effective guardian for the coronaught hive.

Standing at around 8 feet tall, the Spawnskull Sentinel's body is a twisted fusion of human and avian features. Powerful, bat-like wings sprout from its back, granting it the ability to fly for short distances and swoop down on unsuspecting prey. Due to its increased size, this is a short-term option only, and is primarily a glide-based attack. Its head is a nightmarish amalgamation of human and bird, with multiple, milky eyes that can see in the dark and a razor-sharp beak filled with jagged teeth.

The Spawnskull Sentinel's skin is a mottled patchwork of human flesh and chitinous plates, with writhing vurms visible just beneath the surface. These parasites grant the Sentinel incredible regenerative abilities, allowing it to shrug off wounds that would kill a normal human.

Beware: Spawnskull Sentinels are highly intelligent and tactical, able to coordinate their attacks with a level of strategy not seen in lesser coronaught creatures.

Abilities:

Flight: The Spawnskull Sentinel can fly for short distances, allowing it to quickly close the gap on enemies or escape dangerous situations.

Regeneration: The vurms infesting the Sentinel's body grant it powerful regenerative abilities, allowing it to heal from most wounds quickly.

Screech: The Sentinel can emit a piercing, sonic screech that disorients and stuns nearby enemies.

Weaknesses: Fire, Ice, and Lightning Magics
HP: 800/800
Stamina: 1000/1000
Mana: 200/200
Speed: 7/10
Level: 6
Special Abilities: 3/3

HP: 800/800	Special Abilities: 3/3

I ordered the wraiths to divert, to meet the dozens of spawnskull sentinels. We'd seen the vaguest of outlines of things like this when we'd been trying to peer in from the outer limit before.

Now they were here, and they were clear.

Where the seagulls had been converted, along with the remnants of men and other creatures, into something that had looked more like a pterosaur, now that simpler, terrible form had been upgraded. Before, the mouths had been a mixture of beak and human—more broken feral mess than anything—now these looked to have been designed to give dentists nightmares.

Fangs that had to be inches long warred with back-curved carving daggers that reminded me of sharks. And the head was just… Imagine a human one; then grab the jaws and drag them out into a muzzle as far as they'll stretch, then add in another head at that point, then drag it out again.

The end result was an abomination of melded flesh and jutting teeth, exposed bone and drooling vacuous imbecility.

One launched itself out from the goddamn wall, straight into a support beam, impacting with a crunch of breaking bone. Then it fell, slamming into the ground mere meters away. But those that managed to fly?

They were beating the air and making straight for the wraiths.

Deathbolts hurtled free of the wraiths and slammed into the oncoming sentinels. Those that hit heads or the pinions of the wings took out their targets in screaming, dissolving messes.

The others, though, where it hit non-lethal points, the creatures just kept coming.

Maws agape, they latched onto the wraiths, biting down and crunching through bone. Both creatures crashed into the floor with the sound of breaking bones ringing out.

Screams filled the air as both sides rocketed into each other. Behind them, the corpse lords fired heavily into the twin upright titans. I triggered Examine again and snarled.

Flesh Titan Coronaught	Mutated Creature

Flesh Titans are the ultimate abominations created by the coronaught queen, each one a massive amalgamation of dozens of human bodies twisted and fused together by her dark power. These lumbering horrors tower over the battlefield, standing between 15 to 20 feet tall.

The Flesh Titan's form is a grotesque patchwork of human limbs, torsos, and faces that writhe and moan in constant agony. Its skin is a thick, leathery hide that pulsates with the movements of the countless vurms that infest its body. Pulsating sacs of writhing parasites dot their hide, ready to burst forth and swarm any who dare to come too close.

Despite their size, Flesh Titans move with an unsettling speed and grace, their misshapen limbs propelling them forward with terrifying strength. They are living siege engines, capable of smashing through fortifications and crushing armored vehicles with ease.

Beware: Flesh Titans are not only immensely strong, but also incredibly resilient. Their regenerative abilities allow them to heal from grievous wounds in a matter of moments.

Abilities:

Vurm Sacs: The Flesh Titan is covered in pulsating sacs filled with ravenous vurms. If these sacs are ruptured, they release swarms of the parasites that will attack anything nearby.

> *Regeneration*: The Flesh Titan's body is infested with coronaught vurms that grant it powerful regenerative abilities, allowing it to quickly heal from most wounds.
>
> *Smash*: The Flesh Titan can use its immense strength to smash through obstacles and crush its foes with devastating force.
>
> **Weaknesses**: Fire, Ice, and Lightning Magics
> **HP**: 1500/1500
> **Stamina**: 2000/2000
> **Mana**: 0/0
> **Speed**: 5/10
> **Level**: 9
> **Special Abilities**: 3/3

HP: 250/250	Special Abilities: 3/3

The mottled flesh and chitinous plates that made up the titan's exterior seemed to ignore the barrage of incoming .50 cal rounds, or at least ignore the effect. Their skin was chewed up; plates were shattered and the impacts staggered them—but the one thing they didn't seem to do was hurt the fuckers.

They just straightened up, the shredded flesh becoming almost molten, as they flowed and joined again.

I started to guide the ASM skeletons into position, determined that they'd not ignore those fuckers, when one of the nearby sentinels jabbed its head under the boxer and snapped at me, trying to latch on.

Cursing, and with no time to figure out where the hell my damn rifle had gotten to, I yanked the handgun free and unloaded two rounds into the side of the head, punching holes through it and sending it twitching to the floor.

Then, as I twisted, thinking to make sure there was nothing on the other side trying to get at me, it started to shudder and jerk. I rolled back, lifting the gun, then hissed, rolling away and frantically crawling in the opposite direction.

The body looked like it was trying to be sick, but what was coming out of holes in the shattered head wasn't vomit. It was vurms.

I crawled as fast as I could. The pommel of my blade, still jutting out from over my shoulder, caught on the underside of the vehicle's door jamb and jerked me to a stop, making me choke as the strap seemed to garotte me.

Reaching up, I yanked it down and crawled the last few feet out, grabbing the side of the vehicle and standing—only to come face-to-face with another as it landed, then opened its mouth as wide as it could.

I felt the force of the screech, the waves of sound, of pressure that it was forcing out, as well as the overlapping secondaries, as that apparently set all the others off doing the same thing.

More than half the wraiths were already down. As I lifted my handgun and pulled the trigger point-blank into the face of this new intruder, more crashed into the walls and floors, stunned.

The three holes I blew in the back of the sentinel's head were clearly unexpected as it simply collapsed backward. Blood and vurms sprayed, and I grinned through bloody lips, even as I tried the door to the boxer.

I was deaf, thanks to the shite that I'd already gone through and slamming my own ear into the pommel as I had. That turned out to be a blessing, as unexpected as that was.

The queen had taken her species' one great weakness, sonic attacks, and had turned it into a strength, learning to use it as a weapon. I, on the other side, had done the exact thing most of her species did, in that I'd discarded my hearing, to defend against it.

I yanked the door into the boxer open and jumped in, slamming it shut behind me as the first waves of vurms slithered out from under the vehicle, in search of me. And damn was I glad to see the biological hazard confirmation tags, as I hammered the latch, locking the door after me.

This was a vehicle that could be used as a refuge from a literal bio-attack, meaning that there was no chance those little bastards were getting in here!

I clambered into the back, peering out of a thick glass window and focusing, sending the message as hard as I could, to get the closest undead moving.

Chris was already backing out of the doors. The big bastard had his rifle in one hand, firing at the incoming sentinels, and had hold of the back of Kilo's armor while he left, dragging him backward.

The nearest skeleton, one of those tasked with carrying ammunition for the rockets, dropped it all suddenly and spun, darting forward to grab Kilo...and Chris promptly shot it in the skull.

"Fuck!" I shouted, taking control of another.

I sent it forward, this time pointing at the wounded and dying kobold, and then at Chris, before finally pointing up the passage back to where we had control.

He hesitated and then nodded he understood. He let the skeleton grab Kilo, taking over dragging him out, while Chris dumped the rifle, and instead unslung his snub-barreled HMG.

The two corpse lords that had been at the back were in the middle of things now. Their grenade launchers were too indiscriminate to use here, as much as I wanted to—somewhere down here were nukes and bioweapons—so they dumped them and waded in, fists swinging.

As they did that, the first of the rocket skeletons stepped up, aiming its ASM. I figured that although a grenade was marked "to whom it concerns," a rocket at least had a fucker's name attached. And in this case, as the corpse lords' HMGs ran dry in concert, it was time to test it out on the flesh titans.

I'd listened to the warnings I'd been given with the rockets and spread them out, but it was time to share the love now. The first of the skeletons pointed the barrel and pulled the trigger.

It was the farthest to the right, as I looked back at the door. Fortunately, the partly closed door was between it, Chris, and Kilo. But the detonation as the rocket failed to fire?

The fucking boxer vehicle bounced as the second, closer and slightly angled escort vehicle was shoved bodily into the side of it.

I bounced as well; my head ricocheted off armoring and stunned me again. I fell, hitting the floor and laying there for long seconds as the darkness in here was for the first time truly banished.

The flames that were everywhere lit the room up. I struggled back to my feet, staring out of the glass, before swallowing hard.

Most of the undead were gone, just piles of bones now, and at least half of the enemy were as well, where the wraiths had been…nope.

They'd been spread out around the room, but most were now just shredded. A single corpse lord was trying to fire, its HMG still clutched in its upper hands as the belt clicked, empty already. Without some guidance, though, it just stood there; burning debris covered it, one upper arm gone and the two lower having to help take the weight.

The flesh titans hadn't escaped unscathed either, though. One of them was currently running, streaming flames, across what had to have once been a motor pool.

Now, it was a breeding ground.

With the flames finally banishing the darkness, I could see. And fuck me sideways, what I could see was terrible.

The room was square, perhaps only thirty meters on a side, with the farthest wall from the entrance having a series of doors and windows in it. The right-hand side wall also had a door and a single window. But at a glance, I could see that was a security post of some kind.

That would have been enough to mark it out as a standard underground kinky-shit nuclear type base—the additional security, the weird ass yet logical layout, and the heavy doors. But what turned it from that into a goddamn nest of monsters was the thing that half hung from the ceiling in the far corner.

Some forty meters up, the ceiling arched in toward the center, and up there, secured amongst the air circulators and more, was a mass of flesh that had sealed itself to the walls.

Bulges here and there showed that more creatures were incubating. Another huge one, almost big enough to hold a titan, was already shuddering as the queen worked to bring some new horror to term.

The flames covered a solid third of the room, though, and I could see the queen, staring dead at me, thanks to the reflection of those fires, in dozens of dead-black eyes.

On all sides, there were shivering holes, like reversed pyramids of flesh. I knew instinctively these were the source of the dampening fields, the song, the sounds, or whatever was causing the issues.

She was suspended in the middle of the bulges, her flesh sealed to the walls. Dozens of slick, writhing sacs around her pulsed in some bizarre rhythm, and I stared back at her, seeing the true queen for the first time.

The last one I'd seen had been a mass of tentacles and a maw that appeared ravenous. Beyond that, all I remembered was knowing that she was trying to kill me and everything I'd ever known.

There'd been a hunger, though; a mindless driving need was all that had filled her. This fucker? This was awake. This was aware…and it knew where I was.

I was barely able to sense the dungeon; still, I knew it was there, even through the suppression. I dove in, queuing orders and ignoring the frantic, distant queries of the others.

Then I felt it, and I couldn't help but grin as I did. The damage to the queen— the injuries and the flames—had distracted her enough that the barrier was down. And right by the door, we had a fragment of influence!

It was tenuous, but I quickly spammed a single skeleton to appear and crouch there, building the influence out and forcing it to grow enough to be useful.

While it did that, the corpse lords that shimmered into being back at the cutoff started sprinting as soon as the last polished bone appeared, passing the smaller skeleton as it dragged the dying Kilo back.

I reached out, ordering the damaged corpse lord to cast the gun aside, to reach down and snatch up the nearest grenade launcher. The smaller hands latched onto it easily as the larger straightened out the ammo links, and I grinned ferally.

I'd not intended on using this, mere minutes ago, as indiscriminate as it was, but fuck it.

I was having a shitty day, and it was time to spread that around.

The corpse lord pulled the trigger, hammering an impact-fused grenade into the side of the nearest reeling titan.

It staggered. Flesh and blood, bones and gore exploded free as the others turned to orient on their attacker, who fired again and again.

The incoming eight passed a wounded but awake Chris. He was already using a focal orb on himself, healing the wounds he'd taken, and they kept going, picking up speed.

I'd ordered eight of them, and the first four were already forming into a wedge formation, heads down as they raced full tilt toward the queen.

Their greatest ability wasn't one that could be used much, or even one that should be used, outside of emergencies. I didn't want anyone coming up with a counter, after all. But as the two outermost peeled off, diverting to run at the flesh titans, I grinned to myself in my secure little metal box.

The first corpse lord slammed into the nearest leg of the titan, wrapping its arms about it, clinging on tight and triggering the ability.

Ability:

Suppress!

The Corpse Lord can suppress the Abilities or Spells of others, provided it maintains eye contact or direct physical contact.

As it triggered that, the flesh titan staggered. Its abilities and powers might not have been fully understood—certainly, I didn't know what they were—but the one thing I did know was that they were all being controlled by the queen.

As the corpse lord triggered its suppression field, the flesh titan floundered, windmilling as, for the first time in its life, it lost contact with the controlling sentience.

The second corpse lord hit its target, and that too fell. Though, in its case, it hit a wall, bounced, then landed atop the flaming remains of its dying brother.

It too started screeching and thrashing, kicking out, and the corpse lord that held its leg was catapulted into the wall, shattering on impact.

The remaining four corpse lords had paused as they entered the room. Two grabbed ASM launchers and the other two grabbed the rockets; then all four started to run again.

The first two had almost made it to the queen by this point. As they closed to the last few meters, the largest and most mobile of the pods tore open, the queen clearly panicking and determined to stop them.

The creature that fell free was barely half formed. Pulsing veins shone against pale-white flesh. Wet, black chitin and sopping hair covered most of it. As it hit the floor, it did so with a sound like a steak hitting the sidewalk.

The nearest corpse lord leapt atop it, arms wide, only to be smashed from the air by a fist that broke half its bones, before breaking itself.

The creature mewled, shaking its arm in the first display of pain I'd seen. I stared, stunned as the queen started to rip herself free of the wall.

The smaller creature tried to drag itself aside, until the next corpse lord hit it, wrapping its arms around the creature...to absolutely no effect.

I froze, confused, wondering whether the corpse lord's ability was flawed somehow, until the queen shrieked something, and the smaller one—the *princess*, I suddenly realized—replied.

It dragged itself toward the nearest door in the wall, presumably trying to get to somewhere, while the old queen, who was now gushing fluids as she finished ripping herself free of the wall, set herself up to fight for her progeny's life.

The second batch of corpse lords were almost there when the queen ripped the corpse lord free of her spawn and hurled it across the room. It hit the wall and detonated, shattering into hundreds of pieces.

She turned back around. Her flesh split and twisted; great tentacles unwound as she prepared to fight, drawing herself up to her full height...

"Get some, motherfucker!" Chris bellowed out. The mad bastard stood in the remaining small gap between the open doors, his cut-down HMG held in both hands as he pulled the triggers.

The entire belt of chain-fed .50cal ammunition screamed across the room in seconds—slamming into the queen, the wall, across and up halfway to the roof—before he got control and guided it back down onto the fleeing princess.

The first massive round hit her in the back, punching a hole through and out the far side. But the following twenty were what really left a lasting impression.

Where the queen was massive enough to take the hits and keep coming, for a short while at least, and the flesh titans had their insane regeneration to keep them together, the princess had neither advantage.

Riddled from behind, the princess fell, her half-formed body shredded and already failing organs torn asunder. As she fell, the queen went insane.

The holes that had been projecting the suppressing sonic attack went into overdrive, blasting out a cacophony of sounds that, even inside the boxer, and with my eardrums only beginning to heal, I flinched at.

Chris staggered back. His hail of fire was cut off by the release of the triggers, with barely a handful of rounds left to be fired. Then he apparently saw what the corpse lords were carrying, and he spun, diving aside, trying to get behind the doors.

The first of them hit the queen hard. A rugby tackle, that would have killed a lesser creature, only served to infuriate such a large one—right up until it triggered its ability, and her sonic attack cut off entirely.

The dungeon rushed back into my mind, and I reached out, frantic, as the second and third corpse lords hit the queen, latching on.

I was outside of the dungeon's radius—only by meters, but I was. And I desperately needed to not be. I could neither move, nor move the dungeon to me, but I had the influence still, the ability of a Dungeon Lord and his minions to affect the world around him.

I used it, pushing harder than I'd ever done before. I grabbed the field of the dungeon's closest infringement, and the slowly growing patch that I stood atop of, and I heaved.

The world around me seemed to shake, shuddering as I seized both sides of my influence and dragged them mentally closer. A thin line stretched out from me and inched closer and closer to Chris, even as the fourth, and final, corpse lord leapt.

In its arms was the second launcher, the missile pointed unerringly at its brother corpse lord.

The trigger was pulled as it flew. The chemical propellant fired true—instead of exploding on activation—then hurtled the missile over the few feet between its launcher and the armload of missiles the other corpse lord clutched.

Then the missile punched straight through the fucker, hit the floor, and ricocheted into the side of the queen, before cutting out. The missiles in the arms of the other corpse lord clattered to the floor as I screamed in fury.

The world around me grew dim as I strained. My breaths came in heaving pants, as the nearest point of my influence was dragged toward the door.

The queen screeched and roared. Her tentacles smashed down as she turned, locking eyes on my vehicle. Then she picked up the remains of the nearest flesh titan and hurled it at me.

It hit the boxer. The ATV bounced, lifting to the side with the impact and then crashing down again on all wheels as the queen dropped to her tentacles and headed for the door, glaring in at me as she roamed past, clearly intent on revenge.

"Fuuuuuck!" I whimpered, heaving harder. I could sense others there suddenly; even though they didn't know my plan, they worked to help, and the dungeon's influence grew.

I could almost reach, stretching out, and felt the hint of the dungeon mere inches away, as I strained.

My nature slipped free; contained in the compartment of the boxer, the first flare of lightning sparked to life, then more.

The spark begat others. Dozens crackled free, pushing into the vehicle and grounding out, the smell of burning plastics and rubber rising.

Inch after inch was claimed. And just as the queen was about to reach the door, presumably for revenge or to escape, he was there.

Chris, the mad bastard, stepped right out in front of her, firing his now reloaded HMG at point-blank range into her face. The great .50 cals ripped holes and sunk deep, smashing her internals and sending her flinching back as she raised tentacles to cover her face.

Then came the others.

As soon as the field had dropped, they'd started to summon, seeing when I'd managed it. They fell to work, and a dozen more corpse lords raced into sight.

Some leapt atop the queen, triggering their signature ability and suppressing any ability of hers, while others grappled onto her.

One skidded to a halt close by the nearest of the now-dead titans and triggered another ability.

Ability:

Raise!

The Corpse Lord can sacrifice its own health to raise the dead around it, replenishing its master's forces when needed.

The corpse lord collapsed, the bones losing all cohesion. But as they did so, a wash of green and blue light poured outward, rolling across the titan and the dead sentinels nearby.

Only the one titan rose, though several of the sentinels twitched and thrashed, before falling quiescent again. Two more corpse lords raced over, as more came all the time through the doors. As these two leapt atop nearby bodies, disassembling themselves to power their former enemies' new rebirth, this time the energy took root.

The first titan was rising still, as the second and third of the sentinels thrashed, trying to rise as well.

A pair of corpse lords appeared nearby, running from out of sight, and grabbed the nearest sentinel, hefting it and spinning, as it cracked its jaws wide obligingly.

Then they ran with it, as another yanked out one of the queen's tentacles, holding it taut.

The corpse lords and their improvised "jaws of life," as the fire department would have called them, clamped down, biting deep, then shifted. They started to carve sections free of the queen, even as others summoned weapons as soon as they found areas the dungeon could summon into.

I'd just reached the door with the influence, and I barked orders, barely able to see through the strain.

"Seal it!" I got out. "Seal the doors!"

Chris was on the far side still, his gun empty again. Blood ran down his right leg to pool on the floor, looking more than the worse for wear. A tower started to rise near him, the crackling of healing light getting his attention as a wall started to spring up across the doors.

"Matt...!" he shouted, before cursing and diving into the dungeon sense, searching.

I reached out to him, sagging. The electrical bursts died away as I collapsed into the seats before making a face at the smell of burned cushioning.

"What the hell, dude?" he asked me.

I let loose a groan, before closing my eyes, as I slid into the dungeon sense fully, my head hammering.

"It's okay," I assured him, as the first wall lifted into place around my refuge as well, making me grin evilly.

"What did you do?" He sounded exhausted.

"Survived," I said. *"How's Kilo?"*

"Touch and go," he admitted, before wincing. *"Hey, dude, better call off Jack!"*

I cursed, reaching out to grab him mentally. The big robot bear skidded to a halt, almost smashing full speed into the new wall that covered the old doors.

As it finished summoning, and the second layer began to coalesce around my vehicle, I looked tiredly to Kelly and Aly, sensing their arrival, as well as that of others as they, too, took advantage of the dampening field being torn asunder with the queen's release.

"What do we do?" Kelly asked.

The corpse lords, now in their dozens as more and more were summoned by the second, grabbed onto the queen. She was pinned now, no ability able to be activated, and thanks to the titans that were finally upright, pressing down on her and holding her in place, she was going nowhere.

"We kill her," I said.

"You don't want to try to negotiate?"

Aly said it because it needed to be said, I knew, not because she wanted me to do it.

"Fuck no," I growled, reaching out.

Two more corpse lords grabbed up the remaining ASM missiles, the grenade belts, and all the explosives we'd been carrying, then started slapping it atop the queen.

"How do we make it fire?" Kelly asked me. *"I mean, the last rocket went off and didn't..."*

"It's lodged inside her." I nodded. *"The fuckers must have a minimum arming distance. The other one that went off had just deteriorated to the point it wasn't stable anymore. So, instead of that being a flaw, it's going to become a feature."*

"What?" Kelly asked.

"In IT, when something goes wrong, and you want to bullshit your way out of trouble"—I grinned weakly at her—*"it's not a flaw...it's an 'unexpected feature.'"*

Then the first corpse lord lifted its new hammer.

They were simple creations: a short handle, remarkably like a sledgehammer's haft, and at the top, it was sealed to a missile, about halfway down.

His companion to the right of him hefted his own. Then, in unison, they both lifted their shields.

"Ready?" I asked, unable to help myself as I examined the new weapons, then shared their specs with the group.

Ka-Booooom	Tool

335

A single-use hammer, one that's guaranteed to do catastrophic damage to whatever project you're working on, this creation represents the peak of human ingenuity, and insanity.	
Durability 13/100	Charge: 1/1

Then the pair swung their hammers at each other's shields, using their hammers for the first, and last, time.

CHAPTER THIRTY-FOUR

"So explain that again, and this time make it like you're trying to explain it to him," I said slowly, pointing a finger at Chris, who slumped nearby, glaring at the other half of the table.

We were in the new command center of the north dungeon, one that had been shifted, as far as everyone knew, along with the second dungeon core, to the heart of the base.

It hadn't. The meeting room had been set up here while the core was currently slowly sliding deeper, surrounded by enough lead and steel to make a battleship.

It gave a little extra security, though, and Aly had even created a dummy core above it, just in case it was ever found.

The command and control room that we had set up in the Newcastle dungeon had been replicated here, now that we had full control over the area, and an option to pair the tables had popped up, which we'd accepted.

Now Chris, Patrick—he'd been found with the last group, and had apparently held out until only a day before we arrived—Sergeant Reed, Warrant Officer Sanderson, Captain Griffiths, Mike—our captain of the guard—Sergeant Rhodes (who I'd already decided was getting a promotion when I could figure it all out), Sarah, and Jo sat around our table.

On the other side were Kelly, Aly, Finn, Becky, Tulio, Clarissa, Ashley, Dante, Markus, Colonel Ptolemy, and Barry.

Both sides had the advantage of access to the dungeon. Although we all felt like we should be pretty damn fucked up right now, the healing towers had created the odd effect of making our bodies feel incredibly healthy, while our minds and souls felt like garbage.

"It's really not that complicated, Matt." Aly sighed, before smiling and reaching out one hand, catching a cup as it appeared, the top covered with whipped cream and marshmallows. "Whatever the rules are around absorbing things, we just need to be incredibly careful, that's all. We could break the nukes down and absorb them individually, but it's just not a good idea."

"I got *that*," I snapped. "I meant about the research!"

"Oh, sorry." Aly smiled, then took a sip of her hot chocolate as she gathered her thoughts.

"So the five 'suitcase nukes' that you found are part of the nation's arsenal. We're not going to ask where they came from or why, but what we do know is that they need to be maintained incredibly carefully. As it is, they've obviously not been, and neither have the seals on the bioweapons section. The first thing we need to do is absorb them all, making damn sure we get them in one go, rather than say, taking the shielding apart, and setting the nuke off accidentally."

"Yeah, nuclear explosion on the level directly below where I'm sitting: *bad.*" I nodded. "Again, I get that."

"Uh-huh, well, you said explain it so that Chris can understand it, and let's face it, he gets bored and wanders off a lot, so I wanted to make sure we're all on the same page. Moving on. We absorb the five nukes all at once, to keep it as safe as possible, and if we're all here thirty seconds afterward, we'll have basically jumped in tech from the Renaissance to the Information Age."

"How?" I said slowly.

"We don't know exactly how much mana we're going to get from this." Kelly took over as she saw how annoyed I was getting. "But we know that the more complex and denser a piece of technology is, the higher the returned mana value. There's not really anything that we make as a species that'd be more incredibly dangerous, nor powerful than nuclear weapons, especially the kind that can be broken down and carried in a suitcase. I thought they were the basis of crappy spy novels, not real."

"Uh-huh." I nodded. "So we're playing it safe then. We queue up several layers of tech, and we see what we get."

"Yes and no." Aly took over again. "We know that when you attached a storm to the dungeon and basically drained it, we got well over a million points of mana. This is an order of magnitude more powerful, and yet we're not actually triggering them. We might get a pulse of power. We might be catapulted all the way to the top core—or we *could* be."

"Or we might get a few hundred to a few thousand," Chris pointed out. "We'll get that from the biologicals at least."

"We will," I agreed. "What are you thinking for the research?"

"We just need to have a plan is all I'm saying," Aly said. "And we need to make it now, and start right away. Because, if we screw this up, the consequences are…well, they're death."

"Because the suit-nukes could go off at any time," I said. "Fine, let's hear the plan then."

"We've started on the rare converters already." Aly scratched the side of her neck as she thought. "That's as we'd hoped, and worried. A million points of mana for the rare tier, and it's likely to mean that the legendary, which is the last in the row, is just plain out of our price range.

"It does mean, though, that provided we go from here to Steel mana converters instead of Bronze that we've been working on, and start that path, then even when we go to Glass, we can still continue with this.

"What we need to do, though, is queue up the research, to make sure that if there's a ridiculous excess, we don't miss using it. So we have the rare converter, then the basic Steel one, followed by the—" She broke off to check something.

"Yeah, sorry, the research we've gotten done to the storage so far is up to the uncommon level; that's ten thousand in cost at that point. The next one is advanced—that's ready to go. That'll cost us a hundred thousand, and we think net us fifty thousand mana a pop. We research that next."

"Should we work on that first?" I interrupted her. "I mean, get the mana storage up to the point we can actually really store some, and then upgrade the stores?"

"If we had the time?" She nodded. "I'd say yes, every time. The issue is that we really don't. Colonel?"

"I don't have the experience, and none of the survivors do either, but we do have one EOD tech available. He's taken a look at the nukes inside the dungeon sense," the colonel said. "I'm sorry that I couldn't answer questions about it before, and yes, I'm still extremely limited in what I can say now, but there's the issue of national security, and then above that, on my oaths is protecting the realm. If these go off unexpectedly, the realm is rendered uninhabitable, as would be a significant portion of the world, due to the possible knock-on effects, so yes. This grants me some…let's call it wiggle room." He looked around the table.

"Tinson, the EOD tech, isn't happy, and—"

"I'm sorry," Clarissa interrupted, holding one hand up. "For the non-military amongst us, what is that?"

"E-O-D." The colonel said the letters clearly. "Explosive Ordnance Disposal."

"Bomb squad," Mike added helpfully. "Balls of steel, brains of mince, generally."

"They're actually some of the most intelligent people I've ever met," Griffiths corrected, and Mike snorted.

"They literally take bombs apart, knowing they could explode at any second. That's not intelligence—that's madness on a scale so grand it's noticeable from orbit."

"Well, regardless, Tinson isn't happy," the colonel repeated. "He's not rated for nuclear work, but he's all we have, and he's been extremely clear that we're all dead men walking, as of yesterday."

"So no option of holding on a few days?" I glanced from face to face. "Any chance he's overreacting?"

"He started drinking immediately after seeing the condition of the weapons, and claims we're all dead anyway as he can't see a way to disarm them."

"He's EOD, and he's given up?" Griffiths asked skeptically. "Most of them are so gung-ho they're insufferable."

"As agreed, I didn't give him any information on the capabilities of your dungeon, beyond accompanying him through the system to reach the nuclear containers," the colonel explained. "He doesn't know how you could absorb them, and believes that it's only a matter of time before they destabilize and detonate, and that nowhere in the country will be safe."

"The radius on something this size isn't that much…" Griffiths muttered, thinking, before closing his eyes and taking a deep breath. "Fuck's sake, there's more, aren't there?"

"Two more sites," the colonel agreed, holding my gaze. "Should we successfully disarm this one and make safe the weapons, then I'll share their locations."

"And you'll expect us to go deal with them, I take it?" I said coldly.

"Yes."

"Matt, I don't see that we've got a choice," Kelly said softly after a few minutes. "If we leave it, they'll go off eventually. And the damage...whatever's left of humanity won't survive long if the nukes start going off."

The colonel and I continued to stare at each other, until finally he had the good grace to look away. I grunted, agreeing with Kelly, but hating that I was being railroaded into this.

"Fine," I muttered, before taking a deep breath and straightening up. "Fine, we'll do it," I repeated.

"Thank you." The colonel sagged in relief.

"Aly, if we could hold on, what would be the plan?" I asked, before holding my hand up to the colonel as he opened his mouth to speak. "I need to hear it," I snapped.

"Mana storage up to rare, if not legendary, then restart that on Steel level. Work the next few days frantically to get that as high as possible, then we upgrade all the storage."

"What about doing one level then upgrading the storage?" I asked.

"Honestly, it's not worth it." She tapped her nails on the table as she worked out the numbers. "We've got a hundred and sixty storage nodes, and they're at five hundred a pop currently, that's...eighty thousand."

"Right." I nodded.

"If we wait until the next one—we think that's going to go to fifty thousand—that gives us eight million, *if* the jump is as we think..."

"It won't be." That was Dante, speaking up suddenly.

"What?" Aly asked, totally confused.

"The cost-to-storage ratio, it's wrong," he said diffidently, as if embarrassed to be contradicting Aly. "You've said the jump originally was ten, then went to twenty, then twenty again. Probably because the entry-level tech was done in Stone?"

"I think we researched it in Bronze...yeah, this is the Bronze line." Aly frowned.

"Well, I don't know why it's showing as ten for the first one. Maybe the line just starts at ten regardless if you do it in Stone or not, but the first one was worked out on a multiple of ten. The second and third are both a multiple of twenty, so unless the fourth breaks the pattern, they'll come in at a cost of a hundred thousand for this one and get us five thousand points of mana storage per unit, then the next will be..."

He quickly checked the numbers and nodded to himself.

"A million mana at rare and fifty thousand storage, then ten million at legendary and half a million in storage." He looked up from his working out and winced. "Sorry."

"Don't be." I sat forward, looking at him. "Can you predict the next ones?"

"Ummm, maybe?" he hedged, scratching the back of his neck as he thought. Then he scribbled on a piece of paper that Ashley wordlessly summoned for him and slid over. The pen he held was a fountain one, and as he worked, he smudged the lines regularly, drifting back and forth as we waited.

"Okay..." he said after a long minute. "I think I get it. So the research is carried out on each tier. You didn't do any in Stone, so the first one has to start at a cost-to-storage of ten, as that's the basic. Then, because it was Bronze, you get a cost-to-storage or CTS of twenty.

"Moving from uncommon to advanced using that math, you get the hundred thousand cost, and the five thousand mana gained. If we go higher than that, we get fifty thousand storage for a million, then a million for ten million. I'd suggest we stop at one million. It'd be great to do it all, but the next tier is probably going to follow the same pattern as the converters do—then the storage will eventually become insane. As an example…"

He fiddled with things for a few seconds, then two tables appeared before us.

Mana Storage		
Tier:		Bronze
Level:	Cost:	Storage Gained:
Basic	1,000	100
Common	5,000	250
Uncommon	10,000	500
Advanced	100,000	5,000
Rare	1,000,000	50,000
Legendary	10,000,000	500,000
Artifact	100,000,000	5,000,000

Mana Storage		
Tier:		Steel
Level:	Cost:	Storage Gained:
Basic	100,000	20,000
Common	500,000	50,000
Uncommon	1,000,000	100,000
Advanced	10,000,000	1,000,000
Rare	100,000,000	10,000,000
Legendary	1,000,000,000	100,000,000
Artifact	10,000,000,000	1,000,000,000

"Okay, now, remember this is literally going off the data we have, nothing else, so it might be totally wrong. But if the pattern stays the same, then the gained storage doubles from the last tier with each new one, from Bronze to Steel—as we missed out on Iron—we get double the last level. I've capped the research at 'advanced' in Bronze, then worked this out on that as the starter point for the next level."

"I…" I started to speak then shook my head and lapsed into silence. It was just too much, too much "if this, then that," and everything moved all the time. "Fucking aliens," I muttered.

"Basically, yeah." Dante grinned. "There'll be a reason for this, but what it is, and why they cap it and follow these patterns, I just don't know."

"Okay, so we do the advanced level of research, then move on," I growled, my head hurting. "So, what else? Let's get it all laid out, people. We need to be very sure about this."

"We've used the tokens you gave us to reach out to the dungeon fairies, getting a response from one called Lysander."

"Lysander…" I muttered, trying to remember which one that had been. "The Chinese pair? Uh…Kai and Leilani?"

"That's right." Aly smiled at the memory. "Well, you were busy, so Ashley, do you want to take over?"

"I activated the scale token you were given." She straightened slightly. "When Aly, Kelly, and I discussed it, we decided that as I was there, it might be better if it was me who they saw. So when I pressed it to the nexus gate, it activated and opened a portal to their side…though it was shielded, we think."

"A blue film over their side, and Lysander had to deactivate it for Ashley to step through."

"You went through?" I asked Ashley, who nodded.

"I was only there for ten minutes, but yes. They gave some advice, though they said that for any more, there would need to be a deal struck."

"And the advice they gave?" I prompted.

"It was pretty much what we already knew—research everything you can for the lower levels before you move on," Ashley admitted. "The points we'd figured out about the line remaining viable until you start the next tier, then locking down was confirmed as well. And when I started pushing in that direction, the fairy got concerned. She claimed that if we've damaged the core, then we might not be able to advance beyond Glass, and as such might have to start a new dungeon."

"With a seed?" I asked.

"Apparently so. You can link to an existing dungeon with one, as you have with this, or create a totally separate one. We could even, from what she hinted at, possibly set up the new one right alongside the existing, and gather stores for it, then power-level it."

"Power-level it in the short time to start again at Stone," I muttered, rubbing my chin as I thought. "Then what? Get all the tech we can low down, and jump it each time?"

"Exactly," she said. "But she warned that if we tried that, we'd most likely lose a significant amount of time. We'd lose the nexus gate, and we'd have to start again from an influence point of view."

"Also, we think that means that all the things we've built, such as the accommodation, would have to be rebuilt from scratch," Aly added sourly. "So although we could do it, it's only a case of us being able to do that if we had unlimited time. We'd have to create stockpiles of food, equipment, and high-value items to break down, and it'd take a few months with each level of core to get to the point that we 'should' level it up."

"So how the hell did they get to Steel before us?" I asked. "Or at the same time anyway?"

"Selective upgrades." Ashley shrugged. "Lysander said they were willing to discuss that, and possible sharing of technologies, but not with me, and not for free. Any further information would need to be met with us sharing the same."

"They want us to share all our tech?" I asked.

"Ultimately, probably yes. But for now, they want to know what we have and haven't done, and the condition of the core, which they'd need access to."

"Not going to happen," I said firmly. "If I'm not going to trust a dungeon fairy that's essentially blank and summoned with a bond in place to me, to access the dungeon, then I'm sure as shit not going to trust another dungeon's fairy to access it."

"Is it that big a concern?" Colonel Ptolemy frowned.

"A dungeon fairy interfaces with the dungeon on a deeper level than any human can," Aly explained. "If they were to access the dungeon, there's a good chance that they could lock us all out."

Then, apparently remembering that the person she was speaking to was an uncertain ally, she went on hurriedly.

"They'd then be able to allow the other humans they were bonded with to access the dungeon. They might decide to share it with them, or to kill everyone. The one dungeon fairy we'd dealt with separately from all of this was psychotic."

"There's just no way to be sure." I sat upright and tugged my top straight as I thought. "So let's move on. Was there a reason you mentioned them?"

"Yeah, getting to that," Ashley admitted. "Sorry. So they said that there are medical suites that offer more advanced facilities, and yeah, they're gained through higher levels. Once we reach Glass, the medical suites we have access to will get an upgrade, and they'll be able to provide access to scanners, directed healing and more specialized medical procedures, like midwifery and so on. For now? We're basically in the Dark Ages with that, so if we can, we really need to get a move on with that."

"Especially as Michelle is literally days away from giving birth, and right now? The only healers and medical teams we have are either a paramedic with very limited magical experience, or here, where we're not allowed to return to the dungeon until we've proved that we're all clean." Jo spoke up. "Aly, please can you give Michelle and Ian my apologies? I know it's not much, but I'll be there as soon as I can."

"They know it's not ideal, but again, they understand," Kelly said. "The risk if one of the vurms got into the dungeon is too great."

"It is," I agreed. "So, we're all agreed that we're going for the Glass level. So let's make this formal. Aly, you've got advanced mana storage in research now, followed by what?"

"Okay..." Aly started, and I settled back with the others to wait, listen, and plan.

CHAPTER THIRTY-FIVE

"Y̵ou were quiet in the meeting."

"I didn't feel that I had much to add to it, sir," Colonel Ptolemy admitted.

He'd asked for this meeting as we finally got to the end of the last one, and I'd been damn surprised when he asked for it to be only himself, Griffiths, Mike, and Sanderson, the highest-ranking survivor of the battle for Otterburn Camp.

"Okay, well, it takes a lot to try to get your head around this shit." I grunted, rubbing at the back of my neck, before summoning a coffee and sipping it.

"You're all welcome to summon what you like," I said again, having made the point twice already in the meeting to them, though only Mike hadn't needed the prompting. "You want to tell me what this is all about?"

"Rank," Ptolemy said. "I'm the highest-ranking officer here, though Major Stevenson, who is currently still missing, may choose to contest that."

I glanced from him to Sanderson, then back. "Have you explained that—" I started, only for the colonel to nod, cutting me off.

"Sanderson is an old friend, and well aware of the issues that I've had with the major. He served with him in a former position, and is..." He paused, glancing at the senior NCO, who took over.

"I'd not trust him to command a box of chocolate, sir," the warrant officer said. "He gained his rank through connections, and kept it through the same. There were a few like that, but thankfully he's not here now."

"I had one as well," Griffiths volunteered. "Though he grew up before the end."

"Then I'm sorry for your loss, sir," Sanderson said. "The major was incapable of growing up, and frankly, had he been here on base, I suspect an accident would have removed him from the chain of command shortly after power was lost."

"Now, now." The colonel smiled faintly. "As much as we'd all like to dream about that at times, he was a fellow officer, and is now MIA. Let's not speak ill of the dead."

"Fucker better be dead." Mike grunted, having had the time to learn exactly what had happened back home by now. "I'll shoot him if not."

"And that brings us to the point of this meeting, sir." The colonel turned back to me. "I've been careful to keep this from my people and yourself until now, but I'm in the late stages of cancer. And frankly, with my wife and children gone, I have no desire to continue. Your healers have offered magic healing, and I've refused."

"All right..." I said slowly. "Are you sure? I mean, your wife and children might be..."

"They were flying back from the States when the end came," he said. "At that point, I'd been watching the plane some ten minutes before, and due to the location…" He shook his head. "I believe the end would have been quick, like many who were aloft when the change came. They would have had little chance of surviving a landing. As they were, over the Atlantic? No."

"I'm sorry for your loss," I said truthfully.

"Thank you." He nodded. "As it was, the soldiers under my command were all that kept me going. But the situation had been resolved to the satisfaction of most, and I've spoken with several of your people." He glanced at Griffiths and Mike, before taking a deep breath. "As such, I'm willing to make you an offer, to smooth the way, so to speak."

"Go on."

"Your captain of the guard, Mike Jefferson, is as we've discussed, a skilled man. However, he is no graduate of the military academies, and frankly, although he is a gifted soldier, I would suggest another takes his place."

"No." I glared at him. "You don't get to tell me that—"

"Matt, hear him out," Mike interrupted me, and I glared at him as well. "Please."

"What the hell?" I looked from one to another.

"Thank you, Captain," the colonel said wryly. "Matt, please, let me say my piece and then consider it. That's all I ask."

"I'll listen," I agreed after a long glance around, though I wasn't happy at this, starting to feel ambushed.

"Mike came to me, asking me to consider taking his place," Griffiths said.

I twisted to look at him incredulously, then back to Mike. "Mike?"

"I fucked up, Matt." He shook his head. "Griffiths refused because he says he did as well. But at the end of the day, the dungeon's safety was my responsibility, and I fucked up. I took all our most experienced people and we marched off into a trap. I lost the fight and left the base open to that tool of a major to attack. At the same time, you were locked in the trial dungeon and I…I shouldn't have left. Griffiths tried to take command of the group, asking me to stay at the dungeon, explaining the risks, and I refused."

He shifted uncomfortably, then leaned forward and braced himself on the table, looking at me.

"I fucked up and it nearly cost us everything. I've got no real experience in large-scale fights. I'm good with the special forces, and in small skirmishes, sure, but I don't know enough. I want to step down, and I want Griffiths to take my place."

"I told him that I wasn't willing to consider it until he'd explained himself fully, and I need to point out that I went with him," Griffiths added when I glanced back at him. "And, frankly, I don't *want* the job."

"Nobody in their right mind would." The colonel snorted. "But here we are. My suggestion—and my offer, Matt, if you'd consider it—is that you restructure your military. You already have a significant force, and now, with gaining control over the camp and my own soldiers, you have the opportunity to grow by a massive margin."

"The issue we've got is that my soldiers don't know you," Sanderson said suddenly. "You're a civilian with highly limited experience of command. You've been catapulted into this position…we get that. But you've got experienced officers and NCOs who aren't being used to their full potential. Add to that, if you encounter other bases, they'll have the same concerns when they experience your chain of command, and you start to see some of the issues."

"There's a solution, though," Mike offered.

I settled back, folding my arms and trying not to feel like I was being railroaded into this as I listened.

"I'll step down as captain of the guard," Mike went on. "I'll move to create and train my own special forces contingent. They'll be there for the real sticky missions. That gives us somewhere to put those with the right skills, and frees me up to do what I do best. At the same time, Griffiths takes my place as captain of the guard, and under him, we fold in Warrant Officer Sanderson and his people."

"This keeps my current ranks and structure more or less intact, while giving people both a sense of continuity and enables a smoother chain of command," the warrant officer said.

I started to open my mouth, to point out that I didn't know most of these people from shit, and the colonel went on.

"Then, I'll bind them all to the dungeon and you, by an oath."

"What?" I asked.

"An oath," he repeated. "You've agreed that you'll try to protect the Queen or king and their direct heirs. The family who you can reasonably reach and protect, you agree to offer protection if you can, providing them with a place of security When Coldstream find the Queen and her family, you already agreed to protect them. In this situation, you'd agree to listen to the advice of the soldiers under your command, when appropriate."

"That bit's in there so no one can try to fuck you over by enforcing the oath at stupid times." Mike grinned. "I recommended that."

"It is. So you agree to try to save, as well as protect, the royal family. You agree to listen to your soldiers and treat them as your citizens, and their families, should you be able to rescue them, with all the rights and advantages they would naturally receive. In exchange, they agree to transfer their oaths of allegiance over to you. I'd write the oaths, though I'd do it with you or another of your people to help me," the colonel said. "Matt, this removes the concerns you have to be feeling when it comes to the soldiers here, and it provides them with surety that they've got a future."

"Matt…" Mike started, but the colonel held a hand up, taking a deep breath before going on, watching me as he did so.

"And, in exchange for all of this, when I bind them to you, I'll do so using a focal orb, granting you the ability to offer oaths yourself even once I'm gone, but with a single caveat."

"Which is?" I asked after a few seconds of consideration.

"We will have an oath, between you and me, that you cannot use the oath to enslave, nor use my ability to force your attentions or those who are under you upon another. You seem to have a well-defined sense of right and wrong, Matt, and it matches my own, so we will simply let that be your guide, with those caveats to ensure it doesn't change."

I glared at them all, then forced myself to speak, feeling very much ambushed now. "I'll consider it." That was all I could promise. But that was apparently enough, as the others all nodded and started leaving the dungeon sense, until eventually it was just Mike and me, followed by Kelly and Aly appearing a few seconds later.

"Did you know about this?" I asked Aly as she settled in again, then glanced at Kelly.

"I did," Aly admitted calmly, sipping at her hot chocolate again. "She didn't."

"What's this?" Kelly frowned.

"Mike wants to step down," Aly said before I could. "He feels responsible for some of the losses we've taken, and he's wasted as a captain of the guard, when he could be building and leading a special forces squad."

"Who'd take over?" Kelly asked. "Not the colonel…"

"No," I agreed, annoyed by the way it'd all been done. "He's dying of cancer, and his family died in the fall. He doesn't want to be healed, just wants to make sure the soldiers are safe—then he's out. He wants Griffiths to take over."

"He's a good choice," Kelly admitted. "Mike, are you sure?"

"I am." He looked at me. "Matt, mate, I didn't want to blindside you, but the sheer amount of shit we've got going on? I didn't think you'd listen if I just told you. And, honestly, this way we know the soldiers are solid."

"It folds in the entire army camp under your command," Aly said, "as well as providing a legitimate and formal structure for others to join under. The issues we've had from the major and the way the base looked at us to start with…that wouldn't happen if we've got the army folded in formally like this. And it'd mean that we've got people with real experience of things like logistics in the right places."

"So…what do you think?" Kelly asked me.

I tried not to snap, taking a deep breath and forcing myself to look at it.

"Honestly, I don't like it." I held my hand up as I went on. "No, let me finish. I don't like it, but that's because I feel like it was a done deal before you came to me. I'm not liking that you decided all of this without me, and now I'm trying to get my head around it. Yeah, it makes sense, mostly. It just feels…"

"Like you're losing control?" Kelly asked me shrewdly.

I hesitated, then nodded. "Yeah, basically." I sighed. "Look, that really makes me feel like a bit of a dick. It's just a surprise, that's all. Are you sure this is what you want, Mike?" I asked him.

"It is, mate," he said.

"And you're happy to turn it over to Griffiths?" I watched him. "Knowing that he'd then be in charge overall, and you'd be under him?"

"Aye." He nodded, then grinned. "The way I'm thinking is that he'd be in charge of the conventional forces—under you, of course, and Kell—but he'd lead the army and keep the ball rolling there. He'd be responsible for training and all that shite, but I'd take the best and brightest and make a second force, one that's outside of the main chain of command, and that'd be your primary squad moving forward."

"Mine?"

"Your mad plans, your missions that always go tits up? That'd be me and my people. I can't lead that and be in command of the dungeon's forces. Barry? He's good, but he was a fighter like me. Markus? He's learning and he's good at tactics for holding somewhere, but crap at assaulting it. We'd restructure the dungeon's forces into the army. The training cadre would be firmed up and made responsible for feeding into the army. And then I'd have my special forces that are responsible for fucking shit up and being generally awesome.

"All jokes aside, I can run that a lot better than I can the general army, and when we come across some general or whatever, Griffiths can talk to him a lot better than I can. With him as the dungeon's captain of the guard, meetings with other armed forces are going to go a lot smoother than they will with just you and me."

"And the oath?" I asked.

"We get Kelly and the colonel to write it, though I've got no idea how he thinks he can bind *everyone* to it."

"Fine. And I think, as long as he has enough mana, he can probably do it. We'll just have to figure out a feeding mechanism." I sighed. "Kelly, can you do that, please?"

"Of course." She nodded. "It's an oath he swears or...?"

"Sorry." I facepalmed as I realized I'd not explained that part. "He's offering to bind all the soldiers to an oath to obey me, and for me to look after them."

"Got it." She nodded again, making a note. "I'll speak with him. So, you're happy with what we sorted out in the last meeting? The research plans?"

"I am," I said quickly, quailing internally at how long and involved that meeting had gotten.

The end result was that the mana storage, the mana converters, and conduits were all to be brought up to advanced; the first level of each was to be researched in the Steel pathway, before it switched to the Glass core. Those were followed by the individual remaining crafting stations to be researched, finishing with another dungeon seed being produced.

I had no doubt that we'd get that far, but we couldn't queue up technology we didn't have access to yet. And unless we upgraded all the mana storage research to artifact, then upgraded all the individual units already built to that level, we just weren't going to be able to spend it if there was too much overflow.

I was gloomily convinced everyone was going to be really disappointed when we got fuck all from the nukes and the tech around them and had to go back to doing this manually.

The next few hours were filled with Kelly and the colonel arguing over terms and meanings, before the day culminated in a hailstorm that reminded everyone here that we really needed to get the place sorted out as a priority.

We'd spent the last day and a bit in the small command area of the camp underground, but for the vast majority, there was no such luxury.

We'd found that of the original complement of the camp, and those from the surrounding villages for about ten miles in all directions, the survivors had been gathered here.

That, thanks to the size of the camp, the nearby roads and population, was almost two thousand people.

By the time the fight with the queen was won and the survivors had been gathered up, there were a little less than thirteen hundred.

That was a horrific number of losses, and even worse was the fact that so many of them had died since we tried to liberate the camp. The queen had been melding all those who she could into new forms to protect her, and we'd come to the heartbreaking conclusion that had we attacked full-on, and just opened fire on those who tried to stop us, instead of trying to save as many as we could, we'd have hit the queen faster and harder and would have quite possibly saved more in the end.

The barracks at the top of the base were absorbed into the dungeon and pulled apart, as were the dead, those huge piles of the dead that were so heartrending.

The aboveground buildings that we'd judged—with the help of the local people and Griffiths—to be of no real use were replaced with a three-floor apartment block, similar in style to the ziggurat layout that we'd done in the Newcastle dungeon.

Between the three floors, and with the understanding that most of those who lived here currently were single, the building layout was much simpler than the others.

The ground floor was split into the family rooms. Two- to five-bedroom apartments were built side by side, each with at least one bathroom, frequently two for the larger ones, and a communal living area in each apartment. There was no need for a kitchen, after all, so we did away with that.

The next two floors were all single apartment layouts: one bedroom, one bathroom, one living room. They were boring, but that was life in the new world.

Then we created some large communal areas in the apartment block, and a main canteen. That was it. At first people looked impressed by the magic, but unimpressed by the layout offered.

Then they realized that the showers were hot, the food was fresh and pretty much unlimited, and the walls could take a hit from an RPG, and everything changed.

By the following morning, as we were ready to start the oath taking, the details had all been hammered out, and I was reading over the oath in amazement.

"It's a bit...pompous?" I said, feeling really self-conscious.

"It's what the people expect," Kelly corrected. "It's written by the army and they're swearing to serve for a year and a day. Beyond that, everything is fair game, but it covers us for now."

"Why a year and a day?" Aly asked.

"That's the longest he can make it effective," Kelly replied. "It's down to how many people there are, and it's going to kill him, even with the mana we're going to be feeding him."

"That's a concern," I admitted.

"Not for him it isn't," Kelly said. "He wants this. It gives his people safety, and it gives us a huge population explosion of people we can really trust."

"And in a year and a day?" I asked.

"You've got a year and a day to earn their loyalty, and they have to earn yours. Considering who you are, I'm thinking that'll be an easy win."

"Nah, he's a dick really." Mike grinned. "You ready for this?"

"Not in the slightest." I snorted. "You?"

"Gods yes." He grinned. "Can't wait!"

"Dick."

"My wife loves it, yes."

"I can do without it," Aly said dryly. "Though hopefully when the new core comes online, we'll be able to get technology working again and I can replace him anyway."

"Oh, yeah, I miss mine too," Kelly admitted, before grinning as I looked at her askance. "Don't you worry about it, honey," she promised me, kissing my cheek. "You're the best *ever*," she added in a really fake voice, fluttering her eyelashes.

"I don't like this conversation anymore," I muttered.

"Me neither." Mike grunted. "Right. See you out there, boss."

I closed my eyes and slid from the dungeon sense back into my own body, stretching. I gathered my clothes and started to dress, making sure the armor looked the part.

It'd been cleaned and repaired—again—and I shrugged, getting it to settle into place more comfortably, before sighing and heading out of the small room I'd claimed for myself.

I was in the middle of the underground area, about twenty meters from the secure zone where the nukes were currently hidden behind layers of stone. As I headed up the passage toward the armory, I couldn't help but mentally mark spots where we'd had to fight on the way down.

The walls were a strange mixture of spotless because they'd been repaired where they'd been badly damaged, or absolutely filthy, where they'd been intact and hadn't needed any repairs.

Passing them, I remembered the monsters we'd fought there, and that they'd once been human.

Many of our people were back now, rescued and proclaimed "clean" by Jo, but we still weren't taking any chances. Fully a third of the survivors weren't soldiers, and after we'd told everyone the plan and made them the offer, almost a hundred people had refused the oath.

They had left last night, heading on their way with a backpack each full of supplies and a single magazine of ammunition for their weapon of choice.

That they weren't willing to swear the oath but had been proclaimed clean was a concern, but that was life. I wasn't going to turn this into a prison.

They'd be back, I was sure.

Striding through the armory, now secured at all times by a pair of corpse lords on watch, I nodded to the few soldiers about, hurrying through the gentle snow toward the parade ground.

That was what Griffiths had called it, anyway. It was a fucking parking lot a week ago. But considering we had no working cars, it wasn't really needed for that anymore.

The soldiers and civilians had gathered, and I picked up the pace, jogging over, before snorting and lifting into the air, flying across to the raised platform with my cloak whipping in the breeze behind me.

Standing atop it were Colonel Ptolemy, Captain Griffiths, Mike, Rhodes, and Warrant Officer Sanderson, who I'd learned rarely spoke, but when he did, it was generally time to shut up and listen. Lastly, the new representative of the civilian population of the new dungeon, a local man named Arend-Jan, stood smiling out across the crowd, joking with a few in the front row.

All around us in the dungeon I could feel the others—the soldiers of Newcastle who hadn't come with us, and who now stood ready to swear the oath, though I had no clue whether they would be able to, through the dungeon's filters.

I just had to trust.

I landed next to the others on the platform, and they greeted me. The colonel in particular seemed more cheerful and energized than I'd seen him in the entire time I'd known him.

"Are you sure you want to go through with this?" I asked him quietly. "There's other ways. Hell, I didn't need the damn oaths from the others!"

"No, you didn't, but the major screwed that up and there'll always be a disconnect in trust from my people and your own thanks to that," he countered. "Add in that the new soldiers will see that and won't be sure which side they should choose...this solves it all nicely. And it makes sure that moving forward, everyone is able to trust each other."

He took a deep breath, then let it out, staring into my eyes. "Matt, I need to do this. This gives my end meaning, and a gift to my soldiers that nobody else could give. It's what I want."

"I..." I straightened. It was time to start acting like I was the damn Dungeon Lord. He'd made his decision, and I now had to get on and deal with it. "Thank you, Colonel," I said formally. "Your sacrifice will not be forgotten."

"It is my honor, sir," he replied, before turning and nodding to the warrant officer.

Sanderson stepped forward and roared into the early morning sunlight, "ATTEN...*SHUN!*"

The military personnel stiffened and silence fell, as even the civilians quieted, ready to take the oath. I stepped forward, my mouth dry. I cleared my throat before starting.

"Thank you all!" I called out. "We are gathered here, to make formal the arrangement that the colonel and your own Warrant Officer Sanderson made with us. I am Matt, the Dungeon Lord of Newcastle, and I rule there." I let that hang in the air for a long while as the snow gently fell.

"I rule there not because I want to. I rule because someone has to. The dungeon can only have one master, and I created it. It is me, and I am it. Within its walls, as you are here, in a new outpost of the dungeon, you will have safety and security, or as much of both as I can offer.

"The people who live within the dungeon all contribute to its growth and safety. Some protect its borders and look to expand them and protect others through force of arms. Others carry out research. Still more provide teaching to the children, training to our forces, or grow food. Why do we grow food, when we can summon it?" I asked.

"We grow it because it is better to always have excess, to have a level of safety, and so that we can trade and help others. We grow it to raise up greater and stronger lines of crops, herbs for alchemy, wheat for bread, and a hundred other crops.

"That will be this outpost's function, to raise steadily improving crops, and to act as a safe place that our forces can train. We will create a gate here, one that permits instantaneous transport to the heart of Newcastle. That will enable us to be linked together and to make sure that you are as safe as can be. But all of this costs, and it costs resources, instead of gold, as the old world had it.

"Some of those who were among your number…some tried to take advantage of the situation. They attacked me and mine, and they killed members of the dungeon's forces and citizens. Without warning, they murdered my people, and as you'll understand, that's a hard thing to get over for anyone, let alone someone who's responsible for the safety of thousands.

"That is where Colonel Ptolemy comes in. As much as I dislike the necessity of it, I have accepted his offer of his ability, his class and his power, to create a binding oath between us, you and I.

"You have all been given a copy of the oath, and will now swear it with me. If you choose not to, I understand and will respect that decision. You will, however, not be permitted to remain inside the dungeon's borders. You must leave, and seek your fortune elsewhere. Does anyone wish to go?"

Silence rang out, and after waiting a short while, I nodded and went on.

"Thank you all. I feel, as I'd imagine many of you do, a little uncertain about this oath. It ties me as solidly as it ties you, but as we get to know each other, I hope we'll all remember the man who made this level of trust possible.

"Colonel Adrian Ptolemy is going to use his ability, as I've said, but it will kill him—"

"Soldiers!" he barked, stepping forward and interrupting me. "As you can tell, the choice of me administering this oath was not a popular one, primarily with young Matt here! He thinks of this as me committing suicide, while I think of this as me moving on to join my wife and children. I move on with my honor intact and having done all I can to preserve the heart and soul of the British Army. As such, I ask that you all follow direction, as we take the oath!"

The colonel stepped back, then turned and spoke to me in a lowered voice. "You were making it clear you weren't happy, and trying to talk them into—or out of—what has to come. They're soldiers, most of them, and villagers used to living with soldiers. They like straightforward things, not floundering around."

"So much for my increase in fucking charisma," I muttered to myself, before nodding. "All right, let's get this over with."

"About time." He nodded grimly. "Come, Matt, it's your turn."

I stepped up to the edge, feeling it as the colonel used his ability to link to me, and then out to those around us, hearing the grunt as he barely stayed upright. His right hand clamped over the dungeon conduit node that Kelly had grown especially for this, and the left set atop a focal orb, one that would hopefully retain his magic when he passed.

I pulled up the oath as they'd written it, holding it in my right hand. I read it aloud, pausing occasionally to look out across the gathered faces, making eye contact as I recited.

"I, Matt, Dungeon Lord of Newcastle, hereby solemnly swear on my honor and life to uphold the following oath to the brave soldiers of Otterburn Camp and

Newcastle, and the civilians who have agreed to integrate into my dungeon and serve as part of its defensive forces or regular citizenry, for a year and a day:

"I pledge to lead these people with integrity, fairness, and respect, always considering their well-being and valuing their lives as I would my own, and any of my citizens.

"I vow to make every honest effort to rescue and protect the royal family, understanding the importance of this mission to the soldiers and the kingdom they served.

"I promise to utilize these new citizens' skills and bravery wisely in defense of the dungeon and in our expeditions, never wasting their lives needlessly or recklessly.

"I will strive to provide for the citizens' needs to the best of my ability, ensuring they have adequate shelter, sustenance, and equipment to fulfill their duties and maintain their morale.

"As we venture to the south, I will always consider the search for the citizens' families, understanding the importance of reuniting them and providing safety for their loved ones.

"I will lead the expedition with courage, strategic thinking, and a commitment to minimizing casualties, considering peaceful resolutions when possible but standing ready to fight when necessary.

"I acknowledge that this oath is valid for a year and a day, during which time I will serve my new citizens to the best of my ability, and they will serve me in return.

"By my power and word, I hereby bind myself to this sacred oath, promising to lead and serve with honor, loyalty, and dedication. May our alliance be strong, our cause just, and our victory certain."

At the end of the speech, and with sweat rolling down my back and pouring into my butt crack, I stood straighter, staring out at the gathered people before me, as they began, slowly at first, in ones and twos, then in dozens, and finally hundreds, to reply.

"We, the surviving soldiers of Otterburn Camp and Newcastle, and the civilians who have agreed to integrate into the dungeon, hereby solemnly swear on our honor and lives to uphold the following oath to Matt, Dungeon Lord of Newcastle, who has sworn to lead us with integrity, to protect the royal family, and to prioritize our well-being, for a year and a day:

"We pledge our loyalty and service to the Dungeon Lord, integrating ourselves into the dungeon's defensive forces and obeying the commands given to us, as long as they align with the Dungeon Lord's oath to us.

"We will fight bravely and skillfully in defense of the dungeon and on our expeditions, or how so ever we can best serve, always striving to protect our comrades and fulfill our missions to the best of our ability.

"We will respect the hierarchy and structure of the dungeon's forces, working with our new allies to ensure the safety and success of our collective goals, and to protect our families.

"We will maintain our discipline, honor, and commitment to the values that define us as soldiers and citizens, even as we adapt to our new circumstances and roles within the dungeon.

"We will trust in the Dungeon Lord's leadership and strategic decisions, providing our input and expertise when appropriate but ultimately following the orders given to us, trusting in him, and those he places over us.

"We agree that this oath is valid for a year and a day, during which time we will serve the Dungeon Lord and those he places over us to the best of our ability, and they will serve us in return.

"We make this oath freely and willingly, understanding the gravity of our commitment and the importance of the tasks before us.

"By our words and deeds, we hereby bind ourselves to this sacred oath, promising to serve with courage, loyalty, and honor. May our alliance with the Dungeon Lord be strong, our cause just, and our victory certain."

By the time the last voices trailed off, the colonel was shaking, his right hand flat over the focal orb and node access. Light was building in him; his eyes, his mouth, ears…his skull seemed to blaze with it. With a final gasp, he collapsed, his body converted wholly into energy to fuel the ability, locking the spell into the new focal orb at the same time.

Silence fell. Then, as a group, we all gasped, the oath taking hold of us. To me, it felt like a web was laid over me, one made of steel strings. From each string, I sensed a single pulse of awareness, and it ran out from me to that individual, then back again, both sides aware of the touch of the other.

Then I hissed, as did all the others, as the string tightened, before vanishing.

Unlike the others, I had, thanks to those who had sworn through the dungeon as well, gained several thousand strings, all at once. I sagged to a knee, feeling like I'd been flensed from the inside out, before sucking in a deep breath and straightening, eyes widening.

All around me, I could feel them, and even as the sudden rawness of the sensation faded away, I cursed under my breath.

The colonel had been brave and honorable, but damn I wished I'd managed to talk him out of this. Having this ability, it was a link, one that formed to each and every person who had sworn it. Even from here, I could sense several in the crowd who were here only to line their own nest.

Their intentions were far from honorable, though they too now knew that thanks to the oath, but they had to act like they were for a year and a day.

It was almost a form of slavery, and I didn't like that. But for groups that I didn't entirely know nor trust? It was perfect.

"Up and at 'em, big man," Griffiths whispered, helping me to my feet.

I grunted, sensing the oath string that led to him, and the sheer determination that filled him.

He'd sworn, despite not needing to. As I looked around, I saw that everyone else up here had as well. So had the others; even Jimmy and Andre, the two men-mountains who now followed Rhodes around like lapdogs, had sworn.

I almost laughed as I felt their simple devotion. And then I sobered, recognizing for perhaps the first time just how deep the gratitude to me for taking them in was.

I'd come for them—yes, for others as well—but I'd put myself at risk to come for them, when for their entire lives, they'd had each other and the girls they loved, nobody beyond that, they could rely on.

Staring at them, I felt the realization that passed through them, that they were loyal to me, and from them, that they now knew I was loyal to them.

It…it made a difference in how I saw them, all of them. I stood straighter, realizing for the first time that I'd been in real danger of growing too hard in my heart, too untrusting.

Now, though…now I knew that we were back on an even keel. And damn it lifted a weight from my shoulders I'd not even recognized I was carrying.

"Thank you," I whispered, before clearing my throat and trying again, louder. "Thank you all!" I shouted. "I will do my best for you, each and every one. Now, a few last things, then you can all get back into the warmth! This is Captain Griffiths, now Commander Griffiths, Commander of the Guard!"

I felt the flash of the notification as it started and I smiled, moving on.

"He has agreed to take over the forces of the dungeon. Under him will be Captain Mike Jefferson, who will be taking over as leader of the special forces; Captain Rhodes, who will lead the training cadre; and Captain Sanderson, formerly warrant officer class one, who has agreed to lower themselves to a mere captain's rank to fit in with the new structure."

I said that last bit with a wry twist on my lips, as a load of grins and a few laughs greeted that.

"Next is Arend-Jan. He's going to be taking over the civilian side of the northern dungeon. Where Griffiths will be running the military and will be bouncing between both sites, Arend-Jan has spent most of his life here, farming the land, and will be responsible for its management." I paused, eyeing the grinning older man, as he raised one hand, nodding and waving.

"Apparently we all need to watch him as he's originally Dutch, and if there's any cheese left around, I've been warned he'll have it before you can blink."

He shrugged, clearly accepting that was a fair point, then grinned again.

I smiled.

The farmer had been brought to me earlier, along with a truly impressive list of requests. He'd found out about some of the abilities of the dungeon—it wasn't exactly a closely guarded secret, after all—and he came back with a plan to take the entire surrounding area under cultivation.

There were to be mana converters, rows of irrigation, redone soil, the hills to be raised and lowered… The list had gone on and on, but when I'd asked him what the hell he was doing, he'd said it simply.

"I'm a farmer, Lord Dungeon." He smiled faintly. "I've been a farmer all my life, and my family before me. Gods willing, my grandchildren will be farmers. All of this is a plan for the years to come—decades, centuries even. What will this bring, though? I can grow you anything, if you can do this."

"Anything?" My mind had leapt straight from wheat or whatever to potion ingredients.

"Anything." He'd nodded. "With time and love, the land will give us all that we need. Your ability? It makes things possible that a farmer could only dream of. Let me help you, and I'll turn these barren hills into a garden of life."

I'd thought about it, looking over his plans, and then I'd made the decision, for us all. With magic so easily accessible and prevalent, we hadn't really worried about growing crops, focusing on specialist variations of herbs and more.

If, though, this unassuming man—always smiling, weathered skin and worn, recovering from the infection of the coronaught as everyone else was—still had the energy to come up with all of this? There was no way I'd waste the opportunity.

"Then *you* do it," I'd said. "You'll have access to the dungeon and the land around here as it's claimed. Build this and run your farm. Coordinate with Griffiths for the military, and Aly and Kelly for the dungeon. But you're responsible for your own mana budget. You want to use the dungeon's stores to make things? To eat into the hills and create whatever? Fine. You do it, but you and your team make that mana back.

"Think of it as I'm investing in you. You need to bring the dungeon back two things: a much better crop, and a profit in terms of mana. Aly will be able to help you figure it out."

That'd get me a cold shoulder later on when Aly found out she'd been volun-told, but fuck it. If he could do this, grow mana-infused crops, magically boosting the yield or whatever, at the very least we'd be able to set up huge potion reserves.

At best? Snacks that healed you. A sandwich that could cure a stab wound. Cows that were raised on grass that was the healthiest it could be and infused with healing magic, enabling a steak to be truly life changing.

The risk was worth the reward, I'd judged, but I'd still be watching the dark-haired, smiling farmer in the short term.

The bugger was just too damn cheerful. Had to be crazy.

"We'll be providing more structure and clarity as things move forward, but for now, you know who leads each respective side of our forces, and who to go to, or avoid, if you have a problem."

I focused, concentrating and letting Aly know it was time. To the right of the impromptu stage, the air was suddenly lit by the shimmer of motes, even as the clothing that had been left behind by Colonel Ptolemy was absorbed into the dungeon.

The mixture of motes and the shimmering glare made it appear that they were joining together, and although it wasn't true, it looked the part.

As the seconds passed, the new memorial tower—a single five-meter-tall onyx pillar, four-sided, that had the names of those we knew we'd lost in this fight, and others, to date—appeared.

It shone in the dim light of the snowy morning, gleaming black, with each name picked out in red marble, to ensure that they'd live in remembrance forever.

As the pillar climbed higher and higher, the lower sections solidified, darkening and seeming to settle into the world. The lights of creation died away slowly. The tip grew smaller and smaller, until at last it was complete, and I stared at it with everyone else. Too many of the names on that pillar had been friends of mine, and too many more were on it, instead of standing with me now, because of my mistakes.

Kevin and his wife Alison were together in stone again, and Ramnik's name was by the side of her brother at last, though that had been heartbreaking to find out about.

She'd been found melded into one of the spawnskulls a few hours earlier, her face unable even in death to smooth away the look of horror, bound there eternally by the last days of her life.

I swallowed the lump in my throat and gave Sanderson the nod.

"Company!" he bellowed. "Atten-*shun!*"

Like they were a single entity, the military in the crowd saluted with a snap, each and every movement having been polished until it was nigh-on perfect.

The civilians, like me, seemed unsure what the correct response was. Did they salute, even though they didn't know how to do it properly and they had no right to that gesture, or did they stand and just watch? Neither seemed right to me, and I guessed to them, so I reacted on instinct, lifting my right fist, clenched tight, and pressed it to my chest, thinking of all those we'd lost.

The gesture slowly spread, as more and more repeated it, feeling strange, but at least they weren't being expected to pretend to be military if they weren't.

"Company, stand at ease!" the new captain bellowed, before looking at me. I nodded, and he went on. "Dis-*missed!*" he roared.

And just like that, the gathering was over, and the northern dungeon had been stabilized.

CHAPTER THIRTY-SIX

The first thing that we did, when we got back inside, was to take a few minutes to reach out to those we loved, to center ourselves, and to basically get our heads in the game, before our very own newly recruited EOD Technician Tinson reached out to the nukes, getting ready to earn his place in history.

As the first EOD tech to have ever—to my limited knowledge, at least—have taken apart an actual nuke, let alone a nuclear suitcase, and five of them at once, Tinson was both excited and terrified. As he'd joked before, normally, if he screwed up it was only he who would have a very bad day, after all.

He didn't usually have so much of a chance to share the love around.

I watched, keeping quiet and seriously reconsidering allowing him to do this by the second. If it was to be anyone who did this, it really should be me...

When they all vanished at once, breaking down into a light so bright, my first thought was that it had gone nuclear and we were all fucked...up until three seconds later, when I cracked my eyelids. We were all still there, and the mana counter for the dungeon was going *insane*.

The mana storage research was done almost before I could register it, as were the conduits up to advanced, then it...it blurred. Everything that had been set as a "better get this started" job fell away in a barrage of "complete" notifications, before the entire system was switched to feeding into the Glass core. The dungeon shivered.

I was halfway across the dungeon before I'd even consciously registered it, flashing through the air and down to the actual hidden core location here in the northern dungeon. Staring in horrified amazement, I found that the core was wrapped in blazing light.

The conduits that led out of the ceiling and down into the core were all glowing like the sun, casting crazy shadows as they flared and dimmed repeatedly.

The core was now the size of a bowling ball, and appeared to be molten gold. It spun and twisted, rolled and gleamed; waves of light flowed from one side to vanish around the other.

Layers started to lift from deeper inside, forming shapes that looked suspiciously like continents, before fractal patterns appeared and the lines resolved.

Dozens of sections lifted free, hovering above the core, before transitioning into new alignments and dropping back down.

More lifted in their place, twisting and linking together like some kind of Rubik's Cube on acid. As the seconds passed, I felt the difference before I saw it.

The core was cooling, *adjusting*.

It'd take time—I knew that instinctively, as the dungeon core started to shift into a new pattern—but what was happening here was the formation of a new core layer, one that was building up and out, before dropping into place.

The gold took on a hint of pearlescence; a tinge of green shivered across the molten layers, followed by reds and blues, before the yellow and gold came back.

I shifted again, this time flashing to the Newcastle dungeon's core, appearing before it in a heartbeat, then stared as its own imperfections were made painfully obvious.

Where I'd forced the core to grow in previous times, the layers were uneven. Yes, I'd tried to fix them, and I had managed it to a certain extent; the core surface itself was stable again, and there was a solid foundation for more advanced layers to build atop now. But as the core gleamed and shone, the interior becoming visible as upper layers grew translucent, the imperfections were revealed like never before. Entire sections that should have formed smooth supports to the next stage were instead misshapen.

I shook my head in frustration at seeing them laid bare so clearly.

Reaching out with a mental hand, I plunged down to the core. The large ball grew larger by the millisecond, until it hung before me like a world.

I hovered there above its surface, my hands smoothing the gleaming gold and glass as sections shifted and altered.

Here and there, I found patches, areas that were incomplete, and I worked frantically to bring them together, to heal the fault lines as they appeared.

Hours turned into days, though I had no concept of time, buried as I was into the business of fixing the core, of keeping ahead of the constant flow of need that the core had. I simply dealt with what was before me.

I knew, at an instinctive level, that there was only so much I could do with this alone. I also knew, that as much as I loved Kelly, and I trusted Aly, neither of them could help me with this.

Nor could Dante or any of the mages I had access to.

This was a magic problem, and more and more, I grew certain that we'd be stalling at the Glass level, if I couldn't address it. There were too many sections that I just didn't understand. Although I had some information left over from the dungeon fairy's soul, it was hints and vague notions, some of which I knew had to be either impossible or wrong, from the other things her soul had left me.

Hints like passing through the upper layers of the core when doing a core upgrade to perform preventative maintenance were clearly bullshit. I'd tried directly touching the core only the once, driven by the needs of that fucking soul, and I'd had my arm charred to the bone in reaction to the discharging power levels.

I knew not to touch the fucker, not physically, but there it was clear as day...the instinct to slip into the core *physically* and work on it from the other side as well.

Well, fuck *that*.

I was tempted to reach out to the other dungeon fairies, but honestly, I just didn't trust them enough yet. Their bonded dungeons were their priorities, and if they got too much information from me, I was betting that they'd just love to absorb my core and feed a fragment of it to their own charge.

Then, add in their companions? Nope. I'd liked them, and gotten on well with the few I'd spent any real time with, considering that Bryan had been ejected into the cold of space along with the other two monstrous fucks.

Either way, though, there was just too much going on right now for me to go running off and...

"*Matt!*"

It was Kelly, appearing next to me in the dungeon sense, and staring around in utter confusion. Then gasping as I pulled at her, dragging her down and to me.

She'd appeared there in the dungeon sense, which was a bit weird to explain even to myself. You had no body, and yet you did; there was no physical self, but you could touch and feel—to a limited degree; we weren't going to be getting down and dirty through this—but I could feel when she kissed my cheek, for example.

There was something that the others, Aly especially, had taken to referring to as "residual self-image," which was a fancy way of saying that you thought of yourself like "this," so that's what you created out of the data and magic you remade yourself as in here.

That was why she'd known I was here, and could feel me, and yet when she appeared, she was confused to buggery because she couldn't see me.

I'd shifted my reality to be hovering tiny over the core; with a thought, I dragged her into the same condition, holding her there with me until she adjusted.

"Matt..." Kelly breathed, staring up at the core, before reaching out a hand, only for me to yank her backward.

"Don't," I told her firmly. "I don't know what the effect would be."

"Okay, sorry," she whispered, still staring wide-eyed at the core. "This is what it's like for you?" she asked. "Seeing the core?"

"Yeah, pretty much." I nodded distractedly. "You okay? What's up?"

"I..." She blinked and shook herself, then deliberately turned her back on the core and looked at me. "You said earlier about the doctors at the old QE hospital...with everything that's been going on, I just didn't have the time to deal with them. Do you want to make any last-minute changes before I dispatch Ashley and a team there?"

"What's the plan?" I muttered, squinting at a recalcitrant section of the core that refused to smooth out, no matter what I did, wondering how far we'd gotten in the conversations. Then I remembered that yeah, I'd wanted to make some changes after all.

"You said to send Ashley to them once it'd started to get really cold. Things were just too busy before, and too manic. But now that they've settled, slightly, I was thinking we could send her up and start building some bridges?" she suggested. "It's looking like another storm front building."

"Yes, definitely," I agreed. "Look, I need to focus on this as much as possible, but if you could get—" I broke off, and focused on the outside world, summoning a chocolate bar onto a nearby table outside the core area, just to make sure everything was still working.

"What was that about?" Kelly asked me suspiciously, as Amy, who'd been sitting in our small private common room, picked the bar up and cheered, offering a random thanks to whoever had summoned it.

"With the first few upgrades, we lost access to a lot of the dungeon's abilities," I explained. "I was just making damn sure that hadn't happened, as it'd have been embarrassing to go to the hospital and offer aid, then not be able to deliver."

"Good point," she agreed. "It's all okay then? I mean, Matt, you've been in here for two days...you know that, right?"

"I don't know about everything. I know the main research systems are linked to the core and are locked out, for example, but if we can summon things, we can build. That's all we need," I answered, before blinking. "Wait, two *days*?"

"Since you last took a break, yeah." She rested a ghostly hand on my arm. "Matt, you need to rest," she pressed.

"I...no." I straightened mentally and shook my head. "My body is resting— that's as good as it gets right now. There's still issues with the core and during the upgrade process, I can fix things in ways I couldn't before. We need this. I'll rest soon."

Glancing at her and seeing the genuine concern on her face, I smiled as reassuringly as I could. "I will, I promise. Just give me a few more hours."

"So, the hospital?" she prompted after a few seconds of clearly wanting to force me to rest, and knowing it'd not work. "And if you aren't out of here in two hours, I'm sending Jo in to hook up an IV."

"I've been stopping for toilet breaks," I assured her, snorting. "But thanks, Mum, and yes, I'll remember my juice box as well."

"You better," she whispered, before prompting me again. "Anything you want to add?"

"Yeah, send Ashley up there, get her to offer some support—you know the stuff...food, somewhere solid to live. They don't have to come to us, though we'd like it if they did. Either build a much smaller apartment block there for the people, provided they're willing to help us, or at least make somewhere they can get in out of the cold. Ideally, they move to the dungeon or the park, and we turn the hospital into a small outpost, somewhere with a tower so we can see for miles. It's at the top of a hill, after all."

"What do we want in exchange?"

"Expertise," I said. "We're going to have access to the medical technology side of things soon, but we desperately need those doctors, nurses, and more. I don't know how the hell this didn't occur to me before now, but there must have been people giving birth the last few months, and that can't have been good without a midwife and a doctor. They agree to help us. They do the rounds and offer the non-magical side of medicine to our people. They help with all the things that we just can't do, like delivering a baby, because beyond healing the wounds, I don't think a healing spell is doing anything we want with that!"

"Gods, I'd not even considered that," Kelly whispered, horrified. "What if the magic considered a baby a parasite? I mean, it is, if you look at it in the right—or wrong—way."

"Exactly." I nodded. "So we send Ashley. She can charm them all, though honestly, even though she's got great tits, I think they're going to be more interested in the heat and food at this stage."

"Behave yourself…no looking at her tits," Kelly admonished me, and I snorted.

"You know I'm not really looking, but that's the point. Her usual tactics aren't going to be needed here, and she's going to need a whole different approach. Time for her to start planning for that."

"She'll manage it. As you say, though, this might be a training wheels exercise—it should be that easy. Damn, I really hope they're okay."

"Go check," I suggested, looking back to the core. "I can do this, and you can get that sorted out, and if—worst case, I know—but if they're all dead, then we don't send Ashley."

"Matt!" Kelly sighed. "Please don't say things like that. We really need them."

"You know I'm not serious," I countered. "They know where we are, and where Barry is. If things were that bad, they'd have sent someone to him."

"Well, it's still a crappy joke."

"It was being realistic, but yeah, fair enough." I nodded. "Okay, you happy to go check them and I'll get on with this?"

"What are you doing?" She glanced up at the core. "And don't just fob me off Matt, please."

"Advanced repairs." I shrugged, then smiled. "I got a flash of inspiration from the dungeon fairy's memories, something about doing repairs when the upgrade goes through. I know there's issues with it, but I also knew that I needed to check on the core, so fuck it. I'm not desperately needed in the dungeon at the minute. The skeletons are doing the majority of the absorbing and influence expansion work, so it's not like I'm needed there either. And as for the local management, it seemed like a good idea to leave them to sort themselves out, while being close enough if they needed me, I'm here."

"True. And the overall plan for the dungeon is going well. We've got the conduits going through the physical upgrade process now, and all the mana that comes in is being sucked into the core to power the upgrade. While we need to keep producing so that we've got food and power and so on, there seems to be a hard limit on the intake."

"There's a what?" I frowned.

"If we have more than a hundred thousand in the bank, the core drains the excess into the Glass upgrade, making it go faster," she explained. "Or at least that's what we think. It's one of the things I was going to ask you about, though clearly you didn't know about it either."

"Why?" I asked. "How come we didn't know about this before?"

"I think it's literally speeding up the upgrade. And as to why we didn't know…well, we never had the kind of levels of mana coming in that would effect it before," she admitted. "The higher we upgrade the core, the more we preserve functionality during the upgrade.

"When it first happened, you said the core was basically offline, that was it, because the entire core needed to be upgraded. Now, as we go higher and higher, it seems like the last level of the core is maintained. So even though we're in the middle of the upgrade, the lower levels of the core are still working fine. It's just the top layer, or at worst the next down as well, that's offline."

"So while we can't carry out full research, because that's a core function, anything like production and food and so on still works fine…nice." I nodded.

"That's a relief. I'd worried about us ending up drifting in space or something if we triggered the Neutronium core update and everything shut down."

"Space?" Kelly asked, eyeing me. "Why…you know what, I don't think I want to know. Do I need to know?"

"No." I smiled. "Just thinking aloud, that's all."

"Fine. You get back to work, and I'll go check on the hospital staff." She sighed, before smiling and kissing my cheek. "I miss you."

"I miss you too," I said softly, kissing her back. Then I took a deep breath and got back to work as she vanished. "Right then, you fucker…" I muttered to myself. "Where was I?"

The next hour was a busy one, but by the end of it, I had a solid feeling for what I was doing with the core, and the melding repairs I was accomplishing.

It wasn't much, but essentially where I'd sealed the top layer of the core before, and then I'd had to smooth it all out and fix it, I'd accidentally left sections where the lower levels of those "smoothed-out zones" were. As new sections lifted free, they tended to drag a few fragmentary sections with them; a little focus, some smoothing, and voilà. It was repaired.

After an hour more of it, though, and without anywhere near the levels of difficulty nor effort required as before, I was growing progressively more and more brain-dead, and definitely needed a break.

The core was stable, and although I knew it wasn't fixed, there were a lot less issues springing up as I worked. My Lightning affinity seemed to blend well with the core as I worked to smooth sections and repair them.

I'd been desperately pushing, because somewhere, at the back of my mind, I knew that this time, the heartbeat between the cores settling and solidifying, granted me a chance to repair things that I couldn't do at any other time.

Now at least, if the core solidified in ten seconds' time and I lost the chance to do more, I knew I'd done all I could be expected to have done.

"Right, let's deal with you buggers as well," I muttered to myself, pulling up the notifications I'd been ignoring since the fight. Maybe I'd wake myself up and get rid of the fuzziness I was feeling, then do one more hour on the core, before bed.

I knew there weren't likely to be any level-ups, though…

You have completed a Quest!

Otterburn Camp (2):

You have succeeded in your assault on the base, though the losses incurred were higher than you expected. The Queen has drawn a line in the sand, this far and no further, she proclaims. Will you accept that, in the interest of preserving life, or will you decide to eradicate her presence, root and branch?

- **Inhabitants rescued: 1297/1843**

-FAILED-

Due to the losses incurred, this quest reward earned has been downgraded.

For completing this part of the quest, you receive the following bonuses:

- **Additional Forces/Inhabitants**
  - **2̶ - 1 Skill Point**
  - **5̶0̶ - 30,000 XP**

Optional Additional Quest Completed:

Otterburn Camp (3):

You removed the threat that the coronaught queen posed to you, your forces, and your species. As many have before you, you chose the safer option, resolving to never know the advantages of using hive-enforced obedience.
This comes with a significant advantage, however: You remain both alive, *and* in command of your own mind. Those who have encountered a coronaught queen and have remained in this condition are far rarer than many would like to believe.

Note: You have gained a Bonus Title: Hive Harvester
For killing your second coronaught queen, and gaining through the destruction of her hive, you have gained the title: Hive Harvester. You gain 10% bonus to any resources gathered inside the former queen's claimed territory.

By eliminating the coronaught queen, you have completed this final part of the quest, and receive the following bonuses:

- **+1 Class Skill Point**
- **+1 Tech Upgrade (Random)**
- **25,000 XP**

I couldn't help but be seriously pissed at the recognition of how many possible lives I could have saved, though, in reality, I had no clue how I was supposed to have done it.

As soon as the queen had died, so too had all her vurms. That was a bonus in two ways. First of all, apparently the psychic shock of the death of their queen explained why she was so desperate to get her daughter out of there. In killing her, we'd wiped out the local hive entirely, and we now knew that a surgical strike option would be best in the future.

All those who had been under her control had basically keeled over, flat out unconscious. Although the next day had been a nightmare of building healing towers and dragging people into shelters, the majority of that had been done by the undead, and at least we'd not had to fight people again and again.

The second bonus was that after the first queen we'd killed, Rhodes had warned us that the vurms would try to hide and infect people. We'd sealed off the sections of the dungeon that led into those areas that we'd believed were contaminated, and we'd sealed them away. But that we'd never seen anything had always rankled a bit with me.

I'd been worried that at any time we might have to face a burgeoning threat inside the dungeon, but I'd never been able to stop long enough to come up with a plan, beyond keeping our eyes open.

Now I knew that it wasn't a threat and we could move on with things.

The next notification was a painful one.

Congratulations!

You have killed the following:

- **11x Coronaught Warrior drones, Levels 2-11, 4,030 XP**

Total XP earned: 4,030 XP

—Due to the nature of this quest and the threat to your dungeon, you as Dungeon Lord receive full XP from all enemies killed—

You have led your forces to eliminate the following:

- **92x Coronaught Warrior drones, Levels 2-11, 22,646 XP**
- **27x Coronaught Spawnskull Sentinels, Levels 2-5, 10,040 XP**
- **3x Coronaught Flesh Titans, Level 1, 1,530 XP**
- **1x Coronaught Princess, Level 1, 240 XP**
- **1x Coronaught Queen Level 27, 1,430 XP**

Total XP earned: 35,050 XP
Total XP awarded: 39,080 XP

Current XP to next level stands at 104,463/55,000

Congratulations!

You have reached Level 28.

Current XP to next level stands at 49,463/60,000

You have 9 unspent Stat Points and 1 unspent Skill Point.

You have gained additional Stat Points in the following areas through constant effort.

- **+1 Constitution**
- **+1 Endurance**
- **+1 Strength**
- **+1 Wisdom**

Continue to work hard to increase these or other stats...

That...well, that was a nice one. I'd gained a level after all. I'd not expected to gain full XP for the kills. I had no clue why I had, but I'd damn well take it.

That, combined with the XP I'd gotten for completing the quest, despite the losses we'd suffered in those we'd been trying to save, meant I'd almost gained two levels. As I looked my stats over, there was no difficulty in deciding where to spend the nine points I'd gotten.

Charisma had been a bust. I'd had a chance to talk the queen into serving me, apparently, but I had no clue how I'd have managed that. Especially considering she literally wouldn't even speak to me until the very end there, and then was just intent on melting my brain.

So, reading over the details, I slid all nine points, nice and straight forward, into Wisdom, before finally, *finally* getting the prompt I'd been hoping for, for so long.

Congratulations!

Between your Arcane Dungeon Lord class, your earned statistics, and your natural affinities, you have reached the second level of Arcanist through natural advancement!

Arcanist (2):

Arcanists are the wielders of Mana and knowledge in the Multiverse, searching out power wherever it can be found and seeking to grow their knowledge above all else.

Arcanists gain the following one-off bonuses at the second rank of their specialization:

- **+ 2 to Intelligence**
- **+ 2 to Wisdom**
- **+ 1 Spell**
- **+ 1 Class Skill Point**
- **x2 Mana Regeneration**

As a Second-level Arcanist, your mana regeneration has been doubled. Beware, Arcanist...should your hunger for power and knowledge grow too great, always remember that the universe is a place of checks and balances...

"Fuck yes!" I roared, then looked around guiltily, remembering that Amy was in the common area at the end of the corridor, and then grinning when I remembered that it was fine because I was in the dungeon sense and she wasn't, so fuck it.

Reading and rereading it, I bit my lip as I figured my way through the meaning as well as the words. I'd gained access to the class upgrade, not through the normal means—I was due a new class advancement when I hit level thirty, after all—but because I'd earned the class through point advancement alone.

That meant that others were possible to unlock.

That concept just blew my mind. Earning a fighter class, for example, could unlock abilities that were seriously useful—though not highly useful enough that I was willing to forgo a class advancement in other ways.

Learn enough healing magic and in theory, I'd gain a healing class, even if I only invested in other things at my class choices.

That was incredible.

I pulled up my stat sheet and couldn't help but smile. I finally had a realistic way of regenerating my goddamn mana.

It'd take just under four hours, admittedly, but some of my spells only cost me a hundred points and were lethal. This could be a game changer.

Name: Matt, First Lord of the Storm				
Host Powers: 1 (Enhanced Regeneration)				
Species: Thunderstorm			Bonus: None	
Level: 28			Progress to next level: 49,463/60,000	
Stat	Current Points	Description	Effect	Progress to Next Level
Agility	42	Governs dodge and movement	Heightened chance to dodge attacks 84%+20%= 104%	88/100
Charisma	41	Governs likely success to charm, seduce, or threaten	68% more likely to succeed in events that require seduction, persuasion, or threats (10%+ (31x2) = 68)	89/100

Constitution	53	Governs Health and Health Regeneration	HP: 53x60 = 3,180	11/100
Dexterity	45	Governs ability with weapons and crafting	+45% Increased chance of improved result +17 to melee damage	30/100
Endurance	47	Governs Stamina and Stamina Regeneration	Stamina: 47x50 = 2,350	4/100
Intelligence	64	Governs base manapool, standard intellectual capacity	Mana: 64x70=4,480	19/100
Luck	45	Governs overall chance of bonuses and critical hits	+70% increased chance of positive outcome	66/100
Perception	44	Governs ranged damage and chance to spot hidden items/traps	+34 to all ranged attacks	9/100
Strength	41	Governs damage with melee weapons and carrying capacity	+62 to all damage with Melee weapons	2/100
Wisdom	59	Governs mana regeneration	1180 mana regenerated per hour (*Arcanist class 2 boost*)	1/100

After that, there weren't many more notifications to read: a redundant repeat of finding a member of my dungeon team, in Griffiths as captain of the guard, and a few skill upgrades—though, as usual, if it wasn't one that earned me a real bonus, I simply checked it and slid it away, uninterested.

Then finally, with the core revolving before me, golden light filling the room as I returned to normal size, Kelly reappeared. The smile on her face was a rictus, as she clearly tried to decide which news to share first.

"So…" she said uncertainly. "I've got good news, and bad…"

CHAPTER THIRTY-SEVEN

"**B**ad," I said instantly. A migraine spiked as I fought down panic. "Always give me the bad first."

"There's a group a few miles from the hospital. They're armed, and they're hunting people who are desperate for help and some safety."

"Of course there are!" I muttered, rubbing at my face in tired frustration. "Well, I'm a bit too far outta town right now, sorry."

"You are," she agreed. "But that's where the good news comes in."

"How can 'I'm too far away to help' ever be considered good news?" I cocked my head to one side.

"It can be, because it looks like the survivors got away clean in the snow, and the group hunting them are heading home."

"Right, so what's the problem?"

"The survivors," she said. "We need to help them, and we need to hunt those who were hunting them. But at least you've got time to get here and help with it."

"Go on."

"Okay, let's roll this back a bit." Kelly took a deep breath, and shifted us to the command room, standing near the table, and activated it to show the entire area. "God, I love that ability," she murmured, smiling.

"Well, I fucking don't," Aly snapped, and the pair of us spun around. "I practically shit myself when you both appeared."

"Sorry, Aly." Kelly chuckled, barely able to keep it from becoming a full-on laugh before she turned back to me. "Okay, so here we are..."

The map that covered the entire table drew back. The local area of Newcastle was drawn in light on the table, as the POV of the map drew smoothly up to show more and more of the region.

Where it'd started, it showed simply the dungeon as it was: the buildings, the pool, and then surrounding it all, the wall.

The dungeon's influence was shown as an area of color that surrounded the dungeon, while that which wasn't under our control was shown in gray.

As the point of view slid smoothly upward, it showed more and more of the surrounding area—the dilapidated remaining buildings, burned-out parking lots, collapsed apartment blocks, and more—before it finally reached the River Tyne, and the three bridges that crossed it that were in locations that we controlled, more or less.

As we'd claimed territory, we'd installed influence generators, and they steadily pushed outward. The first bridge crossing had been done manually, pushing the influence across it meter by painful meter; once that was done, someone had created secondary spokes out from that point.

Then, every so far along the route, they'd added an influence generator, and boom. They moved on, and the influence slowly spread outward hour by hour, day by day.

The lower swing bridge—barely above the water and formerly capable of being literally swung to the sides, the central point staying fixed with the arms pivoting from (more or less) north–south to east–west to allow for river traffic—had since collapsed.

The upper two bridges, which included the closest to us—the "high-level bridge" and the Tyne bridge—were still there, though the Tyne was getting close to needing repairs to keep it up.

The cars that had been crossing the bridge when the power went out had generally simply drifted to a halt, staying where they'd stopped and cluttering up the place.

Since then, though, lightning strikes, mischievous shitebags, and who knew what had resulted in most of those cars being set alight, and the damage was clear.

As Kelly slid the point of view along the road toward the hospital, she continued to lift it upward. The civic center that we'd taken over a few weeks back now towered over the few remaining buildings that had once surrounded it.

I noted a small team gathered outside, getting ready to start the trek home, having clearly recently finished a dungeon run. Beyond them, under the watchful eye of a party of kobold warriors, a handful of dogs were being trained.

I frowned, wondering what was going on.

Kelly, seeing where my attention was focused, gave me a rundown. "You remember the dogs?"

"Beta's mount? The mutant ones?" I asked, and she nodded.

"Yeah, well, they're still insanely big, and the traps that you set up started drawing more and more in. As she couldn't help with your trip to the camp, she and a bunch of others are working on training the dogs, so that they'll have cavalry options when the time comes."

"Is it going well?" I asked. "How are the kobolds doing with the snow? And have the lures turned up anything?"

"They're okay. We limit them to no more than half an hour in the cold. And once the dogs are ready, that'll be more than enough to do a constant patrol. Aly set up a few maintained stop-off points—heat and water, that kind of thing—and they're back to running full patrols.

"The lures are sort of working. They're drawing in dozens of smaller creatures a day, most of which we'd never seen before. But the occasional larger one that's drawn in as well then eats them and tears the lure apart, before moving on. I think we need a rethink on that side. That's not what I need you for, though."

"Go on." I sighed.

"You remember the conversations we had about the prison?" She glanced at me as she scrolled the viewpoint along and up the long bank leading to the hospital.

"Yeah, that there's one on the other side of Washington, the next town along, and we'd need to deal with it when the time comes." I nodded. "It was some of them who took over the hospital, wasn't it?"

"We think so, an outlier group that tried to set themselves up." She nodded. "Okay, so we kept talking about needing to do something about them, but we've been so busy it's just not been realistic to consider it."

"And we still are," I pointed out grimly.

"We are," she agreed. "But that's the point. Because we've just been handed an opportunity to take the prison out and gain a serious amount of new citizens and territory, for minimal output."

"I don't like the sound of this," I grumbled.

"There's nothing new or unusual about that." She smiled. "Seriously, though, Matt, I think we've got a real opportunity here to make a difference, and it's without that great a risk or cost. If we can make this work, we have a chance to pacify the entire area.

"Once that's done, we can finally start to really work to bring things into line. The people we'd gain would jump our population up to around ten to twelve thousand, and that's a small *town*."

"Is that important?" I frowned. "The number, I mean?"

"No, or at least I don't think so." She shook her head and brought the viewpoint to a halt above the hospital. "My point was more that once we reach that, we've literally got a town of our own. That's thousands of people available to help us—skilled workers, fighters, planners, cooks, artisans, artists, and craftsmen.

"There's going to be thousands of people who can help, with everything."

"Thousands of new people to teach to play nice, and that they have to work and contribute," I complained.

"Hundreds of innocent kids," she added, trying a new tack. "Kids who are going to starve, and many already are."

"I hate kids."

"Says the man who came out of hiding to rescue Amy and then assaulted a park to free her mother," Aly added in. "You can't fool us, Matt."

"I never said I liked them though," I countered. "It was just the right thing to do, that's all."

"And this is too." Kelly swung the viewpoint around until I finally saw what had gotten her attention.

It was a sign, one that had been summoned by us, I instinctively knew, and a small area that had already been set up, no doubt by Aly or Kelly, as a heated and secure zone.

People were crammed into it, and more were being wheeled in by the second. The hospital gurneys squeaked along corridors by the remaining orderlies as doctors and nurses tried to keep the last of their patients alive.

"I thought they lost all their patients?" I frowned. "I thought the gangs had killed them when they took over?"

"They killed most of them," she said. "The last few were kept around to keep the medical staff in line, sort of a 'you do as you're told or we kill them' situation."

"And the rest?"

"Hidden, I'm guessing." She sighed. "We didn't even know they were there or we'd have long since done more to help them. As it is, we've made this a small protected zone, set up the communication board, and a healing tower is being built in the corner."

I glanced over and nodded to myself, seeing it. "So, what's the story?"

"Well, when I came looking to see what condition the hospital was in, I created the board where one of them could see, and a pen to write on it. Inside of a few minutes, they'd gotten a few of their people here to write on it, and this small security force to watch things."

"You think they're more bandits?" I squinted at the woman who sat with a short length of pipe across her knees and a mismatch of homemade armor covering her.

"No," Kelly said. "They're survivors of the bandits, and they're why we know as much as we do."

"Which is?"

"This is Robin, and she's the leader—reluctantly, I think—of a small group of fighters and refugees who escaped from Washington. They set off to try to make their way to Newcastle, found the hospital, and hid there from the weather. The medical teams shared a little food with them, and apparently told them about us.

"The plan, from what I can gather, reading the details they're writing on the board anyway, is to make a deal with us, one where we provide them arms and training, and they go back and wipe out the prison."

"That…sounds a little more doable," I agreed thoughtfully. "That's where they came from then?"

"No, they came from Sunderland, which is now a ruin, to Washington, and it's there that the prisoners have taken over."

"The town?" I asked.

"More or less." She nodded. "From what I can get, they run the town as their personal fiefdom, and they drove these out. There's only so much I can get from the board, but they're begging for backup, weapons, armor, healing and magic—whatever we can get, essentially. The group just want safety, somewhere to live, and in exchange are willing to agree to pretty much anything. But Robin and a few others? They want revenge. They're telling us that the ex-prisoners are a fractious bunch, so it might be possible to take them out before they get any more organized and expansive."

"The taking in of them—I'm assuming the hospital isn't looking to join us?" I changed what I was going to say and looked at her.

"I think they will," she corrected. "This Robin and her people will have made them aware that with us, they have a much better chance than independence, I think. And then, setting all of this up?"

She gestured to the area, then sighed. "I'm going to have to expand this out, aren't I?" she muttered, seeing the way people were cramming into the corners.

"Yeah," I agreed. "Start it now, making it a little bigger so they see you can, then stop. Send Ashley and an escort. Let her do a hearts-and-minds mission, then get back to me…let me know what's going on, and what they can offer, and want."

"The hospital or the refugees?" she asked, and I sighed.

"Both." I knew what was coming. "We can't come back to the dungeon until we're declared clean, I know, but if I took Jo and a team to the hospital, then as soon as the Glass upgrade is done, we can set up a medical suite there. They can examine us and make sure we're clean. Then that should be good, right?"

"It's probably the best we can hope for," Kelly agreed. "Matt?"

"Yeah?"

"I know this is crap," she admitted. "All of it, asking you not to come home yet…but you know why I'm doing it, right?"

"Because if I come home and I'm carrying something, it could spread everywhere." I shrugged. "We could be handing control of the dungeon to a creature that would use it to take over the world, and even if I'm not infected—which I don't think I am—we can't be sure about the others."

"Exactly," she whispered. "I still feel shitty, though, in saying no to you."

"To me coming home?" I asked, and she frowned and nodded. "Well, that's okay…you can just say yes a lot when I get back." I winked at her, and she snorted and shook her head.

"Like I ever say no, even when you want to…" She commented, before Aly cleared her throat pointedly. Kelly colored, breaking off what she was going to say, and gestured at the sign, as the woman we guessed was the lead doctor started to erase the words. "Looks like she's got something to say."

It proved to be a list, one that was mainly food, but also had a lot of medical terms on it. Three were underlined, and "Please help, URGENT" was written on the board.

"Do we even have those?" I asked. "Or access to them?"

"I don't think so," Kelly replied, reading it over. "That one is a diabetes medicine, I think…that's insulin…the others are—I think—broad spectrum antibiotics."

"Why do they want them?" I asked, confused. "I mean, I get the need for people with those conditions, but can't we just heal them?"

"I think so?" she muttered. "I mean, Jo's going to be the best to ask, she's our resident healer, but it might be that their genes and genetic coding means that they can't be healed? Honestly, I don't know."

"A life node would go a long way to helping these people as well," I thought aloud, only to have Aly step in and shake her head.

"Honestly, I don't think that's a good idea," she said. "If we give them everything they need and want, why would they then join us?"

"Well…" I bit my lip then nodded. "Yeah, good point. Send Ashley as we agreed, let her check things out and get the full story. Then, if they're willing to join us, we can look at either maintaining an outpost here, but moving them into the dungeon or not. But as much as I want to, you're right. We're not responsible for everyone. And if we just support them all the way, but they refuse to help us and contribute even now, there's no way they'll do it once they've gotten everything handed over."

"It's a shitty situation," Kelly agreed, straightening. "But if they're not going to help us at all, they can't expect us to help them. I'll get Ashley moving, along with a team. Matt, what are you going to do?"

"I'll get things in motion here." I knew what she was getting at. "Then I'll put together a team, and we'll get ready. Then, if you need us, we can set off at a moment's notice. Remember the distance, though. It's at least a full day's travel from here, and that's without the weather. If the snow gets bad…" I left it unsaid, and she nodded.

"The team we found that had been chasing them…shit, I don't even know if that's what's going on," she admitted, reaching up and trying to tug her hair into a neat ponytail by habit, before realizing that she was in the dungeon sense and her body was, well, imaginary.

"I went up high, and I saw them slogging back through the snow." She went on. "This Robin was writing that there was a group chasing them, so when I told them that the group looked to have lost them and given up, the relief was clear."

"How did you tell them that?" I asked, curious.

"The second board."

I looked over, seeing the other board and that it was blank.

"How…?" I started to ask, only for Aly to shush me, pointing as Kelly got to work.

The board was magnetic, I guessed, as some of those simple letters that my friends with kids used to cover their refrigerators started to appear one by one.

Sending someone to talk.

That was the message that was painstakingly assembled, and I nodded, admiring the ingenuity.

"We tried writing the message out first, then absorbing it into the dungeon and reproducing it, but honestly, it was a pain in the ass," Kelly admitted once she was done. "It also means that anyone who looks can see the messages. There's nothing that needs to be hidden, but there eventually will be, and leaving copies of every message we send in the system is just annoying."

"So you couldn't just summon paper and pens, have them write it out, then absorb it into the system and recreate here?" I asked.

"We could." She nodded. "But then we end up with a thousand letters absorbed, and all the system sees them as is paper. It can't tell the difference between them or a normal trash letter that's been absorbed into the dungeon, so trying to find the right damn one was a pain in the ass. This way we can see what we need to, and once they join us, or don't, we can make a decision about allowing them access to the dungeon sense."

"Good plan." I stretched. "Okay, you deal with this, I guess, get Ashley and her team moving, and I'll make some plans here."

"Matt?" Aly asked; I looked over and nodded for her to go on. "Maybe bring some of our people back with you?" she suggested. "Then we can run them through the medical facility as soon as it's ready?"

"That's what I'm thinking," I assured her, grinning. "And yes, Mike will be one of them."

"Thank you," she whispered, clearly relieved.

With that, I slid out of the dungeon sense, opening my eyes and taking a deep breath, before getting up and going looking for Mike and the others.

Not that I couldn't have dragged them into the dungeon sense easily enough. With the changes to our bodies, we didn't need as much sleep or rest. But after spending two days exercising mental muscles, if I didn't do something now, I'd be flat out soon enough.

The body still needed exercise, though, and regularly, and I needed to stretch my legs.

It didn't take long to find Mike, nor Rhodes, who was sitting with him, arguing over the plan for the next stage.

"But we need it!" he said to her. "We've got access to a shitload of soldiers here, people who are already trained, experienced and skilled. As much as it's shitty to say it, they've been honed to a point by the coronaughts. The weak were killed off and used as raw materials or they died. We're left with the Steel core, and…"

"And they'll die if you push them hard," Rhodes growled. "We need them to heal, to get over this, and to come to terms with what's happened. *Then* we can do this, not before."

"They're already going to need to retrain…" Mike wheedled, pointing to a sketch he'd been working on, only to have Rhodes crumple it up and glare at him.

"No, Mike," she said firmly. "We agreed—the troops are mine. You get to command them, but I get to train them, to look after them. You're an officer now, and you'll damn well treat them as resources…you have to. But to me, they're my boys and girls, and if you try to break them, I'll stop you."

"Fuck's sake." He groaned, covering his eyes with his hands and rubbing at them. "Rhodes, you know I'm not like that!"

"This plan will break at least a third of those we've got left. You'll lose them to burnout, and we all know what that looks like for a soldier, especially one who's lost their family and so many of their friends. No, Mike, and that's final. If I have to take this to Griffiths, I will."

"Just—" he started.

"No!" she snapped. "When they've recovered? Yes, fuck yes. We push them and we do it harder and further than they've ever been pushed. We make them into squads and we level them, and do it hard. For now, though, no, not until they've all healed and had some downtime."

With that, she stood, nodded in greeting to me, and walked off, her back ramrod straight. Had she been a cat, her tail would have bristled and swished.

"What the fuck did you just do?" I asked Mike, sliding into the recently vacated seat in the small base cafeteria.

"I was suggesting a change to the training regimen," he said, before rubbing tiredly at his face. "It's all right, man. She's right."

"Oh?" I asked. "Why'd you push her then?"

"Because I want her thinking about it," he admitted, then shot me a sneaky grin. "As it is, I knew she'd not go for the all-in plan, but now she'll be a lot easier to work with when I suggest my real plan in a day or two."

"Because she'll feel she's already worked you down to this level?" I asked, and he nodded. "You know she's a career NCO, though…you're not going to pull one over on her."

"So am I, mate. Believe me, she knows the game, and she'll be looking to play it and get me slotted into place with her as well. It's all part of us settling into the new structure."

"Okay…" I shrugged, just accepting that he knew what he was doing, and I didn't need the grief. "Well, I trust you fuckers. What's the plan, highlights only?" I asked.

"We give them a day to rest and recover, then we start them on jobs, easy ones at first, then exercise—start them training and making sure they're too busy to think, and to mope around. Then we get them split up and integrated as best as we can, create some mixed sections and squads. Get them used to working with the kobolds and the cats, then we start pushing them against each other, squad by squad."

"Like you were before?" I asked. "Damn, I feel like we just did that."

"We did." He nodded. "We just more than doubled our forces, though, so we need to get them on the same page. We reform the existing companies under the new structure and maybe add a few more to the roster. Just scale it up, you know?"

"Sure." I sighed. "So, you've got this in hand?"

"Yeah, why?" Suspicion suddenly clouded his eyes. "Oh, fuck's sake, Matt, now what?"

"Well, don't blame me." I snorted. "It's your damn wife and sister's fault."

"Fuck me, now I'm even more concerned." He groaned, lowering his head to the table and banging his forehead off it gently. "I'm not ready for this."

"How'd you like to go home?"

He stopped, raising his head enough to glare at me. "That's not funny." He growled. "You know we can't, and neither can anyone else. I'm not letting you put Aly and Amy at risk."

"Fuck Kelly, though, eh?" I joked, and he snorted.

"Kell's a big girl. She'll break you if you think otherwise and she can look after herself, so don't try that shit. What's going on?"

"There's a mystery group at the hospital. Looks like refugees, and…" I explained, covering the basics and the reasons it could be good—or bad—and what we needed to do.

"A small strike force then." He grunted. "Strong enough to do damage, and to eliminate the criminals if that's what's going on, but not large enough to leave the base undefended."

"I was thinking two hundred—" I started, and he shook his head.

"First off, for you to get two hundred of these ready for a full day's march, in the depths of winter, you'll need at least three days. They need to rest and recover. Hell, Matt, I feel like shit. All I want to do is sleep and eat, and I was only held for a few days. For most of these? Months!"

"I know. I was thinking—"

"You were thinking we take the teams that we sent up here already, the best we had, and now all we have who are combat-capable?"

"Well…"

"They're needed here," he refused flatly. "Griffiths will tell you the same. An army of toddlers could overrun us right now. Their bodies are healed, but their minds and hearts are broken, as well as them being drained to the absolute limit by not being fed and being puppeted till they dropped."

"We could—" I tried.

"We could lose them all, and not just to someone else marching in and killing them. We could lose them to suicide and worse. No, Matt—a small team, a surgical one? Yeah, a strike force we could do. A big one? No chance. Hell, add in that if we take a load of our people back, and basically straight past the dungeon, as that's the route we'd need to take, and then not let them check on their families? How many do you think would slip away first chance they get?"

"Okay." I settled back and summoned a burger and fries, then an energy drink. "So, what could we take? Realistically?"

"Ten to twenty, at best," he said. "Maybe, and I mean maybe, thirty, but I'd really recommend we don't."

"What if we take Scepiniir?" I suggested.

"What, them and the humans or just Scepiniir?"

"Both."

"As many as you can summon, I'd guess." He shrugged. "But why are you asking that?"

"I wanted to make sure there wasn't an angle I was missing," I admitted. "If we take a force of just Scepiniir, anyone we rescue is going to freak out. But we've got the weapons here, and they won't have the same issues as the kobolds do with the cold."

"What about the huts?" he asked, stealing a fry and getting a glare.

"We build them when we get back, see how many survive," I tried, before shaking my head. "That sounded better in my head, though we've got the ones we built for the last lot still."

"I hope it did." He shook his head in disbelief. "You're getting *cold*, Matt."

"Just realistic." I took a drink and glanced around. A handful of people moved around the canteen, but for the number of people on the base, that wasn't much. "Where is everyone?"

"I think most are in their rooms."

"Recovering?" I guessed, and he nodded.

"Honestly, Matt, you don't know how fucking hard that was," he said after a few seconds of silence. "Think of the worst hangover you've ever had, then add in a hospitalization, where your muscles are atrophying, and a flu or covid hit as well. We've been essentially puppeted around by the queen, a creature that doesn't understand human limits, the food we need, or the breaks. Every muscle hurts, still, because the way they made us walk—just as an example—isn't the way a natural human moves.

"Then add in things like if you had blisters, you were just kept walking on them. Broken limbs? Keep going. Nail in your foot? You've got it. Almost everyone had, at the very least, serious infections. Then add in the long-term physical damage from walking with say, a stone in your boot for three months straight.

"People are getting things cut out of them and then are being laid to recover, a process that's maddeningly slow because the body doesn't have any reserves to pull on. Seriously, Matt, I don't know how we survived as long as we did. We should be dead. That's the real reason the queen was rebuilding us into those monsters. She used those who were failing, falling apart, and saved the rest of us for regular soldiers until she had enough of the others made. Another few weeks? We'd all have ended up like poor Ramnik."

"Were you aware?" I asked him when he fell silent. "Of things going on, I mean?"

"No, not really," he whispered, then sniffed and sat upright, clearing his throat and forcing a smile. "It was more like a dream, you know? Bits you remember, but most of the time it was just…wrong, and you couldn't figure out why."

"I'm sorry, mate," I said softly. "I shouldn't have gone in the dungeon."

"Maybe, maybe not." He shrugged. "You went in for the right reasons, and I did what I did for the right reasons. I feel shitty enough about it without second-guessing myself, so let's just move on, eh?"

"Okay, so…this expedition?" I prompted. "I don't know if we're going to be needed, but if we are, as shitty as it sounds, I think it needs to be mainly humans. If the people arc used to being fucked over around the clock, and we march in with non-humans, they're just going to freak out. It'll be a step too far."

"So we take a small team of non-humans, the Scepiniir and Kilo, maybe some undead, the wraiths?" he suggested.

I shook my head. "Fuck the wraiths," I said. "You weren't in that last fight, and you didn't see how fast they turned on us."

"I heard." He nodded. "Chris talked about it."

"Well, it was touch and go." I set my burger down, half eaten, feeling sick as I spoke. "Right at the very end, when I couldn't figure out how the hell I was going to get the ASMs to trigger, I got 'creative.'" I lifted my hands and said the last word with my fingers making air quotes.

"I heard," he repeated. "Single-use hammers, eh?"

"That got out?" I grinned. "Yeah, some of the missiles were unstable; some were still locked to the arming settings. I guessed that was down to the lack of maintenance that others had worked, so I made the corpse lords hammer the missiles together. After I'd sealed the walls, door, and around my vehicle."

"And then you basically turned the inside into a hellhole and roasted her with fuel, explosives, and missiles." He nodded, then looked pensive.

"What?" I asked him.

"You know the vehicles?"

"Yeah?"

"They're military ones."

"Yeah, it was the camo patterns." I nodded. "That gave it away."

"Yeah, well, they're also set up to run without electricity." He smiled. "A lot of them, anyway. You know, in case of EMPs or whatever. They'd need some work, though, as the shielded parts that were needed are still fucked."

"You tried that before, didn't you?" I asked him. "I mean, on your way home from down south?"

"I did." He nodded. "But I'm not a mechanic, and with all the broken-down vehicles that covered the roads, there wasn't much point in a car. That's why I made do with a bike."

"And?" I asked.

"And I don't understand why the electricity stopped." He shrugged. "But a basic internal combustion engine should still work fine, as long as we can ignite it. Fuel still burns, after all."

"How the hell would we do that?" I asked, and he shrugged.

"No clue," he admitted. "As I say, I'm not a mechanic—get one of those mad bastards to come up with a solution. The roads up this way were pretty clear, after all. Sure, in the city and past it would be a nightmare, but get something that can go off-road, and we can absorb and clone it, right?" he suggested.

"And then we can clear the streets nearby." I nodded. "The dungeon can absorb the cars that are in the way, and we can have corpse lords pushing the fuckers to areas we can reach to strip them and absorb them into the dungeon. Dammit, why the hell didn't I think of this?"

"I could say it's because you're an idiot who thought a clip and a magazine were the same thing, but I like you, so I won't." Mike grinned. "But only because I like you."

"Yeah, thanks." I gave him the finger. "So, what kind of vehicle?"

"No clue, but I think it's time we got looking." He pushed his chair back. "We could start with Griffiths, Rhodes, or Sanderson. One of them will know if we've got a mechanic around."

It turned out we had two mechanics at the camp, as well as another who had run a successful civilian garage the next village over, and although the same thought had occurred, the solution, without an ability to machine the parts they'd need, had been beyond them.

They'd apparently already gotten three motorbikes up and running, having been working on getting enough together, scouring the local area, to try to send a small team south with the bikes to reestablish communications.

The bikes were gone, though, and nobody knew where or when they'd been taken.

When we talked about it, we came to the conclusion that anyone who got that kind of transport working in the very early days would have had them either confiscated by the local surviving government systems, the police, the army, or whatever. If they then were attacked, the vehicles would have been lost.

Alternatively, gangs would have been working to get them, and so would individuals, desperate to get to their loved ones. Then add in the creatures, monsters, and that any such vehicle would most likely be a diesel one, and loud? With people not getting levels for sometimes weeks after the fall, such things would have drawn fatal attacks like flies around shit.

Lastly, nobody in their right mind would have tried to get into Newcastle on something like that. If they got a working vehicle, they'd have gotten their family and headed for whatever they considered safe, such as the hills, farms, or the sea.

That was why, where we were, we'd most likely not seen anything. And the drive of the last ten years to phase out all the older vehicles in the UK in favor of electric and "low pollution" models had essentially seen all the simpler, older cars that might have still worked scrapped.

Mariusz, the lead mechanic, had tried to explain the issues that he would have with making anything we needed to start the vehicles again. After ten minutes, I'd given up and just took him to the research node, showing him how to access it, and left him to it.

An hour later, we were all being subjected to a rapid-fire barrage of barely intelligible English by the highly excited dual-nationality Polish and English soldier as he showed off the new engine design.

It'd need a lot of work, but essentially the current engines were to be ripped out of the vehicles we wanted, and a new one installed.

These new designs were diesel-based still—which came with more issues as in the months since they were in use, the diesel would have separated, apparently—but they were also hand-cranked.

We'd need a lot of muscle power, we'd been told, as the crank was going to be hard to start. But eventually he'd be able to design one that would operate with a lot less strain.

I simply summoned a corpse lord and showed it to him, explaining that it didn't need breaks or rest, and his answering grin nearly took the top of his head off.

By the time I was summoned back into the dungeon sense by Kelly, we had the beginnings of a plan, and at least the base mechanics were happy about things, even if nobody else was.

"Is everything okay?" I'd asked her straightaway, getting a grim shake of her head.

"No, you need to get the others, and get to the command center," she said.

And just like that, the building good mood was ruined.

Twenty minutes later, we were all gathered, listening as the latest newcomer to the dungeon, a hard-faced and muscular young woman named Robin, told us all her tale.

CHAPTER THIRTY-EIGHT

"**S**underland burned," she said grimly. "All of it, from one end to the other. Once it caught, there was too much, too close by to stop it spreading. By the time I left, there wasn't much standing, and the smoke could be seen for miles."

"Shit," I muttered, thinking back to when she'd estimated it had been. By that point, I was probably still setting up my dungeon. Or maybe we'd just started fighting Dickless? Either way, it wasn't that long ago in terms of days, but forever in terms of events and stress, and despite it being something we should have seen, we'd missed it.

"I left on my own, never really been one for the big crowds of friends…" That was said with clear understatement, judging from the way she was glaring around. "But I tried to help a family out, and when someone started stealing from people, people who had nothing? I don't know. I just had to do something."

"What did you do?" Chris asked, and she glanced at him, before answering.

"I hit him, with this." She held the pipe up, then started as it morphed into an extendable baton, seeming to be surprised that she was holding it.

"In here, you can bring anything," Aly said in explanation to her. "But the only thing you can affect is yourself, unless others want you to. If you hit one of us with that, it'd be about as effective as hitting us with bad language. It's all based on your self-image, so that you brought that here shows how attached you are to it."

"Okay." She sounded both embarrassed and small, as if she shouldn't be where she was and she knew it.

"Robin…" Kelly said, and she waited until the big woman looked at her before going on. "It sounds like you did the right thing, and none of us here haven't done worse, believe me, so please, go on."

"Okay." She took a deep breath and continued with her story. "We headed inland—didn't know what else to do, not really—but by the time we hit Washington, there were streets closed to us. The people who were still there didn't want us, and I don't blame them. We were like locusts, just stripping the area, anything we could use was taken, and there were thousands of us."

She held the baton in both hands and squeezed as she went on.

"We were found by the police, though they were a mess. They said that if we wanted to stay there, we had to live by their new rules. We'd split off, a band of us hurrying around to try to get ahead of the main stream of refugees, and when they offered us that…well, we didn't like it, but it was what we needed. Safety, food, though only if we helped, and a roof over our heads while we figured things out."

"Sounds good." I nodded.

"It wasn't." She glared at me. "They weren't the police. They weren't the army, though some of them were wearing their uniforms. They were the prisoners from Durham prison. They'd broken out, killed their guards, and they stripped Chester-le-Street, though we didn't know that until after.

"Then they took everything they'd gotten and they killed the police and everyone else in Washington who stood up to them, and took over the Galleries shopping center."

"The shopping…" I muttered then closed my eyes. "Of course. The food."

"Yeah." She nodded. "With only them having the weapons, and them having control of the food, people just did as they were told. For most of us, that was all we could do. But if you tried to leave—" She shook her head. "We couldn't. And anyone who asked for more food? Kids who were starving? If you didn't work, you would starve. If you had kids and they couldn't work, you better have something you could offer to pay for their food."

"Like what?" Chris asked.

"Like your ass," Robin snapped. "They took what they wanted, and either you put up with it, or they beat you and did it anyway. Then, if you survived their 'fun'? Back out to try to toil in the fields. Huh, it was a parking lot, not a field, but we were all smashing it up to try to grow crops."

"Motherfuckers," I growled.

"Rape." Chris closed his eyes, swallowing hard. "I'm sorry, Robin. I didn't think…"

"Nobody does," she snapped, then bit her lip. "I'm sorry. But nobody ever does, and it's not just the women. There's a lot of women in who are as bad, taking what they want, and men raping men…it's a snake pit. And when I found *him*? I found a kid, literally, a little kid. He'd gone looking for food to save his family, and they'd killed him and dumped him like he was nothin'. Just left him with all the other garbage."

"So what did you do?" I asked.

"Four of us started it. We told the others, anyone who wanted to run, to get ready, and to be waitin'…sent them to the other side of the barriers, and we picked a fight, tryin' to get to the weapons."

"And?" I asked.

"And others joined us, ten more, maybe twelve, and that's the only reason I didn't die in the first minutes. They had guns and they had magic, and they used them." She refused to look at anyone now, staring down at the pipe in her hand. "We fought, and then we ran. They killed everyone, but the five of us who made it out…five that found the others, and we all ran. Some of us got caught, and the…the screams weren't right. The things they were doing? I… I'll never sleep again!" Tears streamed down her face now, as she twisted the rod in her hands, shaking her head, fighting back choking sobs.

"You got the others out, though, and you lost them in the snow," I said softly.

"Yeah." She laughed—a short, bitter sound. "Fat lot of good that did. We made it here, and we're just eatin' their food, takin' space that they need for people who're sick."

"So what do you need?" I asked her directly, and she looked up.

"You'll help?" she asked, the hope and disbelief in her voice hard to hear.

"Maybe," I hedged. "Tell me what you need and what you're offering." I saw the way her face fell at the last word, and I cursed myself internally before going on. "Not like THAT!"

"Robin," Kelly said softly, "we're a community. We're growing and we protect each other. We bring hot food and all the old luxuries, showers and as much safety as we can manage, but we all work. You might not be able to help in some ways. You might not want to fight, or serve food or whatever, but we all have to help. Do you understand that? You'll never be expected to do *that*, though—nobody is."

"And you?" Robin asked me suddenly. "Is that—all that—is it for show?" She gestured to me, and I frowned, looking down, then snorting as I realized I was wearing my armor.

"No," I said, actually amused. "It's not for show."

"Can you help us?" she asked after a few seconds, noting the way the others were all smiling at the thought of me just playing dress-up. "We'll join you," she offered. "All of us, if you can help."

"At the hospital?" I asked, and she shrugged.

"They might, but at the citadel? They'd do anything if you could help. The people, I mean. They'd join you in a heartbeat."

"The citadel?" Griffiths asked.

"That's what they call it." She looked at him. "It used to be the Galleries shopping center. Now they've got a mage, and we had to pile all the stone up against the walls, so he could make them into walls, getting higher and stronger."

"How high?" Griffiths asked. "How thick? What are the capabilities of this mage? Are there others? How many of them have guns, magic, swords and spears?"

"I don't know," she admitted.

"You said you needed weapons and you'd deal with it," Kelly said. "You asked for help, but said that if we couldn't—or wouldn't—help, you could do it yourself with a few decent weapons."

"Yeah..." she whispered. "I'll try?"

"So that was more along the lines of a desperate plea." Griffiths sighed. "Matt, I can't spare the troops. Not won't..." He held up a hand to forestall the response as both Kelly and Robin opened their mouths. "I *can't*. Most of those we've just rescued are barely being kept alive currently. If you take the forces we have and storm this citadel, chances are we'll be overrun by the time you get back. We don't have so much as a goddamn wall around the base right now."

"We could use dungeon-born," Kelly suggested, looking at me in clear plea.

"We could." I sighed. "I'd need some humans, though, as leaders if nothing else. With the cold, it'd have to be Scepiniir, as the kobolds won't be able to help for long, and they'd need time to understand the situation, the non-combat and civilians and...well, everything."

"What if we do a small team?" Mike suggested, glancing over at me and Chris. "A small strike force, heavily armed, and we attack without warning. Storm the base and just wreak havoc?"

"Sounds suicidal." I grunted. "Hard pass."

"It might be the best choice," Ashley said, and I looked over at her, getting an evil smile in return. "You know, if we did it right, anyway."

"Oh fuck," Dante whispered, closing his eyes, and I glanced over at him.

"You've got something to add, Dante?" I asked.

"Just that when she smiles like that, I get scared," he admitted, before going bright red as she lifted a perfectly manicured eyebrow at him in question. "Not that I'm complaining!" he added hurriedly.

"Robin," Kelly broke up the conversation, "I'm going to remove you, and we'll discuss this, then come back to you with a decision. So if there's anything you think we need to know, now's the time."

"Ah!" she spoke quickly, looking panicked. "There's, uhm, about a hundred of them? The ex-prisoners, I mean. But there's only maybe twenty who fight; the rest aren't combat classes. And we'll help."

"How many?" I asked.

"Four?" she said. "I can't ask the others to leave their bairns alone, not when they'd not have a parent if they didn't come back. But we'll fight. We'll do anything you ask. And the people there? They're desperate. They'd do anything if you'd just help us."

"If we did this," I said firmly, "and believe me, Robin, I mean *if*...then we'd be taking charge of the citadel and the area. As much as I want to promise we're altruistic and doing this because it's the right thing to do, we'd also be doing this to remove a threat. I won't permit another to rise in its place. We'll bring security, food and shelter, and the rule of law. But make no mistake...everyone will have to work again."

As I said it, a quest popped up in my notifications, and I silenced it, determined to get this sorted first.

"It doesn't sound right like that, so let's try it again." Aly spoke up. "Robin, we'll bring healing magic. We'll train people in whatever we can, as well as teaching them magic if they have an aptitude for it. We'll bring heat and food, luxuries where we can, and nobody would be forced to do anything wrong. Nothing like *that*. Nobody will go hungry and we'll all fight for you and those people, but everyone has to contribute. The fall, we call it, but when all the electricity failed? That wasn't a random event. It was done *to* us."

"Who by?" Robin asked, her eyes goggling.

"A race called the Cinthians." She blew a hard breath out as she shook her head. "The story isn't a good one, and I'll be happy to tell you it later. But there are other races out there, and believe it or not, they did it to try to save us from another. A war-like species of orcs. They're literally assholes, and they're conquering the galaxy, slaving and murdering entire worlds. We're in their path, and we've got a very limited time to get ready. There are other dungeons out there raising armies, but every time we turn around, we're getting attacked. That's why we say that we might not be able to help, and why if we do, it'll be to conquer and remove a potential threat. We'll bring stability only if we can without risking our overall mission. Do you understand?"

"If you don't help us, then what's the point?" Robin asked shrewdly. "If you let us die, are you any better than the orcs?"

"And that's the point we're considering," I finished for her. "So, you're happy to help, but you have limited resources, and no fighters—sorry, four fighters," I corrected myself. "You think that the people of the citadel would welcome us with open arms, but you've got no control over them. You don't know how many enemies we'll face, nor how many of them are mages nor what their capabilities are, and no say in how things go after the fight. That about sum it up?"

"I'll fight with you," she said after a few seconds of trying to find her words. "You say you need to make the area safe? You need to take the citadel then, and you need these people. They're desperate, and if you come in and rescue them, the first thing they'll do is thank you. Then they'll panic because there's nobody there who's not one of the prisoners who's in charge.

"Everything will have to be started from the ground up, so if you can bring hot food, and showers? People will worship you. You want fighters? You want people you can trust to do the right thing? How about saving them, and earning that trust and devotion?" By the end, she was clearly pissed but trying not to sour the conversation.

"And that's how we ended up where we are," Kelly said with a gentle smile. "We've rescued thousands already, fought in wars against more undead than you can imagine, and monsters that are, frankly, the stuff of nightmares. If you knew how many of our forces were left bedridden after the last fight, you'd be horrified—and that doesn't include the creatures we fought. Trust us, Robin, we know what you want, and we're trying to figure out if we can do it. If we say no, it won't be because we're lazy or afraid."

"I know but—"

"We'll come back to you soon," Kelly said firmly, before removing her from the dungeon sense. "Ashley, leave for a minute, but pretend to still be in here. See what you can hear and then come back," she ordered, and Ashley nodded, before vanishing.

"You're with her, right?" I asked Dante, who nodded.

"We're in a room next to Robin, but with the dungeon-born watching over us all."

"Good." I nodded. "Gives us some protection for you both, just in case."

"You don't think she'd attack us?" Dante whispered, having clearly not considered it.

"No," I replied honestly. "But I don't want us relying on chance here. Okay, people, what do we think?"

"I think its genuine," Aly said, followed by Kelly nodding.

"What is this 'Galleries'?" Griffiths asked, and I scratched my chin, thinking about it.

"It's a shopping center," Chris said. "I used to live near it. Basically, a great big sprawling thing. The gangs were already getting bad when I left there, but it never occurred to me it'd get this bad. It's like one of those American malls, all laid out over a massive area, with great big parking lots that ring most of it. Then secondary shops, like great big supermarkets and bowling alleys dotted around the outside. Then it's all surrounded by residential areas past that. Uh, the west side of the main building is a great big bus center, set into a lower section alongside the shopping center, with a couple of bridges that lead over it. Like if you pushed two hills together, with a car lot on the west side, a valley in the middle with the buses in it, then the shopping center on the hill to the right. Then you squish them together, making the gap from one side to the other only a hundred meters or so.

"It'd make sense if they closed off the lower areas like the east side with solid walls. The whole thing is laid out on a north–south axis, with the north and south having solid walls, and access roads looping around them. The parking lots are smaller on the west side, split between the shopping center and the nearby tax offices. Then on the east side, there are the bigger main car lots as well as the entrances to most of the biggest shops.

"Then, inside there's a load more shops, and it's spread over a few levels. Plus, she said they were being made to farm, right?" He looked around to see whether anyone else had caught that, and when we nodded, he went on. "Well, that'd make sense. The parking lots were massive, couple thousand spaces, so push the cars out—and it all went down overnight, remember, so there wouldn't have been many in there anyway—and then you've got great big areas to grow crops.

"Across the road from the west side, farther on from the hill that dips down to the bus station, there's a big old tax building, massive thing that overlooks the whole place. If we could get in there, unseen, we could check the place out from above?"

"Sounds good." I nodded. "You think there could be many people in there?"

"Honestly?" He shrugged. "If you set it up with bunkbeds or whatever, you could fit a good few thousand inside. But I don't know…depends what you're doing."

"Robin said there weren't many combat classes," Griffiths mused. "You think we can trust that?"

"Maybe," I said, before looking over at where Ashley had been. "Ashley should be able to—" I broke off as Ashley reappeared. "Speak of the devil."

"And I shall appear." Ashley smiled, but the smile poured off her face as quickly as it'd come. "She's not talking to anyone. She's just sitting there, tears running down her face," she said. "I think she thinks we're going to say no and she's failed."

"Robin?" I asked, and she nodded. "You think she's genuine?"

"I've tried everything I can think of to catch her out, including using my skills and abilities," Ashley said. "I think she's telling us the truth."

"That settles it then." I grunted. "How do we do this?"

"Are we doing it?" Griffiths asked, looking at me carefully.

"We are," I said firmly. "First of all, it's an obvious enemy that's too close to us for comfort. Washington is a big place, don't get me wrong, but it's only a little over twice the distance from the dungeon's heart to the park, and it's right on the path we'd be taking south to try to reach your families.

"Add in, even if they didn't attack us as we passed them, if they figured out where we'd come from, they'd then come knocking as soon as we were out of sight. Lastly, as much as it might not be the fashionable thing to do, nor the sensible one, I'm not letting a bunch of murdering, raping son-of-a-bitches set up and act with impunity when I can do something about it."

"Amen, brother," Chris said, and a bottle of lager clinked as it appeared on the table next to my hand, a second one appearing in his grasp.

I picked it up, clinked the bottom against the bottom of his and then took a swig, before going on.

"You say your forces are too fucked up to help?" I asked him, before nodding. "If that's the way it is, then I'll do it with just me and him, if need be." I nodded to Chris, knowing he had my back.

"Damn right." The big druid grunted.

"Not necessary," Griffiths said just as firmly. "We'll send our fair share. As always, you're the boss, but you need to understand the risk and that there aren't going to be as many to help as any of us would like."

"How many?" I asked him bluntly.

"Not many," he repeated, before looking over at Rhodes in question.

"You want to know who I can spare or...?" Then she grinned as she apparently saw something in the resigned look he gave her. "Ah, yeah, I'm going." She nodded. "So are the chuckle brothers."

"The twins?" I asked, and she nodded again.

"They're not the brightest, but I'd take them any day of the week in my squad. There's no quit in either of them, and I can work with that. The three of us weren't taken and used up."

"Me too." Chris glanced over at me. "And you?"

"Of course," I agreed. "Though I think I'm going to be taking a step back soon, trying to deal with things as the Dungeon Lord more than a fighter."

"Bullshit." He snorted. "You live for this shit, same as me."

"Yeah, fair enough." I grinned back at him, knowing that in all honesty, I did.

"I'm in," Ashley said. "I'm good with a rifle and a sword, and if need be, I can distract and charm people."

"Me too," Dante said quickly. "Uh, I'm going, I mean, not that I can charm or distract... I can cook them, though!" He perked up at that thought.

"They're humans," Aly pointed out warningly. "Not skeletons or monsters."

"No, they're not," he replied, sounding older than his years as he looked back at her. "They're rapists and murderers. They've given up what it means to be human."

"Fair enough," I agreed. "Anyone else?"

"Kilo," Chris added. "And Jo. We'll need a healer and..."

"And me," Mike said firmly. "Patrick?"

"Yeah, I'm in," agreed the big martial artist.

"I'd suggest you don't take anyone besides Robin," Kelly added suddenly, making us all pause and look at her.

"What's up?" I asked.

"I think that if there's just the one of them, and it's her, you can watch over her and make sure that there's no risk from her. If this somehow all turns out to be a scam—and to be clear, I don't think it is...I'm just being careful—then you're better off with just her there."

"That works," I admitted after a second's thought.

"I think we should take them," Ashley disagreed.

"Go on?" Kelly prompted.

Ashley drew a deep breath, then went for it. "First, if there's just one of them, it opens us to possible disbelief—maybe we did something to her, forced her to endorse us, etc. Beyond that, if we only take her and we add her into the group, then she gets a share of the XP, and that means that we're basically going to be power-leveling her."

"And you think that's a mistake?" I frowned.

"No, actually." She shook her head. "I think only doing that with one of them would be, though. Think about the kind of XP you get in the low levels for quests? We could get her and her team five or even ten levels with a fight like this. It gives her a chance to become devastatingly useful, and it indebts her to us.

"We come off as heroes helping them to grow…as rescuers, rather than overlords—which, frankly, we're at risk of appearing. After all, none of them would be able to stand against us as it is. A few powerful uplifted people they all know who also feel they owe us a debt? And who their people already may feel indebted to? That could make a massive difference."

"Good points there," Griffiths said.

"And lastly…" Ashley added, wincing. "If she dies in the fight, and there's just her with us, who's to say we didn't kill her? If there's four of them, there's a much better chance one will live and see why they need us. I'm thinking long-term strategy here."

"That's a really good point," Sarah added, and I looked over at her, seeing the pained look on her face. "I want to go, but…"

I shook my head, seeing the state of her and most of the others.

"No," I said firmly. "Seriously, Sarah, you need to recover. I'm only taking Mike on the condition that he agrees to be a sniper and stay the hell out of the way, rather than trying to get up close and personal. We've got enough people, and I'll make sure Jack's with us as well."

"Agreed." Griffiths nodded. "It'd be a mistake to rely on any who had been held here, at least for any kind of physical fight."

"I can go," Jo said resolutely. "I can make it. And you're going to need a healer. We all know it."

"We do," I admitted. "I don't like it and I'd leave you if I could, but yeah, if the shit hits the fan, we're going to need a healer, not just the spell."

"You should probably take a small team of dungeon-born as well," Sarah added, clearly not happy that she wasn't going if Jo was. But as a healer, Jo was recovering far faster than she was.

"We will be," I assured her. "In fact, thanks to Mariusz, we might be able to take a bit more than just that…"

"Oh gods, he's trying to be sneaky again." Chris covered his face with one hand, and I snorted, waving a rude gesture at him, before glancing over at Kelly and Aly.

"What I'll need, though, is a lot of your creative side, and a lot of help from you, Ashley, because this is going to take a lot of trust…"

CHAPTER THIRTY-NINE

"**I** still can't believe I let you talk me into this," Rhodes muttered, making me grin at her, as on the far side of her, Dante was busy glaring at anyone who looked even vaguely in his girlfriend's direction.

"It'll be fine," Ashley assured her, smiling sunnily. "And you look great!"

"I feel like a whore," she muttered.

"More like meat." Ashley reached up, adjusting her hair to make sure it looked artfully messy. "Remember, we're the *bait*. These idiots will see what they want to see, and if they're looking at your tits, they're not seeing the real you."

"That's fine for you to say," the older sergeant snapped. "You're ten years younger than me, and yours are fake!"

"And you think they'll care?" Ashley said coldly, as her mask slipped for a second, showing the steel beneath the satin. "All anyone sees when they see me is my tits and makeup. They underestimate me, and I make them pay for it. We do this, we pull this off? If we can get inside without anyone stopping us? How many lives is that worth?"

"Any," Rhodes admitted, deflating slightly. "Doesn't mean I like it. But you're right, even though you make me feel like old mutton dressed as lamb next to you."

Ashley smiled; the mask slipped back into place, making her seem a naive young girl.

"Don't worry, Sarge!" Jimmy said suddenly from a few seats further along. "If we wasn't married, we'd totally go for you, wouldn't we bro?" His brain apparently then caught up with his ears, and a look of horror crossed his face.

Rhodes's glare as she turned to regard him was like being caught in the sights of a tank's main cannon.

I winced, knowing what the cheerful guy had been trying to say, and why, as well as the fact that he might never recover from the tongue-lashing he was about to receive.

"Thank you, Jimmy," Rhodes growled, before taking a deep breath and letting it back out again. "I know what you were trying to say, so just…just let's forget this entire conversation happened."

"Yes, Sarge!" he almost screamed, sounding strangled. "Sorry, Sarge!"

"Damn…" I shook my head. "Never seen someone put both their feet in their mouth at once like that."

"I have." Chris snorted. "Dude, you do it like, all the time."

"You really do," Patrick added from the driver's seat, clearly enjoying needling me.

"Really, you think the sarge is hot, too, boss?" Andre asked, looking relieved.

"I mean—oh fuck it, I'm staying out of this one." Patrick, who was driving, cursed and turned back to staring out of the front window, as Andre caught the look Rhodes was giving him and quickly fell silent.

The snow was coming down again, but this time it was gentle, if constant. We'd had to detour around more dead vehicles than I'd expected, considering the time in the morning when the fall had occurred. But as we got closer, we'd pulled over and settled in to wait for recon.

Mike had jumped out and had gone ahead with two of the freshly summoned Scepiniir, while the rest were in the back of the troop transport with us. We'd given him nearly two hours to make it to the top of the tower, then back down and back to us, and it'd been worth it.

He'd made it about an hour before sundown, and he'd entered the tower maybe thirty seconds behind the pair who were swapping over for sentry duty.

Following them all the way to the top had taken half an hour, mainly because the pair were in such a lazy mood. When they'd gotten to the top, Mike had watched a fight break out between the two "shifts."

One of the four men had been stabbed to death by another, and that the only interest hadn't been "what do we do now about explaining why he's dead" and instead it'd been a scramble to search his body?

That convinced Mike that the best option here wasn't just to hide and let both sides go on their merry way.

It was to question the three survivors; then, when he had everything he needed, he killed them, set them out so that it looked as if they'd killed one another, and left again, silent as a ghost.

The two Scepiniir, Vars and Riski, had highly approved, and enjoyed the time they were given to "discuss things" with the mouthiest one, before jointly deciding with Mike that throwing him off the roof, gagged, was the best thing they could do with him.

That might have sounded cruel, callous, and disgusting even, right up until Mike explained the conversation about the "fun" that one had been bragging about having before his shift started.

Then the death was agreed as having been very well earned.

Mike had clambered into the bed of the covered truck transport and spoke quickly when he got back.

"There's thirty-three combat classes," he advised. "Ten are on constant duty, patrolling the area and killing anything they judge is a threat to the camp during the day, back on the inside at night. Five more are on security in the citadel. Three of those are watching over the armory, one on the entrance to the food halls, and one watching over the prison.

"Beyond that, there's two on the tower to watch out for anything coming in—though what they thought they'd see at night and in the snow is fucking anyone's guess—and the rest are split between two more in each of two watchtowers and the guard post, with the rest on downtime."

"Downtime?" I'd asked.

"Basically getting pissed and having fun." He snorted. "That's the combat classes, though, not all the criminals. There's over a hundred of them, scattered about the base, with five mages. One is an Earth mage, a…" He paused, trying to think of the term, only for Dante to give it.

"A terramancer," he supplied.

"Yeah, one of them." Mike nodded. "Anyway, two Fire boys…"

"Pyromancers," Dante corrected.

"You know? I think I'm gonna start callin' pyros all 'spicy boys' if you keep interrupting me? That sound fair?" He glared at Dante, who shut up immediately. "Good choice. Now, next is a necromancer," Mike said. "The last one, though, is a wrinkle in the plan. The others are terrified of him, as he's apparently a real sick fuck. He makes things out of flesh, and not in a good way."

"There's a good way?" I asked grimly. "The necromancer makes stuff out of flesh?"

"No, the necro is just accepted as a weirdo. He's the Goth kid they can't kill, too powerful, but also none of them trust. No, the worrying one is some kind of a flesh mage—takes people and carves them up, makes toys out of their dead bodies…that kinda shit."

"You didn't think that was important?" I asked Robin, who stared open-mouthed.

"I didn't know!" she'd hissed. "They said they took the dead for burning, because of the risk of plague!"

"More likely they're building a force," I growled. "That makes it more fun."

"Anyone seen anything with the necro?" Mike directed the question at Robin.

"No. I mean, the dead?" She shook her head, horrified. "I never saw anything like that."

That'd been true as well, I'd guessed, considering the way she'd looked at the corpse lords when I'd summoned them, having them fold themselves up as carefully and small as possible, then making a box around them, sealing them away as "trade goods."

"Though," she'd added after a few seconds, "some of our people who tried to give us a distraction, they just vanished, so maybe?"

"Might be they fought the undead and were killed." I sighed. "Okay, so that's the combat classes. What about the boss?"

"That's a different story," Mike admitted. "Nothing he would say except that the boss was a massive fucker, and that nobody messes with him. No matter how hard I pushed, he wouldn't, or *couldn't* say anything. Might be genuine terror, might be a skill or magic. Not sure."

"Fair enough." I grunted. "Any last-minute changes to the plan?"

"*Plan* is generous," I heard Rhodes mutter, before she shook her head, pretending not to have said anything. "No, sir. All good on my side."

"Good." I glared at her, then avoided looking at what she was wearing as she tried to pull the cloak tighter across herself. "You got everything you need?"

"I've got everything I can hide," she said, dispirited. "What I need is my battle rattle and my assault rifle."

"He's got it." I nodded to C'tan, the big Scepiniir next to her, armed to the teeth. "You ready for this?"

"I'm as ready as I'm going to be." She sighed. "So let's do it."

"Okay, Mike, get going." I nodded to him, and he reached out, offering a fist bump.

"Good luck to us all." He jumped back out and started to run.

"Do two laps of the area. Let the sound of the engine carry and see if they spot us," I told Patrick, who was driving the truck, while Jimmy drove the boxer behind us. "Act like we're just exploring and looking for someone to negotiate with."

He nodded, and beside him, the slimmer and fastest of the Scepiniir, Saros, huffed out a laugh. "This is going to be *fun*," she said. "I can't wait!"

"Me too." C'tan growled, before looking down at Rhodes and giving her a wink. "Behave yourself now, 'slave,' or I'll not bargain much for you."

"You're brave," she replied, staring up at the huge Scepiniir. "Just you wait till this is all done. You and me, boy? We're going to have a chat."

"Sounds fun," he repeated Saros' words, before winking again.

Human facial and tonal impressions clearly weren't getting through to him much, but that was fine. I figured if he survived this fight, he'd soon have a reason to learn, considering he was unaware he was currently basically propositioning his boss, who I happened to know was a psychopath as a trainer, and as far as I knew wasn't into furries.

For the purposes of this little illusion, he was the leader, and there were eight Scepiniir in total. Patrick, Kilo, Jimmy, Andre, and I were all guards and drivers, and we were very much subservient to the Scepiniir. Ashley, Dante, Jo, Robin, and Rhodes were our prisoners, and we were looking to sell them.

We also had the other three that Robin had promised: Jakob, Katee, and Laurence. Although we'd shared the quest with them, we'd also made it clear that they were to stay the hell back from most of the fighting.

I was betting that the fact we had not one, but two working vehicles was going to be the main interesting point to get us in the door, but fuck it. I was reasonably confident that they'd let us in, and then they'd try to kill us, taking everything we had. And seeing as that was pretty much my plan for them? No hard feelings all around.

We'd replaced the headlights in the troop truck and the boxer with mana lights like the ones we used in the dungeon. They weren't as bright as normal headlights, but they were more than enough, when combined with our own improved eyesight, that we could drive in the dark safely.

We'd spent a day resting up and getting as ready as we could be. Mike, Jo, and all the others who had been captured spent most of that time on IV drips and resting. Then we'd set off, timing it as well as we could so we arrived here not long before dark. By the time Mike and his people were back from scouting, it was a few hours after dark, and we'd settled in, giving them time to relax and let down their guard.

Now, heading around the Galleries center in a wide loop, we acted as if we weren't sure what we were seeing, before rolling up to the entrance, making sure that while Jack was staying back far enough he was out of sight, he was still close enough to be useful for when we needed him.

Mike was right in that the main entrance to the building itself seemed to be the one that could only be reached by driving over a narrow single-lane bridge. But before we could get there, we had to get through the front gate.

The western side had the smaller parking lot for the shopping center, but at the entrance to what had once been the parking lot was now a sloppily constructed wall, one with a tower that looked in danger of collapse at any time, and a single guard standing over the gate, watching out.

The idiot even had a torch that was sputtering in the drifting snow right next to him, guaranteeing that he couldn't see much in the darkness.

We practically had to honk the horns and flash the lights to get him to stop staring in shock. And when he did? He went running to the tower, vanishing from sight a few heartbeats later.

"Know anything about him?" I asked Robin, who shook her head.

"I didn't get a good look at his face, but with all the clothes he was wearing, and being out there, he was probably just another low-level criminal. The bosses don't mark much of a difference between us and the lower-leveled ex-prisoners. If you weren't one of 'them,' then you were prey. That he was left on the wall in the snow means he must have been someone they didn't care about."

"Fair enough," I said.

We started to wait, expecting it to take less than thirty seconds for the "real" guards to be summoned. In reality, it took almost ten minutes, and by the time the pair arrived, I was cursing.

"Whosh tha'?" one of them slurred, bracing himself on the wall and staring down blearily.

The second guard had tripped and fell, coming out of the tower, and had literally face-planted the wall, apparently knocking himself out.

"Are you fucking kidding me?" I asked the world in general, rhetorically. "We put in all this effort for…that?" I gestured up at the utterly smashed-off-his-face guard who was half slumped over the edge of the wall, squinting and clearly unable to focus.

"Who you?" he got out after a few more attempts, and I sighed.

"You know what?" I shook my head. "I don't know why I bother. C'tan, you want to try the act?"

"I am C'tan!" the big Scepiniir boomed, stepping up and smacking himself in the chest with one balled fist. "War leader of this band, and I come to trade human females!"

"Wha'?" was the only response he got.

"Women!" Andre bellowed up at the guard after a brief pause. "You want to buy any?"

"Wha'?" came the response again.

I snarled. "Fuck it. Saros?"

"Yes, boss?" she answered cheerily, leaning out of the truck door.

"Get up there and make sure there's nobody playing silly buggers."

"And the guards?" She stepped down, almost seeming to dance from one foot to another in anticipation.

"Kill them." I grunted, before turning to the back of the truck and waving toward Ashley, who'd been "dragged" out of the back of the wagon, putting on a show of being terrified.

"Look!" I shouted. "Want to buy her?"

"Please!" Ashley cried out, trying to cover herself—she wore a crop top and torn jeans, an outfit that she said was actually considerably less revealing than most she'd worn on nights out, but that would be all she needed to go with for this. She pulled the sides of the cloak—one that she'd designed and made herself—in close, but couldn't quite cover herself, ending up flashing the bright red of her top through it. "Please, sir, help me!" she called up. "You don't know what they'll do to me!"

"Huh?" He leaned out so far on the wall that she apparently had a fit of inspiration, and "broke free," running to the base of the wall and calling up to him to help her, that she'd do anything…

And then he leaned out too far in his drunken state and fell, face-first, crashing into the snow with a cry and a wet *smack*.

Silence fell as we all looked at the bleeding and dazed drunkard on the ground, and then back up at the wall. The single guard, wrapped in all the layers of clothing, peered out of what had to be four or five hoodies inside of a jacket.

He glanced from the guard on the ground next to us, and then off to the side, presumably at the other guard, and then out, before turning and starting to run for the tower.

He made it three steps before a suppressed shot rang out, and he fell from sight. I turned, seeing Rhodes straightening up and glaring at me.

"Do we still need the charade?" she asked, and I snorted.

"No, I guess not," I admitted. "Sorry, Rhodes. I honestly thought it'd have been needed to get us inside."

"I'll probably forgive you, once I'm dressed." She grunted. "With your permission, sir?"

"Go," I agreed, before turning to Ashley. "You too, Ashley. Better to be in your armor, I think. And thank you."

"It's fine." She smiled. "I wore less than this on a night out to get free drinks. Using it to get us inside wasn't a problem, and Rhodes will forgive you," she assured me, heading past me and toward the back of the truck.

"She volunteered for it!" I pointed out, but in deference to the fact I wasn't a complete idiot, I said it very quietly.

She had, in fact, volunteered for it, as had Jo, and, in the end, Robin—with Dante insisting on doing it as well so that he was close to Ashley and in case the guards swung that way.

My original plan had been to have Ashley act as a traveling courtesan, one who had us all as guards. But as she'd pointed out, first of all, these weren't the type of people who bought and paid; they were the type to just take. And if she were really living that kind of life, she'd have been doing it with a much nicer vehicle to live in, even if it was just in terms of decorating the truck out.

Then she'd come up with the whole selling slaves angle, and had argued it gave us more of a reason to have the Scepiniir in charge, supposedly.

I was still pissed, though, because I'd thought my plan was a stroke of goddamn genius. We even had a single corpse lord ready as a "sample," and a stack of them in boxes that were strapped to the top of the boxer and inside it, as well as in the truck.

That plan had been that we were selling them with one acting as a sample, and that they could be claimed by letting the morning sunlight touch the crystal on the box's lid—it was just glass, but hey—then the corpse lords would be ready to serve their new masters.

I'd been sure that would get us all inside. Then, when I was ready, we'd have struck: the corpse lords bursting free of the boxes and us opening fire, Ashley using her skills to distract and charm the boss, and the rest of us basically killing anyone we needed to, and Jack eating someone's face no doubt.

It was a masterful plan, one that was only enhanced by Jo, Rhodes, and the others volunteering when Ashley asked them to "play dress-up" with her.

Now I was left feeling insanely fucking stupid, as Saros appeared on the wall, having run to the side when all eyes were on Ashley. She'd then scaled the small wall and had snuck back along, only to find that she wasn't needed at all.

"Here's one!" she called down cheerfully, pitching the other one, who had apparently slipped on the stairs, over the side of the wall.

He hit the ground and bounced, before letting out a faint groan, one that was quickly silenced by the nearest Scepiniir, who stepped up and drove a dagger into the back of his neck.

"So, I guess we need to open the gate, then drive right in." I sighed, waving to the vehicles. "C'tan, sort that out, please," I ordered him, climbing up into the truck's front seat and sitting next to Andre. "Everyone else, stay away from the back while the ladies change!"

"And me!" Dante responded quickly. "Can I get dressed?"

"Yeah, but if you try to do it while they're dressing, I'm not responsible for them stabbing you in the face." I sighed, then closed the door. "You know what? I'd like a plan to go all the way through, just once," I commented dryly to Andre, who chuckled

"Could be worse." He shrugged. "I ever tell you about us getting engaged?" When I shook my head, he grinned. "We went all out for it on the girls' birthday, you know? Flowers, the ring, everything! Even spoke to Jimmy to make sure he was ready, both of us planning to take the girls out to different places, to make the proposal really special. He was ready and was doing the same, but we wanted it to be different. Most things we do, we all do together: meals, holidays, birthdays…all that stuff. I wanted our proposals to be different, to be separate, special even."

"Yeah?" I prompted him, nodding that I understood. A clang rang out from behind the gate, and Riski started to drag it back, as Vars waved us through.

"Well, I was so damn nervous, I blurted it all out to Jenn that I was going to propose and I was shitting myself—showed her the ring and everything—asked if she thought Emma would like it."

"And?"

"And it was fucking Emma." He slapped the steering wheel and shook his head as if he couldn't believe it. "She was wearing one of Jenn's tops…knew I'd like it, so she'd borrowed it. They're identical—I mean, I know which one is my wife, and then, my girl, all right? There's a million ways they're different. But hopped up and terrified? I ruined the whole thing. Just fucked it up."

He drove us slowly forward, the snow crunching under the wheels as the rumble of the diesel engine filled the air again.

"Seriously?" I asked him, trying to hide a laugh.

"Yeah, man, fucked up my proposal…she was too busy shouting yes and shouting to her sister to come look. I even fucked it all up for Jimmy and Jenn as well, because she gave him *that* look as soon as she got downstairs, and he just pulled it out and nodded to her."

"You romantic fuckers." I grinned.

"Yeah, well, we were both shitting ourselves. Biggest decision of your life, you know? Anyway, everything turned out right in the end, and we ended up just going out clubbing, after, well, you know. Saved us both an expensive meal, too. But if I could do it again?" He shrugged. "I wanted to make it special for her. Something that was just for *her*, you know? I wish it'd worked. Same thing with your plan. Maybe we get up there and we can use some of it still. They can't all be idiots, right?"

He was wrong. They were all definitely idiots.

The Scepiniir ran ahead, with the two vehicles crunching and bumping inside the gate, then coming to a halt. The snow-covered attempts at fields, making it clear there'd be no quiet way to get from here to the bridge, so we dumped them as soon as Saros returned.

"The bridge is empty." She grinned. "There's a tower to watch over it, and the guard was asleep."

"Is he still asleep?" I clambered down from the high cab, getting a frown from her.

"No, he's dead," she replied, confused. "You want me to leave them to sleep? They're your enemies."

"No, I just wanted to be sure." I nodded at her. "So the bridge leads over to the main entrance…there a guard there?"

"It's chained shut from inside." She looked annoyed. "I need the cutters."

We'd tried to anticipate as much as possible, and one of those plans had involved us pretending to sell equipment as well, including the bolt cutters.

"Damn, well, at least they're not complete—" I started to say before Vars jogged up.

"All good! They left the side door unlocked." He grinned.

"Idiots," I finished. "Fuck's sake, did we really even need to come for this?" I asked the world in general, before peering across the scattered fields. "Robin, is this likely to be a trap?"

"I don't…think so." She stepped up to my side. "We were always kept inside, locked away in one of the shops in groups at night. The only way we were let out was if we 'volunteered' to help 'lift the guards' spirits.'" That last bit was said with a sneer, and she spat on the ground.

"Prostitution?" Rhodes asked, and she nodded.

"Basically. It wasn't for money, obviously, but those who did it generally ended up with better jobs and more food, provided they were kept."

"Kept?" I asked.

"Most who did it were used a few times, unless they really worked hard at it. A few were kept as favorites, but most were just used and then sent back. A few were chosen every night, fought over even. Like you." She nodded to Ashley.

"They'd have fought over you. But for me? I didn't, but even if I had, I doubt they'd have taken me more than once or twice."

"You'd be surprised," Ashley replied, shaking her head. "Different people like different people. And don't be so hard on yourself."

"Whatever." Robin grunted.

I deliberately didn't comment. She looked good, but certainly a lot better now in armor than she had when we first picked her up, as well as when she'd been dressed in the clothing Ashley had picked out for her and the others.

Robin was tall and broad shouldered, with thick arms and legs earned through hard labor. At some point, she'd hacked her hair short, leaving her with an image that was more masculine than Ashley's carefully presented one. But in armor?

Where Ashley now wore her usual armor and looked more like just another fighter, even if a pretty one when she wasn't wearing her helmet, Robin had been *born* for armor.

It wasn't customized to her, but considering the fight we'd had ahead, Aly had done all that she could, creating layered armor in dark grey, leather, and steel that just fit her frame *right*.

Add in the rifle, the handgun, and dagger, as well as a mace with a bladed tip that she'd demanded, and she looked every inch the warrior goddess.

We were back in helmets again—I had no clue what'd happened to my last one—but the new ones were impressive. A slit carved across the front—an inch thick, two high, and that ran from ear to ear—gave us great visibility. And even if it did tend to fog up when we breathed too hard, the dark tint to the glass meant that nobody could see our faces.

Add in the overall look was more space-bounty-hunter mixed with Greek soldier, and it was awesome.

It was also well padded and should take a few hits, hopefully saving some lives.

We set off as soon as everyone was fully dressed—Ashley and Rhodes had gotten Robin dressed first, her armor being unfamiliar to her. With the Scepiniir watching the doors and, I damn well hoped, Mike still on overwatch in the tower that overlooked the compound, we started for the bridge.

Behind us, waiting in successive rows, were the twenty corpse lords we'd brought, their boxes scattered as they'd been ordered to get ready. They now stood silent. They were too big, too obviously wrong and too loud to be able to use yet, so the decision had been made to leave them there. When the shit hit the fan, they'd be pulled up to fight.

The drop from the sides of that level to the bus area below wasn't that far, perhaps ten meters prior to the fall. But the sides of the raised platform had been added to, with rings of barbed wire scavenged from somewhere, and sloppily built stone walls angling outward.

The overall impression was good from a distance; certainly, it looked on its way to becoming a real citadel. And as a regular human, especially in the fucking apocalypse, it'd have looked downright wonderful, as a place that might offer you some protection.

In reality though, as we got closer, we saw it was just a mess.

The walls were haphazardly moved into place and apparently melted together as the stone was softened somehow, before being pressed into place and re-hardened.

Barbed wire was hung carefully in some sections, making sure nobody could climb up…and in others, it was loosely draped.

At one point, bloody remains that had apparently been chewed on by something dangled more than halfway to the ground below, and I swallowed hard. The frozen entrails were in various shades of discoloration. Although the torso was large enough, I couldn't make out whether it'd been a man or woman, or even whether they'd been human at all.

I jogged with the others across to the main gate, pausing and peering through the old glass doors I remembered. Piled stone behind them cut the six glass doors, side by side, to a single pair in the middle.

Squinting through the damn gap left between the ill-fitting doors, I could just make out the metal chains that were looped around and secured by a padlock, and I nodded.

The doors could probably be pushed back far enough to get the bolt cutters through and to cut the chain, but trying to free them would make a hell of a racket.

The side door was a staff entrance to an inbuilt supermarket a few dozen meters farther ahead. The metal goddamn security door had been blocked from locking properly by someone stuffing stones into the latch.

I had no clue who'd been literally that much of an idiot that they'd do this, but they had, and the Scepiniir were already inside, waiting.

"What did you find?" I asked in a hushed voice as we trooped in, glancing along the passage to where, at the far end, the gleam of fires shone through a crack in the door. A pair of Scepiniir stood ready by it.

"This was the end of the easy bit," C'tan grumbled. "This leads to a set of metal doors. They don't lock, but beyond them is a bonfire, a big one, and others sitting around. They drink, they shout, some sleep the sleep of the drugged, but there is no way to get past the fire without being seen."

"How many are there?" I asked.

"Thirty, maybe more." He scratched at a cheek. "Most are to the right. Seats are set there, and the smell of burning meat."

"Hope it's burgers," Chris quipped, and Rhodes looked at him and slowly shook her head. "What?" he asked.

"You see any cows out there?" she suggested. "Let's make this easy. Robin, were there any farm animals?"

"No," she replied. "We just got vegetables, no meat."

"And anything that was fresh or frozen would have gone bad in the first few weeks, if not days." Rhodes looked around. "That means that they need a regular meat source, something they can raise, and easily maintain. That leaves us with monsters…or people."

"You thinking what I'm thinking?" I asked her, and she nodded.

"Flesh mage."

"You're kidding me?" Chris looked sick. "That's…"

"Long pig." Rhodes nodded. "Smells like it, anyway."

"Fuck no."

"Well, look on the bright side." I rolled my shoulders, then gestured to the dark passage ahead of us. "It wasn't like we were planning on making nice with them."

"True, but still, man…that's just nasty."

Any further conversation was cut off when the Scepiniir at the far end—Saros, I think, though it was hard to tell at this point with the darkness and shitty illumination from the fires shining through—gave a low whistle.

It was carried by the other Scepiniir without hesitation, and C'tan grinned at me as he lifted his rifle, nodding in that direction.

"It begins," was all he said, before a staggering drunk yanked the door open and stood there, peering blearily into the passage at all of us assembled there.

CHAPTER FORTY

Saros slashed her claws across his throat before he had the chance to get a shout out, grabbing him with her other hand and yanking him into the passage. But someone had clearly seen something, as a shout rose.

"Fuck! Go, go, go!" I shouted, starting forward, only to be left behind as the Scepiniir raced ahead. Jack bounded after them, Kilo fell in behind me, alongside Chris, with Dante and Rhodes, then Ashley and Jo, before finally Andre, Patrick, and Jimmy, who brought up the rear.

Whatever else they might be, the assholes on the far side of the door were clearly used to fighting for their lives. As soon as the Scepiniir Riski burst out of the passage, he was taken down, with Vars and another right behind, all going down in a hail of bullets.

Saros was down as well. Two bullets had hit her, but she'd used the body of the man she'd just killed as cover, and was apparently still alive, if badly wounded as she returned fire, yelling as Jack leapt over her, taking several hits and shrugging them off like water off a duck's back, then starting mauling.

C'tan was just ahead of me. The small shield he'd asked for was on his left arm, and the rifle drawn tight against his chest. The doors swung crazily; bullets hit the walls and bounced, skipping off the floor and screaming past him, until they slammed into my shield.

I ran just behind him. The shield flashed as each hit cracked into it. Ahead, the doors crashed closed. Bullets pockmarked the inside as a sound like the hail of the gods echoed around us.

He reached the doors and kicked them open, before throwing himself into a roll, hitting the ground, then coming to his feet, rifle blazing.

I was behind him still, barely ahead of the others, but the fire was directly in front of us—a collection of shopping carts all lashed together and filled with anything flammable.

They were blackened and twisted, piles having burned through them to crash to the faux marble floors, creating a layered bonfire that made it hard to see anything, especially when we were running toward it and the enemy were sprawled around.

I saw movement and fired on instinct, then cursed as I jerked the barrel left at the last second, barely missing tagging C'tan in the back of the head. He was up again—I'd missed that—and he was sprinting around the fire to the left, shooting as he went.

Bursting from the passage, my mana down by a third to three thousand one-fifty-two, I skidded into sight, turning to the right. A trio of figures aimed at me from behind overturned seats.

I fired. A three-round burst tore into the seats, doing fuck all beyond making them duck, but that was enough.

I triggered Incinerate, roughly aiming for the area the middle one had been and not having time to lock it in any better. There was a scream, then I was hit by a staccato rhythm of shots. Handguns, rifles, and a shotgun fired seemingly randomly as the others of the group had finally gotten into gear, and my mana dropped dangerously.

Not daring to drop the shield, I sprinted along the wall to the right, firing repeatedly even as I blindly triggered the spell again at the small group I had pinned. Screams burst out this time. A gun was flung aside, glowing hot; I might not have hit one of them directly, but I'd apparently caught a gun's barrel with the last spell.

The others were behind me, racing forward and spreading out.

Kilo blanketed the flames in a sudden wash of ice. Hissing, spitting clouds of steam erupted in all directions, adding to the madness. It was a good plan, a cold and calm part of my brain noted; changing it from what they were used to, to a mad mix, evening the playing field.

Chris flung out his left hand, shouting something. A pair hiding behind a battered planter were suddenly grabbed by surging vines that poured over the side, wrapping around their limbs.

As they were dragged up into view, Jack leapt on them, teeth biting, claws flashing and blood spraying as he took them out.

Rhodes was a terror, racing forward. A glowing red light surged around her as she picked up speed, yelling something and leaping high, firing in fast, accurate bursts.

Dante came next. Where Kilo was spraying ice into the fire, suppressing the enemies' advantage when it came to the bonfire blocking our view, he was hurling fireballs that hit and exploded.

Figures were already screaming, writhing as they burned, and the fight went on.

I fired in rapid bursts, my accuracy good, but not great. Shards leapt from the stone benches another pair were hiding behind as I hit it; their handguns were jammed through the slats carved into it, returning fire fast.

Bullets hit my shield over and over. After a brief hesitation, I cut it. I needed to save my mana, and decided to rely on my armor. I instantly regretted it as the pair who were left from the original three I'd targeted both managed a hit on me, sending me staggering into the wall, before bouncing off as I returned fire.

One of the shots had been a shotgun, and I hissed in pain as at least two pellets of birdshot announced their arrival to my body in the worst way.

Ashley made an appearance. Her voice reverberated as she shouted something, before one of the pair behind the stone bench stopped firing, his mouth dropping open.

He struggled to his feet, only to catch a round fired by Andre full in the face. He hurtled backward in a spray of blood.

The brothers stayed back in the doorway, I saw with a desperate glance, as I dove behind a pillar, leaning out to the right and left and firing from as much cover as was available, trusting in Rhodes to take out those she could on the far side.

It was bedlam. The chatter of semi-automatic fire rung out. Distant and close-in screams. An old air-raid siren suddenly filled the air with its wail; I flicked out my left hand in its direction, seeing a filthy figure, grinning through an unkempt beard as he cranked it over and over.

My lightning bolt filled the air with its blue-white radiance, before hitting him in the chest and sending him hurtling back, spasming reflexively even as his heart was obliterated.

I twisted back around, lining up on the remaining figure behind the stone bench, planning on taking him out, before I was hit by a three-round burst in the back from the far side of the bonfire.

I staggered. My armor did its job, but I dropped to one knee, before another shotgun blast hit me full-on from the left. I snarled, throwing myself forward, and trusting the twins to take out whoever just shot me in the back. At the same time, I reached out to the corpse lords and sent a simple message: *"Come."* I fired a rapid burst ahead; the figure behind the bench had stepped out from behind it to shoot me, taking the burst in the thigh, crotch, and gut.

He collapsed, screaming, and it only added to the bedlam.

I tried to rise, only to hiss, my back twanging and shaking. Something hit me, a spell of some kind. The muscles in my back writhed and twisted as I frantically tried to keep from falling over.

Pain…pain filled me. I went from hissing and annoyed into a full-throated cry as it felt like my back muscles were being ripped apart. My arms sagged. I could barely stay in the crouch, straining to stand, to dive from the exposed position I was in.

Five seconds later, the twisting, writhing pain vanished. But even in the absence of the spell—as that had to have been what it was—I could barely move.

The air was filled with the snap of bullets, howls of pain, and the crack and zip of spells. Hissing cold enveloped the side of the bonfire, dropping it to a point that was finally low enough for me to clearly see the far side, between the banks of drifting fog and smoke that now filled the place.

My muscles shook, my legs straining to lift me as if I'd gained a thousand kilos, and yet, I couldn't! I felt the snap as atrophied muscles gave way. I fell to all fours, gasping for breath, my throat hoarse. I dragged lightning from my core and into my body, frantically using it like a goddamn Band-Aid as I forced my head up, looking around, searching for the bastard who had done this.

We were at a crossroads, or near enough. The back passage that we'd used to get in had brought us along between the outer wall and the inner wall of the supermarket. There'd been stairs leading down that we'd ignored, running past them when the fight broke out.

I'd guessed that they led to the actual staff areas, because the metal doors that we'd entered the main complex through were clearly a reserve fire exit or something similar.

The crossroads before us was where the three separate "legs" of the shopping center met up. The one to the left, or the west, led to the main entrance that I'd found chained shut before, then looped around to the north in a general path that led around the inside of the center.

The other two came from almost dead ahead and to the right, where an escalator led down to the lower floor of the supermarket.

Dante suddenly unleashed a huge fireball. His arms windmilled as he summoned it, compressed it, and sent it screeching through the air into the remainder of the bonfire. A blast of flying flaming pieces pushed the whole thing backward, and screams from the far side rang out.

"Yeah, baby, yeah!" he shouted, terror and elation clear in his voice, only to scream as he was hit with something bone-white that hurtled through the guttering flames from the far side, to punch into his armor.

He wore lighter armor than the frontline fighters, mainly leather with a layer of scale over the top. But whatever hit him was driven with the power of a spell.

It punched into his upper right shoulder. He tumbled backward with a howl of pain, before then really screaming, as what was revealed to be a bone spur, attached to a glistening black string, started to drag him along the floor.

Ashley was there a heartbeat later. Her sword, worn across her back, whipped out cleanly and severed the thread joining Dante to whatever lay in the darkness ahead, even as Jack roared and raced into it, searching for the foe.

I had a momentary thought, wondering how her sword could be drawn so cleanly, before a healing spell hit me, and I groaned in relief as Jo made her presence felt.

"Come on, up and at 'em." She grabbed me under the arm as I struggled back to my feet. "No time for lounging around, don't cha know."

"Thank...you..." I grunted, twisting as my back suddenly released. Whatever damage that had been done fixed itself with a series of clicks and pops. "Holy hell...that *hurt*!" I dragged in a deep breath, then squinted around, shifting to put my armored form between Jo and the rest of the room.

"I bet." She grinned. "Okay, how about we get out of the line of fire?"

"Yeah, then I need to find whoever did that," I agreed, before glaring as I saw finally, illuminated by the scattered flames, that the rest of the combat classes were coming.

They were using abilities, that was clear. One was glowing like a supernova, sprinting across the faux marble, a blur left behind him. I blinked and he was gone, only to reappear a heartbeat later; he'd covered at least thirty meters, leaping into the air and kicking out with both feet.

Chris was sent flying, colliding into the wall and bouncing off to crash to the floor, stunned. The speedster twisted, jumping back in the air, seeming to fall almost in slow motion; a pair of handguns came up, locking on Ashley and Dante.

He opened fire. The first shot hit her helmeted head and staggered her slightly, followed by three more hitting her before he touched the ground. His left pistol clicked on a dud round, or empty. Rather than mess with it, he dropped it, opening fire with his right. Two bullets hit Dante, only to be stopped by his armor.

They chewed it up badly enough, though, that the third hit punched through. He cried out, twisting as he tried to roll out of the line of fire.

Ashley was already racing forward, her sword dropped. She gripped her rifle in both hands and fired: two three-round bursts, as we'd been taught by Mike, aimed for center of mass. Then there was the shock of having him step aside, grinning as the shots passed a hairsbreadth from him.

The second to arrive was some kind of warlock, his face painted and carved with glowing lines. Blood ran freely from them, and yet he seemed unaffected. Howling as he ran forward, he pulled at his flesh and filled his hands with blood, before casting it ahead of him.

He threw himself down, landing hard and rolling to slap both hands on a nearby corpse. Each blood spot that hit the ground—and there'd been dozens—opened a hole almost half a meter across.

Through that hole, hands with stubby talons reached out, along with the smell of sulfur and the hiss of escaping heat.

He grabbed the body, beginning a chant. A manic grin stretched his cheeks enough that the white of bone could be seen through his presumably self-inflicted carvings. Then he collapsed backward, and blood sprayed from the hole in the side of his head as Rhodes ran forward, firing.

The holes in the earth suddenly snapped shut. Truncated screams hung in the air as sections of limbs collapsed to the ground on this side of what had to have been portals to another realm.

Glass vials arced through the air from another figure. Where they landed, virulent green smoke billowed forward, seeming to be driven by a great breeze from behind.

That smoke suddenly split, rolling to the sides and backward as Kilo hissed a single word and gestured, a great icy wind sweeping from his hands.

All around me, the fight raged. I grabbed Jo, half throwing her toward Dante, as a pair of new enemies raced at me.

The one on the right looked terrible, his flesh sunken and sagging, barely seeming able to move, and yet his eyes gleamed feverishly. I snapped a single round at him, thinking to remove the weakest piece from the board, as I focused on the second.

He carried a shield and axe, as well as some kind of ornamental metal cosplay kit. But as soon as I fired, the first guy leapt in front of him.

The bullet hit him, punching into his stomach, making him stagger, then grin as the area around what should have been a wound rippled, bulging upward.

I stared for a second, shocked, then fired again, a three-round burst. I cursed as he took all three hits, his body rippling and seemingly growing haler and healthier with each impact.

I switched to the other, firing another burst, only for the intercept to happen again. I snarled, before repeating the process, while simultaneously firing off an Incinerate at the running armor-clad figure.

I couldn't see him, thanks to the figure before him that was growing larger and larger by the second, so I hit the one thing I *could* see: his knee as it came into view.

The armor-clad figure screeched, falling sideways and grabbing at his leg, only to accidentally put his hands into the Incinerate field, as I kept it going.

His hands blackened, a thousand plus degrees causing blood to boil, flesh and clothing to spontaneously catch fire. And the metal of his armor?

Well, nobody was going to be wearing the parts that were in the field, ever again.

"Parts" were also apparently alarmingly close to the other end of a section of armor, and as the saying goes, his nuts were toasted.

Regardless, though, inside of three seconds he was dead. And the now much larger other figure prowled toward me as I straightened, releasing my rifle to fall to my chest, the restraining strap catching it.

"Come on!" he screamed. The former applicant to "Famine Survivor of the Year" was now seemingly at least three hundred kilos and climbing, though all of muscle.

I reached over my shoulder, both hands grabbing both hilt and grip, as I dragged the rail gun shotgun free and half managed to draw my longsword.

Cursing, having to shift my grip and half hop to clear the blade, I eventually ripped it free and grinned at the incoming figure, hoping I was right about this.

Watching him, none of the bullets seemed to have actually hit him. Instead, it was like the momentum of the bullets had entered him and had become a part of him, somehow swelling his body to store the energy.

As he lumbered the last dozen feet toward me, I brought both weapons around, and got ready.

He couldn't do this for long, I guessed; there was just no way. Touching anything would result in it being pancaked if he could store the energy indefinitely, and why would he do a Skeletor impression if that was the case? So he had to be able to *selectively* release. That implied a cap on the energy he could absorb—to my mind, at least.

Well, to test that theory, enter the rail gun.

I fired all three barrels. The shots screamed out and hammered into his flesh. In the quarter of a second before I fired, he'd actually grinned, clearly thinking he had me now.

Then the first of what was a veritable wall of fléchettes hit him, tore through and broke the sound barrier as they decided to explain physics to magic.

Rule One: don't fuck with physics.

Rule Two: there's no need for more rules.

There didn't need to be, to be fair, as whatever energy field he'd been using to counter and store the impact was massively overcome, causing a rupture.

He'd have screamed if he had the time, I've no doubt, but he didn't have that. So, instead, he detonated.

Literally, a tide of blood and fragmented flesh and bone hit me, my armor and helm suddenly inundated.

I reached up, dragging the back of my hand across the front of my helmet, clearing enough of the bloody mess to be able to see something at least. With that fucker dragged clear, I had a half second of vision and I turned, just in time to take a spinning kick to the face.

The speedster was still up, and I flipped sideways. The world revolved around me, until I crashed down. Half of the team were out of action; in the few heartbeats it took me to focus on them all, he blurred from side to side, ripping guns out of hands and deflecting blows.

I hit the ground right at the base of the wall, slamming my helmeted head into the floor, ringing my bell and leaving me stunned, before I twisted on hard-earned instinct. I rolled left, slapped both hands down under me, and pushed off as quickly as I could to pop back to my feet—before nearly falling over again as my center of gravity and still spinning inner ear disagreed on what was where.

That was when I saw the barrel of my rail gun pointed at my helmet, and knew things weren't going well.

That—oh fucking thank you, God—was when Patrick entered the fight, though.

The warrior monk kicked the barrel aside at the last second. The blast ripped past me close enough that I later swore I'd seen them in flight.

The speedster punched outward…and Patrick swayed aside, the blow missing by a hairsbreadth. The pair of them blurred. Their hands and feet moved too fast even for my advanced perception to keep up with, and yet…somehow Patrick was still going after a few seconds, then ten, then twenty.

He wasn't as fast—nowhere near—but he *was* that skilled, I suddenly realized. Where the rest of us had invested in massive power strikes, skills that could bitch-slap God and more, he'd been steadily building himself into a martial arts monk from the movies, complete with floating steps and hovering and shit.

Every blow slid past. It was as if no matter how fast the speedster was, he was just choreographing the move so far ahead to Patrick that it didn't matter.

Sweat rolled down both their faces, and the speedster dropped the shotgun, needing both hands to try to keep up with Patrick.

I saw the second that realization hit them both—that he knew that he needed to, and the sudden fear that brought. I also saw that although he was drenched with sweat, there had to be a limit that the human body, even an enhanced one, could dissipate heat, because he had gone from red to darkening purple and he wasn't slowing.

I looked around quickly. A dozen more were incoming, but the others were climbing to their feet now. From behind us, I could hear the clatter of the corpse lords running down the passage.

The fight had started out bad, then had evened out. Now, as I saw Dante climbing to his feet and throwing his first fireball back at an enemy, even as Jo collapsed, exhausted, I knew the tide was turning.

A figure shouted something, unleashing a horrific blast of pressure that sent Rhodes flying, hitting the floor and rolling. Her rifle dropped as her hands came up to cushion her ears. Even where I was, standing well out of the line of attack, I felt the power of the sonic attack. But she rolled back to her feet, spit blood on the floor, then ripped the ring pull from a grenade and tossed the grenade roughly at the attacker.

The fragmentation grenade went off. Dozens of fragments punched through him and the closest of his allies, many of whom never got off a single shot or attack before being torn apart.

There were others coming now, a few of them armed with more than swords or bent metal, but they were coming.

So too were the volunteers on our side. For a heartbeat, I wondered whether we were about to be betrayed, until they opened fire into the ranks of their enemies.

I saw them coming as well, the next wave, and I took a deep breath before reaching down deep inside myself. I searched for the buried path to power, dragging the lightning upward through my body again, this time getting ready for a heavy strike, thinking to take them all out at once.

There were more and more coming, and behind them... The corpse lords burst from the passage behind me, and I ordered them forward, all but one.

That last I ordered to lock his gaze on the speedster and trigger his ability.

The sight of a corpse lord staring at you was hard to ignore when you knew what they were, and their abilities. I bet that having one lumber over and just stare when you were in a fight had to be disconcerting.

I didn't blame the speedster at all for glancing over. But when he did? That most wonderful suppression ability kicked in for the single heartbeat their gazes met.

Time seemed to slow for the fucker. He was already shading to black, he was moving that fast, heat building in every muscle. And when he slowed, his ability suddenly snuffed out, Patrick didn't miss the chance.

A fast blow to the center of his opponent's chest, followed by one to the left knee, buckled it sideways as the kneecap shattered. Then he caught his opponent's right wrist, bent it back, shoved downward, angled the arm across his throat, and stepped behind him, twisting and pulling his own arm back to choke him.

The speedster tried to twist, to dodge and free himself.

Patrick simply pressed his left hand onto the left shoulder from behind, then pulled and pushed at the same time with opposing hands.

The speedster had gone all out on the speed build, relying on the inability of his enemies to touch him to keep him safe. As his neck was broken, that mistake came back to haunt him, followed sharply by Patrick stepping forward as his enemy fell, to stomp on the back of the neck to make damn sure of things.

I gathered up my mana. More and more it built, and I ground out the words.

"Kilo!" I barked. "Give them a taste of the storm! Dante!" I gritted my teeth, pulling harder as I glared at him. "Give it a second then melt it!"

The pair did as they were told. Kilo dropped to his knees as the loyal kobold channeled everything he had into the fresh blast of Winter's Memory he hurled ahead into the oncoming path of the thirty or more enemies.

Several simply froze, though most just staggered and kept coming. Their flesh turned blue, frostbite blackening extremities...

Then Dante sent a great whoosh of fire, like the roar of an angry dragon, straight down the center of the shopping district.

Anything frozen was flash boiled. The snow that had been coating everything turned into water, boiling in a heartbeat, before the flames broke apart.

Dante collapsed alongside Kilo.

From the distance, over the screams of the dying and burned, those half frozen and cooked at the same time, there came a chuckle.

"Oh, I like you..." the voice ground out. "I'll have a special place in my harem for you two, and you, and..." The figure stomped out into view.

Jack saw him at the same time I did, leaping at him, only to be caught, making me stare in shock. The huge bear had reared up to use its massive weight and reach advantage, and instead of crushing the figure that was half hidden by the darkness, he was caught, his paws gripped by hands like catchers mitts.

Then there was a 'wumph' as something hit Jack, sending him crashing sideways into a wall, one that folded around him like dough.

"Hold him! I want that head on my wall!" The boss roared with laughter, and so did a bunch of his minions, still out of sight.

I gritted my teeth, holding on. I had only one shot with this, and I needed to damn well get him now rather than the pack that were pretty much wiped out already.

Damn, that pair had really brought their 'A' game, which was good as, considering the boss, we were going to need it.

The first corpse lord to reach him was smashed from its feet almost contemptuously, the bone construct hit with a stone bench and smashed into smithereens. The second caught the bench on the backswing, though half of his bones broke and his head was ripped free before he could do more than catch it.

The third and fourth were caught by magic. One had its head ripped back around on itself and then crushed into fragments by an unseen force, while the other was caught by a wall of flesh that poured over and around it, enveloping it.

I ordered the remaining corpse lords to fall back, losing two more as they complied, and I stared at the figure as he moved closer.

He was huge, not merely "big." He was a literal giant, one that was clearly used to his size, and knew the effect it had on people. At nearly four meters tall, and almost the same across the shoulders, he towered over normal humans. And his belly…it bounced with every step he took. There was only one description for him.

As I continued to hold the power, a quest suddenly popped up.

You have generated a new Sub-Quest!
Quest!
Ogre's repose…or is it dispose?

Once a human, one who has fully embraced both the nature and nurture side of being an ogre, this remnant of humanity has reformed himself utterly into a terrifying example of what is possible.
Though following the possible permutations of the system, draining and eating his fellow sentients and a collection of beliefs and actions that even disturb inanimate objects, this being has sunk to a level few believed possible.
As the first pure, mana-born sapient ogre in decades, he presents both an intrinsic challenge, and an opportunity.

Eliminate or gain control of the Ogre Boss to receive the following bonuses:
- *+1 Class Skill Point*
- *Possible new Dungeon-Born*

- **5,000 XP**

It took me a second to make sense of what I was seeing, the prompt and the massive humanoid, and then it clicked.

I knew that there were ways to create other species, and not just through the dungeon. I mean, I'd seen goblins and more out there, evolving naturally.

Now, though, as I saw the ogre, I realized that it was possible to "lean into" the system and double its effect.

The system had clearly offered him an ogre class, and he'd gone for it. He must have been investing everything he could get into whatever he needed—like constitution and strength, I was betting—because he looked about as attractive as a bag of hammers and half as intelligent as Baldrick.

I huffed out a breath, pulling my lightning around, up from my core, through my shoulders and down both hands. Crackling sparks leapt from my fingers as I built the spell over and over. A small ball of blue-white light appeared between my palms as I pushed them closer together.

The ogre ducked under a support and then straightened as he stared down, towering double the height of most of us. Then he smiled, and it was one of the most disturbing things I'd ever seen.

Most of the now ex-prisoners in here wore "new" clothes—filthy, but in a state of more or less good repair…if frequently stained with the blood of others.

This monstrous figure was barely kept decent by a loincloth, and a tattered one at that. His head was pointed, more or less, with the ridge of bone across his scalp the narrowest point on his body, and his chin wide enough I could have used it as an anvil.

His lower jaw had almost double the teeth of the upper, and they were crooked enough to give a dentist nightmares and an orthodontist an orgasm as he contemplated his bank balance.

Add in eyebrows a sheep could have hidden in, and enough curly chest hair to make even a seventies' porn star swear it was time to hang up the medallion, and that was all I needed to see.

This abomination had to die.

Others were gathering around him now—a handful of mages, I guessed. One was wrapped in bandages and grinning through them, making me think of a mad plastic surgeon. The other was a grossly fat figure, dressed all in black, with the makeup and hair that just screamed Goth, leaning on a skeleton's supporting arm.

There were others—a handful more that looked powerful, compared to normal humans, and a dozen at least that looked just broken and twisted—but none close to the size or threat of the ogre.

I compressed the ball of power down smaller, concentrating the lightning, before letting it loose with a roar, as the ogre started to tell Dante the things he was going to do to him.

Dante had been looking back up at him, a sick expression on his face, before the lightning bolt screamed past, slamming into the ogre's chest and… staggering him slightly.

That was it.

"Ho!" the big fuck bellowed, then laughed. "That was a good one!"

He had a single spot on his chest—a pink glossy bit right where it'd hit, and the surrounding hair was burned clear. But beyond that and a still expanding ripple in the layers of fat, there'd been almost no effect!

I stared in disbelief. I'd hit him with a blast strong enough it should have put a hole thicker than a beer can through him and out the far side!

"Magic!" Dante whispered, then shouted louder. "He's resistant to magic!"

"Immune!" The ogre belly-laughed, before slapping his gut hard and sending it shaking. "Immune I be, little one. And you'll have a long time to learn that, while you warm my bed, eh?"

"Shoot!" I snapped.

Those who had their guns to hand jerked them upright, opening fire in a staccato ripple.

Only to have them slam into a disc of bone that suddenly leapt ahead of the boss, snapping into place as more and more bones were layered together, and…

I grunted as I saw the bodies on the ground. Those we'd killed were being torn apart to feed it.

The pair of mages were gesturing now, hands sliding this way and that as they directed their magic.

The one that was all wrapped up in bandages and an operating gown looked to be splitting the corpses, ripping the flesh from them and directing it to one side. The other, the Goth necromancer, was forming half the bones into the shield for their master, and the other half were assembling into new minions to fight for him.

Well, that was just fine, because I had fucking minions as well.

The corpse lords stepped forward, not running to fight, but instead triggering their abilities and suppressing those of others. The necro looked horrified as the bones collapsed from the air, his own summons clattering apart. The flesh mage?

He screamed in fury, then started to gesture, before thrashing as he apparently tried to force the magic through sheer outrage.

"The bones, Lord!" the necro called over the gunfire that now punched through the falling shield and hit the ogre. "They have power!"

"Fool!" the ogre bellowed, swiping at the bullets and glaring as dozens of holes opened in his flesh, before knitting back together. "Stop them!"

"I can't!" he wailed, only to catch a backhand for his failure that sent him into the nearest wall with a meaty *thwack*. The stain left behind as he slid to the floor suggested he'd not be getting back up.

The corpse lords stood silent, staring at the big fucker. But even with three of them on him, and one on the flesh mage, it seemed he wasn't being affected, as the wounds closed over in seconds.

"Anyone else?" he growled, as the fire slacked.

I glared right back. "Dante?" I half asked, half ordered.

"Enough for one more firebolt," he admitted, and I cursed that we'd still not gotten mana potions out of the trial dungeon. "I think this one… I think this needs swords!"

"Kilo?" I asked, then shook my head as I glanced over at the exhausted kobold, taking into account the drained look on his face and the greyness of his scales. "Looks like—" I started to say, before Chris interrupted me.

"Looks like you're all mine, handsome!" He took something out of a pocket, then dropped his rifle to the floor, pulling free armoring and dumping it on the ground.

"I'm in." I grunted, standing and walking forward, rolling my shoulders then snapping loose the rifle as well, dropping it on the ground.

"Me too," Patrick called, stepping up.

"We want a piece too…" called Jimmy, before being grabbed by Rhodes, who shook her head at the brothers warningly and started speaking in a low voice.

I didn't know what was being said, but I guessed it was something along the lines of "Get ready to take advantage of the distraction" or "You can only piss with the knob you've got, son; leave it to the big boys."

That was a fair point, though, I decided, as I settled my sword into my right hand and my hammer into my left. The magic coursed through me still, and I fixed the big bastard with a glare.

Patrick had demonstrated he was frankly terrifying as a martial artist. Chris was a damn tiger-man when he could get it up. And me?

Well, I was the god of the storm, baby. It was time to show that off.

CHAPTER FORTY-ONE —

THE LAST CHAPTER

"Come on then! Let's have some fun!" the ogre boomed, clapping his hands together and grinning as more of the local scumbags behind him spread out to watch better, jeering.

The shopping center was spread across two levels, and although nobody had been stupid enough to try to attack from the top before—it was "protected" by a series of clear glass plates, that was all—more and more were making their way up there now to watch.

"Whoever manages to draw my blood gets a nice cuddle tonight..." The ogre grinned.

My lip curled in disgust as I triggered Examine.

Ogre	Humanoid
Ogres are reviled creatures. Where once they were known both for their culture and strength, a descent into rampant barbarism gave rise to a new breed of the once respected and mighty warriors.	
The Ogrya were a people of legend. Their solid determination and unwavering bravery saved many worlds, but as the tide of battle turned, and their limited numbers dwindled, they began to demand more and more as their due for their protection.	
Soon, worlds were as terrified of their "protection" as they were of the enemy, and then more so. As the smaller races banded together for protection, the last of the Ogrya stood against their more feral cousins, and were lost.	
In time, only the bestial ogres were remembered, and a once great race of protectors was lost forever. Then finally, driven by their own lack of interest in their technology, past, or any form of study—which they viewed as beneath them—they lost the ability to travel the stars.	

Note: **The last known ogre died in the Arcturus sector three hundred and eleven stellar cycles ago, and none mourned the passing of the race.**

Ability:
Berserk! **The ogre's chief ability, beyond their impressive magical resistance, is their ability to drive themselves into a murderous rage. One that allows them to ignore all wounds, supercharging their already impressive healing ability.**

Ability:
Resist! **The ogres were famous for their incredible magic resistance, and the rapid healing that they could trigger at will, though in exchange for this seemingly wondrous ability, they cannot sense mana in any form, nor learn to wield it.**

Weaknesses: Maximum mana capacity/dissipation.

HP: 2000/2000
Stamina: 3000/3000
Mana: 0/0
Speed: 5/10
Level: 17
Special Abilities: 2/2

HP 2000/2000	Special Abilities: 2/2

I read it and called out the details at the same time, as the massive figure grinned and slapped his belly again, then his thighs and shoulders, apparently psyching himself up for the fight and loving that he'd been seen for what he was.

I'd never seen the maximum mana capacity mentioned before, nor the dissipation marker, and listened with half an ear as Dante called out his thoughts on it.

"He probably isn't able to ignore magic, not really. Just absorbs it into his skin or something, then it dissipates loose. If we hit his maximum threshold, it'll probably go the other way."

"Make sense!" Rhodes snapped as she circled to one side, rifle held ready. "What does that mean?"

"He'll stop being resistant and start being vulnerable!" Dante guessed, waving his hands in a gesture of helplessness. "I don't know! It might be a million points of mana a second or something. I'm guessing here!"

"Then let's find out," I suggested, before seeing the way that Robin and the others were stepping forward to help. I caught Rhodes's eye and nodded to them; she nodded her understanding and moved to intercept.

This wasn't a fight for the under-leveled.

"Here…we…goooo," Chris growled. The last of his upper body armor came off and was tossed aside. He grabbed his under armor top and ripped it down the middle, nineties wrestler style, his body changing as he spoke.

Whatever he held clutched in his right hand—I was guessing it was a token from Simo—it crumbled to dust as the changes rippled through him, muscles surging as hair pushed through the skin in waves.

He gained several inches, if not more, and although he was powerfully built anyway, more and more of his body twisted and surged, altering to match his needs.

As a human, he was already massive: solid muscle layered over and over…a bodybuilder's wet dream. But as a tiger-man, he was clearly much more attractive to the surviving Scepiniir as Saros gasped in shock and apparent admiration. Now, instead of bulking higher in muscle, he seemed to slim down in some areas, widening in others.

The tiger heritage was clear as well: the black and white stripes, the widening of his face, the characteristic "chuff" as he let out a laugh. It was incredible. I had to admit the eight-pack of solid abs looked even more insane on him. And having met the Scepiniir and seen what actual naturally evolving cat people were like?

Yeah, he was straight up destined to be their god.

Patrick moved with a grace that made me feel like I was a lumbering mess, but I moved to the right. The other two took the middle and left as we all squared off against the ogre.

"Anyone want to beg me to be gentle?" he boomed. "Want a pillow to bite?" He grinned. The mass of mismatched slabs that he called teeth granted a fresh bouquet of halitosis to the area at large. "No? Fine then!"

He lashed out, darting forward with surprising speed for something of his size, and tried to grab Chris with his right hand, who twisted aside and slashed claws at his forearm as it brushed past.

Chris's hand came away with thin trails of blood lifting into the air as he grinned. "What…you thought a tiger'd not have claws?" he growled, raised one hand and flexed them in demonstration.

I stepped in, stabbing out in a straight lunge with the blade aimed at the back of a massive knee, just as Patrick jumped to grab his extended hand, probably planning to do some kind of judo throw or something.

Instead, the ogre lunged again. His right hand reached after Chris a second time, driving my friend back, as his left went for Patrick.

My blade hit the back of his knee, and I grunted. The tip barely dug into the thick, practically *armored* skin before he half hopped and twisted, lashing out a hand in my direction instead.

I took a few steps back quickly, then slashed my sword across his skin, aiming for the back of his wrist as he tried to grab me. I activated Void Blade ability, then cursed as instead of eating through the bastard's flesh and bones effortlessly, it bounced off without even the minor damage I'd gotten before.

"Magic weapons don't work," I called to the others automatically, before grinding my teeth as I realized that it really didn't matter to the others, considering the claws and unarmed techniques they were using.

"Magic, eh?" the ogre boomed. "That little pigsticker?" Then he burst forward, running at me, arms spread wide as he tried to catch me.

415

I took a step to the right, then dove, tucking myself into a roll, trying to avoid the kick he aimed at me.

Twisting to lash out, he stumbled, crashing into the wall and bouncing off. The jeers and cries of his supporters as he bounced, seemingly uninjured and came after me again, with me on the ground scrambling to get up, really pissed me off.

"Take his arms and legs out," Patrick called. "Fast blood-letting blows."

"It's like rhino hide," I called back, squinting up at the big fucker.

He started to circle us, his gaze flicking from one to another as he picked out his next victim. "You look fun," he told Patrick, before trying the same, arms-stretched-out lumbering run that he'd just tried on me.

Patrick backed up, moving almost as fast backward as he did forward, but damn, those long legs ate up the distance. He saw he wasn't going to make it, and instead of trying to dodge, he stepped in, ducking down under the right arm as it came in, his own right coming up and deflecting.

He slid to the left, skirting the ogre's clumsy swing, and stayed in close. His fists pounded the behemoth's side over and over, aiming for the short ribs, then the side of the knee.

The boss laughed, swinging back around and trying to catch him, making it look like a grown man trying to play at catching a toddler.

"Here, little man, come to Daddy!" he called, before booming out a laugh as he went on. "Cootchie-cootchie-coo!"

"What the hell?" Patrick whispered, eyes wide. He backed up, shaking his fists and staring at what should have been a dozen broken bones, if not outright death.

"What?" the ogre asked. "You don't want to play? Fine!" That last came out as a roar as he suddenly went from joking and bumbling around to racing to his right.

Chris was there, having circled and been moving in, claws extended.

Instead of being able to attack a distracted ogre, he suddenly faced one in full-on rampage mode. The huge creature darted in and grabbed him, picking him up and twisting, throwing him through the air to slam into the remaining corpse lords, shattering and scattering them like bowling pins hit by a cannonball.

I lunged in, stabbing into the side of the ogre's thigh. The blade dug in an inch or two at most before it stopped. I yanked it free in desperation, twisting and jumping aside as a hand sailed toward me.

I landed and spun to build momentum and brought the hammer whistling through the air to impact the other hand. The flat head slammed into the knuckles as he tried to punch me.

Instead, there was a cracking slap, as if a body dropped from on high to the sidewalk.

He howled, pulling his hand back and cradling it. "You DARE?!" he roared, all playfulness gone as he rubbed at his injured hand. The bones creaked and cracked as he hissed, glaring at me. "FINE!" He stepped to the side and, with his injured hand, grabbed a stone bench from where it sat against the wall.

I'd seen that thing before. Hell, years ago in this place, I'd sat on one of them, and I'd tried moving it out of curiosity. I'd barely managed to drag it an inch.

He picked it up one-handed. His eyes pulsed with a sudden gleaming redness as he hefted it over head.

"DIE, BUG!" He brought it up and over, then slammed it down, aimed at my head.

I dove to the side, hitting the floor and rolling, before forcing mana into myself and darting forward, not using the magic to strike but instead to power my flight. I shot forward, twisting and skidding as I brought myself upright again, then grinned.

Blunt force worked just fine against him, so it was time for me to play as well.

The bench had smashed into the floor. The faux marble covering shattered as the bench exploded into fragments. I tossed the blade aside and switched my hammer to my right, squinting as I decided the best way to play this.

He was big, and his skin seemed impossibly strong. The cuts we'd given earlier were healing already. The stab I'd managed into his thigh was scabbed over. And the slice across the back of the knee? I could see the smeared blood, but no wound.

Fine. If the skin was too thick, the bones clearly weren't. Maybe the rest of the internals were similarly weaker than outside.

I triggered Incinerate, aiming at his head, hoping to boil his brain, compressing it down to a tiny space and force the spell through, only to have it totally fail. No reaction.

"Okay, so the skin isn't all it is. It's some kind of field. Nothing gets through, eh? I can work with that," I muttered to myself. The void blade hadn't worked, but again, that was in trying to get *through* the skin. I really wished I'd had the time to enchant the hammer, damn I did, but still, that was life, and physics was still a wonderful equalizer.

I backed up as he glared at me, turning to follow, before snatching up a fragment of bench that was at least a meter long and half that thick. He snarled, throwing it at Patrick, forcing him to skip back and abandon his attack. Then he leapt forward at me, lifting both hands above his head and bringing them down in a hammer fist.

Shoving mana into my ability, I jetted backward ten feet, landed, and skidded a few feet. Then, as the massive figure impacted, his fists crashing into the floor, he glared at me, only to find I was already in motion.

I rushed through the air toward him. His eyes widened in shock as I drew the hammer back in both hands and swung. My magic hurtled me past him, as I swung the hammer into his right shoulder.

The sound of the joint breaking rang out, and he howled in pain and outrage. I twisted, pushing more mana in and lifting into the air. The hammer came around for another blow as I soared upward…

CRACK!

PAIN!

I flipped end over end, to smash into the floor and bounce, sliding as heat, impact, and pain screamed up from my left knee. As I came to a halt and glanced down, I found it had been almost demolished.

The bullet that hit me had to have come from a high-powered rifle. My end-over-end somersault meant I lost control of the mana, surging more into it than I should have, in shock.

I'd come to a halt almost pressed against a wall, and both sides suddenly devolved from watching spectators into a full-on war again. I grabbed at my leg, dragging the lower section closer to the upper, getting it back into alignment, and looked over for Jo, only to see her barely aware and propped against a wall.

She'd drained herself to such a point that she was probably just about capable of healing me of a nasty attack by a head of wet lettuce, and blood was gouting from the wound.

My armor had slowed the high-impact bullet, but it'd not stopped it. Half the knee was just gone. As I looked over, I saw the ogre lifting a slab of the bench and menacing Patrick with it.

Chris was nowhere to be seen. The impact with the corpse lords and the wall behind them had clearly done a lot more damage than I'd realized. Patrick was backing up quickly, but if he didn't get some help soon...

"Here!" Ashley was there, skidding to a halt next to me and dropping down to one knee, pulling out the healing focal orb she'd been entrusted with. She pressed it to my leg, and started to cast, forcing mana into me.

I hissed as the mangled flesh started to reknit and regrow. The scales of my armor and the links that they sat atop had been shredded, forced into my leg along with fragments of both my clothing and armor, as well as shattered bones and the remains of the round itself.

Rhodes and the twins laid down suppressing fire. The difference in assault rifles in the hands of a sergeant in the British Army and her two protégées, compared to scavenged and poorly maintained weapons stolen and handled by escaped prisoners was clear.

"You need to lie down!" Ashley snapped at me, looking over the wound in panic. "Matt, lie down. We need to get your body level! We need to reduce the blood loss!"

I struggled. Magic fucking healing shouldn't work like that, but for all I knew, the fusion of real world and magic might work better. And I sure as shit wasn't going to be doing anything if she couldn't stanch the bleeding, so I started to move.

The enemy were falling fast, but as Ashley shifted, trying to help hold my leg together, a second boom rang out.

This one took me high in the chest on the right side, slamming me sideways as the fresh impact ricocheted off, only to strike the wall as a fractal pattern of cracks radiated out from a new hole punched into the stone.

I hissed out a breath, now staring up at Ashley as she shouted out in shock, then started healing me again. Her face took on a wan and exhausted tinge as her mana was torn free to power the spell.

I was on my back, I realized. Pain flared through me from what was going to be incredible bruising in the chest and from the hole in my goddamn knee, as I tried to figure out what the hell had just happened.

A combination of the reinforced plates and the angle had somehow helped to deflect a high-powered round—blind luck, I guessed, as Ashley had been helping me to lie down, or it'd have gone through the armor and probably out the far side.

Either way, though, as the world started to swim for me, my blood loss weakening me even further, I saw Saros slide in from the side. A squeal filled the air as she apparently used her claws to slow herself, before shoving something into Ashley's hands.

"Herrrre!" she growled. "Sssave him!" Then she was off again, the air all around torn by bursts of bullets ringing out as both sides went to town with their remaining ammunition.

"Fuck, I'd forgotten about this. Stupid...!" Ashley cursed herself, before biting down on the cork of the healing potion, pulling back and spitting it out, then pouring half over my knee.

The glass of the vial was then jammed into my mouth forcefully enough that for a second I was convinced she might have chipped a tooth. Then I was swallowing and trying not to drown.

The high-grade healing potion that Soras had apparently given her was one of only two. The decision had been made that more fighters were a better outlay of the mana we had.

That had nearly backfired terminally, but the potion's effect was incredible.

Where the spells tended to strip the body to power the healing, rebuilding mass, fluids, and flesh from your own body in a way I couldn't explain, the potions did all of that, while also bringing some of the good stuff with it.

I'd lost a horrific amount of blood, I knew. One glance at Ashley as she pulled the vial back made that clear. She was soaked in my claret, as was the stone all around me. But the bubbling of the flesh and surging bone, combined with the healing from the focal orb, was fixing all of that for me.

Ashley was drained to her limits, I could see, swaying as she tried to continue to help me, despite the risk to herself. I grabbed her, dragging her across me and to the ground as I saw a glint of a reflection on the upper floor behind her.

I rolled, throwing myself atop her, and pressed the two of us against the wall, as a fresh high-powered round hit the ground where she'd been kneeling.

It'd have gone through her, and into me, had I not seen the fucker a half second before. I twisted, glaring back along the path of the round, seeing a patch of inky darkness that shimmered slightly as a rifle barrel shifted.

Whoever was up there was cloaked by an ability, one that surrounded them. But the tip of the barrel snuck free of the bubble, and that was all I needed.

"Incinerate!" I snarled.

I aimed it for just behind the barrel, not knowing whether they were standing or crouching, and not daring to miss.

The only thing that had saved us so far was that the rifle was a single-shot one, reloaded quickly each time.

The scream that rang out made it clear I'd hit something. A half second later, the bubble popped to reveal a woman who lurched to her feet, her hands cradled to her chest as she spun, trying to run.

The second spell was much better aimed, catching the back of her head in a six-inch spot that ramped up to a thousand degrees instantly. Her hair along the edge burst aflame; fluids were flash boiled, and the bones, flesh, and whatever else was reduced to charred carbon.

She collapsed from sight, and I snarled, pushing myself up, then glancing down at Ashley. "Are you...?" I started to ask her, hoping she'd not been hit by a ricochet or anything, only to yell as my ankle was caught in a giant meaty fist and I was yanked backward from her.

"Naughty!" the ogre bellowed, lifting me into the air and holding me upside down. "No breakin' my toys!" He grinned, then spun me around and hurled me into a nearby set of windows with a crash of shattering armor and glass.

I hit the ground and bounced, rolling to a halt, before coughing out a wheeze. Then I shook my head, coughing blood into my helmet from where I'd bit the inside of my lip.

"My toy!" the ogre growled at me, before looking down at Ashley and smiling crookedly. "Now you're mine as well..." he started, reaching down with one hand.

"Get away from HER!"

A new voice entered the fray, and I snapped my gaze to the side as a firebolt slammed into the ogre's face, poofing into sparks and smoke, blackening his cheek but doing little else. "She's not yours! She's her own, and you'll never get to hurt her, never!"

It was Dante. But with each step, he was changing. Flames rippled across his flesh; his clothes erupted into greasy smoke as skin and hair were replaced with living, breathing fire.

"MINE!" the ogre roared, stepping over Ashley and lumbering into a run, hands reaching out.

I forced myself to my feet, shaking glass free and staggering to the door. My knee clicked and clacked, grinding, then finally settled back into place properly.

The massive ogre swung a fist at Dante, and I almost shouted to him to dodge, only for it to be too late.

Then the fist passed straight through, as if he were composed entirely of insubstantial dancing, swirling flames. Then Dante was solid again, sliding to the left, punching into the ogre's side with a handful of clearly ineffectual and untrained punches.

The ogre snarled, twisting and trying to slow, before staggering and almost falling over. He caught himself on a pile of scrap, then staggered again as Dante followed him, punching and flailing at his bigger opponent.

The fire wasn't harming him—it left sooty patches across his skin, that was all. But with each blow, the massive figure flailed more and more wildly as apparently more of the heat got through with each hit.

"Kill him!" he screamed to his supporters. "Kill the demon!"

"I'll kill you myself!" Dante roared back, punching out faster and faster as the ogre slapped at him and tried to grab the flames.

The gunfire around me was slackening off. The limited ammunition that the enemy had made its lack apparent as gun after gun ran dry. They were backing away now, I saw, starting to run. Jimmy and Andre moved up, directed by Rhodes to take one side, as she took the other.

The skylight overhead shattered and a high-powered shot came through it, hitting the ogre in the shoulder, the same one I'd hit before and that had apparently healed, getting him back in the fight. But now?

Blood fountained free, as he grabbed at it, howling in rage and shock.

That had to be Mike, I realized. The poor fucker was up on the tower, watching over so that we had him if we needed a path cut through for us to escape. The angle must have been just right for him to finally lend a hand, and damn, it'd been a great shot.

The fucker's head exploding would have been better, of course, but as the ogre staggered back, shouting for help, it couldn't have been more perfect.

He looked up at the skylight, making sure he was out of the way of whoever was on the far side, not knowing that Mike was well out of angle now, when Dante hit him in the face with a fresh firebolt.

He screamed, the resistances apparently dwindling as he clawed at his own face, before another voice rang out.

"You can't!" he screamed. "You're nothing! Weak! My slaves!"

"LIAR!" Robin bellowed, running forward, mace held high along with her shield. She'd apparently discarded the rifle, and something about her... She was...glowing?

"Murderer!" she roared, slamming the shield into the ogre's right leg, knocking him backward through sheer outrage.

"Monster!" She swung her mace, the head of the weapon trailing a bright blue-white glow as it impacted. A burst of light surged from the impact as the sound of bones breaking rang out.

The ogre screamed, both in pain and outrage, but it was nothing to the echoing roar of Robin.

"Faithless!" She shoved him with her shield, no longer with the advantage of momentum, without the weight of all her armor behind it. Still, the ogre, twice her size, lurched.

"Defiler!" The shout rang out as the mace landed again. By now she was truly glowing. The seams of her armor gleamed and shone, lightning sparked across her plate, and the light flared again.

I stared in shock. A notification frantically pulsed for me, and on instinct I opened it, freezing in my shock.

Congratulations!

You are the first of your nascent brethren to have a Paladin pledge their life to your own. Do you accept the life bond of [Robin] as your first Paladin?

Yes/No...

I hit yes, of course. I didn't know what kind of a difference it'd make, nor how the mad bugger had done it. Shit, I'd barely exchanged a dozen words with her since we'd met!

As soon as I did, though, a second prompt appeared, and I read it fast.

Congratulations, First Lord of the Storm!

As the first leader of a Local Pantheon to raise and unlock your own Paladin class, you have been granted the following Boons!

- **+10 to a single Stat of your choice**
- **+2 Spells**
- **+2 Class Ability points**

Followed by:

WORLDWIDE ANNOUNCEMENT!

**THE FIRST LORD OF THE STORM HAS PUBLICALLY
ACCEPTED HIS FIRST PALADIN, RAISING UP A NEW CLASS OF
WARRIOR WORSHIPPER AND BEQUEATHING HIS ESSENCE TO
THOSE HE LEADS!**

**KNOW THIS! THE ONLY LIMIT ON YOU IS THAT WHICH YOU
PLACE UPON YOURSELVES. GROW, ADVANCE, *LEAD*!**

I stared in shock, feeling a connection to Robin that I'd not had a second before. And the effect on her?

She flared brighter than a lightning bolt for a brief second. The light seared the image of her lifting into the air, enveloped in a beam of bright light, into the eyes of everyone nearby.

When I could see again? Robin stood there motionless, her mace in one hand, her shield in the other, both lowered, as she panted, the shoulders of her armor heaving.

"Die!" the ogre bellowed, bringing one fist around in a desperate blow.

Robin's head snapped up, as did her shield. The metal flared with a bright light just as the blow landed, and the crack of bones resounded.

The ogre cried out, staggering back, cradling his broken knuckles, as Robin shrugged off the blow, then shouted in return.

"For Peter!" The first blow of her mace caught the ogre's hastily outthrown left arm, and the crack of bone rang out again.

"For Mark!" She thrust with her shield and sent a fresh flare of light bursting out from the impact as she drove the much larger foe backward.

"For Dianne!" she yelled, as the mace caught the upraised arm again, breaking the bones fully and making the ogre scream as his arm fell limp.

"For Jonnie!"

The shield drove him back another step; then the incoming mace blow landed at the side of the huge knee.

The scream torn from the ogre made me nod, having recently felt the pain of something similar. He crashed to the floor, before lifting his other hand, the broken right one, trying to shield himself from her. "W…wait!" he tried.

"Defiler!" Robin cried. "A thief of hope! Of life! Of dreams!"

With each pronouncement, she struck. Her mace and shield shattered bones, and I gasped, suddenly realizing just how weak I felt, as I sagged to one knee.

"Mercy!" he screeched, sounding less brutish and filled with terror.

She flared brighter than the sun as she raised her mace a final time, standing over his broken body.

"You deserve no mercy!" she declared, before slamming her mace into the center of his forehead with a bright flare of light.

I collapsed to all fours. The world around me spun as a new notification flared before my eyes.

Beware, First Lord of the Storm! Your Divine Core is unestablished, and as such, drawing on your essence to empower your worshippers can be fatal...

New Quest Discovered!

Establish your Divine Core:

As a divine being, you may choose to gift your burgeoning divine essence to those who please you. This can be done through the path of religion, through empowerment of artifacts, or directly, but beware!

The path of organized religion offers a safety net, a buffer, between the god and their followers, but currently you have no such protection!

Create and fill the first level of your Divine Core to gain access to the following rewards:

- Unlock the Priesthood of the Storm Questline
- Unlock the Paladins of the Storm Questline
- Unlock the Defenders of the Faith Questline
  - Level One Artifact Creation
    - Survival...

It was the last reward that really got to me, as I pitched forward, the world blacking out around me.

Survival?

Fuck's sake, I wanted, just once, to be told "Well done, that's it—have a beer" as a quest reward.

And with that stupid thought, everything vanished.

EPILOGUE

"You're sure about this?" Finn asked Kelly, looking at the latest prompt that had arrived only a few minutes ago.

"It's the only thing that fits." She sighed, glancing at the door that led to her and Matt's shared quarters. "When he discovered that you could empower your supporters, it's started a whole new arms race."

"I guess," Finn whispered, unsure. "But, I mean, what the hell do we do now?"

"We try to help him figure it out." Kelly forced herself to look away from the closed door. "We help where we can, and we all double down. Lightning is his gift, and as much as it's not for everyone, we've got a real chance here. He's the first Lord of the Storm...if anyone can guide more of us to ascend, it's him."

"It's all on instinct for him, though, isn't it?" Finn shifted on the small couch and summoned a hot chocolate, then winced as he sipped at it. "I miss the syrups I used to get." He glanced down at the cup reproachfully.

"I miss massages and the beach more." Kelly snorted. "I don't know if it's this week or next, but Aly and I were supposed to be flying to Tenerife, a girls' week with Amy, the three of us by the pool. It doesn't matter, though, because it's all gone now." She straightened up, rolling a hand theatrically and summoning a yellow cocktail into one hand.

"I miss the old world," she went on. "But it's gone, and we're still here. Matt's still here. And yes, it's all on instinct for him, but although you're worried about that, I think that's our best chance."

"How?" The crafter squinted at her, before banishing his own drink and summoning another. "Ferrero Roche cocktail," he admitted, sipping at the sugar-encrusted lip.

"Everyone else is following him," Kelly said. "Where he leads, they're trying to figure out the path. Sure, some will surge ahead, and it's going to be hard for him to teach us all the things he just does without thought. But if he can?"

"You think he's special?" Finn shook his head, snorting as he realized what he'd just said. "I mean, you know, beyond that whole being a god, being a Dungeon Lord and your boyfriend."

"I don't know," Kelly admitted after a few seconds, smiling. "Honestly, I think so, but I don't know how much of that is me being in love with him and the madness of everything that's happened. Sure, he was in the right place at the right time, and he's managed some incredible things. Some of that has to be blind luck, sure, and the knock-on effect, but that can only take you so far. He keeps doing this consistently, and yeah...I think he is special. I think he'd have done some of this, if not all of it, even if he'd not found the core."

"Well, what's the next step?" Finn asked her after a few seconds.

"We brought him home," she said. "I was terrified when I found out that he was hurt, that they couldn't wake him. And when he did finally wake, and we realized it wasn't a vurm or a relapse or whatever, but that the stupid bitch had broken him? I didn't know what else to do." That last was added with a cold glare in the direction of the dungeon main buildings overhead, and the woman now bonded to her boyfriend.

"I don't think she did it deliberately," Finn offered quietly. "It was all in the heat of the moment."

"Most cheating is," Kelly whispered, looking back down at her drink, then setting it on the table with a sigh, before starting to pick at her nails. "Don't bother." She gestured as Finn tried to explain.

"I know what you meant," she said. "I just don't like it. And knowing she's bonded herself to him? That she can do that, that she can drain his life? I mean, what if she's hurt? Will it hurt him? What if she does another smite or whatever in a fight?"

"She doesn't understand it any more than he did," Finn pointed out. "She hit her level choice, and was offered the Paladin class. What does it say about her that, as far as we know, she's the very first to have achieved it, and she chose to select him as her god?"

"That she wants him," Kelly muttered.

"No," Finn said firmly. "Kelly, you need to get your head out of your arse and wake up."

"What?" She looked hurt. "But she—"

"She's not interested in him!" Finn snapped. "Hell, I don't even know if she's into guys or not. You know what she said when I asked her?"

"What?"

"That she wanted to protect people." He stared into Kelly's eyes as she flinched. "Now who does that sound like, eh, Kelly? All she wanted to do was to protect those who were being hurt, and to smite the bad guys. She was taken prisoner. She and all the others there were held against their will by some of the worst scum that those prisons had held.

"Then those same prisoners got control of the only food source around and basically ran riot over everyone else. Kids died, *little kids*, because of the shit that happened there. And when she found out about us all, she had the chance to blame us for not coming to her aid before.

"She could have blamed us, just like we blamed the police and the army. Instead, she accepted that we were doing our best. And then, when Matt decided that we'd fight for them, and when she found out he was a god? When she was offered the chance to become a Paladin, she was offered the choice of her deity. She could choose anyone who had already declared themselves a god, so of course she chose him! Who wouldn't?"

"I know, but—"

"But you don't like that she's gotten a part of your man, and you don't," Finn stated. "Well, that's life, Kell. Sorry, darling, but now you know how I feel. I mean, Patrick is this insane hunk of a man already, and me? I craft. I make pretty bags, armor. I help out teaching those who want to learn about sewing and making things.

"He fights ogres. I'll never have that side of him, because I'd last all of five minutes out there in a fight. You're the Dungeon Mistress, the Mistress of Minions, and if anything happens to him? You'll take over the dungeon. You know it, and so does everyone else."

"If the dungeon survives."

"You know it will." Finn scoffed. "Come on, that lie was useful when we were just getting started. But as we learn more about the shit that's going on out there? There's no chance a race that created these is going to let the dungeon just break down if its bonded lord dies. It'll go to the next in line, mark my words, and that's you. He named you that, and it's because he knows you're his equal, honey.

"He knows that you're the person he trusts the most to take over if everything goes tits up. I'm sorry, but no matter how good you are at sucking his dick, that's not something he'd have done if you weren't the right person for the job."

"I guess."

"You know, and so do I." Finn snorted, pointing a finger at her in reproach. "What he's given her was as instinctual on his part as everything else he's done, and knowing him, it was the right thing. You? He made you the Mistress because it was right, and you know it. You're scared about the shit that's going on…you're terrified that you can't live up to it all."

"Is it that obvious?"

"Honey, you think I'm not?!" Finn laughed. "Damn, I'm terrified! I constantly worry that Patrick's gonna meet someone else, that someone I teach is going to overtake me, that tomorrow some gnome or elf or whatever is going to rock up and be a master crafter and I'm going to be replaced. You know what? If that happens, I'll deal with it, but it's damn unlikely.

"Everyone's living every damn moment with imposter syndrome, and when I realized that, that was when I came out. I stopped hiding myself, stopped listening when people told me I was wrong, and instead I started standing tall. It's time you did the same. You're the Mistress of Minions—get out there and show us minions what you're capable of!"

"You're no minion." Kelly rolled her eyes, but she couldn't hide the smile as Finn grinned back at her.

"I am," he replied proudly. "We all are. We're dungeon minions. The natural and the dungeon-born…we're all his minions, and yours. And now that we've got the ability to swear oaths, I think we're going to explode."

"Why?" Kelly cocked an eyebrow in question. "Matt's terrified people are going to think he's some tinpot dictator wannabe."

"Because we'll know who we can trust." He smiled. "Literally, anyone who's sworn to him, to the dungeon and those oaths…for a year and a day, we all know we're safe from each other. No assaults, no rapes, no danger of getting screwed over. No matter how shitty things are out there, in here? We're in literally the safest place in the world, and it's all because of him taking anything that could be used against us and making it part of the dungeon."

"I guess—" Kelly started and he cut her off, sitting forward quick enough he slopped his drink.

"No, Kell!" He shook his head emphatically. "You don't get it! That's it…that's all the things in the area that we were terrified of, and he's settled them. He's converted them and we've got the chance to grow now! The upgrade to the Glass core is going to be finished soon. Sure, it wasn't as much mana as we'd hoped from the nukes, but it's leapt us so far ahead it's unreal! We've got the chance to grow, to figure all this shit out, and to get ready."

"For the war." Kelly nodded. "You're right. Matt said that the undead are still coming, that they're moving more to the south. They're heading to the tunnel…"

"Fuck the boney bastards." Finn laughed. "Kelly, even if they all ran all the way, it'd be days before they could get here, never mind that they need to find their way through the Channel tunnel, then up the country and slog all the way here. They're going to be fighting every inch of the way, while we're getting ready. You think a bunch of damn skeletons are going to be able to stand up to us once the core is online?

"Think about it! We've got a Paladin. Soon, we'll have more. We've got healers and soldiers—hell, we've got an army! Just let that boney fucker show his face, because I guarantee he's going to be shitting himself right about now!" Finn lifted his cocktail and grinned.

"A toast," he offered. "To Matt, to the dungeon, and to tearing the undead, the Orcan, and the fucking aliens a new arsehole!"

Kelly smiled, lifting her drink as well. But inside, she doubted it was going to be anywhere near as easy.

She knew it couldn't be, not really, all thanks to the single last prompt that Matt had shared with only her, after swearing her to secrecy.

Beware Dungeon Lord, First Lord of the Storm, and Arcanist...for you rise too far, too fast. Always remember, the nail that stands highest is hammered hardest.

The Alliance of Lords has been convened, and their purpose is singular: to prevent their annexation, they declare their enmity against you.

Dungeons rise in prominence, armies are taking the field, and the other lords and ladies of this world have not missed that you gain while they do not.

Abilities and armies are being harnessed, and not all believe the warnings issued about the threat that even now approaches. For your race to stand a chance, the Age of Conquest approaches!

Rise up, First Lord of the Storm; Rise up, Arcane Dungeon Lord; Rise up, One Who Is Yet To Be, for the night is falling, and not all will see the rising of the dawn.

THE END OF BOOK 6

THANK YOU

Hi everyone! Well, that's the Age of Glass complete! Hopefully you've all enjoyed it? I know it was good for me to return to this world, I'd genuinely missed it. Now though, comes the hardest part.

For the Rise of Mankind, I'm going to be writing books 6, 7 & 8 all one after another; by the time you read this, I'll be working on #8, as #7 is already in edits (jump to the Patreon side if you can't wait until its release) but once these are done?

Well then it'll be time for UnderVerse again.

My intention is that I'll jump back to UnderVerse for 2 books, then back to finish this tale off with its last two books, before returning and finishing UnderVerse as well.

Once all of that is done? Well, there's a lot of tales left to tell, and maybe, if you look hard enough, you'll find a hint here and there of what's to come.

For now though, I just hope you've enjoyed the ride so far, and please, if you did? Leave a review or a rating. You'd be amazed at the difference two minutes of your time makes.

Thank you all for your support, and your trust.

-Jez
12/09/2024

PATREON

By the time this launches at the end of Sept? Some of my Patreon supporters have already finished book #7, and have started #8. So, if you want to read it perhaps 4-6 months ahead of release? Come join us on the dark side!

There's several of those wonderful supporters out there that I have to thank personally as well; ASeaInStorm, Mischa, Kevin, Lex, Simon and Wesley thank you all!

https://www.patreon.com/Jezcajiao

Rise of Mankind 7: Age of Expansion

By Jez Cajiao

The Age of Expansion dawns, but will humanity rise or shatter beneath its weight?

Matt's journey from desperate survivor to Dungeon Lord has forged him in blood and terror. With the Coronaught Queen vanquished and his domain flourishing, the days of scavenging scraps are over. But as his towers pierce the sky and his followers multiply, the drums of war beat ever louder.

Far to the south, an undead horde swells, their relentless march spanning continents. As Matt races to unlock the true potential of his abilities, rival dungeons declare their allegiances, not all siding with the living. The line between ally and enemy blurs, and every decision exacts a toll.

Now, Matt must transcend mere leadership. To shield his people from the coming storm, he must become something more – a beacon of hope, a force of nature, perhaps even a god in truth. But in a world where loyalty splinters like glass, how much of his humanity is he willing to sacrifice?

Step into the Age of Expansion, where every triumph balances on a knife's edge, and the fate of humanity hangs in the balance. Will Matt's dungeon become the stronghold of humanity's last hope, or just another tomb in a world of the undead?

Note: This is a Dark Fantasy Epic LitRPG. Expect graphic violence, strong language, and morally complex themes. Reader discretion is advised.

Preorder on Amazon

THEFT OF DECKS

By Lars Machmuller

When the deck is stacked against you? Change the game!

In the frontier town of Isarn, Chase will never be more than the lowly Darkborn thief he is. Banned from training, banned from acquiring better cards, if the Lightborn had their way, he'd be banned from life itself.

He's not alone though, and the one thing he and his friends have is determination. Losing a hand to a brutal punishment only fueled his obsession to get access to his own amazing, reality-bending cards.

That is the path to power and a future for them all. Nobody cares where you came from when you're rich enough. For now, though, they're facing both established powers, churches and age-old prejudices. It's time to get to work, and if the Lightborn won't share and play nice?

Sometimes the only way to get dealt a better hand is to steal the whole damn deck!

Buy on Amazon

QUEST ACADEMY

By Brian J. Nordon

A world infested by demons.
An Academy designed to train Heroes to save humanity from annihilation.
A new student's power could make all the difference.

Humans have been pushed to the brink of extinction by an ever-evolving demonic threat. Portals are opening faster than ever, Towers bursting into the skies and Dungeons being mined below the last safe havens of society. The demons are winning.

Quest Academy stands defiantly against them, as a place to train the next generation of Heroes. The Guild Association is holding the line, but are in dire need of new blood and the powerful abilities they could bring to the battlefront. To be the saviors that humanity needs, they need to surpass the limits of those that came before them.

In a war with everything on the line, every power matters. With an adaptive enemy, comes the need for a constant shift in tactics. A new age of strategy is emerging, with even the unlikeliest of Heroes making an impact.

Salvatore Argento has never seen a demon.
He has never aspired to become a Hero.
Yet his power might be the one to tip the odds in humanity's favor.

[Buy on Amazon](#)

WANDERING WARRIOR

By Michael Head

A divine quest to deliver justice.
One year to accomplish his mission.
After nineteen planets, there's something different about this one.

James Holden has reached the maximum level there is for a human. That's perfect, since he's the only one of his kind. A wandering warrior, without control of his destination, tossed between universes by gods who've failed to tell him why. James is the lone Judge on a new world in need of someone to balance the scales. He isn't afraid to do so with extreme prejudice. As the Chief Justice, he has to right the wrongs the innocent can't fix themselves.

As James quickly discovers, the roots of corruption run deep. Guilds choose to protect themselves rather than the people. Monsters roam the wilderness unchecked. Judgment is usually a decision between right and wrong, but nothing is ever that simple. This time, being the strongest human won't be enough to punish the guilty. James might have to recruit some new blood, even if he prefers to work alone.

On his twentieth world, he is going to win, no matter the cost. James will have to find a way to break past the limits of the system if he's going to have a chance at making a difference.

Buy on Amazon

KNIGHTS OF ETERNITY

By Rachel Ní Chuirc

When Zara awoke in chains she thought she'd gone mad.

She was Zara the Fury - mistress of flame and fear. Her name was whispered across the land, from ramshackle taverns to the royal court. Even the heroic Gilded Knights thought twice before crossing her path.
She was feared—*respected.*
Now she was curled up on a dirt floor on her fiancé's orders. Valerius, leader of the Gilded, mocks her cries for help. And the kingdom is on the brink of war over the missing Lady Eternity…
But that wasn't why Zara thought she had gone mad.
The reason why is that the last thing she remembered was blood, an arcade screen, and the gun that changed everything.

But no chains can hold the Fury, and when she gets out?
The world is going to *burn.*

Buy on Amazon

SCARLETT CITADEL

By Jack Fields

Gormon Hughes is 19, thin as a broom, and has—not for the first time in his life—been swept into the path of trouble. Poor, recently heartbroken, and indebted to the sort of people who file their teeth into needle points and devour wriggling bloated spiders for fun, Hughes sets his sights on salvation.

That salvation is the Scarlet Citadel, a wealthy organization of pageant fighters, monster hunters, and secret keepers. With the aid of strange oracles, rare good fortune, and a unique power that bubbles like champagne in the core of Hughes' being, he must join the Citadel and advance himself.

But the ladder of progression is harsh and dark. The rungs are slippery.

And falling means disaster…

Buy on Amazon

FACEBOOK AND SOCIAL MEDIA

If you want to reach out, chat or shoot the shit, you can always find me on either my author page here:

www.facebook.com/JezCajiaoAuthor

OR

We've recently set up a new Facebook group to spread the word about cool LitRPG books. It's dedicated to two very simple rules;

1: Let's spread the word about new and old brilliant LitRPG books.
2: Don't be a Dick!

They sound like really simple rules, but you'd be amazed…

Come join us!

https://www.facebook.com/groups/LITRPGLegion

I'm also on Discord here: https://discord.gg/u5JYHscCEH

Or I'm reaching out on other forms of social media atm, I'm just spread a little thin that's all!

You're most likely to find me on Discord, but please, don't be offended when I don't approve friend requests on my personal Facebook pages. I did originally, and several people abused that, sending messages to my family and being generally unpleasant, hence, the author page:

www.facebook.com/JezCajiaoAuthor

I hope you understand.

BATTLEFORGED: CONQUEROR

By M.H. Johnson

Battleforged: Conqueror

It was time for Eric to show what one man with a few dozen oversized warthogs and an extradimensional storage space can do against an army of bloodthirsty orcs who think the Northeastern United States is already theirs.

Join Eric on a wild ride of non-stop action and deadly peril as he shows the entire world what happens to a Necromancer's enemies when they dare to threaten the people he loves!

Buy on Amazon

LEGION

Okay everybody, if you've not yet seen or heard, well, the secret is out! My wife Chrissy, and our friend Geneva and I have launched the Legion Publishers! We're taking on new authors, as well as experienced ones, focusing primarily on the LitRPG side of things, but we're open to anything really, with one very clear rule that guides our company:

Don't be a dick.

That's it. Our contracts aren't hidden behind layers of legalese, you can find them here:

https://www.legionpublishers.com/legioncontract

If you want to reach out and ask any questions, get an idea of the support we offer, and possibly become part of the family? We'd love to hear from you, just tap the link and fill in the form:

https://www.legionpublishers.com/contact-and-submissions

Hope you're having a good one!

-Jez, Chrissy and Geneva

RECOMMENDATIONS

I'm often asked for personal recommendations, so if this book has whetted your appetite for more LitRPG, please have a look at the following, these are brilliant series by brilliant authors!

The Ten Realms by Michael Chatfield

The Land by Aleron Kong

Challengers Call by Nathan A. Thompson

Quest Academy by Brian J. Nordon

Wandering Warrior by Michael Head

Endless Online by M H Johnson

The Good Guys/Bad Guys by Eric Ugland

God of the Feast by Kevin Sinclair

The Wayward Bard by Lars Machmüller

LITRPG!

To learn more about LitRPG, talk to other authors including myself, and to just have an awesome time, please join the LitRPG Group

www.facebook.com/groups/LitRPGGroup

FACEBOOK

There's also a few really active Facebook groups I'd recommend you join, as you'll get to hear about great new books, new releases and interact with all your (new) favorite authors! (I may also be there, skulking at the back and enjoying the memes…)

https://www.facebook.com/groups/LitRPGlegion/

https://www.facebook.com/groups/GamelitSociety

https://www.facebook.com/groups/LitRPG.books

https://www.facebook.com/groups/LitRPGforum/

Made in the USA
Monee, IL
25 January 2025

10951112R00243